Yawada /08

Order this book online at www.trafford.com/06-3182
or email orders@trafford.com

Most Trafford titles are also available at major online book retailers.

Note for Librarians: A cataloguing record for this book is available from Library
and Archives Canada at www.collectionscanada.ca/amicus/index-e.html

Printed in Victoria, BC, Canada.

ISBN: 978-1-4251-1423-7

*We at Trafford believe that it is the responsibility of us all, as both individuals
and corporations, to make choices that are environmentally and socially sound.
You, in turn, are supporting this responsible conduct each time you purchase a
Trafford book, or make use of our publishing services. To find out how you are
helping, please visit www.trafford.com/responsiblepublishing.html*

*Our mission is to efficiently provide the world's finest, most comprehensive
book publishing service, enabling every author to experience success.
To find out how to publish your book, your way, and have it available
worldwide, visit us online at www.trafford.com/10510*

www.trafford.com

North America & international
toll-free: 1 888 232 4444 (USA & Canada)
phone: 250 383 6864 ♦ fax: 250 383 6804
email: info@trafford.com

The United Kingdom & Europe
phone: +44 (0)1865 722 113 ♦ local rate: 0845 230 9601
facsimile: +44 (0)1865 722 868 ♦ email: info.uk@trafford.com

10 9 8 7 6 5 4 3 2 1

ONCE A PROUD CANADIAN

AN HISTORICAL
(And Educational)
NOVEL

BY: JAMES T. SAWADA

Woven into the storyline is a STUDENT HANDBOOK ON LIFE

"IF YOU READ ONLY ONE NOVEL IN THIS LIFETIME...

READ THIS BOOK"

James T. Sawada

THANKS

Thanks to my wife Norma and to my son Joe and my daughter Shelly for their suggestions and feedback.

DEDICATION

To: Joe, Shelly and Norma

James T. Sawada

CONTENTS

PART ONE

IN PURSUIT OF HAPPINESS

There is no way to happiness…
Happiness is the way.

Thich Nhat Hanh

CHAPTER ONE

It was not Little Boy who shattered my life.

"Little Boy?" you ask, intrigued by the name, "Who was Little Boy?"

Little Boy fell from an opening on the underbelly of the Enola Gay directly over Hiroshima on August 6, 1945 at precisely 8:15 in the morning, killing 140,000 people instantly.

"Little Boy did that all by himself?" you respond with your mouth open. "Sounds like you're talking about an atomic bomb! Well now, if it wasn't Little Boy who shattered your life, who was it?"

It was actually Fat Man – not Little Boy – who plummeted like a stone from the bowels of a U.S. Superfortress B-29 called Bock's Car, which was named for its usual commander, Frederick Bock. Funny how these details have stayed with me. I was told so many times to "forget it", but I just could not. How do you forget something like that?

On the fateful morning of August 9th, 1945 it was not Frederick Bock, however, but a young twenty-five-year-old pilot named Major Charles W. Sweeney who climbed into the cockpit of Bock's Car and took off from Tinian Island with his specially trained crew and fat passenger. The navigator did a superb job and at precisely 9:44 a.m. he had reached his primary target: the industrialized city of Kokura which contained one of Japan's largest arsenals. But by luck, good karma, or both, Kokura was blanketed in a protective haze of dense smoke which had drifted in from an adjacent city that had recently been hit with conventional bombs. This is probably the only instance in recorded history where smoke pollution actually saved lives! Due to impaired visibility Bock's Car changed direction and proceeded, with the third atomic bomb ever to be detonated, to the secondary target.

"What about the other two?" you ask with a quizzical frown.

The world's very first atomic detonation was a plutonium implosion device with a yield of 19 kilotons or the equivalency of 19,000 tons of TNT. It was secretly developed as the Manhattan Project in a lab in Los Alamos, New Mexico. The director of the project was a theoretical physicist named J. Robert Oppenheimer. The first detonation was called the Trinity Test, and was conducted by the United States Army on July 16th, 1945 near Alamogordo. Brigadier General T.F. Farrel, deputy commander to General Groves, described the test as follows:

"The effects could well be called unprecedented, magnificent, beautiful, stupendous, and terrifying. The lighting effects beggared description. The whole countryside was lighted by a searing light with the intensity many times that of the midday sun. It was golden, purple, violet, gray, and blue. It lighted every peak, crevasse and ridge of the nearby mountain range with a clarity and beauty that cannot be described but must be seen to be imagined."

J. Robert Oppenheimer was much more succinct; he simply quoted a passage from the Bhagavad-Gita: "I am become death, the destroyer of worlds."

The world's second atomic detonation, the first to be used upon a civilian population, occurred three weeks later at Hiroshima on the sixth of August. Three days later, the third atomic bomb, the second ever to be exploded on a civilian population, was headed for its fateful destination.

"What happened?" you ask with bated breath.

At 11:02 a.m. Major Charles W. Sweeney was flying at an altitude of 1,650 feet above the beautiful port city of Nagasaki. The sky was slightly overcast, but visibility was good enough to drop the atomic bomb. At that height the people looked smaller than ants, if you could see them at all. Over 80,000 of them scurrying around like worker ants under the morning canopy of the rising sun. It was then that Fat Man struck with the unforgiving fury of 22,000 tons of TNT. He did not care. When you burn out an anthill, who cares how many ants are killed or maimed? Only the ants care. I was one of those ants. I cared.

"Really?" you say, your rising curiosity suddenly deflated by a disturbing feeling of unease. "After the passage of such a long time why bother to regurgitate such sensitive matters?"

I know why you might feel that way. I know how embarrassing this topic can be. Out of sheer stupidity and ignorance we continue to add war and terrorism to a world reeling from a plethora of natural disasters. What happened to common sense? Have we learned nothing? It is so frustrating. How can you stand it? Be honest. We have to be brutally honest with ourselves. We need to dare to share, if we really care!

I have kept quiet long enough. I was told by my father, who was under the influence of the Japanese mafia called the Yakuza, to keep quiet. To keep my big mouth shut. That to speak out would be bad for business. I felt that no one really cared – except me.

I care. Damn it. I care because it happened to me. To me! Such things should never be allowed to happen again. Not to anyone. Never again! But you know as well as I, that it could.

"God forbid," you say, "God forbid!"

* * *

From the outside they said it looked like a giant clenched fist, or a mushroom cloud. But from the inside? The light engulfed me like a womb. It was a living thing. It was pure energy. Absolute. It was everything. It consumed me with its brilliance. So utterly brilliant! It was beyond exaggeration. A hundred thousand zillion lightning bolts fused into one dreadful strike, striking me dead! But I lived, as if in spite. In spite of what? Who knows? All I know is that it happened to me. And I lived!

"What can I say?" you mutter.

Roll all the swear words you know into one god-almighty expletive. That is what you would probably say in retrospect. But at the time I was speechless. It was overwhelming, but God let me live, because I did not deserve this. Damn right. I had done nothing to deserve this. I should not even have been there!

Oh God, the light! It was all-consuming, and yet, blinding as it was, I could see, hear, smell, taste and feel it! I became the light. The light and I were one, one living expression of energy. One plutonium atom split into an infinite universe. That universe personified became an experience. I personify that experience. A human experience.

"What other kind is there?" you ask rhetorically.

I am not an ant. I am a human being who has spent nearly a lifetime trying to make sense of that moment. That singular moment when Fat Man descended from the sky while I just stood there staring up at the grimy factory windows that reached up to the tin roof under which someone yelled, "Bansai! The Emperor's planes are flying on to victory!" And then the walls became transparent and the light and I became one.

I am not a saint – nor am I a sinner. Who needs those moralistic value judgments? They are all so subjective. I cannot say I am religious, but I am spiritual. Who would not be if they had seen the light? Laugh if you like. Laughter is good for the soul. But it was not a laughing matter to be enveloped in a nightmare and wake up to see nothing but a desert of desolation, a wasteland, and perched upon a distant knoll like a foreboding reminder of the impermanence of all things worldly, the charred hulk of a once truly magnificent Catholic Cathedral, the church of Saint Francis Xavier, Saint Paul Miki, and all the *Kakure Kirishitan*. Did I say I was not religious? Perhaps I am religious after all. See how I waffle? Spiritual? Religious? What is the difference? Why split hairs? This is a very hairy predicament, this predicament called "life". Someone should write a handbook, a simple guide to help us confused souls find our way in the shadows as we grope our way through life.

In spite of the light I felt the dreaded darkness, and I knew I was not dead. The living fear the reality of such darkness; it was all-pervasive. It kept me alive, shivering like a frozen leaf on a barren limb. I could feel, taste, and smell it as it enveloped me in a dreadful cocoon. The icy claw of fear massaged my feeble heart and kept it racing as if in adrenaline shock, while my breath wheezed in and out. I stumbled along like one of the living-dead, passing shadows in a deserted wasteland. I cannot remember much. The darkness was too great and the fear overwhelming. But it passed! It passed like the darkest night fades into the bleak grey of dawn. Somehow I had survived, and my survival filled me with a devastating sense of utter despair. It consumed me with sorrow. I wept for days. For days. I hope you understand. I could not help it.

It seemed as if time had frozen solid and then began to melt in dribs and drabs. It was confusing. My memory recorded light years in mere seconds. When the walls became transparent, I became translucent. The material world became immaterial. Who knows why I just did not vanish like so many others? Do you believe in miracles? I do.

My identity, which endured like the Great Chain of Being, could not be extinguished. I was immortally mortal. I became an oxymoron. Remove the "oxy" and what do you have? Make sense? Even morons like me have a purpose. Do you understand? A purpose. I cared. Shall I repeat that? I CARED. It was the caring that grounded me to my historical roots, the roots of my ancestors. It was the caring that kept me real, that made me cry real tears, tears that gave meaning to a sorrow so profound it felt eternal. And then as if by magic I heard a voice. It said, "Tutomu?"

I stared in utter disbelief as the voice took form. "You look like a ghost!" I declared

"So do you!" was the reply.

Who believes in ghosts? I really did not turn into a ghost. I just looked like one. No doubt I was white as a sheet. But like I said before, I lived.

What is more important than living? Dying? Perhaps they are interconnected in some curved or circular manner we the living will never really understand, a paradox that we spend our lifetime pondering. After a zillion rebirths and reincarnations what do we know? After the detonation of three atomic bombs how much clearer is our understanding?

We look at a mushroom cloud from a distance and say, "awesome". Do we really understand the significance of that atomic blast? The ramifications? The horror? Are we naïve enough, or should I just say dumb enough, to do it again? And again?

Obviously the clarity of our understanding is limited by our ignorance, which is relative to our karmic disposition. Some of us with average intellectual endowments frequently attempt to connect the dots that represent our two dimensional understanding. We cleverly connect dot A to dot B in a linear fashion and get a straight line, no-brainer. We connect B to C and C to D and fashion a rectangle, remarkable. Then we add a third dimension: depth. Wow! Three dimensional space with perspective. How much clearer can it get? Why not add yet another dimension, time, and what becomes manifest? A reality rooted in three dimensional space and one dimensional time, combined into a Four Dimensional Space-Time. Miraculous.

However, this space-time reality is slightly curved in accordance with Einstein's General Theory of Relativity, in a way which encodes the gravitational fields of all distributions of mass density, each mass density minutely affecting the space-time curvature relative to its mass-density. Can our understanding fathom this concept of curved space-time? It throws a curve into the mechanical logic of Quantum theorists who mostly choose to ignore it at their peril, even though the tiniest change in such curvature can have enormous effects on the very rules of Quantum Mechanics. Curved space-time! It is the "curving" that is so challenging to straight-thinking scientists, and a revelation to armchair philosophers and those attempting to see beyond the bend. Does the curving imply that ultimately the end result has to be spherical, a whole, oneness?

"This is rather mind-boggling stuff!" you interject.

The ramifications of a curved four-dimensional space-time are so mind-boggling they even boggled the mind of Albert Einstein. But this is the dimension that we all live in for better or worse. It is difficult for a creature to truly understand the medium it is immersed in and which constitutes the "reality" that surrounds it. It seems we are captives of the four-dimensional reality we are ensconced in like goldfish in a bowl. Would it seem rational if the goldfish deliberately polluted the water in their own bowl, and then complained about the water being dirty? Sometimes it is difficult to see causal relationships when you are the goldfish. Often we are only aware of the end result: we jump from A to D and overlook C and B. Is there a connection between Saint Francis Xavier's landing at Kagoshima in 1549, Pearl Harbor, and the subsequent atomic bombing of the beautiful port city of Nagasaki? All of these events came to pass, did they not? Were they isolated historical events? Is it possible to connect the dots between them?

"Good point, or rather good question," you commiserate, pretending to understand the scope of the problem. "Perhaps an illustrative example may help to further illuminate." you suggest.

Sometimes on warm clear nights I like to lie back and stare up at the vast universe of stars. It is difficult to see how every star relates to all the other stars, how they are all connected as if by some grand design. Some people have made a science out of connecting the starry dots. In a four dimensional reality connecting the dots often clarifies the understanding and helps us to see the bigger picture.

Dot by dot I have doggedly attempted to make sense of the linear shallowness of my life and gain a deeper appreciation of my existential status. The more dots I connected, the more connected I felt to my amazing cousin Penelope. She lived in Canada. She was, how should I say, a precious jewel in the sands of time, a tiny glimmer of something marvelous. Her husband, Larry, was no dullard either. He had a Masters degree in Philosophy like her. He was a very lucky fellow. I was happy for both of them.

The dots did not end there. Eventually they led all the way back to a gaunt, hairy Ainu from the northern island of Hokkaido, who centuries earlier had painstakingly crafted the priceless samurai swords which my father had bestowed upon me with the words, "Be worthy of them!" I have tried. Believe me. You have no idea how hard I have tried.

You know, I think one reason I tried so hard was that way back in '42 when we left the place of my birth, someone yelled: "Good riddance!" I felt unworthy. I was just a kid back then. I cried in secret.

* * *

Memories, memories, memories. How they fill the lives of the elderly with "significant moments" of a lifetime spent accumulating such. Such poignant memories of mistakes made and vital lessons left unlearned. Are they worth sharing? Is there anyone out there who really cares what a dying old man whose life was shattered by Fat Man has to say? Anyone, anyone at all?

CHAPTER TWO

There was something about the samurai swords that rested upon a black lacquered stand at the foot of the bed that caught the eye. They looked so deadly earnest, as if they were there for a purpose, a purpose that brought back memories that spanned generations. If one squinted both eyes and looked very carefully, one could see a small squiggly symbol just below the hilt on both swords. Who put it there? And what did it represent? The black silk threads on the handles were shiny and worn smooth from the sweaty hands that once proudly wielded the finely crafted swords. Whose hands? For what purpose? How did such swords come to rest at the foot of a hospital bed in which lay a dying man withered with premature aging? Although they were considered to be antiques, the *daisho*, or paired big-small samurai swords, commanded a timely presence. The swords were just as relevant and just as mysterious as the old man to whom they belonged. Two old relics, both reminders of ages past and the relativity of time.

The old man rose like a somnambulate from his thirty-nine inch hospital bed with starched white sheets into a sitting position. Although he appeared to be half-asleep his sinewy arms reached, as if in anticipation, in the direction of the samurai swords at the foot of the bed. His eyes were fixed upon them. He nodded his head and broke into a toothless grin as if in agreement with the image in his mind's eye.

Who would have thought that those derelict old swords pre-dated the Spanish missionary Francis Xavier's arrival at Kagoshima in 1549? On his twenty-first birthday, the old man's father, Kasuzimo Miki or "Kas" or "Kaz" for short – who could tell the difference? – had presented him with the family's heirlooms that were practically as old as the family heritage, at least the part that was still remembered.

"In Canada you would now be of legal age", his father had said. "You are my only son. I have nothing much of real value to give you but these. You are a man of the future, and I of the past. All of our hopes rest with you. To look at me you would never know it, but you are the end product of a long line of courageous samurai. If these swords could speak, they would tell you such a tale! Be worthy of them." With that his father paused and cogitated for a solemn moment. Then after a heart-felt sigh that reverberated all the way back to the *Katan Korakura* of Tomakomai, he drew in a breath so heavy it sagged him back on his seat. He gazed with ageless eyes at his only son, and in a hollow voice that echoed down through the centuries, he began to regurgitate everything he had ever been told about the Great Chain of Being that gave meaning to the surname: Miki.

The old man was a Miki. He dangled off the end of the Great Chain of Being that unraveled like an invisible thread through an historical novel that spanned oceans, continents, and centuries tying together seemingly disparate events and lives link by link, chapter by chapter. Toward what end? Was there any significance and meaning to such an individual's existence that was worth sharing?

"Please don't try to attach any labels on me," the old man would say whenever the nurses pried for personal information that would more clearly identify and individualize the withered carcass that passed for a living, breathing human being. He lay in a relaxed state upon his sanitized hospital bed, his dark eyes gazing meditatively up at the ceiling. His hair had turned pure white as had the closely cropped beard that curved around his jawbone, accentuated by a moustache that still retained a few black hairs giving it a grayish appearance. The moustache drooped about the orifice that served as his mouth providing the illusion of a perpetual scowl. It was not the impression the old man wanted to give; it gave credence to the saying, first impressions can be deceiving.

Some people are timid, shy, reserved and very difficult to really get to know. To really get to know such unique individuals and to appreciate what they have become, one needs to go back link by link along the Great Chain of Being and walk in the shoes that left the historical footprints.

* * *

It was 1478, the very year that in Spain the Monarchy was inaugurating a devious plan, a plan whereby, in the name of the Lord and Savior, the Monarchy could suppress any inkling of hostility or negativity toward God, King, or Country. Witches, heretics, political opponents, or any persons of learning who dared venture an unflattering opinion about anything not in accord with the opinions of the established powers were fodder for the Inquisition's insatiable appetite for sadistic piety. It was while innocent men, women and children were being tortured and burnt alive at the stake in Spain, that a hairy Ainu drifted in on a water-logged sampan from the northern island of Hokkaido and landed on the shores of Nagasaki Bay.

He was a tall, gaunt, bony caricature of a human being. Fine black hair covered the exposed parts of his face, arms, and legs as if he were some kind of a throwback to more primitive times. His coal black eyes glistening under a ridge of black eyebrows conveyed an awareness of things vaguely primordial. His skin was weathered like wrinkled parchment and his nose protruded bluntly like a beak above a droopy moustache and a dense, bushy beard. He looked very old for a youth of twenty. In some ways he resembled some of those dark-haired *hakujin* from Portugal or Spain, and in a dim light during the winter months when he had been working under the protective cover of the forge, could have been mistaken for one, except he spoke nothing but Japanese interspersed with a spattering of Ainu slang.

His ancestors had roots as deep as the *Jomone* culture that harkened back to southern Sakhalin and Kuril Islands. No one else knew for sure just where they had originated from, but he knew. They were the only true aboriginal-natives to inhabit Japan, the only indigenous peoples who could claim that they belonged there, because this was their *Ainu Moshir*, their homeland. The divine *Kamui*, or spirit that inhabits every human being, had placed them there. They were given the name "Ainu", because it meant spirited person or human. They were, and always had been, the only people who had the right to call Japan their homeland. Descendents of the powerful Yamato clan that dominated Honshu acted like they owned Japan, but only the Ainu could legitimately claim to be aboriginals. They were proud to be called Ainu – instead of *Nihongee*.

His name was Tsutomu Sawada (pronounced Tsoo-toe-moo Sah-wah-dah). He came from a small village called Tomakomai, on northern Hokkaido. A generation ago the once proud hunters and gatherers had been reduced to farmers and artisans so they could more easily be enumerated for taxation purposes by hordes of better-equipped Japanese invaders from Honshu. The invaders considered themselves to be superior beings and the Ainu to be primitive. Yet none of the invaders could fish salmon or hunt bear like the Ainu. None of them could survive in the wilderness of the Hokkaido forest in the dead of winter without the assistance of Ainu hunters. Perhaps for these reasons they treated the *Katan Korakura*, or village master, with a certain degree of deference.

Tsutomu's father, Kahei Sawada, was the Katan Korakura. He was selected by the warrior priests, who accompanied the occupying hordes, to assist with the prestigious task of sword-making due to the never-ending demand for more and better swords. The instruments for dispatching souls had to be fashioned by people of higher spiritual status. It was a rarity for anyone other than Japanese priests to be trusted with the knowledge of how to make a samurai sword. Because of his graciousness, his noble bearing, and his spiritual aura, the Katan Korakura of Tomakomai was the only non-Japanese priest to learn how to make divine swords.

When the warrior priests left the primitive village and ventured south looking for more civilized places of worship, Kahei Sawada was the only one left on the entire island of Hokkaido who knew how to make samurai swords. Such knowledge was not to be foolishly squandered. It was to be passed on from father to son like a precious heirloom. The Katan Korakura had learned his craft well. Every sword was rigorously tested on the dead carcasses of man or beast to insure that it would slice through flesh, sinew, and even bone, with ease before it was deemed fit to be etched with the Sawada "S" just below the hilt. Discerning samurai traveled from more civilized areas all the way to Tomakomai just to purchase a Sawada sword; after all in the heat of battle, what good is a sword that shatters with the first ferocious impact?

Tsutomu grew up at the forge. As a young child it was his job to help fuel and stoke the red-hot coals of the charcoal furnace wherein the molecular structure of the iron became impregnated with molecules of carbon to produce various grades of carbon steel. Who knew why this happened? It just did. It was one of the closely guarded secrets that made the making of samurai swords such a specialized craft. Tsutomu did not mind the long hours of hot, sweaty labor just as long as his father was there to pat him on the head occasionally and say: *"Yoi, yoi."* That was all the encouragement he needed to keep his spirits up and his unflagging admiration for his father unblemished. Whenever he grew tired he would lie down on the little cot his father had fashioned adjacent to the water trough and rest. At such times his father was inclined to smile as he recalled a question he once heard a wise old Shinto priest ask: *What is more endearing than the innocence of a sleeping child?*

Tsutomu was a curious, clever, and perceptive child who wanted to know everything. His dark glistening eyes watched intently as his father hammered and folded the near molten carbon steel over and over, beating out the impurities and fashioning a lethal weapon out of a harmless piece of iron. By the age of thirteen he already knew more than his father did about making perfect swords. He was much more willing to improvise and adapt new techniques with the old; it suited his temperament and his creative spirit. Still, his father always made the long two-handed *katanas*, while he perfected his technique on the shorter *wakizashis*. To his father, good as he was, sword making was just specialized work – to his son it was an art. There was a world of difference in the end product.

By the time Tsutomu was seventeen, samurai with a critical eye would politely ask the Katan Korakura if he would allow his son to make their katana. This was not good for his father's self-esteem. It was not good to see a proud Katan Korakura humble himself before his son. It was disheartening to see one's own father wither with shame from within every time some insensitive samurai would demand with a haughty attitude of disdain: "I want the boy – not you – to make my swords!" Tsutomu always refused to make the katanas, but it nearly broke his heart every time his father, without looking up, would shuffle off into a dark corner and pretend he was making something else.

It was not easy to make good swords under such circumstances. One tended to make inferior swords so as not to disgrace one's own father. One was inclined not to do one's best, to retreat behind a mask of mediocrity, and pretend one was not aware that one's father was that important. But he was. And so when he turned nineteen, Tsutomu resolved in his mind that in order to be true to himself he had to leave Hokkaido. For a whole year he saved all that he could from the payment he received for making mediocre swords, swords that were not quite as refined as his father's, so as not to tarnish the good name and reputation of the Katan Korakura of Tomakomai.

On the day before he was to leave he told his father: "You are the greatest sword-smith in all Hokkaido. Now that I am a man I must leave and make my own way. I thank you for everything you have taught me. I am proud to be a sword maker. I am proud to be Ainu. I am proud to be your son."

The next day he left on a rickety old sampan operated by an old Chinese sailor. They sailed down the coast as far as his money could take him, all the way to the southernmost part of Kyushu. There, the old Chinese sailor said, "Get off or pay me more!" He was practically broke so he got off and wandered into a little village on the outskirts of Nagasaki called Kogi. That village later became famous because of his sword-smith shop, the shop where he made his famous Sawada swords etched with a small "s" – as opposed to the large "S" on his father's swords – barely visible just below the hilt. Sometimes people got confused and gave his father credit for swords made by his son. That did not bother Tsutomu in the least.

Those experts familiar with the highest quality swords ever made by human hands were not fooled. They knew that the swords etched with the modest little "s" were swords that could make the difference between life and death. They were swords made by Tsutomu's own secret forging techniques. Inside the hardened outer carbonized steel, he meticulously folded in a softer, more malleable inner core. It took days – not hours – of patience, patience, and more patience, until the desired outcome was realized. It required the fortitude and mentality of a perfectionist. The result was a sword of superior tensile strength and fabulous flexibility. They were swords like no others in all Japan. They never snapped in half like punk steel, and they held an edge as sharp as a razor. They were magical swords, and soon the tiny village of Kogi became as famous as its swords. A Kogi sword made by the "Magician of Kogi," was worth a man's life.

Tsutomu was not a magician; he was just a relocated Ainu from Hokkaido doing what he could not allow himself to do back at his hometown forge. It was just common sense to him. The swords had to be malleable with impossible strength, and alive with intensity. To Tsutomu the swords vibrated with life. Each ringing hammer stroke instilled a determination as strong as his will. In the hands of its owner, it lived vicariously. Every sword was therefore unique; it seemed to take on the character and personality of the samurai whose life depended upon it. This was not magic. It was simply the product of a master artist, a humble craftsman who just happened to look more like a magician than a sword-smith.

In due time Tsutomu took a wife, a tall and angular, kind-hearted woman. Although she was not Ainu, she was, unfortunately, socially snubbed almost as much as he was because her father was an immigrant from Korea. Tsutomu had nothing against Koreans. In fact he liked Koreans because they were so open-minded like his wife. That was why he found her to be so compatible; they were both open-minded individuals trying to do their best under trying circumstances. They did their best, and in the attempt produced two sons and three beautiful daughters. Each girl was endowed with flawless pale skin, delicate facial features, and fine black hair that shone with highlights that were the envy of mothers whose offspring sprang from far less despicable lineage.

It seems that the raising of children is such an enrapturing experience for some, that the years are condensed into a fairy-tale with a happy ending. This is what occurred to Tsutomu and his family. When his eldest daughter matured into an intelligent and exotic creature of incredible beauty, a proposal of marriage was received from a highly respected military man by the name of Handayu Miki. It was an unexpected blessing for the humble family of a sword-smith to be so honored. It was a very proud day for the entire village when the marriage took place, for on that day the name Sawada became linked irrevocably with that of Miki, and vice versa. The prestige of the one made the magic of the other more respectable than ever. After that who cared if Tsutomu was a hairy Ainu from Hokkaido and his wife was of Korean descent?

* * *

The sweat dripped from Tsutomu's forehead blurring his vision. The fierce heat from the forge almost blistered the exposed skin on his forearm which protruded from a leather glove which held the tong that thrust the carbon-steel deep into the white hot coals. In the other hand he held a heavy steel hammer which dangled loosely at his right side. When the carbon-steel was red hot he swiftly removed it from the forge and placed it upon an iron anvil and hammered it relentlessly: turning, folding, and pounding metal on metal, creating and re-creating the stuff of nature into a creation that would not exist in the natural world, if it were not created by a sword-smith. To see that sweaty, lean, muscular refugee from Hokkaido standing before that fiery forge with sparks flying, and the red hot steel ringing out with the sounds of re-creation as the hammer rose and fell over an unmovable anvil as solid as the good earth upon which it stood, was an awesome sight. The concentration, the determination, the relentless pursuit of excellence with every hammer stroke, with every turning of the near molten metal, epitomized an artist in search of perfection in an imperfect world. To create, just once, something that was as unique as his existence, as immortal as his mortality. In this small way Tsutomu emulated the Creator, by making real something that once existed in his imagination: a gift fit for the prestigious military family of Miki.

Perhaps it is the fantasy of all truly great artists to attempt to immortalize themselves in their creations, creations that could live on long after they have passed on, like the seeds of their regeneration. When Tsutomu began hammering that inert slab of metal on the third week of April, 1529, did he have an inkling that he was creating something much more than just lethal weapons? Did he have some vague impression, some premonition that the set of samurai swords he would so carefully polish and hone to a razor's edge would one day be made famous by a grandson who bore his name? Would it have been possible for him to dream that works of art fashioned from the basic elements of the earth by his two hands would follow his seed across the vast expanse of the Pacific Ocean and provide the karmic impetus required to magically inspire a distant relative, with just a hint of real Ainu blood, to undertake the writing of something as daunting as a handbook on life? Who would have predicted that over four hundred years later a priceless katana and wakizashi, with his still identifiable imprint just below the hilt, would end up on a black lacquered stand at the foot of a sterilized thirty-nine inch hospital bed, upon which lay a dying old relic of a human being who had been there in the forgotten city when the church of Saint Francis Xavier, Saint Paul Miki, and Father Petitjean, along with the largest concentration of Christian souls in all of Japan, evaporated with hardly a trace from the face of the earth in the twinkling of a ferocious eye? Who could have anticipated that the way of the sword and the cross would be fraught with such danger? At that far-flung moment in historical time when a tall, sweaty, sword-smith, whose father was the Katan Korakura of Tomakomai, gazed with the piercing eyes of a Creator into the fierce fires of his red hot furnace, who knew then, exactly what he was creating?

It took months, but the result was unbelievable. Such magnificent swords were seldom if ever seen, simply because they were so rarely crafted. Every detail was meticulous, from the gleaming blades to the delicate cross-woven silk so painstakingly wound around each elongated handle by the sword-smith's dutiful wife. Who deserved to possess such perfection, such a labor of creative excellence? Such swords created out of the imagination of the Magician of Kogi, and willed into existence from the base elements of fire, water, air, and earth, were gifts to be passed on from the creator down through the ages, father to eldest son, generation after generation.

Tsutomu Sawada's gift to his new son-in-law was a set of the finest samurai swords he had ever made. He could never duplicate that feat again. It happened just that once. Who knew they would turn out like that? It was magic.

When he received the precious gift, Handayu Miki bowed with the deepest respect and humility possible, for as a military man he knew first hand the value of such swords. On the field of battle they could represent the difference between life and death. Never before had he hefted such finely balanced swords, such lethal weapons that looked like works of art. He was filled with such admiration he said, "You honor me too much. I am not worthy of such magnificent swords," but he held on to them covetously, because they felt so naturally a part of him.

"You protest too much," his father-in-law replied, "I made those swords especially for you. They are a small token of my esteem for you and your family name. May they serve you and all future Miki progeny for as long as they last."

Handayu accepted with heart-felt humility, even though at that precise moment he was inundated with a vague feeling of unworthiness. Perhaps in the future there would be others who would be worthy. He humbly accepted on behalf of those others.

Handayu wore his new swords with great pride. They looked good on him because he had the build of a swordsman, tall, lithe, and wiry. When he strode imperiously about the compound in his slow, loping stride, the hilts of the swords would sway with the motion of his body in such an undulating manner as to underscore their lethal potential. Few would wish to meet such an individual in mortal combat. Handayu looked every inch the image of a samurai warrior. But looks are not everything.

Although he descended from a long line of great military leaders, Handayu Miki was cast from a slightly different mold. He had the prowess and skills, but not the temperament. He was not given to ruthlessly destroying the property and lives of others without pangs of conscience. He was a sensitive and creative soul who enjoyed crafting things with his own two hands, an inclination which heightened his admiration for his father-in-law. Rather than being haughty and ostentatious like others of his status, he was gentle, amicable, and humble. In an occupation where ruthlessness and indifference were accepted as necessary attributes for individuals in such positions of power, Handayu suffered from the lack of such traits. He suffered inwardly to save face. This made his suffering all the greater. Still he carried on, because he was expected to.

Handayu once handcrafted a beautiful wooden bench which was placed in a prominent place near the front entrance to his house. It was the only material thing he was truly proud of, because he had created it himself out of nothing but scrap lumber. He loved to sit on it and admire his handiwork after a tiring day of strutting his stuff before the envious eyes of his military subordinates. It was a role that was wearing tediously thin. It no longer suited him. If his name had not been Miki the respect would have faded along with his zeal.

Fatherhood came late to Handayu. He was not expecting it. It just happened. And just like that, his whole life took on a depth of meaning that he could never have anticipated. It was shortly after his one and only son was born, and the occasion upon which he had donated his precious bench to the Buddhist temple as a sign of gratitude, that he humbly stepped down from his military duties and relegated himself to the position of "advisor". Such a move would have represented a tremendous loss of face to others, but to Handayu it was simply a great relief.

Being a parent was very important and very fulfilling to Handayu. He could never forget the magical moment when his son uttered his first cry and drew in his first breath of life. It was such a relief to be able to devote much more time to the raising of the child who represented the outer fringe of his mortality. He never felt so useful and so responsible in all his days as a military leader. He was the father of a newborn soul with a karmic destiny that required much care and attention. It was instinctive and very personal. It gave Handayu a renewed purpose and a gratifying feeling of self-importance. That little child owed his existence to him. In all of Japan it would have been difficult to find a more doting father.

It is amazing how the indulgences of the parents mitigate upon their offspring like the past upon the present. The raising of a soul from infancy to adulthood is filled with hopes, dreams, and expectations that lie just out of reach, in the future. Unfortunately, Handayu would not live long enough to witness the day when his son, Tsutomu, would grow up to be baptized as "Paul", after Saul of Tarsus, by a Jesuit priest who felt that there were uncanny similarities between Saul's conversion to Paul on the road to Damascus, and Tsutomu's experience on the road to Nagasaki. However, to Handayu, his son, named after his grandfather the famous sword maker of Kogi, was just "Moo-chan" (abbreviated from the last syllable from Tsutomu) as he endearingly called his only child, the raison d'être of his earthly existence. Some nights when he tucked the little fellow securely into his bedding, he wondered, "How could I go on living if Moo-chan were taken from me?" At such times he was filled with such an outpouring of love and gratitude it was almost unbearable. However, exemplary as it was, it was all just taken for granted by the handsome little boy sleeping peacefully upon a miniature handmade futon lovingly decorated with tiny pink cherry blossoms by his mother.

Such was the early childhood of Moo-chan, Tsutomu, a.k.a. Paul Miki. A child of destiny raised on a diet of kindness, love, patience, understanding, and compassion. It was precisely the kind of early childhood needed to compensate for the desperate years to come.

CHAPTER THREE

Lassitude in all its human expressions knows no respite from the desperate lessons of history. What is important is the thread of growing awareness woven through a segment of existence, through then and now linking past to future in the present, creating meaningful moments as poignant as each breath drawn to sustain a beating heart palpitating within a confused and bewildered human being attempting to connect the dots that span oceans and circumscribe the world with lessons learned from past mistakes, leading to somber moments of illumination. As a connector of dots, where should one begin? From then to now? Or from here to there? It is an existential dilemma. Who has seen the end result when all the dots are connected to form a single image in the grand scheme of things?

It was very difficult for a Japanese-Canadian family recently evacuated from the West Coast of British Columbia to figure out how to connect the dots in a meaningful manner in southwestern Canada in the nineteen-forties. Particularly in the vicinity of the city of Lethbridge, Alberta populated with Mormons, Hutterites, Mennonites, United Brethren, and devout Christian sects of all variety and type, each claiming like the Catholics to be the only true church in Coaldale, Raymond, Taber, Picture Butte, or any of the other towns in the area. Into this divine mixture of Christianity was introduced a handful of Oriental pagans, mostly Buddhists, from the Pacific coast: untrustworthy and inscrutable *enemy aliens*, fit only for cheap labor on sugar beet fields, or if one were skilled, to cut hair, cook, launder clothes and such. It had been a long and difficult journey into near oblivion for a family with roots that could be traced as far back as the Katan Korakura of Tomakomai.

How in God's name did that ancient Ainu seed get scattered that far? It required a human spirit daring and foolhardy enough to challenge the mighty Pacific. It required a vision grand enough to see beyond the horizon, and the courage to follow a path, just like the Haida, Nishka and Inuit had done in times long forgotten, when ancient footprints across the Bering Strait were obliterated by cataclysmic forces. It required an undaunted free will, an imagination that soars on the wings of eagles, and a desire for freedom that knows no limits. That is how a tiny seed can span oceans, continents, worlds and universes.

* * *

On January 29th, 1913, the two Miki brothers were living on the bayside of Nagasaki on their own. They were tall, strong, hardworking, responsible young men in their early twenties, descendents from a long line of Mikis. Their grandparents were stout *Kakure Kirishitan* (or Hidden Christians), and their parents were lapsed Kirishitan with a leaning toward Buddhism. The taller and elder was a trained carpenter and fisherman named Kasuzimo, and his slightly shorter brother who was younger by two and a half years, was a net-mender, fisherman, and sometimes cleric called Hideo. At that particular time their respective lives did not hold much promise for excitement or adventure in a society nearly moribund with tradition. However, in the spring of that year an adventurous fisherman, who had been abroad for five years, stepped off the deck of an old Chinese fishing trawler that had been converted into a steamer. He caused quite a commotion on the dock. A substantial crowd gathered around him to hear first-hand what he had to say.

He was a flamboyant character with a flair for the melodramatic. He had returned from a faraway place called Vancouver to find a wife whom he planned to take back with him. He told a fabulous story of a land of freedom and endless opportunity where there was so much land it was practically free for the taking, and the fishing was absolutely incredible. Perhaps he was exaggerating, but the two Miki brothers just stood there feasting on every word he uttered.

The imagination is a powerful motivator. How they had dreamed! How they had spoken in wistful tones in the late evenings after a hard day of back-breaking labor that did not yield even the tiniest hope for future prosperity. How they had longed for an opportunity to try something new and challenging, something as daring as leaving the security of their homeland and, dare they even think it? Crossing the mighty Pacific!

What did they know about the perils of such a voyage? Who were they? They were Mikis, descendents from a long line of courageous samurai. They stood tall. They looked each other in the eye. They nodded and bowed respectfully to each other, and then they made a fateful decision. Some might call it rash, or even foolhardy. It was a decision that would forever change their lives. They too, would go to Vancouver!

It was impossible to find passage on a ship bound for Vancouver at that time of year. The only ship heading in that direction was the old converted Chinese trawler, and the Chinese captain was not taking on any more passengers. It was a quandary. What to do? In desperation, the night before the ship was to disembark Kasuzimo and Hideo packed their canvas duffel bags, and in the cover of darkness stealthily made their way down to the docks. With trepidation they leapt aboard the steamer's deck and hid in the dingy space behind the engine compartment. It took a great deal of courage and daring, or perhaps just plain foolhardiness, to do what they had just done. Now, more than anything else, what they needed was just plain, ordinary, unpredictable, dumb luck.

Fortunately, luck was on their side. The Chinese captain was an understanding old sea-dog who knew how to roll with the waves and compensate the ups with the downs. "Not the first time this has happened," he observed upon discovering the stowaways late the following morning as the steamer chugged across the open waves. "Lucky for you I was too frugal to hire any extra deck hands. Now I have enough cheap labor to make this voyage less strenuous on all of us."

In spite of the aggressive imperialist mentality of a few over-zealous Japanese military fools who thought they were still shoguns with a patriotic duty to *subdue the barbarians*, which over the years had created some animosity between the Chinese and Japanese, the captain displayed an attitude of kindliness and generosity toward Kas and Hideo that made the long and arduous journey across thousands of miles of treacherous water seem more like an exciting adventure, rather than a perilous battle for survival. It took over a month, with stops along the Hawaiian Islands, but at long last the old steamer chugged toward a distant shoreline that danced and shimmered like a mirage upon the horizon.

"Must be Vancouver," Kas said excitedly to his brother, as the faint outline of a harbor loomed up ahead.

"Must be," Hideo replied as he leaned over the bow to get a better view. "We made it!"

"*Domo arigato gosaimashita,*" Kas mouthed looking up at the sky. It was always good to be thankful.

Kasuzimo and Hideo had not heard of Steveston until the Captain yelled: "Vancouver is too busy; we will dock at Steveston instead." And so the old steamer turned south and crawled a few kilometers along the coast until it reached the mouth of the south arm of the Fraser River. The current from the river slowed the old trawler down even more as it chugged laboriously toward its destination: a large L-shaped building with a wooden wharf which projected out into the river. A hand-painted sign in block letters read: Britannia Cannery. The old steamer glided up against the forgiving timbers, and dock workers deftly caught the thrown ropes and secured the new arrival to the moorings. The gangplank plopped down and the captain strode across with a satchel stuffed full with official papers. After the paying customers had disembarked, Hideo and Kasuzimo struggled off carrying heavy loads of cargo. When they set their respective loads down on the wooden wharf, they both glanced up simultaneously.

"Is this Steveston?" Hideo asked.

"Yes. We have arrived," Kas replied.

Steveston was a bustling cannery and fishing village strung out along the marshy flats that formed the estuary to the richest salmon spawning river along the west coast of British Columbia. Dozens of canneries had sprung up along its shoreline attracting thousands of workers from a variety of ethnic backgrounds creating a veritable cultural mosaic. It was a mosaic into which Kasuzimo and Hideo blended quite unnoticed. There were hundreds of Japanese, Chinese, European, and Native workers all intermingling and working amicably together.

Almost as soon as Hideo and Kas had set down their loads and secured their own belongings from the ship, an elderly Japanese-speaking dock worker approached them and asked, "*Nihongee des-ka?*"

"*Hei,*" they replied in unison.

"Welcome to Canada," he said graciously, showing off his English. He introduced himself and politely invited them to his humble abode, as if they were his long lost relatives. Refusal was out of the question. He took them in and helped them to become familiar with their new community. His name was Masao. He had arrived in 1898. He took it upon himself to act as Canada's ambassador of good will. *Ogeesan*, as he was known, had generously welcomed dozens of Japanese immigrants over the years. He did so because when he first arrived, no one had welcomed him. He had stood on the dock alone, bewildered and confused, surrounded by strangers who were too busy to give him a friendly nod or a helping hand; he had stood there feeling totally overwhelmed with excitement, and no one to share it with.

"What is mine is yours," he said to Hideo and Kas once they were settled in. "Just help yourself."

In the years to follow, Kas and Hideo took it upon themselves to follow in Masao's footsteps. When ships arrived from Japan, they went down to the docks and made the new arrivals feel welcome in their new land. And it never failed; their kindness and generosity was always repaid with interest.

Soon after their arrival in Steveston, Kas and Hideo found temporary employment as fishermen and net menders. Their skills were in great demand, and they discovered that in this new land people were willing to pay them a lot more than they expected for doing the same work they had done in Nagasaki. They were hard workers who kept their eyes and ears open for better jobs and new opportunities. At first they associated mainly with other Japanese immigrants like themselves, but as time passed they intermingled more and more with Europeans, Chinese, and Native Indians. The common language of discourse was English, and consequently Kas and Hideo challenged themselves with the task of learning it as quickly as possible. To make it easier, they made up a competition with each other to see, on a daily basis, who had learned more new words and phrases. In this way they learned English very rapidly, so rapidly in fact that Masao, who prided himself on his English, said, "Vely good Engrish," whenever he heard them practicing on each other.

Three months after their arrival on the sturdy Britannia Cannery wharf, Kasuzimo, the elder Miki brother with the carpentry skills he had honed building wooden houses in Nagasaki, strode eagerly down the roughly hewn planks of the walkway leading to the

Cannery. It was from here that, according to Masao, fourteen years earlier on July 1899, the two hundred foot clipper called the "Titania", had set sail for the United Kingdom with the first direct shipment of Pacific salmon: caught, gutted, cleaned, cooked, and canned at Steveston. Kas was there to meet a fellow by the name of T. Atagi. He did not know what the T stood for. Everyone just called him "T. Atagi". A few days earlier when he had inquired at a fishing supplies shop about finding gainful employment as a carpenter, a total stranger who had overheard him interjected: "If you have carpentry skills, try T. Atagi. He builds the finest fishing boats on the west coast. He has a place up there past the Georgia Cannery at Garry Point where he flies the Japanese flag. You can't miss it." Kas took the stranger's advice and had arranged to meet T. Atagi at noon on the Britannia wharf.

It was twelve noon precisely when a small, slender, frail-looking fellow wearing a black felt cap and blue fisherman's vest sauntered up to Kas. "You are Kasuzimo Miki, I presume?" he inquired in Japanese.

"I am," Kas replied, glad to be able to use his native tongue. He carefully scrutinized the Oriental who stood before him. The little man looked slightly Chinese. Some Japanese look more Chinese than others; others look more Korean; and some look somewhat like native Indians. It all depended on the slant of the eyes and the shade of their complexion.

"I walked all the way down here from Garry Point to meet you because I need a man who has carpentry skills."

"I am a carpenter as well as a fisherman," Kas stated proudly.

"Have you ever built boats?"

"To be honest, no, but I can learn."

"Don't worry; all boat-builders are carpenters first."

"I'll do my best," Kas responded hopefully.

T. Atagi pondered the situation by rolling himself a cigarette from makings removed from his right vest pocket. When he had licked the paper, stuck the crumpled cigarette on the left side of his mouth, lit it with the deft sweep of a wooden match, and inhaled thoughtfully, he stated reflectively: "I can use you for three days a week to begin with." He paused to exhale, and through the smoke he added, "Perhaps you can also find part-time work at the Scotch Cannery."

"Scotch Cannery?" Kas puzzled.

Atagi flicked the ash from his cigarette, sighed as if weighted by a ponderous duty, and began, "Let me tell you a little about Garry Point... " he began. He methodically spouted off facts as if he had memorized them for the benefit of newly landed immigrants. He informed Kas that in 1905 he and his family had started a boatworks at the head of the northwestern part of the estuary called Garry Point, which consisted of a marsh-tidal-flat that passed for a slough. One drawback of the location was that the boats had to be built bow forward so that, when completed, they could be dragged through the marsh to open water. Some called the area Scotch Pond because in 1889 the Scotch-Canadian Cannery was built on the outer perimeter. It was an imposing structure built upon pylons on the water's edge.

"On the right side, from the land view, it is flanked by bunkhouses," Atagi pointed out.

"Very handy for the cannery workers," Kas noted.

"It is only accessible by a raised boardwalk that snakes through the soggy tidal-flat marshland," Atagi continued. "Prior to 1890, the Musqueam Indians had a settlement there. Always treat the native peoples with respect," Atagi commented after he had completed his history lesson. "This is their land. All the rest of us are immigrants."

"I understand," Kas replied with a humble bow.

"You can start on Wednesday," Atagi announced. "You can help me to build boats worthy of our craft."

"Wednesday," Kas confirmed.

On that day, Kasuzimo, carpenter, metamorphosed into Kasuzimo, boat-builder. Who knew such a thing would happen in Steveston, British Columbia, Canada?

* * *

Hideo Miki's path led in a different direction. It was not that he disliked hard physical labor; he had done plenty of that. It was his sensibilities regarding the nature of work. He liked work that had an artistic bent, work that required less brute physical strength and more of a delicate touch. Consequently he was attracted to a small sign in a barbershop window that read: "Apprentice needed."

The barbershop belonged to a Scotsman aptly named Scotty. It seemed everyone liked him because he was nice to people, genuinely nice. That was an invaluable trait for a barber. His only shortcoming, if it could be called that, was a nervous tic around his left eye which occasionally embarrassed some extremely prudish women who thought, perhaps wistfully, that he was winking at them. This tic, along with his many philanthropic interests which required a great deal of his personal time and energy, led to his decision to hire an apprentice.

When Hideo walked through the door of his barbershop, Scotty was busy shaving the face of a miner who had been in the bush for at least six months. Hideo sat quietly on a chair in the corner anxiously composing a sentence in his mind that would make sense in English. The barber glanced over curiously toward the young man in the corner as he shaved the coarse hair which was quickly dulling the edge on his razor.

"Are you here for a haircut?" Scotty asked, as he turned to re-sharpen the razor on the leather razor strops hanging below the counter.

Hideo shook his head, saving at least one spoken word from having to be uttered. He nervously arose from the chair as a sign of respect. "I-I," he stammered, "I have come to inquire about the applenticeship," he enunciated in near perfect English. His face turned slightly red when he realized he had made the dreaded error of mispronouncing an "r".

Scotty studied the young man between strokes of his razor. He liked his demeanor; he exuded a certain degree of eagerness and that vibe was refreshing. "I need an apprentice," he said as he rinsed off the razor at the sink.

"I start anytime," Hideo said hopefully.

"How about now?" Scotty replied as he wiped his hands on a towel.

"Light now?" Hideo asked in surprise.

"I thought you said anytime," Scotty responded with a grin.

Hideo took off his jacket and hung it on a coat hook. "I'ma ur-ready," he said with emphasis on the ur.

It was six-thirty when Scotty arrived home. "Guess what?" he announced to his wife.

"Your eye stopped twitching?"

"Close. This is going to relieve the stress."

"You hired someone?"

"You must be psychic."

"Who?"

"A young fellow by the name of Hideo."

"Sounds Japanese."

"It is."

"Good for you. Those people are decent folk."

"It was uncanny. I was shaving the hairy face of an old miner with skin like leather, when in comes this shy, young fellow and sits down in the corner chair. Call it intuition, but I just knew. I can't explain it. I just knew that young man was meant to be a barber."

Hideo became the first Japanese barber in town, and the best. His shaves and haircuts were done with artistic finesse. Barbering was something like cooking a meal; it is the cook who turns salmon and plain rice into a gourmet meal fit for a king.

The Scotsman had a lovely wife with humanitarian sensibilities by the name of Penelope; a name which she always felt compelled to explain was associated with some obscure mythological Greek legend. It was this tireless explanation that seemed to add an extra dimension of allure to a name that was alluring enough in its own right. Hideo first met Penelope when she dropped by the barbershop to clean out the cash drawer, and pay him his wages. It was obvious who held the family purse strings. She was frugal but fair, but that was not the quality that set her a cut above the ordinary. It was her kindness combined with an attitude which conveyed her belief that all human beings were created equal. Her presence in the shop always vibrated like a breath of fresh air in a stale room. She took an immediate liking to Hideo, and on that very day invited him and his brother over for supper. It was an evening that forever changed Hideo's and Kasuzimo's attitudes toward *hakujins*.

Penelope was a respected school teacher and a self-taught student of classical Greek history with a specialized knowledge of the Trojan War, in addition to being a marvelous cook and homemaker. Scotty, the barber, who was on occasion lovingly referred to by his wife as Ulysses or even sometimes as Odysseus, was a very lucky man and he knew it. In his clumsy way he heroically attempted to help out with the household chores in any way he could. He really tried, for the benefit of his guests, to at least appear to be useful for something else besides pouring drinks. He was more of a hindrance than a hero, so after he accidentally bumped into Penelope and spilled the *shoyu* on his new pants, she politely suggested that he retire to the living-room and concentrate on pouring drinks for the guests.

"Do you like Scotch?" Scotty asked his guests. He had heard that Japanese men loved good Scotch.

"Isa za Pope Cathoric?" Hideo responded, using a clever reply he had learned from one of his customers that meant, "Yes".

"That calls for a double," Scotty retorted, impressed by Hideo's quick uptake.

His doubles were more like triples, and soon Scotty found that the redder their faces got, the more jovial his guests became. He had no idea that the Japanese had such a fine sense of humor.

After a sumptuous meal, during which they communicated using a low grade of broken English, combined with many hand signals, the Scotsman's wife, on the spur of the moment, offered to teach Hideo and Kasuzimo conversational English. She did it out of the goodness of her heart.

"Conversational English will be of real benefit to you, Hideo," she explained, "because as you know, barbers have to keep up with all the latest gossip."

Later, try as they did, Hideo and Kas were not able to cross her palm with even one single penny for all her time and effort. "No," she would say stubbornly, "you need the money more than I do."

Penelope was an excellent teacher and after only a few months Hideo and Kas were able to more casually integrate themselves into the greater Canadian society using their newly acquired communication skills. They found that there were many others like the Scotsman and his wife who were kind, decent, tolerant folks, and that it was the ignorant who created the inequality, the prejudice, the intolerance, and the inhumanity.

"The world need more people like you anda your husaband," Hideo once told Penelope, showing off his much improved English, when she dropped by to clear out the cash drawer.

She blushed self-consciously and humbly replied, "And like you... and Kasuzimo too."

Except for such instances, unfortunately, their lives in their adopted homeland did not unfold like an idyllic adventure. Rather, in the harsh light of day, it unraveled like an historical documentary full of eventful details that in retrospect would fill the pages of historical texts with footnotes and anecdotes of man's inhumanity to man. It took on this depressing, stagnant aura because it was fashioned in an era where men and women lived awkward lives filled with left-over misfortunes from ages past. Mistakes were made, as if on purpose, to amplify the self-evident, so that later generations could analyze them and say with a tinge of embarrassment: "How could anyone have been that narrow-minded, that intolerant, that ignorant?" It provided a wonderful opportunity for human beings to learn from their own mistakes, providing they were aware enough to acknowledge them as mistakes, and had the integrity to correct them.

CHAPTER FOUR

On May 22nd 1916, Kasuzimo and Hideo Miki, being proud descendents of samurai stock, thought that with the First World War raging out of control in Europe, the patriotic thing to do was to enlist in the Canadian Armed Forces. However, to their chagrin and disappointment, they were both rejected and told they were not needed. Nobody would exactly explain why, although something was mumbled about Japs having poor eyesight. Anyway they kept their rejection papers as proof that they were as patriotic as the men in uniform were, and just as willing.

Rejection did not sit well with the Miki brothers and the feeling amplified an inner yearning for companionship and family life. Two years later at the age of twenty-eight and a half, Kas, who had saved a sizeable bundle of cash, booked passage on a steamship bound for Yokohama. He had been in correspondence with an uncle in Nagasaki who knew of a family who had a very pretty daughter who had seen his photograph and was willing to take a chance. Arrangements had been made to meet at the port in Yokohama, where, if all went according to plan, Kas could return to Canada the proud husband of a twenty-three year old bride called Yutsko. He took the opportunity to procure the precious samurai swords he had inherited from his deceased father, invaluable heirlooms that he carefully wrapped in many layers of burlap bags and secured with coils of rice-straw binding for the arduous trip back to the west coast of Canada.

When Kasuzimo returned to Steveston, bride in tow, to his amazement, his younger brother had gotten married in his absence. It was a wise move on Hideo's part because his older brother would probably have had serious reservations about such a marriage, since it was to a Métis girl of Scottish-Haida parentage named Joyce Greenaway. "Her father is a big white man with a bushy beard who talks like Scotty. Her mother is Haida," Hideo explained.

Two days after Kas had left for Yokohama, Penelope dropped by the barbershop to clear out the cash drawer as she usually did. As she was leaving she paused and said, "Would you like to come over for supper?"

"Of course," Hideo replied.

"I just hired a housekeeper. She will be cooking her first meal for us. Having a guest will make it extra special."

"Maybe I no come."

"Why?"

"I probably make her nervous. I remember my very first shave and haircut. Just havin' Scotty hoverin' around make me extra nervous. Imagine a guest being there to uh, sample her first home-cook meal! She can do without any extra stress."

"My, your English has really improved," Penelope commended Hideo, and as he blushed self-consciously she added, "Don't worry, she'll be just fine."

"You sure?"

"Of course. She's an experienced cook. I'd like you to meet her."

And so Hideo went and was smitten. What impressed him the most about the new housekeeper was her sensitivity combined with a subtle sense of humor that seemed to twinkle in her eyes as if she found almost everything he said to be humorous. At first Hideo thought it was his less than perfect English that caused the mirthful twinkle, but then as the evening wore on he noticed that it was still there whenever Penelope or Scotty were speaking. The twinkle, he surmised, represented something much deeper than mere humor; it reflected an underlying timidity, a shyness and vulnerability which masked an inner insecurity. It was far better than a scowl or a foolish grin.

It was not obvious to Hideo, but oddly enough, he had that same sort of twinkle in his own eyes, and he was not laughing at anyone in particular. Perhaps he was just amused by the situation in which he found himself, by the irony of his existence, then and there, in that moment. He thought he had free will – but there she was, and he had no free will at all. It was fait accompli.

What a memorable evening it turned out to be. The meal was excellent as far as Hideo was concerned, and he wasted little time in expressing his gratitude for being able to partake. "One of the best meals I ever had," he said politely. "I'm so grad you invite me over, Penelope."

"By the way, pardon my absent-mindedness," Penelope gushed, "Hideo, this here is our new housekeeper, Joyce Greenaway."

Joyce blushed. She shyly brushed a strand of loose hair from her face. She was standing to Hideo's right, and was about to pour him another cup of green tea, when Hideo turned to greet her. Perhaps it was written in the stars of his ambiguous horoscope: a trivial accident will prove quite fortuitous. Hideo's right elbow accidentally bumped the teapot causing the hot tea to spray over his new three-piece suit. In near panic Joyce rushed to the counter, grabbed an absorbent towel, and hastily began toweling off the wet spots on Hideo's jacket and pants.

"It's nothing," Hideo protested, "just a little tea. Don't wolly, it will dry soon."

"I'm so sorry, so sorry," Joyce kept apologizing as she continued mopping off Hideo's new three-piece suit with the single lapel.

Scotty and Penelope sat and watched like amused bystanders. What looked like a comedy of errors was actually the beginning of the human comedy. That is probably why both Hideo and Joyce had that twinkle in their eyes.

Hideo was a frequent visitor at the house after that. He'd drop around after supper on the pretext that he was helping Joyce clean up the supper dishes, but mainly he'd just hang around chit-chatting. They did not actually date as such; they just walked up and down the rickety boardwalk in the evenings holding hands and being happy.

Hideo never told her, but one of the reasons he was so attracted to Joyce was that, in his own mind, he thought she looked somewhat like an Ainu – not that Hideo was an expert on the physiognomy of Ainus. But nevertheless there was that magnetism that was undeniable. The magnetism was so powerful that it actually caused Hideo to suffer to such an extent that he could neither eat nor sleep. He agonized for weeks before he timidly asked Penelope for her opinion.

"What should I do?" he asked in anguish.

"Why are you asking me?" she responded.

"Because I respect your judgment," he replied, "and I have already experienced enough rejection to last a lifetime."

"You are afraid she may reject your offer of marriage?"

"Yes."

"If you are that afraid, then do not ask."

"What?"

"Is she not worth the risk?"

Put in that perspective, Hideo mustered up his courage and proposed. To his everlasting amazement and joy she said, "I thought

you would never ask." Hideo was at that moment, the happiest man
in Steveston.

Hideo's marriage to Joyce was a simple affair. They stood
together in the alcove of the United Church of Canada accompanied
by Penelope and Scotty, along with Joyce's mother and father. Hideo
was twenty-six and his blushing young bride was all of twenty-one.
The open-minded minister, the Reverend Peter C. Johnson presided.
When he said, "I pronounce you man and wife," Penelope shed a
quiet tear. She was such a sentimental humanitarian. The fusion of
Japanese, Scottish, and Haida bloodlines would no doubt produce
prodigious offspring full of hybrid vigor.

"Look at the hybrid roses, how they flourish, while the common
ones wither and die!" Penelope had remarked to Joyce the day before
while they were picking roses for the wedding.

Joyce Greenaway considered herself to be a Christian. Her
mother was Catholic and her father was Protestant. She preferred the
Protestant faith because it was a little more liberal, especially the
United Church. When she asked Hideo about his religious faith, he
had casually replied: "Whatever." What kind of an answer was that?
It sounded indifferent, but she could tell by his eyes that he was only
trying to be accommodating. Hideo was like that. He usually
attempted to head off problems before they arose. He was the least
abrasive person she had ever met, and the nicest. After further
probing he finally declared unequivocally that he considered himself
to be a "Christian-Buddhist".

At first Joyce thought Hideo was kidding, but he was not. He was
dead serious.

"Christian-Buddhist?" Joyce had inquired tentatively, not
intending to offend her husband-to-be, "What kind of a religion is
that?"

"It is more of a faith than a religion. I know this will sound
somewhat convoluted to you, but it is a faith unique to Japan. It was
the faith of my parents, my grandparents, and my great-
grandparents. They were Kakure Kirishitan. That means 'Hidden
Christian'. They were so hidden they passed for Buddhists. That is
how their predecessors had survived generation after generation
when they were being persecuted in Japan – by pretending to be

Buddhists. Later generations pragmatically integrated the useful features of each religion creating a much more functional and accommodating faith. They did not have to pretend so much after that."

"Ahhh – so," Joyce replied, mimicking her fiancé. "You are a Christian-Buddhist." She paused and reflected upon the incongruity of such an amalgamation. It boggled the mind in so many ways. The juxtaposition of the exclusivity of Christianity with the inclusiveness of Buddhism was certainly unique, to say the least. "I like that," she remarked with a slow grin. "I like it a lot. Maybe you can teach me how to become a Christian-Buddhist too."

Hideo smiled. Joyce was such an intelligent person, and yet, because she was Métis she had learned to express herself in a very modest manner, as was expected at that time in the social consciousness of a large segment of society who considered her to be inferior.

Shortly after Kasuzimo returned from Japan with Yutsko, his bashful young wife, he insisted that at some future date his younger brother be married in a proper Temple by a legitimate *Sensei* or Buddhist priest. Unfortunately at that time there was no *Bukkyo-kai* in Steveston, and so they had to wait until September of 1928 when the first Buddhist Temple was officially organized under the guidance of Toda Sensei of Vancouver, and the first President, Mr. Jiro Matsu. The Temple was constructed with the help of both Hideo's and Kasuzimo's volunteer labor on Second Avenue in Steveston. When the Temple was completed the stage was set for Hideo's and Joyce's "real wedding", but by that time Hideo had fathered two healthy sons. That made it all the more of a big deal.

It was a big deal. A very big deal. In those days there were not very many big deals for Canadians of Japanese ancestry to participate in, and so when the opportunity presented itself, everyone became excited with anticipation. Never before had a Japanese married a non-Japanese in a Buddhist Temple in Canada. It was a unique union and a singular opportunity to attract some good karmic vibes by demonstrating whole-hearted acceptance of this unique marriage. Almost everyone of Japanese ancestry, Buddhist or not, or whether or not they even knew Hideo or Joyce, expected to be there, because they were *Nihongee*.

All of Joyce's friends and relatives were welcomed, and nearly all attended. Ultimately it turned out to be a cultural smorgasbord of fishermen and cannery workers. Any person who had a shave or haircut from Hideo or Scotty, or said "Hi" on the docks to Kas, felt they were friends, and therefore entitled to attend. And so the little Buddhist Temple on Second Avenue was packed when Joyce, wearing a beautiful flowery, red and white silken kimono, with handmade caribou skin moccasins decorated with pearly white beads on her dainty feet, and Hideo, reserved in his three-piece single lapelled black suit and tie, knelt on a dais in front of the altar, and were properly married by Toda Sensei from Vancouver.

Afterwards a great deal of sake, beer, and Scotch whiskey, along with sushi, was consumed. Many red-faced little Oriental gentlemen, normally very shy and reserved, gave fabulous orations of affection in both Japanese and broken English to the bride and groom. It was almost a love-in, but with subdued good taste, of course. Whoever knew that Buddhists could have so much fun? Such a worldly wedding could probably never have taken place anywhere else in Canada. It was certainly a moment to be cherished.

The essence of that moment was caught in an old black and white photo that Hideo kept with him until he died. It was a photograph of Joyce standing by herself looking absentmindedly toward a window. The light cascaded over her like a blessing from heaven. She was so beautiful she looked supernatural. It was her bearing. Regal. Like Royalty. That is how Hideo treated her. Always. Like royalty. She was the Queen, and he was the Queen's husband. He was proud of it.

* * *

On January 13th 1926, over two years prior to Hideo's and Joyce's wedding at the Budddhist Temple, Kasuzimo's wife Yutsko had given birth to a seven pound three ounce baby boy. He was to be their only child. He was proudly named Tsutomu Paul Miki; Tsutomu after the maker of the precious samurai swords that Kas had brought with him from Japan, and Paul after a distant relative who was a famous Samurai and Jesuit Priest. However, by quirk of fate or simply poor phonetics, a simple spelling mistake was inadvertently made in Steveston, British Columbia that created a brand new made-in-Canada name: Tsutomu without the "s" metamorphosed on a parchment birth certificate into "Tutomu," a unique, one-of-a-kind persona. Would it auger well for his future?

After the birth of his son, good fortune seemed to follow Kasuzimo Miki around. Even in trying times, with his carpentry skills, he always found gainful employment. He was not one to simply take things for granted. Experience had taught him that those who were ungrateful attracted bad karma. Consequently over the years he had developed the habit of going down to the seclusion of Phoenix wharf in the crisp cool of the mornings and quietly exuding an aura of thankfulness in every nuance of his demeanor, as the early shafts of golden sunlight rose above the trees to the southeast and sparkled like shimmering diamonds upon the wispy waves as they washed in from the Fraser estuary. Such moments often reminded him of the early mornings he had spent as a youth fishing off the pier near his home in Nagasaki. It was a very clean feeling, a feeling of aliveness, of good health and well-being, of being centered in the moment.

After giving thanks, he liked to wander down to the Phoenix Cannery where he worked seasonally as a fisherman and net-mender. As an employee, he had been able to rent one of the duplexes in a cluster of sixteen weather-beaten two-story buildings just upriver. The second floor was used for storage and net mending while the lower level was furnished as living quarters. The entire cluster was known as the Japanese Duplexes, as they were rented mainly to Japanese employees. Kitty-corner across the boardwalk, where his Musqueam friend Tyrone lived, housing was provided for Native workers. The First Peoples House was constructed in 1885 and consisted of walls of vertical red cedar with batten siding, capped by a gable roof with wooden drainage gutters. Like the Japanese duplexes it was perched upon pylons to insure its dryness. The Japanese and native workers got along amicably. They were both beholden to the Caucasian owners and managers for employing non-whites at the canneries.

Being a carpenter, Kas was astutely aware of the architecture and construction of the various wharves and buildings that made up cannery row. The sturdy dock where he stood was constructed of thick, roughly hewn timbers set upon red cedar piles driven deep into the murky river bed. The dock hooked out into the south arm of the Fraser in such a fashion that it allowed large boats to easily moor and load up with cargoes of freshly canned salmon.

The cannery itself was a sight to behold. From a carpenter's view it looked simple yet pragmatic. It consisted of a large rectangular wooden structure about a third of a block in length with a steeply pitched roof that soared high above the shoreline. Perched precariously upon the apex of the A-frame roof as a precaution against fire sat dozens of wooden barrels filled with water. They were more symbolic than effective. They gave the workers inside a false sense of security. It was always hot and steamy inside with the humid air perfumed by the odor of uncooked and cooking salmon. The mixture was tolerable. It gave Steveston a distinctive scent of its own. To B.C. Packers it was the scent of money.

The scent of rotting fish guts wafted up from under the dock and filled Kasuzimo's nostrils as he stood on the cannery wharf and gazed upriver. He admired most of the old wooden structures. As a carpenter with a critical eye, he usually found fault with the buildings he encountered. "I would have done this or that differently," he would say. There always seemed to be room for improvement.

Adjacent to the wharf a small unobtrusive building held the title: Kishi Boatworks. It was just a shed in comparison to the mighty cannery. It was a modest beginning, but it was a beginning for many such enterprising Japanese immigrants. Ever since 1877 when the first Japanese immigrant arrived, Japanese fishermen and boat-builders had found Steveston to their liking. There was something about the confluence of river, ocean and land that gave the place a special quality. It was something like the melding together of yin and yang, producing a feeling of gestation, of pending parenthood imbued with hybrid vigor. It was like a magnet to all who gravitated there. "Nowhere on earth can compare to this," Kas breathed to himself. "*Arigato*," he mouthed to the illuminating sky above, "this humble carpenter thanks you most humbly for his many blessings."

"I hear you are a carpenter."

The voice startled Kas out of his meditative reverie. He turned around and saw a gaunt, withered-looking fellow wearing a leather apron with a visor cap perched upon the back of his head. "You heard correctly," he responded.

"Scotty, the barber, told me you were a carpenter. Do you know him?"

"Yes. My brother, Hideo, works for him."

"So that's your brother; I thought he looked Japanese."

"Japanese, Chinese, Korean, Native-Indian, Métis, sometimes it's hard to tell, eh?"

"My name is Otokichi. You can call me Otto for short, like my *hakujin* customers. That's my place upriver," he pointed toward the Britannia wharf, "across from the shipyards. I work there."

"What do you do?"

"I'm starting up my own business, I call it Murakami Boatworks," he said proudly.

"I wish you luck."

"I need more than wishes; I need a skilled carpenter to assist me from time to time. You know how it is with those heavy beams? They have to be planed to perfection and set just right."

Kas looked the slender boat-builder over with a heightened sense of interest. The sun reflected off a tanned face that appeared to be chiseled out of seasoned Douglas fir; the grain was weathered by a kindly demeanor. In a way he looked slightly native. He looked like he should be part of the landscape; the water, the dock, and the boat-builder blended together as if they served a common purpose. It was a common purpose that inspired him to reply: "Perhaps in my spare time I can be of some use. I have done some work for Atagi. Do you know him?"

"Of course – who doesn't? He is one of the best. His well-crafted fishing boats are famous up and down the west coast. That you have worked for him is the finest recommendation a carpenter can have."

Kas felt flattered by Otokichi's comment. "I am willing to try. I will do my best," he said humbly.

"When are you available?"

"My weekends are free. How about Saturday?"

"Good," Otokichi responded with a profound bow of gratitude. "Come up to my place after work, and we'll drink some sake and talk. My wife Asayo and I rent house number forty from Phoenix Cannery. I have built a *furo-ba* which you are welcome to use."

"You are too generous," Kas replied.

"It is I who is beholden to you. Together we will build splendid boats," Otokichi remarked enthusiastically, "splendid boats which will glide through the water with barely a ripple. I look forward to seeing you this evening," he added as he turned to go.

Kas watched as Otokichi walked away. He drew in a deep breath of appreciation. Good fortune smiled upon him, and he smiled generously in return. Sometimes things just worked out for the best. Kasuzimo Miki, fisherman, carpenter, and boat-builder, felt as useful as he had ever felt. It was good to get up in the morning and have a purpose, to be able to do something that made a difference for other people, to be a contributor, to help shape the community. That is why he liked to give thanks. Giving thanks made him cognizant of the gratitude and love that was his to share. It was his simple way of acknowledging "God's" blessings. He kept his religious notions to himself. He did not feel the need others did to seek comfort in numbers.

Whenever Kas was asked about his religious faith, he generally would respond by saying he was a "Buddhist". He did not like to say he was a "Christian-Buddhist" like his younger brother, because it required such an elaborate explanation, which in the end neither the listener nor he, himself, really understood. If the truth were told, he would have to say that his religion was the "no-name-brand." Yes, indeed, the no-name-brand! It seemed to Kas, as far as he was aware of such matters, that whenever a proper label was affixed to any religious faith, it tended to become fixated in the mind of its believer as the "one and only true faith". This led to an undesirable attitude which often resulted in a certain self-righteous form of exclusiveness that provoked hatred, animosity, and occasionally even war, all in the name of a label or brand-name that was supposed to represent God's abiding goodness, mercy, and compassion.

From convoluted reasoning like this – which seemed very logical to Kas – he professed, only to himself, to be an adherent of the "no-name" brand of faith. No wars were fought with self-righteous zeal; no one was tortured and killed with sadistic piety; no one was condemned to eternal punishment for being a pagan or infidel; not a single person suffered or was diminished in any way because of his religious faith. Kasuzimo felt blessed. There he was alive and healthy in the land of opportunity, Steveston, British Columbia, Canada, a free man standing alone on the shoreline where earth, water and sky merged, with gratitude in his heart for the good fortune that had brought him to that miraculous moment.

To look at Kas you would never know that he was such a deep thinker and a poet. In his private time he liked to indulge himself. It was natural to him. He took no credit for it. That was just the way he was born. It always amazed Kas, when he was a teenager, that many people did not do very much thinking. It seemed that their brains were in neutral most of the time, while his was busy cogitating over anything worth cogitating over. Because his brain was always engaged and open, he became the beneficiary of what he referred to as intuitive thought. Simple ideas and even the most complicated, esoteric concepts sometimes just came to him full blown, as if his brain were plugged into a Master-brain of which he was not conscious.

Once he awoke in the morning and said to himself: "I wish I could write a beautiful poem like that!" and then he realized that he had just dreamed the poem and that it had not yet been written, so he wrote it down and began to recite it. People who knew him asked, "Another one of your new poems?" To which he always felt the need to explain, "I never wrote it; a woman read it to me in a dream, and I just copied it." Someone else must have written it; some poet who had preceded him down his karmic path. Kasuzimo knew that if he had sat down with the intent to write that particular poem, it would have been an impossible task. It always amazed him that he could do stuff like that, while others could not. That is what made him into such an exceptional individual.

The years leading up to the Second World War were eventful. Kasuzimo built a lovely home near the water and continued work as a fisherman, carpenter, and boat-builder, while doting on the son who was destined to carry on the family name. On the other hand, his younger brother Hideo purchased half interest in the barbershop, bought a large older house nearby, and spent all his spare time raising four healthy children. Through the late twenties and thirties the Miki brothers had persevered and succeeded because they felt they belonged to their adopted homeland. They worked hard, sacrificed, scrimped and saved, as was befitting fledgling entrepreneurs, and were justly rewarded with a semblance of material wealth. It was a heady feeling to be part of the cultural mosaic that made up the Dominion of Canada, the true north strong and free.

CHAPTER FIVE

It was one of those incredibly ridiculous dreams that begged to be interpreted because it was so outlandish. It occurred in the spring after Hideo's fourth child had uttered his first distinguishable word. Kasuzimo had brought over his precious samurai swords and asked his brother if he would store them at his house for safe-keeping while he was in the process of enlarging his home. Knowing how important they were to his brother, Hideo had been reluctant to place them on display in case they were stolen.

"I'll keep them under my bed," he had said.

"Don't be silly," Kas had replied. "They are our family heirlooms. We share them. Put them on your fireplace mantle. They will look nice there."

But Hideo had not placed them on the fireplace mantle. Instead he had carefully slid them under his bed and placed an old rug over them for extra protection. It was directly over those ancient old relics that his fifth child was conceived. It was just prior to the evacuation and Hideo was approaching his forty-ninth birthday. He remembered it because of the strange dream he had around that time. He had woken up early in the morning and the dream was there in his mind as vivid as if he had actually been there.

The dream left positive and negative vibes floating freely in his conscious and semi-conscious mind, a mind grappling to make sense of the seemingly nonsensical. He dreamed that it was a beautiful fall morning. The sun shone gloriously in through a small, single pane glass window in the dusty prairie shack in which he had awakened. There was a feeling of despair and latent hunger, as if starvation was lurking inside the empty breadbox. The air in the small, cramped room that surrounded him smelled of the lingering scent of decaying prejudice combined with a pervading odor of injustice endured. It made him feel groggy and a bit nauseous. Then there was a noise beyond the flimsy, vertically slatted wooden door, a heavy muffled sound like the rolling of a prodigious weight. It stopped just outside the door.

Hideo crept out of bed, cautiously opened the door, and furtively peeked out. And behold, there, blocking the entrance was a gigantic, golden-orange peach, so round in circumference that it appeared as if it would barely fit through the doorway. Hideo was dumbfounded. A giant peach! Unbelievable! But there it was, plain as day, blocking the entrance.

Hideo leaned over the giant peach and ever so carefully rolled it inward so as not to bruise its perfect complexion. He rolled it gently over the doorstep and gingerly into the tiny house. Once inside the dingy room it radiated a golden aura that vibrated with a sense of hope and adventure. Suddenly Hideo's wife, Joyce, materialized beside him, and with her assistance, he managed to maneuver the gigantic peach onto the largest bath towel in their possession. And then, they just stood back and stared in utter disbelief.

After a prolonged moment of stunned silence, in which Joyce appeared to be bowed in prayer, Hideo mumbled, "Ah-men," as if the uttering of that word was somehow appropriate for the circumstances. Like a zombie, he shuffled off toward a narrow counter that served as their kitchen, and procured a large carving knife. "Perhaps we should taste it?" he suggested.

Joyce nodded. "We could cut it up and make many jars of canned peaches. There is enough, not only for us, but for all of our friends and neighbors. We must share the bounty."

Hideo tentatively held the knife above the crevice that indicated the divisional line of its two symmetrical halves. For some reason it reminded him of the mounded halves of the female genitalia. There was a distinct flavor of eroticism and latent orgasmic pleasure. The hand that held the knife quivered and shook as if in anticipation. With a grunt Hideo pressed down on the blade. The instant the blade was inserted the giant peach cracked open, ripe and juicy. But there in the center – instead of a peach stone – was a tiny infant, curled up fetus-style and sucking its thumb!

Both Hideo and Joyce cried out in unison: "My God! What is this?"

Joyce could not help herself. She immediately knelt and scooped the little baby from its peachy womb and cradled the babe in her motherly arms. It was a girl with an aura so powerful she actually shone with a shimmering halo of light. It was she who gave the peach its radiant glow.

Hideo gazed incredulously at the beautiful baby girl, and as he did, she began to grow and mature before his very eyes into an angel without wings. She danced and sang, and wherever she went people gathered to see her dance and hear her songs. Her lyrics had a profundity of meanings. They mirrored the depth of her personality. People listened as if enraptured. It was a unique union of poetry and music. Such resonance! It was a heavenly experience.

And just as Hideo felt overjoyed with gratitude for his special blessing, an ominous cloud began to gather overhead. The air grew dense and heavy as if perfumed with smoke. He struggled to draw breath. He coughed and coughed and his lungs felt as if they would collapse for lack of air. And then, as if by magic, the skies cleared and his gasping lungs ballooned with a fabulous gasp of freedom – and he awoke to find himself curled up fetus-style in bed next to his sleeping wife.

Later that same day when Kasuzimo dropped over for a visit, Hideo took the opportunity to share his strange dream with his older brother. Kas was always quite good at deciphering the undecipherable. He listened indulgently, nodding his head knowingly from time to time. He was a good listener, for an older brother. He rarely gave unwanted advice unless it seemed essential.

When he finished describing his dream, Hideo asked, "Well, what do you make of that?"

"Ahh," Kas began with a sage-like demeanor, "remember that children's story our mother used to tell us when we were little, the one about the peach-boy?"

The light of recognition flashed across Hideo's face. "Momotaro-san!" he expostulated. "That was one of my favorites."

"Yes, the little boy who popped out of a giant peach and became a heroic swordsman."

"Ah-so, Momotaro-san, the peach-boy," Hideo reflected, a boyish grin spreading across his face like a happy memory.

"Your dream appears to be a variation on that theme," Kasuzimo further explained.

"What about the part where I cough and find it difficult to breathe?"

"Perhaps a premonition of things yet to come," Kas suggested in a sympathetic tone. He knew that was not what his younger brother wanted to hear, but there it was in his dream. "At least your dream ended well," he declared with a smile. "Don't worry," he added, getting up to take his leave, "after all, it was only a dream."

The next day Hideo removed the samurai swords from under the bed and displayed them proudly on the fireplace mantle as he should have in the first place. Still he had this feeling that stayed with him. It was just a notion embellished by the fact that Kas always claimed those old swords had magical powers. Perhaps it was nothing – but how could it be nothing? Were not those old swords something? Something crafted by the Magician of Kogi?

Sometime later after he had been informed that Hideo's wife, Joyce, was expecting, Kaz dropped by to pick up his swords. He predicted with the mystical conviction of a psychic: "Perhaps it was fortuitous that you placed those old swords under your bed. A child conceived over such auspicious relics will be gifted with the fighting spirit of a samurai. Do not belittle the power of these swords; that child could be a child of destiny."

* * *

Some days are more memorable than others. It was one of those warm autumn Sundays that both Kas and Hideo took for granted. At that time they thought there would be many more such days. But much later when they thought back to the good-old-days, it proved to be a day like no other day. What made it particularly nostalgic was their heightened awareness at that time. It was Penelope who had informed them with her school teacher's charm, that a knowledge of history makes each moment that much more memorable. She had emphasized "each moment," as if she was psychically aware that something momentous was pending. And like good students, Kas and Hideo had taken note. They could not help it. History was all around them in the old and new canneries, the wooden walkways, the wharves, the fishing boats that lined the Fraser, and the buildings of every vintage. They became aware of all of this, the details, the significance of dates, who had done what and when. They absorbed it like sponges absorb water and felt that they too were part of the ongoing history of Steveston.

It was Sunday, September 27th. The warm autumn sun reflected off the wobbly boardwalk that served as the main thoroughfare of the bustling cannery village. "This place has a good feeling to it," Kas remarked as he and Hideo began their customary evening stroll down the narrow wooden walkway that connected Phoenix Cannery near Phoenix inlet to Britannia Shipyards a few blocks upriver. Both sides of the raised three and a half foot wide cedar plank sidewalk were lined with weather-beaten fisherman's houses with tin or tarpaper roofs, shops of every kind, rows of net-drying racks, and a hodge-podge of structures required to provide services for a busy community of fishermen and cannery workers. They were all there for a purpose, to help the mighty conglomerate known as B.C. Packers, one of the largest fish processing plants in the world make money for its investors.

"Local history is important," Penelope had informed the Miki brothers the previous week when they dropped by to deliver some fresh salmon Kas had caught. She had been preparing a study unit for her class and the information she had laboriously collected from old newspapers and pamphlets with faded pictures of bearded men in fancy suits, needed to be shared, because it made one more aware of those who had passed on ahead, so that those behind could follow in their footsteps down the rickety old boardwalk to the future. "Come on in," she had insisted, "and take a look at some of the materials I have gathered. You will find it quite interesting."

They found out that originally the Pacific salmon canning industry was established around 1870 further upriver near Delta and New Westminster. However, by 1887 it had arrived in the better situated community of Steveston. At that time there were dozens of individually owned and operated fish packers operating up and down the Fraser. Harry Doyle, one of the bearded, well-dressed fellows in the pamphlets, the son of an American dealer in fishing supplies, got together with a clean-shaven enterprising easterner named Aimelius Jarvis, a Toronto investment banker, and formulated a clever plan to consolidate the many competitive individual fish packers into one single entity known in 1905 as the B.C. Packers Association. Forty-two individual packers were condensed into just fifteen large operators. By 1928, four years after the C.P.R. Cannery at London Landing had burned down, and B.C. Packers Association became B.C. Packers Ltd., they controlled over fifty percent of the fishing and cannery activity on the mighty Fraser River.

It was the outfit to work for. When the salmon were running, Japanese, Chinese, native Indians, and Europeans of all nationalities earned good money making B.C. Packers Ltd. very profitable. Inside the steamy canneries women worked alongside the men. Some women even kept their babies with them as they slit open the salmon, pulled out the guts, and severed their heads with razor-sharp knives. B.C. Packers Ltd. created hundreds of jobs for hundreds of workers.

"Thank God for salmon!" Kas exclaimed as they strode leisurely toward Britannia Shipyards, an impressive wooden structure built originally in 1889 as a cannery.

"This place sure has changed over the years," Hideo pointed out. "Remember the 1918-19 fishing down-turn?"

"The salmon stocks on the Fraser were devastated. It was a disastrous year for the canneries."

"It was disappointing to see Britannia Cannery converted into a shipyard."

"In some ways it was a good move," Kas reflected, "because now they have big contracts to repair and maintain the Anglo British Columbia wooden boat fleet. I did some work for them once. The pay was quite good."

"You have done well over the years, Kas."

"So have you."

"We have been lucky. Things have worked out," Hideo commented as they turned to walk back down the boardwalk.

"Why don't we stop by Murakami's on the way back?" Kas suggested. "Asayo has grown such a pretty flower garden."

"A nice reprieve from these drab surroundings... Yes," Hideo agreed, "let's drop by. Otokichi and Asayo will be glad to see us,"

After a delightful tea at the Murakami's, Hideo and Kas casually made their way back along the undulating boardwalk toward Phoenix Cannery. The declining sun spread orange and red fingers across the copper sky. Sunday was aptly named: sun day. It felt like a special day, a day to remember when times grew bleak from lack of sunny moments, in times when memories were all one had to warm the heart and refresh the soul.

Kas and Hideo slowly made their way west past Phoenix inlet toward the colossus of all canneries: the imperial pride of B.C. Packers with a footprint of over 38,000 square feet, built in 1903 entirely over pylons from twelve inch cedar boards in an elongated L-shape with the short side projecting out into the south arm of the mighty Fraser: a river full of hopes, dreams, adventure, and of course, salmon.

When the old navy cannon was fired to herald the start of another salmon fishing season, a grand spectacle of fishing boats raced out into the lucrative fishing grounds. The returning sockeye salmon gathering in large numbers as a prelude to their migration up the south arm of the Fraser River and beyond in order to spawn and reproduce their species provided the incentive for the fishermen to stake-out their spot and ensure their fair share of nature's bounty. Kas and Hideo had participated every year since 1916, except for the disastrous 1918-19 season. They had caught their share of salmon, and along with the other fishermen, had pitched the freshly caught fish directly from their boat into the receiving bins conveniently located on the riverside of the dock.

The fish were gutted and cleaned right there, with the waste dropped through a hole in the floor of the covered reception area, directly into the murky river waters below. When the fillets were cooked, packed into cans, and decorated with an assortment of fancy labels, the product was loaded onto tall ships and steamers for worldwide distribution. The best salmon in the world was canned at Imperial Cannery, the mother of all canneries.

The sun was setting. It had indeed been a glorious day to be alive. Kas and Hideo grinned at each other. What had they done to deserve such a good life? They felt blessed.

"You know?" Hideo remarked as they made their way homeward. "I don't feel so – so Japanese anymore."

"You don't?"

They walked on in silence in the shade of the large, elongated shadow cast by the Imperial Cannery. As they emerged into the sunlight which snaked down the boardwalk like a river of bronze, Hideo finally replied, "More and more I feel like...." He paused, searching for the appropriate phrase, "I feel like a real Canadian."

"A real Canadian?"

A fish jumped in the nearby ripples and landed with a belly flop. A slight breeze pushed a wisp of black hair over Hideo's weathered face. He brushed it aside thoughtfully with his right hand and pushed his left deeper into his trouser pocket as if searching for an answer that had been misplaced there. "Sometimes," he began, "I-I feel like my wife Joyce feels. I feel I belong here."

The setting sun revealed a look of understanding and empathy on Kasuzimo's deeply tanned features. He looked decidedly native in the glowing sunlight. "So do I," he admitted timidly as his face broke into a self-conscious smile, "So do I."

The Miki brothers stood and stared at one another. What were they saying?

"Joyce thinks we look somewhat 'Haida'."

"She does?"

"Yes."

"I wonder why?"

"Her father told her that it is remotely possible that the Haida may have originated from northern Japan."

"Perhaps that is why we feel like... ah-ah, aboriginals."

"Yeah... real Canadians."

CHAPTER SIX

Racial prejudice is an ugly thing. With the outbreak of World War II it emerged from the cesspools of humanity and the foul odor was offensive to all it affected. In anticipation of expected criminal behavior, all Japanese Canadians living on the West Coast were fingerprinted, photographed, and required to carry a registration card at all times. In January of 1941, (nearly a full year before Pearl Harbor was attacked) a prominent BC politician named John Hart increased the stench by persuading the federal Liberal Party to invoke the War Measures Act in order to persecute all Canadians of Japanese ancestry (as Japan was part of the Axis coalition along with Germany and Italy). The Prime Minister was moved to action by the obnoxious advice received from Hart and other like-minded citizens such as Federal Minister Ian Mackenzie, who proposed the catchy slogan: "No Japs from the Rockies to the Seas." Mistaking the obnoxious odor for perfume, the Prime Minister passed an Order-in-Council in early 1942 removing all people of Japanese ancestry living within a radius of one hundred miles of the Pacific coast to internment camps. (The Germans and Italians, mercifully, were not included.) On March 4, 1942 all Japanese Canadians residing within that radius were given twenty-four hours to pack up and vacate. How long does it take to pack up a lifetime of precious memories and possessions? There was great anxiety and haste. What to pack in two suitcases? The order was so sudden no one was ready, not even the government agents. Where could they relocate thousands of "enemy aliens"? The "filthy Japs" were incarcerated temporarily in dirty animal stalls at Hastings Park Track in Vancouver. It resolved the immediate problem – but created a living nightmare, and set yet another racist stain on the magnificent landscape of "our home and native land".

When he received twenty-four hours notice to vacate his newly built home, Kasuzimo was furious. "This is so unfair! So unjust!" he ranted.

"I too have received the same notice," his younger brother replied angrily. "These politicians have singled us out because we are a visible minority. The war has made them into racists!"

"We cannot be held responsible for the arrogance of the Japanese military. We are Canadian citizens!"

"What recourse do we have? It is the law of the land. The RCMP is bound to enforce it. We have no option. We must comply as law-abiding citizens."

So Kasuzimo and Hideo, like most Japanese Canadians, accepted their fate with a quiet stoicism that would have made Diogenes the Cynic smile. These stalwart folks who came to Canada seeking freedom and happiness became the victims of hatred as old as mankind. It was not new; it was not an isolated Canadian creation; it was not even unexpected. It was as abhorrent as anti-Semitism, and as ancient as man's conception of sin. Framed by the great evil of war, it seeped out against the hapless Jews in Nazi Germany, and the defenseless Japanese in British Columbia. It oozed out of the pores of humanity like a cleansing, a scouring of every resentment, every jealousy, every unfulfilled act of vengeance, every drop of unrequited hatred that had fermented in the cesspools of human nature for millennia. It percolated to the surface and the stench was overpowering in its intolerance. The foulness oozed from the heart of darkness and engulfed a tiny enclave of innocent Japanese Canadians with a suffocating blanket of dread, just as it had done to an innocuous enclave of French-speaking Acadians, evacuated from the opposite Coast for no particular crime except being French, nearly two centuries earlier.

The vastness of the odor spread all the way from the Prime Minister's office down to the next door neighbor's outhouse; the stench was that pervasive. There was no escape. None. By November of 1942 all persons of Japanese ancestry, like the Miki brothers and their families, had to swallow the bitter taste of federally and provincially mandated racial prejudice and injustice. It was legal. It was the law. Twenty thousand eight hundred and eighty-one men, women, and children, of which thirteen thousand three hundred and four were born and raised in Canada, were rounded up as "enemy aliens" for temporary internment in animal stalls at the Pacific National Exhibition Grounds. All property, houses, farms, land holdings of any kind, businesses, fishing boats, and all personal belongings too large to carry or stuff into suitcases were seized, and later sold to the public for next to nothing. What happened to all the money raised? Most of it was used for the diabolical purpose of interning the hapless victims! That was known in the vernacular of the day as poetic justice.

There was an unmistakable desire by the Prime Minister's Office to make Canada "Jap free". Consequently every subterfuge was used to persuade the "enemy aliens" to go to Japan. Those who agreed to go were rewarded by being housed in better internment camps and given paying jobs while they awaited deportation. Some who could neither read nor write English signed up by mistake without knowing what it was they were told to sign. No one wanted to break the law. After much soul searching, Kasuzimo at the age of fifty-two, unlike his younger brother, decided that for the sake of his son Tutomu, he would do as he was advised by government agents, and return to Japan. But before he signed up he went home and discussed it with his wife Yutsko.

"This is no place for our son," he had rationalized to his spouse.

"But he dearly wants to stay." Yutsko had replied. "He said that we should just tough it out. He said, 'I'm Canadian; I was born here – and I will die here!' He was that adamant."

"He is only a sensitive teenaged youth, too immature as yet to understand what is going on here. The prejudice will warp his good nature into something hateful and vile. I have seen it happen to other people. It is very sad. Bad as things may be in Japan – can it be any worse than this?"

"We will be humiliated, perhaps even ostracized and treated like foreigners if we go back."

"My uncle knows some people in the Yakuza who still have some samurai honor, even if it is amongst thieves. They will provide for us until the war is over."

"Honor amongst thieves! What about our son?" she asked raising her voice. This was the first time Yutsko had spoken in such a tone to her husband.

Kasuzimo bowed his head in silence. Never had he been faced with such an agonizing decision. He had aged ten years. His face was creased with worry-lines, and his black hair had turned grey. Perhaps his wife was right. Perhaps they should stay and tough it out like his brother. Did he not tell his brother that he felt he belonged here?

"Perhaps, we should stay?" he asked with such uncertainty and despair etched upon his face that his wife burst into tears.

The moment devastated them both. They were on the brink of a desperate decision forced upon them by a government that considered them to be an unacceptable liability. What was the wise thing to do? They meditated together in silence, their heads bowed with humility. It would be the last time they would sit together on the comfortable old sofa in the living-room of the home they had so lovingly created in which to bring up their precious son.

Yutsko slowly raised her head and spoke in a voice that trembled and broke, "As you have said," she got up and walked over to the handcrafted shelf built in beside the picture-window and picked up a black and white portrait of Tutomu standing proudly beside their new fishing boat, "for the sake of our son," she nodded sadly as she wiped her tear-stained face with the back of her hand, "we must go back to Japan."

Kasuzimo and Yutsko hastily packed what meager belongings they were allowed to take with them into two large metallic suitcases. They had acquired so much over the years that it was very difficult to pick and choose. But most of all they were deeply depressed over the impending loss of their house, the house they had both slaved to make into the comfortable home in which they had planned to live out their declining years. But that was not to be the case. Not in Canada.

Kas drew in a remorseful breath as he carefully rewrapped his precious samurai swords in the same burlap bags he had brought them to Steveston in, and secured the package with the same rice-straw binding that had traveled so far. They inspired him to carry on with the indomitable spirit of a samurai warrior.

"Are we ready?" he asked Yutsko as he sat down wearily on a wicker chair

"I-I don't know," she replied hesitantly.

"Did you pack Tutomu's trophies?"

"No, he said he gave them to his friends who never won anything like that."

"Oh, he was so proud of them."

"He was crying last night, I think. When I peeked in his room he looked up and smiled, but I could see the wetness there."

Kas got up from his chair, shuffled over and tenderly placed his right arm around Yutsko's hunched shoulders. "God only knows what we have done to deserve this, but we shall survive one day at a time."

It was a cold, overcast November morn when the iron-clad freighter left the harbor. The ship was jammed full with hundreds of forlorn looking returnees. Kauzimo held his wife's hand securely as he looked about for his teenage son. A slight moment of panic struck him as he gazed searchingly over the milling throng. And then he spied him, standing alone by the railing facing the shoreline.

The breeze whipped Tutomu's hair into a confusing mess as he clutched the tubular iron rail with his left hand while waving longingly with his right to the craggy rocks, the spiky evergreens, the shiny tin roofs on the wooden houses that dotted the shoreline. He closed his eyes and visualized his uncle, Hideo, his cousins, and friends, waving goodbye at the pier. He looked up at the sky above the receding shoreline and bade a silent farewell to the land of his birth.

Tutomu looked so singular, so solitary, so isolated. Kasuzimo stared up at his only son with a lump growing in his throat. "Oh my God," he thought with a sudden sense of panic, "What have I done? That boy is a Canadian!" Tears of remorse slowly trickled from the corners of his eyes as he turned and hugged his wife so tightly she could scarcely breathe.

* * *

In the midst of this terrible cascade of unfortunate events, like a candle in the darkest night that flickers precariously, yet steadfastly refuses to be extinguished, Hideo clung tenaciously to his dream, his hope for a better life.

That tiny flame of hope was ignited unexpectedly in 1941 in the House of Commons, Ottawa, Ontario when the vote was called, for the invocation of the War Measures Act. Only one political party dared to vote against the invocation. It was the CCF or the Canadian Commonwealth Federation, which later became the New Democratic Party. A small, frail-looking, bespectacled human being rose up alongside his colleagues M.J. Coldwell and Angus MacInnis. It was the one man whom Hideo admired above all the other politicians, the Reverend T.C (Tommy) Douglas, the man who later as a provincial

Premier would bring Canada its first Medicare program. On that fateful day, the diminutive Presbyterian minister from Weyburn, Saskatchewan rose up with the integrity and honor of a hundred courageous samurai, and stood up on principle along with his brave colleagues, to be counted.

Hideo fondly recalled the uplifting words spoken around that depressing period by the courageous CCF member from Vancouver-Kingsway, Mr. Angus MacInnis: "We must always keep in mind that most of the Japanese in British Columbia – the people of Japanese origin – are not Japanese; they are Canadian." It was the tiny spark that ignited the flame of hope in Hideo's heart. After that, when the vote was restored to him, he always voted CCF or NDP. Always. It was a matter of principle.

It is amazing how long the offensive odor lingered. Some say that even today one catches a whiff of it now and again. By 1946, over a year after the war had ended, Canada's American neighbor, the folks who had had their Pacific fleet decimated at Pearl Harbor on 7th December 1941, had already allowed their Japanese-American citizens to relocate back to the West Coast, where their properties which had been held in trust, were restored to them. However, north of the forty-ninth parallel, the sentiment was quite different. The Japanese-Canadians were not allowed to return to the West Coast. It was not enough that their properties had been confiscated and sold off to pay for their internment. In addition, they had been dispersed helter-skelter across Canada effectively preventing them from developing any semblance of community. Although the war was over and the West Coast of Canada had not been attacked, yet the awful stench of racial prejudice persisted at the highest level of government. The Canadian Prime Minister, William Lyon Mackenzie King, signed an order (in 1946) belatedly deporting ten thousand, or the majority of the remaining Japanese-Canadian population in Canada, back to a bombed-out, war-torn, defeated Japan. Had not the Japanese-Canadians suffered enough?

Apparently the general population thought they had. After many were hastily deported (for no other reason other than being law-abiding *Japanese*-Canadians) there was a huge public outcry. The public was far more enlightened than the Liberal Prime Minister. Mackenzie King relented to public pressure and rescinded the nasty order.   However, those who had already been wrongly deported were out of luck, and their Canadian citizenship was not reinstated until the Redress agreement was signed in 1988. It was not until 1949, three long years after Japanese-Americans in the U.S. had been allowed to return to their west coast properties, that the federal government grudgingly allowed their Japanese citizens the freedom to move back to the West Coast. Years later classified documents confirmed that before, during, and after the war, Prime Minister Mackenzie King had been privy to information that clearly indicated that the military and the RCMP had not found a single act of sabotage or espionage by a person of Japanese ancestry living in Canada. The Japanese-Canadians were law-abiding citizens.   Out of fear, insecurity, and prejudice, a tiny visible minority suffered the wrath and racial intolerance of the majority of the citizenry of a democratic society, for being peaceful, law-abiding citizens in their own country.

"What is the use of complaining?" Hideo liked to say, "Things could be worse!" His attitude was contagious; it affected many of the susceptible Japanese-Canadians with a kind of blameless stoicism that enabled them to endure the lingering offensiveness of the odor. From 1946 to 1967, a period of twenty-one years during which hundreds of thousands of new immigrants and refugees were welcomed to Canada – all Japanese were excluded. How the smell lingered. However by 1967 there was a noticeable change in attitude. There was a new Canadian flag, and the world was invited to Expo '67 in Montreal by Prime Minister Lester B. Pearson, winner of the Nobel Peace Prize. It was a long time coming, but sometimes good things just take time. For the first time since the war, Japanese immigrants were considered to be trustworthy enough for citizenship in Canada.

"This country is still young," Hideo advised those with less patience, "in time it will mature into the paradise we dreamed it would be." His attitude never changed no matter how long the stench persisted. "Why do you think we are here?" he would ask the doubters. "Why is all this happening to us?" And without waiting for a reply he would answer: "We are but cogs in a greater wheel, the karmic wheel of justice. It will come around. You can count on it. Think of this as a learning experience, a growing awareness. Each of us will be stronger and wiser for it. All Canadians will be stronger and wiser for it. We all shall become more aware. Be thankful you can play a small part in such a grand undertaking."

Lofty as Hideo's vision remained, there were times when he could feel it slipping away. Frequently, seemingly fair-minded Canadians would attempt to justify the injustices heaped upon the defenseless "Japs". Whenever he heard that word it felt like a slap in the face. No matter how often he heard it, it always had a vicious sting. "The Japs," they would say with a grim look on their face, "not only bombed Pearl Harbor, but also committed terrible atrocities all over south-east Asia. Thousands of innocent men, women, and children were killed; villages were sacked and burned to the ground. Inhuman behavior! Prisoners of war were tortured and badly treated; the list goes on. This is not just hearsay; it is documented fact!" And they would stare accusingly at poor Hideo, with a knowing grin masking the latent hostility lurking beneath the surface.

"But-but," Hideo would feebly begin to protest, as he had done so many times before that it grew as tedious as it was ineffective, "that was not us." That was the sum total of his argument. Sometimes in exasperation he would raise his voice a decibel and add: "Don't You Get It? THAT WAS NOT US! We are Canadian citizens, just like you."

And as he sadly walked away, he would say to himself, "Not exactly like you. I would never treat my fellow-Canadians, like this."

Difficult as it was, life was not unbearable in a little town on the outskirts of Lethbridge, Alberta, Canada in 1942 for a beleaguered family of six uprooted from their coastal paradise and plunked down in Coaldale like a yellow plague on the fringe of a sterile white society. What would be the purpose of bringing a new life into the midst of such a desperate situation? Were not things desperate enough? Who would want to be born into such a family, in such circumstances? Who?

At that time it was difficult to foresee, but for Hideo Miki, his family of four children, and pregnant wife, it appeared as if their luck was about to change. There was a distinctive shift in the ebb and flow of duration that colored the spaces with a rosier hue. On the horizon there was a hint of optimism. In such instances in the grand scope of historical time, a ray of hope often shines through like a shaft of golden sunlight reflecting off distant hills on a gloomy and overcast day.

The world is full of signs and portents with various meanings. Who knows the way? The way of the flesh, the way of the spirit, the way of the world, the way to help make the earth a better place for humankind? Perhaps some day, out of all of this human folly, someone with a modicum of common sense, inspired by the bushido of a samurai warrior and fortified by the indomitable spirit of a Jesuit priest, will find a way to illuminate the long and winding path that meanders between the ominous shadows cast by the sword on the one hand, and the cross on the other.

CHAPTER SEVEN

The old man opened his eyes and gazed, as if awestruck, at the mystery of sunlight as it streamed in through the narrow window on the east wall of his hospital room and struck him full in the face. He looked down and admired the old relics at the foot of his bed. He felt much attached to those old swords. In spite of his vast wealth they were the only earthly possessions that he considered to be worthy of passing on. He remembered his father, Kasuzimo, saying to him: "Be worthy of them." How does one be worthy of such old relics in this day and age? The only thing he could do was share, share with anyone who would listen, what he had learned since acquiring them. He had learned a lot about his roots, and was seldom at a loss for words, because, strange as it seemed, those old swords spoke volumes.

He rang the bell for the nurse, unaware that it was 5:30 in the morning. The nurse on duty arrived in ten minutes looking tired and annoyed as if she had just awakened from a nap. She yawned sleepily and asked, "What do you want?"

"What time is it?"

The nurse squinted at the electric wall-clock and said, "Can't you tell time?"

The old man glanced sheepishly at the clock and replied, "I meant to ask, what day is it?"

"It's Monday."

"I mean what day of the month is it?"

"What difference does it make?"

"It makes all the difference in the world when you are as old as I am."

"It is the twenty-third day of August."

"Did you say August?"

"Yes."

"Just last week it was the twenty-third of July. You sure it's August?"

"Sure as I'm standing here answering your questions."

"How time flies when you're old!"

"Yeah," the nurse commiserated, "How time flies!" She reached over and closed the Venetian blinds on the window. "Why don't you go back to sleep for a while?" she suggested.

The old man curled up fetus-style, "I'll pretend I'm Momotaro-san and this bed is a giant peach," he said sticking his thumb in his mouth.

The nurse smiled, "Good idea," she replied, "it will be so nice and cozy in the peach, you'll be asleep in no time."

"Momotaro-san," the old man mumbled.

"Yes," the nurse whispered, "the peach-boy."

The old man closed his eyes, and in a few minutes he was sleeping like a baby inside a giant peachy womb, waiting to be born.

* * *

It took a scream and an excruciating contraction to force the fetus out of the cozy, warm womb into the cold atmosphere of reality set at precisely sixty-eight degrees Fahrenheit. It was quite a shock, being expelled like that after being nurtured for nine heavenly months. Prior to birth there had been so many choices, so many footprints leading in all directions. It was confusing, but the time was right and conditions were sufficient for manifestation. There were real concrete alternatives as substantial as the chromosomes that finally came together when a tiny sperm penetrated an ovum, and the future extended into the past giving rise to the present. And there she was dangling on the end of the future in the present tense, the latest link in the Great Chain of Being. One would have thought that such a chain would be anchored by something prodigious, something worthy of being the end result. Nevertheless, prodigious or not, it was connected to a six pound fourteen ounce, nearly hairless human being with a greenish sheen in the crevice of its rounded buttocks. It was connected to a soul as old as the Great Chain itself, and whose mortal existence gave the Great Chain its raison d'être.

When she was born an optimist might have said that she was a blessing to her grateful parents. On the other hand, a pessimist might have thought that she was just another mouth to feed, an additional encumbrance upon a struggling family consisting of three older brothers and an older sister. In any case, to honor the wife of Scotty the barber, who had been such an inspiration to her parents back in Steveston, they decided to name their newborn daughter Penelope. However, sentimental as the name was, it was rarely used. Instead, for practical reasons, and most certainly not an indication of her worth, she was known by all who knew her as "Penny".

Penny's parents were not wealthy. Her father, Hideo, was not the "Wealthy Barber," although he was indeed a barber. He felt pride when customers who had previously been to other barbers, came to him to have their crooked haircuts fixed. Sometimes in an attempt to inject a bit of humor into the situation he would ask, "Did your wife cut your hair?" or "Did she forget to use the bowl?" when he noticed a particularly ragged cut. Perhaps at times his humor was taken as sarcasm and customers with thinner skin would rather suffer with an inferior haircut than put up with such ridicule.

In down times business was slow and the family had to resort to penny pinching in order to make ends meet. The little village of Coaldale, just a few miles east of Lethbridge, was a tough place for a barber to make a living. Things might have been better in Lethbridge, but at that time relocated Japanese-Canadians like Hideo and his family were not welcome within the city limits. It was consoling for such newcomers to be able to find comradeship at the newly established Coaldale *Hopi Bukkyo-kai*.

The first Buddhist service was held on January 31st, 1943 in the Teramura home, a converted general store. The "little giant", Reverend Kawamura, presided. Throughout the war years services were held twice a month with the permission of the BC Security Commission and the RCMP. Who knew what subversive acts might be concocted under the guise of a Buddhist prayer service?

In 1945, the Reverend Gordon Goichi Nakayama was appointed by the Missionary Society of the Church of England in Canada to minister to the Japanese-Canadians who had been sent to southern Alberta. Gordon arrived in Canada in 1919 at the age of eighteen after he had learned English in Kyoto at Ritsumei School. He was welcomed by the Akagawas, a missionary family. Mrs. Akagawa was his great aunt, and her husband was a Methodist missionary. In 1942 Gordon and his family of four were relocated to Slocan City, B.C. and lived in a rustic log cabin during the war years. On August 1st 1945 the Nakayamas arrived in Coaldale where Gordon was given the opportunity to pursue his calling.

Gordon was a devout and hard working Christian, but given the times, a little deception was required for him to do the Lord's work. Because the relocated "Japs" were considered to be "enemy aliens" by the government, Father Nakayama had to use the good name of the Anglican Diocese in Calgary to purchase a lot in Coaldale. And then the industrious Father arranged to have an old building abandoned by the evacuees in Slocan City dismantled and shipped by freight car to Coaldale where it was reassembled by volunteer labor as the Anglican Church. Imagine the wonder of it? From internment camp to Church of God! God most certainly works in mysterious ways. In his first ten years in Coaldale Father Nakayama baptized over three hundred people.

Penny was not one of the people baptized by Father Nakayama. She was three years old when he arrived in Coaldale to save the souls of the recently evacuated. Would it have made any difference if she had been baptized at birth? But that would have been impossible since the good Father was probably still back in Slocan City then.

Immediately after Penny's birth, life in Coaldale took on a more austere appearance for the Miki family. With four energetic children and a newborn baby to raise, Penny's mother, Joyce, who took in never-ending loads of laundry from wealthy *hakujin* families to help raise additional income, was always occupied with one task or another. When money was scarce and food was scarcer, she would sneak out at grey-dawn and pick fresh dandelion greens before the sun came up, with the face-saving hope that no one would see her. She did it so that there would be food on the table when the cupboards were bare. She rarely complained. She just did her best with what turned out to be her lot in life.

It was during one of those austere, meager moments, a few months after Penny arrived home from the hospital, that Penny was involved in a near death experience. It was all the more significant and meaningful because it just happened to be her own.

At the time, the family was really scraping the bottom of the barrel in order to find a penny to pinch, and due to a lack of milk in the house and a fatigued mother, Penny was sometimes given a mixture of water and flour, which at least looked like milk. Consequently, it would seem to be unfair to hold Penny responsible in any way for her suicidal response. With hunger pangs ravaging her tiny body, she wailed with all her might for nourishment. Everyone was too preoccupied in the back room helping out with the oppressive loads of laundry that had to be washed, hand-rinsed, and hung out on the clothes-lines in the back yard to notice, so she cried and cried as if her life depended on it. Unfortunately her efforts were ignored, and her crying took on a desperate edge. It was a thin, high-pitched whine, so high-pitched it was almost inaudible. And then with a quick intake she coughed and a blood vessel ruptured, and a thin red blood mixed with mucus began to splatter from her mouth. Her crying took on a crazed desperation. It was a cry for life!

If only he had heard it sooner! That thin, high-pitched sound like the whirring of angel wings, that sound which haunted his dreams forever. "Joyce!" Hideo yelled at the top of his voice as he scooped the little baby from the crib.

How much blood is there in an eight and a half pound vessel of flesh and bone? Enough to dye a faded blue and white cotton baby's gown crimson red. Enough to give the panic-stricken parents time to rush Penny to the hospital, where to the Doctor's dismay her thin, anemic blood would not clot!

What thoughts and experiences were then locked indelibly into Penny's subconscious memory? When her life hung by a thread of divine hope, did she hear her father's fervent prayer?

"Please dear God, the God of all Gods and of all religions, please spare the life of this child and I will gladly forfeit ten years of my remaining life so that she might live a lifetime."

Was her infant life worth ten years of a mature adult's life? At that moment in time was it worth anything at all? Given the unexpected outcome, perhaps she should have been aborted months ago and thus spared her parents and herself this terrible ordeal?

However, if one has abiding faith sometimes miracles do occur. Is there a difference between a pagan soul and one that has been "saved"? Perhaps it all depends upon the sincerity of the prayers and the love, gratitude, and compassion that resonates within the human heart and within the Cosmic Consciousness that makes us all One. Through the marvel of blood transfusions from her mother and injections of Vitamin K to clot her blood, Penny's vital signs gradually returned, and her father's fervent prayer was answered.

Some say that life on the "other side" is infinitely better; it is like comparing heaven to hell. So why would anyone want to come back? Did she have a choice? Was it her call or her father's? Whatever the case, Penny clung to life as if it were everything.

Thus began Penny's existential journey into early life. As a toddler she seemed aloof and detached, as if she were in the world, but not of it. And as she grew older, she would lie on her bed and stare fixedly at the water stains on the ceiling for hours. The ceiling and the stains dissolved into a white tunnel of light, and she was whisked away on the magic wings of her imagination to the "other side", which always turned out to be "this side" turned face up. When she wanted to sleep without dreaming, Penny usually turned sideways.

There is an instinct for self preservation in traumatized children that is remarkable. When the world seems excessively harsh the tender soul turns from the extrinsic to the intrinsic world. So, even as a small child, Penny began to turn her thoughts inward to find the solace and serenity that seemed so natural to her.

In 1946 the city of Lethbridge lifted the restriction that prevented Japanese-Canadians from living within the city limits. Those living on the fringe, like Hideo, and had a specialized skill, looked to Lethbridge for greener pastures. Many skilled workers from Coaldale, and in particular Picture Butte, relocated to various areas within the city limits in a dispersed fashion so as not to draw unnecessary attention to the so-called "black heads". In the spring of 1949 when Penny was almost seven years old, Hideo at the ripe old age of fifty-seven, moved his family to south Lethbridge, near Henderson Lake, because an opportunity arose there for an experienced barber.

Penny remembered '49 fondly because on July 31st of that year she attended her first *Obon* service at the Rainbow Hall on the north side of Lethbridge. The service was conducted by the same diminutive – even by Japanese standards – minister who had presided at the opening of the Coaldale Bukkyo-kai, the indomitable Reverend Yutetsu Kawamura. How he could drone on and on during prayer services was beyond the limits of Penny's considerable patience.

On that particular occasion, she squirmed about so much her mother whispered, "Why don't you go outside and play with the other kids?"

Penny glanced over at her three older brothers and older sister. They were all too shy to go outside. "Kitchen Tarzan!" she taunted. It was a phrase the family used to designate a person who was only brave in their own kitchen. She wrinkled up her nose and quietly went outside to see what was going on. She returned ten minutes later and sat back down. "What is happening outside?" her sister asked on behalf of her brothers. She smugly replied, "Plenty for boys, but not much for girls."

In the evening the hall was cleared in preparation for the *Obon* dancing. Penny suffered from a slight stomachache from pigging out at supper time on too much *mochi*, even though it stuck to her teeth like chewing gum. Consequently she sat on the sidelines with her brothers and sister and just watched. She was fascinated by the colorful *Obon* dancers: women dressed up in their most beautiful kimonos dancing tirelessly around and around the hall smiling timidly with grace and pride. Some braver men, who weren't "kitchen Tarzans", joined in as well, and looked every bit as happy as the women. But most Japanese men suffered from *enyo*, a self-inflicted form of reticence that incapacitated them – even though they enjoyed the dancing thoroughly once someone dragged them onto the floor.

When they arrived back home, Penny badgered her father so much he finally broke down and bought her a small flowery kimono, which she wore at the following year's *Obon*. Shy as she was, because she had such a lovely kimono to show off, she got up and danced. It was mimicry at its finest. She was so cute, with her long black hair drawn up in a neat bun held in place with decorative combs, that Hideo could scarcely conceal his pride. "*Kodomo duh-keh*" he mumbled. Just a kid.

When Penny began her public school education in Lethbridge, her teachers said she was smart, but that she was wasting her time and her intelligence day-dreaming about non-essential matters. So in acceding to their wisdom she became a scholar: a person who knew the facts, and could regurgitate them orally or on paper. She studied hard, and her parents and brothers and sister who were also smart, were happy that she was not letting the family reputation down. However, being smart did not make her any happier; in fact, being smart simply led to rising expectations by everyone. The smarter they thought she was, the more they expected of her. It seemed like a "no win" situation. No one was ever completely satisfied about anything, including herself. But life continued to move on from year to year, and before she knew it she was on her way to the big Junior High School.

Penny's recollections of her teenage years were not all that pleasant. Just when she wanted desperately to be at the peak of her physical attractiveness, her hormones played a nasty trick on her. She became slightly overweight and her complexion was ruined by a few unsightly pimples. She had read somewhere that happiness consisted of seeking pleasure and avoiding pain. How could she do either? It was all very humbling and humiliating. It was the price of vanity.

Penny did her best to seek pleasure along the path that wound though her adolescent years. When she thought she was enjoying pleasure it was always fleeting, and even when it seemed to last longer than a moment it always ended with a vague feeling of dissipation. During this time the most unforgettable memory that seemed to stick in her mind like hardened chewing gum, was the time her good friend, Janice, whose parents ran a convenience store, invited her to take a walk with her around Henderson Lake. She remembered it because it was the beginning of her unexpected addiction to nicotine. It was a cold, windy Saturday in late October when the leaves were falling and winter seemed to be coming early. Penny had worn her blue nylon-shell jacket, and the cold penetrated right through it as if she were naked. For warmth they huddled under a giant cottonwood to seek shelter from the incessant wind. In order to generate extra warmth, Janice produced a nifty flat-fifty of cigarettes lifted from the storeroom behind her parents' store, and they shivered and smoked and chattered just like real adults, swearing and saying, "f... this" and "f... that" for emphasis. And then, out of pure generosity, Janice produced a full roll of chocolate-covered cookies from her ragged pack-sack and they munched and smoked, and smoked and munched in earnest because it was "so darn f... cold".

It was this combination of acrid cigarette smoke and sweet chocolate, as a defense mechanism against the teeth-chattering cold, that drew Penny, against her better judgment, into the inner circle of hardcore cigarette smokers who gathered in basements, attics, and old vacant buildings to "shoot the shit" and "f... the dog," figuratively speaking. These clandestine get-togethers were always highlighted when someone remembered to bring the chocolate cookies. Smoking and eating chocolate cookies at the same time made a few of the girls look pale and nauseous, but they toughed it out because it was important to be part of the clique. Who knew then that smoking something as innocuous as a bit of tobacco wrapped in thin white paper could lead to cancer and premature death?

Eventually one of the sickly-looking girls actually was brazen enough to refuse a cigarette. It was obvious they were making her feel queasy, especially when combined with the chocolate chip cookies that were on hand. Penny vividly remembered that occasion. The girl, whose name was also Penny, but was called "Pen" to avoid confusion, had said: "To be truthful, I really don't like the taste of cigarettes anymore; in fact, I never did like them."

This was a statement of utter heresy because the cigarette companies had brainwashed nearly everyone into believing that cigarettes were actually good for them. After that, it seemed to Penny that her namesake was shunned as if she had some dreaded infectious disease that would cause others to develop the same distaste for cigarettes. It was like the addicted huddling together to defend and reinforce their own addictions. On the last occasion that Pen showed up, Penny remembered going over to where she stood apart by herself. She was just about to say, "It took real courage to say what you said," but before she could speak, the girl looked her straight in the eye and said, "I hope you're having fun," and turned and walked away. That was the last time Penny ever saw her. In later years, when she reflected back on the path she had taken then, she often thought with considerable remorse, "Too bad that hadn't been me."

As a juvenile, Penny gradually drifted into a kind of hazy hedonistic despair bolstered by a cursory reading of an anthology of western philosophy by Bertrand Russell. Sex and the power of alcohol and other mood-altering drugs set her off on a journey of experimentation and exploration. She wanted to investigate the pragmatic parameters of hedonistic happiness. After all, both Jeremy Bentham and John Stuart Mill could not be entirely wrong. There had to be something profound about the "hedonistic calculus" by which one could monitor one's true state of happiness. However, it was difficult to ascertain, even in retrospect, whether five minutes of intense pleasure more than compensated for five months of remorse and guilt. Still she tried and was happy to note that such learned men as Bentham and Mill had trodden this path before her and had unselfishly left behind text-books filled with their wisdom in order that people like her could benefit from their passing.

Of course, her smartness gave Penny a decisive edge over her less-intelligent peers, and following her graduation from high school, she became obsessed by the sense of power this gave her. Being young and full of optimism, given the social milieu in which she was ensconced, she was filled with what turned out to be unrealistic expectations. To her credit, despite her youth and inexperience, she applied for and competed successfully for the highest paying jobs she could find that gave her a sense of power and control over others. Once she had a few years of experience under her belt, surprisingly, better paying junior management jobs came her way in spite of the prevailing bias against placing young women in such positions. She worked harder and smarter, so she thought, than any man she competed with. She enjoyed being the boss of others, for this made her feel like something more than an ant in a gigantic anthill.

Luck followed her in her personal pursuit of power in the capitalistic world. People liked her for her shy and demure ways. Chauvinistic male bosses found her to be not only intriguing, but also dedicated and trustworthy. She worked long into the night to please her superiors. No one worked as hard as she did. Time flew by unnoticed because each new promotion consumed every minute of the day.

In her mid twenties, opportunities for middle management became available in the oil rich city of Calgary, famous for its Stampede. It was smart politics as well as good public relations, even in those days, to employ a visible minority or two in high profile positions. The opportunities were there, if she played her cards right.

Penny examined her cards carefully. It was a mediocre hand. What did she expect? A royal flush? No, she did not know exactly what she expected. Even if she had a good hand, she probably would have thrown it in, because late one night as she lay alone on her forty-eight inch spinster's bed, it just dawned on her that being powerful and important did not equate with happiness. Her underlings both envied and feared her, while her peers looked at her with jealousy. The stress of continuing competition, of always needing to become more important and powerful, provided the impetus she needed to examine some of the other signposts along the pathway she was treading.

She noted with curiosity and excitement one evening as she was reading *The Outlines of Mahayana Buddhism* by D.T. Suzuki, that one of the signposts she had all but ignored until then, pointed to a path that originated in the Orient, and was extremely well worn by the footprints of fellow travelers who had preceded her to that moment. "Were they too in pursuit of personal happiness?" she wondered. "What had they discovered?" She was amazed to discover that even Orientals like Lao Tzu and Confucius, had passed this way and had left pages of wise sayings behind them. In her spare time she eagerly studied these pages and admonished herself for being so full of herself that she had not noticed them before. "Better late than never," she rationalized, as she set foot down a pathway that filled her with an exhilarating sense of destiny.

Penny was not a gambler – but for once in her life she decided to "Go for Broke", like in that old movie starring Van Johnson. She had everything to gain and nothing to lose. It was a sure bet. She had no qualms whatsoever when she calmly walked into her office in the tallest building in Calgary, the office that brought back poignant memories of her romantic infatuation with the previous manager, the sensitive young man who had hired her and who had been transferred to Edmonton, and solemnly typed out her resignation. How she had slaved and sacrificed to get that office! Now it felt like a cage. The air was heavy with the perfume of the office secretary; it smelled like captivity, a camouflage for something stifling: a loss of freedom. "I just need to get out of here," she explained to her boss. It was an inadequate explanation. "Sorry," she apologized humbly, "I know it probably sounds a bit rude, but I just need to get out of here."

Penny felt like a winner. "Win a few – lose a few," she used to say to depressed junior managers. But she had to admit, winning was nice. She had won her freedom back, her mental and spiritual freedom: the freedom to be herself!

To celebrate her new-found freedom she went camping with her good friend, Janice, near old Fort Whoop-up on the banks of the Old Man River. It was on this occasion that Penny went into one of her rare trance-like states which occurred from time to time when somehow she was able to tune in to the vibes of those who had gone on ahead. It could have been the shimmering waters of the Old Man River that caused Penny to stand there as if mesmerized....

"I can see them," she whispered, "there in the ripples!"

"See what?" Janice asked.

"The whiskey traders," Penny replied, "horses, wagons, barrels, guns, bags of colorful trinkets, blankets, tin pots and pans and...."

"You're daydreaming. Snap out of it!" Janice interjected.

"They are so dirty. Filthy! And smelly, like rancid urine and dried feces. Phew!" Penny exclaimed with a look of disgust. "They're in a hurry to get away. They are afraid!" Penny continued. "They are heading for the border."

"Afraid of what?" Janice queried, her curiosity mounting.

"You can see it in their eyes and the grim looks on their unshaven faces. They know the red-coats are coming. Look how anxious they are!"

"Red-coats?"

"Yes, the North West Mounted Police are coming to close down their operation."

"Really?"

"I can still smell that musty odor of stale sweat and damp whisky barrels," Penny asserted as the trance wore off.

"Smell?" Janice questioned, "I didn't think you could smell things in daydreams."

After that Penny began to keep a journal, and in it she faithfully recorded all the amazing insights that she could remember that had come to her in sudden bursts of illumination. In the months after she quit her job and languished in her tiny apartment with nothing else to do but think, the journal became her outlet for an unlimited stream of creative energy that flowed through her in the still hours of the evening. At times she was dazzled by her own brilliance and her immodest ego puffed itself up with unwarranted vanity and pride, a reaction not uncommon for the young and ambitious enamored by the creations of their own intellect. As a tribute to her age-old mentors, she had scribbled in bold print across the top of the first page, "The Way of the Sage in the Modern Age." Under that title she had neatly printed in smaller letters: by Penelope Miki. It was an auspicious beginning for an intelligent young woman aspiring to be a sage.

* * *

Penelope Miki gazed at the title page of her journal in the evening light that filtered in through the west facing window of her somber Calgary apartment on the last night she was to spend there before heading to the University of British Columbia where she hoped to further expand her limited knowledge. In the solitude of the moment she was suddenly overcome by an emotional outpouring that left her feeling withered and ever so humble. It began with a feeling of excitement that filled her with a pregnant anticipation that gave birth to a fabulous exuberance, the kind of emotional high an aspiring young actress might feel when unexpectedly presented with an Academy Award for best actress! It was a heady sensation: to be so selected, to be the chosen one. And then it dawned on her as the exhilaration wore off, "I am only a simple scribe attempting to make manifest words of wisdom that have already been thought by many wise people who have preceded me down this mortal path. Who am I to be taking credit for the wisdom of the ages?"

The question subdued her. "Who am I?" she asked feeling ever so small and unimportant. It was a question, the answer to which, would consume the rest of her natural life.

CHAPTER EIGHT

Penny was somewhat of a late-comer to campus life. Over the years she had diligently saved all the money her father kept sending her every month, even though she knew he could scarcely afford it. "It's enough that Dad gave up ten years of his life for me!" she often thought when the cheques arrived in the mail, but she kept them. These, along with the extra funds she managed to put aside during her dalliance amongst the semi-rich and semi-powerful became the "nest egg" which allowed her to attend the University of her choice, and to choose the courses that interested her without the pressures of economic expediency.

Her academic path wound through the dusty archives of libraries where Socrates still lived through Plato's pen, and Aristotle strode with the gait of a truly magnanimous person. In their wake, Penny began to feel ever so insignificant. Her vain sense of power and self-importance vanished, and like Socrates, she would tirelessly reiterate: "You know? The only difference between a wise person and an ignorant person is that the wise person knows he is ignorant."

Hardly a day passed without Penny discovering something truly remarkable to discuss with her many new friends and fellow seekers at the University of British Columbia. She was indefatigably animated by the light of knowledge; it shone through her like sunlight through a window, illuminating the vast stores of information lurking in the shadows of her mind. People said she looked transfixed with radiant happiness, but she was unaware of how she looked because she was enraptured by what she discovered along the pathway of knowledge.

And then one day, when she was nearing her twenty-ninth birthday, something happened that forever changed her perception of space-time. She was out for a refreshing meditative walk in the early morning near the coast when suddenly a dense fog drifted in on the coat-tails of a mysterious swirling wind that surrounded her in a fine mist. From the corner of her eye she caught the ghostly image of a person just disappearing out of sight. When she hastened to catch up, the person had vanished into the mist. "Who was it?" she wondered. And then, as the fog cleared, it struck her like something that was so self-evident that she was completely dumbfounded! All these wise and gentle people who had so enriched her life and made her journey along the path she had chosen so much more rewarding and fulfilling by unselfishly sharing their knowledge and life experiences with her, had one and all trod this mortal path, just like her, one step at a time. And, all of them were ahead of her – not behind her! She was behind them! Both the Buddha and Jesus of Nazareth were thousands of years ahead of her. The Buddha was approximately 2500 years ahead of her, while Jesus was about 2000 years ahead. "How could we have gotten our perspective backwards!" she sighed. "And all these years, I have been looking into the fog of the dead hand of the past as if I were the one on the cutting edge of the future for all mankind. My God, I thought I was first, but I am actually last! Everyone who has ever lived has preceded me down this path. I am behind them. They are all ahead of me! It seems so self-evident. How could I have been so unaware of something so obvious?"

Penny paused for a long moment to reflect upon this amazing insight. "Up until now," she thought, "I have been looking in the wrong direction for information and inspiration. When I used to think of my grandparents, I always thought, 'How can they help me? They are so old-fashioned and out of date!' Now I realize they are at least a hundred years ahead of me. And if one is not aware of this, one dismisses this source of information as being worthless, out of date and archaic, of no value in determining what lies ahead. How can these people who have gone on ahead of us share their wisdom with us when we are close-minded? How can we receive their vibes when we have tuned them out and turned our backs on them? Every human being who has ever lived," Penny reiterated to herself, "is ahead of me, and my ego put me first instead of last. How inconceivably vain of me! I have always had the wisdom of the ages at my fingertips – instead I chose to wallow in my own egotistical ignorance. Pooh on me!"

From that moment on a new awareness dawned upon Penny. Her attitudes and beliefs regarding time and perspective were significantly altered. She felt liberated from the shadows of the dead hand of the past. It was as if all this time she was only tuned into the AM frequencies received by her five receptor senses – and now she was able to receive the extra-sensory frequencies represented by all the FM stations as well. And it was all a simple matter of changing her attitude toward the past. "You cannot receive the signal," she reflected, "unless you tune it in."

* * *

It was one of those dull, grey days when she was feeling dull and grey that Penny walked into a little bookstore to browse amongst the volumes of stimulating titles on display. She had looked around for about half an hour and was about to leave when she spied a red and while colored paperback book sitting by itself on a nearly vacant shelf near the door. She absent-mindedly reached up and took it down. On the cover was a picture of a handsome young man with rich long hair. Perhaps it was his hair, long and shiny like her own, that enticed her to turn back the cover of the book entitled: *Autobiography of a Yogi.*

The book was written by Paramahansa Yogananda (January 5, 1893 – March 7, 1952). She looked on the back cover and discovered that a lot of wise and intelligent people had said a lot of wonderful things about this book. So she took it up to the cashier and bought it, thinking, "This will be a good day to curl up on the sofa and read."

Once she started reading she could not stop. This man was truly ahead of his time. He was the most authentic Christian thinker born in the modern world – and yet he was a Hindu from India. Amazing! "He knows God in a manner that every Christian should know God," Penny thought. "If only they knew God in that manner they would be able to transcend the minor differences and nuances that create barriers of mistrust, prejudice and hatred among the various denominations, and among the various religions of the world. His mission to the Occidental world was truly inspired."

The part in the book that most intrigued Penny was the section concerning a householder guru by the name of Lahiri Mahasaya (1828 – 1895). Lahiri's encounter with a re-appearing saint called Babaji was legendary. It was precisely the kind of encounter that Penny could identify with. It was as if she had been there and done that. She was so fascinated she wrote to the society founded by Paramahansa Yogananda in California, called, "Self Realization Fellowship", and ordered a color portrait of Lahiri Mahasaya. After it arrived, she had it framed and promptly placed it upon the kitchen table where she liked to work. Shortly thereafter an amazing thing occurred: a diamond stud appeared in Lahiri's left earlobe. "It's just Lahiri trying to look mod and get my attention," she rationalized at the time. The stud had since disappeared, but ever since that happening, she felt that he was just ahead of her, somewhere down the path, nodding his head in approval and beckoning her to follow.

Paranormal happenings are certainly not new phenomena, but at first Penny was very reluctant to share her experience with anyone because she was a very sensitive and intelligent young lady, and she was quite aware that to many people, anyone who had a paranormal experience was considered to be strange if not weird or both. However, shortly after this episode, another unexpected thing happened that Penny found to be personally illuminating. She had misplaced one of her fake diamond earrings. It was a stud, something like the one that had appeared in Lahiri's earlobe. She had looked everywhere and could not find it. The frustration drove her to look even harder. The day after the stud magically disappeared from Lahiri's portrait, she took a wool blanket she used as a cushion outside to shake out the dust. After she had shaken the blanket vigorously, she glanced down at her feet, and there it was sparkling in the setting sun! He had returned it. Had she not been so frustrated and so anxious to find it, perhaps he would still be proudly wearing it!

"Thanks Lahiri," she whispered looking off toward the distant horizon where the earth met the sky, "thanks for being so considerate."

Perhaps she was reading more into it than was actually warranted. Or was it another illuminating sign on her pathway stretching onward toward the horizon, turned golden by the haze from the setting sun, where, if she squinted her eyes and concentrated with all her might, she could bring into focus those microscopic figures disappearing into the cosmos. Were they aware that a kindred spirit was plodding along behind them, struggling valiantly to stay in tune with the higher frequencies of their vast experience?

CHAPTER NINE

The sterile white vastness of the far wall was marred by the presence of an electric clock. Its roundness was accentuated by chrome trim. In the foreground black hands stood out like sentinels against a sky-lit background, marking the journey of man through space, while a thin red second hand rotated around an eternity of duration one second at a time. It was a constant reminder to the old man that he was mortal, and that mortality was everything. There was no stopping it. All he could do was endure, as he had been doing for such a long time. Perhaps it was ingrained in the dharmic pathway he had trodden, one step at a time, just like everyone else. In lucid moments when he reflected upon such matters, the old man was always overwhelmed with incredulity: to be mortal in an infinity of immortality! And to be aware of this mortality! It was amazing. It was beyond amazing. It was miraculous. It gave meaning to a meaningless state of existence: it gave longevity to life, and made death seem natural. It linked dharma with karma. It turned zero into one. It made nonsensical thoughts like this make sense. It was taken for granted by almost everyone else because it simply was the way of all life.

When others prayed for immortality, the old man gave heartfelt thanks for his mortality. When others looked forward to leaving this miracle planet for some imaginary far-away paradise where they would live forever and ever, the old man marveled at the incredible life cycle of all mortal creatures, and saw in the evolutionary biology of their DNA the secret of the ages. When others wore their mortality like a dreadful suit of rusty armor pulling them prematurely into a black hole as fearful as a grave dug as deep as eternity, the old man rejoiced at his miraculous existence. Each day was a miracle; he opened his eyes and voila! Mortality surrounded him like a mother's love for her only child. And the older he grew, the more convinced he became, in spite of all the scoffing and insensitive comments about his senility, that mortality was indeed everything. Everything. Most people thought he was just a blubbering old fool, lost in his delusional world of fantasy, but those few who took the time to really listen had second thoughts. Some were even reduced to embarrassment and hidden tears. This old man was something else, and what he had to say transcended conventionality. It felt, rather than sounded like, the wisdom of the ages.

"In the entire universe," the old man liked to point out to the young Doctor when he dropped by to examine his medical chart in the morning, "there is only one cosmological constant that cannot be denied; it is awareness, awareness of being aware. The mathematical formula for this is moronically simple. It is $0=1$. Isn't that unbelievable? Does it not fly in the face of logic? And yet, and yet, you do exist do you not, my good Doctor? You exist as if in spite of the logical fact that something cannot be created out of nothing. Perhaps you are that something that exists in spite? Have you not always existed in some form or other, and could that be why you continue to exist now in this particular moment of eternity? You must be the cosmological constant that allows mortality to be created out of immortality. You represent the formula of your own mortal awareness: $0=1$. You are the One who is aware of the Zero... you represent the equality, the resonance, the unity, the equation that gives meaning to the paradox... the cosmological constant."

"My, but you are lucid today," the young Doctor would respond with a puzzled smile on such occasions, but he often left the room wondering, "Could that old man be right?"

At first glance the old man looked just like any other bed-ridden senior citizen, but upon closer scrutiny there seemed to be something special about him, something acutely enigmatic. Physically, he appeared to be much older than his chronological age. It was the cumulative effect of a lifetime of unrelenting stress and anxiety. He melded in with his sterile white surroundings, an impotent old man personifying a wasteland of devastation and destruction. It was all there encapsulated in that decrepit bag of withered flesh and bones, living memories of the horrendous experiences that made his life into a tragic comedy of errors.

A month after his arrival at the hospital the head nurse had formed the opinion that the old man was at certain times "delusional". Her opinion was based not only upon her professional training as a therapeutic nurse, but more importantly, upon her personal observations. When she first heard the old fellow talking to himself, she dismissed it as being relatively common behavior for a person of his advanced years. But then to her amazement she discovered late one evening that the old man was not talking to himself, he was talking to an audience, an invisible or imaginary audience! Now that did seem a little odd at first; however the longer this behavior persisted, the more natural it seemed. In addition to this eccentricity, there was a singular incident that seemed to further substantiate her opinion.

It happened on the third of October, six months after the old man had been admitted. She remembered the date because that night in the solitude of her comfortable apartment she had written a memo about it to the young Doctor, whom in a bashful fashion she secretly admired. She had expressed herself in a professional manner she thought, on a perfumed piece of note paper embossed with her initials on the lower right-hand corner. The following morning she had carefully attached the memo to the clipboard tied to the foot of the old man's bed. She had been hopeful that the young Doctor would want to speak to her about the incident, but he always acted as if... as if he was not aware of who had written it. Perhaps he had missed her initials? The embossing was quite innocuous. Or perhaps he did not know whose initials they were? Did he even know who she was? The head nurse sighed as one who is smitten sighs when disappointed. The disappointment kept the incident fresh in her mind.

It occurred around 7:30 pm when she dropped by the old man's room to collect his supper dishes. And there he was, holding the empty tray over his head and quaking with fear beneath it. There was terror in the old fellow's dark eyes as they darted hither and thither about the room. The dishes and cutlery were scattered about the bed.

"What are you doing?" she blurted out, and then immediately realized that the situation called for a therapeutic response. "Can I be of any help?" she asked in a compassionate tone.

"Has the black rain stopped yet?" the quivering old man asked apprehensively.

The nurse glanced about the room and replied, "Yes it has."

"Don't drink it!" the old man cautioned, "It will kill you."

"I won't," she replied, playing along.

The old man shuddered and put the tray down. "Dry yourself," he soberly advised, and began toweling himself with the sheets. "Get that black death off of your body."

"I am," the nurse replied empathetically, pretending to dry herself while keeping a wary eye on the old man. "Thanks for warning me about the black rain."

"Don't ever drink it!" the old man reiterated as he sank back into his pillows, "It is a horrible death."

"I know. It killed thousands. Believe me, I know," she commiserated. "The black rain has stopped. It is safe now. Why don't you get some sleep?"

* * *

The nurses whispered amongst themselves in guarded tones; it was "absolutely miraculous", they said, that anyone who had withstood such a massive overdose of radiation poisoning in his earlier years could still be alive. But miraculous or not, there he sat, propped up in that sanitized hospital bed, a scrawny old man with bushy eyebrows and dark sparkling eyes that peered out over an imaginary audience that provided the occasion that justified his peculiar behavior. Some of the nurses, who happened from time to time to comprise membership in the audience, treated him with such reverence one would have thought he was a saint, but everyone knows that charlatans abound in a world that seems to be populated with an overabundance of shysters and con-artists. He was just a mortal being who had lived so long as to be considered by a few to be a sage. And just because he was old and had lived through many decades of human folly, it was generally accepted that his worldly experiences might actually count for something that in the infinitude of time, could just possibly add up to something more than zero. Not that zero is nothing. Zero is indeed one of Man's greatest thought creations, for without it the universe could not be quantified, as is presently being done by some of the greatest minds in science.

All in all, what was most remarkable about the old man was not his longevity, but his aura. It was most prominent when he pontificated before his imaginary audience. Those who happened to venture into his hospital room on such occasions were struck by his radiance. It was truly amazing. He glowed as if he were animated by an invisible source of nuclear energy. He lit up the room. It was electrifying just to be in his presence.

The old man had been patiently waiting to pass on for a long time. How many years had it been since the Doctor had compassionately said: "any time"? "Ha! What do they know of the human spirit?" the old man scoffed, and then stretched, rolled his eyes toward the ceiling, adjusted the pillow behind his back, procured a tissue from the box beside the bed, coughed into it, and drew in a desperately long breath. It was a desperate breath of life. How long had he been breathing thus? At least since he wrote that autobiographical piece about himself just prior – or was it just after? It must have been just before the Doctor had said, "any time". It had been a motivating factor. Anyway, it was a Story of the Times, as he had titled it, and at that time he had felt so good about it he had sent off a copy to his favorite cousin who lived in Canada. "What was her name? It started with 'P' and ended with 'pee'." It would come to him eventually; it always did.

He had visited her once. It was a long time ago when he was still full of brilliant ideas on how to make the world a better place. "Ah," he reflected, "two amazing weeks cooped up in that tiny apartment of hers in Calgary, Alberta. What was I thinking? I could have extended my stay. It was not imperative that I get into that yellow taxi and leave so abruptly. I should have stayed a little longer. We had so much to discuss, so much...." he suddenly brought his left hand up to his forehead and exclaimed, "Penelope! That was her name. She'd always say, 'Just call me Penny'." He turned and looked at the electric clock on the far wall. It read 9:30. The nurse would be coming around soon.

The old man sat up suddenly, jangling the rubber tubes that were connected to plastic bags above his head. He felt agitated. "I should have stayed longer!" he admonished himself. He clutched his chest while his breath wheezed in and out in a laborious manner. "Penny, Penny, Penny," he repeated to himself, and as he did he could see her hunched over a cup of coffee with a cigarette dangling carelessly from her left hand. She smoked with her left hand, a habit she had developed that freed up her right hand to pick up a cup of coffee, or write notes, or do a variety of things, while her left hand was always ready to bring that foul-smelling cylinder of nicotine up to her lips for a puff or two. That seemed to be her only bad habit. He had even smoked the odd cigarette himself just to be sociable while he was there. It made him feel more like her contemporary.

When he first heard from her husband, Larry Petijean – funny how he always remembered that name – about her untimely passing, he was devastated. He could not bring himself to believe it. It was preposterous that she could have passed on before he did. Preposterous! She was much younger than he was. "Too young," the old man said out loud, "Much too young!" He stared up at the electric clock once again. The red second hand rotated around the face, second by second. "We all have our time, time to do what we do. I should have stayed longer. I should'a, could'a, would'a; it is the story of my life!" he lamented.

He reached over and pulled open the drawer on the adjacent bedside stand. After rummaging therein for a few seconds he held up a white card with silver trim. It was a thank you card he had received when their children graduated from high school. It simply read, "Please accept our heartfelt gratitude for sharing. You are too generous. Find enclosed a picture of the four of us. Thanks once again." It was signed, "The Fearsome Foursome."

The picture was a lovely family photo taken on graduation day. Penny stood on the right and Larry on the left with the twins wearing caps and gowns sandwiched in between. It was the only photo of Penny that he still had; there had been a similar photo taken when the children had graduated from junior high that he had misplaced somewhere. As in the earlier photo, Penny looked every bit the proud mother. The children, Jerry and Sherry, radiated with hybrid vigor. It was there in their dark sparkling eyes, and their dark shiny hair. You could tell they were a real family: The Fearsome Foursome! "I should have taken the time to visit them," he chastised himself, as he turned to gaze at the portrait on his bedside table. He had framed it in mother of pearl with gold trim. They all looked so vibrant and full of life.

"To look at me now, you'd never guess that I too was once young, energetic, and full of life," he mumbled to himself. "But that was another lifetime; to most people a lifetime may seem like a long time, but it isn't. It's just a blink of an eye. In the blink of an eye a whole lifetime can flash by. You'll know how it is when you're old. Sometimes you doze off and before you wake up an entire lifetime is there playing over in your mind like a rewound tape. It is amazing how clear it all becomes in retrospect." The old man leaned forward and puffed up the pillow behind him before sagging back. The IV tubes dangling from his body made him look like a withered old puppet being manipulated from above.

"I visited hell once," he whispered secretively as if sharing information that was classified. "It has been rebuilt now. You'd never know it had been reduced to hell-on-earth, but I was there; I know. It turned me into a pacifist, and God knows what else! Speaking of God," the old man perked up, "did you know that the distance between heaven and hell is only that much?" He held up his thumb and forefinger to indicate the size of the gap. "A naval officer once told me that. Strange how you remember stupid things like that – eh? But it really isn't stupid. It just seems stupid when you first hear it. My whole life has been lived in that gap. I did not choose to live there. It just happened. You know how things are?"

"You know – funny how I keep saying that because you probably don't know – I actually have five cousins that I know of who lived in Canada, but I only got to know one of them. She was a real cool smoker when I knew her. I hope she had the good sense to quit. Smoking aside, it was a dream just to have made her acquaintance. She was really quite remarkable, but if you had known her back then when she was still alive, you probably would have said, 'What is so remarkable about her? She looks just like an ordinary, two legged homo-sapien like the rest of us.' Isn't it amazing how appearances can be so deceiving? I wish you could have really known her. But it's too late now, isn't it? Or is it? A very good friend of mine once told me that it is never too late. Never!" the old man expostulated with such conviction that a fine mist of spittle sprayed from his mouth. He procured another tissue from the tissue box and dabbed his lips gently. "If only you could have known her while she was still alive," he reiterated as he relaxed wearily into his starched white bed with a sigh.

The room seemed to close in around him filling him with a vague feeling of pending suffocation. It was moments like this that sometimes gave rise to sensations approximating sheer panic. Panic over what? The inability to draw breath. The old man shuddered and drew in a very deep breath of life-giving air. He relaxed and reminded himself once again: "It is never too late, never!" The reassurance brought a semblance of serenity to the dramatic tragedy being performed on the cerebral stage of his awareness. It was an awareness not unlike that of Hamlet, Prince of Denmark, when he insightfully stated: *To be or not to be; that is the question.*

"You know?" the old man asked rhetorically, closing his eyes and clasping his hands across his chest meditatively, "to paraphrase that greatest of great English writers, William Shakespeare," his voice trailed off to a whisper, "There are more things, between heaven and earth – than are dreamt of in your philosophy."

PART TWO

A THIRST FOR KNOWLEDGE

What is not clear should be clarified
What is not easy to do must be done
With great persistence.

Confucius

CHAPTER ONE

At his age with his experience and education he could have been something much more than what he turned out to be: an old armchair philosopher who had nearly burnt himself out with excessive cogitation. Some people in their eighties look like they are only in their sixties, while others, you would swear, look like they must be at least ninety-nine and holding. The old man was one of the latter. When he was fatigued and feeling listless, which seemed to be occurring more and more frequently, his skin took on an ashen grey pallor, and when he was asleep flat on his back with his hands clasped loosely across his stomach, the nurse on duty was usually inclined to check for vital signs. He was a shallow breather, and if the nurse watched carefully without touching him for fear of awakening the old fellow from a refreshing slumber, she could detect the slight rise and fall of the blanket just above his hands. Ergo, he was still alive!

It was a pleasant discovery the nurses made almost every night when they checked in on the 2:30 a.m. shift. Something kept the old man alive. He had energy: life force. It radiated through him like electricity through a light bulb keeping his feeble lungs breathing and his fragile heart beating. Where did he get such an ongoing supply of energy? He hardly ate a thing. His skin hung on his bony frame like an empty sack, and yet day after day, week after week, month after month he awoke in the early morning to face another day with a smile on his face.

In the early morning the old man was usually at his best. He was hardly ever at a loss for words. He never disappointed his invisible audience. They understood him. They were as patient and as long-suffering as he was. They were there for him. They were compassionate. They listened to every word, as if it were his last.

"An American naval officer once told me that the distance between heaven and hell is about that much," the old man said, holding up his thumb and forefinger to indicate the distance. He cast a bewildered look toward his invisible audience as he roused himself by shaking his head to loosen up the cobwebs. "Did I tell you that before?" he queried with a frown. "Anyway, what I wanted to tell you about is somewhat heavenly as well as hellish. Have you heard about Saint Paul? I mean Saint Paul Miki. He was one of the Martyrs of Japan. See those swords down there?" he gestured toward the foot of the bed, "They once belonged to him, and now they belong to me. I'm one of his long lost relatives. Can you believe that? Me, related to a famous Samurai and Saint! You haven't heard of him? He was a Kirishitan. Surely you know who they were? They were real believers. Let me see if I can remember...." He puffed up his pillow behind his head and stared off into the distance with a pensive sigh. His long-term memory was still very good, very good for an old man on his death bed.

He recalled that on August 15th, 1549, the saintly one, Francis Xavier, had reached Kagoshima along with two stout Jesuit companions, and began to piously plant the seeds of his faith in soil so rich he deemed it to be one of the most fertile of any he had previously encountered in his long missionary experience. Naturally such soil produced the most vigorous and staunch converts to Christianity. The city of Nagasaki was perhaps the most hospitable environment in all of the Orient for such seeds of spiritual redemption, and in true samurai fashion it also produced one of the most heroic examples of Christian martyrdom in the history of Christendom.

The story of this martyrdom had fascinated the old man when he first encountered it, and for various reasons remained stuck in his memory as if there was more to it than he could fathom. He stroked the thinning hair on his head and recomposed himself as if this change in creature comfort would produce a more profound clarity.

On February 5th, 1597, at about ten-thirty in the morning, Paul Miki and twenty-five other faithful Christians who had been forced to walk all the way from Kyoto, staggered under the loads of their roughly hewn crosses up Nishizaka Hill. It was one of those gruesome events that put the name Nagasaki on the map and burned it into the memory of every Christian living in that part of the Orient. It was not so much the brute fact of their crucifixion that made the event so memorable, but the manner in which the unfortunate twenty-six met their untimely deaths. No samurai could have been braver or more composed. These were true believers. They stood up against the persecution and torture heaped upon them, and went to their deaths with prayers upon their lips. Even when the crosses were set upright and came down with a thud into their respective holes, and the iron chains that bound their ankles to the cross bit into the flesh with the sag of their weight, they accepted all with a fortitude that made their martyrdom a formidable force in the mysterious land of the rising sun.

"Is that what it takes to be a true believer, a real Kirishitan?" the old man asked himself. It was the philosophical magnitude of his vast experience that enabled the old fellow to reflect upon the past, and with conviction confirm, "Ah-yes!" out loud to himself as he lay in a restful repose upon his sanitized hospital bed with the morning sun creeping through the Venetian slats dangling from the narrow window on the adjacent wall. "Unfortunate, but true," he lamented regretfully, "It seems we follow in the footsteps of those who have gone ahead without learning from their mistakes." Sad, but true, the history of the rise and fall of Christianity in Japan was sprinkled with many tragic stories of sacrifice, suffering and important lessons squandered.

Many of these stories had embedded themselves into the old man's memory as if they were more than just a recollection of something he had stumbled upon in the dimly lit archives of a university library. By happenstance, when he was a student at the University of Tokyo, he discovered the long neglected, but carefully preserved research papers of Professor Tagita, an insightful academic, who in the 1920's was the first to realize the social, cultural, and existential significance of the *Kakure Kirishitan*, or Hidden Christians of Japan. It was a study that seemed to resonate as if it were an historical part of the never-ending-story that unraveled as his life. It often gave the old man an uncanny feeling as if some distant part of himself had been there and done that, and that the reason he had stumbled upon it was an indication that there was some kind of lesson to be learned that had not been learned. On second thought, the word lesson was perhaps too moralistic; it was more as if a step had been taken, but in an undefined direction. What step? In what direction? It always filled the old man with a distinct feeling of nausea that he knew he could overcome, if only he could take a breath deep enough to exhale the staleness of every breath that he had ever drawn.

The old man recalled the time Penny had taken away his breath by unexpectedly asking him, with a bluntness that caused him to hold his breath: "Are you a Christian?" while staring at him with those curious eyes that made him feel as if he were being interrogated by the Inquisition. It was an honest question from an honest person. It deserved an honest answer, but he had responded by saying: "I'm not that insecure!" It was a pronouncement regarding his psychological and emotional status rather than a direct answer. Why had he been so evasive? The answer was there in the no-name-brand. Somehow he had inculcated that notion from this father. It was a convoluted concept, if it was a concept, of religious faith. How many hours and hours did his dear old father spend, especially when he grew feeble and near death, attempting to rationalize his go-it-alone no-name faith? In the end it made a great deal of common sense. But it was a lonely way to go. Just the three of them understood: his father Kasuzimo, his mother Yutsko, and himself. His father's final words were spoken with a slight smile upon his face. "If you like, you may call me a Christian-Buddhist," he said, "that's about as close as it gets." The old man scratched the right side of his head pensively, and as he did the tragic story of the Kakure Kirishitan rolled over in his memory like a snowball rolling downhill; with every turn it became more significant. He was that snowball: a snowball of attitudes and beliefs growing more aware with each revolution. No wonder he had been evasive when Penny asked him if he was a Christian.

It certainly was not science, but some might call it a paranormal experience, and thereby make it sound as if there was something more to it than a restless night. The night after he first had read about the Martyrs of Japan, he had eaten more than his share of steamed rice and tofu with green onions. He had a small stomach, and whenever he overate he seemed to suffer the consequences. At first he could not sleep. He was agitated by thoughts of people being crucified. He began to perspire and his breath came in shallow gasps, and then he drifted off into a state as insubstantial as the substance into which primary and secondary qualities are embedded, as the famous British philosopher John Locke had surmised. And there he was embedded like primary and secondary qualities in a substance as substantial as the person being crucified!

He cringed when the cross came down with a jarring thud into a narrow hole dug on top of Nishizaka Hill. And there he was staring into the pain-crazed eyes of Paul Miki. The eyes were liquid pools shimmering with agonizing convictions. "I will not recant. I will not recant," he mumbled hysterically over and over.

Not recant what? Give it up. Let it go. Just let it go for Christ's sake! How we cling so tenaciously to beliefs that make us what we are. He recalled the famous words of the Buddha: All that we are is a result of what we have thought. It was a simple concept, and yet he still had trouble comprehending it. It had taken so long just to become aware of it, aware of the entity called, "I".

And there "I" was grimacing with pain. He could see himself in his mind's eye. It made him feel so smug and self-righteous to be aware of himself, of what was happening to himself because of his beliefs. Suddenly it dawned upon him: it was the self-righteous smugness that was the problem. And now it had come to this. Crucified by his own convictions!

Did it make any difference? What difference? This difference!

"Death casts a long shadow," he thought. And then, behind him like a shadow cast from a great distance, loomed the apparition of a black-robed priest kneeling in prayer. For some inexplicable reason he just knew who it was. It was the sixteenth century Jesuit priest, the Patron of all Missions, Francis Xavier!

And then he sat up in bed, as sweaty and as mortal as the man upon the cross. Who did he think he was? And why was he being crucified?

CHAPTER TWO

It could have been a painting: the deep azure-blue sky, the emerald sea, the lush forested mountains spotted with quaint wooden houses. It was just as his Japanese guide, Anjiro, had described it two years ago when he was in Malacca. He had been so convincing: "You must visit Nihon," he had said earnestly, "before you get any older. It is time. The people of Nihon await you. You must bring them the word of God."

He did not feel all that old at the time, but it seemed to him that some Orientals had an uncanny sense about such things. During the rough sailing from Malacca, if it had not been for the skilful seamanship of the Chinese captain, Avan, he could very well have passed on sooner rather than later. But that was yesterday, and today? "Ah, 'tis like entering a magical scene from a fairy-tale," Francis Xavier commented to his two staunch companions as they stood near the prow of the vessel. "Truly this must be the most exotic place in all the Orient."

"They call it the Land of the Dolls," the companion nearest him replied.

The ship sailed serenely into the sheltered harbor at the southwestern end of the island of Kyushu. It was August 15th, 1549, and the culmination of fifteen hundred years of Christian piety was about to descend upon the unsuspecting shores of Kagoshima with the ominous thud of leather-cased feet.

It seemed like a very long journey – not the journey from Malacca – but the journey through Western Christendom that brought Christianity to Japan. It was a long, twisted, and convoluted journey, but alas, it had come to an end. Or was it just the beginning of a new journey?

The ship sidled up to the roughly hewn timbers of the wharf and rubbed up against it with the resultant squeal of wet lumber against lumber. Eager sailors waiting on shore lashed the boat securely into her berth, and stood by as the Captain prepared to disembark. There was a hush like that which exists just before a tsunami comes ashore. Breaths were drawn in and held expectantly, and then exhaled as the Chinese Captain descended the gangplank followed by Angiro and three strange looking *hakujin* wearing long black robes. The prominent one in front had a dark, short-cropped beard, dark bushy eyebrows, and a large protruding nose. Francis Xavier clomped down the wooden gangplank, across the wooden dock, and set foot upon the land of the rising sun.

He had come a long way since his birth at Xavier Castle in the Kingdom of Navarre, Spain, on April 7th, 1506. He always had an adventurous spirit and a questioning mind. He wanted to know things during an era when knowledge was dangerous. He just could not help it; his mind just could not be shut down and told to mind its own business. But in a way that was precisely what he ended up doing, minding his own business: God's business.

"Everything is God's business," he often reminded himself when people told him that certain subjects were anathema to the Church. "Everything is everything," he would say with a determined set of his jaw. What more was there to say? He was not always so adamantly pious. When he first began to study philosophy at the age of twenty-one at the College of Sainte-Barbe in Paris, France, it was his intention to embark upon a career as a scholar to wealthy patrons. His ambition at that time was to earn as much money as possible in order to be able to assist his parents who had fallen upon hard times. It was a noble and worldly ambition that elevated him a cut above the ordinary student, the vast majority of whom were simply there to find ways to heap glory and riches upon themselves. But that was before he met Ignatius of Loyola, a man of great moral and theological persuasion, fifteen years his senior.

It is no coincidence that great minds are often attracted to each other. At the College of Sainte-Barbe the brilliant minds of Ignatius of Loyola and Francis Xavier meshed with the result that the Roman Catholic Church was, in due time, to become the unsuspecting beneficiary of one of the greatest missionary societies of all time.

Francis Xavier received his Master of Arts degree in Philosophy in March of 1530. But what good is a degree in Philosophy when his calling was at odds with his intent? He had planned to profit by catering to wealthy patrons in order to be in a position to help his economically beleaguered parents. It was a difficult problem made even more difficult when his mentor Ignatius asked, "What profit is it, if you gain the whole world and lose your soul?" The question sat unanswered for many days, nights, weeks, and months in the voluminous command center of Francis' central nervous system. He meditated like a Zen monk yearning for Nirvana. It was a delicate balancing act: the whole world on one hand, and his soul on the other.

The free will of Francis Xavier was the fulcrum upon which everything was capriciously balanced. A free will tempered by a keen intellectual penchant for self-importance, enveloped by a labyrinthine ladder of chromosomes that spiraled back into eternity. It was a time of desperate loneliness, of bottomless pits of meaninglessness, and tombs of unforgiving silence where he cried out in his sleep: "Is there any divine purpose to my existence?" Without light the night was pitch black. If he vanished into the night what difference would it make? Why was it important that he make a difference? That he light up the night? What did it matter in the end? Perhaps Solomon was right. It was all just vanity and vexation of spirit. Nothing more.

Francis sank like a stone into the darkest abyss of meaningless despair. In the cold and damp of his austere little room the darkness of the long winter nights was so profound he cried out for a pinpoint of light, just the tiniest pinpoint of light upon which he could focus the spark of common sense that struggled to make a daring didactic leap of faith over the chasms of reason, which separated the nonbelievers from the believers. And then the words came back to him in a blaze of amazing grace: "For what shall it profit a man, if he shall gain the whole world, and lose his soul?" In the instant he became aware of the intrinsic significance of those words, he cried. Tears, unstoppable tears trickled over his cheeks and glistened in the darkness with the translucent light of enlightenment. It was his intellect and soul crying out together in the darkness for meaning and hope. That inner pinpoint of light was everything. It was the light of the Eternal Spirit. God had given him everything, and everything he did would be *ad majorem Dei gloriam*: for the greater glory of God.

In 1534 in a small chapel in Montmarte, Francis, along with seven other disciples who were instrumental in the development of the Society of Jesus, took vows to observe poverty, chastity, and obedience. The militant and autocratic structure of the Jesuit movement appealed to Francis' need for discipline and order in a chaotic world where might was right and anything, anything at all, could be passed off as a holy deed, if committed in the name of the Lord and Savior by someone of royal lineage claiming to been saved. What was needed in such a world were soldiers for Christ, staunch, courageous individuals committed to the highest moral code of honor, and rigorously trained, with no illusions about what their role in life was to be: committed human beings absolutely dedicated to serving God. They would be soldiers for Christ sworn to uphold the only true church of God, the Roman Catholic Church. It was a role that suited Francis Xavier like swords suited a samurai.

Three years later on June 24th, 1537, Francis was ordained as a Priest in Rome. And three years after that, the Society of Jesus was officially recognized as a functionary of the most powerful church on earth. It was organized to support the Papacy and was subject only to the sublime authority of the Pope. Naturally, the Pope of the day, being of sound mind, was favorably disposed. It was one of his finest moves. The Society was committed to supporting the orthodox Catholic faith against heresy, and provided a basis for a far-reaching missionary service, a service that would spread the Roman Catholic faith throughout the so-called pagan world, and in due course, bring millions of tithe-paying converts to the fold. Its first "General" was elected a year later in 1541. It was none other than the founding father himself: Ignatius of Loyola.

Soon after he was elected General of the fledgling Society of Jesus, Ignatius, with intuitive foresight assigned the future "Patron of all Missions" to work in the Far East. Francis was glad to be getting away from the putrid stench of the Spanish Inquisition, established in his homeland prior to his birth in 1478 by the Spanish Monarchy, and operated by the ruthless Torquemada. It was a political as well as a religious instrument that served man in the name of God. The torture, abuse, and persecution that took place in the name of Jesus Christ by men in black hoods wearing a crucifix, was a forerunner of those who would later perform similar acts wearing white hoods in a land across the Atlantic. It was the small-minded ignorance of those involved in such an abusive display of despotic power that most disgusted Francis. How long would the predestined Apostle of the Indies have lasted in such an insufferable environment? It was indeed fortuitous that someone with foresight had set him on a pathway that led to the mysterious Orient where his infectious love of the Deity would spread like a communicable disease.

On May sixth, 1542, after a long and arduous journey, Francis Xavier finally arrived in Goa. From there he launched missionary expeditions to India, Travancore, Ceylon, and Malacca. He eventually ended up in the fabled Land of the Dolls in 1549. It was as if he had finally reached his destination, a soldier of God with a samurai's mentality in a nation where honor was everything.

It was good to feel the scrunch of solid earth beneath his leather-clad feet as he walked along the shore at Kagoshima Bay. Francis Xavier bade farewell to the brave Chinese Captain, Avan, and his crew, and proceeded with his two stout companions and Japanese guide Angiro, toward an official looking delegation which had been sent to meet him. They had been expecting his arrival ever since he had sent them letters almost a year ago expressing his interest in visiting. Francis had on his person the necessary documents he had received giving him permission to land at Kagoshima. He extracted these documents and gave them to Angiro with the instructions: "Show these to the man in charge."

An important looking man dressed in an elegant black and white silk kimono, with a katana with a black silk-wound handle inlaid with gold trim on his left hip and a matching wakizashi on his right, stepped forth. "Francis Xavier?" he asked, pointing toward Francis.

"Hei," Anjiro replied extending the documents and bowing respectfully. Taking this as their cue, Francis and his two companions bowed humbly.

The entire delegation bowed in return. After examining the documents and returning them, the man in charge smiled and said politely, "I take you to see the Lord of Satsuma. Please follow me."

They were led by the imperial delegation of six smartly dressed samurai to a small town called Ijyuin, a short distance away. There they were ushered through the magnificent fortified gates of an imperial residence belonging to Simazu Takahisa, Lord of Satsuma.

The blood pumps through the heart a little quicker and the expectations are heightened when one is confronted with the unexpected. Francis had been in these kinds of situations many times before; he knew that it was imperative that he exude an amicable aura of good will. The invisible vibes overcame the language barrier better than a thousand mispronounced words and a hundred inappropriate hand gestures. It was important that he not offend the Lord of Satsuma, and so as one long accustomed to poverty, chastity, and humility, Francis bowed deeply and respectfully to the little man who sat crossed-legged upon a dais at the head of a long narrow room. On either side of him sat imperious-looking samurai with fierce-looking hairstyles, and very big swords.

"God's blessing upon you, great Lord of Satsuma," Francis said, kneeling graciously before the little Oriental as if he were the Pope himself.

Anjiro immediately translated the greeting to Shimazu, and he smiled agreeably. He was a good-natured and liberal person, rare qualities for one in such a position of ruthless power. For this reason, he did not have to be ruthless in order to maintain himself in power, because the people who served him genuinely liked him. "Welcome to Kyushu," he replied through Anjiro.

Francis reached into an inner pocket in his black robe and extracted an ornate silver crucifix on a silver chain. He had found from past experience that the voluntary presentation of unsolicited gifts usually elicited a kindly response. Such a gesture had the effect of reversing the tables and placed the receiver in the position of being beholden. He drooped the silver crucifix around his clasped hands and in a prayerful fashion presented it to the great Lord of Satsuma. "A small token of our esteem for your Lordship," he said through Anjiro.

An attendant stepped forth, took the silver chain and crucifix, and with a respectful bow presented it to the great lord. "*Arigato gozaimasu*," Shimazu Takahisa responded gratefully, nodding toward Francis, while accepting the gift with equally prayerful hands. The silver cross dangled from his clasped hands like prayer beads, and in that singular moment the dye was set and the stain was cast that would spread over Kyushu like a tidal wash.

The great hall became as quiet as a cathedral during early morning Mass when the cool air refreshes the spirit with the quietude of solace. There was a feeling of reverence, as if something awesome was unfolding as naturally as the rising sun, and the experience sent tiny shivers up and down the spine. It was not cold, but one felt like shivering.

The opportunity presented itself like the first glowing embers of the morning sun. "I would like your Lordship's permission to share the gospel of our Lo... our Savior Jesus Christ with the people of Japan," Francis Xavier requested. He was going to say Lord and Savior, but thought the better of it because Shimazu Takahisa was Lord here in Kyushu.

"We respect all religions here;" Shimazu replied matter-of-factly, "the people should be able to worship as they please." He paused a moment to reflect upon the foreigner's request before asking, "What sort of man is this Jesus Christ?"

"He is a man of God. A man of great integrity."

"An honorable man?"

"Yes, an honorable and good man. He is said to be the son of God."

"Said to be?"

"Who can prove such a thing beyond any reasonable doubt?"

"It is a matter of faith?"

"Yes," Francis replied looking at the questioning little man with surprise, "You are absolutely correct. It is a matter of faith."

This adroit response pleased Shimazu. There was no beating around the bush with vague answers and evasive posturing. He fondled the silver crucifix noting the heft of the solid silver: it had weight and substance. "In Nihon," he began, "some believe that only the Nihongee are of divine origin. Are not all human beings of divine origin?"

The profundity of the question, the egalitarian implications, the opportunity to display one's open-mindedness – or ignorance - was set before him with that simple question. Francis Xavier gazed up at the little man on the dais before him, and his eyes reflected his admiration and respect. He smiled for the first time. It was a radiant smile full of good feelings about a fellow human being. It was a smile that said: you and I are equals; and so, while smiling, he shared a secret that could only be shared among equals. He said, "Yes, they are," and then he lowered his voice and whispered so that only Angiro and the Lord of Satsuma could hear, and added, "But many do not understand this."

Shimazu smiled, displaying his missing left front tooth. He mostly grinned instead of smiling to hide this defect, but on this occasion one smile deserved another of equal quality. This dark haired hakujin with the large protruding nose was nobody's fool. "Tell me more about this son of God you call Jesus Christ."

Francis ruminated a moment then slowly responded. "Jesus was a human being like you and me, and he was of divine origin like you and me."

"What happened to him?"

"He was crucified."

"Why?"

"They did not believe he was of divine origin."

"Too often the enlightened are sacrificed upon the altar of ignorance."

"Sad but true," Francis commiserated. "We take our inspiration from his great sacrifice. He gave his life for our sins, our collective ignorance. We are beholden to his example. We refer to him nowadays as The Christ. He is the symbol of our faith."

"You honor his name and his deed."

"We honor him somewhat in the fashion that the samurai honor their Lord. We even call him our Lord. We worship the Divinity through him just as the Buddhists worship the Divine through the teachings of Lord Buddha."

The Lord of Satsuma leaned back and propped himself up by straightening out his arms behind. "Ah – so," he exhaled, finding the answers to his questions surprisingly satisfactory. It was stimulating to converse with someone who had such a deep understanding of such ephemeral matters. And to think that according to his papers, this man had traveled all the way from a place called Spain, at least a continent away, just to ask for permission, permission to share his faith. Such dedication was admirable. Who could refuse such a simple request from such an honorable man? "This man Jesus whom you call your Lord," he paused to draw in a much needed breath, "seems to be as enlightened a fellow as the Buddha. I would like to know more about such a human being."

Without hesitation Francis blurted out, "I shall teach you!"

A stony silence filled the room. Who did this bearded hakujin with the dark bushy eyebrows and large protruding nose think he was: a teacher of Lords? People with less conceit had forsaken their lives for such vanity. The Lord of Satsuma sat upright. He gazed sternly about the great hall lined with obedient samurai. He could not afford to lose face in front of all of these courageous and loyal men who would be willing to sacrifice their lives for him. He had to demonstrate his power and authority. After all, he was the Lord of Satsuma!

"Ha!" the Lord of Satsuma laughed. He would make a laughing matter of it. Humor would save his face and the foreigner's head. "Ha-ha," he laughed and pointed to the hakujin's head. "We shall call you the teacher-with-the-big-nose." A subdued murmur of laughter filled the hall. Angiro laughed the loudest, his relief was so great.

"You and your companions," the great Lord continued, "shall be free to travel and spread the teachings of Jesus to anyone you like." It felt good to be magnanimous. And as an afterthought he said to an attendant, "Provide the teacher with comfortable accommodations in Nagasaki, and see to it that he is provided with anything he needs. He is our honorable guest."

Francis Xavier bowed with deep reverence and issued such a great sigh of relief it resounded throughout the entire hall and silently resonated off the surrounding hills like an Islamic call to prayer.

CHAPTER THREE

A beautiful Japanese garden with Zen landscaping surrounded the modest shelter that served as home-base for Francis Xavier, his two devout companions, and Angiro, his interpreter and guide. Soon after they were comfortably settled in their new mission in Nagasaki, courtesy of the generosity of the Lord of Satsuma, a Buddhist monk dropped by to welcome them and to introduce himself. He worked part-time as the gardener for the new mission, and it was also his responsibility to see that the Lord's guests were well taken care of. He was a middle-aged fellow, about average height for a Japanese, with a constant smile and a bald shiny head that was as round as any head that Francis had ever seen. He had spent some time abroad seeking enlightenment in places as far away as India and the Philippines, where he had learned to speak English and Spanish quite fluently.

"I will teach you to speak Japanese in no time," Ninshitsu declared soon after meeting Francis Xavier for the first time. And like a sincere Buddhist monk he kept his word. During their many conversations at the mission it became apparent that there really were not all that many differences in the spiritual outlook of the Zen-Buddhist monk and the Jesuit priest. Perhaps it seemed that way because they were both more interested in seeking common ground rather than splitting hairs. Splitting hairs, they both knew from past experience, was a tedious business that almost always resulted in a very bad hairdo, not that that bothered Ninshitsu with his bald head. So they groomed the hairs, meticulously looking only for those hairs that they could coif and uplift into such splendid creations even the most self-indulgent geisha would be proud. By speaking in this roundabout manner they both were able to maintain the integrity of their personal religious faiths while romanticizing the other's. After all, these were intelligent human beings who realized, after all was said and done, that faith was faith, and you either had it, or you did not, and everything else was simply vanity and vexation of spirit.

Consequently, in no time at all they became very good friends. They were able to transcend their religious differences and appreciate the similarities in their chosen lifestyles. Both were human beings who had relinquished the worldly attractions of the sensuous world and devoted themselves to spiritual matters. Both were very humble. Both were chaste. Both embraced poverty. Both sought the enlightenment of the Divine. It was just that the cultural impact of place of birth, combined with the religious metaphors that they had grown accustomed to, seemed to appeal to their respective vanities in such a manner as to make each think he was the one who was the more compassionate, tolerant, and understanding. Of course, in order to be compassionate, tolerant, and understanding, there must be someone upon whom such virtues could be practiced, so they practiced upon one another.

The Zen-Buddhist monks with their white robes with black capes, and shaven heads that gleamed like copper plates in the noon-day sun as they trod along the busy streets of Nagasaki, inspired Francis to refer to them descriptively as "Bronzes." It became a nickname by which he addressed all such Zen-Buddhist monks. They did not resent this, because he said it with such courtesy and respect. Whenever Francis passed them in the crowded streets, their bronze heads bobbing and gleaming in the sunlight, he would say to himself: "The Bronzes are so humble; they would make perfect Christians."

It was in and around the friendly and religiously tolerant city of Nagasaki that Francis Xavier realized his greatest success as a Christian missionary. There was something divinely charismatic about this gaunt, large-nosed teacher who strode about the busy back streets and crowded alleyways preaching with the zeal of a man possessed by the truth. He really believed he knew the truth. It was this belief and this truth that emanated from him like a halo of light when he spoke. He did not just speak words. He spoke truth.

Crowds began to gather whenever he spoke. Twenty-five, fifty, hundreds came to hear the Teacher-with-the-big-nose, as he was affectionately known. Hundreds came and hundreds humbly accepted his words of wisdom. Why? Because his vision of the truth, the way he presented it, the look in his eyes, the fire in his voice – it was overpowering.

Few priests, no matter what their religious persuasion, had the charisma of the Jesuit priest later to be acknowledged as the "Patron of all missions". It was a missionary's dream come true to be so respected wherever he went, to be treated like a conquering hero, a soldier of God. These little doll-like people revered him because he brought them certainty in a world of illusion; he brought them hope and salvation in a life where suffering and death were commonplace. He promised them what no one else had: everlasting life! What more could anyone ask? And all they had to do was accept. Acceptance was very easy for a people conditioned to accept. All one had to do was nod and say with humility, "I accept Jesus as my personal Lord and Savior."

Allegiance to the "Lord" was not really a religious matter – it was an obligation, an integral part of the Shogunate-domain system. The problem was that the Christian missionaries were saying that it was a religious matter, and not an obligation, and they were persuading thousands that they were right. This was a serious matter, this blatant undermining of the Lord's rights and authority. There was something sneaky about it, something capricious. If this were allowed to continue, the foreign priests would command more loyalty from the common folk than even the Shogun himself. These were troubling thoughts. Sometimes they made Shimazu Takahisa feel a little uncomfortable, but he remained true to his word. The Christians would remain free from religious persecution as long as he was Lord of Satsuma. "I gave the teacher-with-the-big-nose my word," he explained to his advisors. "What good is one's word if one does not keep it?"

It was important to him that he personally exemplify the kind of honesty and open-minded tolerance that he expected from the people. The Christians brought a new vibrancy, a new point of view, and a new challenge to the musty old status quo that rejuvenated the mental faculties of the Lord of Satsuma and made him feel like a seeker after truth himself. There was something about the Christian faith that gave him hope, hope for a better life – if not on earth, then at least somewhere else. It was the hope that drew the people, a kind of hope that knew no earthly limits.

Partly due to the Lord of Satsuma's good will, and the overwhelming success his mission was enjoying in finding converts amongst the Lord's loyal subjects, Francis Xavier's enthusiasm was boundless. "Never in all my life have I encountered such perfect candidates for baptism," he confided to his two companions as they prepared for the baptismal service.

"They are so gentle, so courteous, so respectful, and so humble," his Jesuit companions agreed, "They are like ripe fruit, ready for the picking."

In less than three years, thousands of men, women, and children were converted to Christ. It had been a most arduous, but most satisfying task. Doing God's work was always most edifying. There was nothing else quite as satisfying as making a new convert. To feel the emergence of a new-found trust and acceptance reinforced one's own trust and acceptance, confirmed its validity and filled one's heart with gratitude for being instrumental in bringing one more lost soul to the fold.

Success like this had to be reported to his superiors so that others could be inspired. Busy as he was, Francis sat down in a moment when the joy of doing God's work lifted him to new heights of adoration for these little doll-like pagans and wrote: "The best people yet discovered," he paused and added, "a people who prize honor above all else," and he concluded enthusiastically with a flourish, "It seems to me that amongst pagan nations there will not be another to surpass the Japanese." The letter was signed, sealed and delivered.

In spite of his outward enthusiasm, there were some things about these pagans that troubled Francis Xavier. An incident occurred in front of a Buddhist Temple that agitated him long after it had happened. He had personally witnessed it at a short distance. It felt as if he were viewing a dramatic scene from a tragedy.

It occurred in the calm of the evening in the late spring of 1551. It was horrifying. As he was approaching the Temple where he was to meet his Zen-Buddhist friend, Ninshitsu, an ominous looking samurai, who was resting on an ornate bench adjacent to the Buddhist Temple, suddenly drew his great sword, and in a flash slit the throat of a well-dressed man who had paused in front of the bench. Beside the man stood a little boy, probably his son, about six or seven years of age. The crimson blood sprayed over the little boy, dousing him from head to foot; he just stood there watching his father crumple to the ground. He stood there a long time as if frozen with fear with the blood dripping off his face like scarlet tears, before someone came, pried him loose from his father's hand, and led him away.

There was nothing Francis could do except watch. When Ninshitsu arrived, Francis explained what had just happened.

"Pay it no mind," he said with a perturbed expression on his face, "These things happen from time to time. That samurai was probably a *ronin*. No self-respecting Lord wants their services. They bring us shame and dishonor. I will report this to Shimazu."

"Never have I seen one man dispatch another so quickly."

"No doubt he was once a skilled samurai of some repute. It will probably be difficult to find and bring such a treacherous individual to justice."

Francis stared forlornly at his friend. Needless death always filled him with a vague sense of emptiness, a hollow sensation. He was mindful of the senseless torture and killing the Inquisition was justifying in the name of God in his home country of Spain. It prompted him to rhetorically ask, "Is there no justice in this world?"

The question hung in the air as if suspended upon an invisible question mark. Both men were touched in ways that only sensitive humanitarians can be touched. It was another razor-cut into the heart of humanity, yet another imperfection chiseled indelibly upon Man's self image. It diminished mankind. Both men were filled with a helpless feeling of remorse, as if somehow they were responsible, responsible for the far-reaching implications of the question.

The question remained until Ninshitsu looked skyward and quietly said, "In the end karmic justice will prevail."

The tragic incident happened about six months before Francis was scheduled to depart for China. It stuck in his mind. "After I leave," he asked himself with considerable consternation, "what will become of these people?"

* * *

The sun was trying bravely to peek through the sullen clouds that hung over Nagasaki like a fluffy blanket. It was a steely cold day in late November, and Francis had gathered his meager belongings together for his mission to the foreboding country of China. He had serious reservations about leaving. It had been only three years, three short years. But had not Jesus' mission in the Holy Land been only three short years? And look what he had accomplished in that brief span of time!

In the span of three short years Francis had allowed himself to become very attached to the Land of the Dolls and its little doll-like people. He could not put his finger on it; it was something intangible, something mystic, like the way the mist clung to the mountaintops and shrouded the heavens with mystery. He could understand why the inhabitants considered the islands to be a divine creation. He gazed out the doorway of the comfortable abode the Lord of Satsuma had generously provided for him. The mist lifted just above the crown of Nishizaka Hill and the sun bathed the top with a sublime glow.

"Ah," he sighed, "What a magnificent site upon which to construct a grand cathedral, a cathedral to God." But that would have to be someone else's job. Already he felt the pangs of nostalgia. He wished that he could find some way to prolong his mission in Japan, but he knew that he was needed in China where millions of pagan souls were at risk. He just had to go. After all, it was God's work he was doing, wasn't it?

Practically everyone wanted him to stay. Even the Lord of Satsuma had politely asked him if he could use better accommodations. And his old Zen-Buddhist friend, Ninshitsu, had actually knelt down on his knees and begged him, begged him to stay. He was overwrought with emotion, a rare occurrence for a Zen-Buddhist monk. "Please do not go, my brother," he had pleaded, "this is a very bad time, very bad time to travel on the great Ocean." These Buddhist monks had developed a sort of a sixth sense about such things due to their over-indulgence in meditation, and his friend, Ninshitsu, seemed to have an uncanny ability to see events that had not yet come to pass. It was ironic, at least on the surface of it: a Zen-Buddhist monk begging a Jesuit priest to stay. Little wonder Francis Xavier felt uneasy and near to tears with mixed emotions. Some sixth sense of his own filled him with a nagging feeling of dread about leaving, and no matter how hard he tried he just could not shake it off.

On the fateful day, when he was about to step upon the gangplank leading to the sailing-ship, he was overcome with a premonition. It came to him like a silent wave drawing back from a desolate beach exposing the reality of the un-submerged, leaving him feeling lonely and forlorn. He turned and stared back at the land of the rising sun. He loved the little people; he loved their love of honor and their infectious sense of divinity; he loved being one of them. This was his holy-land. Why would he want to die anywhere else?

Francis was not much given to tears, being a Jesuit priest, but nevertheless a tear slowly trickled down the big nose of the teacher and fell to the ground. He wanted so badly to stay, but orders were orders, and obedience was obedience. There was still so much he wanted to accomplish. He had only gotten started. But it was a very good start. The best ever. "Others will come," he reassured himself, "Surely they will finish what I have begun." He walked resolutely up the gangplank like a true soldier of God.

It was the beginning of the last month of 1551 and the icy northerly winds drifted down and drove the little wooden sailing vessel toward Sancian Island. Francis Xavier shivered in his bunk and mumbled once again for a drink of water to cool his raging fever. How was it that a man could be antagonized at once with ice and fire? One instant he shivered like a frozen corpse in sweat-dampened sheets, and the next he was burning up with such a fever he threw off the bedding and begged for water, ice cold water. There was no relief, no respite. It continued on and on like the rolling waves, on and on and on.

There were tiny moments for reflection toward the end. As the killing fever and dysentery consumed his flagging energy, in moments of lucidity he cried out: "Lord, did you really want me to go? Should I have stayed in the Land of the Dolls?" But, had he not been duly warned? Had not his good friend Ninshitsu gotten down on his knees and begged him not to go? Perhaps this was his cross to bear?

It was far too late, far too late by the time the little boat docked at the sheltered harbor on the east side of Sancian Island. Too late to do anything but carry Francis into a decrepit wooden hovel, lay him down upon a narrow cot made of straw and bamboo reeds and pray. Pray for a miracle. Francis lapsed into a delirious state and suffered mercilessly until the third day of December. Mercifully on that day he passed on. It was a relief, a blessing in disguise to be freed from such mortal suffering.

Was it all worth it? Worth the poverty, the chastity, the self-sacrifice, the loneliness, the pain, the suffering, the ignominious death? Was it worth the sum total of souls saved to Christ? Was it worth a mortal lifetime spent? These are the kinds of questions that many who did not see his kindly demeanor or witness his unselfish dedication to his fellow man might ask. They did not see the teacher-with-the-big-nose stooping to pat little children on the head while smiling graciously to the sick and elderly. They did not feel the warmth of his affection for the downtrodden and weak, the rich and the poor. Some empathic converts remember only his wretched passing on a lonely cot in a little hovel on Sancian Island, as in retrospect they dwell obsessively upon the last agonizing moments of their Lord's passing upon the cross. Francis Xavier, like his Lord Jesus, is to be remembered – not for the manner of his death – but for the manner in which he lived his life: *ad majorem Dei gloriam*: for the greater glory of God.

CHAPTER FOUR

"To be able to glorify all your hard work with this pinnacle of achievement is an accomplishment of which you can all be proud," the Dean of the Faculty of Arts intoned as he slid his forefinger along the right side of his nose thoughtfully. It was a habit he had developed from his father who also had a large bulbous nose. It made him look pensive, he thought, the way a Dean should look. While holding that pose he continued to address the graduating class. When he completed his remarks, the graduating students were called up one by one to receive their degrees.

"Penelope Miki, Bachelor of Arts."

It was a proud moment for one who once had more worldly ambitions, and suffered from inherent feelings of being intimidated even in the absence of any obvious intimidator. What she really needed was a cause, a worthwhile cause, a cause that would enable her to rise above her inculcated feelings of intimidation and make a real difference. Such causes were not easy to come by in an undergraduate program at the University of British Columbia.

Penny graduated from UBC at the ripe old age of thirty. She was one of the older students receiving her B.A. with a major in Philosophy. Her years at UBC had given her the discipline and insights she needed to realize that she was indeed a "life long learner." A Bachelor of Arts degree in Philosophy was only the beginning. It provided her with the necessary background on which she could now begin to sketch in the foreground. She was like an artist, with pallet, paint, and brushes, poised to create a portrait of her own life.

To flesh out the picture, Penny decided after a weekend of partying and flirtations, that it was time for her to get serious. She was getting older and most, if not all, of her female and male friends were either married with children, or married and divorced with children. And here she was, single, available, and waiting for that special person. Did he actually exist somewhere in the real world, or was he just a figment of wishful thinking based upon the reading of too many romantic novels and the witnessing of too many Paul Newman movies? The prospects of her ending up an "old maid" – a card game she loathed to play – were about sixty-forty, and Penny did not plan on hanging around in the country of her birth to find out if the odds were in her favor or not. Perhaps in that land of milk and honey with ten times the population her prospects would improve. At that precise moment as the signposts of her destiny became highlighted in the intentions of her conscious mind, an arrow pointed due south.

Penny had her transcripts sent from the University of British Columbia to the University of Oregon where, after two months of impatiently waiting, she was accepted as a graduate student. On the morning she was about to depart, a few of her remaining friends gathered at her place of residence to see her off. She had packed her meager belongings into the trunk of her trusty old Mazda and was standing outside with travel bag in hand.

"Wish me luck – because I'll need it," she said.

They all hugged her and some even shed a tear or two just thinking about this little person, who actually looked about half her real age, venturing forth all by her lonesome into the great big yonder of glamour and glitz known as the United States of America.

Their vibes impacted upon Penny and suddenly she felt very small, inadequate and insecure. But she smiled courageously with the true spirit of a samurai warrior about to undertake a great mission full of promise, adventure, and new opportunities, and set forth.

Being a graduate student was serious business. The professors treated you with greater respect, and even the under-grads looked up to you with that quizzical look that said, "She must have stamina." All this gave Penny a feeling that this time she really knew what she was all about. Of course she majored in Philosophy, but soon found out to her dismay that most of her Profs wanted to talk about "language games," when she was deeply into "existentialism." Still she persevered, and her perseverance paid off for in her class on Symbolic Logic she met the man who would become her future husband, an intellectual-looking character who was interested in just about everything including paranormal phenomena and the unvarnished existence of unidentified flying objects. Was this just a coincidence or what?

When Penny first became aware of her future husband-to-be, she was immediately struck by his sense of self. He seemed to be more in command of himself than other graduate students his age (at first

Penny thought he was older than she was, but as it turned out he was actually younger); it was as if he had already done a lot of soul-searching which had aged him beyond his chronological years, and had come to some sort of a personal, intrinsic accommodation with himself. In short, he seemed to be a work-in-progress of Socrates' axiom: "Know thyself."

He was usually very quiet, and in class he said as little as possible. In the class on Symbolic Logic he did not speak at all during regular class discussions leaving Penny with the distinct impression that he was some sort of odd-ball. This of course piqued her curiosity. She found this fellow who slouched in the back corner seat as far removed from the front as possible, to be quite an enigma. He did not say anything, even when the Prof commented on the brilliance of his paper, suggesting to those who weren't quite getting it, that they might be wise to consult this quiet, non-assuming intellectual.

Symbolic Logic was not Penny's forte, so one day she made up her mind, and convinced herself beyond any possibility of chickening out, that it was up to her to manufacture an encounter with this quiet young man. He usually hung around after class until nearly everyone else had left; then he would go up to the Prof, exchange a few words, and exit as uneventfully as he entered. Knowing this, Penny decided to out-wait the waiter, and after class she planned to go up to the front and have a few words with the Prof herself, about the clarity of his lectures.

On the fateful occasion, she glanced nervously over her shoulder and caught the young man looking at her. He immediately glanced away and began rummaging amongst his papers as if looking for something. Penny returned to her notepad and pretended she was finishing off some notes she had been taking. The Prof had gathered up his materials and was closing his briefcase in preparation for taking his leave. The young man got up quickly and sauntered up to the front of the class. Penny was right behind him.

"That analogy about using symbolic logic to wire a house was right on," the young man commented.

"It helps some students to visualize beyond the symbols," the Prof explained.

"Practical manifestations are easier to grasp," the young man responded appreciatively. "See you next Thursday." He turned to go and ran smack into Penny who fell unexpectedly "flat on her ass," as her future husband would later love to relate whenever anyone asked them how they had met.

Penny was so flustered she forgot the question she was going to ask the Prof. It did not matter anyhow because as soon as she hit the floor, both the young man and the Prof were down on their knees hovering over her like paramedics, their faces empathetic with alarm and consternation. It was obvious they were having difficulty assessing the severity of her injuries. She had landed with a distinct "thud" on the hard concrete floor.

"I-I think I'm okay," Penny stammered, her face red with embarrassment. Things were definitely not going according to plan!

"Just rest a moment," the young man leaning over her said with compassion. "I am so sorry. I didn't realize anyone was behind me."

"Are you sure you are okay?" the Prof asked in a caring voice, cognizant of the University's liability in such situations.

"I'm fine," Penny asserted, sitting up and brushing herself off.

"You're not hurt or anything?" the Prof asked, just to reassure himself that the filling-out of an accident report form was not necessary.

"I'm sure I'm fine," Penny repeated with greater emphasis on the 'fine', unwilling to play the role of the damsel in distress now that her embarrassment had worn off.

"Good." The Prof heaved a sigh of relief and returned to his feet.

"If you're busy, why don't you go?" the young man suggested to the Prof, "I can take care of her."

The Prof excused himself and left leaving the two of them alone on the floor at the front of the classroom.

"My name is Penelope," Penny said formally, "What's yours?"

"Lawrence," he replied, with equal formality, and then as if it was crucially important that she know who he was, he went on jabbering in an uncontrollable manner about his identity. His real name was Petitjean, but it had been Anglicized many generations ago by one of his great-grandfathers into Petty, because petty as it seemed to him, Petty was preferable to Petitjean in those early pioneering days, for a whole lot of reasons concerning race and social status. "As far as I know," he commented, "the original Petitjean who emigrated from England was fathered by an interloper from France. Soon after the birth of his son, the interloper returned to his homeland where he found his true calling. He later became a respected Catholic priest by the name of Father Bernard Petitjean. I have long roots in this country," he concluded proudly.

"What shall I call you?" Penny asked, "Petty or Petitjean?"

"Larry," he said decisively, "Just call me Larry."

"And you can call me Penny. Just plain and simple, Penny."

"Penny who?"

"Miki, like in Mickey Mouse," Penny replied. "I too have long roots. I have traced them all the way back to a famous samurai warrior in the fifteenth century, named Tsutomu Miki."

"I knew there was something special about you," Larry blurted out, inadvertently revealing that he must have noticed her prior to the accident. "You have the spirit of a samurai warrior, and I have the spirit of a priest."

"What a combination!" Penny declared.

CHAPTER FIVE

It happened immediately after the Christmas break. Penny was returning to Eugene, Oregon, after having spent the festive season at her parents' home in Lethbridge, Alberta, when she became better acquainted with the probability of extra-terrestrial intervention. It was a cold, wintry night. Penny had crossed the border at Yahk, B.C. and after driving through some of the worst winter conditions imaginable, had just passed beyond the Umatilla junction when the nightmare began.

Penny was tired and weary from having driven her sporty Mazda six straight hours in treacherous weather. To pass the time she had been weighing the pros and cons of considering Frederick Nietzsche and Soren Kierkegaard joint fathers of modern existentialism, when suddenly she was blinded by what seemed to be very bright lights that appeared over the brow of a distant hill. "Dim your lights!" she muttered to herself. The dark, wet road loomed before her like an unlit airport runway. Without hesitation she zoomed down the runway – but the headlights before her never passed by. Instead they curved away to the left and disappeared. A very strange and frightening feeling came over her when she then felt the bump, bump, bump of railway ties beneath the tires. She gripped the steering wheel tightly and let the car roll to a lurching halt. The engine had quit and it was pitch dark except for the headlights of her Mazda. She had driven down the railway tracks!

Could she have fallen asleep at the wheel? Was this a dream? No, it was sickeningly real. A nauseous sensation coiled like a snake in the pit of her stomach. She drew in a deep breath, closed her eyes, and rested her head against the steering wheel. It seemed like only a few seconds – perhaps ten to fifteen at the most – but when she sat up and rubbed her eyes, the headlights had faded badly and the railway tracks looked surreal in the ghostly glow.

She sat in her car frozen with apprehension. What if a train came by? What should she do? Should she attempt to flag it down? Did she have a flashlight? Did she have anything useful? No, she had nothing. Nothing! She stood there shivering in the cold engulfed with a dreadful sensation of total helplessness. There she was stranded on the tracks in the dead of night waiting for a train to arrive. Penny felt like a lump of coal: a piece of organic matter, petrified. And then fate stepped in and took charge. What else could it have been?

A set of lights appeared as if by magic behind her. She heard doors slamming and out of the darkness loomed four husky men, their faces masked by the darkness. They said they were on their way to work when they noticed the dimly lit taillights of her car, and realized someone had missed the turn and had become stranded upon the tracks. What a stroke of luck! Four husky men looming up out of the darkness just when Penny was feeling like a petrified lump of organic matter.

A single light appeared far down the rail line. They could hear the distant warning whistle of the train. Penny hustled off to the side with the four men and waited with stoic helplessness for the inevitable. A second much louder whistle amplified the magnitude of the impending disaster. The light rushed nearer and nearer and NEARER. The screeching sound of steel on steel rose to an intolerable crescendo. With a "swoosh" and an incredible clatter the train charged by!

Had she prayed? The gods were with her. The train was on the other set of parallel tracks! Energized by a rush of adrenaline the four men managed to push her relatively light car back down the tracks to where they crossed the pavement. The tail pipe had been completely ripped off. Penny hovered around in a mental state of shock. She shuffled about like a somnambulate. Someone gave her a drink of hot coffee from a thermos. She could hear voices talking in the background. "If we can get it started should we let her drive, alone? Perhaps we should take her with us."

"Just give me a push, and I'll be on my way," Penny interjected. "Don't worry; I'm fine now." She had collected her wits about her and was anxious to be on her way, to be back in control of her destiny.

"Okay," one of the men said rather reluctantly, "we'll give you a push to see if your car will start."

A shove from behind brought the trusty old Mazda back to life. The un-muffled roar of the engine sounded like a hundred tanks in the frosty silence. Penny thanked the four mystery men, rolled up the window, and with all due caution drove the remainder of the way to Eugene. She was completely exhausted when she tumbled into bed in the early dawn. She closed her eyes and just like magic the night's experience faded away like a bad dream.

Two days later when Penny informed Larry, her future husband-to-be, about her strange experience, he was beside himself with excitement. "Gosh Pen," he enthused, "you could have had an encounter!"

"What do you mean encounter?"

"Didn't you mention something about losing track of time? Usually in such encounters time is distorted. There is something weird about your experience. I have this vague sense that you could have possibly been abducted."

"Abducted!" Penny exclaimed.

"Yeah, but don't be alarmed," Larry responded with the demeanor of a medical doctor in consultation with a patient. "We definitely will need to check into this possibility." Larry had read practically every book published on extraterrestrial possibilities, and considered himself to be an interested skeptic, until one fateful day he personally saw an unidentified flying object with his own two eyes.

It occurred during spring-break at the conclusion of his second year at college when his intellectual curiosity about anything mysterious was unbounded. Larry and his roommate, an avid and fearless mountain trekker dubbed "Henry the-foolhardy", due to his mountaineering exploits, decided they would get away by trekking up Mount Rainier as far as they could go. It was a clear, crisp evening and they were about two-thirds of the way to the top and had stopped to rest on the brink of a sheer cliff face. Off to the northwest they could see the grand vistas of valleys and other distant peaks. As they sat there staring off into space they saw a shining speck in the distance. Larry said, "Look there, must be a plane or something." They sat and watched it as it hovered closer and closer.

"It's not making any noise!" Henry whispered in awe as it approached the cliff. It was uncanny. Perhaps they should have jumped up and hid in a crevasse. Human behavior at such moments is so unpredictable. Larry and his fearless trekker friend just sat there as if mesmerized as the UFO hovered right up to the edge of the cliff face as big as life, a shiny metallic, oval-shaped flying saucer about the size of a small submarine. It was so close that if they had jumped off the cliff they could have landed on it. Larry was so thrilled he forgot to be scared, but Henry was quite the opposite. He yelled, "We're going to be abducted!" As soon as he yelled the flying saucer zoomed off and faded from sight. Larry was greatly relieved, but to Henry's chagrin, he had relieved himself! Larry noticed his friend's pants were wet while his were still dry. It was simply a matter of self-control. It is one thing to read about someone else's abduction experience; it is quite another to come within a heartbeat of being one of those persons. So his fearless friend had pissed himself. Who knows how one will react at such times?

Both Larry and Henry were in a semi-state of mental shock. Larry thought he wasn't – but he was. The word dumfounded was an apt description of how they looked. They looked like dumfounded twins, the only difference being the wet pants. They hardly spoke to each other on the way back down. There was nothing to say. Once you have seen a UFO, what is there to say except, "I saw a UFO!" And how many times has that ridiculous statement been spoken by unreliable weirdoes?

Penny believed every word that Larry told her, because she knew in her heart that Larry was just not capable of telling her a lie. That was just the way Larry was. So in the end, after some misgivings, she bowed to his greater knowledge in this specific area of paranormal investigation. He was confident that her recent experience of driving on the railway tracks indicated all the "classic signs" of an abduction. Due to his insistence, she reluctantly allowed him to examine her body for any signs of implants, but to her great relief, and Larry's barely concealed disappointment, there did not seem to be any. The only fringe benefit that resulted from this paranormal investigation was that on that particular occasion they both became sexually aroused and consummated a glorious moment of spontaneous combustion.

As a result of Larry's continuing persistence, Penny eventually found herself on the doorstep of a professional hypnotist, Larry's friend Samantha. She was a good choice, according to Larry, because she really did not believe in unidentified flying objects or extra-terrestrial beings of any kind. This added another level of credibility to an incredible process. Under regressive hypnosis, an unexpected thing happened. Penny recalled in vivid detail the horrendous events concerning her near-death experience when she was a tiny infant. At the time both Larry and Samantha were shocked by her revelations. They both thought the aliens must have performed some god-awful operations upon her. Naturally they were both relieved and somewhat disappointed Penny thought, when she told them about her near-death experience as an infant.

Disappointing as the paranormal investigations may have been, they nevertheless set the stage for a glorious relationship that would eventually culminate in parenthood, and later lead Penny and Larry, in early retirement, to undertake the Herculean task of writing a reasonable facsimile of a coherent and meaningful student handbook on life.

"A student handbook on life"? Why would anyone desire to write such a book? And who would want to read it?

CHAPTER SIX

December in Eugene, Oregon was usually a slate grey rainy month with periods of misty sunshine. It never got really cold, like in Lethbridge; it hardly ever got below thirty-two degrees F. This winter though it actually snowed, and a grad student from Hawaii went berserk with excitement, making tiny snowballs and eating them like ice-cream.

"This is the first time I've seen snow!" he yelled at Penny when she passed him on the pathway that wound between the Fine Arts and Engineering buildings.

"Enjoy it," she yelled back, amused by his antics. She had just attended her last class prior to semester break. "One more semester after this," she thought. She made her way back to her off-campus studio apartment, which consisted of one large room with a bed, table, two chairs, a well-worn couch, and a small kitchen. Tucked off into the left corner was a tiny bathroom. It was adequate for one person, and most important of all, she could afford the rent.

She quickly packed a black medium sized suitcase while humming a tune she had written called, "Takehashi Died Last Night." It was one of those strange songs that had come to her in the middle of the night about a year ago. She could still visualize the scene in her mind's eye. A group of people were standing around a campfire on the shore of a lake. It looked like the lake near the internment camp at New Denver, B.C. that she had visited once as a child when her parents went there for a funeral. The sparks were flying out into the night sky when a young Oriental woman with long flowing hair emerged from the surrounding darkness carrying a battered old acoustic guitar something like her own. In a melodic voice she began singing...

Takehashi died last night
Of a very ordinary plight
All her friends who came to pay their last respects to her
They all began to purr.

She thought that she could change the world
Just a very ordinary girl
All her friends who looked at her and bowed their heads to pray
They knew not what to say.

They knew that if they searched the world
They would never find a pearl
With a natural beauty deep within that made it shine
She really was a find!
    And when all the lights were dim
And she felt the earth as kin
All the world of pearl unfurled came shining from within
She really was so thin.
    It really didn't seem quite right
Too young to face the wrath of might
A downy feather caught upon the whirlwinds of the day
And when she heard them pray
She replied stand by, stand by....

It was a song about the evacuation. It just came to her in the dead of night. It motivated her to get up at 3:40 a.m., get out her battered old acoustic guitar, and like the girl in her dream, she sang, "Takehashi Died Last Night." The refrain was her favorite part. It went...

    Stand by; stand by 'neath earth and sky
Stand by to save the day
Our dream of peace must never die
Stand by, take heart I say.
    Stand by; stand by 'neath earth and sky
Like spirits made of clay
When I waken from this dream don't cry
Stand by, take heart, I say.

And then the song concluded with a final verse...

    Takehashi died last night
Of a very ordinary plight
All her friends watched with hope when she opened up her eyes
She smiled at them and sighed
Good bye, goodbye, goodbye
Dear friends.

It was indeed a strangely beautiful and poignant song. "I wonder who really wrote it?" Penny often thought whenever she sang it. "I know it wasn't me – even though I take credit for it!"

That song set the mood for her long journey back to Lethbridge. Surprisingly, just as she locked the door of her studio apartment, the sun broke through the clouds and shimmered off the melting snow like a zillion sparkling diamonds. A translucent rainbow arched just under the vaporous ceiling and touched down from horizon to horizon. The air smelled as fresh as a spring day in May. "Takehashi just smiled," Penny thought, as she opened the door and sank down into the comfortable driver's seat of her reliable old Mazda. The engine roared to life when she turned the key.

She had to get going. It was a long journey back to the place where her dear mother had given birth to her. Back to where her father, Hideo, had said, "Please let her live and I will give up ten years of my remaining life." Back to where her three older brothers, older sister, and elderly parents were waiting for her. Back to southern Alberta, where in 1942, row upon row upon row of sugar beets had to be thinned, and "black-heads" labored from dawn till dusk under the very same sun that created a rainbow of hope in the mist, as she drove north toward the 49th parallel.

The sun was declining like a purplish-red canopy across the western skyline when Penny drove into the city limits of Spokane, Washington. Once the sun went down the afterglow provided an ambiance of quietude and solace. As she drove along at the posted speed limit of 60, she kept her eyes peeled for a place to stop over. A modest place called the Roadside Inn caught her eye. She liked the name. It was very ordinary and unpretentious. However, the stop-over turned out to be far from ordinary.

The Roadside Inn was owned and operated by a middle-aged couple by the name of Jesus and Marilyn Gonzales. Jesus was pronounced "Hey-Zeus," like hailing a Greek god, "but you can just call me Speedy, if you like," Jesus said with a smile, while Penny was busy registering.

"Excuse me," his wife interjected, peering over Penny's left shoulder to get a better look at the registration card, "That name, Miki, must be Japanese, right?"

"Yes, I'm Japanese-Canadian," Penny replied.

Marilyn peered closely at Penny's face, and when Penny finished registering she cleared her throat and queried, "Of mixed blood?" When Penny frowned she hastily added in an apologetic tone, "I don't mean to pry but it's just that you look slightly, how shall I say...."

"Slightly native?" Penny completed her thought. "My mother was half native," she added.

"Was she?" the woman queried as if relieved. "I'm somewhere between one-eighth and one-sixteenth native myself," she declared proudly, "Cree Indian."

"Her grandmother was a Métis from Saskatchewan," Jesus elaborated. "We have a portrait of her somewhere around here." He left and went into a back room.

"Ever heard of Louis Riel?" Penny asked playing a hunch.

"Heard of him!" Jesus ejaculated, returning from the back room carrying a roughly framed picture turned antique grey with age. "There she is, a relative of Louis Riel himself!" He displayed the portrait proudly.

Penny scrutinized the faded old black and white portrait with heightened interest. It showed a wrinkled old woman with long braids curled up on her head, beady eyes, a slightly bulbous nose, and sunken lips drawn over toothless gums.

"I inherited that portrait from my mother. It is the only thing of Grandma's that I have."

"Amazing!" Penny exclaimed staring more closely at Marilyn to see if there were any facial similarities to her Grandmother. She had the same slightly bulbous nose, something like the one Louis Riel had in the picture Penny once saw in one of her high-school Social Studies classes.

"Louis was a school teacher who went up to Canada to help his Métis brethren stand up for their rights," Marilyn explained, "and to negotiate on their behalf with the government."

"Why don't you sit down," Jesus interjected, motioning Penny toward a round table surrounded by four chairs that crowded the corner by the window. "Why don't we put on a pot of tea and get out those raisin-bran muffins you bought for breakfast?" he suggested while looking at his spouse.

"Why don't we," Marilyn reiterated as she left for the back room followed by her husband. It was just assumed that Penny would enjoy a nice cup of black tea along with a freshly toasted muffin.

Penny sat down at the round table and while she waited she re-examined the old portrait Jesus had left with her. Somehow she felt safe and secure in the presence of two complete strangers she had just met. It was their demeanor and attitude that made her feel at home. Thoughts of a cup of hot tea and a warm muffin made her realize that she was actually quite hungry.

"The Métis were a disgruntled and unhappy people," Jesus explained, when he returned carrying a sterling silver tray from which he removed an earthenware pot of tea along with three teacups, three plates, a sugar bowl, a pitcher of milk and three spoons. He set the tray aside, sat down and picked up the faded old portrait. "Look here," he said turning the old portrait over and extracting a faded piece of backing paper. He gently unfolded it. It was an old newsletter dated November 29, 1885. "Let me read a bit from this," he said while smoothing out the paper.

"Better let me read it," Marilyn demanded, honing in, "your eyes are worse than mine." She set down the napkins and toasted raisin-bran muffins and began pouring the tea. When they were all comfortably seated and enjoying their tea and muffin, she turned to her husband and held out her right hand while setting her teacup down with her left.

Jesus passed the creased old paper over to his spouse and she cleared her throat and began to read in a monotone voice. "Louis Riel was born in the Red River settlement of St. Boniface on October 22nd, 1844. He was a well-educated man for his times, having spent many years in religious schools in Montreal. In 1869 at the age of twenty-four, he founded the Comte National des Métis, to protect his peoples' rights. At that crucial period when the Red River area was being inundated with settlers, the Métis were left to fend for themselves without any claim to Aboriginal rights. Louis was very popular amongst the Métis. In 1873 and in 1874, and again in 1875 the people of Manitoba elected him to be their representative to the Canadian Parliament, and to plead their case. It was their democratic right to be heard." Marilyn paused and rubbed her eyes.

"I'll finish reading it," Jesus said, taking the paper back. He read with a little more animation than his wife. "For his troubles Louis was exiled in 1875 from the country of his birth to the United States, where he was welcome. In 1883 he became a U.S. citizen. While teaching at a Jesuit mission in Montana in the early spring of 1884, a delegation from the Métis community from the south branch of the Saskatchewan River approached Louis and asked him if he would consider returning to Canada to present their grievances, once again, to the Canadian Government. Although he had been exiled, Louis returned to Canada to assist his brethren." Jesus halted and looked up at Penny to see if she was still paying attention.

"And then what happened?" Penny asked knowingly.

"In June of 1884, about two hundred frustrated Métis at the end of their patience and stonewalled at every turn by the government of Canada, vented their anger on the authorities at Duck Lake. Tempers flared and shots were fired. Men were killed on both sides." Jesus put aside the paper and continued from memory. "Someone had to be held accountable, and it was not the politicians back east. It was that so-called 'madman' claiming unwarranted rights for the Métis: Louis Riel."

"Poor Louis!" Penny empathized identifying with his plight.

"Six English-speaking Protestant jurists," Marilyn explained, "after deliberating for a whole hour found him guilty of treason. The honorable judge, Hugh Richardson, in spite of pleas for leniency from the conscience-stricken Protestant jurists, sentenced Louis Riel to hang by the neck until dead. Justice supposedly was done in Regina on the 16th of November, 1885 when Louis was led up to a scaffold, and someone opened the trap door."

"What a travesty!" Jesus ejaculated once again.

"Treated like a troublemaker and a traitor and hung for treason," Marilyn scoffed. "He was truly a great Canadian hero, one of a few who dared to stand up for the rights of a small downtrodden minority."

The more Marilyn and Jesus spoke, the more Penny identified with their sentiments. "The Canadian history books do not do justice to the Métis cause," Penny commiserated, conscious of the bland handling of that exciting episode by most historians.

"Most Canadian historians were born with a stiff upper lip," Marilyn rationalized. "They think it is their duty to defend the status quo, to defend the WASP point of view."

"I never thought about it that way before," Penny admitted.

Marilyn had quite an in-depth knowledge of the Métis cause. As a college student she had once written a brief analysis of what she considered to be the main debate behind the uprising. Her college teacher had read it with interest, and had given her an "A". It was the only "A" that she had ever received at the college level. She said, "Excuse me," and departed for the back room.

"Marilyn is going to get her old college paper," Jesus predicted.

Sure enough, Marilyn emerged with paper in hand. She passed it over to Penny. "Take a look at this," she said proudly.

The paper was handwritten with black ink in a beautiful flowing script. Penny swallowed her last bite of muffin and washed it down with the remains of her second cup of tea. She wiped her hands on a napkin and picked up the essay. She quickly read it over while Jesus and Marilyn looked on.

The Métis Cause

Who knows for sure what the Métis cause was back in 1884? Perhaps not even the Métis themselves could adequately put it into words, but I will try, because my grandmother was a Métis, and I would like to understand why she had to suffer so greatly.

The Métis cause was as confusing in the 1870's as the fledging concept of land ownership was to the Aboriginal Peoples of Canada when they signed treaties that deprived them of the freedom to roam the open prairies, and forced them to suffer the indignity of being confined to reserves.

The Métis were intelligent human beings. Just because many of them were descendents from former "courier de bois" did not make them "unworthy", as many pure-blooded Europeans implied at the time. They knew their rights. They had lived on the land generation after generation like their Native relatives. It was logical to assume that if the Aboriginal Peoples had aboriginal title to the land, the Métis, likewise, had entitlement. They had a perfectly logical and commonsensical case. It went as follows.

Originally, all the land belonged to the "Aboriginal Peoples". They had lived on or "homesteaded" the land for as long as they could remember. Then some foreign authority from across the Atlantic Ocean unilaterally issued a charter giving the Hudson Bay Company the right to trade for furs in a vast hinterland they vaguely referred to as "the Canadas". With the demise of the charter, the Government of Canada claimed all the land, as if they were the aboriginal peoples and the Aboriginals were the foreigners. Subsequently, they began selling the land, or giving it away as homesteads to European settlers who were issued pieces of paper that indicated that they had entitlement or right of ownership. All of this was highly confusing to the original inhabitants of the land who did not have such a concept of "ownership", and could neither read nor write nor speak English (the language in which the concept of ownership was legally defined). In addition no one bothered to clearly explain what giving up entitlement to the land really meant. Of course the ones responsible for implementing and perpetuating the Indian Act, were and are, seemingly incapable of recognizing the injustice.

Many of the Aboriginal Tribes were deceived by empty promises and flashy trinkets into placing a crude mark or a finger print upon a piece of paper. That piece of paper became known as a "treaty", the terms and conditions of which were so abhorrently one-sided, no self-respecting real-estate agent worth his or her salt, even in those days, would have signed, unless they had no other option. The signing of the treaties relegated the Aboriginal Peoples to a few miserable acres, designated as "Indian Reservations", and freed up the rest of the land for exploitation. It seemed perfectly logical to the Métis that since they were partly aboriginal, they had the right to a proportional amount of land, or at least the right to the land they had "homesteaded" for generations. They felt strongly that they had far more legal right to the land than any European settlers who now claimed entitlement to the land because they had "homesteaded" it (a term that meant that any European squatter could claim ownership of a quarter section or 160 acres if they could prove they had squatted or lived on it for a few paltry years).

However, the government of Canada argued that because the Métis were not Europeans or Aboriginals, they had no rights and no claim to the land. And to demonstrate its authority, the government sent the newly formed North West Mounted Police into the Red River area to defend the rights of the white settlers.

So-called native/pagan peoples throughout the world have had to suffer through a difficult period known as "colonialism". It was a mind-set the colonists of the time perpetuated because it justified their unjust behavior. The writer Rudyard Kipling dubbed it, "the white man's burden." The sheer weight of the conceit was overwhelming: it reduced a once proud and free people into a bunch of pagans or heathen Indians. From the colonialist's point of view it appeared to be the "white man's burden" – in reality it was quite the opposite! The "white man's burden" was so burdensome to the non-whites, it was oppressive. The Métis rebelled out of sheer frustration and desperation. Who wouldn't have?

(At the bottom there was an "A".)

"I didn't realize the Métis were that badly treated. It seems like they did have a just cause," Penny admitted. "Even after all these years many Canadians feel that the government was justified in doing what they did to poor Louis."

"That's because the federal government is loath to ever admit, even in retrospect, that it could possibly have made a grave error of judgment," Jesus pointed out. "From outside Canada, things look a little different. The stiff upper lip disappears. From our perspective Louis Riel should have been given a medal of honor for bravery over and beyond...."

"He's slightly biased," Marilyn interrupted. "Jesus feels it is his patriotic duty to always pull for the underdog," she explained.

"As if you don't?" Jesus rebutted. "You're worse than I am!"

Penny laughed out loud, amused by this friendly banter. "Hey," she interjected, "I can relate to everything you've said. I'm one-half Japanese, one-quarter Scottish, and one-quarter native Indian myself."

"You're a mixed bag alright!" Marilyn expostulated. They all laughed, appreciative of a moment of comic relief.

After they had collected their wits, Jesus asked, "Were you evacuated during the Second World War?" raising his eyebrows with curiosity.

Penny felt a sudden pang of anxiety, momentarily caught off guard by the sudden change of topic. "Our entire family was evacuated from Steveston, that's just south of Vancouver, to a place near Lethbridge, Alberta. We lost everything," she said matter-of-factly.

"Damn shame!" Jesus exclaimed. "Same thing happened here to some friends of ours, the Kitagawas who were...."

"Not quite the same," his wife interrupted once again. "They did not lose everything. Their property was held in trust by the government until after the war. When the war ended with the dropping of those two dreadful atomic bombs on Japan in 1945, they were allowed to return to the West Coast after Japan surrendered, and their property was restored to them. After all, they were law-abiding American citizens like anyone else."

"Our property was sold for next to nothing by the government to pay for our internment," Penny explained.

"Damned shame!" Jesus remarked again.

"And not only that," Penny continued, "in Canada we were not allowed to return to the West Coast until 1949."

"You'd think something worse than Pearl Harbor had happened in Canada!" Jesus exclaimed.

"Canada is very white, compared to the U.S.," Marilyn observed insightfully. "The Japanese in Canada probably became the visible minority upon whom every vile aspect of racial prejudice could be vented with impunity, something like the way we treated the Aboriginal Peoples and the Blacks."

"And Mexican-Americans," Jesus added.

"Racial prejudice knows no boundaries," Penny noted sagely. "I hope both countries have learned from their mistakes, and are the wiser for them."

There was a moment of silence, and then Marilyn said, "I'm going to give you our best room."

When Penny got out her wallet to pay, Jesus held up his hand and said, "No charge. You are our special guest."

When Penny protested, Jesus smiled and said, "Just give us a big hug; that is all the payment we need." She hugged them both at once. It made her feel teary.

"You remind me of the daughter... we never had," Marilyn said wistfully.

"Americans are wonderful!" Penny thought as she fumbled to unlock the door to unit number 8. It was a beautiful room decorated in an oriental theme harkening back to the Tokugawa era, befitting its special guest.

Penny slept in late. She needed the sleep. It was restorative. Just before awakening she had a short dream about her cousin Tutomu, the one who had returned to Japan along with her father's older brother, Kasuzimo, and his wife Yutsko. He had visited her once in Calgary when she was living there. He only stayed two weeks, before abruptly returning to Japan where he was employed by some big international trading company. He had been born in Steveston like her older brothers and sister.

In her dream her cousin was an imposing samurai. Although he was a samurai, he was a peacemaker – not a warrior. He said, "Never again!" so vehemently it woke her up.

"Why would he say that?" Penny wondered.

It was 10:30 a.m. by the time Penny hit the road. The clouds hung menacingly low over Spokane when her Mazda departed the city limits. A few splatters of rain hit the windshield tentatively as if indecisive about the forecast. "I hope it clears up," Penny thought. About half an hour later, her wish came true.

The clouds parted and blue sky preceded her all the way to the Canadian border, as the winter sun lit up the pavement like a giant grey snake without head or tail. Penny enjoyed driving alone. She was not the least bit afraid of the giant snake. She enjoyed the feeling of being in control, the independence, the sense of purpose and direction. The quiet hum of the engine, the solitude, the sparse scenery rushing by in space-time, set Penny into a somber mood as the Canadian Customs agent waved her through with a "bon voyage" as she left the forty-ninth parallel behind.

Penny rolled up the car window. The wind had messed up her hair. She glanced in the rear view mirror to check her appearance. "It is difficult to see yourself as others see you," she thought. She saw a delicate oval-shaped face with a smooth amber pale complexion set amongst a tangle of rich dark hair. "It must be the Peach Girl," she said to herself suddenly, recalling the story of Momotaro-san, a tale her father had related to her countless times when she was a small child. She adored that story because her father had changed it so that instead of a little boy named Momotaro, it was a little girl who looked just like her, who popped out of the giant peach. She became the Peach Girl, the family favorite. Her father set the tone by saying, "The Peach Girl nearly died – now she is more precious than life." And they all agreed. Her siblings had been there when it happened, and they remembered it vividly because it was a miracle. It was a miracle that their baby sister lived!

The Peach Girl drove down the highway that led to the Crowsnest Pass, and from there to Lundbreck, Pincher Creek, Fort Macleod, and then Lethbridge. The story of the Peach Girl, the way her father embellished it, always ended with her becoming a heroine who spread words of kindness and love to the common people like a great spiritual healer. Her father had such an inflated notion of her importance in the world!

"I'm so lucky," he would say. "I must be the luckiest person in the world."

"Why?" she'd ask.

"Because the Peach Girl lives here!" he would say as he bounced her on his knee.

Penny smiled happily to herself, feeling her dear old father's unconditional love. To him, she would probably always remain the Peach Girl, more precious than life. The memories rolled by mile after mile, and as she headed east on highway number three, the red Mazda turned into a giant peach on wheels, and inside, she was everything her father said she was, and more.

CHAPTER SEVEN

In southern Alberta the sunsets are truly marvelous. In her rearview mirror Penny could see the golden rays of the setting sun attempting to hide, without success, behind a distant outline of purple foothills silhouetted against the rugged peaks and valleys of the Rocky Mountains. It was awesome. It made her pull off into a rest-stop and turn the car around. Somehow those sunsets were locked into a part of her memory and always gave her a feeling of spiritual solace, a calmness, an intrinsic peace that matched the outer beauty. It reminded her of that lyrical line that went: "All the world of pearl unfurled came shining from within." Takehashi would know how she felt.

The truth and beauty reflected in the sunset was undeniable. It drew that reflection from within and forced one to face up to the reality of it. The stark reality of it. What was once submerged as the background became illuminated as the foreground like the rounded foothills and the jagged mountain peaks. It was a revelation. The setting sun revealed their hidden beauty, their sacred self. It was all in the eye of the beholder.

"I am the beholder," Penny thought as she turned the Mazda around and headed back down the highway. It had been a long day. Penny's empty stomach rumbled, reminding her that it was time to get something to eat, as she approached the sign that read, "Welcome to the city of Lethbridge". She hoped she was going to make it on time for the rare family get-together. "What a weird family I have," Penny reflected as she drove north down the road that led to her oldest brother's residence in North Lethbridge where the whole family was to meet for supper. It always had been a concern of hers, the way her family operated. It definitely was not normal. There was something about it that seemed oddly out of sync with the norm. She had been reflecting and agonizing, off and on for years, upon the meaning and significance of it all.

"We care for each other, but we seem to lack that sense of community that other non-Japanese families relish," Penny cogitated. "We seem reluctant to assemble in groups larger than two or three. We are afraid to make ourselves too obvious! Too many black-heads sitting together might give the wrong impression. What impression?" Penny asked herself rhetorically. "Impressions that might confirm their suspicions, suspicions that we were conspirators: enemy aliens! Fear of being singled out again and being split up and dispersed across a vast hinterland with commensurate loss of any sense of community, and more importantly, any sense of personal identity. What identity?" Penny frowned as she zoomed around a corner at excessive speed. "We are practically invisible now, absorbed into the great Canadian cultural mosaic. It would be very difficult to single us out again. We're so invisible you'd think we were one of them!" Penny laughed out loud as the irony struck her. "They did not have to send us back to Japan to get rid of us – we got rid of ourselves!"

The steady hum of the engine and the muffled sound of rubber tires rolling over pavement provided the monotonous conditions required for unrestricted freedom of thought. "They did more to us than anyone could have foreseen at the time of the evacuation. They robbed us of any sense of self-respect and at the same time instilled into every single Japanese-Canadian an intrinsic sense of shame for being a 'Jap'. We did not want to be 'Japs', so we did our level best not to be ourselves. Who wants to be an 'enemy alien'? No one has tried harder to be a Canadian!" Penny exclaimed to herself, thinking of her father, Hideo. "No one."

Tears clouded her vision when she thought about her dear old father, "that little Jap Barber" as he was referred to by some. She took her foot off the gas and let the car slow down while she dug a tissue from her coat pocket and dabbed at the inside corner of her eyes. When her vision cleared she resumed her speed. "We're all hyphenated Canadians," she thought, "like the French-Canadians, the English-Canadians, the Chinese-Canadians.... The difference is that the Japanese-Canadians just want to be Canadians. Since WW II, the Japanese part has had very unpleasant connotations. It was impossible to be a proud Japanese-Canadian when your fellow Canadians referred to you as an enemy alien. You wanted to hide from your hyphenated self. You just wanted to be a Canadian." Penny slowed down once again and quickly blew her nose.

"It was the trying that was so frustrating," she sighed as if she regretted something of gargantuan proportions. "How do you try to be a Canadian?" she asked herself. "Does anyone else have to try to be themselves?"

"What does it mean to be a Canadian?" she asked herself as she drove past a sign that said, "Slow Construction Ahead" followed by a bunch of reddish-orange cones. She slowed to a crawl as the pavement turned into gravel. "I guess it means to be someone like me, someone with no particular identity of her own," Penny sighed once again as she turned right, onto 23rd Avenue. She did not realize it, but she had been hyperventilating. She felt slightly light-headed. "Who am I?" she wondered. It was a monumental question, the answer to which would require an entire lifetime spent. But she did not have that much time at the moment. She almost did not have time to slam on her brakes and make a sharp left turn up the driveway that led to her brother's residence.

Penny's oldest brother had a modest home although he could have afforded a much nicer house. It was not good for a visible minority to be too opulent; it might lead to jealousy and resentment. It was much safer to be inconspicuous. The sting of racial prejudice is ever present, and the memories of such are never forgotten.

The old Mazda purred up the driveway and halted three feet in front of a brown single-car garage door. Penny got out and walked up to the front door of the house carrying a large plastic bag loaded with an assortment of gifts. She rang the front door bell and let herself in. "Merry Christmas everybody!" she yelled.

The funny thing about Penny – if you could call it funny – was the vociferousness in her own mind. She had the kind of mind that hardly ever stopped thinking. "Does it ever actually stop thinking?" Penny pondered as she sat at the dining table with her parents and four siblings, clutching a fine crystal glass filled to the brim with a vintage red wine. Since she had graduated from high-school and secured her first serious job as a behind-the-scenes penny-pincher for the Royal Bank of Canada, all her siblings had found their professional niches in the world of free enterprise. They were all very smart and had done very well for themselves, thank you. Her three older brothers were, in order of descending age, a dentist, a civil engineer, and a chartered accountant. Her sister was an elementary school teacher. All of them had graduated with distinction from the University of Alberta, and in their modest ways were proud of it. The University of Alberta gave them all an equal opportunity to achieve according to their merits. What more could they have asked?

Penny's siblings always treated her with consideration partly because she was the baby of the family, but also in part because whenever they got together her second oldest brother inevitably felt compelled to reiterate, with saintly empathy, how that "brave little soul" clung to life when it seemed her tiny body was almost bereft of its last drop of blood. "It was a miracle!" he would conclude, and everyone would feel compelled to get up from their padded chairs and give their humble little sister a generous hug. Perhaps they just liked hugging her. If he forgot to tell the story, someone would remind him.

"She always was the quiet one," her sister was prone to point out between mouthfuls of sushi as she monopolized the conversation, as she was also prone to do. Yes, Penny did appear to be the quiet one to them, but in her own mind she was anything but quiet. She was a thinker, and thinkers like her are like omniscient narrators speaking in the first person. They are vociferous in their own mind.

It may seem ironic, but thinkers like Penny are forever being invited out to parties and social gatherings whenever they return home because it is assumed that such quiet, shy, and unassuming persons must be leading a very boring life. On the contrary, for such chronic thinkers the timeless words of the Buddha resonate with existential authenticity: "All that we are is a result of what we have thought" and Penny's thoughts were far from boring. In fact, the genesis of some of her most exciting ideas occurred to her just after her second oldest brother had said, "that brave little soul clung to life as if it were everything." The phrase "as if it were everything" incubated in her mind, and when she went to bed that evening Penny felt strangely elated; she felt as if she had just discovered several pieces of an overwhelmingly difficult puzzle, and the pieces seemed to fit!

When she awoke the next morning the profundity of her realization was withering. She felt like crying. Never did she feel so overcome with humility and gratitude: to be so informed, so privileged, so rewarded. It was too much to expect from an unheralded female graduate student, but there it was full-blown in her mind: a logical explanation of what is, and why things are the way they are. Who would have ever thought that an ordinary person like her would be capable of piecing together all the extraneous bits and pieces of information she had gleaned from hundreds of esoteric books filled with the wisdom of the ages, past and present, and rationalize them in such a manner as to make sense?

"Who thinks about this stuff except sages and wise old people? I'm far too young!" she exclaimed to herself. "Perhaps I am just too enamored by my own thoughts, my own intelligence, my own brilliance inflated by my egocentric vanity! Perhaps my reaction is a sign of my immaturity?" Consequently Penny thought that it would be prudent to file these ideas away for future reference when her advanced age would lend a degree of credibility to her insights. She secured a yellow notepad from her oldest brother's wife, and sat down at the old bedside desk that was in her room, and set pen to paper. With furrowed brow and a determination to get it down right, her nicotine-stained fingers moved the ballpoint pen back and forth across the paper, pausing now and again for just the right word or nuance, and flew on again, page after page until she had written fourteen pages of condensed prose. When finished, she sighed with relief, flexed her fingers, and put the pen down. It was done. Done for the sake of doing. She picked the pen up again and wrote, "For Posterity" across the top of the first page, stapled the pages together with a little stapler she found in the desk, and placed all fourteen pages into her brown leather briefcase. Little did she know – or did she know in the deeper recesses of her mind – that posterity was lurking around the corner?

* * *

Practically a whole year compressed by the stress and strain of term papers, intensive study, and exams slipped away as if it were only yesterday. "Gad, how time flies when you're too busy to notice it!" Penny exclaimed, "And here I am thirty-two going on thirty-three." Penny could hardly believe she was that old already. She did not feel nearly that old. And in fact she looked as if she were under-aged, and many an embarrassed bartender had returned her ID with profuse apologies. It seemed she had barely gotten started on her existential pathway, and presto! the moment for her graduation was at hand. Her second degree: a Masters Degree in Philosophy was about to be bestowed upon her like an academic baptism.

"A Masters Degree in Philosophy," Penny reiterated in her mind, "Isn't that something!" She felt proud of herself for sticking with it when others her age were off living the good life with their children and wealthy husbands. But instead she had studied long and hard soaking up knowledge like a dry sponge that could never be saturated. She thirsted for knowledge for knowledge's sake. She had read or studied most of the Occident's greatest thinkers. She even had looked extensively into Eastern philosophy and religion, and was intrigued by the life story of Gautama Buddha or Siddhartha, and the ageless wisdom of Krishna as found in the Bhagavad-Gita. But what amazed Penny as much as any of the great works she had studied, was the subconscious information she received late at night or early in the morning when her mind was open to the cosmic universe of pure unlimited potentiality. The reception of such information was just natural to Penny. She did not have to ask for it. It just came to her unsolicited as if those who had gone on ahead wished to share their insights with someone with an open mind. Perhaps they could feel her mortal vibrations, and they knew that a kindred spirit was still there, still stoically trudging along behind, struggling valiantly to keep up with the higher frequencies of their vast experience.

Larry, with his vast knowledge of psychic phenomena, was particularly intrigued by Penny's natural talent in this area. "It really isn't all that unique," he commented knowingly when Penny first mentioned her secret source of esoteric information. "There are many others who have tapped into the same or similar sources. Have you ever heard of Edgar Cayce or Jane Roberts?" he asked.

"Yes, but those two had special psychic abilities far beyond anything I have experienced."

"Perhaps it is just a matter of degree. It is possible that we all have some degree of psychic ability, or at least the potentiality to experience psychic phenomena, but are just not aware enough."

"I suppose it could be a matter of degree," Penny acknowledged.

"You sound a bit skeptical. Why don't you elaborate upon your experience?" Larry suggested.

"To me it's as if there is someone up ahead in the space-time continuum who is aware, and sort of indicating the way, like an invisible guide. It's hard to explain. It is sort of like following the tail-lights of a car that is way up ahead in a heavy fog when you can barely see the road. Every once in a while you catch a glimpse of those red lights through the fog, a flicker here, a flicker there. If you focus on them, they can give you a sense of direction. It keeps you going."

"It keeps you from going… in the ditch!" Larry laughed. He had that type of quick wit that could change a serious conversation into human comedy. "I know the feeling," he confirmed sagely. "Good analogy," he quickly followed up, spying the scowl forming on Penny's expressive countenance. "Most people probably have had a similar kind of driving experience because fog occurs all over the world, and people drive in the fog all over the world, and follow flickering tail-lights in the fog all over the world. I guess we're all in the same foggy soup."

Penny smiled her Mona Lisa smile and not to be outdone added, "You could say most of the time we're all in a fog."

"Yeah, a mental fog!" Larry clarified, happy to see that Penny was smiling once again, and in a more serious tone continued, "But usually we travel a foggy road without any tail-lights to guide us, so we either creep along at a snail's pace searching for the side of the road, or charge ahead foolishly hoping for the best. Fortunately for the rest of us, there are a few people who are able to see those flickering tail-lights even in the densest fog. Those people are far more adept at using their extra-sensory perception than others. I suspect that because of your near-death experience and natural intuitive abilities you are much more open, much more receptive to incoming frequencies." Larry gazed at Penny with a look that conveyed his respect and love. "You are a very special person," he concluded.

This conversation made Penny feel very special indeed, and she gave Larry all the credit he deserved for enabling her to feel that way. He seemed to be able to empathize with her. Could it be that they were actually kindred spirits? Soul mates ensconced in a four dimensional reality wherein the biological clock was relentlessly ticking? It seemed to be as good a time as any to get married, settle down, and reproduce the species. But was good old salt-of-the-earth Larry, with his head in the clouds and feet treading water, up for it?

CHAPTER EIGHT

There are many experiences that challenge one's abilities and create adventure out of the ordinary everyday tediousness of earning a living wage. Some are up for the challenge and some just complain. There was no doubt that Larry was ready for the challenge. A few years before he met Penny, when he was still an undergraduate student, he had an eye-opening summer experience that, amongst other things, prepared him for the prospect of marriage. It was eye-opening in that he realized that there were other Americans out there who had very different points of view regarding specific American religious practices than he had. Having had quite a sheltered upbringing as the son of a Presbyterian minister, he had not previously encountered anyone before who was so sarcastic when it came to certain very popular televised religious programs. For the most part such passing experiences probably do not amount to much more than interesting memories to be harkened back to at social gatherings where small talk is all important. But sometimes such experiences are not only eye-opening they can also change one's attitudes and beliefs in subtle ways that are unforeseen.

Larry's recollection of one such eye-opening experience usually began with the conclusion. Just after "the accident" his friend Linc had said, "When you get married, have at least two kids, one for you and one for me." He did not know it at that time, but those words were prophetic. After the twins were born, Larry spent many a night worrying about the health and well-being of his friend, and about what he had said.

He remembered that particular summer vividly. He had secured a job as a swamper on a D-8 Cat at a logging camp north-east of Portland. He did not know much about what a swamper did, but he accepted the job because the pay was good, and they said he could learn on the job. When he arrived at camp with his duffle bag dragging behind him, a tall, muscular young man with a likeable smile on his face strode out to meet him. He grabbed Larry's duffel bag as if it were stuffed with feathers, slung it over his left shoulder and extended his right hand.

"I gather you're Larry," he said, "Just call me Linc with a 'c'."

"Guess I'll be working with you," Larry responded as they walked over to the bunkhouse trailers.

"Yeah," Linc confirmed, "I drive the cat, and you get to do all the grunt work. It's kind of a division of labor thing. You'll learn as we go. It is very basic."

As it turned out Linc was three years older than Larry, and had dropped out of university at Portland after the second year because he was just too restless to sit in classes all day listening to "boring lectures", as he put it, that had nothing to do with everyday life. "Who cares how many angels can dance on the point of a needle?" he would ask whenever some unnecessary or redundant matter was brought to his attention. He liked to paraphrase old clichés and recycle them as folk wisdom. It gave him an air of being in the know.

During lunch and coffee breaks he showed Larry the ropes regarding the general maintenance of the D-8. He was pleased at how adept Larry became at hooking up and releasing logs, and giving him the appropriate hand signals when teamwork was required. The most nerve-racking times as far as Larry was concerned occurred when they had to work on widening hair-pin turns on new logging roads. Sometimes it seemed to him that the Cat was just teetering on the edge of sliding into the precipice below, but Linc was always in control, and seemed to relish pushing the Cat to the very brink of no return. During these moments Larry asked himself: "What in God's name am I doing here?" Of course compared to this, getting married would be a piece of cake. Perhaps that was one reason he was there.

During the evenings Larry found Linc to be a very stimulating person to converse with. Linc was one of those young men who could be described as being an all-round productive American citizen. One day when mail was delivered, Larry discovered why Linc would always say, "Just call me Linc – just Linc." Linc had received a letter from his parents, and after opening it he had folded the empty envelope and tossed it toward the garbage can, and missed. When Larry picked it up to put it in the garbage bin he noticed the name: Mr. Calvin Lincoln Washington Smith. "A true American," Larry thought, "no wonder he insists on being called Linc. Besides being short for Lincoln, it seems to link all these names together as one person."

One flaw, if you can call it that, that Linc had, was his near addiction to watching televangelists. He took great pleasure in watching these TV programs, but "for the wrong reasons," Larry had pointed out to him. This innocuous comment on Larry's part gave Linc the opening he needed to deliver his state of the union address on this subject.

"How can you be so gullible!" Linc had responded, rising to the occasion. "You know Karl Marx once said that religion is the opiate of the people? Well in America, televangelism is the opiate of choice. It provides people with the euphoric experience that allows the charlatans masquerading as priests and ministers of God Almighty to fleece them of their life's savings in the name of their Lord and Savior! The bald-faced nerve of them! Right there on television in broad daylight in front of millions of intelligent American citizens. It is a national disgrace!"

Larry was stunned, and he looked it.

"Every year these televangelists fleece millions of hardworking American folk out of millions of dollars. Tax free! It is better than the drug trade because it is condoned by the government." Linc waxed eloquent.

What could Larry say? There seemed to be a modicum of truth mixed in with Linc's statements of fact, or was it opinion? It was stunning. Perhaps, even stupefying!

"Every week these so-called televangelists can afford to buy prime-time spots on national broadcasting networks worth millions of dollars. They get on TV like life insurance scam artists, and sell spiritual security to all those poor, insecure folks watching. Did you get that? Like life insurance scam artists!" he repeated.

"People are not that gullible," Larry argued.

"Where do you think these ministries get all their money?" Linc challenged.

"I don't know," Larry confessed. Linc did have a point there.

"Selling spiritual security is big business," Linc stated with emphasis on the 'big'. These charismatic preachers are adept at persuading the average person that they too can be forgiven for their sins, and furthermore, have their name inscribed for all posterity on a whole life insurance policy guaranteed in the name of the Founder himself! 'If only they could spare a little seed money for the prayer table,'" Linc mimicked a popular televangelist.

"It's not all that bad," Larry protested.

"It's worse!" Linc retorted, "At least you can collect from your normal insurance policies. But these scam artists never have to make a payout. Never! That's why they get so rich. Think about it. I'm serious. Think about it. They never have to make a payout," he repeated, his voice rising to a crescendo for emphasis. "What have they insured you against?" He paused to give Larry a moment to consider a proper response.

Larry was stunned into silence.

"Against your fears, doubts, and insecurity," Linc continued. "They sell you what you dearly want and need for your own peace of mind, and never have to deliver the goods or make a payout during this mortal lifetime. Now that is what I call a perfect scam! And it is all legal and tax-free. Religion, my friend, is very lucrative."

"I think I get your drift," Larry conceded reluctantly. He had never thought of televangelists from that point of view before. His faculties of reason gave him pause, while his religious upbringing urged him to yell, blasphemy! He had to make a distinction between regular ministers like his father who had lived frugally all his life, and these televangelists who always seemed to be very rich. How else could they afford to purchase such expensive prime-time spots? Still Larry could not help but defend the televangelists because by definition they were also ministers of the faith. Consequently he cautiously replied, "But you must admit, these televangelists do provide their customers with hope." He did not mean to say customers; it just slipped out, and before he could retract it Linc had pounced.

"Customers! Precisely my point," Linc asserted vehemently, "Hope springs eternal in the human breast. What better sentiment to prey upon – I meant that with an 'e'. These scam artists know which buttons to push, and every once in a while they hit the jackpot. Some lonely recluse who has scrimped and saved and hoarded a lifetime's worth of material wealth through acts of frugality, selfishness, and greed, is brain-washed – some call it conversion or being born again – and is led to believe that a one-way ticket to heaven can be purchased with American dollars. Hey, if the Popes could sell indulgences, why can't these guys sell hope?"

"That was a long time ago," Larry interjected, alluding to the Popes.

"Some of the very infirm," Linc continued, after nodding at Larry to indicate that his point was well taken, "with nothing to lose, frequently change their wills and make these televangelists the beneficiaries of their entire life's savings. Why not? They can't take it with them anyway. So why not hedge their bets? What do they really have to lose? Money talks! If ten such people leave an average of one hundred thousand dollars each, that's a cool million just like that!" Linc snapped his fingers. They made a sharp "crack", and somewhere in the porcelain smooth veneer of Larry's dogmatic beliefs a tiny crack appeared.

Linc seemed to have garnered quite an in-depth knowledge about televangelists, and Larry came to suspect that perhaps in some way he possibly could have been associated with them in the past. It seemed odd that someone without some personal axe to grind would be so obsessed.

While watching this "religious entertainment," as he liked to call it, Linc would get so agitated he could hardly control himself. "What a con artist!" he would mumble under his breath while watching a popular televangelist grovel and repent on live telecasts, after he had been caught procuring illicit sex. Larry surmised that perhaps Linc's own parents may have been "fleeced" in some manner, because he never tired of reiterating how a glib husband and wife televangelist team, whom Linc referred to as "sanctimonious real estate agents," were charged with fraudulent dealings with regards to their grandiose housing development, and sent to jail after fleecing the "gullible public" out of over one hundred and fifty million dollars. It was a national disgrace that provided talk-show hosts with fodder for months; and still, according to Linc, televangelists prospered. "Put some sanctimonious salesman on prime-time TV," he sarcastically intoned, "selling nothing but snake oil and hope, and you can bet your bottom dollar that millions of gullible suckers will rise to the bait."

On some occasions Linc got so carried away that Larry was not quite sure whether he was just exaggerating or simply making up outrageous examples to challenge his credibility. It was during the last televangelist program that they witnessed together that Larry felt that he should proffer his friend some friendly advice. As usual, Linc was so agitated he had to get up and pace back and forth in front of the television set. Every once in a while he would exclaim: "Did you get that? Seed money for the prayer table! What are we seeding here? Money?"

When the program was over, Larry quietly said, "You know, you do have some valid points." He paused long enough to allow Linc to calm down and for the comment to sink in. "People would be much more open to your point of view if you presented it in a more subtle and diplomatic manner." He paused again to let this comment sink in alongside the other. "There is no substitute for reason and common sense," he gently advised, "and what you have been ranting about does make a great deal of common sense." He was on the verge of saying something else, but changed his mind. It was better to be brief, than long winded. "That's all I have to say."

Linc calmly walked over to the chair he had been sitting on, and sat down. "You know, Larry, you do have your own succinct way of putting things," he said thoughtfully. And then in a tone reminiscent of a Presidential state of the union address, he concluded: "You can fool some of the people most of the time, and most of the people some of the time – but you cannot fool the American people all of the time."

Aside from his rather negative opinion of televangelists, Linc was one of the most generous and caring persons Larry had ever met. He would literally give the shirt off his back, if anyone was in dire need. He treated Larry as if he was his younger brother, and in spite of their differences of opinion, Linc's rather unique religious views actually seemed to draw them even closer together in invisible ways. Once a brash new recruit blatantly confronted Linc with: "Are you an atheist, an agnostic, a black heathen, or what?"

He probably could have made mincemeat of the fresh recruit, but instead Linc calmly replied, "Don't attempt to attach any labels on me; just call me Linc." Larry really admired him for that very cool response.

Shortly after Larry had returned to University, Linc was involved in a serious accident. His D-8 Cat had overturned when the soft shoulder of the road he was working on gave away. Although he was thrown clear he had been impacted across the lower abdomen and a loose cable had nicked him across the throat. The logging foreman had contacted Larry at Linc's request.

It was the evening of September 28th when Larry arrived at the hospital. Linc was in room 209. He was sleeping when Larry entered the room, so Larry just sat down and waited. Linc's throat was heavily bandaged and he looked pale and anemic. The nurse dropped in to check his charts and said, "He can talk, but he's not supposed to."

When Linc awoke he just smiled and nodded to indicate he appreciated Larry's presence. After awhile he said in a hoarse whisper, "I guess I'm not quite the man I used to be... yet."

When visiting hours were over and Larry got up to leave, Linc touched him on the sleeve. His voice was barely audible and he had to make a real effort to say, "You were the closest person to a brother that I ever had. There's a chance I might not be able to have children now. Just in case, when you get married, have at least two kids, one for you and one for me." He attempted to force a laugh.

Larry nodded, "How can I refuse?" he said. As he turned to leave he noticed that Linc's strained face still retained the boyish grin that reminded him of perpetual youth, and he remembered the time that Linc and he had gone into town one weekend for a few beers, and two local girls had joined them at their table. Suddenly this tall, handsome, glib young man became very shy and tongue-tied. Larry had to carry most of the conversation by himself. At the end of the evening after the girls had taken their leave, Linc had looked over at Larry with a bemused twinkle in his eye and confided, "You know? Someday you will make a very good husband for some fortunate young lady. You're like a father already. You just need some kids."

"You just need some kids," Larry often reminded himself afterwards as he sat at the back of many a classroom looking over the available females. Perhaps he was just fussy because few if any ever really appealed to him. They all looked so – how do you express blandness? – so unsatisfactory from his perspective. Some tried hard to look sexy by wearing short skirts with tight sweaters, but to the son of a Presbyterian minister that was not an essential criterion. What he was looking for was something else, someone who was not your bland, everyday, run-of-the-mill type female student who sat with her legs crossed and her nose in the air. He was looking for a woman who had that special quality. He would know it if he ever saw it. But in all his undergraduate classes he never found it. It was not for lack of trying. He was probably one of the most sexually-deprived, or as his macho-male associates occasionally pointed out in jest, "horny" young men on campus. It was frustrating to say the least. He might just as well have been a Catholic priest. At least then being chaste would have meant something other than just being hard-up; it would have had some spiritual significance. When he was feeling hard-up and far from spiritual, he frequently reminded himself of the advice his dear old mother had given him: "Look deep beneath the surface veneer, beyond race, religion, or the tincture of her skin. Look into the purity of her heart, if you wish to find a worthy soul-mate."

PART THREE

IN SEARCH OF SECURITY

Poverty is not a burden, but excess is.

Tolstoy

CHAPTER ONE

Fatherhood can be a daunting prospect for some, but for Handayu Miki it came as a welcome relief to a tedious life. To be the male parent of a baby boy bursting with latent potential made his life all the more worth living. This infant was his, his to raise, to teach, to nurture into maturity. It was a responsibility he relished. When he held his son in his strong samurai arms, he felt at peace with himself, at peace with the world, at peace with the universe. Everything he valued was wrapped in swaddling clothes pressed securely against his chest. There was no other feeling like it. That tiny lump of living, breathing humanity looking up at him with eyes filled with infinite trust gave Handayu a greater sense of satisfaction than anything else he had ever experienced. He did not have to will it; it just happened naturally. That child, just for being, became the beneficiary of his unconditional love. It was just there. Perhaps it was always there submerged in the murky depths of the procreative instinct. And now it blossomed in all its glory: father and son, connected by an invisible bond that was stronger than the steel of any samurai's sword.

It was in the spring of the year 1550, and the air was perfumed with the scent of cherry blossoms. In a comfortable wooden house on the outskirts of Nagasaki with an open cooking pit in the back surrounded by gnarled old cherry trees, a man and a small boy sat on bamboo tatami mats on the adjacent porch, and conversed in a seemingly adult fashion.

"Remember, appearances can be very deceiving," Handayu reminded his young son. "You must be ever vigilant not to allow yourself to be deceived by the illusionary world of appearances. There are all manner of charlatans, fakers, liars, and cheats in the world around us." It was a rather difficult concept for a young boy of five to grasp, no matter how intelligent, so his father decided to illustrate his point with a story that his father had passed on to him when he was a small child. It was a simple tale about a mongoose that would appeal to a young boy's sense of curiosity.

"There is a little animal about the size of a small dog called a mongoose. It is a predatory animal that feeds on small birds that survive on figs, nuts, seeds and such. Most of all the birds love to eat the sweet tasting figs."

"But how can the mongoose catch such swift flying creatures? The mongoose can't fly – can it?" the little boy asked, his eyes wide with wonder.

"An excellent question," his father replied, impressed by his son's astuteness. Intelligence was such an ephemeral thing, but the vast majority struggled along without the intellectual ability that brought Handayu such immense joy. When Tsutomu's eyes lit up with curiosity Handayu knew that his son was intellectually aware. Every time it happened, it was like sunshine bursting through clouds of opaqueness. It was astounding how aware a five year old could be. "Even you or I would have great difficulty capturing such birds, but not the mongoose." Handayu paused to let his son ponder upon the mystery of it.

"Surely the mongoose can't fly – can it?" the little boy repeated looking perplexed.

"The mongoose does not have wings. Obviously it cannot fly, but neither can we, and we could probably figure out ways to catch birds if we really wanted to. Right?"

"Yes, but how does the mongoose catch the birds?" his son asked, squirming with impatience.

"By deception."

"By deception?"

"Yes, by simple deception. By pretending to be a fig." The statement just hung there and decayed into the consuming silence. After an appropriate passage of time, Handayu glanced at his son to make sure he was rapt with curiosity, and continued. "The mongoose is endowed with an anus that looks just like a fig," he smiled, recalling how that inane statement of fact struck him when he first heard it as a child. He could see the look of incredulity flash across his son's face so he stressed, "...looks just like a fig."

"Of course you're kidding!" Moo-chan laughed, picturing in his mind how ridiculous that would look.

The joy of the moment radiated from Handayu in a smile so fabulous his son came over and hopped onto his knee. "I kid you not," Handayu responded. "The mongoose's asshole looks exactly like a dee-licious fig," he added with emphasis on the "d".

"Dee-licious, you say. Amazing! So how does the wily old mongoose catch the swiftly flying birds?" his son asked, jumping off his father's knee and accosting him face to face with his hands on his hips.

"When there are birds around, the mongoose, with the stillness of a statue carved in stone, displays his anus. The fig-loving birds swoop down and hover close behind the mongoose expecting a tasty meal. And then, quicker than the eye can see, the mongoose twirls, and snap! No fig. No bird. Just a satisfied mongoose licking feathers from its jaws."

"Incredible!" his son exclaimed, jumping up and twirling around as if he were a mongoose.

Unfortunately, Handayu did not live long enough to appreciate how profoundly that simple story would affect his son. A year later, when his son, Tsutomu (a.k.a. Paul Miki) was a lad of six, his doting father took the family into town to participate in the Cherry Festival. It always was a festive occasion. Usually the weather was sunny and warm, and the people came from everywhere to celebrate the positive life energy represented by the blossoming of the beautiful cherry flowers. Taiko drums were beaten in dynamic rhythms, and in such an up-beat atmosphere it was difficult to remain sullen, even if one were that way inclined. Tsutomu's mother, who usually remained somber and reserved whatever the occasion, woke up in the morning and said, "*Ohio-gosaimusu*," which set the tone for the day. It was the spring of the year, 1551, the year that the beloved Teacher-with-the-big-nose, was slated to set sail for China. There was an air of joyous expectation in the morning breeze.

In town, next to the Buddhist Temple, on a beautiful wooden bench that Handayu had patiently hand-crafted and proudly donated to the Temple on the occasion of his son's birth, sat a sullen-looking swordsman. He slouched there looking very morose and ominous as he dozed in the warming rays of the morning sun. No one knew what he was doing there. Around his neck, dangling from a silver chain, hung a silver crucifix. It was an odd thing for a samurai to wear. He was actually a rogue *ronin*, a master-less samurai who had forsaken his code of honor and resorted to thievery and acts of disrepute, symptomatic of his weak character. Perhaps he had stolen the crucifix, or perhaps he had been converted into one of those Kirishitan.

In any case, there he was, dozing on the beautiful bench handcrafted by Handayu, on the one occasion that the Miki family paid homage at the Buddhist Temple, even though they considered themselves to be Shintoists. They were in actual fact Shinto-Buddhists. Accommodation was one of Handayu's greatest strengths. He had this enviable capacity of finding common ground where others found contradiction and chasms of egomaniacal self-righteousness. "Buddhists, Shintoists, Kirishitan?" he would say, "they are all just ordinary people trying to make sense of what they find every morning when they awaken from dreamland. Before we are born we are nothing. After we are born we are everything. And after we die what happens to everything? It is the mystery that makes mortality so worthwhile."

It was a simple act of simple-minded vanity that made Handayu, with his little son in tow, pause in front of the ornately carved wooden bench to admire his own handiwork, while his wife went on into the Temple. Perhaps it was his cough, the cough that had persisted since he had come down with a nasty cold over a month ago, combined with his close proximity to the dozing swordsman, so close that his shadow actually fell upon him and blocked the life-giving rays of the sun from shining upon a human being in dire need of warmth. Perhaps it was the residue of every fearful, life-threatening experience that culminated in that moment and impinged upon the shadowy awareness of the slumbering ronin with a suddenness that startled him into an instinctive act of self-preservation. In a micro-second, his right hand, which had been resting on the hilt of his great katana, arced upward in a graceful semi-circle, and scarlet blood sprayed like a festive fountain from the jugular of Handayu Miki. The crimson blood covered his only son like a shower of death as he stood by his father's side, clinging with all his might to his father's limp hand. He stood there frozen like a marble statue, as his father's body slowly crumpled to the ground

A short distance from the Temple, a black-robed Jesuit priest observed the event with alarm. The dark orbs of his eyes bulged from his head and his breath was frozen. It was the price of admission to a human tragedy. He stood rooted to the spot with his hands clasped in front of him as if in prayer. A Zen-Buddhist monk joined him and they conversed in low tones. There was nothing they could do, except empathize. "What will become of that little child?" the one with the big nose asked compassionately.

* * *

Sometimes things happen that mould one's character into a shape so out of tune with the true nature of the fledging-self that the dissonance so created yields a sort of intrinsic psychological schizophrenia. Little wonder that from the age of six Tsutomu Miki became an unusually quiet and introspective lad. He had much to cogitate upon, and the older he became, the more he began to resent those righteous souls who wandered about wearing metallic or wooden crucifixes around their necks as if they were important symbols of faith. To Tsutomu they represented something else, something associated with his father's gruesome death.

His only respite from a never-ending inner dialogue with himself occurred when he picked up the swords he had inherited from his father, and in the universe of his mind, transformed himself into a samurai warrior. It was cathartic. He became a real somebody. He had a real identity. The inner dissonance momentarily vanished. He became an attitude, a mind-set, a rigid system of beliefs. All questions and doubts were held in check by the strict discipline and moral code of the samurai. Honor was everything. Loss of face worthy only of *seppuku*, an act whereby one slit one's belly from side to side, and hugged one's entrails stoically as life seeped away, fulfilling one's commitment to an honorable discharge. It was the code of honor, or *bushido*, of the samurai warrior.

But was it the way for a sensitive, introspective young boy? A lad who matured into a young man with long black hair pulled back and tied with black ribbon, with a neatly trimmed black beard that outlined the determined set of his jaw, and brooding black eyes inset under bushy black eyebrows as foreboding as the wrath of God?

CHAPTER TWO

A peephole into the unknown. *An AWARENESS with ten toes and fingers, two legs, arms, ears, eyes, and one brain, all quantified by an invisible soul. You do the math. Does it add up? Does it make a whole?*
"Impossible! As impossible as zero equaling one."
But nevertheless… there it is.
"Ridiculous!"
But there it is peering through the peephole, breathing as though… as though….
"It actually exists. My gawd! It's alive!"
Who said zero could not equal one?
"I don't believe it!"
But there it is peering through the peephole like-like some peeping Tom.
"Embarrassing!"
You said it Tom – or is that tu-Tom-u?
"What's it looking at?"
You.
"It can see me?"
Just as if you were real.
"Real?"
You know? Substantial; as if you actually exist and have an identity of your own.
"Unbelievable!"
It seems that way because… well because you have a unique tendency. Yes, a definite tendency to-to… to pretend.
"I do?"
Yes, indeed you do. You love to pretend that you are not pretending.
"No kidding."
Yeah. You're doing it now. Pretending is your modus operandi.
"It is?"
Not only is pretending innate, instinctive, and natural – in so far as you are concerned it is… super-natural.
"Pretending is that powerful?"
It is beyond powerful; it is miraculous.
"Okay. So, let me get this straight: If I am 'real', ergo, it logically follows as day follows night, that I must be manifest?"
You are.

"I've been exposed?"
Apparently.
"Shit!"
Shit happens.

The old man pinched himself as he was wont to do in such circumstances. "Ouch!" he winced. Who pinches themselves in dreams? "It's real alright," he confirmed just before he woke up with a smile of relief upon his face and a twinkle in his eyes. The twinkle was real.

When the old man was in an effervescent mood his dark eyes inset under bushy gray eyebrows twinkled as if he were on the verge of bursting into mirthful laughter. It was a family trait. His father had that same ironic twinkle in his eyes. And so did his favorite cousin, Penelope – at least she did the last time he saw her. She had not said anything, but he knew she was in a good mood just by the way her eyes twinkled. It really was an endearing quality.

It is amazing how family traits can be passed on from generation to generation, preserved, so to speak, in microscopic strands of DNA. If Tsutomu Miki while in the service of Toyotomi Hideyoshi, had not formed a sexual liaison with a sensuous young geisha called Aiko and fathered three healthy sons, it is reasonable to assume that the old man would not be there along with the twinkle in his eye. But both the old man and the twinkle in his eyes had been salvaged from oblivion, a testament to the logical biological fact that every new link in the Great Chain of Being is actually the latest link on an endless chain of being stretching back into antiquity like an invisible beam of energy passing along the fibrous roots of a single plant drinking in the energy from the Light that connects the living to the dead, long forgotten in the dead hand of the past.

Of all the people who presently existed, the old man was one of the few who had become aware of this, and thought about it night and day. "Why?" he asked himself, "Is there some larger purpose behind these esoteric ruminations?" Perhaps it was merely the fact that such thoughts required the perspective of old age to be grasped, if they were to be grasped at all. Did the composite of his life experiences mould him into an individual destined to understand with profundity what others simply took for granted? There was so much to consider, so much to reflect upon and re-examine, so much to make sense of, so much to share. He had only a lifetime of mortal memories to call upon, but they seemed endless. Fortunately his long term memory was able to delve back into the murky depths of the hard-drive of his vast memory banks and retrieve clear images of things past, even though his short term memory was as fleeting as the next moment.

"What is consciousness?" the old man asked himself with a quizzical smile. More and more he felt like an omniscient observer of the passing-parade of his soul's mortal sojourn upon the miracle planet called earth. Was he the portal to a Cosmic-Consciousness which became evident when his cytoskeletons excited by a cascade of coherent tubulins gave emergence to a quantum coherence within the cellular structure of the neurons firing in his brain and voila: one dimensional time gave duration to a three dimensional space that due to the mass-density of his brute existence surrounded him with a four dimensional level of awareness? Such an awareness! Whose was it? His?

Or was he just the unique biological vehicle that gave expression to its existence, and the conduit through which it passed?

"Those were the days!" the old man exclaimed suddenly. "Sundays in Steveston," he sighed reflectively. He grinned as he recalled getting up early Sunday morning by himself while his parents slept in, and shivering in the quiet stillness of the unfinished wooden house which he, in his energetic childish way, was helping his parents build adjacent to the Fraser River. There was something about being an only child that made such moments particularly solemn; it was always just him, just himself alone in the cool of the morning air, getting up from his single cot with a tired yawn and getting dressed in the Sunday-best which he had laid out the night before. "There is a lasting significance in the slow movements of a little child getting dressed in the solitude of the silence," he thought. It is a silence that nobody else hears as time endures through a childhood spent.

When one is an only child the "only" rhymes with "lonely" in ways that are beyond mere poetry. The singularity provides a uniqueness of existence that is quite solitary. Sharing is not an automatic instinct; there are no siblings to share one's thoughts and things with. It was his own decision to attend Sunday school at the

United Church, because in Steveston that is what the other civilized Canadian kids were doing.

His parents did not mind his attending Sunday school at the United Church since they had many Christian friends, and quite a few of their offspring participated in Sunday school there. "It's okay with us," his mother said, "This is Canada, and here most of the people are Christians." So at eight forty-five he hurried off to Sunday school at the United Church, along with the other neighborhood kids. Somehow he felt good about that. There was acceptance there. He was one of them. He seemed to belong. It was a long time ago, and he was just an innocent little Oriental boy attempting in his own way to fit in. He recalled sitting in the basement of the local church back then, looking forward with the other impatient children to the upcoming Christmas concert.

And there was Miss Robertson, the Sunday school teacher, dressed in her neat blue-grey, Harris-tweed suit, with white bobby socks protruding above black leather low-heeled shoes, saying: "Christmas is a time of sharing, and the season to wish all people of all races, peace on earth and good will to man." He was one of three visible minorities in the class, but rarely felt conspicuous unless race was mentioned. Miss Robertson was very considerate when it came to treating every member of her class with equality. She was, perhaps, ahead of her generation. Sometimes there are individuals like that, individuals who rise above the mentality of the common herd and make a difference. It made a difference to him. Much later he often wondered: "Was she really aware of what she was doing?" In that Sunday school class, he was the equal of anyone else there; Miss Robertson would not have it any other way! That was just the way she was.

But that was before the war. Before – and after. What a contrast! Like day and night. "Too bad there weren't more people like Miss Robertson around at that time," he often thought. But in a democracy, the majority rule, and the majority was guided by the herd mentality of the times.

"Ahh-sohh!" the old man sighed in acknowledgement of the unique role Miss Robertson had played in his early life. Yes indeed, once upon a time he was just a curious young child growing up amidst the wonderment of the marshlands, canneries, and fishing boats, with an exhilarating sense of freedom discovered in the hustle and bustle that was Steveston, British Columbia, Canada. Who could imagine that an old codger like him actually had a happy childhood? There were so many precious memories like that stored in the command center of his central nervous system, memories that made him into the old man who now lay practically comatose with premature aging upon a sterile thirty-nine inch wide hospital bed.

Who exactly was this hilarious old caricature of a human being who pontificated like a sectarian preacher before a phantom audience as if he really was somebody worth listening to? This singular individual who looked out at the world through dark twinkling eyes as deep and as mysterious as the cosmos? It would be laughable, if he was not so darn serious! What did he care? So long as the last laugh was on his side?

CHAPTER THREE

Penny laughed when Larry popped the question. She thought he was just joking around. But he wasn't. The joke was on her. It was not funny, although it had the potential for hilarity.

Penny said, "Are you up for this?"

Larry said, "Yes, I've been up for this for some time."

"For some time?"

"For years."

"You certainly have staying power."

"I've been patient."

"I thought you'd never ask."

"I took my dear old mother's advice. I looked beneath and beyond, and there you were sparkling in the sun like a precious jewel."

"Your mother must have given you very good advice."

"She gave me you."

"What can I say?"

"Just say, 'yes'."

"I thought I did," Penny replied feeling flustered. "Didn't I say yes?"

"You said, 'Are you up for this?'"

Penny gave Larry a great big kiss and said, "Yes."

The wedding was held a month after they both graduated with Masters Degrees in Philosophy. On the marriage certificate was written: Lawrence and Penelope Petitjean.

Larry had changed his surname back to its genesis. It made him feel more authentic – not that Petty was not a perfectly authentic name for thousands of others – but to him it seemed rather phony, as if he were misrepresenting himself. "I really don't feel good about the name Petty," he had confessed to Penny shortly after they first had met. "Do you think I should change it back to its non Anglo-Saxon roots?"

"It seems to me that your real name is Petitjean," Penny replied with emphasis on the 'is'. "To me you look more like a Petitjean than a Petty," she declared with a laugh.

That was it. The next day Larry phoned the government agent's office to inquire about the process of changing his surname from

Petty back to Petitjean. He was comforted by the fact that his father who called himself John Petty – which ironically was a complete reversal of his original surname – had once told him that just prior to getting married he had seriously considered changing his name back to Petitjean. Now it was up to Larry to set the record straight.

The wedding was supposed to have been a low-key, under the radar, small time affair, that would be "no big deal" as Larry put it. The plan was to simply rent an inexpensive room in Las Vegas, and get quietly married in a little chapel nearby. For entertainment, they would take in a few free shows and gamble at the Golden Nugget. At least that was the plan at the beginning, before Penny made her one, single, fateful phone call.

Larry's parents, unfortunately, had passed away a few years back, and consequently were only able to attend in spirit. On the other hand, Penny's family members were alive and able to attend in the flesh. They were all looking forward to coming to Las Vegas: Hideo, Joyce, all three older brothers with their spouses and nine collective children ranging in age from seven to seventeen, plus her older sister and husband, with their four hyper or *yuncha* kids, for a grand total, count them: twenty-three people!

A month before, Penny assured Larry, "They will be devastated if I don't at least call. Just one quick call, just to let them know. I can't imagine them wanting to come all the way down to Vegas. Don't worry."

The call was quick all right. Like a quick call to the Fire Hall. They were prepared. "We've been looking forward to this day for, how long? At least fourteen or fifteen years, since your older sister got married," her mother, Joyce, replied excitedly when Penny called. "We'll all be there. You can count on us."

"But-but," Penny stammered. So much for their low-key, under the radar, no big deal, wedding.

They all stayed at the Golden Nugget. Expense was no obstacle. The bridal suite was reserved for the big night. Arrangements were made for an adjacent chapel. Banquet facilities were booked and meals decided upon. The youngest brother, the accountant, looked after it all. "Don't worry, it won't cost you a cent," he assured the bride and groom.

On the wedding day, Penny wore a gorgeous traditional white wedding dress. It was actually her older sister's, taken in at the waist and shortened. Her sister insisted she wear it. After all she was the matron-of-honor, and it was her duty to look after the bride.

Larry wore a black three piece suit with a double lapel, that matched the one worn by his best man, Henry, the fellow trekker who wet his pants when they saw that UFO on Mount Rainier. He was most cordial and had the makings for a first class master of ceremonies with his laconic wit and easy drawl.

"How do you plan on paying for all of this?" he asked the groom during dress rehearsal.

"I'll borrow the money," Larry replied.

"I could lend you a few bucks if you need it."

"Don't worry; Penny and I can handle it."

Still the best man worried about his buddy's welfare, because that is what makes the best man best.

Everything went off as smooth as the silk doilies on the banquet tables. A fabulous time was had by all involved, including the kids. The food was tasty and the hard drinks flowed like water. After all, how often in one's lifetime does this happen?

Still the best man worried. He approached "the accountant" as the banquet was wrapping up and casually asked, "I feel, that as best man, I should help pay for some of the expenses."

"Nonsense," the accountant remarked, with a red face compliments of the Johnny Walker's Red Label Scotch. "It's all taken care of. Don't worry!"

A family portrait was taken at the end, with Larry and the "baby sister" sitting in the middle. It was a strange feeling for Larry to be surrounded by so many Orientals, but he handled it well. He just pretended he was Oriental himself; who knows, perhaps in a previous incarnation he was! Everybody liked him, especially the kids. It made Penny feel ecstatically proud of him. And she had worried that he would not be up for it!

After the picture was taken, they all stood around and enjoyed fifteen minutes of small talk. When it was time to go their separate ways, Penny's second oldest brother sidled up to Larry and timidly asked, "Did you know that Penny just about died when she was a tiny baby?"

"Yes," Larry responded soberly, "Penny told me all about it. It was a miracle she survived."

"That is why she is so special to all of us," he explained. "I know she is also special to you," he said, and excused himself.

Larry sauntered up to where Hideo and Joyce were standing. He wanted to thank them for everything, but especially for their daughter's hand. He had a phrase worked out in his mind that did not sound too flowery, but then this strange feeling of guilt crept in and emboldened him to say, "It is not fair that you and your family pay for all of this."

There was an awkward moment of silence. It was as if he had suddenly transformed himself unwittingly into a *hakujin*, a foreigner. It was Joyce who stepped forth and quietly said, "It is not a matter of fairness. It is a matter of honor. It is an honor for us. Please accept this small token of our esteem. We have all been honored by your kindness, sensitivity, understanding... by your presence here."

Larry bowed humbly. Never had he felt so honored in all his life. His eyes watered as he gratefully said, "*Arigato gozai-masu.*"

Hideo clear his throat and expressed his heartfelt sentiments: "Take good care of Penny. She is more precious than life."

* * *

Mr. and Mrs. Petitjean spent two weeks honeymooning along the beautiful Oregon coast, frolicking in the sand dunes and swimming in the refreshing waters of the Pacific Ocean. It was a magical interlude, a time to be fondly recalled in quiet moments when the sunlight caught the nuance of that instant when Penny skipped lightly down the beach, throwing her hands up to the sky and shouting, "Never has there been such a perfect moment. I could burst with joy!"

And in that fabulous instant Larry knew in his heart he had never seen anything so poignant or so perfect, and tears clouded his eye because he felt so privileged to have been able to share in that moment. What had a mere mortal like him done to deserve such perfection?

However, all such fleeting moments of near perfection must flow into other more mundane moments, and even though the days seemed endless, the economic reality of the work-a-day world kept impinging itself upon their consciousness. What were they going to do to earn a living? Was anybody hiring educated beach bums with Masters Degrees in Philosophy?

Who ever heard of Ludwig Wittgenstein in the everyday world of trade and commerce? What economic value did Logical Positivism have on the marketplace? After they pondered such pragmatic questions over and over, the road leading north seemed more viable than the ones leading anywhere else. In a lesser developed marketplace like Canada, perhaps their hard-earned degrees might still be of some small advantage in securing gainful employment.

Thus it came to pass that Larry and Penny Petitjean packed their meager belongings into the trunk of the reliable old Mazda and headed to Vancouver, British Columbia, Canada, to begin their married life together. It seemed to Penny as if she was making a U-turn, but to her husband, the road north was a whole new experience.

Americans, in general, are more than welcome in Canada, especially those with big companies and lots of US dollars to spend. But Larry had neither. Consequently when he arrived as a landed immigrant, he had considerable difficulty qualifying for a work visa, even though he was "married to a bona fide Canadian citizen," as he repeatedly impressed upon the disinterested bureaucrat who raised her eyebrows and calmly said, "I can assure you I am not deaf."

In due time the bureaucracy did the necessary paperwork, and Larry, with his penchant for reason and common sense, managed to secure a job as a management trainee with a business machines company that was just starting up. It was a bit of a calculated risk in such a fledgling operation, but Larry opted to buy-in, as part of his employment package, thereby making himself part-owner of a company that looked to have a very bright future. The buy-in left Larry with very little disposable income with which to support his wife, even in the frugal manner to which she had become accustomed. Consequently Penny was obliged to look for gainful employment to keep herself and her husband at a comfortable standard of living commensurate with their lowered expectations.

After a short job search, Penny thought herself very fortunate, due to her previous contacts at UBC, to be offered a union job as Library Clerk at that bastion of academic excellence. The male personnel officer told her in strict confidence that they preferred to hire "overqualified women". It was good to know that her Masters Degree in Philosophy was good for something.

Penny enjoyed her job because it allowed her the time to take some courses on the side. "I might as well begin work on my Doctorate; then perhaps some day I might be able to teach the odd class or two here," she explained to Larry, who was all for the idea. However, no sooner had she been approved for candidacy in the Doctoral program, when her missing period moved her ambitions from the fast track to the very slow track.

The prospects of parenthood encouraged their nesting instincts. Never was an unborn child so loved even before it was born. The nursery was the nicest room in the small two bedroom apartment. The entire apartment looked and felt more like a home.

Larry suddenly became much more responsible both at home and at work. At work he put in longer hours without complaint and so impressed his co-workers and superiors that they elevated him to the lofty position of "Manager of Public Relations", which was an impressive way of saying "sales rep". Incredibly, as the months passed, sales and service increased geometrically, and in spite of his humility, Larry was once again singled out for praise. Not only did his wages go up, so did the value of his stock. It was a good thing because Penny was informed after the fifth month was nearly over, that she was carrying twins. Costs were rising along with their expectations.

When she found out she was going to have twins, Penny applied for and received maternity leave. Waddling around like a duck in the library was fatiguing. At home she could lie back and put her feet up while Larry waited on her hand and foot. He cooked; he washed and dried the dishes; he did the laundry; he vacuumed the floor. He was very concerned and very excited about the prospect of having twins.

"I hope we have a boy and a girl," he said. "That would be so perfect."

It turned out just as Larry had hoped. He had been squirming impatiently on a black vinyl couch in the waiting room for over two hours when at long last the Doctor came in and said, "The first one was a girl, and the second one was a boy. You may go in and visit your wife now. She is resting, but you can sit with her. We'll be bringing in the babies as soon as they are cleaned and presentable. They are both healthy and well-formed. Should be no problems. Congratulations!" Larry gave him two Cuban cigars.

What a picture it was to see Penny nursing two babies at once. The day she became a mother the magnitude of her aura changed. It overlapped with those of her two offspring. When she was nursing them they were three in one. Larry felt like an outsider. However, as the babies grew and matured, they became individuals, and Larry felt the magnetic attraction of fatherhood. And for the first time he understood what Hideo meant by, "...more precious than life."

CHAPTER FOUR

Parenthood disguises the relentless passage of time. Who cares how old the parents are when the children are happily celebrating one birthday after the next? Time stands still for the parents and races ahead for the offspring. And before the bewildered parents grasp what is happening, their precious children are grown up and leaving home. Suddenly the parents feel their age and the house feels like an empty nest.

It happens like this most frequently in civilized nations where both parents have careers to salvage and preconceived ideas about what a nuclear family is supposed to consist of. Sometimes such families explode like a nuclear bomb and the fallout hits the front pages. It is not the best way to raise children but it happens everyday in crowded cities all over Western Christendom where the Protestant Work Ethic evolved into the Spirit of Capitalism. It is not a spiritual phenomenon. It is more of a religious doctrine manifested. God smiles upon those who become rich, an obvious sign of favoritism. It rationalizes our irrational behavior and makes it seem reasonable. That is probably why we continue to subconsciously perpetuate it in spite of the dire consequences that may result in the prophesied Doomsday scenario.

It was into this type of modern, capitalistic, civilized society that two innocent souls emerged. When their proud parents left Vancouver General Hospital with the baby twins wrapped securely in fluffy flannel blankets – a pink and white one for the girl and a blue and white one for the boy – they were oblivious to everything except their unconditional love for their two precious offspring.

In many, many ways they were very lucky. The twins, whom they had named Sherry and Jerry respectively, were healthy, well-formed, beautiful, cuddly infants. They actually shone with a shiny glow. Perhaps there was some hybrid vigor there. What more could they expect?

It is the expectation of most intelligent parents that their offspring reflect at least the same or higher level of intellectual capability as their own. Sometimes, however, in accord with the law of averages, intelligent parents give birth to offspring of mediocre intellect. Unfortunately, many such parents feel somewhat hard-done-by, with the result that such offspring are often treated with an unconscious disdain they do not deserve.

As Sherry and Jerry grew from infants to toddlers to pre-schoolers, it became evident to their doting parents that they had been blessed with twins with remarkable intelligence. This was particularly important in a University environment where intelligence is so highly appreciated; it reflected positively upon the parents of such precocious youngsters. If the offspring were smart, was not this proof positive that the parents must be at least above average?

By the time Sherry and Jerry, who were the "nicest kids you ever saw", were ready for kindergarten, Larry's good fortune with the business machines company in which he had invested, rose to an all time high. His stock went up a considerable amount from the original purchase price. It was a good thing too because as it turned out with his growing young family, he needed more living space. He never told the company bosses that his wife had been hassling him mercilessly for nearly two years about purchasing a "brand new house" near the University.

"This tiny two bedroom apartment is just too darn small," Penny would say as she prepared breakfast in a six by six kitchen and served it in a six by six dining space that flowed into a slightly larger living-room. "The bunk-beds have served us well, but I think it is time the kids had rooms of their own. When they start school they probably will want to have friends stay overnight once in a while, just for fun. You know how it is."

"I never had anyone stay over when I was a kid," Larry argued feebly. "However, I guess that is no excuse for depriving our kids," he relented.

"The kids should not have to suffer the same deprivations that we did."

"Thinning sugar beets might be good for them once in a while!" Larry joked.

"If you had to do it day after day, week after week, month after month under the hot blazing noonday sun, I doubt if you would be making a joke of it," Penny replied soberly.

"Yeah Dad!" the twins both jumped in, siding with their mother.

"Three to one is not good odds," Larry relented. "I guess I'd better retract that statement for my own good."

"Why don't we sell off some of our over-priced stock and buy a house?" Penny continued.

"Yeah, why don't we, Dad?" the twins sided with their mother once again.

"We can afford it," Penny asserted. "If we sold it all, we probably won't even have to have a mortgage."

"What do you think, Dad?" Sherry asked wrinkling up her pug nose.

"Well, let me think about this," Larry cogitated. "What do you think, Jerry?" he asked, looking for an excuse to give in.

"Well, Dad," Jerry pondered mimicking his father, "I think we should take a vote. All in favor of selling the stock and buying a house raise your hands."

Everyone raised their hand including Larry.

"It's unanimous!" Jerry announced.

"Where did you learn that word?" Larry asked in surprise.

"From me," Sherry took credit.

"Smart kids – eh?" Penny remarked smiling somewhat smugly, like the Mona Lisa.

Larry could not bring himself to sell all of his prized stock, so he cautiously relinquished eighty percent and kept twenty for future considerations. In hindsight he should have sold it all, but who could have predicted that years later it would come crashing down? Consequently they had a small, but manageable mortgage on their beautiful three bedroom bungalow with full undeveloped basement, two car garage, and ample lawn and garden space out back. It was their dream home. It was located fairly close to the University and situated in a quiet cul-de-sac with minimum traffic. It was a great place to raise a young family.

Everyone was ready for the move. The whole family was energized. Not one single complaint was heard. Joyous anticipation bubbled beneath every act of drudgery as they happily packed all their precious belongings into cardboard boxes and stacked them in the living-room, ready for transport. The kids were very anxious to help in any way they could without getting in the way. It was an exciting time for all.

Larry rented a twenty-four foot Budget rent-a-truck on the day the big move took place. Three of his co-workers volunteered to help him move. In less than two hours the truck was loaded and ready to roll. Three hours later it was unloaded and returned to the place from whence it was rented. Penny made sandwiches and the whole crew sat around in the large new living-room and drank beer and ate. The kids drank milk and ate. The move was complete. The Petitjeans were installed in their very own house at last.

The next day Penny checked out the neighborhood schools while Larry checked out the recreational facilities. The house was close to everything. They were elated.

When they gathered in their spacious back yard for the first time, Penny declared, "What a fabulous place!"

"Almost too good to be true!" Larry responded.

"Boy, are we lucky!" Jerry exclaimed.

"*Arigato-gosaimusu*," Sherry said showing off one of the few Japanese expressions that her father knew.

It was indeed the correct sentiment, adroitly expressed, by a little girl of five on behalf of a family dreaming of the good life. In a world in which so many people go to bed hungry, and often must subsist on a small amount of rice and worry about contaminated water, the Petitjeans were very fortunate to be living in one of the few democratic countries in the world where dreams of the good life had every possibility of being fulfilled.

"Thank you," Penny said humbly, realizing that her daughter had instinctively vocalized a sentiment that resonated throughout the centuries in the hearts of those overwhelmed by good fortune, "thank you very much for this wonderful new home." She bowed her head, and reminiscent of a dutiful Japanese wife, repeated with heartfelt gratitude: "*Arigato-gosaimusu*."

"You're welcome," Larry responded awkwardly, his face flushing with embarrassment.

"I don't think Mom was speaking to you, Dad", Jerry politely pointed out with an insightful sensitivity rather extraordinary for a five year old.

CHAPTER FIVE

One of the amazing things about Larry was that he turned out to be such a "free thinker". His parents, especially his father, were more or less straight-laced Presbyterians. In public his father, the Reverend John Petty, presented himself as a fire and brimstone type Presbyterian preacher who believed staunchly in the inevitability of Armageddon, but in the private confines of their home he displayed a more lenient attitude.

Being an only child in such a family had both its upside and downside. The upside was that every Sunday Larry got to dress up in a handsome little three piece suit and sit in the front pew with his mother, who never wore anything but black dresses, and listen to the finest sermons his father could deliver. Larry was always impressed by how animated his father became when he described how powerful the sins of greed and lust could be. It seemed to Larry that his father really knew whereof he spoke; when he stood in the pulpit with the Bible in his hand he was so convincing.

Because Larry always sat so still and looked so attentive, his father began to believe that as he grew older and was able to make up his own mind, Larry eventually would be "called" to follow in his own footsteps. This belief, along with a natural parental affection, filled Larry's father with a wonderful sense of pride. To see his only son sitting there Sunday after Sunday with his eyes looking up at him as if he were God Almighty, filled Larry's father with such a deep-seated feeling of appreciation for this wonderful "gift of life", that he frequently had to turn away while he was preaching because he became so choked up with emotion. The congregation could plainly see that God was working through him and became all the more devout.

The downside to all of this was that all throughout his public school years Larry must have heard at least a thousand Presbyterian Preacher jokes. If the joke did not originally include a Presbyterian Preacher, it was always modified in such a manner that the Presbyterian minister ended up being the butt end of the joke. This type of ridicule rarely fazed Larry. He developed a defensive strategy where he would ruin the jokes by telling them first, in such a lackluster fashion that they were more boring than funny. Sometimes he would reveal the punch line prematurely and laugh hilariously, making the others feel that they must have missed something. Usually the last laugh was on his side.

With such an easy-going attitude, Larry made it through unscathed to Presbyterian College where it seemed natural that he would study Theology. Ironically, it was the study of Theology that illuminated his gift for logic and analytical thought. He could see right through the dogma and the doctrine to what, in his mind, constituted the logical conclusions. And they were often at odds with the preconceived outcomes. "It has to make logical sense," he would complain to the instructor conducting the seminar, "Otherwise what is the point of the discussion?"

"There are some things you must accept on faith alone," the instructor would say.

"But only after you have exhausted all attempts at reasonable explanations," Larry would counter. "It seems to me that reason and logic constitute the bridge from which the didactic leap is taken."

"Why don't you take the course on classical Greek philosophy?" the frustrated instructor candidly suggested. "I think it may be more to your liking."

That was probably the singular piece of advice that forever changed Larry's outlook on life. It was a revelation to discover that in Philosophy reason and common sense took precedence over dogma and doctrine. The only begotten son of a Presbyterian minister was on his way down a path no one in his family had even considered to be a remote possibility. He felt like a pioneer breaking trail for the first time in virgin territory as old as the mysterious universe.

Larry apologized profusely to his father on the day he returned home, full of apprehension and anxiety, to inform him that he was no longer interested in pursuing a career in Theology, and was switching his major to Philosophy. He could see by the withdrawn look in his father's eyes that he knew his precious dream was not to be realized during this lifetime. He did not say anything, but he looked as if he wanted to cry.

Larry's mother, who was very intuitive, came over and placed a comforting arm around her husband's sloping shoulders. She gazed meaningfully into her spouse's eyes and spoke in a calm soothing voice: "It is Larry's way."

At that precise moment the unnoticed became apparent. It was the humble acceptance, the quiet tone of his mother's voice when she said, "It is Larry's way," and the almost imperceptible nod of his father's head. It was then that for the first time Larry understood with profundity the true meaning of "unconditional love."

* * *

It's funny how some things can go unnoticed, and then one day it just comes to you because it is so obvious. Penny noticed that there was something truly unique about her daughter, Sherry, at a very early age. She seemed to radiate a healing vibe. Not only did she display a keen intellect and an independence of mind that indicated to her parents that she would one day march to the beat of her own drummer, she also had that special quality that attracted people to her like a magnet. It was like being attracted to the sun on a cold and miserable day. Sherry's sunny disposition was like a golden ray of sunshine. She was like a placebo that caused people to heal themselves. Since Sherry's birth no one in the family had been sick. It was uncanny.

When Sherry visited her sick friends, they always felt much better the next day. It was as if this seven year old child was a magic healer, and was not even aware of it. "It is a natural gift," Penny thought. "It is there because she is not aware of it. It is natural and uncontaminated by her self-awareness. It flows through her unimpeded. It will last as long as she is unaware of it, but once she becomes aware of it, it will change because her awareness will make her self-conscious, and her natural healing vibes will be contorted by her anxiety to heal."

It was a fascinating insight. There was no way to verify its authenticity. Perhaps it was just a mother's wishful thinking. "Just let her be," Penny told herself. "The world is a better place because of her. She is just like a tiny bud that will grow and mature, and one day she will blossom into the most beautiful flower the world has ever seen. But will the world appreciate her presence in their midst? Will her growth be stunted and her blooming go unnoticed in a tangle of noxious weeds?"

Such thoughts were a prelude to Sherry's Junior High School years. "We must encourage her to be strong and true to herself,"

Penny reminded her husband, the night before school was to recommence after summer break, "Junior High is whole new ball game."

"She'll hit a home run," Larry said confidently.

One night when Jerry was in grade three, Larry went into Jerry's room to help drill him on a few basic math facts that he was learning at school. He was always amazed at how quickly someone so young could calculate such complex mathematical problems in his head. "Incredible intellectual ability there," he often thought to himself, but he never made this too obvious in case his son became conceited. He merely made up harder problems that challenged and expanded Jerry's ability to see other possibilities.

"Anyone can see the obvious," Larry would say, "but it takes a real brain to grasp what has not yet been seen."

And the boy would outdo himself to grasp the ungraspable. He would say things like, "Numbers are easy, Dad, because they really don't exist anywhere except in our heads." And one time just as he was about to fall asleep he whispered, "Numbers don't make any sound."

But the singular comment that most impressed Larry occurred when he asked his son, "Why do you like math so much?"

Jerry looked up at the ceiling and said, "Numbers are magic. They are nothing, and yet they can account for everything. We can build the whole universe out of numbers. They are the toy building blocks of the mind."

Larry could visualize that little boy stacking up those numbers like building blocks and building mansions in the sky. He was reminded of that phrase his father so liked to use in his sermons, "In my father's house are many mansions." He did not think his father really understood what Jesus was getting at, because he was not very good at math.

After he would leave his son's or daughter's rooms at night, Larry would go to bed and think how lucky he was to have such marvelous children. He could not imagine life without them. They meant everything to him, especially at a time when they were so young and dependent upon him. He vividly recalled one particular time when a classmate of Sherry's had been run over in the school zone crosswalk and killed by a reckless driver.

"How do parents withstand such pain?" he thought, "How is it possible to continue to live when life has become an empty vessel?" That very night when Larry looked in on Jerry and Sherry he said, "I must be the luckiest person in the world."

They did not have to ask him why. They knew.

CHAPTER SIX

One of Larry's and Penny's more fun activities was camping. When the kids were both in grade four and full of boundless energy, an opportunity arose that provided the family with one of their most fun-filled summer holidays. The vice-president of Larry's business machines company had decided to move up in the material world by purchasing a semi-new class C, twenty-six foot motor-home. This made his semi-old hardtop tent trailer, fully equipped with stove, two-way fridge, and port-a-potty, available to his good buddy and business associate, Larry. And the price was right!

Prior to the purchase a serious family discussion took place, and after the supper dishes were cleared a vote was taken. It was unanimous. The purchase of a tent trailer entailed camping duties. Jerry said he would help with the dishes and be in charge of the campfire. Sherry said she would make the beds and help with the dishes. Larry said he would help with the dishes, cook, chop wood and draw water, put a trailer hitch on the Honda, and arrange to pay off the new purchase over the next six months. Penny said that as it looked like everything was being done, she would just supervise. As it turned out later, she had the hardest job.

When school was out on June 30th the entire family was ready and chompin' at the bit. The itinerary had been carefully laid out with input from everyone. They would leave early on the morning of July 1st and drive directly to the provincial campground at Scotch Creek on the northern shores of Shuswap Lake. They would stay there for three or four days and then head down through Salmon Arm, Enderby, and Vernon, and camp out on the sunny shores of Okanagan Lake near Kelowna for two or three days. From there they planned to take it slow and easy while winding their way through the Monashees to the Kootenays, and play it by ear from there through the historic Crowsnest Pass where the kids were looking forward to seeing the Frank Slide, to Pincher Creek, Alberta, where Penny's hard-smoking friend, Janice, was living with her hardworking rancher husband. Since they could camp out there free of charge while the kids learned to ride real horses, they decided to stay there for a whole week and take an excursion to Waterton Lakes National Park.

From Pincher Creek the highway led east through the Brocket Reserve to Fort Macleod and from thence to the city of Lethbridge where Penny's parents, siblings, nephews and nieces resided. When they arrived at Penny's parents' home the twins reverted into being such timid creatures in the presence of their aged grandparents that Larry felt slightly embarrassed by their reticence and Penny was reminded of the term "Kitchen Tarzan". However the twins soon lost their shyness when Penny's three older bothers and older sister arrived with their respective families and a laid-back party atmosphere developed in the beautifully landscaped and shady back yard. Country and Western music reverberated from an oversized boom-box, and wide assortments of sushi, sandwiches and other refreshments materialized. The adults relaxed by standing around or sitting on folding lawn chairs imbibing unusually large amounts of ice cold Lethbridge lager straight from the bottle, behavior that seemed not only excusable, but reasonable, considering the sweltering weather, while the younger kids drank orange punch and ran around laughing and shouting with such glee that soon Jerry and Sherry felt right at home. By the end of the first day the twins were on a first name basis with all their relatives. By the end of the second day everyone was pals with everyone else. When they left on the morning of the third day all their relatives were sad to see them leave. "Come back again soon!" they shouted. And it was obvious they meant it.

On the way back the Petitjeans were scheduled to make stops at Calgary (but unfortunately not in time to see the Stampede), Red Deer (where there should have been a red deer somewhere), and Edmonton (where they just missed Klondike Days). From Edmonton, they planned to take a leisurely jaunt through the magnificent mountain landscape of Jasper National Park, to Kamloops, and from there, through the Hell's Gate Canyon back to their home sweet home.

It turned out to be a most memorable camping trip. One of those once in a lifetime summer activities, that at the time, passes unnoticed in the hectic melodramatic rush of a plethora of fun activities. When they got back safe, sound, and exhausted, the kids said that next year they should rent a houseboat at Sicamous, shoot through the Roger's Pass, and camp in Banff National Park. The reason they wanted to go to Banff was that most of the road signs along the Trans Canada Highway indicated that the next stop was Banff, even though it was hundreds of miles away in Alberta, and they were just looking for the next pit stop.

Anyway, it was nice to get back home and go to sleep in their own nice beds.

It was while they were camped out in Pincher Creek that Larry came to comprehend with greater clarity and understanding, Penny's somewhat ambiguous attitude toward his Christian heritage, a heritage with which he was constantly attempting to come to terms. It was late at night, the kids were in bed and the campfire was glowing red embers. Larry was sitting hunched over the fire pit with a cup of warm coffee in his hands.

"You know," he said to Penny, "your attitude is contagious. It took a while, but now I think I've got it figured out."

"You have?"

"It's like you said, the main difference between Christianity and Buddhism is a matter of perception. This perception affects one's attitude."

"You've been thinking all right," Penny responded. "Please elaborate."

"I've been thinking about this for some time, actually."

"Some things take time to sink in."

"Especially into a hard head like mine," Larry grinned. He swished the coffee around in his mug, slowly raised his gaze from the mug to Penny's eyes, and spoke in a ponderous tone. "Christianity has an external God," he paused as if for effect, "while Buddhism has an internal God."

"So?"

"This makes all the difference in the world."

"It does?"

"When God is external or outside of the self and creation, it makes the self and creation – get this – godless. We are here and God is out there. I know this sounds simplistic, but I am talking about a point of view here that translates into a powerful mindset: a particular way of looking at and thinking about ourselves and about creation. Most Christians, in my humble opinion, view themselves and creation from this mindset. They are here in this creation – and God resides somewhere way out there," Larry waved his hand toward the vast darkness of the sky.

"I see," Penny responded encouragingly. "Man and Creation are distinct and separate from their Maker. Man exists here in this earthly creation or reality, and God exists out there, and there is this gulf between them."

"Right on, and because God is external and separate from Man and Creation, this creates an overwhelming yearning in spiritual man to somehow be worthy enough to gain the attention of this external God. How can this be done? If he cries and wails and shakes his fist, will his 'Father who art in Heaven' acknowledge this wayward child?"

"What a predicament to be in!" Penny exclaimed.

"From this point of view, everyone is in this predicament whether they know it or not," Larry continued. "Almighty God is way up there, and puny man is down here groveling about on a God-forsaken planet hoping that somehow he can make a connection with his Maker."

"If he could make that precious connection what a miraculous thing that would be!" Penny enthused, motivating her husband to continue.

"From this point of view that connection is everything. Everything!" Larry emphasized. "Without a divine connection, Man is nothing, as worthless as a cut off bit of hay or the spittle from cattle." Larry was very good at throwing in bits and pieces of paraphrasing from the Bible.

"Could this have something to do with the concept of sin?" Penny offered.

"Yes, of course," Larry agreed. "Man has rationalized his circumstances vis-à-vis his external conception of God. Somehow he has to justify this separation, this sense of abandonment and isolation from the essence of his origins and ultimate identity. So he makes up all kinds of reasons why this situation exists – he has to, because this point of view depends on it. Without such an explanation he would sink into the deepest abyss of nihilistic despair."

"You're thinking about the ancient Hebrew enslavement in Egypt."

"You are a mind reader! If you were born and raised as a slave in a wretched godless society, you'd have to provide an existentially sound explanation filled with hope and intrinsic purpose to your children when they asked: "What have we done to deserve this?"

"A very human sentiment. And the answer is?"

"We are not perfect like God. We are tragically flawed creatures beholden to God for our existence. In our ignorance we foolishly disobeyed God, our Father, and like wayward children we must be punished for our sinful ways. But, because we are the chosen people, God has not abandoned us, although it may seem like it. He is only testing us! And if we persevere through this lifetime of sin, God, who is all powerful, will reward us by taking us up to His Heavenly Paradise, way out there, where we will be safe. And then He will punish the unrepentant and the evil doers!" Larry's voice rose like his father's used to when he stood in the pulpit and gesticulated grandly with his soft white hands for emphasis.

"Aren't you getting a little overly dramatic about this?" Penny cautioned diplomatically, as her husband's face flushed with his increasing animation.

Larry remained silent for a moment to let his blood pressure subside. "Sorry, I guess I started preaching again – didn't I?" Larry apologized with a grin, "but you know how it is with me."

"I understand," Penny nodded wisely like a sage waiting patiently for a disciple to see the light.

"Man had to find some natural mechanism by which he could make and maintain a connection with God, his Maker and Holy Father," Larry continued in a moderate tone. "This mechanism was exceedingly simple: Man had simply to acknowledge through blind faith that, yes indeed, a separate and all powerful God did actually exist somewhere out there. Once this acknowledgement was made, that external God had to be humbly accepted as being the one and only true God of all gods, bar none. This belief became known as Monotheism."

"And the Judaic, Moslem, and Christian faiths are different manifestations of the rationalization of this point of view," Penny added.

"Yes, these three inter-related religions presented this external God as a Being to be feared. To them, fear of God was the beginning of wisdom. Most of their religious dogmas and doctrines were subsequently premised upon this relationship and understanding. It was an authoritarian model. All power and authority was given, through God, to His all-too-fallible representatives on earth. Each institutionalized religious faith claimed to be the one and only true faith. This pitted Christian against Muslim against Jew."

"Three authoritarian religious faiths paying homage to one all-powerful God. If only one of these religions represents the True Faith, then the other two must obviously be misrepresentations or false religions," Penny followed up with her impeccable sense of logic.

"God's wrath upon the two false contenders! 'Vengeance is mine, saith the Lord,'" Larry added for effect.

"Whew!" Penny exhaled. "What have we gotten ourselves into?"

"The authoritative dogma of these three religions was founded upon the notion that fear of God was the beginning of wisdom," Larry repeated for emphasis, "and fear one should, because God was vengeful! What kind of a relationship could one develop with a vindictive God? It fostered a quicksand of irrational fear. It had no real substance because it was based upon blind faith. But this apparent weakness turned out to be its saving grace, because irrational fear is a very powerful motivator! Perhaps even more powerful than reason or common sense."

"I can see why, from this point of view, one would be motivated to conceive of oneself as being 'chosen' or 'saved', or in some traditional or historical fashion included in the good graces of this fearsome God," Penny reflected.

"You can appreciate the power of 'excommunication'," Larry followed up. "In a world filled with fear and insecurity this view of a fearsome yet forgiving God grew like mustard seeds in fertile soil, spawning a vast variety of denominations that over the last two millennia have spread fear, terror, and hope in the hearts of men, women and children throughout the world, in the name of the One and only True God. Reality reflects what it is."

"And what is it?"

"The secular and economic manifestation of this world-view evolved over time and became transformed into a pragmatic way of life presently known as Modern Capitalism. Its *modus operandi* is subconsciously justified by the attitudes and beliefs which underlie and support it, making it quite permissible to plunder, pollute, and decimate Mother Earth for profit. This behavior is condoned, because in the end Man will be taking his leave from this god-forsaken planet to dwell in sublime comfort in a faraway heavenly paradise with his Almighty Father."

"What an amazing story of pathos and glory," Penny rhymed accidentally.

"If it were a darksome fairy-tale told by an idiot, full of sound and fury signifying... " Larry coughed into his clenched fist.

"Who would believe it was actually true?"

A gentle breeze whipped up the campfire coals into brilliant spurts of yellow flame. Larry absentmindedly dumped the remains of his coffee cup on the fire causing it to sputter and smoke. The breeze blew the smoke in his direction causing his eyes to water. "Sometimes we do stupid things," he said.

"I'll say," Penny noted, as Larry moved around to her side of the fire. "And how does the external view differ in substance and kind from other religions with an intrinsic point of view?" she inquired.

Larry glanced at his wristwatch. "It's getting quite late, so I'll try to be brief," he replied. "The intrinsic view places God inside Man and Creation. God is part and parcel of everything there is, because, according to this view, God is everywhere. Therefore Man does not need to seek God outside of himself because God is inherent in all Creation. Through a natural and innate yearning to know who he really is, Man gradually becomes aware of God's presence. This growing awareness leads to self-realization and eventually to a state known as enlightenment, where Man realizes his ultimate Identity."

"I can see why those people have such reverence for life, and foster a sacred relationship with the earth that nurtures and sustains them," Penny observed.

"Yes, because this universe and this Creation is everything to them, because God is here instead of out there," Larry pointed out, while bending forward to stir the glowing embers with a short poker-stick.

"I am impressed, dear, how clear and unequivocal your notion of these two universal points of view has become," Penny assessed, drawing closer to the campfire.

"We've probably discussed aspects of this topic dozens of times before, but-but as you know, I seem to have had this negative mindset of sorts back then," Larry admitted. "This built-in bias prevented me from looking at both sides objectively. Remember how

I always had to argue against you, as if it were a categorical imperative?"

"The traditional view could not have had a more stalwart defender."

"And yet," Larry paused reflectively, "all these insights that I've just presented as if they were my own, were really the fruit grown from seeds you planted years ago."

"You are too modest," Penny replied humbly.

"There have probably been many other seeds that fell upon my hard-headedness and failed to sprout."

"You are much too hard on yourself," Penny commiserated.

"For some reason I was subconsciously defending the status quo, even though I always presented myself as being so open-minded," Larry continued apologetically.

"I admire you more than ever!" Penny declared. "Regardless of the small role I might have played in their formulation, these are your insights. They have a great deal more significance for you because you had to overcome a mindset so powerful, it would have been debilitating for most others."

"I only wish there was some way we could share these insights with others."

"It would be nice," Penny sighed wistfully, "but as you know, there are a whole lot of intelligent people out there with mindsets so powerful, perhaps they would simply be offended."

"I think you underestimate them," Larry countered politely. "They may seem to be so, but believe me, underneath it all, they too sincerely want to know in the cellular memory of their hearts, who they really are! In the end reason and common sense will prevail over dogma and doctrine. I just know it."

"Ah-men," Penny concluded, rising from her camping stool. "For the sake of our children, and all the young people the world over, I certainly hope that you are right."

CHAPTER SEVEN

Penny's positive outlook and imaginative flights of intuitive thought often reminded Larry of a beautiful butterfly soaring high above the mundane world where time is money and money is power, and time and money chased each other around in a vicious circle.

There was a time in Penny's life when she was not able to soar above the viciousness of the circle. It was during her time in Calgary when she was striving to reach her true potential in the cutthroat world of business and commerce that Penny went through a stage of self-metamorphosis somewhat like cocooning, before she emerged as a fledgling butterfly, anxious to try her new wings on the prevailing winds of conventional wisdom. It may seem, to use a tidbit of conventional wisdom, that what goes in determines what comes out. Following this logic, who would ever have imagined that the sluggish creature that spun the cocoon would be magically transformed into a butterfly of such exquisite beauty?

Penny crawled along at a snail's pace through her life during this metamorphic period of savage competition, romance, and devastated hope. It was not that she could not handle it, but rather that she just was not in tune with it. What was militating against her in those days was the potentiality that lay dormant inside her: an innate energy bursting with eons of latent evolutionary wisdom inculcated into the deoxyribonucleic acid or DNA of every single cell that constituted her biological makeup. She was, without knowing it, destined to emerge as a butterfly with powerful wings designed to soar above the mundane and the conventional to heights other butterflies looked up to with apprehension.

This matter of soaring above the mundane and conventional did not just happen overnight. Even if one is born with the potential to rise and soar, this latent ability has to be honed on the slippery surface of everyday life where the nitty-gritty grains of insecurity and doubt dull the nervous edge of the daring and replace the desire to soar with the tendency to burrow.

Penny spent countless hours burrowing as one who is destined to soar, burrows: with flights of wild imagination. She burrowed around the cutting edge of issues that lay buried in the murkiest caverns of conventional wisdom and sought to bring them to the light of day. One sensational issue of the day that caught her fancy had to do with credibility. It separated the believers from the non-believers. It could have been a religious issue, but it was not. It was the most controversial of mundane issues. It had to do with her southern neighbors and the national security of the most powerful country in the entire world. Perhaps it was not all that mundane after all, but to a potential butterfly it seemed rather mundane at first.

What piqued Penny's curiosity about this issue was that the whole thing had the distinctive odor of a rather foul smelling cover-up. Of course this factor immediately triggered Penny's burrowing tendency to get to the bottom of it. The irony that Penny encountered when attempting to uncover the truth about what actually happened at Roswell, New Mexico in 1947, two years after the Second World War had ended was that the "truth" had already been succinctly put forth by the American government's trusted officials who worked for the O.S.S. or Office of Strategic Services.

The "true story" as presented by the OSS, amounted to this: A weather balloon had crashed at Roswell, New Mexico in 1947. Subsequently their modern replacements, the Central Intelligence Agency or CIA, reiterated these facts ad nauseam, and attempted to persuade a disbelieving public that indeed no alien spacecraft or UFO had crash-landed at Roswell, and, of course, it had to follow that no little aliens were found at that site. Weather balloons are not manned by aliens. Was the credibility of the CIA and indirectly the Government undermined by this story? Was there much more to it than a skeptical public was aware of? The matter was important enough for vital information to be classified.. Why? Because national security supposedly warranted it, and anything can be classified by some anonymous high-ranking bureaucrat if it is deemed to be in the interest of national security. That weather balloon must have been really special!

This singular issue consumed Penny's interest for many weeks, which soon became months. It was obvious to her that there was a much greater issue at stake than appeared on the surface. The question that was foremost in Penny's mind was not whether little green aliens existed, but whether or not the government of the world's most prominent democracy would deliberately lie to its own people, for whatever reasons. The feelings of frustration, doubt, and exasperation this issue raised in Penny, aided and abetted her latent tendency to want to soar high above such "Machiavellian machinations," as one of her friends encapsulated it.

The account of this dubious issue that seemed "most believable" to her friends went something like the following. Shortly after the Second World War ended the USA was plunged into a cold war with the USSR. Some Americans who tuned in late to a radio broadcast by Orson Welles mistook a fictitious newscast regarding an alien invasion as being authentic or real. This caused considerable panic. Consequently, when a small, reconnaissance-type UFO crash-landed at Roswell, New Mexico on July 2nd 1947 some high-ranking officials in the Government decided that such news might cause public hysteria, which would be detrimental to the national security of a country involved in a Cold War. Consequently the original report that appeared in the newspaper immediately after the incident and stated that a UFO had crashed at Roswell, was quickly replaced with the official story. The real facts pertaining to what actually happened at Roswell had to be covered-up and a lie concocted that would serve as a plausible accounting of what happened. All pertinent information regarding the Roswell incident had to be classified for the public's own good. They could not handle the truth – could they? A covert operation code-named Majestic 12 (MJ12) began on July 7th with a two fold purpose: (a) to investigate all UFO sightings and, (b) to debunk all such sightings. In spite of the CIA's best efforts to cover up this matter, questions continued to be asked.

Did a small, reconnaissance-type UFO actually crash-land at Roswell, New Mexico on July 2nd 1947? Did a trigger-happy militia shoot and kill/capture the inhabitants of the spacecraft as they emerged? Were the inhabitants discovered to be highly intelligent, greenish-pigmented "humanoids," biologically endowed with a photosynthetic cellular constitution, genetically modified and engineered to withstand space travel? Would not such "humanoids" with a photosynthetic capability similar to that found in all green plant life, have no need for bodily orifices? Would not such little green humanoids look like "fake" humans?

And further, did a high ranking government official in charge of Research and Development secretly distribute the so-called "found technology" like fiber-optics, super-tenacity fibers, integrated circuit chips, lasers, accelerated particle beam firing mechanisms, and other such high-tech inventions to appropriate multi-national companies and allow them to take credit for and profit from them, while withholding (in the interests of the billion dollar petroleum industries concerned) the non-polluting technology that would have made our dependence upon carbon-based fuels like oil and gas obsolete? Did not this "found technology" catapult a mechanical nineteenth century technology into the computerized twenty-first century in a single giant step? Is there still a great deal of "found technology" being back-engineered at a restricted military base known only as "S4" a few miles away from Area 51 which is about 80 miles north of Las Vegas, Nevada? Are those involved secretly attempting to construct anti-matter propulsion systems that produce gravity waves that can be amplified to warp space-time, as indicated in the Theory of Relativity re curved space, and thus make space travel over vast distances possible? Did not the people have a democratic right to know the truth about such a stupendously important encounter with extra-terrestrial life?

But wait just a cotton-pickin' minute! Had not the people been told the truth? It was a weather balloon. Believe it or not, sometimes in the interests of national security, a greater insecurity is created. It lurks in the masquerade of the suspicious mind asking an honest question: "Does anyone dare to tell the truth any more?"

The truth was important to Penny. Lying was foreign to her nature. Anything that was tainted with the scent of falseness made her feel uncomfortable. But this presented her with her greatest problem: What is the truth?

Ah, but at this quaint juncture of her life it was always a moot question to ask, with apologies to Keats: If "beauty is truth and truth beauty" – what is this? It was a fascinating question to which a long and convoluted answer was shaping up in the suspicious recesses of her curious mind. But then one early morning as she arose in time to see the sun rising, it simply dawned on her: the truth is everywhere. In her path as it wound through the busy intersections of office buildings, shopping centers, cozy coffee shops, austere libraries, and dozens of tiny bookstores. Everywhere her path led, there embedded in the ephemeral pursuit of what others called "frivolous" was the poetry that made Keats' poem so special.

Perhaps one, upon first encountering Penny in those days, would have thought, "What a frivolous way to spend one's free time!"

browsing through dusty shelves in libraries and eagerly searching for that special book in dingy nooks in run-down bookstores where who knows what esoteric gems could be lurking? "Frivolous Penny" was the nickname that stuck to her during her sojourn in Calgary. It seemed to the outsider that she was wasting her life moping around searching for something that was not there. It was to all appearances a down time in her existence: a time when life passed by without real significance, because to the young and energetic crawling along at a snail's pace, there is not much meaning inside a cocoon. But miraculously, when the butterfly emerges and takes flight above the mundane and the ordinary, and soars on magical wings to heights undreamed of by the cocoon makers, the mundane world becomes a global village of such exquisite beauty it is truly breath-taking, and one then becomes aware for the first time what is implied by the phrases, "the secret of the ages," and "the wisdom of the ages." It is all too much, too much to be expressed in mere words that can be misinterpreted.

"Penny, Penny, Penny," her closest friends sighed and advised with genuine concern during those melancholic days, "Get a life!" And Penny would smile that demure, almost mischievous smile of hers, and reply, "But I do have a life – it is just not the same as yours." Of course it was not the same, because there was only one Penny in the entire world who thought those thoughts and lived that particular life. It was a life filled with dharmic purpose. Who knew that someone so humble and unpretentious would some day be motivated to write something as ostentatious as a handbook on life?

Who can predict what lies around each blind corner as one cautiously treads down the path that leads to one's destiny? Penny read her horoscope every day. It gave her some cerebral sense of direction. "Who knows," she would say to the many scoffers she encountered, "Are not the stars up there for a purpose? And are we not tiny specks of energy amongst those stars?" She had a way of seeing things that did not require sight.

CHAPTER EIGHT

Penny began to delve into her roots in order to gain a more substantial sense of who she was and where she might be going. Perhaps her ancestors held the key to her future, but how far back is it possible to go? Penny carefully traced her roots back and back and back, and yet the end was nowhere in sight. It was then that she became aware of the Great Chain of Being. She understood that biologically and logically she should be able to trace her roots back to the very source of the life force that enabled her to engage in this exercise in futility.

It was during this exercise that Penny wrote a letter to her cousin, Tutomu Paul Miki, in the land of her father's ancestors, to request whatever information he could provide. To her surprise he sent her a prodigious portfolio of research that caused her to exclaim: "What an extraordinary cousin I must have!"

This extraordinary cousin was the only cousin she had who lived in Japan and could communicate in English. The remarkable thing was that his handwriting even looked like hers! Perhaps not so amazing in light of the fact that their fathers were brothers and their handwriting was similar. Did they assist their children with the fundamentals of writing? It is not surprising to find such remarkable similarities when you realize that this is a global village, and coincidences abound that seem to belie logic, but entail a substratum of unconscious interconnection that gives the global village its global reality, and makes all handwriting similar – but different.

In the global village there are ordinary cousins, and there are remarkable cousins, and beyond both categories, way out there in left field, so to speak, are extraordinary cousins. It was a confluence of unpredictable circumstances and events that provided the opportunity for Penny to experience such a rare individual during her mortal lifetime. It happened at a very opportune segment of her fledgling life. She was feeling slightly insecure and a bit depressed with respect to her self-induced infatuation with her boss at work, when, like a care-package from the homeland, her extraordinary cousin landed at Calgary International Airport with suitcase, carry-on bag, and Nikon camera slung over his left shoulder.

Tutomu Paul Miki descended upon her like a ray of light through the brooding fog of the misty morn. It was beautiful, like Keats' poem. There he was, looking bewildered and out of place. Lost. And Penny found him.

What a find! As soon as she saw him, Penny felt a chill tingle up and down her spine. That face! Those brooding black eyes glistening under a ridge of dark bushy eyebrows. That mess of fine black hair flying in the wind. That gaunt primordial look that harkened back to the aboriginal homeland of the Ainus of Japan. A fragment of her roots stared her in the face. Penny blinked, and four hundred years flashed by, and the Grand Inquisitor, Tsutomu Miki, materialized with deadly samurai swords dangling at an adroit angle instead of camera and carry-on bag. She slowly raised the thumb and forefinger of her left hand to her face and pinched the tip of her nose. And still he was there. A ghostly figure from the past reincarnated into the present. His presence had a culminating effect upon her, just like the epilogue at the conclusion of a novel full of loose ends.

Penny was full of loose ends, ends that dangled impatiently in her mind waiting for a synaptic connection that made sense. The two weeks her cousin spent with her in her tiny apartment were two weeks she would never forget. It was like an instant fusion of the minds. They talked and talked and talked with such intense animation and transference of energy that the room expanded in their presence into a universe of its own. Her elation filled the tiny apartment with an aura that made each evening when she returned from work into a magical session of Alice in Wonderland.

Her cousin was older than she was and more resolute in his outlook on life. In spite of this he was very humble and self-deprecating – to a fault one might say – and yet it was this unassuming humility that made him so endearing. He always thanked her for everything she did for him, for the morning coffee, the breakfast, the supper, the use of the phone, the room he slept in, her graciousness as the host. Everything. He was astutely aware that everything cost money, and that time was money, and that he was there as a dependent upon her generosity, and that made him feel beholden, because Penny absolutely refused to accept one penny from him.

"Your flight here and back will cost you a fortune," she proclaimed. "This is the least I can do."

This business about time and money was Tutomu's sole obsession. When he experienced the work-a-day world from this mindset, it gave him a sense of purpose and accomplishment. It made reality concrete and substantial. He could relate to it. He could own it. Ownership was important to him for unfathomable reasons that often made him feel desperately uncomfortable, as if he were somehow living on the edge of a precipice that symbolized its own downfall. He felt vulnerable, like a Samurai without swords.

In those days, for the sake of argument, Penny liked to play the role of the devil's advocate, so she blithely asked, "When do you think you will ever have enough money?"

"Never!"

His definiteness astounded her. "Never?" she echoed, "I suppose when you are a millionaire you will just naturally proceed to becoming a billionaire?"

"Naturally."

"And when you are a billionaire, you will just naturally desire to become a trillionaire?"

"It follows, does it not?"

"Is that all there is to life – to make as much money as possible?" Penny asked, her voice trembling with a tinge of exasperation.

"Money represents security and power. Do not we all desire security and power in a world where life is cheap?"

"Is not life precious?"

"Gold and diamonds are precious because they are scarce. Life is cheap because it is plentiful. The world population is exploding as we speak. Millions are starving to death because they have neither power nor security. In short they lack money. That is why money is so important."

"When you treat each mortal life like a commodity, it cheapens that precious life. Is not your own life precious to you?"

"Yes, absolutely." Tutomu furrowed his brow and looked up at Penny as if he was burdened with a perplexing conundrum. "There is a tragic flaw in the system we call Modern Capitalism. Although the flaw is self-evident, we have been reluctant to face up to it because the system condones the flaw."

"What do you mean by the system condones the flaw?"

"Greed is condoned. It is an economic virtue. The system justifies greedy behavior. To the capitalist such behavior is natural; it is essential if one is to accumulate more than one needs – especially in a world where hundreds of millions of people are dying from disease, malnutrition and poverty. We know this. Yet we blithely continue to greedily hoard our stockpile of riches like self-deceived misers."

"Self-deceived misers?"

"Like you and I and all those who live in opulence compared to those in third world countries. We commend ourselves for our compassionate thoughts regarding our fellow human beings living in abject poverty in some wretched refugee camp, and blithely continue to live the good life as if it were our inalienable right to continue to do so. We behave this way because the system condones such behavior by giving awards for outstanding achievement to individuals who have accumulated mountains of wealth and give away molehills as charity."

"While the poor slob who shares his last crust of bread with a less fortunate soul is overlooked," Penny chimed in.

"We are only tiny cogs in a very big wheel of fortune. Playing the money-game with skill, luck, and determination can lead to success. It is our modus operandi. It helps provide meaning and purpose to our otherwise meaningless lives. Winning is important, because the winners are always right. And righteousness is the attitude that enables the capitalist to rationalize his behavior. It has religious implications."

"Are you a Christian?"

The question caught Tutomu off guard. It was a fastball, when he was expecting a slow curve. "I'm not that insecure!" he blurted out.

"You're not?"

"I think I know why you asked that," her cousin felt obliged to explain his outburst. "Christians are, existentially speaking, very righteously-insecure folks on the whole. They will do almost anything to be righteously-saved. Being saved means to be safe and secure when the world ends as prophesized. Collectively, their will is manifested by their modus operandi: the Protestant Ethic and the Spirit of Capitalism which is the driving force behind the righteousness. Obviously there would be no need to be saved if they were wrong! There can be no other option; they simply must be right. To insure that they are right, and to justify being saved, the world must end, providing the ultimate proof that they were right. Make sense?"

"Subconsciously and unconsciously they could be moving the world in that direction, without being aware of what they are actually doing." Penny added solemnly.

"There are basically three world-class religions in which being 'saved,' is imperative. All three pray to the same extrinsic God who will save them from a fate worse than death. All three believe in the absolute infallibility of their own dogma."

"What are these three religions?"

"Judaism, Christianity, and Islam. All three have the same dogmatic derivation, and all three claim to be God's sole messengers of truth. Unfortunately, because they are exclusive instead of inclusive, the authenticity of one necessitates the in-authenticity of the other two. Consequently, the conflict is mainly amongst these three related combatants."

"Is it imperative for all three of these powerful world-class religions that the world ends?"

"Unfortunately, yes – otherwise, what is the point of being saved? Perhaps amongst themselves, they are acting out their own self-fulfilling prophesy of doom. Just look at what is happening in the Middle East as we speak."

They lapsed into silence, stunned by their own realizations.

"Can anything be done about this?" Penny asked with consternation.

"If they are not aware that 'what we are, is a result of what we have thought'," Tutomu responded by paraphrasing the Buddha, "then it is possible that the conflict in the Middle East could escalate into a terrifying world conflagration."

"Those three religions are so dogmatic!" Penny declared. "What can you say to stalwart converts who believe in the righteousness of their cause? Stop being so gullible? The rest of us do not want the world to end!"

"Gullibility is a very common human trait."

"It seems to me that people are looking for ways to help make the world a better place for all mankind."

"They need to become more aware of what is happening. They need to find a common solution to this dire predicament we find ourselves ensconced in."

"They need to become less gullible!"

Tutomu remained silent for a moment before sprightly responding in Shakespearian fashion: "Aye, there's the rub!" The creases around his eyes crinkled into a wry glimmer of a self-deprecating smile. "I must admit," he declared dramatically, "that gullibility is one of my own greatest weaknesses."

The honesty impaled Penny with its forthrightness. "And mine too," she confessed.

"What is needed is some kind of a guidebook for the gullible," her cousin suggested with a smile.

"A handbook of sorts that would illuminate the way, so to speak?"

"Yes, for the gullible ones, like me, who are prone to stumble and fall along the way."

"You are very humble," Penny complimented her cousin.

"Is it possible to be too humble?" he wondered.

"Too arrogant, too vain, or too self-righteous perhaps, but not too humble. The problem is that we are not humble enough. Our ego always makes darn sure of that!"

Penny got up from the sofa and went into her tiny kitchen to make a pot of green tea. She felt stimulated and challenged by the ideas they had been discussing. She took down her two nicest teacups from the cupboard and proceeded with them back into the living room. "It will take a few minutes for the water to boil," she announced while settling back down on the sofa.

Tutomu stretched his arms up toward the ceiling. "You have a way with words," he said, "You get them to say what you mean." He bowed his head as if he were in the presence of royalty, and suggested after a thoughtful pause, "Perhaps some day you should write a book – not an ordinary book – a handbook, a guidebook for the gullible, or something like that."

"Who would be so pretentious as to consider themselves worthy to write such a book?" Penny challenged, feeling incompetent.

"You," her cousin grinned as if vaguely amused.

"I appreciate your vote of confidence, but it requires a much more knowledgeable person than I will ever be."

"You are very intelligent, gracious and humble; that is why you are a suitable candidate."

"What about yourself? Perhaps you could write such a book."

"I'm too jaded."

"Too what?"

"Jaded. I do not have the proper attitude toward life. You do. You have precisely the right attitude."

"I do?"

"Yes, definitely, and I say that with all due respect."

"Wow! I am flattered beyond words." Penny slumped down comfortably and leaned back against the padded backrest. After a moment's rest she said, "You're quite extraordinary, you know?" She got up, walked thoughtfully into the kitchen, and returned carrying a steaming pot of green tea which she gingerly poured into the two teacups on the coffee table in front of them. Her cousin picked up his teacup and blew on it before trying a sip.

"Pretty good tea," he appraised.

Penny picked up her teacup and imitated her cousin, "Not bad," she said.

"Speaking of Christians," Tutomu began reflectively, "Have you ever heard of the Kakure Kirishitan of Nagasaki?"

"Can't say I have."

"Kakure means hidden, and Kirishitan is the Japanese pronunciation of Christian."

"Hidden Christians? Who ever heard of them?"

"Very few people have, especially in Canada."

"Not surprising, if they have been hidden," Penny quipped, "and furthermore, who even knew there were any Christians existing in Nagasaki of all places, let alone hidden ones."

"Like I said," her cousin plodded on, chalking up her wisecracks to a lack of understanding of a topic that exuded a foreboding undercurrent that was far from humorous. "Very few Canadians," he smiled at her, "have heard of the tragic decimation of the Hidden Christians of Japan." He paused dramatically.

"Please continue," Penny responded, her eyes wide open with curiosity.

"Where shall I begin?" he asked himself rhetorically.

"At the beginning, of course," she prompted.

"Ah – so," he began, leaning back and rotating his head as if to increase the blood circulation to his brain. "In 1549, the Jesuit missionary, Saint Francis Xavier, landed at Kagoshima on the southern tip of the southernmost of Japan's three major islands, just north of Okinawa."

"That would be Kyushu, right?" Penny validated.

"Yes. Francis was welcomed by the Japanese leaders of the time, and found that part of the country to be most receptive to his message. In fact in his enthusiasm he had written: '…it seems to me that amongst pagan nations there will not be another to surpass the Japanese'."

"Sounds like he hit the missionary's jackpot."

"Indeed, the Japanese people were already somewhat conditioned, so to speak, to accept the view that they were special and therefore worthy of being saved."

"Did they not already believe that they, as a people, were of divine ancestry?" Penny asked.

"The myth was that the islands of Japan along with the original inhabitants were a divine creation. Divinity was therefore found in everything: the wind, the water, the earth, and all life forms. It was the basis of the Shinto religion."

"Really?"

"Yes. Life is divinity being expressed." Tutomu paused to let that concept sink in. He could tell by his cousin's facial expression that she found it interesting. "Everything is an expression," he continued. "The Shinto religion is an expression of this expression. From this viewpoint worship itself is a divine expression that acknowledges the presence of that which is natural. Such an acknowledgement makes all human expressions, moral expressions. It is a difficult notion to explain precisely because it is basically a feeling of divinity, a sacred feeling of being part of a divine manifestation."

"And yet the Christians refer to the Shintoists as pagans."

"The word pagan has such negative connotations these days, especially in Western Christendom. Wherever it is used, it sounds like a put-down uttered with moralistic disdain. It self-righteously elevates… by putting down, a sign of conceit and hidden vanity. But that aside, the so-called pagans of Japan were a missionary's dream come true."

"Easy pickings for Christian missionaries, eh?"

"Yes, and due to Saint Francis Xavier's success, many other Christian missionary groups began arriving, foremost amongst these being the Franciscans. They were very zealous, and soon the numbers of converts to Christianity in Japan mushroomed to over four hundred thousand devout souls."

"Four hundred thousand saved! An amazing feat at a time when communication was strictly by word of mouth," Penny acknowledged.

"The rate of conversion was so rapid that it had a destabilizing social effect which raised the ire of the ruling class. In due time it led directly to a political backlash. In 1587, a scant thirty-eight years after Francis Xavier landed at Kagoshima, the head-honcho named Toyotomi Hideyoshi, issued an edict expelling all Christian missionaries from Japan. However, due to its unpopularity, this edict was mostly ignored and missionaries carried on unperturbed for another ten years."

"And then what happened?"

"The opinion of a single human being, a Spanish sea captain, regarding the insidious influence of Christianity on the integrity of the Shogunate-domain system, turned the tide of events against the Christian missionaries. Who knows, if that Spanish sea captain had kept his mouth shut, Christianity might have swept over Japan like a tsunami wave. Instead it alarmed Toyotomi so greatly, he decided to enforce his edict by making an example of twenty-six innocent foreign and Japanese Christians. They were crucified, on his orders, at Nagasaki, and became immortalized as the Martyrs of Japan. One of the crucified was a distant relative of ours called Paul Miki."

"Really?" Penny's ears perked up. "When will we ever learn!" she empathized.

"After that the persecution was relentless throughout the entire Edo period, which lasted from around 1600 to 1868. Hundreds of Christians were burnt at the stake, crucified or dispatched in some other gruesome manner."

"Like the Spanish Inquisition – only in reverse," Penny commented.

"By the eighteen hundreds it was thought that Christianity had all but been eradicated from the very soil which once had proven to be so fertile. However, persecution makes the persecuted all the more defiant, resilient, determined, and resourceful. Unknown to the authorities, hidden away in secret enclaves in the hills around Nagasaki and on tiny secluded islands, the Hidden Christians or Kakure Kirishitan clung desperately to their faith as if it were everything. In the absence of any printed material, which would have been folly to possess, the entire body of doctrine and liturgy was passed on by word of mouth. They managed to survive, and pass on their religious faith secretly from one generation to the next for over two hundred and forty years. An amazing feat of perseverance and devotion."

"Hard to believe!" Penny exclaimed. "Imagine hiding out for two hundred and forty years. Talk about your true believers!"

"What resulted was a very unique and fascinating form of Christianity relevant only to the Kakure Kirishitan themselves." Tutomu paused to clear his throat by coughing into a handy tissue. After blowing his nose he continued, "A small enclave of Hidden Christians continued to practice their distinctive form of secret Christianity in Nagasaki until 1945."

"You would have thought that the Kakure would have integrated back into the bosom of the Catholic Church and resumed the relationship that existed prior to the repression."

"After two hundred and forty years of persecution it was necessary, for the sake of their survival, that they develop a way of life based upon secrecy and self-sufficiency. And later, when this modus operandi was no longer necessary, they still clung to it because it defined them and gave them their special status."

"Something like the Israelites," Penny interjected the comparison, "who after being led out of the bondage of slavery by Moses, still clung slavishly to the religious dogmas, doctrines, and rituals that, while necessary to their survival as slaves in Egypt, were no longer required of a free people."

"You are well informed for one so young," Penny's cousin praised her. "I have heard a variation of that idea from disenchanted Jews who are attempting in vain it seems, to free their religion from this slave mentality that holds them moribund in the dead hand of the past."

"It is amazing how stubbornly the established religious authorities cling to the status quo that gives them the power and authority to perpetuate outdated dogmas and doctrines that are detrimental to the good of their own people."

"They are defined and legitimized in their own minds by the obsolete dogmas and doctrines that they cling so tenaciously to. The Kakure, like the Israelites, were unable to put the past behind them.

In the past their survival and raison d'être depended upon secrecy, self-sufficiency, and deception – because their religious views had been forbidden, punishable by persecution, torture and death. These practices became part of the Kakure mindset. It made them into who they were: *Kakure*. It gave them an identity. How could they preserve that identity if they allowed themselves to be swallowed up by mainstream Catholicism?"

"So what happened to them?"

"They survived two hundred and forty years of persecution and proudly retained their religious identity, only to be decimated by the atomic bomb that leveled Nagasaki in 1945. There is something disturbing, something so – so… I really do not know what to say. It just makes me very, very sad." Tutomu stopped talking and sat in prayerful silence. He looked like a Zen Buddhist monk with his head bowed forward and his deep dark eyes staring into the empty space that separated the foreground from the background. He picked up his teacup and slowly drank down the rest of his green tea. "Today a few still exist as Hidden Christians in small pockets on the islands of Sotome, Goto, and predominately in Ikitsuki."

"It would be a shame to see them pass away after such a valiant struggle to survive," Penny lamented.

"They pass on before us as notable examples of survival under the direst circumstances. It is not lamentable. It is applaudable. They do not pass away. They pass on…."

And so the dialogue continued into the late hours of the evening, day after day for two solid weeks. They discussed the most controversial, mundane, intellectual and sublime subjects known to both of them, and were delighted at each other's responses. What impressed Penny the most was her cousin's profound understanding of both western and eastern philosophies and religions. He possessed a photographic memory and was able to repeat phrases and passages verbatim as if he were reading from the actual texts. It was at times, overwhelming.

If she had known then that many of those disparate topics would later form the nucleus of a handbook on life, she would have taken extensive notes or tape recorded every evening's conversations so she could give credit where credit was due; but she had not, and the inexorable passage of time blurred things in her memory, and her cousin's ideas blended in with her own. Consequently she was loath to take credit for hardly anything, even if she deserved it. It was perhaps her own sense of inadequacy that made her prefer to be the background that made the foreground so prominent, and consequently like magnanimous old Socrates who managed to extract pearls of wisdom from the most unlikely sources, she questioned and probed and via the discourse gave form and voice to seedling ideas that her cousin had planted in her mind in the dusky evenings of long ago.

It was via their profound intercommunications that Penny became intuitively aware of a deeper psychological basis for her cousin's obsession with what she considered to be a rather shallow, Pavlovian and dogmatic response to his focus on money. It seemed to her that it was only a camouflage for a much deeper survival instinct, an instinct that made him mimic the shallowness of those who wielded the manifestations of power and security that enabled them to frequently determine the fate of the less fortunate, and to... to beat them at their own game.

Unfortunately, just when Penny felt she was really getting to know her cousin, the two weeks he had allocated for his vacation came to an end. Apparently he had "deadlines and commitments" with a large international trading company that he was loath to put off. "Time is money," was his only explanation.

On the evening of the second last day before his scheduled departure he casually mentioned something that made her ears perk up and the hair on the back of her neck tingle. He said in the apologetic tone that one uses in a confessional: "Sometimes it is one's fate to experience things that should never have happened in the first place, things too horrible for even an intelligent and open-minded person like you to imagine, too horrible even to be contemplated, things that must never ever happen again on the face of this sacred planet we call Mother Earth, things that no human being deserves to experience."

"Huh?" Penny exhaled instinctively, stupefied by the gravity of what was being shared.

He drew in a deep breath and looked down at the floor as if ashamed of his confession. "There is a phrase..." he proceeded hesitatingly as if uncertain whether or not to continue, "that used to puzzle me, but now I understand what it means."

"What-what is it?" Penny stammered in a voice that was barely audible.

He hung his head and shuffled his feet as if tempted to walk away. After a long silence he looked up at her with dark fearful eyes and said quietly with deep emotion: "After such knowledge!" his face grew pale and withered – "What forgiveness?"

Penny was mystified by his response, but it was late in the day and she could tell by his body language that he did not wish to elaborate. However, the next morning when he was preparing to take his leave, she impulsively embraced him and whispered empathetically, "I forgive you," and kissed him on the cheek.

Unexpectedly he began to tremble, and tears slowly trickled over his cheek where she had kissed him. He stepped back and gazed at his little cousin. His grateful eyes sparkled with a melancholy as profound as the tears that glistened beneath them. "You are very special," he responded in a choked voice. "I have been blessed to have made your acquaintance," he bowed humbly, raised his head, smiled graciously and quietly added, "Arigato gozai-mas...." Then he abruptly turned and entered the waiting yellow taxi-cab that took him back to Calgary International Airport.

After her cousin left, Penny felt an acute sense of abandonment, as if her mentor had deliberately left her to fend for herself. There was no one else with whom she could carry on such exhilarating conversations. No one else who stimulated her to rise to such great heights of intellectual curiosity and creative thought. No one else who made thinking into, not only a great adventure, but an art form! Without it, life seemed drab and petty. When she returned home to her small apartment after work it seemed as solemn and quiet as a tomb.

And then one solitary evening as she was tidying up the cushions on the sofa where her cousin had slept, she found a crumpled piece of paper wedged in the crevice along the back side. She smoothed out the paper, and to her surprise it contained a simple little poem hastily scrawled in handwriting that reminded her of her own. She examined the scrap of paper carefully, "I wonder if he could have written this?" she asked herself. She read the poem over several times. At first it seemed trite and even childish, but with each re-reading it began to take on an ominous emotional life of its own. It was as if her cousin was sitting once again on the sofa hunched over that cup of green tea and staring into the greenish liquid as if it were a crystal ball, contemplating his predicament.

The poem was entitled, "The Boot," a jack-boot no doubt, the kind worn by those who like to stomp on things with impunity.

I am an ant...
My name is "I"
I cannot jump and I cannot fly
I sought the light
And loathed to lie
And then one morn
From way up high
There came a *boot* out of the sky
It stomped and stomped and made me cry
I hung my head and wondered "why?"
I said my prayers
And closed my eyes
It stomped and stomped
And stomped and stomped
And stomped...
Until I died.

"That's my cousin alright," Penny whimpered, halfway pleased with her find. She neatly folded up the poem and placed it securely in the side pocket of her purse. She carried it around with her for months. Some days, when she felt just like that ant, she got out the paper and re-read the poem. In some strange fashion it always made her feel better. And never again did she knowingly step on an ant.

CHAPTER NINE

How the good years flew by! Before Penny and Larry realized the irreversibility of what had happened, the twins were young adults, and both Penny and Larry were considered by them to be seniors. They did not feel old, but relative to the younger generation, chompin' at the bit to demonstrate their independence, they were nearing obsolescence in a throw-away economy. What happened to those two little kids with boundless energy tearing around the house wrecking the expensive furniture? How quickly childhood fades into adolescence and adolescence into adulthood. In the blink of an eye, the present becomes the past, and all that is left are memories of the way things used to be.

"We should have gone on more camping trips," Larry once lamented when the twins no longer wanted to go camping with their old parents anymore. Nostalgia became a pleasant feeling, nostalgia for happy moments squandered without due appreciation at the time.

"Do you have any regrets?" Penny asked one evening, as Larry sat on the couch looking wistfully through an old photo album. A picture of the old hard-top tent trailer with the kids standing proudly in front holding up the trout they had caught near Pincher Creek, caught his eye.

"I should have taken more time off when the kids were that age," he held the picture up so Penny could see it. "It's the same old story I'm afraid, too late smart," he commented as he slowly turned the page over.

After the twins graduated from high school, and courtesy of some unexpected financial assistance for the twins' post secondary education from a wealthy benefactor in Japan, Penny and Larry were able to retire from their respective jobs. By then Penny, who had given up on completing her PhD, had been teaching an undergraduate course in Philosophy in addition to maintaining her part-time Library duties. Meanwhile Larry had risen to the lofty position of Regional Manager in a business machines company that had expanded into the lucrative computer and software business, and through deft management had survived through the lean times and now commanded a fair slice of the marketplace. Larry's co-workers were truly sorry to see him retire because he had become such a fixture around the place.

Although Larry did not have a pension plan at work he had saved up a tidy sum in his registered retirement savings plan, and the income from this combined with Penny's Union and Staff pensions from the university, provided them with more expendable income than they needed for their frugal lifestyle.

Retirement brought much more leisure time for the whole family. But after the initial rush of travel and sightseeing wore off, Penny declared that it was time to begin their "second career," their real career, and Larry concurred.

What was their real career? It was the career they had been subconsciously preparing themselves for from the day they were born. It had nothing to do with making money. It was the magnet that drew them to study Philosophy when others were preparing themselves for more lucrative careers. It was posted on invisible signposts along the way that illuminated the path that wound through the synaptic connections of their minds revealing vistas so grand it was not only inspirational, it was edifying. It was a career that they had spent nearly a lifetime preparing for. Now that they were finally free to do whatever they wanted, what should they do with the precious time remaining in their mortal lives?

One evening after a leisurely supper, Penny said, "I think we should do something really useful. I think we should endeavor to share the insights and wisdom we have gleaned from our long sojourn down this pathway we have traveled by writing some sort of joint dissertation about life."

"A dissertation you say? Sounds rather academic and stifling to me," Larry replied.

"I agree. That word 'dissertation' has a rather stifling connotation. I was thinking of something more like a guidebook of some sort," Penny clarified.

"You know, Penny, there are a plethora of guidebooks and self-help books out there written by qualified authors on practically every possible subject."

"I wasn't thinking of anything... uh-uh that mundane. I was considering the possibility of writing something unique, something original, something that hasn't been written yet... as far as I know."

"Well if it hasn't been written yet, it must be something that is not worth writing about, or beyond human comprehension," Larry responded in a skeptical tone.

"Sometimes your skepticism can be quite demoralizing," Penny complained. "Sometimes you just have to take a chance. You have to dare... to dare to share!" she retorted.

"What exactly are you thinking about?"

"Some kind of a - a handbook... a student handbook... on life," Penny clarified with a beseeching look toward her husband.

"Hmmm, a handbook on life, you say," Larry cogitated. "Well now, who would want to read such a work?" he queried.

"When I was an undergraduate student, I hungered for such knowledge, and in the undergraduate classes that I've taught, I could see that hunger, that need to know what life is all about." Penny paused reflectively, "But, as you know, such knowledge is scattered hither and thither everywhere along the path, a penny here and a penny there. And now, are not you and I existential millionaires?"

"A fine analogy," Larry appraised, brightening up. "You make a good point. Yes, from our opinionated point of view we may feel like existential millionaires, but such an evaluation is purely subjective. Do we dare to even pretend to be qualified, let alone share whatever paltry knowledge we may have as if it were of any value to anyone but ourselves?"

"Your reticence is understandable," Penny acknowledged with a prolonged sigh, "But we must dare to share if we really care! Do we care enough to share what little we do know, even in the face of pompous critics who might ridicule the legitimacy of our efforts because we only have a few academic letters to tack onto the end of our names?"

They sat in stony silence for a long time, looking at each other for some inadvertent signs of encouragement, while listening to the sounds of impatience captured in every sober breath that wheezed in and out into the space between them. Penny raised her dark eyes that glistened like pools of infinite wisdom and stared steadfastly at her husband. As he gazed at the mirthless twinkle in the depths of Penny's eyes, every drop of Larry's reticence disappeared, and with the timidity of the meek and humble he quietly replied, "I suppose... it is the very least we can do."

And so they started working at night and early in the morning on the rough draft of a manuscript they hoped would someday be of some benefit to other seekers after knowledge. To begin with they made an exhaustive list of all the ideas they thought would be relevant to their project. Then they discussed each concept at great length, and after that one or the other of them would volunteer to laboriously write it out in long hand for the other to critique, and when they were both satisfied it was their best work, they typed it out on the computer.

It was an inspired labor of love. When they were working together on the manuscript time flew by and disappeared into the void as if it never existed. Weeks, months, and years shot by as if only days had passed. And as their brainchild gradually took form and shape, they felt like genuine creators. To be able to pluck out of the infinite vastness of pure unlimited potentiality such manifestations of knowledge gave them a real sense of accomplishment.

Penny and Larry were confident they were doing what they were supposed to be doing. It was fun because it was natural. Preparation was minimal. They had spent practically their entire lifetimes getting ready. There was no question. They could feel it in the marrow of their bones. Yes indeed, this was their real career... their *karmic-calling*.

PART FOUR

ORIENTATION

A journey of a thousand miles
Starts from beneath one's feet.

Lao Tzu

CHAPTER ONE

It happened the way it did because that *ronin* was wearing a silver crucifix. Perhaps if it had been made of wood or something less noticeable it would not have had such an impact. The silver glistened in the morning sun against the dullness of his unwashed skin. It became seared instantly like a white-hot poker into the six-year-old mind of a frightened boy, and then the blood fell like crimson rain. Tsutomu Miki was petrified. Petrified by a shock so great he froze solid like a block of ice. His father crumpled to the ground beside him. He clung to his father's hand with all his might, holding on for dear life. For dear life! He clung to a hand that suddenly became limp and lifeless. And still he held on. What else could he have done? Could this have impacted upon his destiny? Was he predestined to become a great samurai?

Much later, some would nod their heads and knowingly say, "It was his Karma," as if that simple statement explained the whys and wherefores of the making of a legend. Perhaps it did. In any case, on the legendary day concerned, Tsutomu Miki dressed himself slowly and meticulously. It was very important. He wrapped a narrow waistband twice around his mid-section and tied it securely. Just above his right hip bone he inserted the scabbard for his short *wakizashi* or backup sword, the blade of which was precisely nineteen inches long. On the left side he secured the scabbard for his two-handed *katana*, the blade of which was exactly thirty-three inches. There were blades that were slightly longer or shorter, but none were honed to such a razor's edge and gleamed with such deadliness even as they were being sheathed, cutting edge up, into their resting place.

These were not ordinary swords. They were Kogi swords, a gift from one of the greatest sword-makers who ever lived: the Magician of Kogi. Tsutomu trembled as he recalled his mother's words on the day he inherited his father's precious swords.

"These swords were made by your grandfather, Tsutomu Sawada, after whom you were named. See that little 's' just below the hilt? These are the finest swords ever imprinted with that trademark. They were a gift to your father on our wedding day. He wore them with such pride. No one else had such magnificent swords. They gave him a distinct identity: Handayu Miki, Samurai and Military

Leader. Those swords were much more than just lethal weapons;
they had a magical quality hammered into them by the Magician of
Kogi. Somehow your father felt almost intimidated by them. He
once confided to me that he never really felt worthy of them. As you
know, he was not wearing them on the day he was slain. Make sure
that does not happen to you. Be worthy of them!"

Over the years Tsutomu had grown so used to wearing his *daisho*,
or paired big-small swords, that without them he felt out of balance.
They were as much a part of his body as the clothes he wore. On
those public occasions when he did not wear his swords he always
felt slightly uncomfortable and ill at ease, as if he were incompletely
dressed.

Tsutomu Miki had the physique and nimbleness of an acrobat,
lithe, wiry, and balanced. He was like a cat with two fierce claws.
When he drew the slightly curved blade of his two-handed katana
from its scabbard, it was always with a graceful sweeping arc that in
the field of battle would continue into a circle of three hundred and
sixty degrees, as he pivoted like a ballerina upon the tips of her toes.
When he was poised like that, frozen in action, he looked so fragile,
so vulnerable. But no one who had seen him in action dared stand
within the radius of that deadly circumference. Side-lungers and
back-stabbers alike, all hung back, wary, that in a split second that
terrible blade might circle, slash, arc and descend upon them
wherever they stood. In the chaos of even the most intense battles, it
was awesome to see how he moved with such consummate grace and
agility like an artful dancer in a battle scene in which he had no fear
of death, swooping, pivoting, leaping, crouching, a dynamo of
continuous circular movement. It was the efficiency of the circular
movement that was the secret to his success, a movement that had
neither beginning nor end. Circles and more circles carved out in a
continuous acrobatic gyration of body and sword. It was
mesmerizing even on the field of battle to witness such a deadly artist
at work. Inept swordsmen lunged and stabbed with an awkward
thrusting action that proved futile against the seamless sweep of a
sword that sliced with effortless grace. It was an art form that
Tsutomu Miki had honed to perfection, just like the edge of his
deadly swords. There were many copy-cats, but none could equal
the original. He had that air of invincibility.

When persuaded to elaborate upon his special technique, he would ask with a twinkle in his eye, "Have you ever heard the story of the mongoose, the fig and the bird?" If they had not, he would tell it just as his father had told it to him. And "...snap!" he would conclude, "no fig, no bird – just a satisfied mongoose licking feathers from its jaws." Many thought he was just kidding, and would get up and walk away with a haughty laugh. But those who remained heard him say, "All actions are embedded in the limitless potentiality of inertia. It is where all actions begin and where they must end. In a circle where is the beginning or end? There is no separation."

Because his father had once been a proud military leader, it was natural, after his demise, for his mother, Chi-ecko, the eldest daughter of the Magician of Kogi, to direct her only son toward the well-worn path known as the Way of the Warrior. The *bushido* that stressed honor, duty, loyalty, and above all, freedom from fear, proved to be very alluring to a youngster anxious to prove his worth.

As a child, Tsutomu loved to hear his mother relate the story of Jimmu Tenno, the original samurai warrior who embodied the fighting spirit that resulted in the path that became immortalized as the Way of the Bow and the Horse. Tsutomu could imagine himself racing across the battlefield at full gallop with the horse's mane whipping in the wind, fearlessly arching his bow and shooting arrows on the fly, just like Jimmu, the divine warrior, who brought honor and respect to the Yamato clan and rose to become the first Shogun, or Barbarian-subduing General. It was a title that Jimmu Tenno richly deserved, unlike many who attempted to follow in his footsteps down through the centuries. The Way of the Bow and the Horse evolved into a way of life for an entire social class. It eventually became known as the Way of the Samurai.

Who can blame a young boy who had witnessed the slaying of his defenseless father by an unscrupulous rogue samurai from dreaming of becoming a Divine Warrior like Jimmu Tenno? The samurai's life, he was told by his uncle Daiyo, was like a cherry blossom's: beautiful and brief. For the samurai as for the blossom, death followed naturally, gloriously. Just as the sun rises, it also sets with equal majesty. Such is the life of a Divine Warrior. Such was the life much coveted by a young boy who had stared death in the face – and lived.

One did not become a samurai warrior overnight. It took years of meticulous training in the martial arts. Years and years. Hojo Nagauji, who had lived from 1432 to 1519, was often quoted to Tsutomu by his mentors: "Consider that which exists to exist and that which does not exist to not exist, and recognize things just as they are. With such a frame of mind, one will have divine protection even though he does not pray." But the quote that was dearest to his heart was really not a quote at all. It was just advice given on the last occasion, Kamio, his father's oldest brother dropped by, two weeks prior to his glorious death on the battlefield. He was a truly magnificent samurai warrior. His death was a true warrior's demise. It brought great honor and prestige to a prestigious family name. The evening before his uncle departed he sat down beside his nephew, and like a great actor rehearsing his lines, said, "When thunder rumbles ominously in darkening clouds – strike like lightning! And in the aftermath give thanks. Always give thanks. Be thankful that you are able to be thankful."

Tsutomu Miki was very thankful for his good fortune, the good fortune that allowed him to remain alive when his comrades perished in mortal combat. He always gave thanks in the aftermath of battle. He would stare up at the sky and whisper to no one in particular, "Thank you, thank you, thank you." He did it without thinking. It seemed natural, instinctive. One was always so thankful just to be alive, in the midst of so much death.

Strange as it may seem, it was not Tsutomu's heroics on the field of battle that inflamed the imagination of the masses and led to his legendary status. It was an event that happened when he was still a relatively young man hoping to make a name for himself. There are basically two accounts, told and retold, of the singular event that turned an unknown samurai into a hero. The two accounts are basically the same except for the starting position of his two-handed sword, his katana. The incident occurred when Tsutomu was nearing his twenty-third birthday, strong, lithe, wiry, and lethal as a mongoose amongst fig-loving birds. Already his services were being sought by many reputable Daimyos who wanted only the best to serve in their personal entourage.

Throughout Kyushu there were many skilled samurai from respected military families whose credentials were impeccable.

Among them a kind of natural pecking order of excellence developed based upon personal reputation. Included in the handful at the top was Tsutomu Miki. He was frugal and reserved in contrast to some of his peers who dressed up in extravagant samurai outfits and paraded brazenly about in public. His skinny frame draped with a worn grayish-white cloak that looked more like a Buddhist monk's outfit than a samurai's, projected the deceptive appearance of a misfit intermingling amid the elite of the samurai class. It would have been easy to have been deceived except for his magnificent swords that he wore low-slung on his left and right hips. Vanity calls attention to itself and consequently it was to be expected that being among the elite would create a certain amount of jealousy and envy amongst those to whom honor and fame were elusive.

Thus it came to pass that not one, not two, but three despicable rogue samurai, or ronin, aspiring to infamy conspired to empower, enhance, and enrich themselves by dispatching the most vulnerable of the young samurai. Greed, slothfulness, and a cowardly disposition made them unfit to be samurai; still all three were skilful swordsmen and that combined with their deceit made them particularly treacherous. Over the years they would come and go intermittently from the village. They were known simply as the "three ronin". Their reputation for foul and evil deeds followed them wherever they went. It was always a great relief when they disappeared. Three days before the Cherry Festival of 1567 they appeared out of nowhere and lounged about under a large shade tree near the village entrance. Their filthy unkempt appearance and malevolent leers struck fear and insecurity into the hearts of any passers-by, who nervously hurried along keeping a wary eye on the adversaries.

They skulked about stealthily on the fringe of the compound sizing up and discussing the strengths, merits, and weaknesses of each potential victim. It was their cunning and advanced planning that made their villainous activities so successful. In the past they had occasionally argued tooth and nail when differences of opinion prevailed and often ended up nearly killing each other in a drunken stupor inflamed by vanity and frustration. However, for once there was very little argument. Of all the young samurai there was one who stood out from the rest. He was something of a loner which made the decision all the easier. It was unanimous. They laughed with glee and slapped each other boisterously across the back in anticipation of their foul deed to come. Whom had they selected?

They picked out the quiet reserved one, the skinny weak-looking one, the one who went to sit meditatively from time to time on a weathered old ornamental bench located in front of the Buddhist temple, the solitary, introverted one whose father had died on that very spot in front of the bench years ago without so much as a whimper. The frail, melancholic one with the "priceless swords" and drab looking outfit. That one would be easy pickings.

Perhaps it was sheer coincidence, or fate, or both, but one of the three conspirators was the same ruthless ronin who had dispatched Tsutomu's father. He was many years older and had grown even more cagey and cunning with age. The silver crucifix still hung around his unwashed neck. Why it remained there after all that time was a mystery. Was it the only valuable item he possessed? Maybe he considered it to be his good luck charm. At any rate it dangled there, swaying with the undulating motion of his body as the three rogue samurai approached the young man sitting alone on the beautifully hand-carved bench located just in front of the Buddhist Temple.

Tsutomu sat meditatively, paying homage to his deceased father. After a hectic day he liked to come and sit on the old bench his father had hand-carved and donated to the Buddhist temple on the occasion of his birth. He sadly recalled standing there on that tragic day before that very bench when his father crumpled to the ground covered in his own blood, while he hung onto his father's hand for dear life. His dear father was the only one who called him, Moo-chan. "Come here Moo-chan, and sit on my knee and I'll tell you your favorite story," he would say, "the one about the mongoose." A pleasant smile creased the edges of Tsutomu's eyes, but quickly disappeared when he heard the scrunch of approaching feet. He spied three shabbily dressed men armed with samurai swords, slowly withdrawing their deadly katanas as they drew closer. He was alone. Their intentions were obvious. He could see the menacing looks on their faces as they drew nearer with their great swords pointing the way. What could he do?

What would a Samurai do? When his dear mother had bestowed his father's precious swords upon him had she not said, "Be worthy of them"? Tsutomu Miki, only son of Handayu Miki, calmly rose to his feet and walked seven paces toward the three approaching ronin and stopped. And waited.

The older ronin, the one wearing the silver crucifix, was the ringleader. He cunningly signaled his cohorts to space themselves strategically around their intended victim so that he could not escape. Not a word was spoken. The temperature dropped. The air froze. Mortality balanced precariously on the cutting edge of immortality. The intent was obvious. The three treacherous ronin cautiously circled the solitary victim with murder in their hearts.

They were hoping to catch him off guard and steal his leather purse that was heavy with silver pieces, along with his valuable swords. They had heard that his swords were made by the famous Magician of Kogi, and were worth more than all the money they had ever stolen. They also knew that such swords could only be removed from their owner upon death.

As the three stealthy ronin encircled Tsutomu, a small group of Buddhists were just arriving for evening services at the temple. It was before this sparse audience that Tsutomu Miki gave his most artful exhibition. Yes, he was like a great artist demonstrating his art, while the small audience stood there in the foreboding shadows tense with apprehension, as if they anticipated something spectacular was about to unfold. Something that would be considered to be unbelievable, if one had not seen it with one's own two eyes.

Tsutomu Miki just stood there. The cool evening breeze fluttered a loose strand of hair that dangled across his forehead and billowed the neat folds of his worn grayish-white samurai's outfit. He looked deceptively vulnerable, like a tasty morsel being presented for the palates of the gluttonous. His sword was not even drawn. He existed in the moment with an awareness that triggered every nerve cell in his body with anticipation. He never moved. He was scarcely breathing. He just stood there waiting for the inevitable.

The three murderous ronin crouched and feinted in and out as they cautiously circled their prey, holding their gleaming swords aloft, ready to dart in and thrust them into the yielding body of a human being whose flesh was as mortal as their own. As if by instinct or an uncanny sixth-sense, something in the stillness of the tepid evening air made them become extra cautious; something in the demeanor of the statue caused their eyes to widen and their hearts to palpitate with a dreadful anticipation. The weak-looking young samurai with the drab outfit and priceless swords waited stoically with his right hand casually resting on the beautiful handle of his great katana, woven and cross-woven with black threads of the finest silk. Perhaps it was the blackness of the threads that made the handle appear so ominous. The statue remained immobile like a slab of marble. Does marble know fear? Tsutomu Miki stood as still as a mongoose amongst fig-loving birds, while the three wily ronin slowly circled clockwise and then counterclockwise, looking for an opening. And then for one fateful moment, they hesitated.

Suddenly there was a flash and a sound, the sound that a sharp object makes when it slices through the air at incredible speed! Two jugulars were slashed, and the ronin who had slain his father lurched forward like a drunk, his arms recoiling upward reactively, and then as if by magic, a thin red line appeared around his neck, and in slow motion his head toppled into his waiting arms. He lurched forward a half step and then sank to his knees holding his head like an offering to the gods. It happened so quickly that few even noticed that Tsutomu had moved at all – except for the flash and the sound, and the undeniable fact that his sword was in his right hand, and the blade dripped droplets of crimson blood.

The second version differs from the first mainly in the matter concerning the starting position of Tsutomu's great sword. It has been insinuated that the story was possibly embellished at a later date by those quick-draw artists who took such pride in the speed with which they could unsheathe such a lengthy weapon. It has become a contentious issue to some. The purists point out that no one could possibly draw a katana that quickly. Defenders of the first version claim that it was actually the correct or original version, and because it seemed so unbelievable, it was later changed so that it would at least seem to be more believable. Such is the stuff of legend! Although it may seem somewhat repetitious, it is included here as a substantiation of the difference.

Gripping the handle of his two-handed katana with his right hand, Miki-san, slowly and methodically withdrew the deadly blade inch by inch as the three ronin watched as if mesmerized. The burnished steel blade, honed to a razor's edge, gleamed menacingly. The older ronin, the one wearing the silver crucifix, motioned his cohorts to encircle their intended victim so that he could not escape. They crouched and stealthily circled clockwise and then counterclockwise searching for an opening. The odds were three to one. No one has eyes in the back of his head. Sooner or later one of them would find an opening!

Miki-san held his great sword at a thirty degree downward slope, with both hands gripping the slender handle, cross-woven with black threads of the finest silk. His right hand was positioned on top of the left and nearer the blade. From this stance he would be able to pivot to the right wielding the thirty-three inch blade in a deadly circle of death. He stood perfectly still. It appeared as if he were posturing, offering himself up as a tasty morsel fit for the palates of three gluttonous ronin, who circled their prey with murderous intent. The air was frozen with dread and icy anticipation. Anxiety and an instinctive fear of death gleamed in every wary eye – except that of a statue posing as a divine warrior.

Suddenly there was a flash and a sound, the slicing sound of a sword cutting through wind. The statue had not moved – had it? Yet the blade dripped crimson blood, and the jugulars of two of the ronin were slashed, while the third staggered like a drunkard holding his own head in his outstretched arms, as if he were presenting it, in a gruesome act of contrition, to his dispatcher.

Whichever version one accepts, it was a sight no one could easily forget. Several years passed before both versions of Tsutomu Miki's heroics reached the ears of Toyotomi Hideyoshi. He was duly impressed. "I prefer the second version because it seems much more plausible," he declared, and ordered his chief advisor Sugiyama Suzuki to locate and hire the young samurai whatever the cost.

Toyotomi needed someone who would be able to deal with the troublesome Christians in the same ruthless manner as the young samurai had dealt with the treacherous ronin. Thousands of his devout subjects were being converted to this new foreign religion. It was undermining the traditional social fabric that maintained him in power. There were probably well over a hundred thousand converts already and the number was growing daily! Something had to be done soon before it was too late. Even his most liberal-minded supporters were alarmed. The status quo was gradually being eroded, but the farmers and artisans were sympathetic, sympathetic toward the missionaries and Japanese-Christians. It was a prickly religious issue that plagued him from every corner of his vast domain. These Christians were like a hoard of nasty mosquitoes. He was being bled dry by their pious lamentations and zeal for gaining new converts. He had to act – but few were willing to take serious action. What was the good of issuing an edict if it was not enforced? It was frustrating. He needed someone who was willing to undertake this admittedly rather loathsome endeavor without pangs of conscience. Perhaps this young fellow, Tsutomu Miki, was the man he was looking for. He had heard from many reliable sources that for personal reasons Miki had very little respect for anyone wearing a crucifix.

And so it came to pass that three and a half years later, Tsutomu Miki was offered the lofty position of apprentice to the senior advisor, in the employ of the most powerful Lord in all Japan. It was a glorious opportunity for a relatively young man to become someone important. It was the year 1572. It would take time and seasoning to turn a novice into the Grand Inquisitor.

Miki-san, as he was affectionately called by his employer, was instructed to use his considerable skills, influence, and reputation to find ways to counteract the insidious influence of the Kirishitan. It was a very difficult assignment for one so young and inexperienced in such matters. There were few if any rules and no precedents to guide him. He was a novice treading a path that led to places he had never been before. As an apprentice to the senior advisor he had considerable latitude to improvise and create. The senior advisor's only advice was: "Always be mindful that whatever you do does not negatively affect our Lord's reputation and honor".

Tsutomu worked doggedly for fifteen years behind the scene learning about his religious adversary and carefully devising ways and means whereby its influence could be curtailed – fifteen years that shot by like an arrow from his quiver aimed impotently at the heart of Christianity in Japan. Toward the end of that time he could tell that Toyotomi was edgy. He spoke in terse, impatient phrases. The number of converts to Christianity had mushroomed to well over two hundred thousand! It seemed everyone with any social status was on his case. He had to do something that would at least appease them for the time being.

During their last confidential meeting Toyotomi had asked with a nervous twitch over his right eye, "What if I appointed a reputable person to specifically handle this tricky issue. Would that satisfy the chronic complainers?"

"It might get them off your back and onto the back of the new person responsible for dealing with the problem," Tsutomu had replied. "Who did you have in mind?"

"You."

"What?" Tsutomu responded, caught off guard by the forthrightness of the monosyllabic answer. He recovered by saying, "Surely there are more qualified men in your employ?"

"I have been grooming you for such a responsibility since the day I hired you. How long has it been?"

"About fifteen years."

"That long? My apologies. That is a long time to be serving in the role of apprentice to the senior advisor. You deserve a much loftier title."

"I am truly flattered."

"I trust you will do what is good for the country. You are one of the most honorable men I have ever had the pleasure to work with. I know I can count on you. This is a very grave and sensitive problem. It requires a man of your integrity."

"I am overwhelmed by your confidence in me, my great Lord," Tsutomu responded with a deep bow of humility.

"Your new title will be *Grand Inquisitor*."

Toyotomi Hideyoshi issued his famous edict in 1587 that called for the expulsion of all Christian missionaries. It was the year in which Tsutomu's second child was born. He named the boy Toyotomi, in honor of his great Lord. He might not have, if the Edict had been issued the year before. It tested the mettle and fortitude of the Grand Inquisitor to carry out his mandate, and to make Toyotomi proud of him. He held the power of life and death over every Kirishitan he encountered who would not recant his or her so-called Christian faith. It was a very heavy responsibility for one who knew all about the evils of Christianity but very little about the teachings of Jesus of Nazareth.

The duties and responsibilities of the Grand Inquisitor were made even more perplexing when Toyotomi undermined his own edict by allowing Spanish Friars into Japan, giving rise to a plethora of complaints from every level of society about the intent and fairness of the Edict. Consequently it was ignored by almost everyone except the Grand Inquisitor who valiantly went about attempting to carry out his lamentable mandate. He felt as if he were a solitary student seeking answers to ultimate questions about religion and life in a book in which the pages were either missing or blank. Each step he took was like a word being written in the book. In the end would the words make a sentence? Would the sentence make sense?

CHAPTER TWO

It was Penny's idea to present the book as if it were open and being read by both the student and authors simultaneously. She thought that this rather informal style would give the student a sense of participation, instead of simply being an interested onlooker. The cover page looked something like this:

A STUDENT HANDBOOK ON LIFE

Join us for a walk along
The Path and the Way....

* * * * *

By Penelope and Lawrence Petitjean

"There is something to feeling the heft of a book in your hands," she told Larry, "that gives one the feeling that there could be something substantial therein."

"Yes," Larry agreed, "and furthermore, a handbook is designed to provide ready information that is available to the student at their convenience. It is something over which they have control and which, if utilized properly, could be a real benefit to them."

"Exactly," Penny continued, "and you know, there is something to be said about the word 'handbook' itself that makes it personal... like you have something that belongs to you."

"It provides a sense of ownership," Larry concluded with a flourish.

"And rightly so," Penny substantiated, "because this book is written for them."

They decided after some deliberation to call the first part, *Orientation*, because as Larry put it, "It's something like getting out your compass and figuring out just where you're at, so that you can get going. It sort of sets the stage for things to come."

The study was pragmatically furnished with a long writing table situated under the window facing into the back garden. The computer desk was located at a right angle to the writing table and took up half the wall on which hung a family portrait of Penny, Larry, Jerry, and Sherry. The rhyming that occurred when their names were strung together gave each of them a sense of being a unique foursome. "The fearsome foursome!" Larry would say at times, when the family had to face adversity together. "We are here to save the world from injustice, greed, cowardice, and stupidity." At other times Penny would add the words "intolerance, prejudice, and ignorance." And once, when the topic was appropriate, Sherry had said, "Yes, and what about moral depravity, cruelty, and man's inhumanity to man?" And usually at the end, Jerry would reiterate the family motto: "We must dare to share if we really care!"

Whenever he pulled up a chair before the computer Larry would gaze up at the "fearsome foursome" and feel inspired to carry on fearlessly. He adjusted the computer chair, which had rolling castors and comfortable armrests, and clicked the mouse on the appropriate icon. The file labeled "Student Handbook" opened up on the seventeen inch monitor screen. Before scrolling down to the section entitled *The Predicament*, he quickly scanned the preface which they had added at the beginning in case the readers thought they were being too vain or pretentious.

PREFACE

The authors wish to clearly indicate at the outset that this handbook only demonstrates the limited level of awareness achieved by the writers, commensurate with their capabilities, relative to the social and scientific advances of the milieu in which they find themselves ensconced. The readers are challenged to examine, question, and expose the limitations and ignorance of the writers. In this way the existential foundation of awareness provided herein will expand with the growing awareness of future generations.

I ORIENTATION

(1) The Predicament

The Start

It is fortuitous that you are reading this sentence because that means you have made a start, and because you have made a start, you cannot go back and "un-start." You must carry on as best you can. Hopefully you will be able to finish what you have started but that is up to you. Still you have made a start. You are on your way.

Life is like a marathon race. You began the instant you were born and instinctively you started to run for the sake of running. Who are you? What are you doing here? How will you finish?

If your answer is, "I don't know," you are in a predicament. But this much you do know: you exist, you are here, and you have started.

The Situation

Your predicament started the moment you came into existence. Others were witness to your physical manifestation into this realm. It all began when an animated sperm penetrated an animated ovum, and life was passed on to life in a biological manner. Nourished by an ocean of life in the womb, you gradually developed the sensate receptivity known as your vertebrate nervous system and became aware of "being." It is as if you were slowly awakening from a dream of which you have no recollection. The only thing you know is that you are aware because you are alive, and you must be alive because you are here reading this, because a few moments ago you made a start.

The physical reality in which you live is called four dimensional. In this material dimension, everything has a start because everything endures through the fourth dimension known as time. This process of enduring is known as duration. All things endure, and because of duration, they change. Therefore nothing stays the same. Everything is constantly changing or in a state of flux. Another more common name for this process of duration is "aging." Because everything in this dimension is time-bound, everything ages, and consequently everything changes. And paradoxically, because everything changes relative to everything else, it could be said that things must constantly change in order to remain relatively constant.

It is because things are relatively constant, that they can be "known" relative to a constantly changing reference point. It is the reference point that allows for differentiation between the relative and the absolute, and permits a world of Idealism. The "I" of Idealism provides the constant point of reference or focal point of awareness that has endured in the persona of "I." This roundabout reasoning may sound rather convoluted to you, but there is actually a word in the dictionary for this point of view. It is called "solipsism." Look it up.

"I" instinctively knows that in order to continue to be manifest as a life-form in a four dimensional reality, energy is required. "I" innately intuits that in order to remain animate a source of energy must be readily available. The main source of sustainable energy on planet earth is the sun. The energy from the sun travels ninety-three million miles through the "vacuum" of space to reach the earth. This energy has neither density nor mass, yet is life-sustaining. Without radiant energy from the sun the earth would be a cold, dark and lifeless planet. As a life-form, "I" is a physical manifestation of vibrant energy. Unfortunately, in spite of billions of years of evolutionary development, "I" is incapable of photosynthesis, i.e. the ability to combine the energy from the sun with inorganic matter to form organic matter. Only green plants have this miraculous ability. In order to grow and continue to survive "I" must directly or indirectly consume organic matter. In a parasitical manner "I" sits on top of the food chain and ingests the vibrant energy from the sun which fuels or energizes "I" with life-force.

Change

In this world of constant flux, there are two types of change: involuntary and voluntary. Involuntary change consists of all activity that occurs without the conscious employment of the human will, such as the erosion of mountains, the rotation of the earth, the beating of the heart, the growth of trees, etc. Voluntary change, on the other hand, comprises all activity that is initiated by the impetus of the human will. It is this type of change that creates the rationalizations that make life meaningful. It is this type of willful change that determines how well the marathon runner will run the race.

There are many self-imposed voluntary activities that can have a negative impact upon the runner. Let us take, for example, three basic human activities: breathing, drinking, and eating. Suppose the runner (a) smokes heavily and becomes addicted to nicotine which floods his body with carcinogens and hampers his breathing; (b) drinks an excessive amount of alcoholic beverage and becomes addicted to alcohol which deteriorates his kidneys, liver, and spleen, and impairs his mental capacity; (c) eats more than he needs and packs on excessive weight that places extra stress on his heart, increases his susceptibility to diabetes, and hampers his mobility. These are all self-imposed voluntary changes.

The question is, if we are going to make voluntary changes, would not it be prudent to make changes for the better? If so, then why do we deliberately make voluntary changes for the worse? The answer is not the least bit flattering. We voluntarily make self-imposed changes for the worse out of sheer stupidity or ignorance, or both. Just look around you and you will find that the world has no shortage of this type of behavior.

Some experts would excuse these people by suggesting that they are just plain lazy. Does it help to be called "lazy" on top of stupid and ignorant? All voluntary change for the better or worse requires will power. The heavy smoker spends a lot of willful energy in order to continue his habit: he wastes his hard-earned cash buying expensive cigarettes and guiltily huddles outside in the cold and damp exercising his right to ruin his health. A heavy drinker likewise wastes his hard-earned cash, but is able to imbibe in places where smoking is not allowed because drinking is a social activity condoned by the great unwashed. A glutton is aptly described by his weakness; he eats and eats to excess even when he is not hungry. It takes a great deal of persistence over a long period of time to become a member of this group. These are not necessarily lazy people. They have worked hard to achieve their condition. Certainly along the way they had other much more healthy options. If they could start over, would they wander down the same path again? Is it possible to learn from our mistakes?

Some claim that we are captive to the collective will of a religiously capitalistic system so pervasive that it brainwashes us into believing that such unhealthy self-imposed voluntary behavior is not only the norm, but the customary expectation the general public has of all racers. It is the status quo that must be followed in spite of the perils. This type of behavior has become known as "socialized ignorance." Although it is often staunchly entrenched in the attitudes of the popular culture, it can be effectively cured by the application of a strong will fortified by wisdom.

There are two powerful inputs which determine to a great extent the type of person we will become. These two powerful inputs are labeled Nature and Nurture. What are they, and how do they affect us?

Nature, the interior input, is represented by the innocent, uncontaminated, biological infant who emerges from the womb into the world of Being as the latest link in the evolutionary chain. The meeting of the sperm and ovum determined in advance the content of his/her deoxyribonucleic acid or DNA, the spiraling strings of which contain the secrets of his/her heredity. Depending upon the donors, he/she could be black, yellow, red, white, or some combination of these four basic races. Every aspect of his/her genetic make-up is inherited: the color, the shape, the size, the intelligence, the five receptor senses, and the innate abilities. Everything not accorded to Nature is accorded to Nurture.

Nurture is the exterior input. Everything that impinges upon the newborn baby, (including external inputs by the mother during pregnancy such as smoking, or drinking which can lead to fetal alcohol syndrome), shape and mould the baby into developing who he/she becomes. The force of this exterior input is constant and relentless. It includes such influences as culture, religion, education, and environment. Everything that impinges upon and is transmitted into the memory banks of the brain accumulates as the effects of nurture. Everything that is not accorded to Nurture is accorded to Nature. This being the case, *how much free-will do we actually have?*

Let us just leave this question dangling for the moment and return to our discussion of voluntary behavior. Accident of birth and place of birth throughout history have determined to a very great extent the nature of our voluntary behavior. In this wonderful multi-cultural mosaic known as the Global Village, Hindus, Jews, Buddhists, Muslims, Agnostics, Atheists, Christians, and every manner of religious faith and belief intermingle. Cultures evolve and patterns of behavior are established.

If you, dear reader, by accident of birth, were born and raised in a luxurious mansion in Dallas, Texas to devout, white, born-again Christian parents who sent you to be educated in the finest private Evangelical schools, and took you to pray for the forgiveness of your sins in the grandest Christian church money could build within a Christian state in a Christian country – there is a 99% chance that you would become, like the people in your cultural environment, a Christian.

On the other hand if, by accident of birth, you were born and raised in a small apartment in Baghdad, Iraq to shop-keepers who were born and raised as devout Sunni-Muslims, and you were educated in a Sunni-Muslim school and prayed daily in a Sunni-Muslim mosque in a Muslim city in a Muslim country – there is a 99% chance that you would be a Muslim.

How much freedom of choice did you have? Did you have any say in the matter concerning your religious beliefs? As a child you most likely had very little input into how your faith would be nurtured in the cultural environment in which you were simply, by accident of birth, born. Do you think it reasonable that you should fight, even amongst sects of your own religious faith, and claim that your particular faith over and above all other faiths that exist in the Global Village is the one and only True Faith? Would you be willing to kill and die, even sacrifice the entire Global Village, for the sake of that incredibly *selfish* belief? Is that what any mature human being representing the end result of billions of years of evolutionary development, and endowed with reason and common sense, would do? Is that what you would do?

A brief digression is in order here with regards to the previous use of the word "selfish". In 1976 Richard Dawkins, a professor at Oxford University, published an insightful and thought provoking book entitled "The Selfish Gene", which due to its unique evolutionary point of view and provocative title, caused a wave of excitement among biologists and the general public. The book has been re-issued many times due to its popularity.

It is difficult to conceive of a gene being personified as "selfish" or man being genetically selfish, mainly because the term "selfish" is a loaded word. It has negative connotations for most people. Who likes being called "selfish", even if it is true? Ironically, it is precisely Dawkins' use of the word "selfish" that perks up the ears of self-serving capitalists seeking an evolutionary explanation that justifies their greedy behavior. Loaded as it might be, the word "selfish" does in many ways seem appropriate when one looks about at the end product of some three billion years of evolutionary progress and sees the worldly manifestations wrought by the "selfish" gene. Could any other kind of genes have produced this?

The human body is the end result of billions of years of evolution. Evolution, according to Charles Darwin, is an orderly and logical process of natural selection based upon the logic inherent in life-enhancing behavior which results ultimately in survival. There appears to be no objective basis upon which to elevate one life form above another; they are all simply "survival machines" (according to Dawkins) striving to survive. Naturally the species most fit for survival survived, giving rise to the phrase "survival of the fittest".

It has been said that the much maligned chimpanzee and the highly esteemed human being share over ninety-nine per cent of their evolutionary history. At base level, at the level of the one thousand million, million tiny cells that represent the survival machine known as the human body, the role of the microscopic "replicator molecules" called DNA, made up of double helix coils of four different kinds of "building blocks" (represented by the letters A, T, C, and G) called nucleotides, provide some clues regarding the mysterious difference.

The DNA contains the instructions required to make a human body, or a monkey's. This vast and complex information is stored in the nucleus of each and every cell. These "genetic plans" are encoded in exactly forty-six thread-like shapes called chromosomes, along which are strung the mysterious bits (of karmic dust) known as cistrons or genes. A gene has been defined as any portion of a chromosomal material that lasts for enough generations as to serve as a unit of natural selection.

The human body represents the "whole" made up of the one thousand million, million cells. The process by which each normal cell, which consists of forty-six chromosomes, replicates itself is known as mitosis. The singular exception to this process results in the need for sexual intercourse in the human species, or "copulation" when monkeys, dogs, horses, cattle etc. are concerned.

Why is such an act (often associated with Original Sin by the human species) necessary? The cells involved in the reproductive process, known as meiosis, produce exactly twenty-three chromosomes (or half of the forty-six required). The ovum from the female donor contains twenty-three chromosomes as do the sperm cells from the male donor. The union (23+23=46) results in the creation of a single unique but normal cell. From this solitary cell the entire thousand million, million celled-leviathan known as homo-sapien is manifested in a four dimensional reality. Consider the undeniable fact that the entire human body including blueprints for the *conscious* brain which is *aware* of itself and capable of *thinking*, developed from one single cell containing forty-six chromosomes! The philosophical question which arises from the end-result of such a miraculous creative process is: *Could the whole be greater than the sum of the parts?*

Advocates of the selfish gene theory support the view that the human body is simply the survival mechanism via which the genes seek to replicate themselves and survive; such a deterministic view which contends that *the body is simply a robot vehicle blindly programmed to preserve its selfish genes* makes the aforementioned question seem to be rather redundant. The sum-of-the-parts over billions of years of evolutionary progress has, through natural selection created survival mechanisms like porpoises, reptiles, fish, trees, fungus, bacteria, etc., capable of promoting the continuing survival of the gene pool of which they are a part.

In an environment like planet earth dominated by the survival of the fittest, what particular life form has successfully risen to the fore? What gene pool has survived and best manifests the ruthless qualities that could be expected of a life form evolved from selfish genes? The answer can be easily ascertained from the following set of questions.

What highly evolved life form greedily plunders, selfishly decimates, and carelessly pollutes the good earth which sustains and nourishes it? What existing species has callously demonstrated that for selfish reasons it is capable of perpetuating a holocaust of death upon an innocent minority of its own kind? What intelligent life form has created weapons of mass destruction and used them on their own species? What earthly life form has multiplied and proliferated throughout the ages, and presently threatens the entire planet with the catastrophic consequences of global warming?

The answer is self evident. The most highly evolved species on the face of the planet: *human beings.* The human gene pool has survived, and now their replicates manifest a reality commensurate with their evolutionary status. What type of humans predominate? The most selfish. How selfish? Selfish enough to sacrifice the entire world in order in order to "save" a chosen few who will enjoy eternal life? Do they truly represent the end product of billions of years of evolutionary survival? Are they the fittest?

There is a fundamental question that arises with regards to the selfish gene's evolutionary purpose: is it simply to "survive"? To what end? Is there a hidden agenda toward which all genes are secretly evolving that goes far beyond simple brute survival? Is it possible that after billions of years of natural selection the selfish genes have been able to approximate the *Source* of their existence by creating a manifestation far grander than anything the sum of the parts could ever amount to: *a conscious, thinking, survival mechanism capable of genuine "altruism"?*

Selfish as a gene might be, the survival machine per se often behaves in ways that seems to be contrary to the selfish interests of the sum-of-the parts. Contraception, suicide, and deliberate life endangerment are notable examples. This type of "willful" behavior by the body which seems contrary to the survival instinct inherent in each microscopic gene, gives further import to the question asked previously: *Is the whole greater than the sum of its parts?* The implications of a positive response gives rise to a further question of equal significance: *Does the "whole" have free will?*

Consideration of a non-scientific concept like "karma" might, without being contradictory, go a long way toward allowing Dawkins to expand the gene's nature from being limited by an all inclusive tautologically defined selfishness, to being "self-determined". In this sense the genes could represent biological units of "karmic information" that reverberate along the Great Chain of Being to the *Source*. Logic informs us that any gene that cannot be traced in an unbroken line to the *Source* would not exist to replicate itself.

All such genes represent positively and negatively charged bits of karmic energy with the evolutionary tendency to aid and abet survival. Positively energized genes would be life-enhancing – whereas negatively energized genes would tend to have the opposite effect. Both are needed to create the evolutionarily stable situation experienced universally as "mortality". All mortal genes vibrate collectively to produce the appropriate incarnations naturally selected for survival in the environment in which they are "fit" to be manifested.

What if, by accident of birth, such highly evolved individuals were born and raised as Muslims in Istanbul, or Jews in New York City, or Christians in Montreal, and grew up believing that their particular brand of faith was the one and only True Faith. Would such people be willing to sacrifice the entire world in order to save themselves? No one can answer on their behalf. Only time will tell.

However, you dear reader, have been reading this handbook and can probably adroitly answer the question that we left dangling: *How much free-will do we actually have?*

"AS MUCH AS WE ARE AWARE OF."

Well spoken, indeed. Can you, my friend, with your newly expanded awareness, transcend the nature and nurture that limits the boundaries of your freedom, and exercise your free will to help make the world a better place for all mankind? Or will you supinely sit back on your buttocks and say: "Let someone else do it." We do not mean to sound offensive, but let's face it, it is personal. What "you" do affects "me" and vice versa. Yes indeed, it is personal. "We" are all in this together. We all live in the same Global Village. We have all survived! Self-serving as you might genetically tend to be, if you read on, consider getting up off your fat, lean, or middle-sized ass and exercise your FREE WILL. This is serious.

"Wow!" Penny exclaimed. "It sounds good, but I think we may have overstepped the boundaries of etiquette just a little."

"We're trying to make a point that requires a touch of sardonic humor."

"There is a bit of self-righteousness creeping in, you know, that opinionated, 'I told you so', attitude?"

"Yes, I'm familiar with it."

"We must try to tone that down a little more in ensuing sections," Penny advised.

"Let's not get ahead of ourselves." Larry cautioned. "If we get too conservative, we'll begin to sound as if this is not important. This is challenging stuff we are dealing with. Challenging for us, and challenging for the reader."

CHAPTER THREE

Larry's fondest recollection of his parents was when the family would go fishing together. His mother would pack a superb picnic lunch and his father would eagerly get out the fishing tackle and prepare two fishing rods, one for himself and the nicer one for his son. On the morning of the fishing expedition Larry and his dad would go down to the little creek within walking distance of their house, with a minnow net they had made from a discarded screen door, to catch some minnows for bait. They would build a "V" with rocks leaving a small opening downstream just large enough to be covered by the net. Larry usually held the net while his father chased the minnows down into it. It was always fun to catch the minnows. It was the prologue to catching bigger fish.

There was a stream about a half mile behind their house, which, in those days, was productive for cutthroat and rainbow trout. His father taught his son how to set up his fishing rod and how to put the bait on the hook. Once Larry got the hang of catching fish he became an excellent fisherman. His father always let Larry go first when they were stream fishing because he so enjoyed seeing his little boy get excited each time he caught a good-sized trout. One time Larry caught an eighteen inch cutthroat. It was the biggest trout he ever caught in that stream. It was a real beaut!

After they had been fishing for two or three hours and had worked their way downstream for one or two miles, Larry's mother, who always wore black rubber boots with red trim, and carried the picnic lunch, would say, "You two men hungry yet?" This reference to him as a man made Larry feel like he was his father's equal even though he was still a child. During such moments he basked in the sunshine of their warmth and affection. He was precious to them and he accepted this as his birthright.

The outdoor lunch along the creek bank always tasted delicious. Larry looked forward to gathering sticks together and making a little bonfire. Sometimes they roasted wieners and marshmallows. Larry's father would take off his hip waders and lean back and soak up the sun while his mother read the book she had brought along. On such occasions his father rarely spoke of religious matters; he was just "good ol' Dad."

One activity that made Larry feel particularly close to his father occurred whenever they had to ford the stream to get to the other side and the water was deeper than Larry's knee high rubber boots. His father would piggyback him across on such occasions. It was always a poignant experience. Larry would cling to his father's back, holding his fishing rod, while his father would tentatively make his way across the rushing stream. He would place one foot carefully ahead of the other in his attempts to avoid stepping upon a slippery boulder and falling down. Sometimes he would falter, and then quickly regain his footing. Whenever this occurred Larry would tighten his grip about his father's strong neck and hold his breath. His father always came through although at times when they were halfway across and the water was dangerously high and swift, especially during spring run-off, Larry would pray, "Please help us to get across," for it seemed to him at such times he was truly in his Father's hands, and the phrase, the same difference, actually made sense.

As great as his father's influence was, the one person who had the greatest impact on his life was his mother. Larry's mother had been born in Germany and was of Jewish extraction. . She was a survivor of the Holocaust. It made her into the quiet, humble persona she represented in the modern world. She seldom spoke of that period of her life but when she did it was for good reason. It was as if she had repressed those memories into some deep recess of her subconscious and placed a lid on it so tightly hardly a word escaped. But from time to time when a family member complained vociferously about something quite incidental she would say, "Oh my, it can't be that bad." It was the way she emphasized the 'that', that elicited the comparison. She was never challenged when she said that because it was understood by her husband and son that she knew exactly what she was talking about.

Sometimes people would say to her, "You don't look Jewish," as if anyone can tell these days what a modern Jew is supposed to look like! She was a slender, rather elegant looking woman, a little on the frail side, with dark brown hair, dark brown eyes, and a refined chiseled profile that could have been a cameo. It was her elegance combined with her quiet humility that so captivated Larry's father. He met her in New York City at a Judeo-Christian seminar for increasing understanding and tolerance. Although she was still in her late teens her face reflected a maturity far beyond her years.

She was there of her own accord, trying in her own way to accommodate herself to her new country. Like many of the other new Jewish immigrants at that time she was willing and anxious to blend in, to become an American. In a subconscious way she was searching for a way to camouflage her Jewish identity that had so traumatized her. She was susceptible and vulnerable to the charms of an inoffensive non-Jewish young man with a hawkish face and an awkward, embarrassing presentation of self by the name of John Petty. Although John was in his mid twenties, his face reflected the innocence of a teenager. He was one of the few, if not the only person there, who was as shy and self-effacing as she was.

Shortly after that seminar they became good friends. And six months after that John, unromantic as he was at that time, actually got down on his knees and proposed. He cried when she accepted. It was slightly embarrassing to his bride-to-be, but she never forgot it. It was an unforgettable moment, a once in a lifetime experience.

This tall austere, self-conscious, and reserved young man who always held his emotions in check and wrapped himself in a cocoon of piety, had allowed her to catch a brief glimpse of his real self, the self he guarded and protected as if he was afraid, afraid to share that which was most sacred: his heart and soul. He had momentarily let down his guard and exposed his vulnerability to a potentially devastating refusal, a refusal that would have compromised his sense of self-worth. He had offered himself up to her like a sacrificial lamb. She could see the innocent look of total infatuation in his grayish-blue eyes: the pleading, the worship.

How could she refuse? When she quietly said, "Yes," he wept for joy. His bony shoulders shuddered, and he kissed her slender hands as if they were the hands of an angel of mercy. "Thank you," he whispered, "thank you very much."

Shortly thereafter, they were married in a quiet civil ceremony that reflected both Jewish and Christian sentiments. John and Anna Petty spent their honeymoon at the Bluebird Motel in Niagara Falls. It was during the honeymoon, when she was a sexual novice and a timid and insecure blushing new bride that Anna received the best marital advice she ever heard. The advice did not come from a professional marriage counselor, but from the cleaning lady, a buxom, matronly, middle-aged woman who had a penchant for minding other people's private business. Her saving grace was her jovial personality and her good intentions. She had a nose for sniffing out newly-weds. Her advice was probably worth millions, but distributed out of sheer generosity to those who looked like they could use it, free of charge.

"Let me share an invaluable secret with you," she said one morning to the disheveled looking bride. "The best way to keep your husband satisfied and from straying from home is to keep him well drained." She paused dramatically to let the profundity of this tidbit of wisdom sink in and take effect. "Drain every drop of sperm his testicles can produce. He'll have no need to look for greener pastures to fertilize when he is plumb out of fertilizer." The cleaning lady peered closely at Anna to see if she properly understood what was being shared. "Know what I'm gettin' at?" she asked as she shifted her weight from one leg to the other. "I lost my first husband because I didn't know any better. He was hornier than a horny owl but other than that he was a real gentleman. He couldn't help himself, believe me; it was purely instinctive and biological." She paused once again and peered closely at Anna. "Imagine for instance, being told to 'hold it' if you had to urinate or defecate in the worst way," she added, hoping this would provide further clarification. "You gettin' this?" she asked quizzically.

"Huh?" Anna responded.

"You know that whenever young couples separate or divorce," the cleaning lady pressed on with a bemused twinkle in her eyes, "the vast majority come up with the vague excuse: 'irreconcilable differences'. Ha! – what they really mean is that one or the other of them felt rejected, hard-done-by, pissed off... and split the sheets. I know. It happened to me. There has to be accommodation, if you get my drift?"

Anna's face was flushed with embarrassment. It made her look healthy and robust. "I-I think so," she stammered.

"I can see you're full of the right juices," the cleaning lady continued. She heaved a sigh of satisfaction, pleased with Anna's response. The tone of her voice altered to reflect the change in her demeanor as she stepped back and philosophically added, "To make a whole the yin must fit with the yang, as the Chinese say. There is a natural reciprocity between male and female. Just keep him well drained, and you will have no problems," she advised with a wink of her right eye as she departed.

Of course it proved, in the months and years to follow, to be such excellent advice that Mrs. John Petty was often tempted to pass it on for what it was worth.

In those days Larry's mother was unsure of herself, particularly of her social status and of the cultural role that was expected of young women in America. Consequently, shortly after their Spartan honeymoon to Niagara Falls, she allowed herself to be included in the Presbyterian congregation her husband presided over. She felt it was her duty to support her husband in his chosen vocation. She was there every Sunday, as faithful a member as anyone else, but her husband knew she had a deeper no-name brand of faith, a faith far deeper than anything written down. From time to time the Reverend John Petty would feel slightly embarrassed when he was standing up there in the pulpit, drained, and pretending to be holier-than-thou. At such times he could feel her dark eyes fixed upon him, and in spite of his best performances, he felt that she really knew how inadequate a Presbyterian Minister could be.

* * *

The most wonderful thing about Anna was her positive attitude toward life, her enlightened point of view toward good and evil, and especially toward her fellow human beings. It was born from an experience that happened to her just before an American relative pulled the strings that enabled her to find refuge in New York City. It happened in Germany near the beginning of the Second World War in a little town near the border with France called Baden-Baden. That was the town where Anna was sent after her parents were killed by an explosion at the munitions factory where they were employed. It was actually hit by a stray bomb, a lucky strike – lucky for the Allies - but at the time was called an industrial accident, to keep the general population from feeling threatened. She was only twelve years old when she arrived at her grandparents' home, dropped off by her uncle Levi, at the doorstep of a narrow two-story house sandwiched in amongst row upon row of similar abodes. She stood there in the doorway with her knapsack and a large brown leather suitcase. She looked forlorn and as stoic as a sixty-year-old spinster whose age was suddenly divided by five.

"Little Anna has arrived," her grandmother had announced to her husband. "Come, make her feel at home."

Nearly four years shot by like the whiz of the Ancient Mariner's crossbow, and the albatross of prejudice hung around Anna's neck in the same metaphorical manner as it had hung around the Mariner's. Except she was as innocent as the bird itself. She had no crossbow, and she had not shot anything. Yet in Western Christendom where anti-Semitism made sense, and some intolerant person had vehemently mouthed the spurious phrase, "Christ Killers," she was singled out for persecution for being who she was. It was unjust and unfair but history is full of lessons that must be hard-learned if they are to be learned at all.

It was the late afternoon of October twenty-ninth when three Nazi soldiers wearing red armbands with black swastikas dropped by Anna's grandparents' house unexpectedly. Anna was in the upstairs bedroom where the golden rays of the sun slanted obliquely through the solitary window adjacent to the double doors of the clothes closet. She was standing before the mirrors on the closet doors brushing her long brown hair when she heard her grandfather's panic-stricken voice rise up the staircase like a pistol shot: "Hide!"

There was no time to do anything but open the right hand door of the closet, scrunch down into the far corner, pull the hanging clothes over herself, close the door, and pray. The entire house was so quiet she could have heard a mouse scamper across the floor, let alone the clomping of heavy army boots. They clomped in through the front door, and she heard an authoritative male voice ask: "Are you the only Jews living here?"

"Yes, just the two of us."

"Take them outside." More clomping of heavy boots.

"Wolfgang."

"Yes sir."

"Go upstairs and check out the rooms up there."

Clomp, clomp, clomp, fourteen risers and fourteen clomps. Anna counted every single one. She heard a door open and heard more clomping in the adjacent room, before the clomping halted at her bedroom door. It was pitch dark inside the musty closet where she scrunched into such a small ball of human flesh and bone she almost disappeared into the fabric of her surroundings, like a quivering fawn with luminous eyes crouches down into the flora and is protected by the camouflage of the leafy forest from the hunter's searching gaze. She closed her eyes and prayed with all her might: "Please, please, please...." She could only wait and hope against all odds. All odds! Who could be so foolish, so crazy as to even proffer odds?

In the vastness of the universe did anyone feel the depths of her desperate plea? Was it lost in the infinitude of time and space where it dwindled into a whimper that disappeared into the nothingness of the void? What else could she do? What else could anyone do but pray and hope against all odds. "Please, please, please.... "

Little Anna, who was not so little anymore, held her breath as if frozen with fear, a fear so great the sound of her beating heart sounded like an executioner's drum roll. She heard the bedroom door open and the army boots clomp in, muffled by the thin carpet on the floor. The boots clomped slowly around the bed and paused before the closet doors.

"Please, please, please...."

What made Wolfgang pause there so deliberately? Was it simply the confident pause of a hunter steadying himself before the final act? Or was it something else? He pulled the left door open and quickly pushed the hanging clothes aside. Nothing. And then he slowly began to open the right hand door.

"Please, please, please, please, please, please...."

From under the clothes Anna could see the brilliant late afternoon sunlight reflect off a pair of shiny black army boots standing a mere eighteen inches away. A uniformed knee came down and touched the carpet, and then a groping hand reached in blindly past a long purple gown and latched like an icy claw onto her left arm just above the elbow.

Anna's entire body convulsed as if she had been electrocuted. She was terrified. Her skin was white as chalk and her dark eyes as large and luminous as a frightened fawn's. She trembled uncontrollably as another hand brushed aside the purple gown, and suddenly, the hunter and hunted were face to face!

Eyes stared into eyes. The recognition was instantaneous! There was a quick and explosive intake of breath that rushed in from a universe of unlimited probabilities. All breathing ceased. In the frozen space between them time melted, and the icy claw gripping Anna's left arm like a steel vice, released and dropped away.

Anna stared into Aryan eyes as blue and as deep as the eternal sky. The two pupils slowly merged and then miraculously fused into one compassionate eye. The fear vanished. She stared into the eyes of humanity!

An eternity passed before Wolfgang exhaled. "Stay here," he whispered, "I will be back to help you escape!" The words flowed from his lips as if that was the natural thing to say. The impulse was instinctive. The risk involved was unthinkable! It was stupendously foolhardy. Yet he felt a tremendous elation because he had dared. DARED! It was a first. His face was flushed with exhilaration. He stood up and composed himself. He never felt so worthy in all his life. The exhilaration lingered as he lowered his head and quietly said, "*Auf Wiedersehen.*"

Anna whimpered. The closet door closed. The army boots clomped across the floor. A voice yelled, "There is no one else up here," followed by fourteen fading footsteps. The front door clicked shut and then all was quiet, except for a sobbing sound and the prayerful vocalization of a simple gratitude so profound, so universal it resonated in the compassionate heartstrings of a departing young German soldier clomping nonchalantly down the road with his comrades in arms.

"Thank you, thank you, thank you, thank you...."

Years later when Anna was safe and secure on the other side of the Atlantic she found many people who spoke of the Holocaust with hatred and vengeful anger. How some of them loved to condemn and blame the Germans. What the Germans had done was unforgivable, "simply unforgivable," they would say.

"I will admit it was a hard lesson," Anna would thoughtfully reply at such times, "but it will be a lesson wasted if we are not able to forgive. It was a very hard lesson for all of us living at that time in Western Christendom." She would pause to let this sentiment sink in, and then she would ask with a determined glint in her luminous eyes, "Are not the Germans human beings? Are not the Jews human beings? Are not the Americans human beings? When will we ever learn that superficial characteristics like race, religion, and nationality are simply secondary attributes? It is our humanity that is the primary substance which is universal to Man and God. Is one man's humanness of any less worth than anyone else's?" Anna liked to question rather than pronounce. It was her style. She did not say much but when she spoke people listened respectfully.

That was Larry's mother, the one who wore the black rubber boots with the red trim when they went fishing. He would not have turned out the way he had if it was not for her quiet presence in his life. She appreciated the fact that anyone with an ounce of compassion for their fellowman could make a difference out of all proportion to that ounce.

CHAPTER FOUR

"**W**hat the world needs is more good Samaritans and fewer self-righteous bigots!" Larry pronounced.

"What brought that on?" Penny asked, caught off guard by her husband's outburst.

"I was just thinking about the Holocaust and all the ignorant behavior associated with it."

"There was a lot of ignorant behavior back then," Penny commiserated.

"Too much," Larry sighed.

"Do you think we are any wiser now?" The question had a relevancy that required a response that combined objectivity with intellectual honesty.

"I suppose every generation thinks they are a cut above the preceding one," Larry pondered. "I guess it all depends...."

"On what?" Penny interjected before her husband had time to complete his thought.

"On how one defines wisdom, and on the number of people who know the difference."

"What difference?"

"The difference between ignorance and wisdom.

"You know? We wrote something about this in the Handbook. I think it is in the section called Wisdom. Remember?" Penny reminded her spouse.

"Ah yes. Now I remember. Let's take another look at it."

The computer screen flickered ominously in the defused morning light that reflected off the west wall of the study. The index finger on Larry's right hand twitched voluntarily and the mouse sent a signal to the computer to open the selected file.

(2) Wisdom

The Difference

Wisdom is the result of knowledge. Knowledge is a result of thought. Thought, which enables man to realize that he might be something more than an evolutionary survival mechanism for selfish genes, transforms the selfish brain into an altruistic "mind". There is a vast difference. Wisdom is the knowledge you need to "know" the difference. If you know the difference, you will be able to change for the better. "What difference?" you might ask. The difference between *knowing* you can transcend your state of ignorance – and *being* ignorant. It is a simple matter of attitude. That is the only difference that matters after all is said and done.

Many intelligent and well-meaning people think they know the difference between good and evil, and are quick to judge others whose views and opinions regarding the same concepts differ from their own. Consequently crusades are organized, wars are fought with self-righteous zeal, and people are murdered by the hundreds of thousands (an estimated six million in the Holocaust alone) because their selfish beliefs and opinions differed from somebody else's. If they really knew what difference the difference made, they would understand why a wise man refrains from pre-judging others.

The Pillars of Wisdom

In order to get a better understanding of why the wise man is nonjudgmental, let us examine the three pillars of wisdom. Wisdom, like all knowledge found in a space-time continuum, "endures" on a sea of self-serving ignorance. This process of enduring obviously takes time. Consequently, the first ingredient of wisdom which stands out of the sea of ignorance like a shining pillar of virtue is patience. Patience, in contrast to the impatience of the ignorant, naturally manifests the second pillar of wisdom: tolerance. Tolerance tempered with patience, in contrast with the impatience and intolerance of the ignorant, creates a third pillar of wisdom: understanding. Understanding amplifies patience and tolerance, yielding an even greater degree of understanding. Consequently, a symbiotic relationship develops among the three pillars of wisdom that bind and reinforce each other, enabling them to rise above the sea of ignorance like an invisible three-legged stool. The seat of the stool is where the wise man sits supported by the virtues of patience, tolerance, and understanding.

The wise man is aware that the stool floats upon a bottomless sea of ignorance, and that the three pillars of wisdom constitute the foreground that defines itself against the background. Furthermore, without a sea of ignorance to keep the stool afloat, the contrast would disappear and he would lose his identity. Therefore, the wise man feels beholden to the ignorant for his wisdom, and consequently is non-judgmental because he knows the only difference between a wise man and an ignorant man is in the "knowing."

Therefore, when you know the difference, you will be able to make a difference. The purpose of this handbook is to help you to make a difference, to help you make a change for the better just like Krishna, Lao Tzu, Socrates, Plato, Moses, Confucius, Buddha, Jesus, Mohammed, and all those other wise human beings who have trod this mortal path ahead of us in order that we may follow in their footsteps, the wiser for their passing.

Penny sauntered back into the computer room after having eaten the lunch that Larry had wisely prepared for her, knowing she would be ravenous after returning from her late morning walk. "Thanks for the salmon sandwiches," Penny said, "it was very thoughtful of you." She sat down in the empty chair beside her husband and asked, "What did you think about that section on Wisdom?"

"I was going to ask you that question before you left for your walk."

"Well, to be honest, I think it could use a little more work."

"I concur," Larry responded, "but let's leave it for now and check out the next section. We can come back to it later."

"Isn't the next section about the Two Universal Points of View?"

"Yes, I believe it is."

"I think that section may spark a little controversy."

"Controversy will be good. It makes people think," Larry replied.

"We have really dichotomized these two views into two simplistic categories as if there is no overlap," Penny critiqued.

"It clarified the fuzziness. I think we needed to be clear-cut in order to get our point across," Larry defended.

"Being clear-cut is one thing," Penny pointed out, "but being rigid and unwilling to compromise is quite another."

"I hear you. That could be a valid criticism of what we have drafted out here along with our references to the Judeo-Christian-Muslim point of view. Let's look it over." Larry clicked the mouse and presto, there it was on the screen.

(3) Two Universal Points of View

Two Views

Patience, tolerance, and understanding have led man to two unique points of view. These two points of view can be labeled (a) the Extrinsic View, and (b) the Intrinsic View. From the Extrinsic View, God (also referred to as the Source or Eternal Spirit) is external to both man and creation, while from the Intrinsic View, God is inherent in man and creation. How do these two points of view affect the way we relate to God, to creation, and to each other? In a world filled with religious turmoil it is vitally important that we have a clear-cut understanding of these two universal points of view because the ramifications are quite extraordinary.

Mass Confusion

These two views have not previously been clearly delineated; consequently, over the years, there has been an increasing amount of confusion and misunderstanding. The problem is basically existential in nature: modern Western scholars who have been raised and educated in a milieu that is predominantly Judeo-Christian-Muslim or extrinsic in view, have gradually shifted their own focus toward the intrinsic view, blurring and overlapping characteristics of the extrinsic view with the intrinsic view and vice versa. The result? Mass confusion.

A Clear Orientation is Important

There is presently a whole generation of students (and young and middle-aged adults) who are curious, open-minded spiritual seekers after truth. They are looking for answers that their parents, unfortunately, were unable to provide, perhaps because like their parents and grandparents, they manifested a world view that is commensurate with the "extrinsic view". This has been the predominant view of the modern industrialized world until recently.

Change can bring confusion, doubt and insecurity. It is our objective here to attempt to untangle the tangled views that confuse and baffle, and hopefully provide the forthcoming generation of spiritual seekers with a little clearer orientation for the journey that lies ahead.

A Changing Focus

It is the observation of the authors that on a universal basis, as man's collective consciousness continues to evolve toward higher states of awareness, the natural evolutionary progress is from the more exclusive and contained view, toward the more inclusive and accommodating view. Just as man's scientific view of the universe evolved from the limited Ptolemaic view to the more accommodating Copernican view, man's view of self and God is naturally evolving from the extrinsic view toward the intrinsic view. The transition will probably take generations, and in the process create a great deal of confusion and existential angst. There will be an even greater need to practice the virtues of patience, tolerance, and understanding.

What follows is an attempt by the authors to clearly delineate in a side by side manner, the ten points of description and comparison fundamental to these two universal points of view expressed in a meaningful vernacular. Hopefully this juxtaposition of the two views will help clarify some of the present confusion. Although we have tried to be as objective as possible, the chart probably reflects our personal biases. The reader is encouraged to modify the chart in any way he/she deems necessary that will further enhance its clarity.

TEN ESSENTIAL ASPECTS OF THE EXTRINSIC
AND INTRINSIC VIEWS OF MAN AND GOD
Direction of Change ->

EXTRINSIC VIEW	INTRINSIC VIEW
(1) God is separate from Man and Creation.	(1) God is inherent in Man and Creation.
(2) Man is "other" directed.	(2) Man is "inner" directed.
(3) Man is not inclined to have reverence for life on earth because Man and the earth are "Godless" as God resides elsewhere.	(3) Man is inclined to have reverence for all life on earth because God is inherent in everything, and consequently life is precious.
(4) The earth is profane, and may be plundered and "used" by Man for the glory of God.	(4) The earth is sacred and should be cherished, sustained, and appreciated by Man.

(5) Man's nature is inherently flawed (by "Original Sin"), consequently his outlook reflects this life-negating attitude amplified by a prophecy of doom in which the earth is ultimately consumed in flames.	(5) Man manifests a spark of divine life upon a sacred earth; therefore it is possible for those who are cognizant of this to reflect a life-affirming attitude commensurate with the degree of awareness.
(6) Man must obey God's "commandments", which are just and absolute.	(6) Karma and reincarnation are God's natural laws of justice, which are relative.
(7) God's authoritarian nature is manifested as an "exclusive" view empowered by a righteous attitude: those who choose this view will be "saved" – those who do not will be eternally "damned", giving impetus to selfish rather than altruistic motivation.	7) The universality of God's presence leads to an "inclusive" view, the realization of which provides its own reward, without dire consequences for those with differing views.
(8) Man acknowledges the existence of "the one and only true God", who is the only God who can "save" him from eternal damnation – as he does not have the moral integrity to save himself.	(8) Man becomes aware of God's inherent presence through a process of self-realization, which leads ultimately to a profound awareness of the unity of Man, Creation, and God, called Enlightenment.
(9) God is forgiving as well as judgmental; consequently God is to be respected and feared.	(9) God is non-judgmental as the Karmic laws apply to everyone uniformly.
(10) Man has free will, and because he has been made in God's image, it is his duty to do God's will on earth.	(10) Man has free will, and it is his divine purpose to resonate graciously, harmoniously and compassionately with God.

CHAPTER FIVE

Larry could still see that look in his father's eyes when he told
him he would not be following in his footsteps as a Minister of the
Presbyterian Church. After that existential moment he had promised
himself that he would do his best to be deserving of his parents' love
and respect. Accordingly he always went back home to visit them on
holidays and long weekends, and on such occasions sternly reminded
himself that he was their only son and it was his duty to behave like
an upstanding Christian soul when in their presence. Although they
never again discussed his decision to leave the Presbyterian Church
and go his own way, he knew it was one of his father's deepest
regrets.

It was not as if he had really left the Christian Church. It all
depended upon one's point of view. The Church would always have
a special place in his life, but on terms he would personally set for it
within the parameters of his newfound attitudes and beliefs which
were greatly influenced by reason and common sense. The Bible
always remained dear to him as a literary source of historical
wisdom. Perhaps it was because as a toddler his mother would sit
him on her knee and read various passages from it, which she would
then patiently translate in plain language he understood. "How
come the man did that?" was his favorite question in those days.
And his dear mother would look into his eyes and say, "Because
Jesus was a good man."

When he was a teenager, Larry took it upon himself to study the
Bible from cover to cover. He knew more about it than the Bible
study teacher at his church, and was often asked if he would like to
conduct Bible study classes. Larry always refused; for some
inexplicable reason he felt that he was an inauthentic Christian
because he found it very difficult to accept every word of the Bible as
the literal truth. "This cannot be the word of God," he frequently
thought to himself in those days, "God is just not that stupid!" It was
blasphemy. He knew it. So he kept quiet.

He often wondered if it showed on his face, because he would
feel hot, flushed, and uncomfortable like a liar must feel when taking
a lie detector test. He found it difficult to hide his embarrassment.
He kept hoping that as he grew older and studied more, these

embarrassing sensations would fade away with his greater understanding of the Bible. However, the opposite happened; the more he studied the more embarrassed he felt about what he was doing. It was depressing. Try as he might, he just could not accept the literal word of the Bible as truth, as his father did. He could not make that "leap of faith" that he knew was necessary in order to bury his free-ranging intellect beneath a tradition of dogma and doctrine. In the end his intellect took precedence, and by the time he began his post secondary education Larry's many debates with his college peers frequently ended with the phrase: "There is no substitute for reason and common sense!"

Still, Larry took the Bible with him wherever he went to live: in dorms, frat houses, or rented apartments. The Bible remained tucked in the lower left hand corner of his suitcase. On occasion he would get it out and re-read his favorite section from Ecclesiastes. The wisdom of Solomon was the impetus that spurred on his intellectual curiosity. It was Solomon who had to discover for himself that "all was vanity and vexation of spirit," before he was able to turn to God with purity of heart. And it was the solemn way that his mother had asked, "Should he cut the baby in half?" that made him realize, even at that tender age, that reason and common sense was Solomon's greatest virtue.

Later on when Larry read the life story of Siddhartha, he was amazed at how similar he was to Solomon in his youth. "Except for time and location," he thought, "Solomon could have become a Buddhist." That is when Larry began to look beyond mere names and labels like Hindu, Buddhist, Christian, Muslim, and Hebrew. He was mindful of that time his old logging buddy had said, "Don't attempt to attach any labels on me... just call me Linc."

After he finished college, Larry took some time off to earn enough money to finance his further education. Although his parents subsidized him, he was always short of cash. It was while he was working as summer replacement in a lumber mill in Northern Idaho that he went to the local library on his day off and loaded up with an armful of esoteric literature. One of the titles was, "The Dead Sea Scrolls."

"What a find!" he said to himself as he settled comfortably on his narrow cot in Lucy's Bunkhouse where the rent was cheap and the meals were adequate. It was the only book he had time to read during the summer. He read it with great interest. It reinforced the new vision of Jesus of Nazareth that was slowly developing in his subconscious mind.

The Dead Sea Scrolls presented Jesus as the illegitimate son of Joseph, a potential pretender for the resurrection of the monarchy, because he was supposedly descended from the lineage of King David. This hope for a resurrection of the Jewish Kingdom of God was passed on to Jesus, and then to his stepbrother, James.

The manger outside of Bethlehem was not a "manger" as we conceive of it in modern times. In those times, a manger designated a location just on the outskirts of town where unwed, pregnant women could give birth. The place was stigmatized as a "manger" because it was considered by the devoutly religious to be "unclean" and therefore unfit to be located in town. This was such a far cry from the Biblical account that Larry had to read it over twice to make sure he had read it correctly.

It was in such a manger that Mary gave birth to her son, Jesus. Her son was considered illegitimate because at the time she was not married to Joseph, although she was betrothed to him. Later on, Joseph married another woman who bore him a son named James, and several daughters. This was the first time Larry had read any information about Jesus that was not contained in the Bible. He found it very interesting.

From Larry's point of view, this new information helped to put a more human face on the man deified as the "Son of God." The more human Jesus became the better Larry was able to relate to him. In the end Larry was still left with two perturbing questions that rolled over and over in his curious mind like a stuck record.

Whatever happened to the three wealthy Wise Men from the Orient, the ones who adorn every Nativity scene as if they were very important people who would play a significant role in the life of the child they had come so far to discover? And where on earth did Jesus disappear to during those eighteen crucial developmental years, an interval that enabled a child of twelve to develop into an adult who would later return as a confident, enlightened, mature thirty year old man with a religious view so radical it would lead to his untimely demise?

"Are the two questions somehow connected?"

The mere posing of these questions to people who Larry thought had considerable knowledge in this area brought the most puzzling responses. Some people just became irritated and reacted as if bothered by a pesky mosquito which a good slap would take care of. Others seemed to consider the questions to be the problem, rather than their inability to answer them. Most of the people just wanted to avoid the questions altogether and talk about the "good news" gospel, as if a newly authenticated version had just hit the headlines.

Of all the people that Larry consulted, a radical old woman with a penchant for speaking her mind gave the most practical response. She stared searchingly at Larry with watery blue-grey eyes, and with a flair for poetic license said: "Let sleeping dogs lie..." hesitated a second then continued, "in their dogmatic kennels growling menacingly in their dreams as if protecting a petrified bone." She drew in a heavy breath and concluded, "Let them have the bone."

It was Sunday morning and the town folk dressed in their Sunday best paraded quietly into the local parish Church. The summer sun glowed warmly over the sleepy little Northern Idaho village, and the people felt blessed that God was still on their side. Larry walked casually into the beautifully decorated Catholic Church with high stained glass windows depicting various religious symbols of faith, and sat down in a pew in the second last row. At the front behind a massive oak altar, rose a larger-than-life crucifix of simulated wood, upon which a skinny man clad only in a loincloth, who looked more like a white Anglo-Saxon Protestant than a swarthy Middle-eastern Jew, was nailed through the hands and feet, crucified. A crown of thorns bled upon his head, his chest was crisscrossed with the reminders of an excruciating lashing, and a scarlet spear-gash pierced his side. His eyes gazed upward penitently. Who was this man? The belated fabrication of a much maligned person who probably would not even recognize himself! Who would want to be remembered thus? Do people who are publicly executed desire to be remembered for the manner of their gruesome deaths – rather than the manner in which they proudly lived their lives?

"That is our Lord and Savior," a regular parishioner pointed out to the stranger in their midst, "Doesn't he look wonderful?" she asked with an adoring smile.

"That is Jesus Christ?"

"Isn't the likeness remarkable?"

"You've seen the real Christ?"

"No, but I have seen pictures of Him. He does not look the least bit like a Jew."

Larry smiled mischievously and said, "Perhaps he was the son of God, and God is not Jewish – is he?"

The parish priest dressed in a black flowing smock with a wooden crucifix dangling at his side like a short sword entered from a side door, assumed his place behind the altar, and began the morning service. His sermon was amply spiced with Latin phrases which made him sound profoundly pious, as if Christ had spoken Latin with the same proclivity. Although he hardly understood what the pious little man was saying, Larry crossed himself at the conclusion of the sermon like everyone else and said, "A-men." It made him feel as if he were one of the flock.

After the morning service was over and all the parishioners had left, Larry politely asked the jovial looking, rather rotund little parish priest if he could spare a few moments of his time. The priest, who was called Father Albert, was very accommodating. He led Larry into his office at the rear of the Church, opened the door and ushered Larry in. It was a plush office lined with shelves of books of every size and layers of manuscripts, pamphlets and loose papers. Larry seated himself in a padded armchair while Father Albert sat down behind his massive mahogany desk.

"What can I do for you, my son?" Father Albert asked looking up at the young man who stood before him.

The "my son" made Larry feel at home. He relaxed and stared quizzically at the little man who represented the most powerful institutionalized religion on earth, and began with a note of renewed hope, "Perhaps you can help me with some questions that I have had a great deal of difficulty finding answers to."

"What sort of questions?"

Larry asked his two perplexing questions, and the little priest rolled his eyes upward and said: "I don't know. No one seems to know for sure what happened to the Three Wise Men, or what happened to Jesus during those eighteen crucial developmental years of his life. You would think that such information would be readily available for one who is so important to our religion. We know what happened to him up to the age of twelve, and after the age of thirty.

But in between?" He threw up his hands in a gesture of frustration, "Who knows what happened?"

"You mean you don't know?"

"It remains a mystery. If only all those precious manuscripts had not been burned!"

"What manuscripts?"

Father Albert stared inanely at Larry, "Those three hundred alternative gospels concerning the life of Jesus that were available at the Council of Nicaea, those thousands of so-called blasphemous accounts of the events surrounding the life and times of Jesus of Nazareth. All destroyed!" He lapsed into momentary silence as if subdued by his own overt display of emotion.

"Incredible!" Larry breathed.

"All destroyed," Father Albert continued, "as if there was something that happened during those eighteen years that needed to be hidden for all posterity. Perhaps something so crucial it had to be expunged from the face of the earth!" The little priest had risen to his feet as if in righteous indignation.

"I think I know exactly how you feel!" Larry commiserated somewhat surprised by Father Albert's sense of betrayal.

"I'm just a small fish," Father Albert moderated his tone. "I'd like to know what happened during those missing eighteen years as much as you do – probably even more! It is the one thing that irks me beyond belief. But the information has been destroyed, if it ever existed, and it seems we must just carry on with the hope that those eighteen missing years do not imply that something important was deliberately covered up," his voice trailed off, "and we have been deliberately misled and misinformed all these years," he concluded soberly.

"I appreciate your remarks," Larry responded, genuinely impressed by Father Albert's openness and willingness to share his views.

"It is not often that I have an opportunity to discuss this issue. Most people do not comprehend its real significance, its crucial importance to our understanding of who the real living, breathing Jesus of Nazareth was. Whenever I think about it I feel – well I think you know."

"I know," Larry empathized. "It makes me feel like I have been presented with a cosmetically pre-packaged, institutionalized facsimile of someone who has become a martyr for someone else's cause."

"You may have a point there, my son," Father Albert said with a kindly smile. "A martyr for someone else's cause, you say – I like that," he said with a reflective air. "Next time I see the Bishop I'll mention it. He's something like me; he should have been a philosopher."

Larry stared at the little priest who was willing to share his inner thoughts. "Too bad there are not more priests with your attitude," he said. "I am truly flattered that you have been so candid with me."

Father Albert shuffled through a bunch of papers stacked in a pile beside his desk. He pulled out a photocopied document. "Here," he said, "you can keep this. I think you may find it," he was going to say "edifying" but changed his mind and said "well, ah, interesting."

Larry thanked Father Albert profusely for sharing his views and for the document. He folded it in half and attempted to fit it in the inside pocket of his jacket; it did not fit so he just rolled it up like a scroll and carried it back to his place of residence. He had nothing else to do when he got back to his sparsely furnished second-story room so he sat down in a straight-backed chair by the window and unrolled the document. What had Father Albert given him?

The document was entitled: *The Council of Nicaea and the Roman Catholic Church.* It was a compilation of many scholarly works regarding the Council of Nicaea that was organized at Nicaea by Emperor Constantine in 325 AD. At that time the question of the divinity of Jesus was splitting the Church apart. A dispute arose called the Arian Controversy, after a priest named Arius, who was supported by a considerable number of rationally minded people. Arius came to a logical conclusion that seemed to undermine the irrational claims being made regarding Jesus' divinity that were vital to those attempting to create a powerful new religion in his name. Using a commonsensical discursive argument popular at the time, Arius maintained that it was reasonable to assume that: if the Father begat the Son, then the Son must have had a beginning, or been created out of the void/nothing like the rest of Creation (which included Mankind). This argument implied that Jesus was really the "son of man" as he personally claimed to be. Most of the documents of the times used that particular phrase. The Judaic high priests were adamant in saying that Jesus was certainly not the Messiah/the Son of God. In fact there was no evidence at all at that crucial moment in history that implied or suggested that Jesus was anyone other than who he said he was: the "son of man." To say otherwise was to fabricate an "identity" in retrospect that suited the purposes of the fabricators. Was Jesus really the "son of man"? The majority of the three hundred and eighteen Bishops in attendance had a much loftier notion in mind. But first Arius and his followers had to be discredited. That was easy. He was simply branded a "Heretic" and his view discarded as heresy.

After soundly condemning the rational views of Arius, the Council was left with the impossible task of wording an irrational alternative. This was no easy matter. The "son of man" had to be ideologically transformed into the "Son of God," and all the subsequent dogma and doctrine had to uniformly support and reinforce this particular point of view. First and foremost it was imperative that they all agree on a word or phrase that was ambiguous enough to convey a meaning that meant that the Father could "beget" a son without that son being conceived of as being separate from the "begetter", such that the Father and son could be One. After much discussion the obscure Greek word, "homoosius" was agreed upon; it demonstrated the creative ingenuity of the Bishops and the lengths they were willing to go in order to create a new religious concept commensurate with their pious objectives. It became the single word that defined the religious faith that provided the cause célèbre for his martyrdom.

The Council of Nicaea proclaimed the famous Nicene Creed in 325 AD. This Creed became the cornerstone of the new holy "Roman" Bible. The Creed claimed that the Son and the Father were *homoosius*. Anyone who doubted this was a heretic like Arius. The Creed was the absolute truth. Who would dare to argue with the truth? Once the "truth" was established as dogma it was imperative that all the evidence be made to support this dogma. The Gospels had to be carefully selected and rewritten if necessary to reflect the truth of the Creed. All other contrary points of view had to be destroyed. The validity of the newly formed Creed depended upon the thoroughness of the purge. The entire life from birth to death of the man called Jesus of Nazareth had to be carefully scrutinized and any information that did not accord with the Creed had to be surreptitiously altered to suit, or be destroyed. The cleansing had to be immaculate. The bonfire burned for days and smoldered on and on until hardly a shred of contradictory evidence remained! A powerful new idea was being hatched whose time had come. It was the idea, rather than the convoluted manner by which it came about, that was important.

This was truly a momentous event in the history of man's sojourn upon that particular portion of planet earth. In the collective consciousness of man in that part of the known world the notion that a puny, flawed, sinful creature like man could aspire to be holy was particularly appealing, especially to a down-trodden population. There was a subtle shift in their sense of self-worth. What was most significant was the concept, the idea, the notion that God actually had a son, and that son had been sent to save them. There was hope for salvation. Man could be *saved* – if only he could bring himself to make a didactic leap of blind faith, faith in the dogma that proclaimed Jesus was indeed the Son of God, and like Christ, they too could aspire to become united with the Father in the hereafter. This was perhaps the most powerful idea afloat in the first millennium.

Man's collective consciousness expanded just enough to grasp the notion of his subservient relationship to an omniscient parental authority. At this collective level of awareness the elation that accompanies such a belief has the effect of an opiate; man became stupefied with edification in his sadomasochistic endeavor to ingratiate himself to the representatives of this higher authority (resulting in the ensuing "Dark Ages" highlighted by oxymoronic "Holy Wars"). But to a perceptive individual like the mighty Roman Emperor Constantine, this new article of faith provided the opportunity to consolidate the Empire under one single all pervasive *Catholic* authority over which he would imperiously preside.

It was not easy for the Council to compile a single coherent Gospel that supported the Creed out of over three hundred different gospels available to the Council, and a vast array of other priceless historical documents concerning the life and times of Jesus of Nazareth. Constantine really did not care much what version of the Bible resulted, so long as there was only one version. As far as he was concerned it was all about politics, power, and control. He just wanted a unified Church over which he could exert his influence. He was not even a Christian! Did it matter if the chief architect of the revised Christian Church was a Roman pagan? Considering the results – apparently not.

In an atmosphere rife with dissension, intolerance, prejudice, bigotry, jealousy, and persecution, the *Gospel* which would be accorded to Jesus of Nazareth, the Son of God, was sorted out. All contrary versions and documents of any kind that did not accord with the Creed or with the biases of the Bishops concerned were burned or otherwise destroyed. Consequently the greatest purge of priceless Christian documentation/writings ever recorded, was carried out. Because it was carried out by the Church itself in order to maintain itself in control of its own religion, this devious behavior has seldom been criticized and never been condemned. It was an immaculate cleansing, as immaculate as the process by which the son of man was conceived of as being the Son of God. In the end, only the information that the Council found to be acceptable was presented to Emperor Constantine for final approval.

Who was this man in whose hands the destiny of the Christian Church was entrusted? He was not the Pope. The Pope at the time was apparently a little known fellow named Victor Sylvester, the last of a disputed succession of Popes supposedly appointed in apostolic-succession from St. Peter, the rock upon which the original Church was founded. The man who commanded the cooperation of all three hundred and eighteen Bishops as well as the Pope was an imperious Roman pagan named Gaius Flavius Valerius Aurelius Constantinus (27 Feb. 272 – 22 May 337 AD), better known as Emperor Constantine the Great.

In 312 AD at the Milvian Bridge outside Rome where he defeated Maxentius in a crucial battle for control of the Empire, Constantine had a spiritual experience to which he credited his victory. Thereafter he paid special attention to the plight of the persecuted Christians within the Empire. In 313 he magnanimously proclaimed the Edict of Milan which bestowed imperial favor upon Christianity. The founder of the Byzantine Empire realized that it would be convenient for the Emperor if there was only one religion, and he was its unchallenged leader. He was the de facto Pope. It was this imperious Roman pagan who made Christianity into the One and Only True Faith. He was the one who called for and organized the Council of Nicaea in 325, and it was to him – not the Pope – to whom the culmination of all the Council's work was delivered.

It is purported that, overwhelmed by the sheer volume of the biblical material presented to him, Constantine, in a fit of frustration, threw the pile of papers toward a small table. It was indeed a vitally significant moment in the much maligned history of the aptly named "Roman" Catholic Church. It was one of those incidental moments that some might call an epiphany or insightful experience, aptly summarized by the familiar old cliché: "Let the chips fall as they may." The papers that missed or fell off the table were discarded. Those that stayed on must have stayed on for a reason! It must have been a sign. God works in mysterious ways. In this manner the New Testament was constituted.

"A sign of what?" Larry wondered as he paused and got up from the straight-backed chair. He limbered up by jumping up and down on the spot and swinging his arms out to the sides in unison. He rotated his head clockwise and counter-clockwise to ease the tension building up in his neck and shoulders before sitting back down. "This is really something!" he declared as he composed himself comfortably on the wooden chair and stared out the window thoughtfully. "Now where was I?" he asked himself as he scanned over the document looking for the answer to his question: *A sign of what?*

The manuscript indicated that it was a sign... a sign that the ascetic and austere Christian Church was to undergo a fabulous pagan makeover. The splendor and magnificence of Roman opulence combined with the piety of the Christian attitude evolved into an Orthodox-Roman Catholic Church deserving of being the official religion of the mighty Roman Empire centered in 330 AD on the newly created city aptly named Constantinople. After the split between the Orthodox and Roman points of view regarding the mystical aspects of God, Constantinople eventually became headquarters for the Byzantium Empire or Eastern Roman Empire. In spite of Constantine's noble effort to unify the Church, after his demise in 337 AD (as unfortunately sometimes happens in the evolution of religious institutions where doctrinal differences become entrenched) two illustrious patriarchs, one situated in Constantinople and one in Rome, simultaneously claimed to be "Pope" of God's only true church on earth. To put it baldly: Which one was suffering from delusions of grandeur?

Each respective Church/Cathedral claimed to be the final resting place for its primary deity, the Son of God. Within the sublime splendor of its cavernous halls the devout came to pay their respects and to pray for forgiveness of their sins before the deceased body of Christ hung pathetically in effigy before them, a worthy religious symbol designed to remind them of the ultimate sacrifice made by their Lord and Savior. It mortified the souls of the converted with deep-seated feelings of remorse and guilt while priests recited glowing eulogies. The setting was most edifying in a magical pagan sort of way: the imagery was bold and fleshy, the rites sensuous and painfully masochistic. It was a religion fit for a Roman Emperor with pagan inclinations. The worst thing imaginable that could happen to a devout Christian was to be excommunicated from such a glorious Church.

However, in 1054 the ridiculous combined with the unimaginable to produce the abominable. The Pope of the Western Catholic Church in a vengeful fit of righteous indignation "excommunicated" the Pope of the Eastern Orthodox Church. Of course the Eastern Pope returned the favor. The pronouncements of both Popes had the authority of being *infallible*. What a predicament for God's only true church on earth!

For 911 years two Christian Churches existed, each believing that with the authentic righteousness of God on their side, they had dealt appropriately with a false pretender to the Papacy. However in 1965 in hopes of once again unifying the Church that Constantine the Great had brought together in 325 AD, Pope Paul VI and his eastern counterpart Patriarch Athenagoras I, met and agreed – in spite of their historical animosity – to simply erase this blot from the memory of both Churches and to cast it into oblivion as if it never happened.

What about the infallibility of public Papal pronouncements? Perhaps they simply serve as enduring examples of how man vainly endeavors to manipulate the "truth" in order to make it palatable to his own purposes. A purpose rationalized in the name of the saintly human being who died in order to free his Jewish peers from the abomination which continues to enslave those who profess to follow in his footsteps with a sin so archaic it has been labeled Original.

In retrospect it could be said that in an era fraught with insecurity, prejudice, fear, and oppression Constantine displayed a tolerance and understanding that made him worthy of the epithet

".Great." In the years following the Council of Nicaea there was a new-found openness and freedom to worship without fear or persecution that attracted people from all walks of life. The appeal was intoxicating! Holiness was available to everyone. To see the humble and downtrodden symbolically eating of Christ's flesh and drinking of Christ's blood in a primitive endeavor to become holy through ingestion, was a reminder of past pagan practices reconstituted to serve a higher purpose. Constantine brought the imperial splendor of Rome to a drab and austere religion, and made it into a truly magnificent spectacle the likes of which the world had never before encountered or seen. He "Romanized" the Christian Church, and set the "Orthodox" tone and direction it was to follow for centuries to come. And for this, one would think, all Christendom would be thankful.

Instead with the inexorable passage of time to dull their memory and a penchant to rise above by putting down, many present-day defenders of the faith go out of their way to disassociate the modern Church from its delightfully mystic and robust pagan influences without which the magnificent Christian Church would most likely have remained an ascetic, austere, uninspiring tomb of perpetual mourning.

The founder of the most powerful religious institution on earth could not have remained a pagan his entire life – could he? It is purported by Church officials that the Roman pagan known as Constantine the Great, was *converted on his death bed*, and during his last lucid moment was confirmed in the faith that in 325 AD made the "son of man" *homoosius* with God.

"Amazing!" Larry thought as he rolled up the manuscript and set it on the window ledge. Learning about what happened at the Council of Nicaea and the role played by Constantine the Great in the development of the Roman Catholic Church marked a turning point in Larry's life. He began to understand the real significance of what Karl Marx had meant when he said, "Religion is the opium of the people." It had a drugging effect. Reason and common sense drifted like smoke into mirrors of illusion. "Poor Arius, with his logical argument," Larry lamented, "condemned as a heretic!" He had identified with Arius. It saddened him that somehow, it seemed as if reason and common sense had been culled out of the Christian version of the Holy Roman Bible represented by the New Testament, and replaced with a powerful and controlling dogma and doctrine based upon a religious Creed established in 325 AD at the Council of Nicaea.

For weeks Larry felt vaguely depressed and disillusioned. It was the feeling of disillusionment that was the most difficult to come to terms with. His father had always considered the Bible to be the one and only authentic source for religious inspiration. "If he knew what I now know, would he still remain such a staunch believer?" he wondered.

"In the world there are many diverse sources of religious and spiritual inspiration," he reflected, "many thousands of books filled with the wisdom of the ages – and most believers restrict themselves to only one, single, solitary source/book, because of their upbringing. It is as if they are wearing blinkers restricting them to one-degree vision. They are only willing to look straight ahead. They think they have the right-of-way and everyone else must yield to their point of view. Like them I used to have one-degree vision, and now I can turn around and view the majesty of it all, all three hundred and sixty panoramic degrees!" It was liberating. The last remnants of the ghostly chains which bound him to the dogmatic faith of his Christian heritage fell away with the shrug of his shoulders. "I'd rather be free – than saved," he thought.

Thereafter Larry looked to other sources for wisdom and understanding. Long before Jesus had been credited with the phrase, Lao Tzu had said: "Treat thy neighbor as thyself," only he had spoken Chinese. The wisdom of the ages filled the libraries of the world with volumes of the most profound thoughts human beings were capable of.

To Larry's surprise not only the wise, but the saintly and despised, the robust and sickly, the affluent and impoverished, the mighty and downtrodden, the creators and destroyers, the adulated and persecuted, the masters and especially the enslaved, all – without exception – seemed to reiterate one singular message like an irrepressible yearning that reverberated down through the centuries and resonated in his own heartstrings: *There is no substitute for freedom... freedom is everything.*

CHAPTER SIX

Reason and common sense are natural allies to an inquiring mind. Like the inexorable rising of the ocean tides, the idea began to germinate in Larry's mind that Christianity, as he had known and experienced it, had a profound effect upon the development of the modern capitalistic system in which he was ensconced, and upon the collective psyche of the modern world. For the first time he began to understand the dimensions of his struggle and why it had been so difficult.

As the rational parameters of his awareness expanded the term "Western Christendom" took on a new significance, and the phrase, "Self-fulfilling prophecy of Doom," seemed even more ominous. He recalled the many times his father had urged the congregation to repent of their sins, for the "Day of Judgment" was imminent. He could feel the anxiety and the insecurity that infected the congregation when his father lowered his voice and asked: "Have you been washed in the blood of the Lamb?" Where else but in Western Christendom would such a question make sense? Although he was only seven years old when he first heard that question, it still embarrassed him to hear it. Actually he was embarrassed for his father. He could not exactly explain why.

It was not as if he had not bent over backwards to accommodate himself to his father's beliefs. Perhaps he had tried too hard not to be representative of that clever observation made by school counselors that, like other children of the clergy, "he is simply in rebellion." It definitely was not rebellion. It was something much more innately profound, some deep-seated yearning that rose up from inside of him like pure spring water rising up incessantly from the depths of a bottomless well. It was a yearning to know who he was and why he existed. It was a yearning to truly know God.

This was the humble beginnings of Larry's slow and patient pilgrimage toward self-realization. This was the origin of the bits of blank verse scribbled on the backs of pieces of scrap paper. This was the genesis of his secret poetic endeavor that he worked on when no one else was around, because it was just too personal and too radical. He was embarrassed for himself when he imagined anyone else reading his work. "Will I ever be able to share any of this with anyone?" he thought. "So why am I writing it? For my personal edification? Perhaps if I wait long enough things will change, and I will have the courage to share it with others. I'll call it "Waiting for the Tide to Turn." It seemed like an appropriate title fit for both himself and his creative work in progress. He imagined himself waiting patiently like Job on the ashes of a misunderstood religion, stoic and solemn, a pillar of virtue and quiet humility. In a way it prepared him for one of the greatest tragedies life could inflict upon him: the unexpected passing of his dear parents.

Exactly four days after Larry returned home in late August from his summer job to prepare for his admission to the University of Oregon at Eugene, a fatal automobile accident claimed the lives of both of his parents. Larry was devastated. What had he done to deserve this? Feelings of guilt and remorse flooded over him. He was their only begotten son. The "only" part weighed heavily upon him in many ways. If only he had done more, if only he had been a better son, if only he had taken the time to demonstrate his appreciation, if only.... Had he ever done anything that would have inspired them to desire to prolong their sojourn upon this planet?

Somehow he had to come to terms with his feelings of abject despair. He had to. There was no one else. He was their only son. He sat on the couch in the living-room like Job sat on the ashes of antiquity and stoically meditated, and gradually the depression lifted and was replaced by an overwhelming sense of gratitude and love for his parents.

Prior to the funeral so many people dropped by the house to convey their condolences, so many fine upstanding Christian souls with genuine affection in their hearts for his dear parents. His parents had worked hard to be worthy of the congregation they served. They were always available if someone in need called. And now they were gone, snatched away prematurely by a drunken driver who broadsided their old green Chevy at an intersection at over seventy miles per hour. The drunken driver was taken to the Emergency ward in critical condition and not expected to live – but somehow he managed to survive, thanks to the miracle of modern surgery.

Practically the whole town attended the funeral. The funeral director was superb. He handled almost everything. "Don't worry," he said to Larry, "I've got it all under control."

Throughout the entire ordeal Larry felt detached, like he was watching a black and white motion picture. He recalled an old newsreel called "The Passing Parade" he had seen at the local theatre. The funeral was something like that. It happened quickly, like counting down from ten, and then zero. The End – except for the flapping of the feed-end of the film on the take-up reel.

In years to come when he visited his parents' grave site he recalled with an enduring sense of loss and sadness the last occasion that he sat down to supper at the round oak table with the beautiful white lace tablecloth. After a delicious supper he had very diplomatically, so he thought, attempted to explain to his parents his personal understanding of what it meant to be called a "Christian". The occasion remained stored in his memory like the last scene from a play he had rehearsed so many times he knew everyone else's lines as well as his own.

It was a solemn occasion. Larry sat on one side of the dining room table while his father sat across from him with his hands tightly clasped in front of him. His face was stolid and void of expression as if he had steeled himself to hear something he had been dreading to hear. In the background Larry's mother hovered about within earshot, her prematurely white hair frequently catching a glint of the evening sun as it shone in at a low angle from the open window on the west wall of the dining room.

Larry cleared his throat and rubbed his hands together as if warming up for a difficult announcement. "I thought it was time to come to a meeting of the minds," he began, "regarding the matter of my religious beliefs," his voice trailed away as he adjusted himself in his chair nervously. He hesitated momentarily, and then added, "Especially concerning my Christian faith." He stopped and looked searchingly into his father's parchment face for some little sign of understanding and acceptance.

"Such a solemn face," Larry thought, "Such a sad and weary face. My dear old father, what have I done?" He drew in a ponderous breath and as he slowly exhaled he spoke with a much softer and kindlier demeanor.

"I am your only son," Larry continued. "I will always be your only son. I am your flesh and blood. You gave me life. You gave me faith. You gave me freedom." He bowed his head humbly and turned toward his mother with a nod of acknowledgement that indicated his remarks included her as well. When she smiled, Larry continued in an even humbler tone, "I can never thank you enough for what you have done for me. I owe you everything. You owe me nothing."

Dampness appeared near the inner corners of his father's eyes and spread slowly to the lines etched alongside his beak-like nose. He nodded his head ever so slightly, but remained silent.

"The spirit of Christ lives in my heart as it lived in the heart of Krishna, Buddha, Moses, Jesus, and Mohammed, to mention but a few of the enlightened souls who have come to be universally admired," Larry plodded on. "The spirit of Christ lives in every human heart. It is as sacred as eternal life itself. I know this to be true as sure as I am alive. Jesus recognized the spirit of God or Christ Consciousness within himself. He gave us his example. He said: 'Follow me'. I have been following him in my own way, as have you. We are kindred spirits." Larry paused, looked beseechingly at his father, and lowered his voice to a whisper. "I just wanted you to know that, Dad."

Again Larry's father nodded ever so slightly, but remained silent. It was the awkward silence of a man who sincerely desires to speak, but is frozen with emotions so powerful he is incapacitated.

"Perhaps," Larry added meekly, "to some who assume the label 'Christian', I am considered to be unfit for that designation." He bowed his head apologetically, on the verge of tears.

The distant sound of birds twittering in the evening glow of the setting sun filtered in through the open window. Larry's mother stoically shuffled to and fro in the background. Tears began to slide helplessly down Larry's cheeks as he hunched over on his elbows at the dining room table.

"WHO ARE THEY TO JUDGE?" The question exploded from his father's lips and thundered around the room. "Judge not, lest ye be judged!" he added authoritatively, his shoulders squaring up proudly as he rose defiantly in defense of his only begotten son.

"A-men," his mother concluded as she approached the table.

Larry's father stood up as tall and erect as he had ever stood. He looked like Moses must have looked when he stood defiantly before the Red Sea. There was a mystical glint in his eyes. He looked at Larry and smiled empathetically. "I understand, son," he said with an affirmative nod of his head. For the first time in years he looked serenely happy.

Larry's mother moved up behind Larry and placed her hands gently upon his hunched shoulders. She gazed toward the sunlight that filled the room with the warmth of its departing rays, and spoke with quiet conviction to no one in particular: "Your father is a good man."

PART FIVE

THE MYSTERIOUS UNIVERSE

When we add up all the numbers...
we will approximate zero.

CHAPTER ONE

Tsutomu Miki thought of himself as a good man, a good man with a noble mission: to suppress the spread of Christianity in Japan. It was a mission nourished by tenuous roots that predisposed an innocent young boy of six into becoming one of the most respected and feared samurai ever to wield a two-handed katana.

Shortly after the fateful day his mother had pried his father's blood-splattered hand from his and led him away from the beautiful wooden bench his father had so lovingly handcrafted and donated to the Buddhist Church, Tsutomu began experiencing a recurrent nightmare. In it a huge dark shape with a brightly polished silver crucifix dangling from its neck chased him down a long and solitary path that came to an abrupt end. And there he was, too terrified to speak or call for help, while the hideous figure loomed out of the night and towered above him wielding a gigantic sword that whirled through the air with the sound of a million darksome wings of death. There he stood, trembling like a tiny leaf on a barren limb. Vulnerable. Exposed. Frozen.

It was his worst nightmare. It kept recurring even after he grew up and became a samurai warrior. There was no way he could stop it. It always stopped him dead in his tracks, frozen solid with fright. That is, until that moment... that moment he stood in front of the Buddhist temple encircled by three murderous ronin. He did not freeze then. It might have looked like he was frozen, but from somewhere deep inside, in a place where he always felt safe and secure, from that quiet inner place where he had retreated when his father's warm blood dripped off his face like a crimson rain, from that haven he struck a blow for freedom, for justice, for life! He did not have to think. It was instinctive, like a bolt of lightning that surged up from that secret place, up through his arms and flashed through the air.

The surge of energy left him drained, depleted, a pale statue of skin and bone covered with a fine sheen of cold sweat, clutching a great sword stained with the remnants of death. After that the nightmare never returned and Tsutomu was filled with such an uplifting feeling of freedom that he offered his services to every Lord with a righteous cause, and fought like a whirling dynamo of death.

He was absolutely fearless on the field of battle. Wherever he stood a space suddenly cleared. Was it a sign of respect, or was it fear? Or both?

It was a time of youthful exuberance when Tsutomu laughed in the face of death as if he had been there and done that. It was a kind of foolishness bred from a feeling of being invincible. When others hung back quaking with fear he strode forth boldly, confident that no steel tipped arrows or razor sharp swords would ever mutilate his mortal flesh. It was as if he were protected by an invisible shield. There was a divine aura about him, an aura that called to mind the image of a Divine Warrior.

Who knew then that the great samurai, Tstutomu Miki, would eventually become a persecutor of those who wore a crucifix, or were associated with those who wore them? What was it that an innocent six year old boy experienced that so imprinted itself upon his subconscious mind that years later as a mature adult with grave responsibilities, he would harbor a secret prejudice?

* * *

The slanting rays of the morning sun crept in and spread across the serene countenance of the Grand Inquisitor. The year was 1591, over four years after Toyotomi had issued his infamous Edict banning all Christian missionaries from Japan – and then in a gesture of good will allowing Spanish Friars to enter. Did Toyotomi have even an inkling of the impossible situation that created? Little wonder the Edict was mostly ignored. Still, it was Tsutomu's job to enforce it. It was frustrating to say the least but nevertheless it was time to rise with the morning sun, say a sleepy farewell to his wife and three sons, and begin his long journey to Nagasaki.

The Chief Regent of all Kyushu had recently commended him for his relentless efforts to eliminate the disruptive influence of the upstart hakujin religion from the *bakuhan taisei* or shogunate-domain system. Even the Shinto priests were becoming alarmed at the incredible rate and the ease with which these foreigners in black and brown robes were able to convert stalwart Shintoists to their new religious views. These so-called Christians were becoming a real menace to the stability of the social and political order of the land; they did not appreciate the simple fact that the sons and daughters of

Nihon were the descendents of the Divine Kamui from which all life originated. Who were they to call the Nihongee "pagans"?

Thus it was on the morning of September twenty-seventh, 1591 at approximately five thirty a.m., that Miki-san rose from his futon, and carefully dressed himself for his long journey to Nagasaki. It was his professional duty to persecute the foreign devils who were corrupting the moral fabric of the socio-political system that made the Japanese people proud to serve their lord and master, Toyotomi Hideyoshi. Yes indeed, it was a very important task, and Tsutomu Miki had been given the authority to carry it out. When his name was mentioned, Christians trembled. He had only to glare menacingly at recent converts and without a word being spoken they would immediately fall to their knees and grovel with clasped hands, begging for his forgiveness. It was pathetic.

It had not taken Tsutomu long to gain the kind of recognition that others labored years to attain. The recognition just naturally came along with the notoriety of his occupation. Not everyone was cut out for the gruesome task of persecuting their fellow human beings because of their religious faith. In many ways Tsutomu did not consider it to be such a great honor to be given the illustrious title of "Inquisitor". Toyotomi probably heard it from some Spanish priest and thought it appropriate. It was a title that conveyed a connotation that ill-suited Tsutomu's personality; it frequently filled him with feelings of self-loathing that he overcame by pretending to be unfeeling and imperious. Toyotomi had sympathetically added the word "Grand" because he thought it would accord him the respect he would need in order to carry out such a lamentable task. Still it was a title, and most important of all, Toyotomi appreciated his dedication and his attitude. Tsutomu had little sympathy for Christians.

The Grand Inquisitor's method of repressing Christianity was simple, systematic, and mostly non-violent. It consisted of three effective requirements. The first was known as *efumi*, or the forcing of all Nagasaki citizens to trample upon any graven images of Christ or Mary. The second was called *sonin hosho seido*, and consisted of giving monetary rewards to persons who revealed the names of Christians, for example, one hundred silver pieces for each convert, and five times that for each priest. The third, *terauke seido*, was perhaps the most effective; it consisted of the enforced registration of all Japanese citizens as parishioners of either a Buddhist or Shinto temple. Of course this latter requirement probably served as a cover for underground Kirishitan pretending to be law-abiding citizens. But at least on paper nearly everyone was accounted for, and the converts who were willing to stand up in the broad light of day and be counted were getting to be very hard to find – even for one as fastidious as Tsutomu Miki.

How long can one endure in such an unrewarding occupation without feeling the ravaging pangs of remorse for nasty deeds done without the conviction of belief or faith? It was one of those jobs that frequently left Tsutomu bereft of any human emotion at all. He had to steel himself to do things that caused his heart and soul to recoil with disgust and revulsion. It was an occupation incongruent with his natural sensibilities, but he carried on with a samurai's stubbornness determined to overcome his obvious "weaknesses". It was this mental toughness that enabled Tsutomu to hold his head up haughtily and carry on from day to day with a perverse sense of dignity.

Such a perverse sense of dignity existed on a diminishing undercurrent of dread and insecurity which manifested itself as an irrational prejudice toward the Kirishitan. Over time, reason and common sense gradually began to make inroads into the subconscious realms of his psyche and caused him to ask, "What have these innocent souls done to deserve such persecution?" It was a question that came to mind more and more frequently each time he looked into the pleading eyes of the persecuted. Wisdom is often simply the accumulation of time endured as experience. It was the experience gleaned over many arduous years of persecuting his fellow human beings that inclined the Grand Inquisitor to secretly ask himself, "Who am I? ...to be doing this!"

Strange as it may seem to those who expect reason and common sense to gradually reveal the existential meaning and significance of one's personal identity, Tsutomu Miki was not always to be identified as "Tsutomu" Miki. On the morning of September twenty-seventh 1591, as he assiduously prepared for his long journey to Nagasaki, he was still Tsutomu Miki, Grand Inquisitor. He was far from being a saint! How far? It seemed he had already traveled a long way down the road that led to his destiny. On the morn of

September twenty-seventh Tsutomu Miki set out with high spirits and high expectations to that bastion of Christian influence, the picturesque little coastal city of Nagasaki, where, with the powers of his divine ancestors to aid and abet him, he would do his best to cleanse Japan of this unwanted religious blight.

Little did he know as he set foot on the well-worn path that wound its way along a rugged coastline that provided the edge that defined the finiteness of the China Sea to the west, that he was following in the invisible footsteps of the Teacher-with-the-big-nose, a fellow human being who had once trodden that very same path, but with a vastly different purpose in mind.

CHAPTER TWO

The sun was beginning to turn a scarlet red, so brilliant and so red it seemed as if the entire western sea was filled with blood. Tsutomu stood on a distant hill overlooking the ocean, "The blood of the non-repentant," he thought. The road appeared to vanish into the sunset as he trod along and the blinding light burned into his eyes, blurring his vision and causing his eyes to water. He squinted and stared ahead down a long shimmering road that snaked its way toward the blood-red sea.

Another long and fatiguing day was slowly drawing to a close. He had walked a long way in nine days. He enjoyed the solitude of walking alone. Others like him traveled in secure groups of no less than three and often as many as five or six. But he was basically a loner. His reputation and fearless demeanor protected him as well as an army. If he anticipated more trouble than he could handle, it was always easy to hire help with the silver pieces in his leather pouch that he had confiscated from Church coffers.

The silver pieces jangled in his heavy purse as he stoically strode along. One hundred for a convert and five hundred for a priest. Bribery was what it was. Greed made it work efficiently. It was not the kind of business that samurai should indulge in. There was no honor in it. No sense of pride. Tsutomu coughed up the road dust from his throat as if in disgust and spat it out vehemently. It was an ugly business, this business of persecuting Christians, especially the Franciscans. The brown robes were so gentle and humble, a complete contrast to the militant, hard-nosed, defiant, overly zealous black robed Jesuits. Those Jesuits would have made superb samurai; they would suffer anything for glory and honor on behalf of their Lord. Tsutomu coughed and spat on the road once again. It was distasteful however one looked at it. He felt suffocated. He paused to draw in a deep chest-expanding breath. When he exhaled with a prolonged whoosh, it felt as if he were exhaling the breath of all those obstinate Christian souls who would not recant.

Why would they not recant? If only they had uttered the words he needed to hear he could have spared them. But they would not. They were so stubborn, so stupid! They just knelt and prayed: "Jesus, Lord, have mercy on my soul," and stared up at him with a look of –

of pity. All he wanted to hear was the words. That's all. He would have forgiven them. He wanted to forgive them for their transgressions. He practically begged some of them to say: "I recant". But they wouldn't. Pathetic!

Tsutomu strode down the dusty road with a determined gait. A self-righteous sense of anger boiled up from within causing him to lengthen his strides. As he hurried along the sense of anger dissipated and was replaced by a feeling of remorse verging on self-pity.

"Who is pathetic?" he asked himself, "That a noble samurai allowed himself to be reduced to this? Persecuting innocent human beings because of their religious beliefs? Did not my father say, 'Shinto, Buddhist, Kirishitan, what difference does it make so long as they are decent human beings?'" It was hot and dry – yet he felt the moisture gather in his eyes. "It is pathetic all right!" The irony hit him, and he laughed sardonically at himself. He had become worse than the ronin that he despised!

It had not been easy this last time to leave his wife, Aiko, and three sons. It seemed the older he got the harder it was to constantly leave his family behind in Kyoto while he journeyed forth to persecute Christians. Perhaps after he returned from Nagasaki he would relinquish his position as Grand Inquisitor and settle for something much more sedate. Toyotomi had once hinted that he considered him a likely candidate for the prestigious position of personal bodyguard and advisor. It was an opportunity worth exploring. "Yes, when I return to Kyoto, I will definitely look into it," he thought as he trod along toward his destination.

The unrelenting heat and dust from the road was beginning to make Tsutomu feel fatigued and slightly light-headed. As he strode along determined to reach Nagasaki in time for the Shinto celebration of Mother Nature's bounty, a weird sensation, something like walking on air, engulfed him. The heaviness of his body seemed to disappear and he felt as if he were floating along effortlessly.

The glare of the setting sun was blinding. The heat rose from the ground in waves making the road shimmer surrealistically. In the distance he thought he detected a tiny speck on the horizon. Perhaps it was a speck of dirt. He rubbed both eyes to clear his vision; yet the speck persisted. It seemed to move in an undulating motion in rhythm with his floating gait. Soon he felt the undeniable presence of another being.

Some stranger was probably treading the same path as he. He hastened his pace to catch up to the stranger. After a while he could hear the distant plop, plop, plop, of the stranger's sandals, and was able to vaguely discern a physical form. Could it be a reflection? A mirage? Tsutomu suddenly felt disoriented, as if he were somehow walking into the mirror of his own mind. Reality turned surreal.

But it was real. The road was real. The dust was real. He was real. Whoever was ahead must be real. Tsutomu half-ran to catch up, and soon he was directly behind the diminutive stranger.

The stranger stopped, conscious that someone was close behind. When the stranger turned to see who was following him, the sight froze Tsutomu in his tracks. What stood before him was a grotesquely deformed person of diminished stature. He had no defined facial features, and his grimy black robe and stubby arms and legs were caked with road dust. The sight of such a grotesquely deformed creature filled Tsutomu with revulsion. He recoiled in disgust.

The creature hung his head in dejected humility as if conscious of Tsutomu's loathing. He said nothing. In the middle of the dusty road to Nagasaki time stood still, until the stranger slowly raised his head. Tsutomu Miki stared unexpectedly into the eyes of a human soul. In an instant he felt the immortal linkage of the Great Chain of Being connect their disparate spirits. In that instant he was overcome with compassion, and as his compassion grew, the stranger grew respectively in size and stature until he stood before Tsutomu, face to face, man to man, human being to human being. He was a hakujin with a neatly trimmed beard like his own.

"Who are you?" Tsutomu demanded, placing his right hand on the handle of his katana.

"See this?" the stranger pointed to his nose.

"You have a big nose, so what? If you are a Christian, you could be smelling trouble."

"I have a nose for smelling out troubled souls."

"You look like one of those Jesuit priests."

"I presume you are Tsutomu Miki, the one so self-righteously persecuting the Christians?" the man with the big nose asked politely.

"I am."

"You will soon become Paul Miki," he stated matter-of-factly. "You will be persecuted as you have persecuted. That is the karma of all righteousness is it not?"

Tsutomu was stunned into silence. The statement simply felt true. He had it coming. It was karma. He deserved his fate. There was nothing to say.

"You have been following me for some time," the entity continued.

"I am not following you. I just happened to be going in the same direction," Tsutomu protested.

"It is easier to go in the same direction. You have more latitude."

"I'm on my way to Nagasaki."

"You have come a long way?"

"All the way from Kyoto. And you?" Tsutomu asked, his curiosity mounting.

"I come from the land from which your title originates."

"From Spain?"

"Yes, the land infamous for its Inquisition. You do not want to follow in that path. In this island of Oriental divinity there is no place for such ignorance and cruelty."

The forthrightness of the statement cut like a knife. Inexplicably Tsutomu was suddenly deluged with deep feelings of remorse and guilt. He stared at the ground and mumbled, "You have spoken the truth!" The truth pierced through to his soul. It was undeniable. In the land of the divine there was no place for such ignorance and cruelty! It was a revelation. "You are a teacher and I am but an ignorant student," he admitted humbly. He fell to his knees in the dirt before the stranger just like so many pathetic Kirishitan had once knelt before the Grand Inquisitor.

The stranger patted Tsutomu on the head as if he were a repentant little child and said, "You kneel before me as I kneel before another who has preceded me down the mortal path of space-time. He is just ahead of us. From his perspective we are all ignorant. It is just a matter of degree. We all make mistakes. That leaves room for improvement. It is a human trait."

"We need to learn from each other's mistakes, so that we need not repeat them."

"Well spoken."

"Who is this fellow who is ahead of you?" Tsutomu asked in a respectful tone.

"He precedes me as I have preceded you. It is a logical condition of the reality in which we are manifested. It is difficult to explain to those left behind even though they may be traveling in the same direction and down the same road. It would be nice if you could meet him. He is just up ahead."

"Your concept of time and space is quite amazing. Perhaps it is my limited awareness that prevents me from recognizing the direction you are traveling, even though it would appear we both are on the same road."

"Time will tell," the entity's voice trailed off as a sudden gust of wind whipped up the fine dust from the road into a fantastic cloud.

It was becoming all too confusing! The sun and the heat drew the perspiration to Tsutomu's brow and caused him to blink his eyes rapidly to clear away the sting of sweat. He held his left hand to his forehead to shield his eyes from the dusty glare of the western sun, and drew in a sobering breath. He momentarily closed his eyes. It seemed only a few seconds, but who knows how many mortal lifetimes can be contained in the blink of an eye? When he opened his eyes the mysterious universe reappeared and behold, the ethereal entity had miraculously metamorphosed once again! This time he appeared to be much older and stooped with age. His hair had turned snow white and his neatly trimmed beard was long and scraggly. He looked like an oriental sage, wise and humble. The unexpected transformation caused Tsutomu to step back timidly. He shook his head vigorously as if to clarify the confusion. It was too much, but what else could he do but continue?

"Are you-you still the same person?" he stammered.

"You see what you want to see. It is all in the eye of the beholder."

"You've changed!"

"To you I have changed a great deal. You no doubt wished to see a wise man or a sage. What do you see?"

"I see someone stooped and withered by wisdom and age. I see someone trustworthy. Someone I can identify with."

"You are very perceptive."

"What shall I call you? You must have a name?"

"Call me whatever you like. I prefer not to be labeled."

"Why?"

"I've learned a lot since my sojourn in the Land of the Dolls, as some referred to your divine country. I used to think that labels like Christian, Muslim, Buddhist, Shinto, Hindu, Jew, and so on mattered much more than they actually do. You can never be a label. You can only be yourself."

"Ah – so. It is karma, neh?"

"It is as it is. You can never be anyone but yourself. Think about that."

Tsutomu stared at the old man as if he were looking at Confucius. "You say you have learned a lot since your sojourn here. You must have had a wise teacher."

"Yes, the fellow up ahead is very wise. He taught me about the labels. If you only knew what they call him now, you would understand his concern. It would almost be funny, if these people weren't so, so serious."

"What people?"

"The people who came after him and called him names. I must confess, I was one of them. There was nothing he could do about it. He just looks back now and then and shakes his head."

"Where did this wise man come from?"

"Everywhere."

"Everywhere? Where is that?" Tsutomu asked as if in a stupor, overwhelmed by his own limited awareness and inability to comprehend the magnitude of what was happening.

"I suppose I should be more specific. About fifteen hundred years ago he was in the land of the Jewish-Christian-Muslims."

"Jewish-Christian-Muslims?"

"At that time only the label 'Jewish' was known to him. The other two labels were fabricated after his demise. During his sojourn in that Middle-eastern land there were not any entities such as Christians or Muslims."

"But now there are?"

"Yes. Now it is the land of one God with three distinct labels, and three recipes for salvation and or disaster. And yet strangely enough, they each respectively call their faith monotheism."

"Sounds like a paradox. Everywhere there are opportunities for salvation or disaster, or perhaps enlightenment?"

"Opportunities that can lead to the illumination of an increased awareness, or the ignorance of a diminished awareness. It is all about awareness."

"Is not awareness relative to the perceiver?"

"Yes."

"Sometimes I really have to struggle to see things that certain others take for granted. It is as if compared to those gifted individuals, I have the intellectual awareness of a primate, and no matter how hard I try to see, my limited capacity prevents me from truly appreciating their grand views," Tsutomu elaborated, feeling compelled to rationalize his own ignorance.

"And how do you feel toward those whose degree of awareness is much diminished from your own?"

"They seem so ignorant"

"And yet you are ignorant yourself as compared to someone more gifted. Right?"

"I see. It is like the ignorant judging the ignorant."

"It is a sign of ignorance to judge others. We must attempt to be morally non-judgmental, especially with regard to our fellow human beings."

"It is my job to judge others."

"You must realize that all human beings have their own karmic destinies, regardless of your moralistic pronouncements, and are the manifestation of the same miracle."

"What miracle?"

"The miracle of Freedom."

"You speak in riddles that are difficult to fathom."

"I know it sounds puzzling," the stranger stepped back and surveyed Tsutomu with a critical eye. I asked that same question of my mentor who is some fifteen hundred years ahead of me in space-time. It was an interesting conversation."

"I wish I could have been there."

The stranger looked skyward and seemed to levitate off the ground as he gazed upward. "You can be," he said adroitly. "Look into my eyes."

The eyes were hypnotic. Time dissolved into space, and space endured into time. Tsutomu felt mesmerized. He heard a voice say: "Close your eyes and the conversation will resound in your mind like an echo from the past". He closed his eyes.

"What miracle?"

"The miracle of Freedom."

"Freedom?"

"I know it sounds puzzling. I have been cogitating on it for over fifteen hundred years. Some things just take time to become clear. Imagine what knowledge and insights you could share if you had the hindsight of fifteen hundred years at your disposal?"

"I imagine that what is puzzling to me is probably self-evident to you."

"Freedom is that great miracle that never really becomes self-evident, no matter how long or how hard one tries to comprehend it."

"It took you fifteen hundred years to realize this?"

"Yes, I was lucky."

"Lucky? Please elaborate if it is possible."

"Freedom is very difficult to explain in words. Suffice it to say, it is something like the Unmoved Mover, the Uncarved Block, a Zen Moment. It is all of those notions put together. It is everything and nothing. It is the is-ness of being, and the mortality in everlasting life."

"Now I see why it is not exactly self-evident."

"We human beings experience Freedom as growth and adventure. We feel it as chaos, harmony, serenity, ecstasy, happiness, depression, and hope. We touch and taste it as disease, starvation, nourishment, health and sickness. We hear it in the music of our moods, and the sounds of nature. We are immersed in it – and yet separate. If we were not separate, we could not experience it. We would be it."

"It is everywhere, but we are just not aware."

"It is inherent in the Human Condition. Ironically, it feels like an encumbrance, like a straitjacket – yet it is only possible because we exist. It is as simple as a movement and a rest."

"It appears to be a paradox. No wonder it has taken you fifteen hundred years to come to this realization."

"Fifteen hundred years is nothing. It is a drop in the bucket. Like I said, I was lucky. It could have taken me fifteen thousand years or more."

"It was not just luck. You were ready. You were aware of the possibilities. You had the right attitude."

"You are more advanced than you give yourself credit for."

"I have always attempted to follow in your footsteps after a fashion. I realize now that my understanding was greatly influenced by the opinions of others. I have many shortcomings. Too many."

"I used to be somewhat like you, full of self-doubt and recriminations."

"You're just saying that to make me feel better."

"Listen my son, I know how it feels to be wrong. I have made far greater mistakes than you ever have. And now I know that I must be daring enough to share what little illumination I have managed to realize."

"And what is it that you have come to realize?"

"All human beings in their own way yearn to be free. Let me rephrase that with emphasis: IN THEIR OWN WAY ALL HUMAN BEINGS YEARN TO BE FREE."

"To be free?"

"They yearn for nourishment and good health, for growth and adventure, for beauty and truth, for significance and happiness, to be unencumbered, to be free."

"That is reassuring."

"It is a profound truth that we must dare to share."

"Dare to share?"

"Yes, we must bolster up our courage and dare to share even in the face of death. I tried in my own time and in my own way, but as you know, my contemporaries were not in tune with my readiness. They were not able to see what I was attempting to share."

The stranger stopped talking and looked over to see if Tsutomu was still in a receptive frame of mind. "Shall I continue with this story, or have you heard enough?"

"You are an artful story-teller. You know when to pause for effect and heighten the listener's curiosity. Of course I want you to continue."

"I stopped there because since my mentor's demise much controversy has erupted regarding his intent and purpose. I had no idea how this singular individual was, and still is, being used and abused by others who came after."

"Used? For what purpose?"

"To create a powerful new religion based upon an abstract notion formulated as a Creed."

"A what?"

"A Creed. A dogmatic doctrine sanctified by the conceivers to be true."

"Was it?"

"I used to think so."

"Your mentor was used after his passing by the creators of this new religion for their own purposes?"

"You have no idea to what lengths some people have gone to disguise the facts."

"Please enlighten me."

The stranger shook his head sadly as if ashamed of his own duplicity in the matter and replied, "How important would you say the years from age twelve to age thirty are to the development of the personality and character of a thirty-three year old man?"

"You are talking about eighteen of the most crucial years that would mould and define such an individual."

"Based on the first twelve and the last three, is it possible to claim to truly know such an individual?"

"One would be foolish to claim that one could really know such an individual based upon such skimpy information. Why do you ask?"

"I am interested in your unbiased opinion. Why do you think that such vital information would be eliminated from the life-story of such an individual?"

"If you wished to distort or fabricate, I suppose it would be in your interest to destroy such important information. Then, of course, your version of who this person is would be difficult to contest."

"I commend you for your insight. And now I will continue. Look into my eyes." In a flash Tsutomu's consciousness expanded to include another time, in another space.

"I dared to share in my own way in my time, but my contemporaries were not in tune with my readiness. They were not able to discern what I was attempting to share."

"Attempting?"

"Yes, I made an attempt even though it was not as clear to me then as it is now. You know how it is when you look into your past with a critical eye. I did my best under trying circumstances."

"You did your best?"

"What more could I have done? I did my best to demonstrate to my contemporaries, my countrymen, my fellow travelers through life, that they too could be unencumbered and free, like me. I tried to lead by example."

"You simply did not say: 'Do as I say' – you said do as I do, 'follow me', be like me."

"I wanted them to be free and unencumbered."

"Free from what?"

"From the most debilitating and suffocating self-inflicted encumbrance of the times. From something called, 'sin'."

"Original sin?"

"An archaic and imaginary human condition conceived of at a particular moment in history to be original, or innate, in order to rationalize an inhuman situation for a subjugated nation of captives whose offspring were born and raised from childbirth, generation after generation to serve as slaves to another more powerful nation. It seemed so unjust. There had to be an explanation for this untenable existential predicament. Why was this happening to them?"

"I suppose they could say that all human beings were afflicted with this flawed nature or original sin, but since they were the only ones slavishly atoning for their innate sinfulness, only they would be rewarded in the hereafter for their penitence and perseverance because God had taken notice of their existential predicament and felt sorry for them?"

"You are indeed perceptive. Yes, it provided them at once with a raison-d'être and a modus operandi."

"A modus what?"

"Operandi... a methodology, a way of life."

"It helped them survive when a lesser people would probably have perished."

"Your insightfulness is impressive... continue."

"They survived by giving themselves a significantly higher and meaningful reason to continue to live, generation after generation – even though they were physically and morally degraded to the life-negating level of existence associated with slaves."

"After the passage of such a long time the rationalization became so deeply inculcated into their psyche that even after they were led to freedom and were no longer slaves, they clung tenaciously to their slave mentality. It defined them in their religious dogma as the Chosen People."

"Don't we all rationalize?"

"That is what we human beings do best. Better than anything else! Remember that. Anyway, I attempted to free them from their self-inflicted religious addiction to this concept of innate sinfulness. I led by personal example. I encouraged them to follow me. They preferred to follow in the comfortable old rut of Original Sin – even though that self-concept was no longer a necessity for survival."

"What a shame!"

"They were not ready to relinquish the slave religion that had served them so well in the past. It is understandable. I underestimated the influence of the high priests whose responsibility it was to maintain the status quo."

"Nevertheless you tried. You did your best for them."

"They were not aware enough at that particular moment. Their slave mentality was still too much a part of their modus operandi and self concept. They were not as ready as I was to let-go."

"Letting-go is a precarious undertaking for many... extremely precarious. It is no little thing. It is as if one is letting-go of something very precious and irreplaceable."

"It was no little thing, especially to a people who owed their survival to its inculcation."

"It must have been very frustrating?"

"It was."

"You were charged with blasphemy and disturbing the peace."

"The high priests were not without influence. As it turned out, as if subconsciously the dilemma had to be clearly delineated in the light of the times, the Roman procurator washed his hands of the unsavory matter by handing the decision back to the people. He was trying in his own way to highlight the disparity, the injustice being perpetrated; he gave the people a seemingly ridiculous but clear-cut choice: the life of a proven murderer – or the life of a man whom he had questioned and found to be innocent. The one chosen by the people was to be freed. I represented freedom from sin, and the murderer represented sin. For a moment there I had this impossible hope. I had this incredibly optimistic hope that, as a free people, given a free choice, they would choose Freedom! I must admit I was devastated."

"I understand. It's only human."

"It was all or nothing. What is one life compared to the freedom of a people?"

"It would take a Messiah to attempt such a task!"

"Super-human attributes can be attributed to any human being in retrospect, by retrospective believers".

"You are very humble. I must admit I became one of the retrospective believers!"

"I am truly embarrassed. The circumstances dictated my actions. I was caught up in the ferment and turmoil of the times. I should have been more aware. It was all about freedom and hope. It is unrealistic to hope too much.

I assume full responsibility for my actions. We all must learn from our mistakes."

"I do not think I could be so, so contrite."

"Someday you will understand. You see, my people were simply substantiating what they had come to believe was the truth. They were being true to their flawed self-concept. Their religion was more important than their freedom."

"That's the bottom line for many people. You have my deepest sympathy. But surely afterward, some of them must have understood what you were trying to do for them?'

"Forsaking me only confirmed to them the sinful nature of man in general. It substantiated the legitimacy of their faith in Original Sin. The aftermath reflected the reality of their state of mind. I did my best – and failed."

"You consider yourself a failure?"

"Think about what happened. Be very honest. What good did I do? Look at what has transpired in the wake of my sacrifice. Like I said, be very honest."

"The Dark Ages, the Crusades, the Inquisition, the prejudice and persecution... who can free them now?"

"They must learn to free themselves. It is so frustrating because in the final analysis it is not about religion – it is all about kindness, love, understanding, compassion, and freedom."

"I am astounded by your wisdom."

"And yet, as you probably know, approximately three hundred and twenty-five years after my demise, at a place called Nicaea, some of them, deluded by their own piety and a desire for power and control, created a new dogmatic Creed that elevated me from being the 'son of man' to being the 'Son of God'! The notion that they crucified the 'Son of God' further encumbers them, not only with a profound feeling of sin, but also with a remorseful sense of an abiding guilt that only the sinful can truly appreciate!"

"Exactly the opposite of what you were attempting to accomplish!"

"The irony of it has not escaped me."

"Alas, it is the irony of ironies!"

"And, as if to compound the irony, guess what?"

"What?"

"They expect a failure like me to 'save' them!"

"They refer to you as their Lord and Savior."

"I am neither. Somehow they must come to realize that I was only attempting to help them to 'save themselves'. The spark of divinity that they have attributed to me is found within each human soul. No single human being is more divine than another. We must learn to love one another, as you and I have preached."

"You said 'follow me'. You wanted them to be like you, free and unencumbered by Original Sin. In their ignorance they crucified you! And now, ironically, they expect you to 'save' them."

"Well spoken, my son, and what is even worse, they worship me! They claim that I was physically resurrected, bones and all, directly into heaven."

"Weren't you?"

"I was only resurrected spiritually – not physically. Our immortal soul passes on and is 'resurrected' according to our karmic disposition. My bones are buried along with my wife and son in a family tomb near Jerusalem. Someday it will be discovered."

"You had a wife and son?"

"I know you thought I was celibate and have been attempting to emulate me. It is normal to desire a wife and to have off-spring - otherwise the human species would become extinct. I only wanted what was best for the human race which included my own people, the Jews."

"You set a compassionate example."

"You and I are much alike – except they worship me."

"Some people, especially the ego-centric type, would probably love to be worshipped. What is it like?"

"It fills me with impotence. I am reduced to nothing. It is the furthest counterpoint to my sense of self-worth. It undermines my humanity."

"You continue to astound me! I am, once again, humiliated by my ignorance. I too have worshipped you. Please accept my most humble apology."

"I understand. You have been a faithful seeker after truth like many others. I did not intend to disillusion or embarrass you, but to enlighten you."

"I still think of you as 'the Christ'."

"I know; many people think of me as such."

"It is a lofty title."

"Some names represent the projected expectations of the down-trodden upon someone whom they hope can fulfill their dreams. I have been giving a great deal of thought to this matter from a safe retrospective distance. At first I was quite depressed by what happened during the interval

immediately after my demise, but I am constantly impressed by the capability of people like you, free-thinking souls with the ability to transcend the dogma and doctrines that restrict and bind the spirit to the concept of Original Sin. Perhaps we should look at this as an opportunity to raise the level of awareness of those who call themselves Christians?"

"How could this be done?"

"What if the term Christ was considered to be a spiritual term synonymous with the concept of Freedom? Would it not follow that all persons who aspire to Freedom aspire to a consciousness of Christ, or a Christ Consciousness? Freedom is innate within every human being. Let Freedom replace Original Sin in the hearts and minds of all Christians."

"That will sound like blasphemy to the converted. Take my word for it. I know. But, what a miracle it would be if it could be realized!"

"We must make the best of what is. As you know God works in mysterious ways. It is never too late. Never! Divine hope is eternal. When they pray in my name, they pray in the name of Freedom — whether they know it or not."

"Whether they know it or not?"

"I am what I am. I cannot be any other. Eventually they will understand what it is that I represent."

"They will know who you really are?"

"They will know who 'we' really are."

"We?"

"We are all manifestations of the same Divine Spark of Freedom. We are all seeking the same illumination."

"There is hope for all?"

"Yes."

The stranger with the big nose sighed and gazed at Tsutomu with a twinkle in his eyes that reflected the unspoken question: Do you find this believable?

"How do I know you are not just making all this up?" Tsutomu protested, feeling compelled to challenge the authenticity of what he had just heard from a perfect stranger who refused to be labeled.

The sage pinched his big nose thoughtfully to indicate that such skepticism was not lost upon him and smiled, gratified that he had read that look on Tsutomu's face correctly. He avoided the question by replying, "You liked that part about Freedom and Christ Consciousness, did you not?"

"It was interesting. Why do you ask?"

"You are in conflict with yourself."

"I am?"

"You are ill-suited for your occupation and that is why you found the part about Freedom and Christ Consciousness so appealing. Someday you will become a Christian." The statement hung there unchallenged. It seemed to be a simple statement of fact uttered without malice or spite.

"I cannot imagine that happening," Tsutomu offered with a baffled smile. The reasoning seemed convoluted in places, but it was not the logic that mattered. It was the essence of what was being shared. Suddenly Tsutomu was overcome with an incredible feeling of humility before the steadfast gaze of this articulate stranger. The glare of the sun was hallucinogenic. The sage seemed to vibrate before him as if he were the fabrication of a pulsating light that pierced through the dimensions of color with colorlessness. Gradually the stranger faded from view and then disappeared altogether, but his voice continued.

"Have you no compassion?"

"Compassion for whom?"

"For your fellow man."

"Of course I do."

"Then why do you persecute those who call themselves Christians?"

"That is my job."

"Are not Christians human beings?"

"Yes, but..."

"What is more important, humanity or religion?"

"Humanity."

"Are not all human beings of divine origin?"

"Yes," Tsutomu acquiesced. The logic was simple and forthright.

"When you persecute others – you are persecuting your brothers and sisters. They are your next of kin. We all belong to the same family: the family of Man."

"We can all ultimately trace our roots back to the same origins?"

"To the same divine origin. Someday we will truly understand that a human being is a human being is a human being."

Tsutomu bowed down humbly before the invisible stranger. "Yes," he replied, "we are all human beings." He groveled in the dirt of the dusty road overcome with an abject sense of sorrow. "Forgive me for not understanding this sooner. Once I did terrible things..."

"Once?"

"Once I murdered my fellow human beings."

"Once is all it takes. One mortal life is one too many. Suppose it was your life? Once is forever."

The stupendous weight of that single statement hung about Tsutomu's shoulders like a dozen decaying corpses. His entire body began to quiver uncontrollably as if he were freezing to death. "I-I am so-so sorry!" he stuttered. "What can I do?"

The disembodied voice pondered his fate. "There is no going back," it stated matter-of-factly. "What is done is done. You must move on."

"I will commit seppuku," Tsutomu resolved with a samurai's heightened sense of duty. "What I have done is beyond redemption."

"Only if you forsake yourself."

"You mean there is still hope for one such as me?" Tsutomu asked staring into the sun.

"Where there is life, there is hope."

"It feels so... so hopeless."

"I know."

"You speak as if you know me. What am I to you?"

"A human being of infinite worth."

"I feel worthless."

"You are worth redeeming."

The voice resonated with such deep compassion Tsutomu lapsed into silence with bowed head. He stood staring into the setting sun with his elongated shadow providing the sensate evidence that proved that he was really there. He did not know what to say or do. He stood there with a growing feeling of gratitude welling up from within.

"You are the only one who can redeem yourself," the voice continued.

"How?"

"By forgiving."

"Whom shall I forgive?"

"Start by forgiving the one who caused you to hate, the one who slew your beloved father, the one wearing the silver crucifix, and all those you have persecuted because of your hatred. Be kind, tolerant, understanding, and compassionate. And most important of all, forgive yourself as you forgive those who have trespassed against you, and as others will forgive you."

"You seem to know more about me than I know about myself! I can only surmise that it is because you have gone on ahead, and looking back, you discovered an ignorant fool attempting to undo the good work you had done, and rather than chastising him, you took pity on him."

"We all make mistakes. Perfection is an imperfect illusion; a vanity of sorts. Imperfection is the genesis of perfection. It engulfs us with an illusion of perfection which is never quite perfect. The search for perfection is endless like a continuous spiral. It goes around and around and around. It is the going around that really matters. Make sense?"

Tsutomu shook his head with bewilderment. "Are you speaking of karma?"

"You reap what you sow. Go now and forgive yourself. It is a start. Even with all your regrets, shortcomings, disappointments, and sorrows, you can do it. Remember a human being is a human being is a human being. You and I are human beings just like everyone else, and in our own way we are representatives of the grandeur of the human spirit... just like everyone else."

"We are?"

"Aren't all *Nihongee*? We are all of divine origin differentiated by our relative degrees of ignorance. It is just a simple matter of acknowledging the obvious. It is actually a blessing in disguise to be mortal and fallible. Remember that, a blessing in disguise."

"I see! That is the essence of the human condition!" Tsutomu suddenly exclaimed as if he had been blind all his life. "Never have I heard anything more illuminating!" He swooned with reverie and was so overcome with self-realization that he fainted.

* * *

It was the sun and the heat, he later rationalized. The sun and the heat created this mirage, this apparition, this likeness of one of the hakujin who had passed on some time ago, probably that Jesuit with the large nose. It was quite understandable – except for the words that kept reverberating in his mind long after he had passed out.

"You are the only one who can redeem yourself... be kind, tolerant, understanding, and compassionate... forgive yourself... you will be persecuted as you have persecuted."

How could he rationalize such words? How can one rationalize the obvious? There is doubt, and then like the falling away of a great weight – there is acceptance.

Some Kirishitan later said it was a spontaneous conversion. It was not. Tsutomu Miki agonized for weeks. He became severely depressed. He returned home and bequeathed his priceless swords to his eldest son with the phrase: "Be worthy of them." He felt he had not been worthy. In his depressed state he considered himself to be a disgrace to the noble tradition. He sent a kindly message to Toyotomi Hideyoshi thanking him for his generosity and requested permission to leave his service. Toyotomi at first refused but upon receiving news of Tsutomu's distraught condition grudgingly gave him permission, out of respect for his meritorious service, to terminate his employment. A bedraggled Tsutomu returned to Nagasaki as if by instinct. He had nothing to do but walk about the busy streets. He behaved as if he was doing penance. Months passed. He lost about a third of his bodily weight. He wandered aimlessly around the marketplaces of Nagasaki with a wooden bowl begging for forgiveness.

"Forgiveness for what?" he was frequently asked.

"I did not know what I was doing at the time. I was so ignorant," he would sadly reply whenever a passing stranger took the time to respond.

Without further inquiry some would place a small coin in his wooden bowl for which he would bless them a hundred times. Eventually he became deranged. He lost his sense of identity. He walked about the crowded streets and alleyways saying, "I am nothing. I have no name. Who should I be? What should I call myself? Who am I?"

On some days the light of recognition would flash briefly in his eyes and he would rage about the backstreets yelling, "Where is that scoundrel who calls himself the Grand Inquisitor? That ignorant fool! That persecutor of innocent men and women! He should be crucified!" It was pathetic. He became the object of derision from other beggars who still retained a modicum of sanity. Normal people avoided him like a dreaded disease. He was reduced to a walking skeleton clothed in filthy rags. It was worse than pathetic.

Who could have predicted that the greatest samurai of his times, the legendary Tsutomu Miki, would be reduced to this?

It was by pure chance that a compassionate Jesuit priest happened upon a derelict shadow of a man wandering the streets of Nagasaki at high noon, and took pity upon the once fearsome tyrant who had persecuted the Christians with a fanatical zeal reminiscent of the Grand Inquisitors of Spanish infamy. He stooped, heaved the living bag of bones over his left shoulder, and proceeded to the mission. "One more soul for Christ," he said prophetically when he arrived at the door.

Some miraculous recoveries take time. It is not easy to convert the damned into the saved without the spirit of Christ being present at every step of the process. It took months but the conversion was immaculate. Christ Consciousness filled Tsutomu like a beacon of light the moment he forgave himself. It was astonishing to the Jesuit priests at the mission to witness the uplifting sense of freedom that burst from the bonds of self-recrimination. It was hard to believe that one who used to persecute Christians could make such a complete reversal. After he shared the essence of the experience he had on the road to Nagasaki with them, they spontaneously cried out almost in unison: "Like Saul of Tarsus!"

Like Saul of Tarsus he had been given a second chance. Did he deserve it? Some people have trouble learning from their own mistakes. Few are given the opportunity to experience a karmic-return during a single lifetime. Was Tsutomu Miki one of the lucky ones?

On the day he was baptized, the eldest priest, Father Perez, presided. He had graciously volunteered because he felt it was a very special and unique occasion. He looked deeply into Tsutomu's eyes and said, "You have been reborn like Saul of Tarsus, my son. He too once persecuted Christians and while on the road to Damascus was converted into Saint Paul." He paused to let the significance of what he was saying impinge upon the other priests who were present. "Henceforth," he continued in a resonant voice filled with inspiration, "you will be known as Paul... Paul Miki."

CHAPTER THREE

History is full of good men who did their best to live morally upright lives in times when good and evil were book ends, and the story in between was a tragedy. History is also full of coincidences, and the future often mimics the past giving rise to events that seem remarkably similar except for time and place. Yet every single event is new, and every experience is a first.

"Ah – so," the old man sighed insightfully to himself as he turned over to his left side. "If only someone had written a simple guidebook on life, perhaps the wheel of life would not have to roll over and over in the same old rut." Over the years the old man had become aware that there was a static quality in the four dimensional vibrations in which he was ensconced that allowed for the repetition of unlearned mistakes to roll over and over until they were learned. The problem was two-fold: first, the errors had to be recognized as mistakes, and secondly, the correct responses had to be learned. Sometimes the error was grudgingly corrected and the learning was inadequate; consequently the same error frequently raised its ugly head in the guise of righteousness. "Righteousness!" the old man expostulated out loud, "righteousness and more righteousness, and – when will we ever learn? When?"

The head nurse, hearing the old man muttering to himself, poked her head into his room. "I wonder what he is talking about tonight?" she asked herself as she reached around to where the light switches were located on the inner wall and cleared her throat to draw the old fellow's attention. "Isn't it time to turn out the lights?" she suggested. "Or would you like me to sit with you awhile?" she asked kindly.

The old man shook his head, smiled, and rolled over to go to sleep. He actually looked much younger when he smiled. It made the nurse feel good to know that she had somehow managed to elicit that smile. As she was about to flip off the light switch, she noticed that one of the old man's ancient samurai swords, the short one, had been removed from the black lacquered stand at the foot of the bed, and lay beside him on the rumpled sheets. She approached the bed, carefully picked up the wakizashi, inserted it in the scabbard, and replaced it strategically upon the stand just like the old man always did, with the handle to the right side and just a hint of the deadly blade exposed.

She switched off the lights as she left the room. And suddenly, for a brief moment the room became as dark as the universe in the old man's eyes. A myriad of tiny pinpoints of light danced in the heavens like a zillion stars from a billion galaxies. A halo of dimensions telescoped into a pinpoint of light that slowly faded from the old man's domain of cognizance, and vibrated vicariously in a membrane of invisible forces. Tutomu sighed dreamily and allowed his mind to resonate with the music of the spheres.

Some mornings were better than others. It was hard to tell in advance what mood the old man would be in. Old age does funny things to some people. Usually the old fellow tried to be chipper and forced a smile even when he was feeling sad. But the head nurse could usually tell when the old man had been crying by the amount of crumpled tissue cast aside beside his pillow. When she dropped in unexpectedly he tried to cover up by pretending to blow his nose. He didn't fool her. She knew.

He reminded her of a traumatized old WWII veteran who had been reliving the terrors of war. She had seen plenty of old vets scarred by the ravages of man's inhumanity to man struggle to find some semblance of meaning in their lonely lives of unmitigated misery. There was something so pathetic about seeing a decrepit old man like him cry. She had seen him through the open door during her early morning shift when she passed by his room. She saw him sitting up in bed with his frail hands clasped together in a position of prayer with tears glistening on his bony cheeks. It was so darn pathetic, she felt like crying herself.

There is something almost instinctive that causes people to clasp their hands together when praying. It just seems like a natural thing to do when communicating with the Divine. And so the old man did it just as if it really was natural. But what the nurse did not know was that the old man was crying – not because he was sad and lonely as she thought – but because he was so very, very grateful. He was so grateful for every precious moment of mortality that led to his self-realization. When he thought about it and gave thanks, he was frequently overwhelmed by gratitude. He had lived a long and interesting life that had brought him great wealth, power, and respect. He had achieved the pinnacle of economic success, but that was only the half of it. It was the other half that led to his realization.

He had been extremely lucky. It had taken him only one lifetime to learn such a vital lesson. It was like climbing a treacherous mountain. When you reach the top you suddenly realize that your objective is to go back down to where the people remained, the people who helped you reach the top.

"Tell us what it was like at the summit?" some curious person representing the great unwashed would usually ask expecting a fabulous tale of power, riches and glory.

The hardest and most frustrating part was attempting to convince them that there was nothing there, nothing at all. The old man was getting weary of informing them that he too would be exiting the world empty-handed just like everyone else. He had reached the top of the economic summit and he knew from personal experience that there was nothing there except empty labels and facsimiles of labels. There was nothing substantial that he could actually take with him, just himself. And for that profound insight he was grateful. All he wanted was a clear conscience and a compassionate soul. It had only taken him a lifetime to realize this. It was something he could take with him. It wasn't much, but it was better than nothing.

When he was alone in the solitude of the morning, the old man often prayed. However, he felt self-conscious if anyone noticed him and when discovered, would pretend he was just meditating. Sometimes, to pass the time, he would look at the portrait of the Fearsome Foursome he kept next to his bed and attempt to imagine what their life together was like. He could pass hours building fabulous mansions-in-the-sky.

The nurse spied him as she passed by in the hallway. "So pathetic," she mumbled under her breath, as she stopped, backtracked, and entered the room. She smiled compassionately. The old man was gazing serenely at a lovely portrait framed in mother of pearl with gold trim. "Relatives of yours?" she asked.

CHAPTER FOUR

Of all the stars in the entire galaxy, as far as Penny and Larry were concerned, there were none more precious than the twin stars that resided in the Petitjean household called Sherry and Jerry. Each child was a star in his/her own right. One of the strategies they used to keep such stars from having to compete against each other while they were in elementary school was to have them placed in separate classes. This worked fine because the school in which they were enrolled was large enough to usually have two grades of each class, and in the sparse years when the enrollment dropped they had split-grade classes. So as it turned out, Jerry and Sherry did not have to "embarrass each other", as Sherry put it, by being in the same class together. That is until two teachers got together and decided to specialize in certain areas of the curriculum. Mr. Taguchi and Mrs. Saunders received permission from the Principal to try out their team-teaching plan. The two classes concerned were melded together and the students were offered a choice of two topics in each subject area. In science, Mr. Taguchi offered a unit called The Mysterious Universe, while Mrs. Saunders offered one called The Sun, Moon, and Stars. Both Jerry and Sherry chose The Mysterious Universe. In Science and Math Mr. Taguchi had the larger classes but was compensated by having smaller classes in the Language Arts. It turned out to be good for the students and good for the teachers. Even the Principal was pleased with the outcome.

One day in early March both kids came home very excited about the upcoming Science Fair. Their favorite teacher Mr. Taguchi said they could work together in pairs, and to their parents' amazement the unbelievable happened, Jerry and Sherry had decided to work together.

"Another small victory for mankind!" Larry mused aloud at suppertime. "And what might our two budding scientists be thinking of as a project?"

"A model of the solar system," Sherry blurted out excitedly. "We've been studying it in class. Mr. Taguchi thought it would make a very nice display."

"I'm glad to hear that," Penny commented.

"Do you know all the planets in order?" Jerry asked his parents.

"I think the first one is Mercury and the last one is Pluto," Penny offered.

"Who taught you science?" Larry scoffed, "Tell her Jerry," Larry asserted smugly, pretending that he obviously knew such mundane facts.

"Mercury, Venus, Earth, Mars, Jupiter, Saturn, Uranus, and Pluto," Jerry rattled off.

"Correct," Larry sagely remarked.

"What?" Sherry interjected, "He left out Neptune. It's the second last planet."

"Just checking," Larry commented, turning a little red in the face. "I'm glad you noticed. Sure, there are nine planets and Jerry only mentioned eight."

"Nice try, Dad," Jerry empathized.

"You have to be on your toes in this family," Penny pointed out with a laugh. "Anything else you wish to share?"

"Yeah," Jerry followed up, "Mr. Taguchi said that if the projects were suitable we could work on them in Art Class. You know, to create the backdrop and other special effects."

"I'm going to concentrate on the art work and Jerry is going to work on the mechanics of the model, and we'll both work on the written report," Sherry pointed out.

"Mr. Taguchi suggested that we might like to visit the Planetarium one day soon to get a better feel for our project," Jerry added.

Penny and Larry sat and listened as the twins elaborated upon their project. Occasionally they smiled at each other and nodded their assent. This Mr. Taguchi or "Mr. T," as he was frequently referred to, seemed to know just about everything knowable in science. It was "Mr. T said this," and "Mr. T suggested that". And if Mr. Taguchi suggested something, then of course, naturally, it had to be done.

"Of course we'll be going to the Planetarium," Penny remarked, "Was there any doubt?"

"There is a special showing all this week," Larry chimed in, "It's about the birth of the universe."

"Can we go tomorrow?" Sherry asked enthusiastically.

"How about this weekend?" Penny suggested, "Then we can all go as a family."

"The fearsome foursome venture forth!" Jerry exclaimed.

"Should be fun," Larry added.

* * *

It was recollections of pleasant memories spent with two dynamic children growing up in a family where the quality of the conversations kept everyone on their toes, and stimulated thoughts that enabled them to reach beyond the stars, that motivated Larry and Penny to persevere with their retirement project.

"This handbook is for their generation," Penny declared as they made their way into the study

"And hopefully for generations to follow," Larry added as he sat down and turned on the computer.

"We started off rather cautiously but now we're on a roll."

"Funny how this handbook just seemed to evolve on its own once we got started,"

"There did not seem to be any other guidebooks of this nature that we could consult, so naturally we had to tread carefully and bolster up our courage and confidence as we progressed," Penny noted.

"We've generated our own momentum."

"The way we feed off each other's vibes stimulates our creative tendencies and inspires us to reach beyond the grasp of our own limitations."

"From baby steps, to giant steps... and now we are ready to make a quantum leap!" Larry announced as the next section appeared on the monitor.

II THE MYSTERIOUS UNIVERSE

(1) A Quantum Leap

There is only one almighty leviathan
And we are but a few of the many cells
That make up its gigantic body...
When it breathes in the universe expands
And when it breathes out the universe contracts

While the beating of its heart gives duration
To its solitary existence as a meditating Monk
Sitting comatose in a cave of silence
Deprived of the pleasures of his five senses
Deaf, dumb, unfeeling and staring blindly
At a spot between his eyes
Transfixed by the soulful bliss
Emanating from the raison d'être
Of his cellular memory
Which in one finite moment of eternity
Infuses every cell of his miraculous mortality
With an inkling of how lonely it can be
To be... the One and Only.

The Leviathan and Us

Each of us in our own way is a leviathan whether we know it or not. The notion is inherent in our limited understanding of the concepts of size and duration, and the relativity of such. These concepts provide the parameters that define our finite, mortal dimensions. They provide the genesis of our notions of eternity, and infinity along with our innate feelings of spirituality.

Man has always had difficulty with the concepts of size and duration because they are relative concepts and only make sense in comparative situations. When we consider the infinitely small, this concept only makes sense as compared to the infinitely large, and vice versa. It is the comparison that provides the meaning even though we have no idea what the infinitely small or large are. All conceptions of duration and size are relative to all other such conceptualizations.

The following illustration may help provide some perspective while exemplifying the relativity involved in the concepts of size and duration. What if the entire universe as we know it was contained within one extremely complex Universal Cell! And further what if this Universal Cell along with a zillion other such cells constituted a single hair on the head of a nearly hairless super-natural anthropoid. This anthropoid along with six billion other such primates looks up at the sky and attempts to visualize the grand universe. However, the universe in which the anthropoids are ensconced is but a single gargantuan Universal Cell that along with a zillion other such cells makes up one of the lovely strands of hair on the beautiful head of an almighty leviathan known as Her Eternal Beingness. Her Eternal Beingness scratches her head thoughtfully, smiles beatifically, and pretends she is just one of the many searching for clues to her real identity.   Her real identity is multi-dimensional. How can it be understood in a four dimensional reality?

The Big Bang Theory

In order to comprehend Creation, Man had to make many quantum leaps of faith. The natural place to begin was where he found himself, on planet earth. From there he peered out into the dark skies all around and began to gradually piece together the vast puzzle that confronted him. At first he thought the earth was the center, and the moon, sun, and stars revolved around the earth (Ptolemaic theory). Soon he learned that the earth was only one of nine planets revolving around the sun (Copernican theory). Then he discovered to his amazement that this solar system of one sun and nine planets was only a tiny fragment of a vast galaxy of billions of stars and planets whirling about at tremendous speed in the shape of a huge spiral. As he peered beyond his own Milky Way galaxy, man discovered galaxy after galaxy after galaxy all whirling away at tremendous speed. Since all the galaxies represented by zillions of stars were moving away from each other, the most brilliant scientists assumed that at one time in the distant past all the galaxies were packed very close to each other, compacted by the force of gravity into one gigantic body. This huge, invisible, primordial mass compacted itself into a singular mass so dense not even light could escape its gravitational pull. Hence it was called a "black hole". Everything was sucked into it. There was absolutely nothing left – zero... until it exploded with a "Big Bang!"

Zillions of fragments flew out in every direction giving birth to the expanding universe of light. The force of the Big Bang hurled the galaxies that were re-created farther and farther apart into outer space. It was surmised that as the impetus of this tremendous force wore off, the speed with which the galaxies were moving away from each other would gradually diminish due to the relative effect of opposing fields of gravity. The sum total of all available scientific knowledge concerning the laws of physics indicated that as sure as the sun rises and sets, the universe would eventually have to stop expanding and gradually begin contracting as the relative gravitational force exerted by each galaxy on all the other galaxies pulled all the galaxies back together into a dense mass once again.

Is Space Empty?

All the logic and empirical evidence of science clearly demonstrated that when an object is thrown upward it gradually loses the force of its upward thrust and eventually reverses its direction and plummets back to the earth attracted by the force of gravity. It seemed to be inconceivable that an object could actually gain speed as it moved away from the source of its initial impetus, because gravity would slow it down. However, surprise, surprise, the galaxies are not slowing down. They are speeding up! Scientists are flabbergasted by their own research. The "red shift", a change in the light spectrum detected from a super-nova is an unmistakable indication that the galaxies in which they exist are moving away at greater speed. How can that be?

At first when scientists stared up with awe into outer space they were confident, based upon their empirical research, that the universe was a macrocosm reflecting everything they already knew about energy and matter. The earth, the moon, the sun, and the stars were composed of matter and energy that could be broken down into subatomic particles like electrons, protons, and neutrons and these in turn could be broken down into smaller particles that seemed to behave according to the known laws of physics. The universe consisted of galaxies of such matter and energy scattered about in space. What scientists took for granted was that all that space between the pinpoints of starlight was empty, that it was void of anything. It was nothing.

Alas, all that dark space is not empty. It is no more 'empty' than say, the background is to the foreground. Without one, the other cannot exist. They define each other. This void of "nothingness" is now believed to be something.

Real Space

There is no such thing as "empty space". All that dark space between the stars is an undefined form of energy. It is this "mirror-energy" that is causing the universe to be expanding against the force of gravity. This dark space is as real as the black squares on a checkerboard are to the red squares. Which is the background and which is the foreground? It all depends on what you are looking at. They are both equally real, and their co-existence gives unity to this checkerboard reality

What scientists are gradually beginning to understand is that what appears to be an expanding universe is really like the outside spiral of an expanding and contracting universe. If the universe is self-contained, as the first law of thermodynamics presupposes, then it must be continually renewing itself in a way that does not create new matter. Perhaps it is something like a rotating double helix. What appears to be going in is coming out, and vice versa. The background becomes the foreground and the foreground becomes the background. It all depends on how you look at it.

Wholesomeness

When Werner Heisenberg attempted to ascertain the position and movement of a subatomic particle (around 1927) he discovered that when he focused upon the position, the movement became unclear, and vice versa. From this experiment the "Uncertainty Principle" was born. It is now used in the vernacular to connote the uncertainty of knowing anything with precision. It has become known as the "perceiver-effect".

There have been subsequent experiments involving photons and other subatomic particles that have demonstrated further scientific mysteries. One of the better known is called the "twin paradox". In this instance twin subatomic particles heading in opposite directions with opposing spins, seem to be affected by each other even though they seem to be unconnected to each other or at-a-distance. For example, when particle A is given an up spin using an electromagnetic field, the twin particle B immediately takes on a down spin even though the two particles are at-a-distance. Since distance per se is a relative concept dependent upon the observer, it makes no difference whether the distance separating the twin particles is a fraction of an inch or a million light years. How can this be?

When scientists and physicists look at one piece of the puzzle they may think they are dealing with that piece in isolation. They are not. They are empirically concentrating upon part of the whole. The "whole" functions as a whole; all the parts are interconnected even though they may appear to be disconnected or unrelated to each other. When one part is affected the effect could be felt anywhere else. Think about acupuncture: when a thin needle is strategically placed in the Leviathan's neck, the pain in its injured knee might disappear. Everything is interconnected in ways that make up the whole.

Dimensions of Reality

Scientists have long been attempting to come up with an all-encompassing theory that would explain why things are the way they are. What they had to work from were two existing theories: (1) a theory to explain the macrocosm called the General Theory of Relativity put forth by Einstein, and (2) a theory to explain the microcosm referred to as Quantum Mechanics. What was needed was a composite or overall theory that could explain everything. After twenty years of individual and collective investigation, scientists came up with a mathematical formula that they claimed was able to explain everything. Consequently it was called The Theory of Everything, or more particularly, String Theory.

What String Theory did was amalgamate and theoretically redefine the function and relationships amongst all the known forces at work in the microcosmic and macrocosmic universe. These forces are Gravity (G) from the General Theory of Relativity, and the Strong (S), Electromagnetic (EM), and Weak (W) forces discovered in Quantum Mechanics. These four forces, G-S-EM-W are created by gravitons, electrons, protons, and neutrons, which in turn are made up of quarks, rays, and an assortment of very small sub-atomic particles. The question was: what did these sub-atomic particles consist of? The answer: infinitesimally tiny "strings" of vibrating energy. It was all in the vibes, so to speak!

String Theory

At first there were five innovative and logically sound String Theories, which in 1995 were reduced to one grand theory by Ed Witten, and called M Theory. Even Ed Witten himself was not exactly sure what the "M" stood for. Some suggestions have been Matrix, Magic, and Mysterious. The wonder of the M Theory is that it is so basic, yet it seems to be able to logically explain both the microcosmic and macrocosmic universes simultaneously. It is able to explain everything in the known universe and more. It is the "and more" that excites the imagination of creative thinkers, scientists, and philosophers alike.

M Theory goes beyond the bounds of the knowable by projecting up to eleven distinct dimensions, seven more than are presently detected by our five receptor senses in our four dimensional reality. The four dimensions of our known reality are length, width, depth, and time. This reality allows for the existence of a three dimensional space through one dimensional time. What if it were possible to add more dimensions separately or in various combinations to the four existing ones?

Just as a three dimensional space is metamorphosed with the addition of a dimension called "time" into a unique four-dimensional "Reality", each more complex "Reality" is a combination of many dimensions, and they all exist right here and now, even though we may not be consciously aware of them. According to String or M Theory, the differential-degrees of "vibration" of strings of energy (known as Strong, Weak, Electromagnetic, and Gravitational forces) that resonate together form a "membrane of forces" identified as a dimension. A "Reality-membrane" is created when one or more dimensions resonate to form a unique "reality" such as the four dimensional "Reality-membrane" we experience as "space-time". This is the reality we all take for granted as being the only real reality because it is the only Reality-membrane of which we are currently "aware". However, with seven dimensions available, here and now, in addition to length, width, depth, and time, the variety and number of "Reality-membranes" possible is indeed intriguing.

It is not clear in what manner these eleven dimensions can combine/resonate to form more complex or higher realities. What is clear is that a vast number of greater realities are possible. Freedom and awareness can only be experienced within the context of these realities; therefore it seems to follow that the degree of freedom and awareness one experiences may be relative to the complexity of the "Reality-membrane" in which one vibrates or exists.

This grand theory of Everything appears to fit in with the notion of karma. We become manifest in that reality that is commensurate with our karmic vibrations. It is nice to know that according to M Theory, with eleven dimensions postulated (and there could be many more) that the number of combinations and permutations of "Reality-membranes" possible, leaves plenty of room for further conjecture, contemplation, and advancement.

CHAPTER FIVE

"**I** must say, that last section of the handbook is rather esoteric, or should I say mind-boggling," Larry critiqued.

"It certainly is a little complicated in places," Penny agreed. "We need to keep this as simple as possible if we want to get our ideas across to our targeted audience."

"Yeah, sometimes we get too enamored by our own insights and take it for granted that others will feel equally as inspired," Larry commented. "We need to apply the KISS formula as rigorously as possible."

"What do you mean by KISS formula?"

"Surely you've heard of that before?"

"Nope."

"It means, Keep It Simple, Stupid!"

"Of course the Stupid applies to us."

"Who else?" Larry responded, "But knowing you, I know it won't be easy because to you everything is simple."

"That's because I'm basically a simpleton," Penny rejoined with equal sarcasm.

"Yeah, right!" Larry expostulated with a disarming smile, happy that they could work together so amicably.

Penny sighed and abruptly changed the subject by saying, "I remember one warm starry night when I was in grade five, I took my sleeping bag and went out behind the house and just lay on my back staring up at the immensity of the universe. I was out there, a tiny speck of consciousness, marveling at Creation. I felt an eternal presence within and without and I knew without a doubt I was part of a mystery so vast it would always confound the most brilliant scientific minds."

"I know what you're saying," Larry concurred. "It seems the more scientists discover about the nature of our space-time phenomenal reality, the more there is to explore."

"Fortunately we are beginning to develop the high-tech tools to help us to begin our journey into outer space."

"Don't forget our journey into inner space," Larry added enthusiastically, giving voice to a topic he was interested in. "Before you know it man will be able to clone himself and the very nature of our identity as human beings will be a moral issue we will have to come to grips with. It seems the more we discover about our outer and inner selves, the more mysterious we become."

"Did you know that if the double helix strands that make up our DNA were unraveled they would reach to the moon and back forty times?" Penny asked emphasizing Larry's point.

"Amazing!"

"And the sequencing of the billions of microscopic strands of that vast double helix genome has been likened to decoding the book of life. At first scientists thought that it would be impossible to sequence such a large combination of probabilities, but as you know curiosity is a powerful incentive, and in 1990 the U.S. government felt that in spite of the serious ethical considerations regarding tampering with our genetic makeup, the advantages were so great in the areas of disease control, biological health, and longevity, that they allocated approximately fifteen billion dollars to fund a public project to map the human genome." Penny rambled on regurgitating an article she had recently read. She glanced at Larry anticipating his input.

"Yes, and because of the huge profits that could potentially be realized from the control of such vital information, private corporations also invested heavily into the task of mapping the human genome." It was Larry's turn to show off his knowledge on the topic under discussion. "And on June 26, 2000, President Clinton announced that in the field of microbiology a quantum leap had been made. Through the joint efforts of public and private concerns, the human genome had finally been sequenced or roughly mapped. The genetic code is unraveling."

"What used to be science fiction is gradually becoming the norm."

"Computer science has greatly accelerated the rate at which information can be gathered, assessed, and categorized. The important question is: is man morally and spiritually evolving in step with the incredible advances in science?" Larry reflected.

"Scientific discovery should always be premised upon an altruistic desire to help make the world a better place for all mankind," Penny responded.

"Too bad altruism is not innate within the human condition."

"Speaking of the human condition, let's check out that section with the KISS formula in mind."

(2) The Human Condition

The three elemental components of the "human condition" as we know and experience it have been delineated in this fashion:

(1) The spirit or pure essence
(2) The mind or metaphysical plane
(3) The body or physical plane.

When we combine those three elemental components we produce a state of "being" or existence known as the human condition. The fusion yields a miraculous paradox in which it is apparent that the whole is greater than the sum of the parts, making the division or separation between the components purely superficial. Of course this adds ever more confusion to a confusing matter.

Perhaps another less confusing way to conceive of these components is as follows:

(1) The creator
(2) The manifestor
(3) The manifested.

These categories expressed in religious terminology can be personified to read:

(1) The Father or Eternal I
(2) The Son or Immortal I
(3) The Holy Ghost or Mortal I.

In terms of the secular world these components can be translated thus:

(1) Creation or the Observer being self-observant
(2) Cosmic Consciousness or the Mind of the Observer
(3) Re-creation or manifestation of the mind of the Observer.

Re-creation is of particular importance to Man because it represents the physical or material plane that gives substance to all manifestations. It is determined by three very important laws that are applicable in a four dimensional reality. They are:

(1) All acts or actions are acts of re-creation which defines creation (universal law)

(2) Matter or energy cannot be created or destroyed; it can only be changed or transmuted (first law of thermodynamics)

(3) For every action there is an equal and opposite re-action (third law of motion).

If all of the aforementioned concepts are deemed to be relevant, and could be molded like parts into a whole, the human condition could be said to be a miraculous combination of being:

(1) A self-conscious observer, i.e. capable of being aware

(2) A re-creator, i.e. endowed with free will

(3) Mortal, i.e. finite.

The human condition is a very difficult if not nearly impossible concept to clearly comprehend as is evident by this multi-level, round-about explanation. Yet it is a "condition" that we all have in common. It makes us human. Who really knows what it is that makes us what and who we are? Perhaps it is the best kept secret of the ages.

Whenever she read the section on the Human Condition, Penny was reminded of that time in Calgary when her cousin sat in the living room of her tiny apartment and gave voice to thoughts like these that had subsequently incubated and grown to fruition in her ever-curious and questioning mind. She could still visualize him sitting there hunched over a cup of green tea with his thick mop of unkempt hair falling over bushy eyebrows, from beneath which peered luminous eyes as black as coal. He looked somewhat like an artist brooding over an unfinished picture of the metaphysical world, a picture which he painted with words instead of paint and brush. He enunciated a philosophical vision in vocal vibrations that gave meaning to his existence, such as it was back in the confines of that existential space in a tiny one bedroom apartment in Calgary, Alberta, Canada.

There he sat, evening after evening, consumed by an intellectual curiosity that knew no limits. It was contagious. She had no immunity. She was susceptible to every seminal concept or idea. There was something majestic about his verbosity when he held forth on a subject dear to his heart: his eyes sparkled with the fire of a billion stars, his face glistened with excitement, and his entire body posture spoke a language which a novice like her found absolutely captivating. It was magical, just two people conversing about esoteric matters that few other people had any inclination to think about, much less discuss.

What gave each moment its magical ambiance was the intellectual music; it was like a fabulous orchestration of the most wonderful melodies. Thinking per se was the music of the spheres and they were both finely tuned instruments. The resonance provided the freedom to imagine, to dream, to create. The resonance of those fourteen days provided Penny with the experience that set her on a path designed for those who have had a taste of intellectual freedom. It was natural for an introspective person like her because thinking is without a doubt the highest activity in which the human species can participate, and to her it was very enjoyable, if not exhilarating.

Even after all the intervening years the resonance remained in the tingling synapses of her long-term memory. It was a pleasant memory of a time when she engaged in a stimulating and prolonged intellectual intercourse that seemed ever on the verge of orgasm.

Thoughts of orgasm stimulated Penny, and her face flushed with a glow that Larry mistook for a radiance caused by his own male proximity.

"You look particularly ravishing this evening," he remarked.

"I do?" Penny responded, feeling a little embarrassed.

"Yes, there is a glow about you."

I was thinking about that time my cousin visited me in Calgary," Penny admitted. "You know, my cousin from Japan?"

"Oh yes, he seems to have made an indelible impression upon you. Even after all these years it's as if he still is conversing with you in absentia. Perhaps you two are linked by a telepathy that spans oceans."

"Did I detect a hint of jealously in that remark?"

"Perhaps just a tiny hint, to be honest, but I was serious about the telepathy."

"You mean something like psychics who can receive impressions from persons who are physically at a distance?"

"There are people who seem to have the ability to tune in to vibes that span space and time. It is a phenomenon that does not fit into our notion of what constitutes reality, so most people tend to dismiss it as being mere foolishness."

"I think my cousin had psychic powers even though he was not aware of it. He had this transcendent presence of mind that seemed rather otherworldly. Sometimes when he held forth on a far-out topic it appeared as if he was in tune with a vibration or frequency that the rest of us are not able to tune in."

"Who knows how many Reality-Membranes are available to those advanced enough to tune them in?"

"And they are all telescoped, so to speak, into a single reality spiritually experienced as Oneness."

"What made you think of that?" Larry asked, impressed with Penny's astuteness.

"It's like my cousin said, "It is all a matter of being in tune with what is."

CHAPTER SIX

It was a warm sunny evening in late July when Penny and Larry retired out to the comfortable lawn chairs on the back patio facing the garden. Larry had just opened a bottle of their favorite red wine and had poured two generous sized glasses full to the brim. "Aren't we lucky!" he stated with contentment as he sipped his wine and stared out at the seasonal beauty of the flower garden.

"We have been most fortunate," Penny responded. "We have the two most wonderful children in the world, we are financially secure, and we have an exciting project to work on that gives us a sense of sharing what we have spent our lives accumulating."

"It almost feels like too much," Larry remarked, "like too much of a good thing, like do we really deserve all this?"

"It's funny," Penny reflected, "how things seem to happen just as if they were supposed to."

"What are you getting at?" Larry asked.

"You know, how everything seems to fit together in time and space just as if some omniscient narrator were telling a story."

"Yeah," Larry acknowledged, "something like an ongoing video or movie that keeps on rolling along toward a preconceived end."

"Not exactly," Penny interjected searching her mind for an illustration of what she was getting at. "Remember that time down at Eugene when we were both in the same grad class on Symbolic Logic at the U of O, and you turned around and accidentally knocked me flat on my ass?"

"You're talking about coincidences," Larry surmised.

"I guess maybe I am, but that word seems to imply that all these events were somehow purely random, just chance happenings, like rolling the dice."

"Are you implying that it was not a fluke that you and I met in that particular manner and at that particular time?" Larry queried.

"Well, I must confess, it was actually my intention to make your acquaintance but not in that particular fashion," Penny revealed turning slightly red in the face as she took another sip from her wine glass.

"Ah-ha!" Larry expostulated, "so that is what you were doing there." He smiled at Penny, feeling somewhat embarrassed by her embarrassment. "But I must also confess I wanted to make your acquaintance too! So perhaps that coincidence was not quite so coincidental after all."

"It became transformed into a golden opportunity for both of us."

"The more we rationalize coincidences, the less coincidental they seem," Larry puzzled.

"I see!" Penny exclaimed as if a light suddenly flashed on in her head. "All coincidences have the potential, relative to the perceiver, to be something else," she rambled on as if receiving information on a higher frequency. "There really are coincidences. These coincidences are manifested by the perceiver from the pure unlimited potentiality of the energy field that engulfs them, and transformed into events that occur as random probabilities in space-time. They remain as random probabilities until they are realized to be opportunities – giving us the distinct impression that there are no such occurrences as coincidences."

"Convoluted but inspired!" Larry acknowledged. "Ah, the power of intuitive knowledge. You have a gift that is enviable, especially to logic-bound, one step at a time discursive thinkers like me who get bogged down in the rhetoric of their own language games. Sometimes I feel like a real ignoramus. I wish there was some way I could develop my intuitive powers.

"We all have intuition, Larry. It is innate in all human beings. It is the basis of all knowledge. All knowing is basically intuitive. Even our five receptor senses are intuitive whether we know it or not. It is just that the extrinsic view of the world, augmented by the scientific approach to just about everything including education and medicine, is dependent upon this outside-in approach. We depend almost entirely upon our five receptor senses to bring in the reality that surrounds us. Consequently we have neglected our extrasensory abilities."

"What you have just said, as if it were just common sense, is so profound it is breathtaking! Yes, indeed, now that you have pointed it out it seems obvious. We just assume that the real world must be experienced 'outside-in', as you say."

"There have been those who have suggested that reality is projected from within, reflected from the inside-out."

"A far-out concept for those of us conditioned to the extrinsic view of reality."

"Think of consciousness. Where does consciousness originate from? Outside? Or inside? Obviously consciousness arises from within and allows us to become aware of what appears to be out there. Consciousness is the light of awareness. When the light fades reality fades with it."

"I get it. Like in a dream. We dream the dream and while we are dreaming it appears as if the dream-reality exists separate from the dreamer. But when the dreamer awakes, he/she realizes the dream-reality that seemed so real was nothing. It had no substance. It was not really real. That being said, we are loath to take that next logical step. *We are dreaming this!* And it will remain real until as you say, the light of consciousness fades and we awaken to a greater reality."

"It is a very difficult concept for those conditioned to the extrinsic view to grasp."

"But not impossible. I got it, did I not? We all dream. We can relate to what you are saying. It makes sense because it makes our dreams make sense. It is amazing how you come up with these profound ideas."

"You know, I'm not nearly as profound as you may think I am. Most of these ideas and insights are not new to me. They have been coming to me for years and years. You know in the early morning when you think I'm asleep? I'm not asleep. I'm wide awake but the electrical synapses in my brain remain tuned-in to the frequencies emanating from the static electromagnetic energy that endures in space-time. I think it is because I am consciously aware that the past and future exist in the present, and this simple but sincere acknowledgement allows me to tune in these intelligent people who have passed on and are somewhere just ahead of us," Penny explained.

"Yes, that makes sense," Larry nodded. "Obviously these people have existed in the flesh and blood, just like we presently exist, but they have simply gone on ahead of us in space-time, just as we will with respect to those we leave behind when we pass on."

"Exactly," Penny agreed, "but unless we acknowledge that they are ahead of us instead of discarded in the dead hand of the past it will be difficult, if not impossible, for us to tune them in because we will be out of tune with them."

"I think you're onto something, Penny," Larry stated after a thoughtful pause. "You really are on to something here that is worth exploring. I've never really even tried to tune in to any other vibes except for those that just came to me haphazardly. Since I was raised with an extrinsic view I externalized the past and future; they were separate from me. However, if the past and future are not separate from me but here right now telescoped into this very instant, it would be natural to be able to tune in to all these existent vibes. Still the logic behind all this is rather confusing. Could you elaborate further?"

"Hmmm, how can I put this? Like I said before, space-time is relative to the perceiver. When you were born space-time began for you. That was your zero year, so to speak. When you were born, Jesus of Nazareth, for example, was approximately one thousand nine hundred and forty chronological years older than you. The universal path that he and you are traveling is as old as the Great Chain of Being. He has been traveling down the path for one thousand nine hundred and forty years already, while you are just starting out. Just as in a marathon race that has a staggered start, some runners are way ahead of others who may just be starting. They are all in the race called the Human Race down the mysterious path of the Great Chain of Being. If you are Human you are automatically in the race. There will be runners behind you and runners ahead of you. If Jesus of Nazareth started the race ahead of you – how could he now be behind you in space-time?"

"Good question!"

"Would it be fair to say that we have difficulty placing ourselves anywhere but at the head of the race, and consequently we relegate all those people who have ever lived, behind us into the dead hand of the past?"

"Yes. To most people Jesus of Nazareth is around two thousand years behind them in space-time. How did they get ahead of him? It is an existential illusion: a mindset that creates a reality commensurate with that point of view."

"Is not that a common conception of space-time?"

"It is like seeing the universe from the Ptolemaic viewpoint when it really is Copernican in scope.

"I'm getting confused. Are you saying that our perceptions are unreal?"

"The universe was real even in the Ptolemaic era. It was our conception of the universe that was not only suspect, but limiting.

Our conception that Jesus is two thousand years behind us is 'real' to those who believe that. However, when they pass on, they will leave their children behind like everyone else, and the loved ones they leave behind will probably relegate them into the 'dead hand of the past' as if they were of no further use. Meanwhile they will actually move on ahead of their children, and shake their heads sadly because from their vantage point they have a lifetime of wisdom to share with the offspring they left behind, but no one is tuning it in because nobody cares. Why should they? What can be found in the dust bin of obsolescence except rotting corpses?"

"I'm beginning to get your drift," Larry acknowledged. "Jesus of Nazareth is around two thousand years ahead of us, and because we are aware of this, Jesus is alive to us – and dead to just about everyone else."

"That is certainly putting it dramatically. I am sure Jesus is alive to most Christians, but only in a religious sense requiring the miracle of a resurrection from the grave. Wouldn't it be wonderful if Christians could tune in their Lord and Savior?"

"They see him there at the front of the church hanging upon a wooden crucifix with a terrible red spear gash in his side, and a crown of thorns upon his head. It would be extremely difficult for them to conceive of him as being about two thousand years ahead of them, smiling graciously and beckoning them to follow. Some might even call such a notion blasphemous!"

"You are too pessimistic. You need to develop a more charitable attitude toward Christians in general. There are all sorts of Christian souls. Probably most of them are more like you than you give them credit for," Penny admonished her spouse.

"My parents were Christians. They are both somewhere up ahead of me in space-time. I wonder what they are thinking."

"Since you're their only begotten son it would be nice if you could tune them in."

"Ah, yes. You know, I've never really tried."

"Perhaps from their perspective they are wondering if it is possible to convince those they left behind that they do not reside in the dust bin of obsolescence but are up ahead cogitating upon sublime topics of universal significance."

"Like 'from zero to unity'?"

"Possibly."

"And we thought it was our idea."

"We wrote it down."

"Let's take another look at it," Larry suggested.

(3) From Zero to Unity

Importance of Zero

At the present time you probably think of zero as simply a number denoting the absence of value or the commencement of a numerical scale. When the Arabs came up with this concept it was the most astounding insight since the discovery of the wheel. The mighty Romans and the scholarly Greeks struggled along without the conception of zero. It is the reason why, prior to the Common Era or C.E., the calendars began at 1 B.C. and 1 A.D. with two years of missing time in between. The man credited with this calendar is known as "Dennis the Short"; his real name is Dionysus Exiguous. When Dennis was improvising the calendar, the Roman numerals with which he had to work did not have a zero; therefore he simply skipped over the zero as if it was non-existent, because to him it really was non-existent. 'So what is the big deal?' some may ask. In Western Christendom time begins with the birth of Christ and is counted from that initial starting point on a before and after basis. So what is the date of Christ's birth? It supposedly lies somewhere between 1 A.D. and 1 B.C., if you trust in the accuracy of Dennis the Short's calculations. Without the concept of zero, historical accuracy was a risky business especially for calendar makers.

When zero was invented, mathematics and all the exacting sciences became possibilities. Today the known universe can be defined in terms of math. What would we do without our precious zero? It has given us a new dimension of awareness.

Zero, as well as denoting a number, also represents unity or wholeness. It is a paradoxical concept representing nothing, but being something. Zero is the genesis of a numerological reification of the cosmos. It is the beginning of the process of quantifying the universe based upon the assumption that the first law of thermodynamics is correct.

In a very short time Man was able to use this idea to develop a macro and micro conception of the reality that impinged upon his five senses. The parameters of his awareness expanded geometrically. What Man could conceive of, he could manifest. Reality reflected man's expanded awareness. Who said that zero was not important?

Time-Space

The concept of zero ushered Man into the age of science. Man was given a logical means whereby he could attempt to rationalize the reality that surrounded him. Mathematics evolved like magic anchored by zero on one end and infinity on the other. In between lay a universe of possibilities contained within the quantifiable space that endured as time. Mundane as it may seem, there are few more important or "far-out" concepts than time. It is an essential aspect of our four dimensional reality and fits the frugal standards set in Occam's Razor: *Entia non sunt multiplicanda praeter necessitatem* (No more things should be presumed to exist than are absolutely necessary). In the mind of a genius like Albert Einstein, mathematics revealed the underlying unity that melded time and space into time-space.

There is an interesting experiment that allegedly took place on October 28th, 1943 during World War II when secrecy, deception and deceit were considered by the U.S. President of the time to be acceptable war-time practices. The top-secret scientific experiment that accidentally revealed the underlying complexities of the energy fields that manifest the fourth dimensional Reality-membrane in which we are ensconced took place at the Philadelphia Naval Shipyards. This alleged incident is known as the Philadelphia Experiment/Project Rainbow. Within the context of the ongoing war, the U.S. Navy was experimenting with various applications of Einstein's Unified Field Theory which postulates the interrelated nature of the "forces" known as gravity, strong, weak, and electromagnetic, in an attempt to find a way to render objects invisible. Invisibility would obviously be a great advantage during wartime for an object like a naval destroyer.

In preparation for this experiment the internal confines of the Naval destroyer USS Eldridge were gutted in order to accommodate four immense generators along with Tesla coils, electron tubes, and miles of inch thick cable that was laid throughout the ship's runways. Previous experiments in which caged animals were "arced" with various materials proved reasonably safe and successful. The objective seems to have been to render a fully manned destroyer invisible to the naked eye by bending or refracting light around it, a rather simple application of a complex theory, so it seemed. On the fateful day the USS Eldridge along with the crew stood ready for the "experiment".

The results are legendary. The reason the word "legendary" is applicable is because both the U.S. Navy and Government deny that such an experiment ever took place – but on the other hand, what would be the point of making up such a convoluted story? It is alleged that on October 28th, 1943 when the four massive generators aboard the USS Eldridge were turned on, the Navy's primary objective was successfully attained. The USS Eldridge became almost completely invisible to the eyes of the naval observers who were aboard an adjacent ship. There was great joy for a moment. Suddenly there was a flash of blue light and in an instant the nearly invisible ship dematerialized and vanished. Poof! Gonzo.

Where did it go? This is where the misunderstood aspects of time-space, as a factor, become evident. The entire ship was "teleported", so they thought, and re-materialized 375 miles (600 km.) away off-shore in Norfolk, Virginia. From there it vanished once again to re-appear back in the naval shipyard in Philadelphia, Pennsylvania! Someone on board had turned off the generators and the amazed experimenters were able to board the destroyer to assess the outcomes. They were horrified.

What did they find? Some of the crew had completely vanished never to be accounted for. Where are they? At least five (the number varies) were "fused" to the deck or bulkhead! Many crew members kept fading in and out of sight until they were touched by an observer, which seemed to ground them. All were in severe mental shock or deranged. Perhaps some panicked crew member had prematurely shut off the generators without giving them time to gradually wind down with the resulting incomplete return to the "here and now". The Philadelphia Experiment/Project Rainbow was immediately terminated, and under the guise of wartime security everything was labeled "top secret". If Project Rainbow actually happened, then there is a great deal for which some individuals or groups could be held responsible and accountable. But at that time back in 1943 few people were aware that a scant year and a half earlier the same combination of Navy and Government had secretly implemented, and covered up, an "eight-action plan" of deliberate provocation and deceit that on December 7th, 1941 propelled an isolationist America into the Second World War. Pearl Harbor was not a "surprise"; it was in fact an infamous "Day of Deceit" (as Robert B. Stinnett revealed over fifty years later, after gaining access to long "classified documents" via the Freedom of Information Act, in his definitive book by that title). In the light of the previous cover-up and deliberate distortion of the truth by the Navy and Government, is the official story offered by the Navy and Government regarding the Philadelphia Experiment credible?

Later theorists claim that what happened during the alleged experiment was that time, which exists in curved space, was electromagnetically warped and curved around to form a temporary "wormhole" through space-time. The "wormhole" momentarily connected Norfolk where the ship had been previous stationed, to Philadelphia where it presently was. There are plenty of amazing theories regarding the incredible qualities of time as it interrelates with all the known "forces".

We really do not know what time per se is, but common sense and reason indicate that time is a relative matter interconnected and inseparable from space. It can only endure in the presence of an Existent-essence (e.g. a Soul) living in the "here and now" who experiences the duration (in Physics this is known as the perceiver-effect). The ongoing fusion of the time-bound concepts of Future and Past creates the Present. When the Future and Past fuse, a "reality" is created that illuminates the Past and the Future in the light of the Present. In the course of our daily lives we are not aware of the micro-second when the Future becomes the Past, because it is in the light of that ongoing fusion that we exist.

The Past only makes sense as it curves back or relates to the Present, and can only be recalled in the Present. In other words, the Past, however far back it may be projected, can only have relevance, meaning, and significance as it is remembered in the Present by an Existent-essence.

The Future, likewise, only makes sense as it relates to the Present. For example, tomorrow can only come-to-pass in today. No matter how far into the Future we project it can only have significance, meaning, and relevance as it curves back and is experienced in the Present by an Existent-essence. In short, in the Present, we are always living the Future and creating the Past.

This explanation implies that space-time is not lineal or cubical – it is curved or spherical. This conception allows for the back and forth movement of time commensurate with the concept of "wormholes" that connect past with future dimensions and vice versa. The essence of time is duration through space which enables the existence of "mortality". This is a stupendously non-scientific notion, because mortality is not a scientific matter – yet it is fundamental to the reality of space-time and the existence of anything or anyone within that dimension. Meaningful concepts like Past, Present, and Future only make sense in the here and now relative to an enduring or time-bound Existent-essence (i.e. Soul).

Let us take a moment of eternity to further consider this spherical model by proposing a crude but concrete analogy that can be visualized by the mind's eye. Suppose the sphere was something like a gigantic ball of infinitely elastic string. The elastic string begins at the center of the ball, at a volume-less zero-point (Soul) from which the elastic (time) is stretched resulting in a vector of direction. The instant the elastic is attached to the zero-point, "immortality" is circumscribed as "mortality". Each loop (dimension) represents the "perceiver-affected" space through which time has traveled. In order to create a sphere or ball each successive dimensional loop must travel in a slightly different direction resulting in a slightly different dimension of space-time. As the ball grows each successive layer of loops (which could be traveling in the same direction as previous layers of loops), is differentiated by being at a higher level i.e. further from the center, representing a greater/expanded dimension of awareness. The ball can keep on growing indefinitely loop by loop and layer by layer as the elastic is looped or wound around the ball.

Since this model is very abstract and exceedingly difficult to conceptualize it is broken down here into seven simple points.

(1) The Zero-point

This is a volume-less, and therefore infinitely elastic or expandable, center, that due to its paradoxical nature of being-and-nothingness, exists theoretically (as a definable concept in this model) as the self-descriptive *Zero-point*.

(2) Extension

As soon as the Zero-point is extended it is changed or transformed. Zero is no longer a point. It is an extended point or a vector of direction. This extension transforms the Zero-point from Zero into One (vector of direction).

(3) The One

The One (vector of direction) is the Zero-point extended. Extension changes the zero-ness of the point into a direction which endures. This duration transforms the vector of direction into a dimension of space and time. Within this space-time continuum the One becomes transformed into a space-time dependent "I".

(4) The "I"

Being space-time dependent makes the "I" mortal, relative to the One. For every directional loop there is a commensurate "I". The number of loops relative to the One (Zero-point) are infinite. Each loop is an extension of the Zero-point. This is an example of the paradox of the One and the Many.

(5) Loops

Since the loops are directions, the infinitely elastic Zero-point can be stretched into an infinitude of directional loops layer upon (karmic) layer. The loops are continuous; there is no end point. The finitude of the space-time continuum simulates beginnings and ends (mortality). Each loop is a microcosm of the macrocosm represented by the Zero-point.

(6) Rationality

This is only an attempt to conceptualize the inconceivable. It may help to say that this model operates according to the first law of thermodynamics that states that matter cannot be created or destroyed, only transformed and changed, and the third law of motion which points out that for every action there is an equal and opposite reaction (e.g. the expanding and contracting universe).

(7) Compatibility

This model is compatible with the Vedic concept of Akasha, the religious/spiritual idea of Cosmic Consciousness, the scientific notion of a Universal Mind, and most modern theories regarding the known universe.

One of the advantages of this model is the connectivity of the "string" of time; it can be followed backwards and forwards.

Through "wormholes" the various layers can be penetrated and instantly one or a million layers can be visited from any "here and now". Something like this could have happened accidentally during the Philadelphia Experiment.

In microcosm, the elastic ball of string is metaphorically analogous to the karmic evolution of a Soul through various dimensions as it grows in awareness. In macrocosm, the elastic ball represents the expanding universe. From the point of view of the here and now, the macrocosm is a projection of the microcosm by an Existent-essence. In an elastic ball of string, that's "reality".

"What do you think?"

"I'm not sure if the average reader will get it. It seems kind of radical and far-out in places," Penny replied. "Perhaps we could have been a little less…"

"Our objective is to be as clear and forthright as possible," Larry interjected.

"We have re-written it four times. Do you think we could simplify it any further?" Penny asked wrinkling up her nose.

"Sometimes you encounter topics that are just plain far-out. That is what makes them intriguing."

"In a Handbook on Life it is important that we do our best to tell it like it is, far-out or not – even if it makes us look like a couple of a-ah…"

"Loose cannons on the deck of the Titanic!" Larry chimed in with a laugh.

"Your self-deprecating sense of humor is timely. It keeps our vanity from overstepping the acceptable boundaries of egotistical self-aggrandizement known as bragging."

"Well spoken. We need to proceed with due humility."

"And yet we must be cautiously confident. We need to have faith in ourselves and in the readers."

"Although what we have written may not be simple, it is direct and to the point."

"I don't think we need to change our tune."

"We just need to stay tuned."

CHAPTER SEVEN

While she was sitting out in the flower garden by the purple and yellow pansies Penny felt the lyrics and tune ease into her mind like sunshine through a wispy cloud. It filled her with a creative glow. The song was entitled "Charlie Wenjack", and it was based upon a true account of the death of a young First Nations boy she had read about. The boy had been forced to attend a parochial institution called Cecelia Jeffery School two hundred miles south by rail from his home, where he was treated like a pawn of the government, and a pagan in dire need of indoctrination and redemption. One cold miserable fall day Charlie ran away. He began following the railway tracks back north to a weather-beaten little shack located on a barren and destitute Indian reservation. He called it "home". Several days later Charlie was found curled up alongside the tracks, frozen to death. The tragic story resonated empathetically with Penny's social conscience and provided the psychic vibe that momentarily connected her with the lad who preceded her down the pathway that led to the true north strong and free. The song turned out to be one of her favorites.

> Charlie Wenjack was his name
> To Cecilia Jeffery School he came
> To share in this democracy
> His heritage with you and me.
>
> They gave him room and paid his board
> That's all this country could afford
> So Charlie sat alone in school
> And played the pawn and looked the fool.
>
> (Refrain)
> O Canada so proud and free
> Thy Native People call to thee
> Take away this misery
> And let them live in dignity.
>
> The light was dim the sky was grey
> The morn when Charlie ran away

And those who stopped to wonder why
Could hear poor Charlie Wenjack cry.
(Refrain)

With hunger a pounding on his brain
He walked through mud and snow in vain
His shirt soaked through with frozen rain
And his soul transfixed with mortal pain.

The night was blowing dark and cold
Around a lad with grief grown old
Beside the railway tracks he lay
And there his spirit passed away.
(Refrain)

(Repeat first verse and end by adding...)
To share in this 'great democracy'
His heritage with you and me.

Writing songs and giving birth was the closest Penny came to feeling like a Creator. There was something about creating new songs out of the vastness of unlimited potentiality that was very satisfying. It was a marvelous feeling to be able to create something tangible out of the intangible, something that was meaningful and poignant out of chaos. Something personal that justified one's existence. All of Penny's songs justified her existence in a similar but microcosmic manner as Creation justifies the existence of the Creator.

Playing her own songs brought Penny a certain amount of acclaim amongst the small circle of privileged friends before whom she performed on rare occasions. Although she had written dozens of songs she only played a few of them in the presence of others. She was actually very shy about playing in public.

The first time Larry heard Penny sing and play her guitar was when they were both grad students at the University of Oregon. Penny was sitting under a sprawling oak tree with her back against the trunk singing and strumming her Yamaha guitar. He had quietly walked up from the opposite direction and had plunked himself down with his back against the hidden side of the tree. He sat there and listened. It was as if he was part of a vast universal audience for whom she was playing. He felt very privileged.

The music seemed to flow out of her soul. It was soul music. Sometimes it was upbeat, fast and joyful, and at other times slow and mournful. It was just Penny being one with her music. Was it the singer or the song? It was both. Larry closed his eyes and listened with both ears. The music swept over him and nuzzled his soul.

After a while Penny became self-conscious. She looked around and although she did not see anyone she sang is a softer voice. She missed a few chords and struggled with the lyrics. Something made her feel uncomfortable. Finally she got up and walked around the tree, and there he was!

"Larry!" she exclaimed.

Larry twitched and opened his eyes. "Hi Pen," he replied.

"How long have you been here?"

"Maybe thirty-forty minutes. I kinda dozed off. I dreamed I heard an angel singing and it was so wonderful I thought I might have died and gone to heaven."

"You joker!" Penny retorted feeling infinitely flattered.

"One of the best concerts I have ever heard," Larry continued. "I had no idea you could sing so beautifully."

"I try."

"I really liked the songs. I have not heard any of them before."

"I'm glad you liked them."

"Do you know who wrote them?"

"Yes."

"Someone I know?"

"Yes."

"Who?"

"Guess."

"Hank Williams Senior?"

"Close, but no cigar."

"Hmmm… how about Hank Williams Junior?" Larry teased.

"I wrote them."

"You wrote them!"

"Yes."

"What are you doing here? You should be out on tour. That's good stuff."

"I have no stage presence. I'm too shy. If I had known you were listening, I would have choked up."

"Practice on me. I'll be the audience. It seems like a real shame to blossom unnoticed in the dark."

Penny took Larry at his word, and practiced some of her songs in his presence. He was very patient and flattering. "You've written some very good songs," he would say, "You just need a little more work on your stage presence."

After a month of practice and encouragement from Larry, Penny lost some of her shyness and performed once in a while in the presence of friends. They were all in agreement with Larry: it would indeed be a shame to see such a talent bloom unnoticed in the dark She would not do it herself, so they volunteered her for a solo performance at the Student Building on November 11th.

"You can do it, Penny," they all concurred. "You have written a beautiful song. It is perfect for the occasion."

So on November 11th Penny summoned up her courage and courageously walked up the front steps of the Student Building carrying her battered old Yamaha guitar in a tattered old black guitar case. She walked confidently in through the magnificent double glass doors and into the lounge. Larry and a small cluster of her friends were sitting there amongst a sizeable crowd of students, faculty members, and patriots who had gathered there for the occasion. A feeble old man with a white beard, handlebar moustache, and wire spectacles complimented by a chest full of important looking medals, shuffled up to the mike and spoke in a gravelly voice:

"Penelope Miki will honor us with a composition she has written for this occasion. She will now perform her song entitled 'Remembrance Day'." The announcer shuffled back to his chair and sat down.

It was too late to chicken out. The die was cast. The moment had arrived.

Penelope Miki carried her black guitar case to the stage. It suddenly weighed a ton. She plunked it down and fumbled with the latches. Snap, snap, snap, they opened. She pulled the cover back and extracted her marvelous old Yamaha. It greeted her like a friend. She strummed a friendly chord: a G-chord. The Yamaha resonated with vibes that said, "I'm ready – how about you?" Penny gazed out

over the expectant audience. She drew in a deep breath, closed her
eyes and imagined she was alone with her universal audience. Her
fingers caressed the strings and her voice resonated throughout the
universe like that of an angel.

> "I remember the day you went away
> You didn't know that I had meant to say
> When the world feels cold and cruel
> Well I'll be there for you
> When the world feels so cold and cruel
> Then I'll be there... for you.
>
> In this world of shadow and of light
> Who knows what's wrong or what is right
> When you're feeling lonely and confused
> Well I'll be there for you
> When you're feeling so lonely and confused
> Then I'll be there... for you.
>
> When sunny days have turned to gray
> And all your friends have moved away
> And you're feeling forlorn and blue
> Well I'll be there for you
> When you're feeling so forlorn and blue
> Then I'll be there... for you.
>
> Where the river flows beyond the bend
> And you search to see where it will end
> Like the ocean hidden from your view
> Well I'll be there for you
> Like the ocean hidden from your view
> I will be there... for you.
>
> I remember the day you went away
> You didn't know that I had knelt to pray
> And the world felt cold and cruel
> But I was there for you
> All the world felt so cold and cruel
> But I was there... for you
> Yes I was there... for you."

Her performance was followed immediately by a one minute silence; all that could be heard was the sound of one-hand-clapping. It was a solemn occasion. Afterward a frail gentleman with a cane hobbled up to Penny. His eyes were bleary with age and his hands shook uncontrollably. He looked like a veteran from World War I.

"I'd like to shake your hand," he said.

Penny grasped his bony right hand and squeezed it gently.

"Thank you very much," he said, "Now I can tell my friends that I shook the hand of an angel."

PART SIX

MANIFESTATIONS OF RELEVANCE

The way is empty, yet use will not drain it
Deep it is like the ancestors of the myriad creatures
Blunt the sharpness
Untangle the knots
Soften the glare
Let your wheels move only along old ruts.

Lao Tzu

CHAPTER ONE

The world felt cold and cruel as the winter winds penetrated the thin wooden walls of the Jesuit mission in Nagasaki. The brethren all huddled together in the rectangular common room for warmth and shivered at the thought of what might happen to Brother Paul if he took it upon himself to go to Kyoto – in spite of their objections to the contrary. But he was resolute, and fearless.

Paul Miki was not afraid. He was descended from a long line of courageous samurai. How many times had he stared death in the face, and lived? His samurai training served him well in his new role as a Jesuit priest. He knew better than anyone else how Christians were persecuted. This knowledge made him invaluable at the mission. He knew more about persecuting Christians than the persecutors did. In the years since his conversion wherever he traveled persecutors were hard to find. His reputation always preceded him. It kept him safe like a guardian angel.

But over time things change. People age, memories fade, and reputations wither from lack of sustenance. Thus it came to pass that an older and wiser Paul Miki prepared himself for his fateful journey. He had come a long, long way since leaving the employ of Toyotomi Hideyoshi. It seemed like another life, a bad dream to one who had been re-born as a Christian.

Everyone at the mission advised him not to go. There was a distinct feeling of dread that hung like a dark cloud over the entire building. It was very difficult to voice an optimistic opinion.

"It will be very dangerous," they said. "If you go, your only protection will be our prayers."

"The times have changed for the worst," Paul admitted, "but your prayers will protect me."

"We must consider going underground like the others. We must hide everything. We must operate in total secrecy. We must become Kakure Kirishitan if we are to survive. Yes, indeed, the times have changed for the worst. It is too dangerous for you to go. Please, we beg you; please stay here where it is still safe."

Paul knew they were probably right. But sometimes there are things that just have to be done. So you do them.

In the morning the sun rose with such solemnity that even the birds refused to sing. It was the morning that Paul Miki rose at first light and donned his worn black Jesuit's robe with a pride and purpose that made every movement poignantly significant. The robe never felt so comfortable and so right. It identified him for who he was: a Jesuit priest.

When news of the captive twenty-five reached him in Nagasaki, he was devastated. How could Toyotomi Hideyoshi turn on them like that? There had to be a good reason. He was after all a reasonable man, and in truth, had been a decent person to work for. He had a certain degree of integrity that few shoguns who had ascended to his position of power and eminence were able to maintain. It seemed out of character for him to engage in something that was usually left to his underlings to pursue at arm's length so as not to contaminate his reputation. But twenty-five at once, at his palace! That was unheard of. It had never happened before as far as Paul knew, and he knew precisely how it used to be. Was he not the very one who as a young man had proudly accepted the grand title of "Inquisitor"? Had he not at one time mercilessly persecuted Christians?

But this was different. He could sense it. Something had changed quite dramatically. All twenty-five had been bound hand and foot and thrown into the guardhouse where they had been practically left to starve for the past few weeks. He knew the routine. They would be asked to recant. He had done it so many times in the past. He shivered and shook his head. It was too much. He had to let it go. The past was the past, and this was now.

They would never recant. He knew it. Two of them were his Jesuit lay brothers, the resolute Spaniard John Goto, and the pious Korean immigrant, James Kisai. The rest were compassionate Franciscan brethren: six timid brown-robed Spanish Friars, and seventeen shy Japanese lay converts. What was Toyotomi doing arresting seventeen innocent Japanese lay converts? Surely he was not that desperate!

"I must find out what is going on," Paul Miki stated resolutely to himself. "There must be some mistake. Twenty-five at once, and Jesuits and Franciscans mixed together. Far too conspicuous!" Even though the Franciscans competed with the Jesuits for converts, he considered them kindred spirits. It was up to him. He was the only one who stood a chance. He was the only one who was personally acquainted with the most powerful Lord in all Japan and to whom an audience would be granted. He was the only one who could possibly make a difference.

One more journey. Just one more. He had made so many over the years. His missionary zeal had taken him far afield. On the southern island of Kyushu he had concentrated most of his missionary work on specific hot beds of conversion: Kagoshima, where the Teacher-with-the-big-nose had come ashore, Nagasaki, the Christian stronghold, Fukuoka and Kita-Kyushu. On the main island of Honshu he had made major missionary efforts all the way from Hiroshima, Kyoto, and Osaka in the southern region, to Edo in the center, and Moioka and Aomosi in the north.

On the northern-most island of Hokkaido where his hairy ancestors still resided and insisted upon practicing their own primitive pagan rites, Paul did not waste much time preaching. Rather, he passed through the homeland of his grandfather, the famous swordsmith, and great-grandfather, the Katan Korakura of Tomakomai, with mute pride. Occasionally his former reputation as a great swordsman would precede him, and someone would whisper with awestruck admiration: "There is the fellow who dispatched six villainous ronin with a single stroke of his katana." The number of ronin dispatched had grown from three to six. The people seemed to need a legendary hero, a super being who represented a force for justice and honor. Sometimes it was a hindrance, but most of the time his reputation guaranteed him a sizable audience of potential converts. Who would not be intrigued by the charismatic personality of a Jesuit Samurai?

All in all, his missionary efforts were well rewarded. He had personally brought in so many converts he had lost count. Ten years ago it had been estimated that there were over two hundred thousand Christian converts, and now? Who knew? It was miraculous. "Too many, too quickly, too easy," Paul thought. It was so easy to get them to switch allegiance from one Lord to another. The earthly Lord offered them a hopeless life of drudgery and serfdom, while the otherworldly Lord offered them hope and everlasting life. In some ways he could understand why Toyotomi would be concerned.

"Perhaps it was a misunderstanding regarding the use and meaning of the word Lord?" Paul cogitated while preparing a frugal supply of food for the journey ahead. "Like Jesus had once explained: 'Render unto Caesar the things that are Caesar's, and unto God, the things that are God's'. It was a clear and simple distinction. Surely Toyotomi would understand. After all he was a reasonable man, a considerate man, an honorable man," he thought.

The sun was beginning to warm up the crisp morning air when Paul Miki set out for Kyoto on November twenty-sixth, 1596, to see his former employer, the great Lord Toyotomi Hideyoshi. The birds had begun to chirp and a slight breeze blew in from the omnipresent waters of the sea. It felt like a good day to be going forth on a mission of hope.

* * *

Fluffy, white, cumulous clouds floated like misty omens of hope in the light-blue sky above Paul Miki's head. Road dust caked his ankles like grey chalk and the bottom of his black robe was tattered and stringy. It had been a long and tedious journey, but at last he stood before the magnificent double gated entry to the fortified palace. He was allowed to enter the guarded gates unimpeded, as he recognized the head gatekeeper, a former persecutor of Christians like himself who had become disillusioned with the inhumanity of the repression and had settled for something less provocative.

"Ah, Mikisan," the gatekeeper said upon recognizing Tsutomu. "What brings you to the Lord's headquarters?"

"I come to beg his mercy on behalf of the twenty-five Christian brethren he has imprisoned."

The gatekeeper left his post and sidled up to his former comrade in persecution. "Do not risk your life on such an impossible mission," he said solemnly. "Things are very different now. Take this as a friendly warning. Leave now!" He lowered his voice and looked around, "Leave quickly before the Chief Attendant sees you. He is a most inconsiderate tyrant." The gatekeeper pushed Paul toward the gate with an anxious glance backward. "Go, Tsutomu. As a former comrade I implore you to leave at once. If I am asked who was at the gate, I will say it was just some old monk looking for a handout that I sent away."

"I am known as Paul Miki now," Paul quietly informed the gatekeeper. "I must see Toyotomi Hideyoshi. I will not leave until I see him," he added resolutely.

The gatekeeper stared into Mikisan's eyes. They were deadly earnest. "You are as foolhardy as they say you are!" he expostulated and returned to his post. "Go ahead," he waved Paul through, "it's your life."

Once inside the ornately-carved wooden gate, Paul found himself within the familiar courtyard of the Great Lord. It was comprised of a large square open area where horses and samurai could be mustered, surrounded on four sides with wooden structures. On the eastern side fronted by a wide wooden walkway bustling with busy workers and artisans, the main residence rose with a magnificent curved roof set upon great wooden posts. It was just as it had been when he was a prominent samurai in Toyotomi's employ; very little had changed except that there was now a Chief Attendant with an entourage who sat prominently on the veranda puffed up with self-importance.

Paul calmly walked over and stood directly in front of the Chief Attendant and his cohorts. He felt awkward standing there alone, conspicuous in his tattered black Jesuit's robe.

Tojo, the Chief Attendant, rose slowly from a long wooden bench. His right hand rested upon the flashy handle of his great katana. "Who are you?" he demanded.

"I am known as Paul Miki."

"I have heard of you. You are that traitor who brings dishonor to all who call themselves Samurai." Tojo spat disdainfully in the dirt narrowly missing Paul's dusty sandals.

"I am what I am."

"What brings you here?"

"I have walked all the way from the Jesuit mission in Nagasaki to plead for the lives of the twenty-five Christian brethren you have imprisoned. I humbly ask permission to speak to my former employer, the Great Lord, Toyotomi Hideyoshi."

A look of scorn seared across Tojo's face. He gazed down at the travel-weary priest who stood humbly before him with bowed head. With a raspy snarl he cleared his throat and vehemently spat out a gob that caught the edge of the verandah and sprayed over the bottom edge of Paul's frayed black robe. "Why waste his time?" he asked rhetorically.

His cohorts surged forward anticipating Tojo's response to his own question.

"Search him for weapons, and then throw him in with his brothers where he belongs," he ordered.

Who knows how long Paul Miki would have languished in the guardhouse along with his twenty-five brethren if the gatekeeper had not sent a secret message to the Great Lord informing him that Tsutomu Miki had entered the gates? Perhaps the outcome would have been much different if he had not sent that note. But the secret message was sent, and when Toyotomi received it he immediately sent for the gatekeeper.

"Someone sent this message to me." He showed the gatekeeper the note. "Do you recall when Mikisan passed through the gates?"

"About five days ago," the gatekeeper replied.

"Why did you not inform me?"

"I noticed that the Chief Attendant apprehended him. I thought he would inform you."

"If it was not for this note I would not have known he was here."

"Someone has done you a favor."

Almost a week went by during which the twenty-six prisoners survived on faith and a few handfuls of brown rice gruel washed down with cold miso soup. It was enough to keep them alive and their spirits up. And then to Paul's surprise, one day Tojo showed up looking very reserved and chastened.

"The Lord wishes to speak to you," Tojo stated matter-of-factly. "He wishes to speak to a samurai – not a filthy beggar or priest." Tojo led Paul to a large bath-house where he was allowed to scrub himself thoroughly in a shallow wash area before sinking leisurely into the soothing hot water of a steaming ofurru.

When he dried off and returned to the dressing area, Paul found a fresh new samurai's outfit neatly laid out on an adjacent bench. He dressed slowly and carefully so as not to look sloppy or offensive to the Great Lord. The only thing missing from his imperious-looking outfit was the daisho. "Without swords a samurai feels naked," Paul thought to himself as he strode majestically about the room listening to the smooth silk whisper against his skin. It had been a long time since he had worn such wonderful garments.

"Are you ready?" Tojo called from the doorway.

"Yes."

Tojo and an entourage of six courtiers escorted Paul, like an honored guest, to the great hall in the main house.

"I wonder what Toyotomi is up to?" Paul wondered as they strode along. He felt conspicuous and uncomfortable being the center of so much attention.

When they reached the entrance to the great hall the entourage stopped and Tojo announced to all within: "Your Lordship, the great samurai, Tsutomu Miki, is here at your request.

Paul Miki was ushered in to the center of the great hall. The side walls were lined with smartly dressed samurai and at the front, sitting cross-legged upon intricately woven tatami mats, was Toyotomi Hideyoshi flanked by his trusted advisors.

All eyes were riveted upon Paul. He felt like some rare commodity on display. The beginnings of a nervous twitch trembled just below his left eye. He hoped no one could see it. The quiver became incessant and he thought his eye might start blinking involuntarily. He ignored it and drew in a deep breath while organizing his thoughts.

"Great Lord Toyotomi Hideyoshi," he began formally, and prostrated himself before the man sitting calmly upon the tatami mats like a living Buddha. "I am so grateful that you have consented to receive me."

"You fool!" Toyotomi retorted. "You were once a great samurai – and now, what have you become? A traitor, a Kirishitan!"

Paul remained silent, shocked by the vehemence of the accusation.

"I consider myself to be as tolerant as anyone else," Toyotomi continued in a somewhat conciliatory tone. "A person should be allowed to practice any religious faith he chooses so long as it is not subversive. I have it on the authority of a very trustworthy Spanish sea captain that it is the function, intentional or not, of the Christian missionaries to insidiously undermine the authority of our social and political system in order that the Portuguese and Spanish can later dominate Japan as they have done elsewhere."

"I have not heard of this before," Paul admitted, dumfounded.

"At first I was skeptical. Of course I was stunned by such an arrogant assertion, by a hakujin of all people. So I challenged him to show my scholastic advisors examples of what he was referring to. And guess what?"

"He was mistaken?" Paul offered hopefully.

"In every single case throughout the entire world where Portuguese or Spanish missionaries have managed to convert the pagans, it has been to the detriment of the host country. In every single instance! My advisors informed me that it appears that the captain could be right. He had little to gain and much to lose by sharing this information with me. He claimed it was his love for the Islands of the Dolls, as he put it. Sometimes there are individuals with great integrity, even hakujins! How do you feel about this?"

'It is very disconcerting."

"The thought of such deception infuriates me, especially when I have attempted to be so understanding and generous toward them. But this subversiveness I cannot tolerate. It is my duty to condemn such atrocious behavior by foreigners in our sacred homeland."

"The Jesuits and Franciscans are certainly not subversive. It is hard to believe that people with such good intentions could be party to such callous political machinations," Paul ventured with a frown of uncertainty. All his premeditated arguments vanished into the space between Toyotomi and himself, filling it with an air of nervous anticipation.

"Hah, easy for you to say," Toyotomi challenged. "You are not responsible for the consequences if he is correct. What if he is correct, then what?"

"You must have faith."

"The astute Spanish captain was cognizant of what I did not see at first. He explained how exclusive Christianity really is, how it claims all divine authority entirely to itself. Entirely. Whatever legitimate authorities that exist that are not subservient are condemned outright as being evil. Have any of the so-called pagan cultures ever flourished under Christian domination?"

"I do not know of any."

"According to the Spanish captain, who has had personal experience with the Spanish Conquistadors and the Roman Catholic Church in other parts of the world, it is the most ruthless and intolerant of any of the religions he has encountered. From his point of view its narrow-mindedness is second to none and its righteousness is insufferable. Who could, in good faith, support such a religion and call themselves Japanese? I ask you, Mikisan, in good faith, to re-evaluate your religious beliefs in the light of this information."

"I am what I am," Mikisan replied calmly. "I am not a traitor. I simply choose to serve another Lord, a Lord who is not of this world and who wishes no ill will against you."

"It is not what your Lord and Savior teaches that concerns me. It is what the Christians will do! If the Spanish captain is correct Christianity is an unrelenting religious force as well as a powerful social and political influence which insidiously undermines and eventually dominates whatever pagan culture it encounters."

Paul Miki was at a loss for words. The saliva dried up in his mouth and tiny beads of sweat began to moisten his forehead. The Great Lord was being so patient and understanding. So reasonable! What could he say? Perhaps the most honorable thing he could do was to simply recant. It would be so easy. He struggled to find the right words.

Toyotomi gazed compassionately at one of the most courageous samurai who had ever served under his banner. He could see the indecision etched upon Mikisan's noble countenance. He sweetened his tone, "I am prepared to give you back everything, to restore you to your former greatness as a samurai in my service, and because of your intelligence and wisdom, make you one of my trusted personal advisors," he hesitated as if overwhelmed by his own unexpected outburst of generosity.

Paul Miki remained silent, his dark eyes glued upon Toyotomi.

"You are a man of unusual courage and honor," Toyotomi resumed, "as noble a man as I have ever known. That is why I make you, Tsutomu Miki, this exclusive offer. Simply recant, and the lives of your twenty-five comrades will be spared along with your own, and everything will be restored to you."

The light of reason grew dim within the cavernous shadows of dogmatic faith that protected Paul Miki like a host of guardian angels. His eyes became depthless pools of unmitigated sorrow. He swallowed hard to moisten his throat. "I-I am very flattered, my Great Lord, very, very flattered," he whispered humbly, conscious that his voice was barely audible in the great hall, "but..." he paused to draw in a much needed breath, "but I am deeply sorry I-I cannot recant what it is that I am."

Not a sound was heard. All eyes were focused upon the Great One who sat like a statue in stony silence with furrowed brow. After a prolonged silence he heaved a heavy sigh as if burdened by the crushing weight of an unavoidable responsibility. "I appreciate your sentiment," he began thoughtfully. "You are a Christian who is concerned about saving your own soul – while I am a Lord who is concerned about the divine soul of a nation comprised of many people. To me the people are everything. I am nothing without them. As you know, without the shogunate-domain system there would be chaos. What I do, I do for the divine good of the people. Do you understand what I am saying?"

Paul Miki nodded. "I understand, Great Lord," he acknowledged.

"People call me 'Great Lord' out of respect for my position, but in my own mind I am not that important, not that vain, not that righteous. I do not ask you to do what I would not do myself," he paused and looked beseechingly at Mikisan. "I urge you, for the good of your comrades and the good of the nation, to reconsider."

It was truly a magnanimous thing to say. What more could be asked? Never had such consideration been shown to a single individual within those walls. Who deserved such generosity, such a humble display of patience and understanding? In that moment in the minds and hearts of all the dedicated samurai present, Toyotomi Hideyoshi rose to the greatest heights of esteem he would ever achieve. What human being had ever before demonstrated such magnanimity? Such statesmanship? The great hall was deathly quiet. Every breath was held. Every ear was perked.

It was the common sense, the reasonableness of what was being asked regardless of who was asking it, that penetrated into Paul Miki's intellect and flooded it with a dizzying sensation of confusion and doubt. The doubt clogged his arteries and caused his heart to palpitate as if it was about to seize up. He felt nauseous, breathless and faint, and yet as if in self-preservation, a breath wheezed up from deep within, passed over his vocal chords, and issued from his lips with an audible sound.

Paul Miki's voice sounded strangely distant and impersonal. The vocal sounds that issued from his throat were semantically modulated into linguistic manifestations of auditory relevance, amplified by a dogmatic faith. That faith presented him with a righteous rationalization that had justified the mortal actions of many an immortal soul down through the ages with a single question: *"What good is it to gain the whole world, but lose your own soul?"*

All breaths exhaled. No one dared to inhale, until the Great Lord spoke.

"Have you not done enough penance?" Toyotomi asked sympathetically, his regal countenance devastated by an emotional surge of disappointment.

He waited solemnly for a reply and hearing none, shook his head sadly. With that motion magnanimity turned to chagrin. The Great One slowly rose to his feet and looked imperiously down upon Paul Miki as if he were a stranger.

"Make an example of them all," he said coldly, and as he turned away he added, "Let their dreams be fulfilled... crucify them."

CHAPTER TWO

A long, winding, indirect route was chosen for the journey from Kyoto to Nagasaki. Each of the twenty-six condemned Christians was assigned to a guardian samurai who walked alongside his charge. The procession made quite a spectacle as it wound its way through a myriad of little towns and villages that were scattered along the way. It was an example to all who came to watch. Twenty-six condemned, bedraggled Christian scapegoats forlornly trudging side by side with twenty-six proud, imperious-looking samurai clad in the regal colors of the Lord Regent, Toyotomi Hideyoshi. The contrast told the whole story.

It took many days to complete the arduous journey. Weeks of being displayed like ohni, or dreadful demons, who were being dispatched because they were considered to be imbued with evil foreign spirits, bad omens, very bad omens for one's health and well being. It did not help that some of the twenty-six condemned were hakujins with strange colored hair, anemic looking skin, large protruding noses, and bulging round eyes that bugged out of their heads. They looked just like ohni! They were scary. Little children hid fearfully behind their mothers' long flowing kimonos for protection, while their parents, unable to curb their curiosity, stared with fascination.

Each day of the march was one day closer to the moment of death. For the twenty-six condemned, each day was a glorious day of life, a day to be exalted in the name of their Lord and Savior, Jesus Christ. They trudged along stoically like sheep being led to slaughter singing the Te Deum and praising the Lord. It was a parade like none ever witnessed before. It seemed more like a religious celebration than a funeral procession.

On the seventh day of the last week, the fatigued, trail-worn procession straggled into Nagasaki and rested at the foot of Nishizaka Hill. A group of women dressed in black garments with black shawls over their heads busily prepared their last supper. The samurai guardians lined up and were served first. They each respectfully accepted a large bowl of expensive washed white rice heaped with an ample serving of steamed sea bass mixed with an assortment of green vegetables, and a cup of green tea. After being served, they hunkered down and ravenously devoured their sumptuous meal, while the condemned watched with hungry eyes.

When all the samurai had eaten their fill, the twenty-six starving Christians were herded together and told to line up in single file. To their surprise each Christian was served the same sumptuous meal accompanied by a sincere display of reverence and respect. At the conclusion of the meal each of the condemned was presented with a small tumbler of sake. The latter was purchased out of their own earnings by the samurai. It was the honorable thing to do.

The next day as the sun rose a pale amber, the color of ripening peaches, over the eastern horizon, the twenty-six condemned were mustered forth and respectively burdened with the symbol of their faith: a roughly hewn wooden cross. It was the task of each of the condemned to pick up a wooden crucifix and drag it up to the top of Nishizaka Hill. One by one each of the Christians stooped, and with the assistance of the samurai, draped the cross-end of the crucifix across their shoulders with the pole-end dragging in the dirt.

There was something surreal about what was taking place, the way the sunlight hit the hill casting long shadows from a distant past. The moment seemed oddly retrospective, as if it had been enacted somewhere once before... to someone else. And now, it was happening again.

The roughly hewn timber inclined awkwardly across Paul Miki's right shoulder as he struggled up the winding path that led to the crest of the hill. Wooden splinters slivered into his shoulder tearing the sheer fabric of his black robe and scouring the tender flesh on his back until it was raw with blood. It was such a fabulous relief when he reached the summit and dropped his heavy burden that he muttered, "Thank you, God." And then after only a minute's rest, he went back down, back down to the bottom to assist a weaker brother struggling with all his might to inch his way upward. He picked up the dragging end of his brethren's crucifix and together they slowly made their way toward the top.

About halfway up they came across a most bizarre but heart-warming sight. Several samurai were helping their charges to carry their heavy burdens up the steep incline. They grunted and sweated but not a word was spoken. Everyone knew what was happening. The courageous were not afraid or ashamed to reveal their compassion. There was a *Great Samurai* in their midst, and they knew it. It was a singular opportunity to demonstrate a kind heart and invite good karma by being of real service to a fellow human being in dire need. It did not show on his sweaty countenance, but in his heart Paul Miki felt a twinge of pride for his fellow samurai. Nothing was said. Nothing needed to be said. They all knew who he was.

When all twenty-six condemned Christians were assembled on the summit of Nishizaka Hill, a Buddhist monk lit an incense burner and began chanting a long dirge, interspersed by mournful intakes of breath accompanied by the clanging of a small brass bowl-shaped gong. Upon the conclusion of this part of the service, two bearded Jesuit priests who had been given special permission to participate, stepped forth and dutifully began administering the last rites and sacraments to each of the condemned. It was done quickly and efficiently while the samurai stood by, waiting to complete their gruesome duties.

One at a time the twenty-six Christians were lashed securely to their respective crosses with chains and iron rings. Amidst grunts and groans the crosses were propped upright, and came down with a jarring thud in narrow holes dug upon the zenith of Nishizaka Hill, where they were on display for all to see.

At the base of the hill a crowd of onlookers, much smaller than had been anticipated for such an occasion, crouched on their knees, their hands draped with prayer beads and their heads bent low with respect. Many of them were Kakure Kirishitan, but it did not matter whether the onlookers were Shintoists or Buddhists, the sentiment was the same. It came from the same source: the human heart and soul. Tears were shed and prayers were uttered on behalf of all concerned. Those who raised their heads were overcome with a reverent sense of awe by what they beheld.

A grand spectacle of twenty-six crucifixes spaced four feet apart fanned across the crest of Nishizaka Hill like a majestic crown of thorns silhouetted against a cherry red sky. It was a scene they would never forget. It was etched upon their memory like a pictograph carved into granite. The date was February 5, 1597.

Upon the completion of their task the samurai squatted down at the foot of the crosses with an uncanny sense of foreboding. The anxiety polluted the atmosphere along with the incense and the dying breaths of the crucified. They wanted to leave but they had to remain until the last of the twenty-six expired. Their orders were to pierce them through the heart with lances after they passed out or fainted. It was the humane thing to do; otherwise they would suffer for days before they expired.

One by one the crucified passed out or fainted and were quickly pierced through the heart, except for Paul Miki. He was in superb condition. His courageous heart beat on defiantly and his lungs drew in breath after breath as if in spite. Hour after hour the impatient samurai kept vigil throughout the tortuous hours of the day, and still the Great Samurai hung on to consciousness with a tenacity rarely if ever seen amongst the mortal.

After the first few hours he became numb to the pain as the iron chains and rings cut off the circulation. To pass the time he prayed, sang, and chanted. Sometimes he grew so faint he seemed on the verge of passing out, but then he would rouse himself by shaking his head vigorously and stare down at the onlookers with a compassionate smile. Sometimes he cried pathetically with a devastating sense of utter hopelessness and despair, a solitary figure crucified upon a cross, stark against the copper sky. What a tragic predicament! What a gruesome end to a mortal lifetime. Where was the beauty and the truth?

It was just a matter of time. Sometimes he wept silent tears of remorse, and sometimes of joy. He seemed to be in the world but not of the world. He was there, just like a person in a dream is there, but where is there? He was up there, up there on the cross, dying for his sins. Some of the samurai fidgeted impatiently with their lances. Someone said, "Let's pierce him through the heart now and put him out of his misery." But someone else replied, "Let him live until he loses consciousness; he cannot last much longer." And so they all huddled around the base of the single cross upon which a human being still drew breath, still struggled feebly to survive as if, as if, there were some purpose in it.

The sun had crept to the zenith illuminating the crest of Nishizaka Hill with a clarity that exposed every nook and cranny to the light of day. The shadow of doubt disappeared revealing a vibrant beauty that resonated in the human heart as a moment of truth. The air was still, quiet, solemn and expectant. It was as if intuitively all twenty-six guardian samurai knew that the moment Paul Miki lost consciousness would also be the moment he passed on. They set their lances aside and gazed up anxiously at the once Great Samurai who now hung pathetically upon a roughly hewn cross that loomed grotesquely against the brilliant sky. It was not an end befitting one who had become a living legend.

Paul Miki gazed somberly down at the samurai with fathomless eyes that were as deep as eternity. Every drop of hatred, every drop of vindictiveness, every drop of inhumanity had drained from them with every tear shed in anguish and remorse. His dry lips quivered and parted.   The samurai instinctively pressed closer with anticipation. A sound resonated from his lips. "I forgive you, my brothers," he whispered hoarsely in a final moment of lucidity. "I know you are only doing your duty as I am doing mine. With all my heart I forgive..." he raised his chin and feebly uttered "you-ooh." Then he smiled beatifically and they could hear his last breath linger and then depart with a wistful sigh like the whoosh of a dying wind.

It was the "you-ooh" followed by that prolonged sigh that pierced into the hearts and minds of the onlookers. To be singled out, to be spoken to directly by a dying man, to hear his final words, to be forgiven – only the truly compassionate could do that. And in the still of the moment when all those present were ready to deify Paul Miki in their minds and hearts, a hush like a white noise fell over the crown of Nishizaka Hill, and unexpectedly a voice filled with the exuberant joy of revelation echoed back as if from a great distance: "*It is not about religion! It is all about love. It is all about freedom. It is all about love and freedom....*"

And then all was silent.

CHAPTER THREE

"**H**e was truly a man of God," Larry thought to himself as he looked up from the book he had been reading entitled, *The Patron of All Missions*. Although he was not a man of God like his own father or like Saint Francis Xavier, he was a good husband, a good father, and above all a good man. He put down the book, and sauntered across the living room to gaze out of the large picture window. The house seemed so quietly empty since the kids had left.

It was so nice to have the kids home on long weekends. Larry would pick them up at the Tsawwassen Ferry terminal and drive them home. They had decided to attend the University of Victoria because most of their friends went there and also because they wanted to get away and be more independent. This made their homecomings all the more special. On such occasions Larry was reminded of his own homecomings when he was a college student. His mother always prepared his favorite meal: roast chicken with stuffing, mashed potatoes and gravy, with lemon pie for dessert. Before the meal his father would say a special grace in which he mentioned how thankful they were for the "gift of life," which Larry represented. It was their way of making him feel special that Larry attempted to recreate with his own children. Although he did not say grace before each meal when the kids returned from UVic, Larry often felt inclined to say a few silent words to himself like, "Thank you for these precious gifts of life."

Even though the kids were actually young adults, Penny pampered them and waited hand and foot on them as if they were invalids. Perhaps that was one of the reasons they both loved to return home on semester breaks and holidays. But the real reason, as Jerry pointed out, was that they were the "Fearsome Foursome". They were a family unit. They had the same outlook, the same intrinsic attitude toward life. Like the legendary Musketeers they were bonded by the silent power of their defiant cry: "All for one and one for all!"

The memories that Penny and Larry cherished the most about those homecomings were those cold winter evenings when the family sat in front of the fireplace and played cards. The competition was always fierce because everyone in the family thought they were winners even if they lost. Once Sherry said, "I learned two very valuable lessons from those games: the art of losing gracefully, and the art of winning with grace."

"Whatever is done gracefully is artistic," Larry clarified.

"Living life gracefully is an art form," Jerry contributed.

"In the end it is the grace that counts," Penny concluded, her radiant smile lighting up the room.

In retrospect, things always seem to make much more sense. The fuzziness wears off with time and the picture becomes more focused. When Penny thought about her children, sometimes a feeling of nostalgia would creep into her heart, nostalgia for her own childhood, a childhood spent just being there and being aware of just being there, surrounded by four boisterous older siblings, yet feeling remotely like an only child. It was not a lonely childhood; it was a quiet childhood, a childhood spent being aware of being aware. As far back as Penny could remember, this awareness of being aware was the modus operandi of her existence. Now as she stood alone at the kitchen sink carefully washing the supper dishes because the darn dishwasher had become plugged and Larry had not gotten around to snaking it out, she reflected upon those singular occasions when she became aware that awareness was everything.

There was a natural incredulity about such awareness. It was like magic. The ordinary became incredible, like standing absent-mindedly at the kitchen sink with soapy hands and being mesmerized by an intricate design engraved artistically upon the handle of a stainless steel spoon. The mundane became amazing. It was hard to explain, but it was something like that.

The first time Penny became amazed by her awareness occurred when she was seven years old. It was a cold winter morning and she had gotten up early to get ready for school. It was still dark outside, so Penny had gone into the kitchen to dress where the light was on and the old coal-burning oven was beginning to warm up. She sat on her own little chair, the one with "Penny" hand-painted on the backrest, and slowly began to get dressed for her second grade class. She stared at the front of the stove, the square plate just in front of where the coal was put in, as she had done umpteen times before – except this time it was not just a square steel plate. It was a marvelously smooth silvery surface with a carefully centered apple-shaped design etched into the hard steel. It had always been there, but she had not noticed it before for what it was: a unique little emblem that drew the eye and made that stove seem warmer and friendlier. It personified the stove and gave it personality. It was a really nice stove and it had been nice all along, but now for the very first time, Penny became aware of its unique presence, just like her own.

That feeling of knowingly being aware never left Penny. It clung to her, just as she had clung to life when her blood ebbed away as she teetered on the brink of being-and-nothingness, clinging to mortality as if it were everything. Was it really everything?

It was this sense of heightened awareness that bolstered Penny's burgeoning curiosity as she matured, a curiosity that was as limitless as the night sky that she stared up at with the comforter pulled up to her chin on cold winter nights when the sky was crystal clear, and her curious mind wandered freely amongst all the stars that made up the horoscopes of destiny.

"Mom? A penny for your thoughts." The kids never tired of using that old cliché even though it mildly irked their mother. Sherry strolled into the kitchen, picked up a dishtowel, and began drying the dishes.

"I've been thinking," Penny began.

"No kidding!" Sherry remarked, "Is there ever a time that you aren't thinking?"

Penny smiled and said, "I've been thinking that a person's childhood is a very precious time."

"I'm fully aware of that," Sherry replied, "after all, I am studying Psychology."

"So you are," Penny responded in an approving manner, aware that her daughter was entering that stage in life where she really believed she knew something.

Whenever the twins left to pursue their respective vocations, the house always seemed so quiet and deserted. "Perhaps it's time to downsize," Penny suggested one evening after the kids had gone.

"Let's wait until we get this handbook completed," Larry replied, "then we'll have more time to look around at alternative life-styles."

"Good thinking," Penny agreed. "What would I do without your good old common sense?"

"Who knows? You have plenty of common sense of your own, but it is nice of you to allow me to put in my twenty-five cents worth now and again without contradicting my input."

"I used to do that a lot when we were younger, didn't I? You were very patient and understanding. I'm sure it was often frustrating for you. To be honest, I really didn't know I was doing it until you pointed it out."

"Like a good wine, you are improving with age."

"Some days I feel my age more than others. I frequently feel this overwhelming fatigue well up inside me, especially early in the morning, and then it passes as the morning wears on. It must be a sign of encroaching old age."

"We're getting older but we still think young," Larry commented. "Working on this handbook has been rejuvenating."

"I had no idea it would be so much fun."

"You know, when we first started out I went along with it just to humor you," Larry confessed. "But once we got started and the ideas began to flow it took on a life of its own. Isn't it amazing how everything just seemed to come together?"

"You have spent a good part of your life 'humoring' me. And in my own way I have done the same for you. That is probably why our life together has been a bundle of laughs, and the Fearsome Foursome have usually had the last laugh on their side. If we could somehow instill some of that compromising spirit into this handbook it would be something."

"Something that would benefit the entire self-righteous world... especially those people in the Middle East whose religious ideals and values leave little or no room for compromise."

"Religion per se is such a sensitive matter to many. It seems to place dogmatic blinders on some people and they cannot see the forest for the trees."

"And yet, they are all human beings just like us. They have a brain, they are intelligent, and they have free will."

"They need to read this handbook!" Penny exclaimed with a laugh.

CHAPTER FOUR

"Surgeons have discovered that patients have experienced out-of-body experiences on the operating table even though all brain activity flat-lines on the monitor indicating that the person is actually *brain dead*!" Penny exclaimed while switching on the computer. "And yet such persons upon being resuscitated are able to recall aspects of the out-of-body experience as if the experience were stored in their memory."

"In what *memory*?" Larry asked, knowing that the answer was on the tip of his wife's tongue.

"Well, if the brain had flat-lined, indicating the absence of all brain activity, the persona who experienced the near death experience must continue to exist in some extra-dimensional or nonmaterial form in which *memory* is still possible."

"Your brain has been working overtime as usual," Larry commented. "Yes, I see the difficulty. If the brain has flat-lined, how is it that such experiences can be *remembered*?"

"Perhaps it is like we intimated in that section on 'Speaking with Silence'; the brain is only the material manifestation of the Mind."

"Let's take another look at what we wrote there."

"Sometimes we write things that make more sense in retrospect than at the time we wrote them."

"Let's see if that is true in this case," Larry suggested.

Penny clicked the left side of the mouse and behold, there it was.

III MANIFESTATIONS OF RELEVANCE

(1) Speaking with Silence

The Human Brain

Man has discovered that the very thoughts he uses to imagine and create are the result of electrical activity in the brain. Electron microscopes and brain scans have clearly shown that this mass of gray matter is a marvelously intricate electrified organ consisting of millions of fibrous nerve cells miraculously interconnected by electronic synapses to form a whole out of many parts. What Master

Electrician could have conceived of and "wired" such an impressive organ? And how many eons of space-time would it have taken?

The brain is the command center of the vertebrate nervous system and sits astride the medulla oblongata acting as the mainframe computer into which all human experience is processed. It provides man with his sense of space-time or "awareness" within a four dimensional *reality membrane*. Amazing as it is, it is nevertheless a finite biological organ with a limited mass, and limited ability to convert, store, and utilize energy. In this sense it is a microcosm of the finite universe in which it resides.

Thinking

Just as man is beginning to understand and unlock the awesome power of the atom, in an analogous fashion he has been able to look inside his own skull and discover a universe of secrets about himself and the awesome power of thought represented by the miraculous process called "thinking". Thinking is the electrical flashpoint which allows man to connect inner space and outer space, or the microcosm to the macrocosm, or the finite to the infinite, or the material to the spiritual. Thinking is the incarnated reflection of the universal constant: AWARENESS. It is conditioned by our attitudes and beliefs, and is the means by which they are manifested in the material world.

Thinking allows man to apprehend the "truth". What is the truth? It is the creation of the brain in its attempt to "rationalize" itself. It is therefore Creation rationalized as thought. The rationalizing process is known as thinking. The truth as apprehended by thought is consequently rational, logical, and amenable to reason and common sense. The truth resonates in the particular/microcosmic brains of all human beings and is relative to the level of awareness attained by each mortal being.

The Mind

Thinking is Man's most sublime activity. It is the single activity that encourages him to consider that he just possibly could be made in the image of his noblest thought creation: the Eternal Spirit/God. Thinking places man at the center of the universe as he experiences it. From the instant he is born all his biological and psychological receptors provide feedback from the nearest and farthest dimensions of the universe to the command center of his biological essence: his brain. When he thinks about the wonderful powers of his brain he is convinced that it must be more than just a mass of gray matter; it must be something more mysterious: it must be a "mind". The mind reflects all the attributes he has religiously attributed to "that in whose image he is created." The mind is omnipotent, omniscient, and omnipresent, just like his conception of the Eternal Spirit/God. Is there a connection between the finite four dimensional brain and the infinite multi-dimensional mind?

The mind is the macrocosm of the microcosmic brain and vice versa. The brain represents mortal/finite consciousness, while the mind represents cosmic/infinite consciousness. There is a natural reciprocity between the two that creates an awareness of the disparity between the two levels of consciousness: finite vs. infinite. In the Vedanta, this notion of cosmic consciousness is referred to as *Akasha*. The *Rishis* of India were far ahead of their time with respect to such concepts, many of which are making increasing sense in the West as philosophy and science delve into such esoteric areas of knowledge.

Thinking puts man in touch with his mind. It is the most creative activity he can indulge in. It is natural and essential to those who are so inclined. It allows a human being to think about himself as if he were an object of his own perception. In out-of-body experiences, where is the brain? It still resides within the physical body in a space-time dimension. With his mind, man is able to understand his own brain via thought and language.

Water

There is a universal medium within which all thinking indulged in by "Mortal I", occurs. That medium is water, a miracle substance consisting of two parts hydrogen and one part oxygen. The human brain is made up almost entirely of water: over 99%. It is like a watermelon encased in a protective skull. As a matter of fact, the entire human body is mostly water. An unborn fetus is 99% water; a newborn infant is 90% water, and a mature adult is about 70% water. Wherever there is water, there is the possibility of life. It could be said that water is to life as soul is to spirit. Water is sacred. It is sacred because it has the innate potentiality to resonate with soulful life-giving vibes.

The mysterious qualities of water have long been overlooked because as everyone knows, water is just a plain old everyday liquid that we drink, wash and bathe in, pollute, and throw away. In the year 2001 Dr. Masaru Emoto published a little book called, *Mizu Wa Kotae Wo Shitteiru* (translated into English as *The Hidden Messages in Water*). It soon became an international bestseller. Why? Because for the first time someone gave credence to the idea that pure water was sacred and polluted water was a measure of our collective ignorance.

Dr. Emoto equates water with life. There is no other more precious commodity in existence. Water is a universal vibratory medium that is capable of absorbing all types of vibrating frequencies. Think about that. Attitudes and emotions are vibrating frequencies as is thinking per se. Water absorbs all impinging vibrations like a sponge, and relative to the vibrations received, empathetically mirrors or reifies in the form of surface ice crystals, the silent messages hidden in the depths.

It has been stated as if it were an empirical fact that no two snowflakes are the same, no two human beings are the same, no two souls are the same, and no two ice crystals are identical. Dr. Emoto perfected a technique for photographing individual ice crystals. He places different types of water in Petri dishes, and under special conditions subjects them to precisely minus twenty degrees C. for three hours. At that temperature the surface tension of the water forms tiny droplets of ice about one millimeter across in size. A crystal is visible when a light is shone on the crown of the ice drop. The extremely fragile ice crystals must be photographed quickly and with all due care. What the ice crystals revealed was not only astounding, but life altering, as Dr, Emoto wrote:

"I particularly remember one photograph. It was the most beautiful and delicate crystal that I had so far seen – formed by being exposed to the words 'love and gratitude'. It was as if the water had rejoiced and celebrated by creating a flower in bloom. It was so beautiful that I can say that it actually changed my life from that moment on. Water had taught me the delicacy of the human soul, and the impact that 'love and gratitude' can have on the world."

(p. xxiv *The Hidden Messages in Water*)

Dr. Emoto discovered that pure water conditioned by vibrations of gratitude and love produced the most perfect and most beautiful ice crystals – but on the other hand, water polluted by hostility, hatred, and rejection, produced deformed, unsymmetrical, blurry ice crystals. Amazing? Yes. But there is more. Human beings are mostly water. Like water they absorb and give off vibes. When they vibrate sympathetically with gratitude and love a powerful resonance can be created that yields harmony, beauty, serenity and peace; however, on the other hand, when humans resonate with hostility and hatred, a powerful wave of destructive pollution results. It is evident everywhere human beings exist. Wise people and spiritualists have been saying something like this for centuries and now the ice crystals are *speaking with silence*. They can only tell it like it is. We reflect what we are. Remember, water conditioned by vibes of love and gratitude produced the most beautiful ice crystals. And in our mortal state we are mostly water. We manifest our own "truth".

Cosmic Consciousness

The universal or macrocosmic mind is what gives commonality to all individual or microcosmic minds. There is one universal mind in which all humankind "participates" microcosmically. It is a profound spiritual concept that great minds over the centuries have become naturally aware of through a process of self-realization. Such enlightened persons have espoused a view consistent with the following ten statements:

(a) The universe is one harmonic whole sometimes referred to as the Universal Mind (or Cosmic Consciousness)

(b) The Universal Mind vibrates with spiritual energy or life force

(c) This spiritual energy is reflected in the mind of Mankind

(d) Man is therefore, via his mind, able to "participate" in, or access the potentiality of the Universal Mind

(e) The degree of "participation" is governed by Man's free-will and level of karmic awareness via the vibratory frequencies of the mind called "thinking"

(f) Thinking is the creative process which allows the microcosm (Mortal I) to infinitely create/re-create *everything-there-is* which allows the macrocosm (Eternal I) to eternally experience *everything-it-can be*

(g) Vibrations that resonate as thinking are experienced as freedom: the freedom to create

(h) The world without is a reflection or exegesis of the world within; therefore one cannot escape one's karmic-self; one's intrinsic level of awareness creates a subjective ideation of *everything-there-is*, making the four dimensional re-creation or manifestation of *everything-there-is* relative to the level of awareness of its beholder

(i) Like attracts like (this is called the *universal law of attraction*); the intrinsic world is the "cause"; the extrinsic world is the "effect", e.g. if one cannot visualize a beautiful world within, a world free from hatred, jealously, resentments, fear, doubt and all such negative thoughts, how can one manifest a beautiful world without?

(j) The universal unfolding of the principle of cause and effect results in natural (karmic) law: you reap what you sow.

Reason, commonsense, and simple logic inform us that we must *exist* before we can *act*; and our actions are dictated by what we have become or are; and what we *are* depends upon our thoughts or what we *think*. In 1912 an introspective American thinker named Charles F. Haanel (1866-1949) published an insightful work called *"The Master Key System"* in which he described, in an inductively logical manner, the intrinsic power of the mind. It was a creative break-though in an era restricted by the religious parameters of an extrinsic mindset. Alas, Haanel was ahead of his time, as is often the case with such innovative and creative thinkers. Consequently a certain degree of secrecy was required to protect the reputations of the open-minded who allowed reason and commonsense to take precedence over dogma and doctrine. In recent times, however, Haanel's work has been revived as "the secret" and the concepts popularized in motivational and self-empowerment workshops and seminars designed to help business-oriented men and women to utilize the intrinsic power of their minds to overcome the debilitating effects of an extrinsic mindset that reduces their potentiality to that of impotent sinners.

Unfortunately, in a materialistic world besotted by greed, the intrinsic powers of the mind conditioned by capitalistic desires reflect a world where more is never enough. There is as yet a lack of awareness, and an unwillingness to share the bounty. The "part" selfishly deems itself to be more important than the "whole". There is ungratefulness.

"It is amazing how we can continue to blithely pollute our precious supplies of pure water in the name of industrial progress, and call ourselves civilized," Penny pointed out with a tinge of exasperation, as she switched the computer to standby.

"I suppose it really does not matter much to those who consider themselves to be 'saved' and guaranteed an after-life in some heavenly paradise far removed from this polluted earth," Larry pointed out. "And furthermore, why should such persons concern themselves with a trivial problem like polluted water when in the end the entire earth will be consumed in flames?"

"Don't get too sarcastic," Penny cautioned.

"Their self-righteousness is insufferable! They'd rather see this miracle planet along with all its life forms be burnt to a cinder – than admit that they could possibly be... uh-uh, misinformed."

"You were going to say 'wrong' weren't you?" Penny laughed.

"I did not want to sound too righteous," Larry admitted.

"Although most Christians probably believe in some version of that doomsday scenario, which could possibly account to some extent for their present rather irrational behavior – it does not preclude them from changing their mindset. Most modern day Christians, Jews, and Muslims are quite capable of using their God-given intellectual faculties, combined with their free will, to do the Good. Like Plato said, 'if you know the Good, you will do the Good.' "

"And what is the Good?"

"The ice crystals tell it like it is. 'Gratitude and love' produced the most perfect and the most beautiful ice crystals. When more and more people resonate with gratitude and love the world will change accordingly."

"I can see that you have taken all of this to heart."

"Really? What makes you say that?"

"I see a beautiful ice-crystal... personified."

CHAPTER FIVE

"The Haida are a beautiful people, as beautiful as the land that they inhabit and the art that they create," Penny reflected in the solitude of the late summer evening as she sat alone with her thoughts on the back patio.   Larry was over at the neighbors evaluating a recent bottle of single malt Scotch that had been purchased on account of a bet he had won while playing golf earlier in the day.   His absence provided Penny with the opportunity to enjoy the evening without the intrusion of his ever present vibe.

Penny's mother, Joyce, was part Haida. It was the part that gave her mother's skin a beautiful bronze tan in the summer and enabled her dark eyes to twinkle as if she harbored wisdom so profound her existence, in the midst of so much unwarranted prejudice, was an occasion for mirth.   It was a twinkle embedded in the cellular memory of her genes that harkened back to the year 1774 when the serenely beautiful islands isolated off the northwest coast of Canada were "discovered", according to Joyce, by a white European explorer by the name of Juan Perez, disrupting over twelve thousand years of peaceful existence by an intelligent and creative people.

Haida Gwaii (a diverse archipelago of over one hundred and fifty islands located just below the Alaskan panhandle) was known to the Haida as the "Islands of the People". In 1787 when the British explorer who called himself Captain George Dixon arrived and dutifully re-named the islands the *Queen Charlottes* after his boat, the population was estimated to be about seven thousand souls. It was as if the re-naming placed a "pox" upon the Haida, for by the year 1830, a communicable disease unknown to the Haida and to which they had little or no resistance called smallpox, devastated the "Indians", as the Europeans referred to the Haida.

The Haida were almost wiped out courtesy of those who had developed some immunity to the disease. Did anyone care? Missionaries arrived instead of Doctors. They did their best to "save" the "heathens". Only five hundred precious pagan souls survived. Only five hundred! That is five and two zeros: 500.

The Haida instinctively huddled together to help each other and combine their meager resources. It was a fight against extinction. Eventually they relocated to two areas known in 1889 as Skidegate and Masset villages respectively. The land was now essentially unpopulated and free for the taking. The federal and provincial governments encouraged settlers to move to the Queen Charlottes and "homestead" the choice low-lying farmland. Fortunately for the Haida the harsh climate, poor access to markets and the commencement of WWI discouraged the settlers, and by the depression of 1930 the homesteads were mostly abandoned and the area later became Naikoon Park.

This was Penny's mother's version of her native heritage as it had been told to her by her parents. Her father was one of those early settlers. When he took a Haida woman for his wife the racially intolerant referred to him as a "squaw man". It was meant to be a put down. Squaws were nothing more than filthy heathen pagans and white men who consorted with them became contaminated. Somewhere Joyce had read an account where a brave Indian-fighter with a penchant for bragging had cut out a squaw's private parts and stretched it over his hat as a hatband. It was difficult to comprehend such ignorant behavior. It denoted the malevolent intent of a sadomasochist's sinful obsession with sex.

Sometimes in her recollections when Joyce reconsidered her childhood, she realized how fortunate she had been to have had such a decent and considerate man for a father. Ted Greenaway could have been a saint if he had been ordained. He was a six foot bushman with a full brownish beard and glistening grey eyes. His empathy for the natives was boundless. "You call them pagans, and heathens, and at best noble savages – I call them human beings," he would inform the politicians whenever he cornered one.

Penny, being the youngest, became her mother's confidante as the shy and graying mother of four grew older and dared to share her innermost thoughts. It was always with sadness tinged with an abiding sense of an irreplaceable loss that Joyce recounted how her parents had left Haida Gwaii and settled near Vancouver. She was only a young girl then; she remembered the feelings as much as anything else.

When Joyce's mother passed away in 1973, she was buried along with her relatives at Qay'llnagaay, or "Sea Lion Town", where the future new Haida Heritage Center (a magnificent 53,000 square foot cedar multi-plex which would enable the Haida to share their culture with the world) was to be located. Joyce and Hideo went to the funeral. When Hideo returned to Lethbridge he said: "Some Haida look more Japanese than Japanese."

"You mean some Japanese like you look more Haida than Haida," his wife corrected.

"Their woodwork and carvings are fabulous. You should be proud. I think in a previous life my brother Kaz was a Haida."

Funny how one's self-concept can be altered by someone else's attitude. It seemed to Penny that after her parents returned from that trip her dear old mother held up her head proudly and smiled a whole lot more.

* * *

Clarity can be a product of time. It seemed like a long time ago but some things do not fade with time; instead they become much clearer. It was a real shock to Larry when he was first given the news of his parents' fatal car accident. He had promised to stay at home and house-sit until their return from a religious symposium in Los Angeles. He remembered the front door bell ringing in the late afternoon. He had been snoozing on the couch and the persistent ringing of the bell had been annoying. He sauntered over to the front door thinking, "Probably Jehovah's Witnesses or such like." But it was not. A very somber looking policeman stood there. He said, "Could I step in for a moment?"

Larry nodded and the policeman entered and stood uneasily in the front entranceway. He looked at Larry's sleepy face and cleared his throat, "I'm sorry. I have some very bad news."

Larry suddenly came wide awake. A cold chill rose up his spine and froze at the base of his skull. "Pardon me?" he asked.

"I have some very bad news," the policeman repeated. He drew in a somber breath and blurted out "Your parents have both been killed in a car accident."

Larry froze stiff. He stopped breathing. He stood immobile like a zombie. The policeman took him by the arm and said, "I think you better sit down, son." He led Larry over to the sofa where Larry sat down. "Just sit for a moment," he said. "Can I get you a drink of water?"

Larry nodded. The policeman went into the kitchen and returned with a full glass of cold water. Larry gulped down half the glass.

The added electrolyte seemed to bring him out of his state of mental shock. "Is there anything else I can do?" the policeman asked.

"I-I don't think so," Larry responded hesitatingly, "but thanks for being so understanding."

The policeman waited until Larry stood up and walked with him over to the front door. "Are you sure you're feeling okay now?" he asked looking into Larry's eyes.

"Yeah, I just need some time to myself," Larry stated as matter-of-factly as he could. He opened the door. "Don't worry, I think I can handle it," he said as the policeman left with a skeptical look on his face.

After the policeman left, Larry returned to the sofa where he just sat and stared at the family portrait that hung above the fireplace mantle. It was a simple black and white picture framed in dark oak. There they were standing proudly on each side of their only son on the occasion of his graduation from high school. It brought back memories that reached back to the good old days when they used to go fishing and his father wore the hip-waders and his mother carried the picnic lunch and wore the black rubber boots with the red trim. Silent tears rolled unimpeded down Larry's cheeks. For the first time in his life he knew what it felt like to be alone in the universe.

Everyone congratulated Larry on the efficient manner in which he had single-handedly looked after the funeral and wound up the family affairs. After funeral expenses there was very little left over by way of inheritance. Their home was a rent-free residence provided by the Church as partial payment for services rendered, and the used car they drove had been leased free of charge to the Church by one of the stalwart members who owned a Ford dealership. Everything had a cost factor and had been regulated in a fashion similar to that of a Charitable Society with a board of directors, and Larry's father was just one of the Society's expenses. One of the reasons many of the more frugal members of the congregation supported Larry's father was that he never asked for a raise in all the years he served as their minister. During that time Larry's father's salary grew in proportion to the size of the tithing membership of the congregation, which was sufficient to cover the rising costs of living. Even though Larry's parents had been very frugal, all that they had managed to save had mostly been spent subsidizing his post-secondary education.

"We'll be lucky to break even here," the accountant who handled the estate had said with a sigh of regret when Larry asked him for the bottom line.

"Don't worry," Larry had responded, "what my parents have given me is beyond money."

"I wish all my clients had your attitude," the accountant replied. "It is amazing how hard-done-by some offspring can be if they think they should have gotten more. And they take it out on me – as if it is my fault!"

"Perhaps if my Dad had been a televangelist he would have made much more money," Larry suggested harkening back to memories of that time when his old logging buddy, Linc, had waxed eloquent on that subject.

"Some of the successful ones make millions. Even the not-so-successful ones drive Cadillacs. But that was not your father's style," the accountant commiserated, and after a brief pause thoughtfully added, "Your father was a highly respected member of the community. No one that I knew ever had a negative word to say about him in all the years he faithfully served the community. He was one of the few Christians that I personally knew who actually lived his faith. He was truly a humble servant of God." He looked soberly up at Larry and sympathetically added, "In the final analysis it's not about money, is it?"

"I've already received more than I deserve," Larry commented as he left the accountant's office, "I only wish I could have done more for them."

* * *

"Death is a subject most people prefer to avoid," Penny thought to herself on the occasion she accompanied Larry to the cemetery in the hometown of his youth to place some new-cut flowers on his parents' grave. Since their passing Larry had been somewhat reluctant to return to the United States except for such occasional visits to the cemetery.

"How long has it been since they passed on?" Penny asked.

"It has been a long time. I was still an undergraduate student then, and now we're retired. How time slips by unnoticed as the years roll by one by one until you are as old as your parents were when they passed away," he replied. "Too bad they weren't more enlightened," he reflected as he carefully arranged the flowers in the ornate stone vase set in front of the headstone.

"That's a rather judgmental thing to say," Penny mumbled under her breath as her husband bowed his head and said a silent prayer.

When he was finished Penny stepped forth and did the same. She could feel a spiritual presence, and somehow she knew that Larry's parents were both happy and contented.

They opened the car doors and sat inside listening to the sounds of nature. A lovely white pigeon flew in and landed on the roadway looking for something to eat. Penny found some leftover sunflower seeds in her jacket pocket which she threw out on the road. A second bluish-green pigeon flew in to join the first.

"They always believed they would go to heaven," Larry reflected. "I'm glad to know they are happy wherever they are."

A seagull swooped in to join the pigeons. There were plenty of sunflower seeds for all. They ate contentedly trusting in the good intentions of the two onlookers.

"Heaven is right here. It is just that you and I are unaware of where it is at. It is not way out there in outer space. It vibrates within this dimension like the third dimension vibrates in the fourth. Can't you feel their vibes?"

Larry sat absolutely still and waited. After a moment he said, "I feel the spiritual presence of – of…"

"Judge not, lest ye be judged," Penny suddenly interjected.

"What?" Larry looked up at Penny with surprise. "Where did that come from?"

"I don't know. It just popped into my head."

"My Dad once said that a long time ago," Larry said sadly.

Penny gazed at her husband with the most kindly eyes he had ever experienced and added, "It is not about religion – it is all about love."

On the return trip to Canada, Penny and Larry decided to head up through Spokane. It was past eight thirty in the evening when they drove into the driveway that led to the Roadside Inn. "I stayed here once on my way back to Lethbridge from Eugene when I was a grad student," Penny announced while turning off the ignition.

"Brings back old memories, eh?"

"It looks likes it's had a facelift."

"Places like this change hands quite frequently," Larry replied. "Enterprising couples buy them cheap, fix them up, and resell for a tidy profit. You want to stay here overnight?"

"Why not?"

"It looks kind of rustic."

"I like rustic," Penny responded getting out of the car. She went up to the Office, opened the door which had a bell attached to it, and sauntered into the dimly lit room. She half expected Jesus and Marilyn to be there behind the counter, but they weren't. "Poor old Louis Riel!" Penny sighed aloud as she pictured Marilyn proudly reading her college essay entitled "The Métis Cause", the one that had an 'A' on the bottom of the last page.

An overweight woman wearing a faded red bandana on her head leaned over the counter, smiled amicably and said, "I'll bet you are Canadian."

"How did you know?"

"I thought I heard you mumble something about Louis Riel."

"Did you know Jesus and Marilyn Gonzales?"

"They sold this place to us. Let's see, must have been about eight or nine years ago by now. Real nice elderly couple. They told us all about Louis. Relatives of yours?" she asked gazing closely at Penny.

"No relation," Penny replied suddenly feeling self-conscious as she fumbled in her purse for her wallet. "I'm partly Scottish, Native, and Japanese," she offered as if she had to explain herself, "I'll take a room for two for one night."

"That will be thirty-nine dollars."

Penny opened her wallet and extracted a fifty.

"We take Canadian dollars at par," the inn-keeper generously offered. "Units six, seven, and eight are open. You can have your choice."

"Which is the nicest?"

"They are all nice, but I think you'll like number eight. It is decorated in a heritage Japanese theme."

"Hmm," Penny vacillated. "Six, seven, and eight you say. Would you mind if I go ask my husband? He's waiting out in the car. I'll let him make the choice."

(2) Contrast, Contradiction, and Choice

Life, in order to have any meaning, must be significant. Adding significance to a life is a subjective endeavor. It begins from the moment of conception and lasts a mortal lifetime. The manner in which a particular life gains significance depends mainly upon the interface that takes place between the subject and the phenomenal world.

Duality

The objective phenomena a subject encounters in this four dimensional reality impinge upon his/her five senses from the moment of birth, and are experienced as "awareness" in the context of background to foreground. At this particular level of karmic awareness the subject is tuned to receive the positive and negative vibrations commensurate with such a karmic incarnation. The reality of such a duality is a manifestation of the paradoxical separation of Existence from Essence. Conditions are sufficient at this karmic level for the subject to realize this particular dualistic manifestation of reality. To the subject, there are no other dimensions of reality of which he/she is initially aware. This creates a common reality of dualism, i.e. of contrasts and contradictions for all concerned.

Meaning

In a dualistic reality what can be known and therefore have meaning exists in the context of contrasting forms or ideas, like foreground to background or Yin to Yang. Neither can have meaning nor make sense without the other. Both are needed to provide the unity which encompasses both and provides the meaning. Between dichotomies like up-down, right-wrong, good-evil, light-dark, life-death etc, lies an infinity of "difference", giving rise to an infinite number of subjective meanings (attitudes), which in turn become manifested as beliefs. When inculcated these experiences add meaning and significance to a subject's life. In the attempt to understand, share, and communicate this meaning, common abstract symbols (words/language) are created to express the relative significance of an experience. Such a language can only approximate the essence of the experience. Words therefore can only allude to the "truth", the meaning of which is purely subjective. The paradoxical essence of the problem is evident *here*, where words are being utilized by the authors in an attempt to share a "truth" that is locked within their subjective experience.

Mindsets

Mindsets are preconceived attitudes and beliefs that precondition an individual to think about things from a pre-set outlook. They color the way the individual sees the world. Most institutionalized religions condition their converts to see the world from their particular mindset. For example, some religions are based upon a belief in a "righteous" God. Such a God cannot admit to errors or mistakes. Paradoxically, being confined to such a straightjacket of righteousness is an existential hindrance; it is an impediment to freedom!

Self-righteous persons have great difficulty admitting to errors or mistakes because they always need to be right. Their freedom is restricted by their self-righteous mindset. Such persons need to rise above their restrictive mindsets and allow themselves the freedom to be wrong and the freedom to learn from their errors and mistakes. In this way they will be able to further perfect themselves and realize their true potential.

As an aside, it is important to be cognizant of the implications and ramifications of the aforementioned mindset on the civilized world. A RIGHTEOUS God is at the heart of the belief in righteousness, i.e. the notion of infallibility, of never being wrong. Such a mindset is at the core of the monotheistic faith represented by the Judaic, Christian, and Muslim religions. This is without a doubt the single most powerful mindset affecting the modern era. When one is ABSOLUTELY right, it is much easier to be willing to die for one's beliefs – and very difficult to learn from one's errors and mistakes.

Consequently righteous nations, like righteous individuals, tend to repeat the mistakes of the past. In a nutshell this partly explains why in the oil rich Middle East for example where billions of "petro" or American dollars are exchanged each year there is still poverty, disease, malnutrition, prejudice, hatred, terror, and war. It is a volatile situation manifested from righteous mindsets and accordingly, righteously justified and perpetuated.

What makes such mindsets seem attractive is that they are frequently rationalized with flattering rhetoric which clothes the righteous with virtuous principles and motives. They talk vociferously about justice and freedom – while pragmatically protecting their social, political and economic interests. They are loath to admit that what they are doing could be construed as possibly being vain, immoral, or even "wrong", an all too human fallibility even without the mindset. From their respective points of view the righteous always consider themselves to be the "good guys" while those who contradict or oppose them are usually referred to as the "evil doers". Unfortunately there is no room for compromise, because in order for the righteous to be right – someone has to be wrong.

Choice

If mankind has free will, then it follows that he/she must also have choice. Free will is innate, which means that it is natural and intrinsic to the subject. Everyone has it. It is the basis of the formation of one's attitudes, beliefs, and mindsets. In a four dimensional reality words and actions conditioned by our attitudes and beliefs define our social behavior. If each of us lived in isolation our words and actions would not have any shared social or moral implications. In a dualistic reality of contrasts and contradictions like right and wrong, love and hate, good and evil etc., moral behavior is all about making good choices. Good choices lead to wise decisions. And wise decisions resonate universally with vibes that promote harmony, gratitude, love, and compassion.

We are free, and we have choice. We must choose wisely.

"Love and gratitude, those words go together hand-in-glove. They have such a nice resonant ring," Penny commented.

"I can feel the resonance in this house," Larry remarked.

"It seems that since we returned from our last trip to visit your parents' grave, you have been much more in tune with your surroundings, and more at peace with yourself."

"I'm just getting ready for the upcoming Yuletide season. You know, 'Peace on earth and good will to man'."

CHAPTER SIX

"Christmas is truly a man-made creation," Penny thought. It was the week before December twenty-fifth. Time was passing. Penny was busy shopping for gifts for the kids and preparing for the festive season.

However, this usually turned out to be a low energy time for Larry in spite of his efforts to perk himself up. It was strange because just when everyone else was getting hyped up and into the Christmas spirit, Larry tended to feel slightly depressed and regressive in his outlook on life in general. Of course he always did his best to hide this unnatural affliction of his by forcing an artificial smile upon his face and pretending to be jovial when others were singing carols and "ho-ho-hoing".

"It must be the Scrooge effect," Penny pointed out sarcastically.

The sarcasm was wasted on Larry who pretended he did not hear her so he would not have to respond. It was just when Larry was entering into the incommunicative phase of his regressive behavior that something occurred that snapped him out of his mental funk. A Christmas card arrived. It was an innocuous occasion that in the context of the moment seemed most unlikely to be pregnant with possibilities. Penny had picked up the mail from the mailbox and had just returned to the house. She was standing at the kitchen table sorting out the mail and Larry was sitting in the living room taking it easy.

"Guess what?" Penny shouted, "You've got mail."

As soon as she said this, Larry got this intuitive feeling that he was about to remember something important from the past. He got up and walked into the kitchen, and as he did he somehow began to cheer up. Penny was holding a white envelope. She held it up to her forehead like a magician attempting to divine the contents.

"It will be a surprise," she said as she handed her husband the letter.

Larry took the letter into the living room and sat back down in the recliner rocker. It was a large envelope with a certain amount of heft to it. He turned it over to see if there was a return address. In small neat print he read the name: Mr. Linc Smith, followed by an address. Suddenly Larry was back in the hospital gazing at a broken man who had said, "Have two kids, one for you and one for me." A lump rose in his throat and he could not imagine why, relative to Linc's situation, he of all people should be feeling down. He had lost touch with most of his American friends since he had moved to Canada. He carefully opened the letter and removed the contents.

Linc had sent him a lovely red and gold Christmas card from which the center section had been neatly removed in the shape of an oval. In the oval was a beautiful photo of three children. Larry opened up the card. There appeared to be a chicken scrawl which began on the left inside flap, extended across the right side and ended on the back of the card. With concentrated effort Larry was able to decipher the handwriting. Furrowing his brow he carefully read the message.

I got better. I'm married to the most wonderful woman who ever walked on her two hind legs. She is very loving and attentive to my every need. As a result I now have three kids. The girls are Joanne and Jackie, the boy is named – you guessed it, Larry! You're off the hook now. I just thought I'd let you know.

Remember that time we had that discussion about televangelists? I have become a little more spiritual since. Last year I had the good fortune to visit India, the land of over a billion souls. I landed in Delhi. It was in India that I discovered the true spirit of Christmas.

Delhi is a dusty city teeming with humanity. When you are a foreigner in the midst of such a teeming morass of goings and comings the culture shock is shocking. You ask yourself: Is it possible to get used to this grinding onslaught of human poverty, misery, and suffering?

After the passing of a few days you begin to harden yourself to the pathetic pleas for food from starving children in rags. You stare straight ahead and pretend you are unaware of the sea of misery that confronts your senses.

One night as I lay sleeping in an air-conditioned room within the opulence of the "Peninsula Grand Hotel" in Mumbai I had a rather disturbing dream. I dreamt I was the "father of humanity" and all of those starving, ragged little kids with their dark staring eyes and hands mimicking the universal sign for hunger were "my children". What kind of a father abandons his children like this? What kind of a father could be so callous, so uncaring? Their father: me.

The dream haunted me for days. About a week later as I strolled pensively down the beautiful beach that defines the western boundary of the region known as Goa (where the body of the Patron of all Missions, St. Francis Xavier, lies entombed and the Spanish and Portuguese influence abounds) I was struck by an amazing insight: All of this suffering is like an accusing finger pointing to the obvious. Look deeply into the eyes of humanity. What do you see? A mortal manifestation of your karmic soul. Suddenly the mighty Arabian Sea turned into an ocean of tears and I was the source. I was encumbered by the suffering of humankind. What could one mortal human being do?

It was then that I caught a glimpse of the Grandeur of the Human Spirit in the twinkling eyes of a scrawny little girl walking barefoot beside me. That is all that is required, just a glimpse. I emptied my pockets; I turned them inside-out. I gave that stoic little girl every penny I had. The Human Spirit knows no bounds. Through the Human Spirit it is possible to reach out to all humanity with vibrations of charity, love, and compassion. This is the true meaning of Christmas. Merry Christmas.

Drop by if you are ever down our way.

Your old logging buddy,
Linc.

"It is the sentiment that counts," Larry reflected soberly. "Good ol' Linc... with three kids of his own!" The thought caused him to rise up off the recliner rocker and begin pacing excitedly about the living-room. "What a wonderful Christmas present," he said to himself as he sat back down and returned his attention to his mail.

Included with the card was a neatly typed note, prefaced in bold print with the statement: "For your continuing edification". The note consisted of an updated version of an old message. Larry leaned back in the recliner-rocker and read with avid interest....

If the present world could be demographically condensed into one global village represented by 100 human beings, there would be: 57 Asians, 21 Europeans, 14 North and South Americans, and 8 Africans. Of these villagers 52 would be female and 48 would be male, with 70 of these being considered non-white or colored, while 30 would be designated as being white.

Now it is interesting to note that 59% of the total wealth of the global village would belong to only 6 people, and all 6 would be citizens of the United States of America. Of these 6, two-thirds or 4 would be labeled "Christians." These privileged few would consume most of the global village's consumable goods, and hoard most of the rest for a rainy day. Their major concern would be for their own security; hence they would possess the village's most impressive arsenal of weapons of mass destruction – while doing their best to keep such weapons out of the hands of anyone else.

Sharing the bounty would not yet be a popular concept amongst the few who hoard most of the abundance. Consequently 80 of their fellow villagers would subsist in poverty and substandard housing; 70 would not be able to read or write, and unbelievably, 50 or half of the villagers would suffer from starvation, disease, and malnutrition.

However, in the spirit of Christmas, one citizen out of the 100 would be attempting to help make the global village a better place for everyone. But unfortunately, the other 99 would be either suspicious or indifferent.

Are you one of the 1?

> *Happy New Year*
> *Linc and Family.*

"Good old vociferous Linc, he has hit the nail on the head again. When we see the big picture, it makes us feel really small," he thought to himself. "If ever there was an American who embodied the noble virtues that have made America great, he would be the prototype. I am indeed glad to call him my friend."

Larry's mental funk disappeared as if it never existed. He got up and walked sprightly into the computer room to work on the handbook singing, "Oh come all ye faithful...."

Sensing the sudden change in her husband's mood, Penny yelled from the kitchen, "Hold on and I'll join you".

(3)   From the Eye of the Beholder

Point of View

Perception is relative to the perceiver. It is a manifestation of attitude and belief. We subconsciously, consciously, and unconsciously manifest these attitudes and beliefs into every instant of reality. We thereby create our own intentions relative to the instant. For example, consider the following illustration. Suppose the letters G to K were arranged as follows:

$$G \quad H \quad (I) \quad J \quad K$$

Suppose you are positioned at (I). From your point of view you could say: (a) I am behind J and K; (b) I am ahead of G and H; or (c) I am in the middle. However, we can take the same situation and present it like this:

(I)

H   J

G   K

From your point of view you might say: (a) I am the king of the castle, or I have achieved the pinnacle of success; or (b) G and H are on their way up or possibly down; or (c) J and K are on their way down or possibly up.

Now consider (I) to be a dot on the surface of a globe or on planet earth. There are an infinite number of meaningful configurations that could intersect that point representing an infinite number of positions. How often have you heard someone ask: "What is your position?" Is not your position determined by your point of view? By your perception of how you perceived the situation? And this perception is your own subjective perception: you created it the instant you became aware of it. If you were not aware of it – did it really exist as a position?

Having a position or a point of view gives meaning to our actions. For example, consider the following three general points of view and how powerfully they impact upon the behavior of those who possess them: (1) The Jewish point of view, (2) The Muslim point of view, (3) The Christian point of view. Now consider the birthplace of these three points of view: the Middle East. Notice how entrenched their respective positions are, and how it provides meaning and rationality to their respective behaviors and modus operandi.

A Unique Reality

The uniqueness of the position that wise and thinking man finds himself in is as difficult to fathom as it is to express, due to the uniqueness of each individual's point of view. This leads to the question: If every point of view is unique how is it that we can agree on anything? There is a commonality in our biological make-up that produces a common reality via our five senses. It is this ground of commonality that produces our common vision, and allows us to distinguish between illusion and reality. Much has been made of this distinction in religious lore. For sake of clarity consider the following simple experiment.

(1) Take two hand-mirrors and place them face to face as if they were fused together. This fusion represents one single point of view, the real, undistorted view. (2) Now separate the two mirrors by moving one face away from the other. Instantly, everything that is reflected in one mirror is reflected in the other at the speed of light or 186,000 miles per second. (3) As the light is reflected back and forth between the two mirrors, multiple unique images result at the speed of light. Each succeeding unique image is slightly smaller and less distinct than the former. What has the light (of attitude) revealed? Which is the real image? (4) This illusionary reality is known as "Maya". The further the two hand-mirrors are separated one from the other, the greater the illusion, and the greater the degree of ignorance regarding the real image. (5) Now move the two mirrors closer and closer together. The closer the mirrors are, the sharper the images. Awareness of what is real or true increases as the two mirrors draw nearer to each other. The fusion of the two mirrors results in the disappearance of "Maya".

What can one conclude from this experiment? When one sees through the illusory world of "Maya" and becomes fully AWARE, one is "awakened" to the real world. Of course this leaves us with the question to which a definitive answer can only be found in the eye of the beholder: What is the real world?

"In the real world it is Christmas time," Penny noted.

"You should take a look at that Christmas card I got from Linc." Larry got up, went into the living room, and returned carrying his mail. "Here it is," he said giving the card to Penny. "There's a note inside. I found it quite interesting. I think you will find it fits in with your perspective of the real world."

CHAPTER SEVEN

There was one thing about Penny; she always tried to make things better. One of her favorite sayings was: "Creation is perfect and it is up to us to learn how to maintain it." She felt the imperfection people experienced and created were manifestations of their own ignorance.

Before she came to this rather sophisticated point of view, especially when she was much younger and trying to fit in, she saw the world through the eyes of those who believed in an external God, a God who was righteous, judgmental, vengeful, and loved to wage war on practically everything. Along with the mindless horde she had jumped on the bandwagon and waged war against poverty, drugs, cancer, rape, despots, terror, and ironically, even against war itself! Without realizing it, she waged war against anything that impeded the free flow of petroleum which lubricated the international marketplace and made billionaires out of millionaires.

She forgot to ask: "Is this making things any better?" She just assumed it must be the right thing to do because practically everyone else thought it was. Because of her willingness to go along with the herd, she nurtured one of her worst habits: smoking. Practically everyone smoked from prime ministers, presidents, priests, royalty to impoverished teenagers and kids. She did not even have an inkling that smoking would eventually lead to her untimely death and ravage the health of an entire generation. This was one of those anomalies against which no one even thought of waging war. Big money and vested interests were involved and took precedence over the physical health and well-being of a nation.

"Sad but true. Big money talks and carries a mighty big stick," Penny thought on the day she quit smoking.

Before the twins were born, Penny used to smoke a pack and a half a day. She considered herself to be a real "cool" smoker. She had worked really hard at affecting all those stylized mannerisms associated with glamorous movie stars who made smoking a cigarette into a pop art form. When she found out that the cigarette-smoking life style advocated by cigarette companies was simply a marketing ploy designed to produce the largest generation of nicotine addicts since man began walking upright upon the earth, she felt not only hard-done-by, but betrayed by the false advertising that bombarded her from every side.

In retrospect it was a real no-brainer, and to think that she had paid dearly for the privilege of polluting her own body with carcinogenic impurities so that the callous cigarette companies in conjunction with business-friendly governments could make vast amounts of money. It made her feel just plain stupid for being so darn gullible.

"What we do to ourselves and to the world in general out of simple gullibility based upon stupidity, insecurity, vanity, and greed is beyond belief!" she complained bitterly to her husband.

"Ah-so," Larry responded, accepting the blame on behalf of the great unwashed. Although he had experimented as a youth in Carl "the rat-face" Jones' basement and in the bushes adjacent to the church after Sunday School was over and there was nothing better to do until lunch time, Larry never became a smoker. He was slightly allergic to cigarette smoke; it made his eyes water and induced a kind of asthmatic attack that made it difficult to breathe. He tried during his teenage years to overcome this disability. Who likes being called a sissy and a homo and other worse pseudonyms for not being a real man? Larry tried and failed miserably because he always felt so much better away from cigarette smoke. To maintain his own good health he even managed to train Penny not to smoke in his presence. It wasn't easy at first, but when she saw his eyes start to water and his breath become labored, she relented.

When she found out that she was pregnant Penny summoned up all her good sense and quit smoking cold-turkey. It was difficult but she was motivated and had the will power to overcome a powerful addiction. Nicotine withdrawal and the habits associated with the culture of smoking made quitting a formidable challenge.

"I have much more sympathy for those who have tried to quit and failed," she said afterward. "There were so many times I thought: What harm could one more cigarette do? Just one more last cigarette!"

Fortunately that last cigarette stayed in the pack along with the other dried up cancer-sticks. To further augment her physical health Penny gave up the consumption of red meats and became a partial vegetarian. The cleansing effect made her feel more like a natural part of nature. The vibes she gave off were much more pleasing to both flora and fauna.

In the right light when Penny stood amongst the flowers in the flower garden behind the house, it seemed as if every little infinitesimal detail was in its proper place. At such times the existential ambiance of her presence inspired Larry to reach beyond himself and to think thoughts that he never knew he felt so strongly about. For example, whenever the topic of smoking came up when they were informally socializing with their friends, it was usually Larry, the non-smoker, who went off on a tirade against the cigarette companies. He regarded companies like these to be symbolic of the self-fulfilling prophecy regarding man's self-destruction.

"Isn't it ironic," Larry would say, "that we spend billions of dollars on our fight against drugs and cancer and further billions on medical and health initiatives, and more billions on encouraging a healthy drug-free life style – while at the exact same time our duly elected governments enable the tobacco companies to rake in obscene profits by creating generation after generation of nicotine addicts destined to fill our hospitals and clinics with an epidemic of carcasses consumed by the cancerous effects of unmitigated greed?" And then, Larry would conclude, his voice rising to a crescendo, "As a show of public concern, the government makes it possible for the victims to sue the hand that digs their grave!"

"Shush, not so loud," Penny would interject at this point.

"It is not the carcinogens we need to worry about," Larry would continue in a more moderate tone, "but the greed. Little wonder our children are confused. We sit around slowly killing ourselves with nicotine and alcohol, and tell them that marijuana is bad for them. Our children are not as stupid or ignorant, or as gullible as we were. We, the gullible, freely participate in our own demise as if we are the chief architects and actors in a self-fulfilling prophecy of doom. Little wonder we callously pollute the world around us in the same manner as we pollute ourselves. It is a reflection of what we are. First we predict that the world will end and then we subconsciously, consciously, and unconsciously go about ensuring that it will happen. So in the end those who have hoped and prayed for this tragic outcome can smugly say: 'See? We told you so!'"

Sometimes Larry would get so animated you would think he was preaching a sermon. He had that self-righteous, ministerial quality about him that was very convincing. It was almost as if he had changed personalities. At such times he exuded a preacher's charismatic presence, and Penny often thought; "If only his father could see him now!"

* * *

The house was very still. Larry had gone out to winterize the roses and other flowerbeds that he thought might need extra protection against the winter cold leaving Penny alone in the house. When the back door closed snugly against the solid frame of the jamb with a heavy thud the reverberation set Penny to thinking. "If only I had not smoked so much," she lamented. "We do so many things out of ignorance that lead eventually to our demise. Life seems to float like a mirage upon a sea of ignorance. We know about as much about ignorance as we know about life. They are in essence like smoke and mirrors. Ignorance is the ocean in which we drown searching for the knowledge which will keep us afloat."

Penny rocked back and forth in Larry's recliner-rocker raising her right leg slightly to promote the action as she had seen her husband do so many times. It was truly amazing how that simple motion stimulated her thoughts which lit up her face with a special radiance that she had often seen on her husband's face on those occasions he had cogitated in that very chair in that identical manner.

"Knowledge per se is the means by which life can be enhanced, and life is the crowning achievement of all Creation. Could it be that without some form of life, Creation per se would seem to be redundant?" she asked herself. "The fact that we are not doing our best to positively enhance life is a measure of our collective ignorance. The potential for positive life enhancement is equal to the potential for negative life enhancement. Emphasis on the latter leads to dying and death; it happens out of ignorance. The fact that we are indeed living longer and more fulfilling lives is a good sign. We are moving in the right direction." Penny opened her eyes and drew in another prodigious breath of life. "It is Man's dharma to seek to enhance life," she thought.

"A penny for your thoughts?" Larry asked.

Penny glanced around at Larry with a startled expression. "Good God, you scared me! I didn't hear the back door close."

"Sorry. I left the door ajar. I just popped in for a drink of water and saw you rocking there in my chair."

"Well, I've been sitting here like you usually do, rationalizing the state of our ignorance."

"No doubt it has been time well spent." Larry smiled that enigmatic smile that reminded Penny of a smug little boy who thought he actually knew something worth knowing.

* * *

Penny was a "saver". She rarely threw anything away that she had written, especially creations that she considered to be inspired. Larry, except for his poetic efforts, had long ago thrown out almost all the old papers he had written during his university days – while Penny had stored hers like a miser under the bed in an old leather briefcase. When they replaced their squeaky as well as sagging double-bed with a luxurious new low profile queen-sized bed, there was no room under it for her old briefcase, and consequently it was exposed to the harsh light of scrutiny when the old bed was removed.

"What's in there?" Larry asked out of curiosity.

"Nothing much, just some old papers of mine," Penny responded protectively as she opened the bi-fold door to the closet and slid the briefcase in.

When Larry went to the Vancouver Canucks versus the Edmonton Oilers hockey game and she was left alone, Penny retrieved the old leather briefcase from the closet and opened it. Inside lay an assortment of file folders. She picked one up at random. It was labeled, "For Posterity". She flipped it open and inside, amongst various notes and memos were fourteen lined yellow pages stapled together entitled, "A logical explanation of what is, and why things are the way they are". She casually picked them up and began to read, and as she did she recalled that magical moment in her past when she had written it, that time when she had thought she had written something quite profound when she was a graduate student on Christmas break in Lethbridge.

"Hmm, not too bad," she thought, "Some good stuff in here but it needs to be reviewed and updated." She secured a pen and began scribbling in changes as she continued to read. When she was finished she sat back proudly and reread what she had edited. "I think we could use some of these ideas in the handbook," she thought. "When Larry gets home I'll share it with him."

It was after midnight when Larry returned home. Penny could always tell when he had been drinking. He had that bloated look about him. As usual he sauntered in casually pretending he was stone-cold sober.

"The Canucks lost three to one," he said and flopped down into his recliner rocker and picked up the newspaper.

"Too bad," Penny commiserated. "They need more speed if they want to match the Oilers."

"I'd have to say you're probably right. If it wasn't for the goalie the score could have been six to one."

Larry excused himself and went to the bathroom to urinate. He left the bathroom door slightly ajar. Penny could hear the recycled Molson's Canadian splattering into the toilet bowl followed by a sigh of relief. When he returned, pulling up the zipper on his fly, he sagged back down into the recliner rocker and said, "That was a relief!"

"Would you like a beer?" Penny asked.

"No thanks. I had more than my share tonight."

"It must be frustrating watching the Canucks struggle," Penny said as she went into the kitchen to get herself a beer. She returned sipping the head off a foamy mug. "While you were out I looked through that old briefcase that was under the bed."

"Yeah?" Larry asked, straightening up.

"I found some stuff that might be useful for the handbook. It needs further editing and updating. I thought it would be better if you looked it over. You'd be much more objective."

"Sure, if you don't mind me reading your personal papers."

"I mind, but what the heck, I wrote it for posterity. And now posterity is here."

Posterity had been a long time coming. Isn't it funny how things happen as if they were supposed to have happened? And what happens has an impact upon what occurs subsequently? Perhaps it was Penny's remarkable cousin's mental objectivity, his ability to rationalize without becoming personally obsessed, that lifted Penny into a similar state. Whenever she thought about that far-off experience, it always seemed as if he were present inside her head and talking to her as he had talked in that crisp and succinct manner of his. She could hear the resonant tone of his voice. How could she forget it? It was as if they were kindred spirits connected by an invisible cord.

It was her cousin who was responsible for the genesis of much of her philosophical thought. He had been the gardener. He had planted seedling thoughts in a mind so fertile they grew and grew and grew, and were still growing. Would they ever reach full maturity? Do such ideas ever reach maturity, or do they evolve on and on just like all life forms? Onward and onward from one epoch to the next, with each epoch thinking it is on the cutting edge, unique and special, creating brand new ideas – which are as old as eternity.

Yes, there was something to be said for her cousin that Penny could not say about anyone else. He was truly unique. He must have experienced something so dramatic, so powerful, and so overwhelming that it transformed his outlook on life. He must somehow have gained an inkling of something so finitely absolute that over time it had withered his soul and filled his heart with such a feeling of dread it fostered a fathomless insecurity. It was the type of insecurity that drives men and women to overachieve in the sensate world of capitalism in a vain attempt to satiate the five receptor senses with an elusive sensation of satiation. In such a world, and to such a person, is more ever enough?

Many a night in the silence of the darkness when universal vibes floated freely about the surface of the planet looking for a receiver tuned to the higher frequencies of extrasensory perception, Penny had lain awake wondering what her cousin could have meant when he said with such solemnity: "After such knowledge... what forgiveness?"

What knowledge? What forgiveness? The questions seemed to resonate with primordial implications, implications that have echoed down through the ages in the minds of those playing out the human tragedy/comedy without a script. It is a drama being enacted upon a thin cracked crust that floats like continental plates upon a massive sea of molten magma. Sandwiched between the crust and an atmospheric sky, the actors, unaware of their predicament, scurry about like tiny ants searching for significance and meaning on the sublime surface of the miracle planet called Earth, struggling dramatically to find their niche in the phenomenal world that impinges upon their five receptor senses with the immediacy of the here and now.

"Ah-soooh," Penny exhaled as she shuffled off to the bathroom in her green flannel pajamas to urinate, wash her face, and brush her teeth. "Ahh-sooh," she repeated as the cool porcelain tiles on the bathroom floor met the warmth of her soft bare feet. "I have so much to be grateful for..." she reflected as she, with a tinge of annoyance, put down the plastic toilet seat that her husband had once again forgotten to return to the seating position.

PART SEVEN

RATIONALIZATIONS

We are the seer
And we are the seen
If there is but one seer
How can the seer be seen?

CHAPTER ONE

Father Petitjean had struggled to find his niche in the world. It had taken a long time to discover his true calling, a calling that was not only intrinsically meaningful, but also made him feel significant, as if his existence upon this miracle planet made a difference.

Bernard Petitjean knew his limits. He was a man who knew his own mind and the degree to which he could use it to curb the insatiable demands of the flesh. Yes, there were times in his youth – before he became a priest – that he had given in to the delights of the flesh. He had even sired a child back then. It had been very difficult, very, very difficult to abandon him like that, especially since his mother was so young and naïve. But, what else could he do at the time? He was called, was he not? Called up from the dregs of the Paris sewer where he had been tossed like a rotten carcass, drunk, beaten to a pulp, robbed, and left for dead. Fortunately an old woman had passed nearby, heard his soulful moan, and took pity on him. She was a Catholic. She wore a silver crucifix around her neck. She said, "Every soul is precious to God," as she extracted him from the sewer, took him to her humble abode, cleaned him up, and nursed him back to life. When he recovered he knew he was called to do God's work. "God works in mysterious ways," he rationalized to himself.

It was a brilliant autumn morning in the year 1865. Father Petitjean, a dedicated Catholic priest, stood proudly beside the front doors of the newly refurbished Roman Catholic Church, the only true church of God in all of Japan. The sun had risen to the tops of the cherry trees to the east of the *Cathedral*, as he liked to call his church. Nearly three hundred years had passed since the Shogunate led by Ieyasu Tokugawa had all but eliminated the blight of Christianity from Japanese soil.

"It is tragic what man will do to his fellow man," Father Petitjean lamented, "Tragic!" Still the Japanese authorities had seen fit, as an act of benevolence, to allow him, a Jesuit Priest, to enter their sacred homeland and begin the process of restoring the old Cathedral in the district of Urakami to its former magnificence. It was more than just a place of worship; it was a symbol of hope and perseverance. In

Nagasaki it represented not only the past but a new beginning. "Like the undaunted phoenix the spirit of Christ will rise once again from the ashes of redemption!" Father Petitjean mouthed aloud in the ripe autumn air.

It was indeed a delicious fall morning in the land of the rising sun. A faint breeze blew in from the sea perfuming the air with a refreshing odor of salty cleanliness. The atmosphere held the crispness associated with newly fallen leaves, and there was a pregnant hush in the air as if Mother Nature were holding her breath in expectation. A dewy mist hung just above the highest peak of the Church giving the magnificent edifice a halo effect emphasizing its holiness.

Father Petitjean drew in a refreshing breath. On such mornings it was a blessing to be alive. Not only alive, but alive in this mystical land where the people reminded him of a quaintness found only in fairytales. It had always been his fondest desire to find himself ministering in a place and time where his sheer presence made a difference, where he was the difference.

It was this deep-seated desire to make a difference that had brought Father Petitjean to the Orient. The Church was a pragmatic vehicle by which he could serve God. It was a two-way deal: he served God and the Church served him. That was not the way it was supposed to be, according to Church Officials, but nevertheless that was the way it was. He made no secret of it. "What is more important?" he once asked a Cardinal, "God or the Church?" It was not the kind of attitude the Church Officials were looking for.

Perhaps that was the reason they sent him to Japan where he would be out of sight and out of mind, hidden away on a little Oriental island somewhere way out in the Pacific. There he could do God's work nearly unimpeded by the sanctity of Church protocol. There he could do almost anything he wanted – so long as it did not make any difference as far as the Church was concerned.

Father Petitjean was first and foremost a seeker after truth. His keen intellect· and insatiable curiosity could not allow him to be anything else. He just had to know things, things that his superiors referred to as blasphemous. However, it was this particular predisposition that enabled Father Petitjean to rise above the pettiness which engulfed the day to day operations of the Church.

He soared high above the dogmas and doctrines with a kind of respectful disdain that was mistaken for reverence by pious Bishops attempting to mind God's business. He saw all the dogmas, doctrines, and infallible truths for what they were: man's feeble attempt to find certainty in a world of flux, to be able to say with absolute conviction, "This is the way it is!"

Certainty, as far as Father Petitjean was concerned, was the Church's greatest problem. It required the restraint of a powerful institution rationalized by the righteous actions of the Bishops at the Council of Nicaea in 325 and sanctified with dogma and doctrine, to provide the certainty that could withstand the revelations made self-evident by common sense.

The growing awareness that predisposed Father Petitjean to come to this realization began when he was an adventurous young fellow filled to overflowing with the reproductive juices of manhood, searching for his identity in the country across the Channel from his homeland, called England. In those early days, before Bernard realized his true calling, in order to relieve himself of an overpowering urge to procreate the species, he frequently masturbated in the dead of night with sinful hands. "You will go blind!" his mother, who was a devout Catholic, warned him on days she washed the sheets. He went to England to get away from the guilty conscience he was developing at home.

His eyesight, to his everlasting surprise, remained as sharp as ever even though he continued to masturbate diligently to relieve the pressure. His eagle eye, ever alerted to finding more natural ways to relieve the pressure, twinkled with appreciation when he spied a comely young English maid called Marion Smith. She was the only daughter of Mr. and Mrs. Seymour Smith, on whose modest farm he had found gainful employment. Marion took a liking to Bernard due to his delightful French accent which she thought was very sophisticated. She learned to say *Bonjour* and *Bon voyage* with the proper inflections. She always hung around when Bernard milked the cows, and demonstrated great curiosity when the neighbor's bull was brought around in the fall. Of course, it goes without saying that Marion had a most disturbing effect upon poor Bernard who fantasized about the forbidden attractions of sin.

Consequently it seemed natural and healthy for Bernard to form a conjugal relationship with Marion Smith. Smith was a common name in that part of England just south of London. What distinguished Marion from the other Smiths was that she had an uncle named Lincoln Alexander Smith, who operated a small cotton plantation across the Atlantic in southern Virginia, and once owned as many as eighteen black African slaves. In his own way her uncle considered himself to be a humanitarian of sorts; he liked to share his seed with his comely black female slaves, especially right after they got back in from the fields all hot and sweaty. They were much more submissive then. It was probably the hardest work he did: "an obligation of the noble", he liked to rationalize in moments when he felt particularly fatigued by the exertion. In a secret back corner of the cotton storage shed he managed to sire six "coloreds" who also took the surname Smith and whom, when they reached puberty, he sold for substantial profit. It was probably the hybrid vigor that gave his offspring such a natural glow of vitality and contributed to the ridiculous prices offered for such magnificent specimens. Marion was very proud of her uncle's accomplishments.

However, when Marion proudly informed Bernard about her uncle and his accomplishments, Bernard nearly hit the roof. "Who ever gave one human being the right to own another?" he fumed. "The arrogance of some people is insufferable!" Marion swallowed her pride and bowed her head timidly. Never again did she mention her infamous uncle in Bernard's presence.

After precisely two hundred and seventy-three copulations, etched on the south wall adjacent to the bed by a precocious lover who was also something of a bean counter in those early days, Marion gave birth to a robust baby boy whom they proudly named, Lawrence Bernard Petitjean. Marion's father was called Lawrence, and he was particularly delighted when his only grandson was named after him. It turned out to be a rather fortuitous christening.

Unfortunately, during that era it was the custom, as it is even today, for some of the inconsiderate to belittle the French. Consequently Bernard was condescendingly referred to as "Little-john" or "Tiny-jean", or just "Tiny" for short. It could have been taken as a joke because there was definitely an element of humor involved. Yes, Bernard could have laughed it off, but he did not. He sulked and felt terribly hard-done-by. His pride was hurt. He found those oxymoronic nicknames particularly irksome. He was not tiny at all. In fact he towered above the average Englishman, and yet they had the unmitigated gall to call him "Tiny".

It was when his sensitive ego was bursting with so much resentment that even the tiniest slur, no matter how unintentional, could provide the impetus to change the course of his destiny, that it happened. It occurred just after his father-in-law dropped in to see his grandson. As he was leaving he casually turned his head and said in a fatherly tone of voice, "See you later, Tiny."

Bernard could hardly believe his ears. He stood there speechless. In that instant he became aware of something quite profound. He was not tiny! But if he stayed in England he would always be "Tiny".

It was an epiphany. He was not sure of who he was, but he knew who he was not. His tiny bubble of self-awareness expanded to accommodate this realization. He knew he could not stay in England. It was not his father-in-law's fault; he was only being his good-old-English self. In fact if it had not been for his father-in-law he might not have come to this profound realization. It gave him an immediate sense of direction. He had to go back to the country of his birth where his surname, Petitjean, had roots and where his destiny beckoned.

Bernard did not leave for France immediately. He incubated upon the notion for months. It was not an easy decision for one who had serious family responsibilities. Subconsciously he was readying himself for his eventual calling. It called to him from somewhere across the Channel. He felt the call in the still of night when his wife lay on her back and snored spastically, unaware that he was curled up fetus-style on the far side of the bed nauseous with dissonance. It lay in the pit of his stomach like a lump of undigested haggis. The dissonance refused to dissipate. He had to do something. The call was vague, but irresistible. He had to go.

After months of indecision, self-recriminations and mountains of guilt, Bernard sorrowfully left Marion and his son Lawrence with his in-laws, adamant that when he reached France and found gainful employment he would send for them. He set out with high hopes and equally high expectations. There was the spring of new-found freedom in his step which foreshadowed a personal weakness: a tendency to over-indulge himself. When he reached Paris he just had to celebrate his return to his homeland by spending most of his savings on wine for all his old friends who were all so glad to see him... buy the wine.

For eleven days and nights he lay in a drunken stupor in a flop house. On the twelfth day as he was making his way back to the flop house with a jug of cheap wine he was set upon by a gang of thugs. They beat him senseless, took his wine and what money he still had, and threw him into the open sewer. His high expectations vanished when the pungent order of sewer gas hit his nostrils and reactively caused him to raise his head above the offal and emit such a long and soulful moan it could be heard for blocks.

Just when his head was about to sink under the murky depths of the open cesspool, a hand grasped him by the hair and extracted him from oblivion. Was it the hand of a compassionate Catholic woman with a silver crucifix hanging around her neck? Or was it the hand of God?

Who could have foreseen this unexpected curve in the pathway to his destiny? There it was: his calling, calling him in this most unexpected manner, to serve. There was absolutely no mistake. Nothing so dramatic could be a mistake. It was God's way of making sure, making sure he got the message: put aside all your earthly belongings, and serve.

On the day that he was ordained as a priest in the only true Church of God on earth, the Roman Catholic Church, Bernard Petitjean put aside his earthly possessions, his dear wife and darling son, and embraced the vows of poverty, chastity, and obedience. Sacrifices had to be made. He chose to serve the most powerful religious institution on earth because with its blessing he, Father Bernard Petitjean, could rise above the cesspool of ignorance and make a real difference.

What can one person do to make a real difference? Is it not like throwing a single pebble into a great ocean?

The ripple effect of the difference Father Petitjean made rolled on long after he was pronounced dead and buried in a simple wooden casket in a small cemetery just behind the beautiful Cathedral in Nagasaki. His faithful spouse, Marion, had predeceased him at the tender age of thirty-three, overcome by grief and consumption brought on by a broken heart that refused to mend. His darling son, Lawrence, dutifully raised by his hardworking English grandparents, eventually stowed away aboard a sailing ship bound for America. Lawrence was only sixteen, and already anxious to carve out his own niche in the New World.

When a pebble is tossed into the placid waters of a karmic sea, who knows where the ripples will end?

CHAPTER TWO

It was with a sense of heightened awareness that Father Bernard Petitjean began his customary stroll around the perimeter of the magnificent Cathedral. He liked to walk around it each morning and admire its stout beams and graceful arches. It was indeed a beautiful work of art crafted by the pagan hands of dozens of skillful Orientals who worked tirelessly under the watchful eyes of the chief architect and engineer, a convert with a penchant for building magnificent edifices.

"God's work is never done," Father Petitjean breathed as he surveyed the manicured gardens of red, yellow, and purple flowers which graced the edge of the walkway around the church. "Divine," he thought, "just like these little people, so gentle and so amenable to conversion. They are like ripe fruit, ready to be plucked and offered to God. They already think they are of divine origin and all they need is for us to confirm it. It really is a matter of confirmation rather than conversion."

The thought made Father Petitjean feel very privileged to be the one selected to rebuild the Roman Catholic Church in Nagasaki. It was the only true Church of God in all of Japan. What a grand opportunity it was to make a real difference! The little doll-like people came so willingly, just like little children. "Suffer the little children to come unto me," he whispered to the flowers. He could visualize them in his mind's eye, smiling and bowing so respectfully.

Sometimes it is not unrealistic to dream dreams in which one is raised to great heights of exultation by one's own ambitions. To be the one chosen to travel halfway around the world to minister to these little pagan folk in dire need of redemption was a dream-come-true. It was a great honor to be the one standing there on such a miraculous morning under the omniscient canopy of He-who-sees-and-hears-all. It was indeed a rare opportunity! The reassuring words of Saint Francis Xavier sprang to mind: "...amongst pagan nations there will not be another to surpass these Japanese."

Father Petitjean greatly admired Saint Francis Xavier, and insofar as possible attempted to follow in his fading footsteps. To think that the saintly one had possibly trod upon the very ground upon which he now stood filled him with a deep felt sense of gratitude. He drew in a prayerful breath, squared his broad shoulders, and stared up at the heavens. "Thank you," he said to the one who had preceded him down this path. Optimism glowed in every crevice of his beaming countenance. It felt so good to be of service to man and God on that glorious autumn morning in 1865.

Although the Church had been refurbished, the congregation was still quite sparse due to the ongoing repression which had not yet been formally rescinded. Even though Father Petitjean had offered all who attended the protection of the most powerful Church on earth, only a handful of recent converts dared to turn out on a consistent basis. Still Father Petitjean was hopeful. It would take time and patience to earn their trust and to restore the Roman Catholic Church to its former position of prestige and grandeur. The repression had all but extinguished the light of Christianity from Japanese soil, but he, Father Bernard Petitjean, was there to rekindle the flame.

He smiled graciously at Michiko Sawada, a petite middle-aged woman dressed in a beautiful black and white kimono with flower-like cherry red accents. She had very delicate and beautiful facial features, and moved with grace and agility on wooden gheetas that made a plopping sound on the wooden floor. She had volunteered to help out with his first baptismal service soon after his arrival. Without her assistance it would have been much more difficult to accommodate himself to the cultural differences that engulfed him. He thought of her as a Japanese nun, sent to help him with his mission in this mysterious Land of the Dolls, as Saint Francis Xavier had called it.

He did not have to convert Michiko because she claimed, with a solemn glance toward the heavens, that she had already been converted. He did not challenge the legitimacy of her claim. It just would not have been prudent. Honor was such a consuming passion to these people. "Strange," he thought at the time, and then let the matter rest, because for a pagan she really did seem to know a great deal about the teachings of his Lord and Savior, Jesus of Nazareth.

Father Petitjean, in his inimitable style which was very endearing, treated Michiko as his equal. It just seemed natural because she knew so much more than he did about what needed to be done around the Church. He was actually dependent upon her expertise in practical matters. However, in spiritual matters he was confident and resolute like the Rock upon which the Church was founded.

As time passed, the natural magnetism that exists between a beautiful woman and a healthy man with powerful sexual urges repressed by dogmatic concepts of Original Sin, came into play. It was unintentional, but the more time they spent together, the more difficult it became to maintain a platonic relationship. As the months passed Father Petitjean developed a particular fondness for Michiko. He could not help himself; she attracted him like a lantern attracts moths.

There were days when Father Petitjean despaired. His iron-will moaned and groaned when temptations had to be consciously avoided. He suffered in silence and displayed a stoic exterior. He resisted temptation with all his might, but in the depths of his most erotic dreams he felt as craven as any sinner who sat in the confessional and laid bare his soul. But who can control such dreams? Perhaps they serve a purpose, an opportunity to free oneself from one's earthly shackles.

Nevertheless, because of them, Father Petitjean treated Michiko with more respect and platonic affection than she probably deserved. It was as if he had to demonstrate to himself that he really was a priest and not just a horny old man in a black robe. The irony of it all was that Father Petitjean was acutely aware of the juxtaposition of these two images in his mind's eye, and he would haughtily admonish himself thus: "You fool. Shame on you. Rise above it. Sublimate!" And he did because unnatural as it was, abstinence was part of the deal he had made with the Church.

Still the fondness never disappeared because it was a genuine fondness of one human being for another. And so they managed to work together in the evenings after the sun had set and the regular day's work was all but done. Michiko knew a smattering of French she had learned from an old French sailor who had served as a handyman around the Church prior to Father Petitjean's arrival. As it was vital that he have a trustworthy translator, due to his very ragged Japanese, he tirelessly groomed her on the nuances of conversational French, evening after evening. She was so patient and such an apt pupil that after awhile Father Petitjean looked upon her with a kind of familial love and affection that he once had bestowed upon the son he had abandoned in England.

Sometimes at night after a particularly tiring day when he was curled up on the rice-straw mattress in his Spartan little room at the rear of the Cathedral, he felt an emptiness that caused his entire body to quake with an eternal longing for something more than prayers. It was then that he usually thought of his earlier days in England. Days that shimmered in his mind like a distant dream vaguely remembered when he was a virile young man carefully carving counters for posterity in the soft plaster with a rusty nail on the south wall adjacent to the bed, while his exhausted young wife lay sprawled out beside him with her nightgown wantonly pulled up to her waist exposing her pale muscular thighs etched with tiny blue veins.

* * *

Michiko Sawada was a proud woman. She was proud because anyone with an Ainu lineage had to be proud in the midst of so much unwarranted scorn. She was proud because one of her great ancestors was known as the Magician of Kogi, a famous sword-maker. She was proud because he had three beautiful daughters, the eldest of which gave birth to a Saint. She was proud because of her religious heritage, and the crucial role women played in ensuring the secrecy of their religious practice. She was particularly proud to be a Kakure Kirishitan in a society where her particular faith was forbidden.

She recalled that dark and fearful night after her uncle, her father's youngest brother, had been taken away for questioning by the authorities, and the lamps had been turned down as low as possible, her mother pulling her up onto her lap and fearfully whispering: "Say your prayers in silence from now on; just move your lips like this," and she demonstrated by moving her lips without making a sound.

"What were you saying?" she had asked.

"Jesus, Lord, take care of this hidden jewel of faith."

She was only seven years old at the time, and in some ways it had been rather fun to be so secretive. The family pretended to be stalwart Buddhists by making small financial contributions to the temple and by attending the most popular Buddhist festivities. But when her uncle never returned everyone became very insecure and apprehensive. Had he talked? Had he given them away? No one knew. He just disappeared without a trace.

In the quiet of the evening as the adults huddled around the eating table, Michiko had sat unobtrusively in the corner and listened to the speculations. Although authorities had not returned to interrogate other members of the family it was suspected that he might have recanted and renounced his Christian faith. Once someone recanted it was impossible to return to the fold. The loss of face and dishonor to the family was best avoided by simply going away like an outcast and disappearing into the void provided by the vast population of some large city. The true believers all agreed that it was better to die than to recant. This was the spirit that kept the Kakure safe and hidden for over two hundred and forty years.

The repression had let up considerably since then but it was still dangerous, too dangerous to be seen praying in a public place, even in the sanctity of the newly refurbished Roman Catholic Church. It was wonderful for the Kakure to secretly visit the Church grounds during visits to Nagasaki and see the magnificent Cathedral standing there like a glorious monument to God. They longed for the day they would be able to venture inside the holy edifice and worship in a true House of the Lord as their ancestors had once done centuries ago. It had been a dream for generation after generation of faithful Kirishitan. It was a dream they held in their hearts and aspired to with hope every time someone said, "I went to Nagasaki and saw the Great Cathedral!" in a tone that inspired wishful thinking amongst the young and impatient. It was a dream that had lasted a long, long time. But sometimes dreams come true.

After a busy day assisting Father Petitjean with various jobs at the Church, Michiko would return home at night and in the secret confines of her family's birth home she would infect the others who had gathered there for the secret evening service with Father Petitjean's sincerity and kindness. It was the kind of infection to which there seemed to be little or no immunity. The hope was so great. The longing was so long. The yearning was so overwhelming. All with whom Michiko came into contact became infected with her enthusiasm for the devoutness, and the trustworthiness of Father Bernard Petitjean.

Did Father Petitjean deserve such trust? How did he know he could make such a difference? It was like a storybook ending that was later modified and told in biblical terms: And thus it came to pass that... seven months after the official re-opening of the "new" Catholic Church, which a paltry few attended, as Father Petitjean and Michiko were dusting and rearranging the artifacts on the front altar, Michiko looked around apprehensively as if fearing that someone was spying on them, and insecurely whispered in simplistic Japanese that she hoped the good Father would understand: "It is safe, Kakure Kirishitan, come to church?"

It was a simple question, he thought, that required a simple answer, so he simply nodded his head in the affirmative giving her the impression he understood completely what he was giving assent to. She looked at him intently, studying the deep-set lines of sincerity etched upon his craggy face. It was an honest face, a farmer's face, a face accustomed to planting seeds of faith.

Michiko reached inside the left side of her kimono and extracted a flattened bundle neatly wrapped in a purple silk bandana. She laid it upon the narrow counter in front of the altar and carefully uncovered the contents exposing a faded and wrinkled picture of a man hanging upon a cross. The portrait was painted upon rice paper, creased and brown-tinged with age, and encased in a thin, unpainted bamboo frame. It looked very ancient.

Father Petitjean gingerly picked up the picture and reverently set it in a place of honor next to a larger-than-life-sized wooden crucifix upon which Jesus agonized in effigy with his soulful eyes staring upward toward the highest point in the vaulted ceiling.

"A wonderful faded old likeness of our Lord and Savior," he commented with a look of delight radiating from his smiling face.

Michiko stared uncomfortably at the delighted Father. She shook her head gravely and reluctantly uttered, "I'm sorry."

"Sorry?"

"That is the rightful place for that portrait, but that is not a painting of Jesus of Nazareth."

"Then who is it?" Father Petitjean asked in surprise.

"It is Saint Paul," Michiko replied with deep-felt reverence.

"Ah, Saint Paul the Apostle," Father Petitjean responded with appreciation.

"So sorry, Father," the words were uttered with humility tinged with disappointment. "You do not know who that is?"

Father Petitjean scrutinized the portrait carefully. He could see the look of bewilderment on Michiko's face beginning to turn to sadness. His heart palpitated with anxiety. There was no one else on earth he so wanted to please. He stared at the faded old portrait in desperation, willing himself to recognize it. The vibrations from centuries past echoed from the crown of Nishizaka Hill and revitalized the portrait with the resonance of that fateful moment: *It's all about love.*

"That is Saint Paul Miki!" Father Petitjean blurted out. "He was recently canonized in Rome, on June eighth, 1862, to be exact, by Pope Pius the Ninth, out of respect for the martyrs of Japan."

"The people will be pleased to see his picture up there with our Lord." Michiko smiled with satisfaction and radiant happiness.

A lump of gratitude rose up and clogged Father Petitjean's throat. He was at a loss for words. Somehow he felt like crying. It was one of those moments.

"*Arigato gozaimasu*," Michiko said gratefully as she left to pass on the good news.

Thus it came to pass that on a warm autumn morning in 1865, three years after the canonization of Paul Miki, as Father Petitjean stood proudly beside the finely carved wooden doors of his recently refurbished Cathedral, a heart-warming miracle of sorts took place. Perhaps it was his perseverance, his unceasing faith in the improbable, his dreams of really making a difference in this world that produced the results.

Father Petitjean and one other lay Jesuit along with Michiko stood by the magnificent front entrance to the Church basking in the warmth of the brilliant morning sun. Father Petitjean liked to stand near the entrance on Sunday mornings, and personally welcome the few brave souls who dared to attend the morning service with words of encouragement and gratitude. However on this particular morning he noticed that Michiko had a rather smug smile on her face that he thought was a little unusual. Perhaps it was due to their conversation of the week before. He had left the portrait of Saint Paul Miki standing next to the crucifix of Christ. It was a prominent location, one that was sure to please those who attended.

Slowly and surely the people began to trickle in. Five, ten, fifteen – incredible! Twenty! In little groups of two to five finely dressed adults, some with little children in tow, the congregation began to assemble. Thirty, forty, sixty, eighty, ninety, one hundred! Where did they all come from? It was surreal, like in a wonderful dream.

Father Petitjean stood near the entrance to the great Cathedral spellbound with rapture. He had dreamed of this! Was he in fact dreaming? Was this actually happening? He glanced over at Michiko. She was beaming and smiling with such a radiant joy she looked positively angelic. Was he daydreaming, or had he actually died, and gone to heaven?

One-fifty, one-seventy-five, two hundred. Unbelievable! And still they came, bowing and smiling respectfully to the trustworthy man wearing the long black robe, to the tall, gaunt Jesuit priest who reciprocated so graciously, so sincerely with a beatific smile on his face while in the most humble fashion honest tears of gratitude ran unimpeded down his shiny cheeks. The morning sunlight revealed the inner soul of a simple man who bowed and smiled ever so reverently because with all his heart he wanted to demonstrate to God that he, Father Bernard Petitjean, could make a difference. No one could have looked more saintly on that occasion.

It was a moment like no other moment in Father Petitjean's entire life. He never shook so many eager hands and bowed tirelessly to so many happy faces ever before. His countenance was flushed with excitement and his eyes sparkled with incredulity. Two-fifty, two-seventy-five, three hundred. Astounding! And still they continued to arrive dressed in their Sunday best.

After two hundred and forty years, isolated in small secretive pockets in the foreboding hills and on isolated islands around Nagasaki, without even a single Bible or any printed material – which would have been far too incriminating to possess – these Christians in hiding had kept their faith, inspired by the twenty-six Christians martyred on Nishizaka Hill back in 1597. And now they had revealed themselves for the first time for what they were, *Kakure Kirishitan*, because they had placed their trust in Father Bernard Petitjean. What difference would this make?

"It is a blessed miracle," Father Petitjean was heard to mumble over and over to himself as the multitude assembled in the cavernous confines of God's only true Church in all of Japan

Michiko returned to Father Petitjean's side after ushering in the last of the stragglers. She smiled that enigmatic smile that so intrigued the fatherly priest. It was as if on a psychic level she vaguely intuited the good years that lay ahead. It was a heady feeling. Heady enough to cause Father Petitjean to cross himself and offer up a humble prayer of thanks. He spoke reverently in Latin, but Michiko understood the sentiment. They both stood there transfixed by the momentous ramifications of the moment, smiling inscrutably with an inner joy that knew no bounds.

Over the years as more and more Kakure Kirishitan revealed themselves, their numbers mushroomed to well over thirty thousand devout Christian souls! It was deemed to be miraculous enough to inspire Pope John II to reward them with his illustrious presence. It was an occasion like no other in the history of the Roman Catholic Church. It represented the magical culmination of over two hundred and forty years of unrelenting devotion, unmatched perseverance, and unshakable faith in their Lord and Savior, Jesus Christ. It was only fitting that His Eminence, dressed in raiments of white and gold to suit the occasion, welcome the Kakure Kirishitan back into the fold of the mighty Roman Catholic Church.

What a great honor had been magnanimously offered to the valiant and stalwart Kakure Kirishitan. What a noble gesture of acceptance and accommodation. It was indeed a pivotal moment in the tragic history of a long-suffering group of "Hidden Christians."

Sometimes the passage of time, like a tiny trickle of water over the polished surface of granite rock, erodes the face and leaves it scarred with the ravages of duration. Similarly the smooth face of tradition is often marred by circumstances to make it coincide with necessity. After two hundred and forty years of secrecy and isolation the Hidden Christians had developed a self-sufficiency and independence that affected their sense of identity. God was protecting them. They were special: they were the favored ones God had saved.

Persecution has a powerful effect upon the psyche of those persecuted. The longer the persecution, the more imperative the need to rationalize one's existent state in such a manner as to insure one's survival and justify one's abysmal existence. There is an obvious common sense and logic in such rationalizations, relative to the dire circumstances concerned, that make them not only believable, but necessary. The necessity gives rise to dogma and religious belief. Long after the persecution ended, the Hidden Christians, like the enslaved Israelites who were led to freedom by Moses, clung tenaciously to their persecution mentality. It gave them a special identity. The hidden Christians came to believe that they, and only they, were "the chosen few." It was a righteous belief that enabled them to secretly survive for over two hundred and forty years under the most dire of circumstances, a belief they were loath to give up.

The unbelievable happened just as if it were natural. The Kakure Kirishitan in a "righteous moment" humbly declined the Pope's generous offer without due consideration as to how this would be construed by the most powerful religious institution on earth.

How, even in retrospect, can such a seemingly irrational response be rationalized? What happened, happened because unfortunately, at the worst possible time one of Christianity's most self-serving features surfaced: exclusivity; the same exclusivity that self-righteously enables Christians in general to believe with impunity that only they are amongst the chosen, saved, or elect. The Hidden Christians behaved like the true Christians they claimed to be. Since they righteously conceived of themselves as being "special", they refused to be absorbed into the bosom of the Mother Church. What darksome forebodings might a sensitive soul have intuited at that turning point in the tenuous survival of the long-suffering "Hidden Christians" of Japan?

Alas, in one of history's most terrible tragedies, at precisely two minutes past eleven on the morning of August 9, 1945, an atomic bomb nicknamed "Fat Man", manufactured by the world's most powerful Christian nation, exploded with the vengeful wrath of a man-made hell above the beatific arches of a magnificent Catholic Cathedral located in the heart of the district of Urakami in the beautiful port city of Nagasaki, and in the twinkling of a ferocious eye, decimated Japan's largest community of Christian souls.

CHAPTER THREE

Penny awoke from a restless slumber. It was one of those nights, one of those sleepless nights when her mind refused to shut down. She glanced at her wristwatch; it was 5:30 a.m. and the sun was just beginning to stain the eastern horizon with a wash of old whiskey yellow. Larry was curled over on his side sleeping peacefully like a baby, having imbibed a liberal amount of good Scotch at the neighbor's across the street the night before. "I'm so glad he is happy and content," she thought. "Funny," she reflected, "how I can be lying right here beside him wide awake, and he is unaware." She stared at her husband. "Perhaps he is dreaming a fantastic dream about us and in that dream I am lying in bed wide awake. He is so unusually perceptive, kind, and considerate. I am a very lucky woman."

In spite of their trusting and loving relationship there was one thing that Penny could not bring herself to share with Larry. It was one of those embarrassments that existed at the core of her being and every once in a while when she thought she had forgotten it, it would appear unexpectedly triggered by a thought or a dream that would leave her with a forlorn yearning and a nostalgic sadness. The fact that it persisted over time gave credence to the depth of its impact. "It was nothing," she would rationalize to herself, "just an infatuation by an immature, lonely and vulnerable young woman with unrealistic romantic notions."

She had kept it to herself. It was too personal. No one else would appreciate the existential indecisiveness she had exhibited way back then when she was an aspiring manager in training. With the passing years it diminished in significance but at the time it was everything. It was a young girl's romantic yearning for something more than a business career. If she told Larry he would probably understand in a cerebral capacity. "Just one more needless thing for him to worry about," she reflected soberly. So she kept it stored in the murky recesses of her memory where it percolated along like watered down coffee grounds.

It was a cool autumn day in October when Penny entered the office building in downtown Calgary. It was in those early years when she was obsessed with the desire to become a powerful force in the business world. The receptionist said, "You must be one of the applicants for our Assistant Manager position?"

Penny smiled and nodded. "Yes I am," she responded confidently, "I'm Penelope Miki."

"Just take a chair; the boss is interviewing another applicant at the moment."

"How many applicants are there?" Penny asked boldly.

"There were dozens, but we've narrowed it down to only seven. You're the only woman on the short-list." The receptionist looked Penny over. She raised her right eyebrow. "The company's policy is to be nondiscriminatory," she offered sympathetically. "We have hired the odd Oriental in the past, but they were all overqualified males; one had an MBA – you'd be the first woman. Good luck."

"I must be the token woman," Penny thought to herself as she selected a chair near the window.

After a wait of about fifteen minutes a solemn looking young man emerged from the Manager's office and left without saying a word. The receptionist came over to Penny and said, "The boss will see you now." She ushered Penny into the Manager's office and introduced her to the boss. "Jim, this is Penny. Penny, this is Jim." She turned and closed the office door quietly behind her as she left.

Penny looked apprehensively at the man called Jim. He was of slim build and average height. A neatly pressed grey gabardine suit accented with a narrow black and white striped necktie matched his shiny black patent leather shoes. A pair of thick black academic's spectacles sat perched upon a thin protruding nose. His sandy colored hair was combed sideways with a neat part on the left. He looked like a typical "organization man".

He smiled. It was a shy, timid, self-conscious smile, the kind that otherwise confident young males sometimes unintentionally display when in the presence of a woman they find attractive. It was that smile that captivated Penny's heart. Was it love at first sight? Or simply a young girl's infatuation with the seemingly impossible?

Jim walked forward, as he did with all the applicants, with his right hand extended in welcome. He found from past experience that shaking hands at the beginning rather than at the end of the interview fostered a more amicable atmosphere of openness and cordiality.

Penny glanced down at Jim's extended hand and was suddenly and inexplicably overwhelmed with a simple child-like sensation of mortifying shyness.

Jim stood there awkwardly with his hand held out in greeting. The pale white hand looked obscenely naked dangling out there by itself. He self-consciously withdrew it with a tinge of embarrassment as if he had been caught exposing himself, and pretended he was just slowly raising it to smooth his neatly combed hair. "Please have a seat," he said briskly as if to cover up his vulnerability. He quickly turned and sat down as if to hide behind his massive stained-oak desk. With a deliberate casualness he slowly removed his spectacles, and as he peered across the desk's vast surface, removed the lid from a yellow felt pen and studiously highlighted the name Penelope Miki on the neatly typed list in front of him.

Penny sat down and attempted to compose herself. She knew Jim could sense her feeling of nervousness in his presence, but there it was, and it was not about to go away. "I'm so glad to be here," she said, smiling that demure smile of hers. "I guess I must be the token woman applicant," she blurted out without thinking, and immediately turned beet red.

It was a pathetic scene. Nothing was going according to plan. All those brilliant answers she had memorized vanished into the confusion of her embarrassing response. Penny could feel the heat drain from her cheeks as the realization of what she so uncharacteristically had done impinged upon her. *I must be the token woman applicant.* What a presumptuous thing to say! What was done was done. There was no taking it back. She sat up primly, smiled graciously and rose, with the face-saving intentions of one descended from a long line of honorable samurai, to excuse herself.

"How did you guess?" Jim asked rising along with her.

"I'm sorry; I really did not mean to say that," Penny apologized.

"But you are right!" Jim exclaimed. "My boss instructed me to interview at least one female to make it look good. But, you know? I would have short-listed you anyway. Please, do sit down."

Penny sat down and composed herself. She had no idea that he had studied her letter of application assiduously and was anxious to meet its author. It was his instinct for honing in on talent that had enabled him to rise so quickly to his present position. *Penelope Miki,* there was something about that name that intrigued him, and now he knew why. It was so natural. She just appeared through the office door like a ray of golden sunshine that filled the room with a sublime aura. It was a first, one of those fluke happenings that occur as if it is supposed to. To Jim she looked like a precious gem, so rare and so exquisite you could spend a lifetime searching and never find another, because she was one-of-a-kind.

"Tell me," Jim asked, sagging back into the comfort of his plush leather swivel chair while forming a thoughtful little pyramid with his index fingers, "Why are you the best candidate for this job?"

Penny got the job. She was thrilled. She gave notice that she would be leaving her old job as a junior management trainee with a large department store chain. She could hardly wait to begin her new job as a junior assistant manager. Penny went out and bought a new wardrobe befitting the new executive role she would be playing. It was a very difficult part, a very complicated and difficult dramatic role to be thrust into so suddenly. Perhaps it was too difficult, too demanding, too much to ask from such a young inexperienced woman.

It was one of those challenging situations with high expectations and intricate personal relationships that only come around once in a lifetime. If the opportunity is not recognized, if the moment is not seized and acted upon decisively, if one is not fully aware of the monumental significance of the existential implications, and if one is blown away with intimidating feelings of self-doubt and insecurity, the moment passes, never to return again. And when it passes, it passes with a whimper as if a crying need is never again to be met in this lifetime. It is as if a hollowness has been created that can never be filled, as if a never-ending sorrow has made itself at home in that hollow space.

Penny recalled that first day at work. She was so nervous and filled with anxiety. All she wanted was to please her new boss. She wanted him to think well of her both as a colleague and as a person. She did her best. She never worked so hard before. And yet it really was not work. It was fun. It was stimulating. It was life.

Jim was the most patient, tolerant, and understanding man Penny had ever met, let alone worked for. He was genuinely kind, polite and considerate. He was too nice not to have a profound effect upon a maturing young lady aspiring to walk in his shoes. He epitomized everything a woman could desire in a mate. He may have had many personal flaws but to Penny he was perfect. Her youthful dreams of love and romance were all rolled into one fabulous person, and his name was Jim.

Each day when Penny went to work she looked forward to seeing Jim but he was frequently upstairs on the fifth floor where he was being groomed for a more senior management position. Sometimes a whole week would go by and Penny would only catch a glimpse or two of him at lunchtime or at coffee break. Perhaps it was this unavailability that heightened Penny's infatuation and deepened her emotional need for human warmth and affection. She had her own office and she was making a good wage but all of this was incidental if a day went by and she did not see Jim.

Jim was eight years older than Penny. He appeared to have a glamorous looking girlfriend who frequently dropped by the office to chat with him. "Why in the world would he be interested in a drab person like me?" Penny would admonish herself whenever she saw Jim in the presence of his sophisticated female friend. But still she could not deny the crying need that overcame her when she lay in bed hugging her pillow at night. "Please God, let Jim fall in love with me," she would pray with an audible whimper, and her heart would nearly burst with longing.

Once during coffee break Jim came over to where Penny sat alone and said, "Can I join you?"

Penny's heart skipped a beat as she said in a pleasant voice, "Sure, be my guest." This was the only non-business meeting that Penny ever had with Jim. She vividly remembered every minute detail of that opportunity. He sat across from her at the round two-seater table and clasped his hands around a shiny black porcelain coffee mug. He seemed a little nervous and apprehensive. He took in a deep breath and seemed to be building up the courage to say something momentous – but he never said it. Instead he shyly stuttered as if in the sublime presence of a deity, "H-how's it going?"

"Oh, fine," Penny responded quickly while gazing at his hands which cradled the coffee mug gently. She longed to reach out and touch his hand. Ever since she had missed the opportunity to shake his hand she had fantasized about the simple touch of his hand, but the opportunity never rose again. And there he was sitting with his hands erotically caressing that porcelain mug as if its smooth surface was the palm of her hand.

"I guess you must be busy – eh?" he asked tentatively looking up at Penny as if she was seated upon a pedestal.

"Of course, I'm very busy," Penny replied hastily, thinking Jim was inquiring about her workload. She immediately realized the possible implications of that particular response regarding her availability after work, and was just about to clarify her response when Jim replied.

"It's nice to be busy." He slowly rose to his feet looking somewhat disappointed by Penny's Spartan response. "I guess I'd better let you get back to work," he said and hesitated a second as if attempting to prolong the moment. He gazed with hopeful anticipation in Penny's direction.

Penny's heart was palpitating so wildly she could scarcely breathe. "Yes-yes," she stammered.

"Keep up the good work," he added reassuringly and slowly walked away as if disheartened.

Penny wanted to run after him and say, "I was referring to my work here. I'm not busy. I'm not busy at all." That night Penny cried herself to sleep. It was another missed opportunity.

Soon after, Jim was promoted to Regional Manager and transferred to Edmonton. On the day of his departure he dropped by Penny's office and poked his head in past the door.

"Guess I won't be seeing you again – will I?" he said in a voice tinged with sadness as if he knew he was on the verge of losing something very precious. He looked tired and disheveled.

Penny just sat forlornly at her desk. Jim was leaving and there was nothing she could do or say about it. She looked up and smiled feebly. The door closed and Jim left.

That was the last time Penny saw him. Since then she had rationalized her behavior every which way. "If only I had reached out and shaken his hand," she regretted, "it might have made all the difference in the world."

Larry yawned and rolled over to face Penny. He rubbed his eyes and said, "What time is it?"

"It's a little after six," Penny replied brightly.

"How come you're so wide awake?"

"I couldn't sleep. I've just been lying here thinking about my younger days in Calgary."

"Want to share your thoughts?"

"Not really. As you know, some things are better left unsaid," Penny replied sitting up in bed.

"I understand," Larry agreed. "There are some things that are too embarrassing for words."

"You are a gem," Penny commented as she slid out of bed and pulled on her long blue velvet dressing-gown. "I think I'll work on the manuscript for a while. Why don't you go back to sleep?"

"I might as well join you now that I'm awake," Larry responded, jumping out of bed. "Let's look at that section on Awareness."

I V RATIONALIZATIONS

(1) Awareness

Awareness entails consciousness. It is the prerequisite for knowledge, and the illumination by which the darkness of ignorance is transformed into wisdom and understanding. It is that which impinges upon the five receptor senses at birth and floods the brain with sensate information. It is the basis of intelligence. It is associated with a self-conscious "I" who peers out from within a mortal identity to find a miracle planet. It is relative to the beholder.

Karma and Awareness

When a pebble is tossed into the ocean, concentric circles radiate out from the initial point of entry: the larger the pebble, the greater the radius of the ensuing concentric rings. It could be said that a newborn babe is like a pebble tossed into the vast ocean of life, and from her/his initial moment of awareness, the circles of awareness have been expanding commensurate with the karmic magnitude of her/his point of entry. One's potential for awareness is relative to one's karmic status at the point of entry; that is why some people are more aware than others. An untold number of years of karmic reincarnation have evolved each individual into the unique persona she/he has become. When conditions are sufficient, then manifestation results relative to the frequencies that resonate to form that particular personality or individual.

An Expanding Awareness

Human beings have been gifted with varying degrees of potentiality with which to expand their level of awareness during each karmic incarnation. Unfortunately many squander the opportunity. For various reasons they do not seem to be able to learn from their mistakes and consequently are prone to repeat them over and over. The human experience is all about learning and benefiting from one's mistakes. No one is perfect. A greater degree of awareness makes one more conscious of one's imperfections. It is relative to each individual persona.

Toward A Global Awareness

As residents of planet earth most humans begin their sojourn as citizens of a specific village or city. They usually start out by limiting their awareness to their immediate surroundings like their house and their neighborhood, and quickly expand it to include the encompassing village or city. As they mature and grow older their awareness expands to include the Province or State, and in most cases the Country. Most people identify strongly with this level of awareness because it provides them with a meaningful identification, e.g. as a Canadian, Australian, Russian and so on. The vast majority of people seem to have reached this particular level of awareness; it is often referred to as "nationalistic patriotism". At this level of awareness the people are willing to make heroic sacrifices for the good of their own country, state, or city.

In the modern era the vast majority of people, wherever they live in the Global Village, have risen to this "nationalistic", self-protective and self-aggrandizing level of collective consciousness and that is precisely why they see themselves as being different and separate from all the others who come from different countries or nations. The cultural and religious differences give each respective nation a sense of patriotic pride which makes them susceptible to militant leaders espousing a jingoistic war-mentality motivated by greed and self-interest. It is a limited outlook that, due to its world-wide pervasiveness, makes it difficult for individuals seeking a greater spiritual happiness to rise above the righteous restrictions placed upon them by inflated egos with narrow minds.

However, an increasing number of enlightened souls are managing to rise above this nationalistic level of awareness during this incarnation. They have developed a "global awareness": the World is their country or nation. They are responsible citizens of the Global Village, mature adults with an expanded level of awareness that enables them to identify with, and feel compassion for, their fellow human beings wherever they may reside. At this level every human being is part of the mosaic that constitutes the reality of their identity and self-concept. They are "Citizens of the World" and "Universal Patriots".

"Citizens of the world and universal patriots," Larry enthused. "Wouldn't that be great?"

"No more nationalistic bickering or jingoistic platitudes."

"We'd all be able to work together for the common good."

"*The common good.* A socialist phrase with communistic implications that strikes fear into the heart of every dyed-in-the-wool capitalist," Penny retorted.

"Did I detect a hint of sarcasm there?"

Penny cogitated briefly before sprightly responding, "Did you know that my father, Hideo, always voted CCF or NDP?" as if that bit of information was pertinent.

"I thought he might have been a Liberal or PC. He always struck me as being very conservative."

"He was a great admirer of Tommy Douglas as were most Issei and Nisei who were evacuated from the west coast. 'It is a matter of principle,' he'd say."

"Tommy and the CCF voted against the War Measures Act that authorized the evacuation of the Japanese-Canadians... right?"

"Tommy Douglas had backbone at a time when the political elite were spineless!" Penny retorted with extra vehemence.

"I'd say your sarcasm is warranted," Larry commiserated.

"It really wasn't sarcasm."

"What was it?"

"The hard truth."

CHAPTER FOUR

"I find the time we spend together working on this handbook very enjoyable," Penny remarked.

"Yes, it is not only mentally stimulating, it is exciting," Larry agreed.

"We have chosen some interesting ideas and concepts that have excited and challenged man's intellect over the centuries."

"The challenge can also be demanding and draining if you don't take a break once in a while," Larry added, turning off the computer.

Penny rolled back her chair with a push of her left heel until it was even with her husband's. "I've been feeling a little fatigued of late. I feel the need to get away for a while," she said with a sigh.

"Why don't you drive out to the Professor's," Larry suggested as he rose to leave the study, "I'm sure he won't mind."

Every once in a while Penny craved solitude; at such times she would drive out to the Professor's house down by the ocean. He had been very kind to her ever since she had begun work on her doctorate. She had a standing invitation to use his guesthouse whenever it was vacant, which was nearly all the time. It was very generous of him because to rent such a place would be very costly.

The guesthouse was a little A-frame tucked back in the cedars beside the main house. It had a lovely view of the ocean. Penny liked to sit out on the front patio and just gaze out at the endless waves as they rolled in one after the other. It reminded her of the phrase, "shores of eternity." She had been coming out more frequently of late because she seemed to be feeling a little more tired and fatigued by her daily routine at home. Perhaps it was her biological time clock telling her to slow down and take it easy. Lately she looked forward to getting away as much as possible and just vegetating at the guesthouse. She seemed to need it.

The last time she felt particularly tired, she began to think about her last will and testament. She had never really given it much thought before because her whole orientation had been toward life – even death meant new life to her. Consequently it was somewhat difficult for her to think about her will. But something told her it was time. It was time to begin to get her earthly affairs in order.

The pen and paper were still there where she had left them on the side table just inside the patio door. Penny picked them up on her way out. She settled into the comfortable lounge chair under the sprawling branches of a giant cedar tree on the north side of the patio. She held the pen poised for action above the surface of the paper; it waited there apprehensively, ready at a moment's notice to scrawl some wriggly lines that would represent the sum total of her material wealth. It was a simple but solemn task. What should she leave to her husband and two children? Everything? She would leave everything to Larry and trust that he in turn would leave everything to Sherry and Jerry. The way those three names rhymed always made her smile. She was so fortunate to be so blessed. There was not much she needed to say. She trusted them to do the right thing.

Beside her husband's name she placed a small asterisk, and near the bottom of the page she made a larger asterisk so that it would not be missed. Adjacent to it she wrote, "Leave at least five thousand dollars to the David Suzuki Foundation on behalf of the Fearsome Foursome. The entire world benefits from his work." Ever since Penny had joined the staff at UBC she had become an admirer of Dr. David Suzuki. He represented all the values that resonated with her notions of what was needed in a world consuming itself with greed and irresponsibility.

Death did not frighten Penny. "It really is a strange word," she thought. "What does it really mean, and why are people so afraid of it? Is it because it is an unknown, and always will be as long as we are mortal? Is it not part and parcel of the definition of mortality? And is it not mortality that gives life its special significance and meaning?" She glanced at the vast ocean. The sun hovered brilliantly above the distant horizon sending shimmering fingers of life-giving energy across the surface of the placid Pacific.

Penny got up, opened the screen door that led from the front patio to the interior of the guesthouse. She disappeared inside and returned with a cold bottle of beer. She sat back down on the lounging chair she had been sitting on and continued with her pondering. "What if we are actually immortal?" she asked herself, "and birth and death are the alpha and omega that make our immortality seem mortal. Being born is the transition into mortality, and dying is the transition out of mortality. Birth and death are like the covers on a life's story," Penny reflected taking a thirsty drink from the beer bottle.

"Each life is a unique story, and mine has been too wonderful for words. I have been so fortunate. I could have died when I was an infant – but I would have missed everything! I have been blessed. I have been blessed. I have been blessed...." Penny kept repeating that phrase over and over to herself like a mantra until she dozed off into a very calm slumber.

Funny how things come to you when the timing is appropriate. When she awoke in the calm of the summer evening Penny felt refreshed and ready for a quiet stroll along the beach. The sun sat poised as if sitting upon the thin edge of reality waiting patiently in all its scarlet-red magnificence for a slender, sleepy-eyed little woman to view the magnificence of its departing rays. It was a moment worthy of being shared with the world – but Penny was alone.

"What have I done to deserve such beauty?" she asked herself as she stepped down from the patio and made her way toward the water's edge. She felt very privileged. For some inexplicable reason she felt the need to do something indicative of her presence; consequently she casually picked up a pebble the size of a small marble and pitched it out into the Pacific with a side-arm motion that caused the pebble to arch high above the surface and descend into the water with a splash that could be seen but not heard.

A cool breeze from the Pacific ruffled Penny's hair as she stared off toward the western horizon where the copper-red of the water met the fading pink of the sky. Out of the crest of the horizon a tiny blip appeared about the size of a lightning-bug that darted left and right as it zig-zagged its way into the field of her observation. "Something is out there!" she thought. Somehow she refused to think of it as an "unidentified" flying object because she knew precisely what it was. It was a highly sophisticated flying disc manufactured and operated by a very intelligent life form which due to its advanced state seemed alien to those unable to conceive of the existence of a higher species. This was not the first time she had spotted one. Mass sightings such as the one that occurred on July 11th 1991 in Mexico City on the occasion of a pending solar eclipse confirmed beyond a doubt the existence of such flying machines. "They are everywhere,"

Penny reflected. "They have been hovering around, possibly flitting in and out of space-time dimensions/reality membranes, observing us ever since mankind as a species became upright and began walking on his two hind legs."

Over the years, since she became interested in the Roswell, New Mexico incident where according to government officials a "weather balloon" crash on July 2nd 1947, she and her husband had been mindful of the ongoing saga of the UFO debacle, especially in the USA where powerful special interests had been able to take control of government agencies and limit public awareness of the phenomena. The objectives espoused by these agencies were twofold: one, to investigate all sightings, and two, to explain away all such phenomena as being either a hoax or some natural misconception – while utilizing all such extraordinary "found technology", such as that garnered from the crashed flying disc recovered at Roswell, for their own purposes. It was, and is, an extremely small-minded and selfish modus operandi that keeps nonpolluting energy-saving technology secret, in order that a power-elite can continue to reap obscene profits from nonrenewable sources of highly polluting carbon-based energy. It was frustrating for those who felt that the official story lacked credibility, and the frustration was being felt far beyond the borders of the USA.

Recently an old photo the government had circulated to debunk the claim that a UFO had crashed at Roswell came back to haunt them. It was taken in the days when the US government produced such photos as hard evidence to back up their claims. Penny had seen the photo many times. It was published in books, magazines, and newspapers, and shown prominently on television as proof positive. In the photo an army officer is clearly shown holding up the remnants of a crashed weather balloon with one hand, while in the other he is nonchalantly clutching what appears to be a small piece of paper on which there appears to be some blurred typing. No one gave that innocuous looking bit of paper a second thought... until recently.

"Sometimes clutching-at-straws, pays off," Penny sub-vocalized. With the aid of advanced photo-image enhancing technology, the blurred typing was deciphered! It was hard evidence. The innocuous piece of paper turned out to be a telegraphed message from a General to the officer holding the memo. The telegram ordered the officer to: *Ship the crashed flying disk and the alien victims' bodies to Houston.*

Penny stooped to unbuckle her sandals intending to walk barefoot in the sand. As she straightened up the blood rushed from her head. She staggered around like a drunk momentarily losing her sense of equilibrium. She sat down on the sandy beach with a thump.

Perhaps it was the dizzy spell; who knows? As she sat quietly on the sand waiting for her head to clear an idea that somewhat explained the ignorant behavior that so frustrated her floated into the realm of her cognitive domain. "It is all about the relativity of our level of awareness. We do not realize how limited our level of cognition is! On a scale of 1 to 10 our pretentious ego always tends to place us near the top because we feel we are as aware as we can possibly become; it is a vain pretence reinforced by our ignorance and limited lower level of awareness. We think we are a ten when we are probably closer to a one or a two. Such vanity and self-deception makes it difficult for us to relate realistically to other life forms with higher intellects and vastly expanded levels of cognition. It provides an explanation for the general lack of understanding and foresight associated with the self-serving mentality that gives rise to the temptation to profit financially from disasters as life-negating as starvation, disease, poverty, sickness, pollution, global warming, and war."

Such thoughts left Penny feeling emotionally upset. She attempted to calm herself down by asking rhetorically, "Who cares what I think?"

The question was humbling, and the answer even more so: "Next to nobody!"

A deprecating scowl seared across her face reflecting an underlying dissonance. "So be it!" she scoffed at the humiliating manner in which she had managed to put herself down. She kicked her right foot through a crested mound of sand and sent it flying into smithereens. "So much for that!" she pronounced out loud.

The outburst sent a slight shiver racing up her spine and flooded her consciousness with such a sudden resolve that she exclaimed: "We just don't get it!" She shuddered and shook her head. It was mentally and physically demoralizing in such a way that it affected her bladder. She felt a sudden need to relieve herself. She hurried back to the cabin, rushed in through the patio door and straight into the bathroom.

While she was sitting comfortably on the smooth hardwood toilet seat Penny smiled and reflected, "Funny how some of our best thinking is done while sitting on the throne or standing in the shower. It seems laughable but it really does happen!" The notion prompted her to laugh out loud and remark to herself, "I might just as well take a soothing shower while I'm in this frame of mind."

She deftly removed her clothing and gingerly stepped into the corner, beige-colored fiberglass shower and pulled the clear plastic curtain carefully over the opening. While she was in the shower with the relaxing massage of the hot water cascading over her naked body like a waterfall in the wilderness, her primordial instincts brought back vivid memories of a movie in which primatologist, Dian Fossey, was depicted living unobtrusively amongst the Great Apes in Africa. The movie was based upon Dian's book entitled *Gorillas in the Mist* which told the story of how she established a research camp in Rwanda in 1967 and three years later made the first gorilla-to-human contact ever recorded.

With the warm water streaming down over her head, the analogy washed over Penny like a stream of consciousness: *We human beings are analogous to the great apes! The gorillas are only aware of their limited jungle habitat and the reality of that habitat. To them it is everything. Into their midst, from out of nowhere, appears this "alien" who sort of looks like a primate, but is pale, skinny and lacks body hair. Where did it come from? It just appeared out of the mist and settled amongst them in the forest. Is it a threat? Should they attempt to kill it?*

Of course the gorillas are not aware that this strange-looking "alien" has an awareness that is vastly superior to theirs. They are blissfully ignorant of the fact that the "alien" is aware that that specific jungle habitat in which they exist is only a tiny enclave in a country called Rwanda which is only a small part of a large continent called Africa, which is one of many continents which make up the land mass on a planet called earth, which exists in the Milky Way galaxy, which is only one of many galaxies that make up the universe. Can the gorillas somehow instinctively intuit that the "alien" means them no harm, and is there to study them in order to find ways to save them from becoming extinct as a species? How can the "alien" communicate this knowledge to the great apes?

The gorillas are only aware of a puny-looking "alien" who sometimes emits strange sounds and waves its skinny arms about. They tolerate it. It seems so weak and defenseless; they take pity on it. After all they are Great Apes – and what is this?

As the analogy soaked into her mind, Penny turned off the water, opened the shower door and grabbed a towel. She quickly dried herself off and secured a fluffy white terrycloth bathrobe from the closet. She slipped it on and proceeded back out through the patio door toward the sandy beach. As she slowly walked along the shore feeling the soft sand squish between her toes she thought: "We are the great apes – and the extra-terrestrial 'aliens' are us!

"They have been monitoring our evolution as a species from the point of view of a vastly superior level of awareness. They see us nearly hairless homo sapiens scurrying about the surface of the earth selfishly squabbling like imbeciles, terrorizing and killing each other, while allowing billions of our own kind to suffer from impoverishment – when we have the technology, thanks to them, to eliminate starvation, poverty, and pollution. My god, a mere month after we manage to construct the atomic bomb we use it on our own species, not once, but twice, and threaten to use it again. We stockpile weapons of mass destruction and intimidate each other with our war-mentality. We aptly manifest the current level of our ignorance; it is commensurate with our diminished level of awareness. What is, exists or becomes manifest, because in our ignorance we create it! Is this representative of our collective karma?

"Are the benevolent 'aliens' hovering about in their magnificent flying machines alarmed by what has transpired on earth within the last century? Can they, with their vastly superior level of cosmic awareness, prevent us from exterminating ourselves? Will they dare to share their greater awareness with a lesser, a lesser that seems to be acting in a most self-righteous, ungrateful, and uncharitable fashion?

"Obviously they must be willing to dare to share. That is why they are here. Charity and magnanimity go hand in glove with a greater awareness." It was this new perspective that gave Penny a renewed sense of hope. She looked toward the horizon. The little glowing spark hovered there like the evening star. Was it a good omen?

"How can we pretend to be so morally and spiritually superior when our behavior is so atrocious? With our large brains we have unlimited potential – perhaps the 'aliens' know this, and our aberrant behavior piques their curiosity – they appreciate our innate potentiality, but do we? When one thinks one is superior one's conceit is one's greatest detriment to progress. Who can reason intelligently with such conceited pretenders who are not even aware enough to be cognizant of their own insufferable conceit, let alone their limited awareness?"

Penny groaned audibly. It was a loud and mournful groan self-inflicted by a new found sense of humility. The groan vibrated out across the vast Pacific where it resonated with the infinite potentialities of the miraculous cosmos. It represented a tiny spark of awareness emitted by a thoughtful little person walking barefoot along the shores of eternity, a single, solitary individual who within the depths of her heart and soul wanted with all her might to help make the world a little better place for all humankind. Was it enough to make a difference?

When Penny returned home from her sojourn of pensive isolation at the Professor's guesthouse, she found her husband hard at work editing the handbook. He was working diligently on the section labeled, Dharma.

"I'm back!" she announced as she strode into the study.

Larry levitated an inch from his computer chair with the comfortable padded armrests while his right index finger involuntarily clicked the left side of the mouse inadvertently highlighting the word, impetus. "Geezus," he exclaimed with a startled expression on his face, "You scared the shit out of me!"

"About time you changed your drawers," Penny responded. "What are you working on?"

"That section on Dharma that we weren't sure belonged in a handbook that attempted to present religious views objectively."

"And you still are undecided?"

"It depends upon the particular mindset of the reader. Some concepts are universal in application, but because certain religions have inculcated them as special aspects of their particular world view, they are frequently associated in the mind of some readers with that religion. But I suppose that is to be expected. I am sure most people are smart enough to see beyond the religious limitations."

"I take it that you have talked yourself into leaving this section on Dharma and the related sections that follow, in the handbook?"

"My consciousness has expanded sufficiently to allow me to rise above petty religious distinctions," Larry declared as he scrolled back to the beginning of the section under discussion.

(2) Dharma

Dharma requires a conscious "I". The "I" is you, and dharma is your path. Of all the paths that exist you have chosen this one: it is your very own. It is your personal past, present, and future all rolled into the Now. It is your Purpose. It is the reason you are here, instead of there. It is the breath that blows out the candles on your birthday cake and determines your wish. It fills the sails of your will with freedom and sets you on a course that leads to your destiny. Do you not feel it with every heartbeat and every breath you draw? It is you: the "you" that you have identified as "I". Being "I" is your dharma.

Historical Roots

Dharma is a very interesting concept that comes to us from the spiritual land of India where it was known as Sanatan Dharma or "eternal religion". It represents the name given to a body of Vedic teachings that later became designated as Hinduism after the ancient Greeks labeled the inhabitants along the banks of the Indus river as "Indoos" or "Hindus." Today the concept has been generalized to mean the eternal principles of righteousness that give direction and purpose to all human endeavor. It is the purposefulness of dharma that provides the impetus towards re-creating Creation according to the principles that order the universe and provide the universe with its essential function or nature. It is the innate purpose of all life to conduct itself in conformity with these universal principles. On a spiritual/ethical plane it provides the individual with an eternal purpose: to seek the way of higher Truth. The seeker is motivated to become a better person, a kinder, wiser, more patient, tolerant and understanding human being worthy of being made in the image or reflection of the Eternally-evolving Self.

Dharma and Vanity

It is one's essential purpose to conduct oneself in conformity with the nature and function of the universe. The impetus comes from within and provides the free-will that shifts neutrality into gear and provides Man with an ego. To consider oneself to be made in the image of one's Maker (or God) is of course the ultimate conceit of a very vain ego. It is the nature of Man to be vain and egotistical; if he were not so he would not have an identity. "I" is ego incarnate. His ego vaingloriously spurs him on to find out more and more about his identity. It provides the curiosity that motivates him to trace his roots, to explore the past, to examine the present, and to anticipate the future. How Man sees and defines himself determines how he will react to himself, to others, to the environment, and to Creation. It will become an expression of his personalized dharma (or self-ordained purpose or calling) and determine how he values his own life, the lives of others, and life in general.

There are two universal points of view that underlie how Man perceives the essential function or nature of all things. The inability to differentiate between these two points of view has added, and continues to add, more confusion to an already confusing situation. Put succinctly the two universal points of view are as follows: (1) the Extrinsic View where God is external to Man and Creation, and (2) the Intrinsic View where God is inherent in Man and Creation.

A person's attitude toward the essential nature and function of the universe can be seriously affected by one or the other of these points of view. Where one believes God resides colors one's entire perception of reality because God is the entity that gives meaning and significance to Man's existence. If one looks at the concept of "purpose of life" from these two points of view, the impact of the difference is staggering.

Dharma and the Extrinsic View

From the Extrinsic view God is separate and external to Man and Creation. This means that God does not reside inside Man or in any aspect of Creation, just as the maker of an idol does not reside in the idol. Man and Creation are therefore God-less because God resides somewhere else. This viewpoint naturally yields attitudes and beliefs that support and reinforce this view of reality.

The term "godforsaken" is symptomatic of this outlook on life. The earth is a godless place commensurate with the notion of "sin" where moral and ethical behavior is beyond Man's capacity. Pain and suffering and a low regard for the value of life are substantiations that God is not here. Life on earth is cheap. Why? Because it is godless. Attitudes condoning war, violence, a lust for power and control, and a disregard for the sanctity of planet earth are outgrowths of this view.

Unless Man acknowledges the existence of this external God, his life will remain Godless and devoid of any moral virtue. Man is incapable of saving himself as he is a Godless creature; therefore he must pray to his external God to "save" him.

Dharma and the Intrinsic View

From the Intrinsic view, God is inherent or inside Man and Creation. This makes a world of difference as to how Man then views himself and Creation. Because God resides in Man and is part and parcel of Creation, all life is precious, and the earth is a sacred place. Why? Because God is here instead of out there. This instills a natural reverence for life. Everything that matters is here and now; and what Man does to himself, to his fellow man, to planet earth and to Creation, he does to God.

Man's Collective Dharma

Everything that has happened on earth since Man's arrival could be considered to be Man's collective dharma. Various prophecies have been made regarding what could be the eventual outcome of Man's sojourn on planet earth. One of the most popular is an outgrowth of the extrinsic view known as the Doomsday scenario or the Self-fulfilling Prophecy of Doom. It is the collective "death wish" of hundreds of millions of religious sinners throughout the world who staunchly believe in the innate power of Original Sin and consciously, subconsciously, and unconsciously seek to justify this belief.

What is key to the realization of this scenario is the "belief" that it will happen. Before a runner can win a race the runner must believe that she/he can win the race; then the runner must enter the race and do her/his best to win. The same is true of all endeavors: first one believes one can do them; then one does them. It is imperative to hundreds of millions that Armageddon or the Doomsday scenario be realized in order to validate their belief, justify their actions, and confirm their place as sinners in a Godless world.

Is this to be our collective dharma? To be able to say as repentant sinners: "We were right!" Would it not be much better for the sake of all Mankind and this miracle planet, in this instance, for the self-righteous to be wrong? Think about it.

The more man in general thinks about his predicament, the more confused he can become. A great deal of the confusion is a result of the overlapping and blurring of the Intrinsic and Extrinsic points of view leading to endless squabbling over what the term "God" really means. What does the term "God" really mean? Could it be our collective dharma to figure this out?

CHAPTER FIVE

"Hmmm," Penny looked inquisitively at her husband. "Don't you think we were a bit repetitive in that section on Dharma?

"Repetitive?"

"Haven't we mentioned that business about the intrinsic and extrinsic views previously?" Penny asked turning sideways to look at her husband.

"Yes, but concepts like those need repetition. It is amazing how much scholarly confusion is simply the result of the inability of various new-age authors to clearly differentiate between these two points of view," Larry commented.

"I agree," Penny followed up, "and we are probably guilty of some confusion ourselves because we too are the product of this confusion."

"Me more than you," Larry admitted. "I have had to do a whole lot of soul-searching to arrive at my present point of view, while you have always had a more positive sense of dharma."

"You may be giving me more credit than I deserve. It is difficult to maintain an unbiased perspective, perhaps even impossible. Our ego constantly asserts itself, insidiously attempting to overcome our humility. It seems that every generation thinks it is the most advanced, the most knowledgeable, the highest point on the evolutionary scale. They think they stand on the cutting edge of the future, that there is no one ahead of them."

"Little do they know," Larry interjected, "they bring up the rear!"

"Most people are unaware that every person who has walked this earth in advance of their generation is ahead of them. Consequently they think they are truly modern and highly civilized even though their behavior indicates otherwise."

"It is amazing how technically advanced we currently think we are," Larry added giving voice to one of his pet peeves. "We still think we need to use brute force to overcome nature. We're still waging war against nature instead of working in harmony with the latent power and energy that is inherent within matter."

"It is a manifestation of our extrinsic mindset," Penny added.

"We waste billions of dollars of the taxpayers' money building crude three-story rockets to put a couple of hundred pounds of payload a few miles into outer space, because we have pitted ourselves against gravity and our mindset stereotypes our approach. All we need to do is apply the third law of motion to gravity itself. I know it is easier said than done but it irks me to see the lengths to which we will go to prove that the inherent power of nature can be overcome by brute external force. Those rockets symbolize our collective mindset."

"Our approach is determined by how we see the world. The reality we create matches our attitude and point of view."

"We have no idea how ignorant we really are!" Larry exclaimed. "We think we are so smart and highly advanced."

"Unfortunately we accord the highest status to those with all the material manifestations of power and wealth. We'd rather be ruthless, greedy, cruel and avaricious billionaires – than poor but highly spiritual and compassionate monks living in India or Tibet."

"Good examples of what we are alluding to are hard to find in this day and age, but there are a few popular individuals, although they are far from penniless, who seem to be at least eliciting the proper attitude."

"Who did you have in mind?" Penny asked.

"Who am I to say?" Larry responded reticently, unwilling to be put on the spot.

"You're not condemning – you're commending. I think I know of at least three well known contemporaries you may be thinking of."

"And they are?"

"Three respected individuals who are still alive and breathing are the Dalai Lama exiled from Tibet, and residing in the country of your birth: Dr. Deepak Chopra and Dr. Wayne Dyer. Of course there are many others, but these three compassionate persons come to mind at this time. Somehow they have risen above the herd mentality that surrounds them. Like you said, they have the proper attitude."

"Your psychic abilities have not diminished."

"Thanks."

"If we were not so puffed up with our own righteous attitudes, we might be able to rise above our collective ignorance."

"Ignorance is always represented by the last mistake, the last desperate question, the last hysterical laugh. It is what spurs us on to make progress. To reach beyond where we think we are," Penny pointed out.

"And like you said, we ourselves are no exception! We are both products of our times. We have been fortunate to have had the curiosity, the motivation, the perception, and the sensitivity to seek answers to questions that required us to reach beyond the prevailing attitudes and beliefs of the day."

"Yes, and if our children and other students and young adults like them are able to reach beyond where we have traveled in our journey through life, the world will be a better place for their passing," Penny added sagely. "It seems we have been the transition generation."

"I think the next generation will be far more illuminated than we were. It is hard to see things clearly when you have to look through a haze of dogmatic opinions, attitudes, and beliefs that have been prescribed for you like a set of tinted spectacles that are ruining your vision."

"When did you last get your vision checked?" Penny asked with a laugh.

"Just last month. Funny thing, when you are near-sighted your vision actually improves with age," Larry pointed out. "I can see a lot more clearly now."

"Clear enough to look over the next section?" Penny grinned at Larry, as she rolled her chair forward to a workable distance from the computer and scrolled on to Karma and Reincarnation.

(3) Karma and Reincarnation

What is Karma?

Put simply karma is the law of cause and effect applied to one's dharma. Karma is the universal law of cause and effect that when applied to human behavior results in a natural form of justice. There is no need for a vengeful and judgmental God to mete out justice. You reap what you sow. If you sow seeds of hatred and violence you will reap the consequences of those actions for in a complete and harmonic Creation the third law of motion which states, for every action there is an equal and opposite reaction, applies to every type of action: physical, mental, and spiritual. There are no exceptions.

In karmic terms the words "opposite reaction" indicate that the action produces an equal action in kind on the opposite side. It does not mean that hate produces love, but that hate produces hatred of an equivalent force on the opposite side. For example, let us say that a free-willed human being projects hatred and prejudice into the world by saying: "I hate all people whose skin color differs from mine." The moment he projects his hatred outward into the world there is an opposite reaction. His hatred mirrors his attitudes and beliefs which are reflected back to him much in the fashion that the images in two mirrors that interface each other reflect the reality of their own reflections. He reverberates in a reality of hatred.

This concept of karma is also supported by the first law of thermodynamics where matter and energy can only be transformed or changed. By our behavior we re-create a reality where the consequences of our behaviors become a part of the reality we created by our free-will. And consequently the actions and reactions produce the foreground and background of a karmic reality in which behaviors and actions set in motion in this lifetime can be transformed and changed, but never destroyed. What goes around comes around. One always gets exactly what one deserves.

And what is it that one deserves? One deserves to be reincarnated into precisely the being one has become. That is why the Buddha said: *All that we are is a result of what we have thought.*

Reincarnation (and Enlightenment)

According to the accepted doctrine of reincarnation human beings incarnate as many times as required, retarded by ignorance and advanced by wisdom, in order to evolve to higher and higher planes of existence until the highest plane of Oneness is realized. The level of one's progress is determined by one's karmic status. One incarnates at a level commensurate with one's level of awareness (or ignorance). Time is not of the essence. This is not a race. It is an eternal journey toward self-realization. Various degrees of awareness of Oneness can be achieved as a state of mind; the greater the awareness, the higher the karmic plane of spiritual progress. An indication that one is on the right path is manifested by the proper attitude.

Many people believe that an enlightened state of mind can be pragmatically self-induced through the physical manipulation of the energy known as "kundalini". One popular notion describes this process as follows: the kundalini which represents the life force rises up the spine passing through and energizing the seven chakras that encircle the spine with life energy. This life energy which is frequently associated with various colors of light continues to rise until it reaches the brain and induces a state of "Samadhi" experienced as a white light of bliss often described as a sensation of pure joy. Entire lifetimes are spent by some attempting to achieve this sensation. This blissful sensation is associated with the feeling of being holy, and although it can be "enlightening" – it is not enlightenment. Why? Enlightenment is the karmic attainment of a very special type of compassionate attitude that leads toward a heightened awareness of "Universality" often referred to as "Oneness".

The best known example in classical Greek philosophy of a proper attitude is found in Plato's "Allegory of the Cave". In this allegory, reality as we know it is compared to existing in a cave. In this cave the inhabitants are fixed in position so that they can see only their own shadow and the shadows of all other things from the world above reflected magically upon the wall of the cave from the fire-light behind them. The light from the fire burns inconsistently and consequently the shadows vary accordingly. Because the shadows are all that they can see, they assume that the shadows are real. They talk about these shadows in the same fashion as we talk about the things we can see. They spend their precious time discussing in animated fashion what they think the shadows represent and when consensus is achieved, a relative form of knowledge results. Eventually they make up a knowledge-game where the smart ones achieve status by being able to correctly identify the greatest number of shadows in the shortest time. Since this world of shadowy illusions (or Maya) is all they know, they refer to it as reality.

Now, suppose one man was to somehow become freed from his fixed position and slowly find his way to the mouth of the dark cave. The way would become his path to freedom. At first, however, the harsh glare of the sunlight would burn his eyes and he would be inclined to turn back into the cave, but as his eyes became adjusted to the real light of the glorious sun he would be amazed at what he saw. For the first time he would see the real objects in the real light of day. Could not such a man be said to possess real knowledge? He would indeed be a very wise man compared to his peers in the cave. But is he an enlightened man?

It all depends upon his attitude and his actions. He could
selfishly indulge himself by blissfully basking in the joyful warmth of
his newly discovered heavenly paradise for the rest of his mortal life
with those who had already found their way there – or he could
compassionately descend back down into the shadowy realm of the
cold, dark cave to *share his illumination* with his fellow human beings.
Is there any question what the "enlightened man" would do?

* * *

Penny knew what she had to do. She had to go back to
Lethbridge. She recalled the event with a tinge of sadness. It was a
dark, windy autumn night when the telephone rang and she received
the news. "I will have to go back right away," she told her husband.
"My dad is on his death-bed."

It was a somber day in mid October, October the 15th 1982 to be
exact, when Penny's father passed away. He had been diagnosed as
having pancreatic cancer three months previously and the doctors
were surprised that he had lived as long as he had considering his
advanced age.

Penny remembered attending her mother's funeral only two years
previously. Although she had been on blood thinners for several
years, she passed away quite suddenly one morning from a heart
attack brought on by a blood clot. She was a nonsmoker but she had
inhaled nearly a lifetime of secondhand smoke that perfumed their
little house with the pungent odor of burnt cigarette papers and stale
nicotine. At that time the surviving family members had decided to
purchase a joint headstone for the parents. Her father's side of the
headstone had been left blank awaiting his eventual demise.

"Death is the only constant in a life of change," Penny thought.
"It is the only event everyone can count on regardless of race,
religion, or nationality. It is the great equalizer."

The service had been brief. Her father had wanted it that way.
He had become a devout Buddhist. The older he got the more devout
he became. "When I am dead," he had said between puffs of his
everlasting cigarette, "cremate my body and scatter my ashes in the
estuary to the Pacific Ocean at Steveston." Hideo had never returned
to Steveston. Since the evacuation he had settled down in southern

Alberta like many of the others who had been sent to work in the sugar beet fields. He had made Lethbridge his home. All of his friends lived there and the people of Lethbridge were very tolerant and accepting of the Japanese Canadians in their midst.

Some of Hideo's ashes were interred alongside his wife Joyce's in the cemetery in Lethbridge. The rest were placed in an earthenware jar and given to Penny since she lived so close to Steveston. She stood alongside her siblings and family friends at the gravesite with her prayer beads dangling from her left hand, awaiting her turn to go up to the headstone and whisper a silent prayer of farewell.

The "Peach Girl" stood before her father's headstone with the prayer beads wrapped around her clasped hands. "More precious than life," he used to say, she recalled. "He could have lived ten years longer if not for me." Tears welled up in Penny's eyes as she remembered that solemn moment in room 201 at the hospital just a few hours before he passed away. He seemed very lucid then in spite of the painkillers. He had motioned for her to lean over so she could hear every word he uttered. It seemed he had something very important to share.

"Instead of 'ten years' – I should have said 'take my humble life, but spare her life', but at that time I was younger and still looking forward to a life of my own. It was very selfish of me, I must confess. Please accept my apology. I am so sorry, so very, very sorry."

Tears were coursing down Penny's cheeks. All those years she had never suspected how this humble man had labored to set things right. All that money he kept sending her which she had taken for granted while she enjoyed her classes at college and university. He had scrimped and saved and done without because he felt he should have been more magnanimous, more unselfish, at that existential moment when her fragile life hung in the balance and he had prayed: *Please God… God of all gods and of all religions… please spare the life of this child and I will gladly forfeit ten years of my remaining life – so she might live a lifetime.*

A cold breeze blew in from the west and ruffled the flowers scattered upon the gravesite. "Thanks Dad," Penny whispered, "to me one day of your life is worth an eternity. *Namu Amida Butsu*," she prayed.

* * *

Premonition is an irrational thing. Sometimes it just comes to you out of the blue. You say to yourself, "It's really nothing," but it is not nothing. It is something quite tangible, something that floods your entire being with a vague sense of foreboding, like a warning signal flashing in the distant fog as you travel toward your destination. Ever since the twins began U Vic Penny had developed an occasional inability to really draw in a deep breath without it being tinged with a sensation of fatigue. It had been intermittent over the past few years, and each time she just shrugged it off uncharacteristically as the effects of encroaching old age. But the sensation became increasingly incessant and at times almost overpowering.

"I'd better watch out or I'll turn into a hypochondriac!" Penny admonished herself whenever the feeling overcame her. Slowly and gradually she could feel her vibrant energy wane with each passing month. She ate more fresh fruits and green vegetables. She consulted her dietary handbook for ways she could enhance her physical energy level. She took vitamin supplements to balance out the healthful elements she thought her body was lacking. She forced herself to go out on long brisk walks in the refreshing air of the early morn.

Then one day she commented to Larry, "You know, I haven't been feeling very energetic of late. In fact I have been feeling quite poorly off and on for some time now. Sometimes I feel bone tired deep down inside and no amount of rest seems to alleviate the fatigue."

"I have noticed," Larry commented. "I think you should make an appointment to see Dr. Lee. You need to have a complete physical exam. Let me make an appointment for you," Larry asserted. There were times when it seemed natural that he should take charge. He walked over to the telephone and began dialing.

"Dr. Lee's office ? Yes, I'd like to make an appointment for my wife. Her name is Penelope Petitjean. She can come in almost anytime, the sooner the better. Next Wednesday is open? Just a sec; I'll check with my wife."

Penny procured her day-planner from the phone desk and saw she had a hair appointment at two-thirty in the afternoon. "Wednesday morning would be fine," she replied.

"How about Wednesday morning? At nine o'clock? Great. Thank you."

Thoughts of Dr. Lee brought a fleeting smile to Penny's face. When their old Doctor, whom Penny and Larry had been seeing since their move to Vancouver, decided it was time to retire he had referred them to a woman by the name of Dr. Lee.

"Most of my old patients are going to her. I recommend her highly." He paused and waited for their response.

"Dr. Lee," Larry had replied, "is that Chinese or what?"

"Or what difference does it make?" the old Doctor responded with an amused smile, "She is an excellent Doctor and isn't that what you want?"

Dr. Lee gave Penny a complete and thorough physical examination and had her undergo a series of tests which she said were routine for a woman of her age. All the specialists were close at hand and very professional. Smears, x-rays, scans, and biopsies were the order of the day. In addition Dr. Lee said she wanted to double check on one more thing "just to be on the safe side"; it had to do with her persistent cough. "I'll call you when the all the results are in," she said.

When Penny arrived home Larry sensed that her aura seemed quite feeble. She did not say anything. After a few minutes Larry asked, "How'd it go?"

"I had to take a few tests. You know the routine. She'll call me when the results are in." She did not say anything else.

Larry could tell by her body language that Penny was feeling a little apprehensive. At such times it was best to just leave her alone. When the time was right she would open up.

Penny went out to sit in the flower garden. She sat on the ornamental bench they had situated under a cedar tree. She sat there and marveled at all the beautiful life forms that surrounded her: the reddish Japanese maple, the yellow roses, the purple pansies, the kaleidoscope of shapes, colors, and auras flourishing happily under the noon day sun.

CHAPTER SIX

There was an old, old woman. She was one hundred and two years old. Her eyes watered, her back was slightly humped, her skin was dry and wrinkled, her wispy hair barely covered her scalp, and she walked with a slow shuffle. They called her *Obasan* out of respect. She deserved respect because she had learned how to be happy. It took her one hundred and two years, but she had achieved what Aristotle had pronounced to be the aim of all life: happiness. How elusive that state of mind can be for some of us who possess practically everything money can buy. Perhaps we should look to the little known country of Bhutan, where the Gross National Happiness or GNH, is more important than the GNP. There the individual happiness of each person is very important because it affects the GNH.

But Penny did not live in Bhutan. She lived in Vancouver, British Columbia, Canada, where the Gross National Product was the measure of the country's economic health and well-being. There her life ticked on one second at a time without anyone asking if and how it affected the GNH.

Asayo Murakami had been attempting to add to the GNH for one hundred and two years. Her husband, Otokichi, had passed on leaving her with ten children: five boys and five girls. The children were all grown up and their former home in Steveston had been restored as an historical site. Even the flower garden had been replaced. Time had been turned back to pre-1942, around the time the Chiyako had floated free as a seagull in Phoenix pond, and the dye was being cast by politicians with a racial bent. There would be no more splendid boats constructed by Murakami Boatworks. Only memories remained, stored in a one hundred and two year old brain perched upon a frail skeleton of a body.

"I met her once," Penny suddenly remarked out loud staring at Larry. "I caught her vibe. She resonated at a very high spiritual level. She shook my hand. I told her my father was a barber and had probably cut her husband's hair. 'Was your Dad's name Hideo?' she had asked raising her half closed eyelids. 'Are you a Miki?' she had inquired further."

"Whom are you talking about?" Larry demanded, slightly annoyed.

"Asayo Murakami. You know, that one hundred and two year old woman in the film we saw at the folk theatre? I actually met her last week at UBC in the student's lounge."

"I'll bet she has some memories!"

"She held my hand like a happy little child. Her vibes really got to me. I must go down to Steveston some day," Penny declared.

"I know. You have been saying that for about eighteen years, ever since you brought your father's ashes home from his funeral. You were supposed to scatter them on the ocean, weren't you?"

"Gad, it can't be that long! It seems like it was just a short time ago that I brought them home."

"And there they sit, perched on top of the fireplace mantel like a conversation piece."

"No one notices except you."

"I've seen others admiring that vase."

"But no one takes it down and looks inside."

"And now it is past the year 2000, and here you sit saying, 'I must go down to Steveston'."

"I guess you could say I have a psychological approach-avoidance conflict."

"You know, Pen, your reluctance to visit Steveston may be due to your sensitivity about the issue of the evacuation. For some strange reason I sometimes detect a tinge of apprehension, perhaps even dread, if that is the correct word, whenever the subject of the Japanese removal from the West Coast is mentioned."

"I do have these amorphous feelings," Penny admitted. "Who knows? Perhaps I feel inferior and ashamed that it happened to us and to no one else."

"Why should you feel inferior and ashamed because of the ignorance of others? Imagine how you and I would react today if all people with so called mixed marriages like ours, and their offspring, were suddenly, without justification, forced to abandon all their worldly possessions and were herded into cattle cars destined for concentration camps?"

Thoughts of such an injustice being heaped upon Sherry and Jerry caused Penny to rise indignantly in their defense. "How dare they?" she declared defiantly.

"We'd be apoplectic with rage and indignation. We would not stand for it! We'd rebel. It would be grounds for justified resistance."

"Civil disobedience!"

"Right on! Civil disobedience!"

"It is important that what happened to your parents never happens again!" Larry stated resolutely.

Penny gazed at her husband appreciatively. She thought a moment, and then replied in a subdued tone. "You know, when you are the victim of racial prejudice it is very intimidating. Very intimidating indeed, especially when the intimidators are in the vast majority and in important positions of political power. It makes you feel insecure and vulnerable, and of very little worth. Your self-esteem approaches zero. It is difficult to be indignant when you are so intimidated."

"Get over it Penny! You are no longer a child. You are a mature woman of infinite worth."

"I know. I know I should be more assertive, but all my life, all my live-long-life, I have felt inwardly intimidated by the racial slurs, putdowns, indignities and injustices heaped upon my parents, my siblings, and myself, for being Japanese-Canadians. I know by now I should have risen above it, transcended these negative experiences and feelings – but it is not easy to change who you are, is it?"

Larry got up abruptly and slouched off into the bedroom. He returned holding a little paperback novel. "You need to finish reading this novel," he stated matter-of-factly.

The novel was written by Joy Kogawa, and published in 1981. It was the first Canadian novel to tackle the sensitive subject of the evacuation of the Japanese-Canadians from the West Coast of British Columbia, and present it in a tasteful and prosaic manner. On the front cover in large white letters was a single word: *Obasan*. A few years ago Penny had started to read the novel, and for reasons unfathomable until now, she had set it aside.

"You need to finish reading this novel!" Larry repeated with greater emphasis when Penny remained silent. "It is a Canadian classic. Every Canadian should read it, especially you."

"I'll read it," Penny asserted. "I promise. I'll read it to the very end." She cast a furtive glance at her husband. He had an uncanny knack of knowing what was good for her. Sometimes it was better to simply acquiesce, pull back her fears and trepidations, and accept the wisdom of his counsel. "I'll do it!" she reiterated with conviction.

Larry stared at his wife as if seeing her in a new light. He leaned toward her with a serious look of consternation etched upon his face. "Someday you must go down to Steveston," he said quietly. "Sometimes you need to go back... in order to go ahead."

* * *

It was a profound day. There was a heaviness in the humidity that blew in from the Pacific and through the open window adjacent to the bed. The air itself had a scent that clung to each oxygen molecule that provided the breath of life for the inhabitants within the room. From the moment Penny awoke she felt it: the profundity. It was all around. Embedded everywhere, even in the way her husband lay curled up fetus-style on the other side of the bed sleeping in rhythm to the ebb and flow of his pulsating heart, in the way the sunlight crept in under the window slats and layered the room with dark and light shadows, in the way the sheets rustled when she crept timidly from the bed taking extra care not to disturb her sleeping prince, in the way she became aware of where she was going. She was going to Steveston.

Penny had never been to Steveston. Her mother and father had told her plenty about it. She could picture it in her mind's eye. But although she had been conceived there, she had been born in Alberta a short time after the evacuation. She had missed it. Missed one of the most tragically historic moments in her family's recent history. In some ways she often felt guilty. All her older siblings could say: "I was evacuated" – but not her. She was only a fetus in her mother's womb, conceived over ancient samurai swords crafted by the Magician of Kogi, and transported in a cattle car bound for Lethbridge. And now, she was going to Steveston.

She had avoided going to Steveston because it represented some very bad feelings: feelings of rejection, of not being worthy enough. Those grainy grey pictures of hordes of inscrutable Orientals standing stoically on the loading ramps at the train stations were depressing. Yes, they looked inscrutable; they had to be. How else could they hide such an injustice and remain accepting? Accepting of being forcibly uprooted and sent to punitive work camps scattered helter-skelter across Canada where the yellow-peril was strategically dispersed upon reluctant communities, because some bigoted politician had mouthed the words: "No Japs from the Rockies to the Pacific."

"Thank goodness the Germans and Italians are white," her father Hideo once had reflected. "Imagine the fiasco that would have resulted if they had been yellow like us!" In a quiet way, so as not to attract any unfavorable attention, the German and Italian Canadians, had radiated vibes of empathy for the hapless "Japs" who were scapegoated mercilessly on behalf of the Axis powers by anyone with an axe to grind.

Her father had lost his barbershop, his house and all the furniture, everything, including his self-esteem. However, he did not lose his faith in his karmic destiny. "Things will get better eventually," he'd always say when food was scarce and the future looked bleak. "People are people; they usually come to their senses in due time."

"Time heals all," a wise man once said. Penny was not sure of the healing, although a substantial amount of time had flowed like the murky waters of the Fraser River, past Steveston and out into the vast Pacific. The word "racist" had taken on a negative bite in recent years alluding to some deep-seated moral imperfection of character. Even in retrospect, after nearly a half a century, it had been difficult for politicians to admit that respected Members of Parliament had acted in such a loathsome manner back then. Better to deny, rationalize, and forget. Let the wound fester and slowly scab over. A simple apology was unthinkable... until 1988 when the Redress issue was finally resolved. Prior to then it had been much easier to wax eloquent about a "Just Society" than to provide closure to a sad chapter of Canadian history. Closure, who needs it?

"I need it!" Penny exclaimed to herself. "Me, a second generation Japanese-Canadian: a Nisei. I need it." It was time for Penny to go back and visit the place where she had been conceived. She strode with a new spirit of determination into the living room and procured the beautiful earthenware jar, kiln-fired with a stunning blue and white glaze which dribbled around it like dripping water. She carefully removed the lid and looked inside. Near the bottom she could see the powdery ashes of her father's remains. "About time I scattered these," she thought with a twinge of guilt.

Like a homing pigeon, Penny drove south from Vancouver until she reached No. 2 Road to Richmond. She made a right turn on Granville and continued to Railway Avenue along which she drove, crossing Moncton Street toward her journey's end a few meters from the wharf along the estuary of the mighty Fraser River where, in the not so distant past, her father Hideo and his older brother, Kasuzimo, had stepped ashore from an old Chinese steamer with all their worldly belongings stuffed in two bulging duffle bags, and took their first breath of the aroma drifting from the cookers inside the Canneries that dominated the shoreline of Steveston, British Columbia, Canada.

Penny parked her red Honda Civic in the parking lot adjacent to Britannia Shipyards where, in an attempt to preserve the authenticity of a colorful history, restoration projects were being undertaken. She picked up the earthenware jar that contained her father's ashes, opened the door of her Honda, and gingerly made her way down to the water's edge.

It was a profound experience to be there. The air felt different. It was easier to breathe, easier to see, easier to hear, easier to feel the texture of the moment. It was all there, every single nuance that created the word poignant.

Penelope Miki walked meditatively along the reconstructed boardwalk toward the old shipyards. Her footsteps sounded much the same as those heard by her father Hideo and his brother Kasuzimo when they came to visit their friends Asayo and Otokichi Murakami at house number forty. The movement was the same and the sound was the same. "Clunk, clunk, clunk," Penny's footsteps resounded through time and space as she clomped along the worn four-wide wooden boards running parallel along the water's edge, back into history.

"My father walked along here, once," she thought, "And now I follow in his footsteps, one step at a time down a pathway that has led me to this moment. Everything that makes this moment so profoundly significant is a result of all those who have trodden here before, one step after the other, just like me. This moment exists for all of us." Penny inhaled slowly, savoring each precious second. As she exhaled she heard a crow cawing in the distance, and saw the shore-grasses undulate to the rhythm of the seas. It was a gratifying experience.

"I'm back!" Penny exclaimed out loud. The words resounded up and down the mighty Fraser River like a defiant cry for acknowledgement and justice: "I'm back... I'm back... I'm back...."

How things had changed, and how they still remained the same. Most of the area was overgrown with neglect. The old dock rotted away along the shoreline. The weather-beaten Cannery loomed imperiously out of the foggy silhouette of Shady Island. And there it was, across the wooden walkway, crouched down in the secluded side-yard like a blush of hope upon a depressing saga of dread and disappointment: Asayo Murakami's flower garden, bursting with renewed life and vigor.

"Seeds of faith never die," Penny reflected somberly. "My father, Hideo, never returned but I am here now on his behalf." She picked a small bouquet consisting of four beautiful flowers that were near at hand. The purple, yellow, red and white flowers shimmered in her tiny fist as she held them toward the sun. "For you Dad," she breathed, "for your older brother, Kasuzimo, his only son, Tutomu... and all those who were forced to leave and never returned." She bent down and carefully stuck the stem of each flower into the rich loam of the garden forming a semicircle of color. "It is only half a circle," she thought, "half a life... half a dream."

She slowly stood erect, turned as if in slow motion and looked out past Shady Island toward the vast Pacific. "Such a long way," she thought, "such a long way to come in search of happiness." The vibes washed over her like a long forgotten memory of early morning risings on a distant shore full of daring hopes and romantic dreams. Who has not had such hopes and romantic dreams in their youth when the spirit yearns for adventure and freedom?

"I have," Penny thought as she stepped gingerly across the sagging boards of an old wharf, holding the earthenware jar tightly with both hands. The out-flowing breeze ruffled her silky black hair and the pungent odor of a decaying past flowed past her nostrils.

It had been a long time coming, but there she was, Penelope Miki, youngest daughter of Hideo and Joyce Miki, standing there alone on the shoreline listening to the sounds of the past echo in her ears. She could hear the despairing voices of those long uprooted souls vibrating like the gossamer wings of wounded angels fluttering in the wind. It was surreal, except for the salty tears that slowly flowed over her cheeks and fell to the decaying cedar planks upon which she stood.

She slowly walked, as if in a meditative trance, to the end of an old wooden pier carrying the earthenware jar that held her father's ashes. Somehow it felt like as if she was participating in an ancient religious rite, and she was a pagan deity presiding over the dispersal of sacred ashes. "It's not about religion," she said as if to reassure herself. She carefully removed the lid and slid it into the left side pocket of her jacket. With a graceful sweeping motion she threw the ashes up into the persistent breeze as it blew out across the mighty Pacific.

She stared up at the translucent sky that mirrored back the sentiments from ages past. "Welcome home Dad," Penny whispered. Through the sparkling sunlight the fine ash glimmered as it billowed up into the atmosphere and disappeared out across the vast ocean, across a generation of hopes and dreams... all the way to a distant island where a hint of sunlight was just beginning to peek above the brooding brow of a foreboding hill where long ago one of her ancient ancestors with his dying breath had proclaimed: *It's not about religion... it's all about love.*

PART EIGHT

IDENTIFICATION

The Unborn mind…
What is it thinking?
And to whom does it belong?

CHAPTER ONE

The young Doctor made his way down the dingy hallway and paused at the open doorway. He could hear the old fella inside talking to himself. He was such a character! Some people thought he was senile; some swore he was crazy; some just assumed he was both. But the Doctor knew better. It was not because he was a doctor with an M.D. after his name, but because he had taken the time to listen, really listen with both ears wide open to what the old guy had to say. And it touched him, a science-oriented intellectual like himself, moved practically to tears by a blabbering old fool who looked as if he could pass on any day. Now he realized it had been a privilege, yes a distinct privilege to have heard the words that issued from his withered lips. He was casting verbal pearls of wisdom before the vast universal audience he so loved to address, and except for himself and one or two nurses, the pearls were wasted.

The Doctor had been in the old codger's room last night. It was marvelous how the old guy's eyes lit up when he realized there was actually someone out there listening. He had so much to share. So very much to share. He seldom knew where to start. Where did he get such knowledge? It seemed to flow through the old man as if he were tuned in to vibes that resonated from a higher frequency of awareness. It puzzled him at first when he heard the old man pontificate about the cosmological constant, as he called it, and how zero could equal one. It was impossible. It flew in the face of logic, but the old man had a way with words that piqued one's curiosity. Afterwards, when he went home and really thought about whatever the old man had pontificated upon it did not seem so crazy. It actually made sense in a weird and wonderful way, a way that had more to do with attitude than belief.

"You've got the right attitude," the old man had told him one evening just before he left the room. "You and I actually have a lot more in common than you are aware of, my son."

The old man frequently referred to the Doctor as "my son". It was a term of endearment that suited the relationship. It allowed the Doctor to pamper the old man without seeming excessive, like a dutiful son caters to his aging father. There was a natural chemistry at work that came together like hydrogen and oxygen and resonated as water. There was gratitude and love involved without those words ever being mentioned. Even during his precious time off the Doctor would often drop in quietly and sit down in the chair against the far wall by the window and meditate along with the old fellow. It felt so soothing to be in the old man's presence. All the discordant vibes dissipated with the slow intake and outflow of breath, and the little room expanded to become a universe of peace and tranquility. After such times, the old man's face always looked so radiant, like that of a guru. "Perhaps he is a guru," the young Doctor once thought, "and I am his pupil."

Once, near the beginning when the old man was teaching him how to meditate the young Doctor experienced something quite extraordinary. It made him feel a little uncomfortable just thinking about it. While he was attempting to meditate he suddenly felt transfixed as if by a powerful electromagnetic aura emanating from the mind-field of the old man's magnetic presence. It was as if their mind-fields had intersected and instantly the young Doctor caught an inkling of something so vast it took away his breath and boggled his mind. It was too much. He could not handle it. It was as if his limited awareness was suddenly confronted by an awareness so vast it was not only mind-boggling, it was intimidating.

It took him nearly a week to get over that feeling, that feeling of having his identity compromised. During the interval the young Doctor consciously avoided associating with the old man. But the allure of the unknown challenged his intellect and piqued his curiosity to such an extent it gradually overcame his reluctance.

And so the young Doctor was drawn back into the old man's presence as if by a magnetic force. He could not help himself. How can a piece of steel not be attracted to a powerful magnet? It was natural. And besides, the young Doctor actually liked the old fellow. It was the combination of the kindness, the compassion, and the humanity that emanated from that solitary bag of flesh and bones that was so endearing. The old man welcomed the Doctor back like a long lost son when he sat down on the side of the bed one evening and said, "How's it going?" There were glassy tears of joy reflected in the old fellow's blinking eyes. It was touching.

To demonstrate his appreciation the old man dared to share his greater illumination. It was an illumination that had increased along with his age. "If only I knew at your age what I know now, I would have done things much differently. Too late smart, as they say – but never too early, my son," the old man had pointed out affectionately. "There are more things between heaven and earth than are dreamt of in your philosophy," he had concluded, paraphrasing a favorite line he had memorized from Shakespeare's Hamlet.

It was easy to listen to the old man ramble on and on, especially for one who was ready and willing to listen. The young Doctor was ready, even though it took a great deal of his precious free time. He had to admit that it often turned out to be quite an edifying experience. The old man was probably ahead of his time, off in a world of his own. It was a world the young Doctor had come to appreciate since he became aware of it. It was a world where, for some inexplicable reason, he felt right at home.

He stopped on his way out of his patient's room to check the medical chart that hung on a clipboard tied to the end of the bed. He examined the data carefully with furrowed brow. His face lit up when he realized that the following day was the old man's birthday: January the thirteenth. "He deserves a birthday cake," he thought, "After all, how many more birthdays will the old guy see?" He left the old man's room and went straight to the cafeteria and summoned the chief cook.

"I'd like to order a birthday cake for the old man," he requested, "a real nice cake with plenty of colorful sprinkles on it." He paused and reflected a moment then added, "Put a bunch of candles on it, as many as possible."

* * *

Perhaps it was the smell of the bouquet of flowers the young Doctor had picked that morning from the small garden plot behind his town-home on the occasion of the old man's birthday that brought back memories of his early childhood. He could not remember much. If his parents had not told him he had been adopted, he would have been happy to believe that he was their natural born son. But he was not. Apparently he was orphaned at an early age near a decrepit old shack within walking distance from a liquor store by a worn out "comfort hostess" who unfortunately had succumbed to a combination of heartbreak and alcoholism. That was about all he knew of his real origins. There was nothing glamorous about it. It was very forgettable. That was probably why, except for moments like this, he never thought much about it.

His mother, so he was told, ended up at the city morgue as just another useless statistic in a manila folder. She was the final product of a city with gluttonous appetites, shamelessly used, exploited, and discarded by a business that hunkered down over her something like a stray dog over a bone: ever watchful, with a low growl in its throat emitted through snarling fangs. She was the bone.

It really was the hunkering that was her nemesis. It was weird; whoever heard of such behavior? It had a sense of parasitic absorption, an insidious osmosis about it that was impossible to describe; it was just something you did out of habit. It became a life-style. The spotlight sought her out, while the heavily drinking customers hunkered around. The customers hunkered down over her, and she hunkered down over everything else worth hunkering over. It was a very unsatisfactory way to live. One hunkered down covetously over anything one thought one had ownership of, especially something one had paid hard cash for. It was instinctive; who knew when an envious adversary might snatch the prize away from right under one's nose?

Most of the businesses promoted this attitude and behavior. It became habitual and life-negating. It was a very shallow and hollow existence, as empty as the desperate look in her eyes. And in such cases of sexual exploitation, never once did she even come close to achieving what one of her close friends referred to as an "orgasm". She just hunkered down like a stray dog over a bone.

The young Doctor's birth mother's only claim to fame or notoriety, or both, was something her face-saving relatives did their best to keep secret. She was a direct descendent from a long line of Kakure Kirishitan. Her last name was Sawada. One of her great aunts had been the hostess for a famous Catholic priest named Father Bernard Petitjean at a magnificent Catholic Cathedral that used to exist in Nagasaki. Other than that she was a nobody. Just another comfort hostess who gave out comfort and received next to nothing in return – except for her son, the little baby boy she had proudly named "Paul", in memory of one of her distant relatives she most admired.

Paul's mother had a Christian name. It was Angela. A decade before he was born when Angela was approaching twenty-nine and a half she had a conscious accident. It was conscious in that she knew what she was doing. She was depressed at the time, which seemed to be almost a natural state of her existence, and weary to the bone with a hopeless fatigue. It was the sense of hopelessness that depressed her beyond endurance and made the fatigue seem endless. She was desperate for sleep, and the fatigue made her frantic with anxiety. She was so desperate for sleep that she purchased some sleeping pills and took more than she needed. She took too many, enough to sleep for an eternity. It was an accident. Somehow she knew it. Just before she fell asleep she phoned her grandmother, the grandmother who had raised her single-handedly after her unwed mother died during childbirth when the baby who would have been her brother was breeched and they crushed his head, but not in time to save her mother's life. Her grandmother, Kane (pronounced Kha-neh) who raised her from the age of three, was not there when she called, but someone else answered the phone and said she would pass on the message.

"Bye Grandma. I love you."

It was the desperate edge in her voice which caused her grandmother's friend to call the police. The police arrived in time to rush Angela to the Emergency room where her stomach was pumped out by a team of frantic interns. The Doctor in charge nodded grimly and said, "Send for someone who knows how to pray." It was his way of saying, "Hopeless." By then she was in a deep coma. She slept as soundly as she had ever slept since her arrival in Tokyo from Osaka.

Tokyo was a lonely city for young women after the war. The young men could dream of becoming businessmen: young capitalists struggling to find the American dream – but not the women. The women lived secondhand lives, used, worn out lives devoid of anything new or fresh. Women like her huddled in dingy bars breathing in secondhand smoke and consuming watered-down drinks with disillusioned GIs too drunk to speak coherently even in English. The neon lights of Tokyo glittered at night with a flashiness that masked an undercurrent of loneliness that was reflected in the eyes of every woman sitting beside an impaired GI with a cigarette smoldering.

That was occupied Japan in those days when the spoils of war went to the victor. The young women were part of the spoils. All the young GIs knew that; and all that the old Japanese folks could say about it was: "*Gummun-steh*", which meant "Persevere and keep quiet!" That was all the young women attempting to survive on the Ginza in post war Japan could do. "*Gummun*," day in and day out in lonely barrooms while the harsh glare of neon lights flashed on and off invitingly.

It was not much of a life, but it was her life. She was the owner. It was like that. You owned things. Things could be bought and sold. You could sell yourself – if you could find a buyer. Everything had a price. People scurried about buying and selling. Tokyo in those days was one big anthill of goings and comings. All the tiny ants were going and coming as if they had a purpose. Going and coming. Coming and going. Busy, busy, busy. Rebuilding. Putting a new face on war-torn Japan. Building modern Japan in the victor's image: Japan Inc. But Angela's grandmother was still old fashioned.

She arrived at the hospital wearing a black kimono decorated with red and white circles. On her feet were wooden gheetas with red thongs. Her arms were filled with a massive bouquet of freshly cut flowers of every hue and color. She was eighty-some. Her eyes watered a lot, but she could see well enough to say: "Where is she?"

She was in a room relegated to those not expected to live too long. It was a nice quiet room with a big window overlooking the city lights. The grandmother shuffled in to see her granddaughter. She was lying comatose upon a thirty-nine inch wide hospital bed with starched white sheets. What could an old woman do that the medical experts could not?

Angela's grandmother artistically arranged the flowers in a large vase on a shelf by the window, pulled up a chair beside the bed, and gazed with watery eyes at her granddaughter. Angela appeared to be scarcely breathing through tubes inserted up both nostrils and connected to a respirator. The old woman reached over and clasped Angela's right hand. The instant she touched her, her body twitched as if in recognition.

Angela's grandmother was a Christian-Buddhist. She leaned towards Buddhism, but she usually prayed in Christ's name. Old age had made her extra-sensitive to discordant vibes. Somehow she intuited that her granddaughter was afraid. She was afraid of going to hell. She was a sinner. She was loaded with guilt. She was afraid Christ would not be able to forgive her. Instinctively the old woman began to recite one of her favorite sutras, and as she did, her granddaughter's fingers tightened ever so slightly.

When she finished reciting the sutras the old woman bowed her head and began to speak in a trembling voice that broke and faltered as she wet her dry lips and struggled to breathe in and out between phrases. "Do not be afraid, my dear," she began, "I am calling upon the Buddha. Did you know that Jesus was also a Buddha? I am calling upon all the enlightened folk to help you cling to the mortal life you have almost extinguished. Did you know that the immortal light of life that exists within you has never been extinguished? We do not die; we just pass on." She paused and mumbled something incoherently under her breath that sounded like "She is too young to die... Jesus, Lord, have mercy."

"You have always been alive in the vibrations that make up your music. You always loved to dance and sing as a child. You were such a beautiful child. You brought beauty into the world. I loved your music. We vibrated together. We both have incarnated as a result of our vibrations into this realm. It is a realm consistent with our animal and spiritual nature. We are without sin. You are not a sinner. Forget all that nonsense the priest told you about the sins of the flesh. You are a fragile flower attempting to bloom. Have no fear; your grandmother is here." She smiled, pleased by the poetic ebb and flow of her words. Again the old woman paused and mumbled incoherently under her breath: "Jesus, Lord, have mercy!"

"We need to mend ourselves, heal ourselves, forgive ourselves, realize ourselves. We are free to be. Conditions are not yet sufficient for you to pass on. There is much more for you to realize, much more love and gratitude. Angela, you are an earthly angel; that is why your mother named you Angela. It is a beautiful name for a mortal being. I know it is hard for you to exist here, but you are here to affirm life – not negate it. You are here to give life and live life in your own fashion. I know things are difficult here in our occupied homeland. You are like a breath of fresh air in a stale room. You have the fragrance of spring flowers in the dead of winter. Times are very hard. Believe me, I know. You are desperately needed to bring a sparkle into the eyes of those who reach out for you in their moments of desperation. You bring them comfort and a facsimile of love and compassion in a space where the soil is barren and flowers are nonexistent. You are a beautiful flower of hope. You are the sun attempting to break through cloudy skies. We need you. Come back to your old grandmother."

It was 4:32 a.m. when Angela awoke. "Best sleep I ever had," she proclaimed to all the medical experts who marveled at her recovery. "Sometimes the wind blows in the right direction," the Doctor in charge sagely pointed out for the continuing edification of the eager young interns.

The wind is not noticeable in downtown Tokyo. Sometimes, however, when one least expects it there is a gust or a swirl and paper litter dances about on invisible currents of energy. Life went on for Angela after her recovery, on and on, year after year as she tripped along with the breeze. She was a dancer, an improvisational dancer. She just followed the rhythm in her head. It was soul music to her. She found it soothing. In her youthful exuberance she danced upon the stage of life until her youth and exuberance faded and she hunkered down and became a comfort hostess. And then unexpectedly she was blessed with a son, and became a loving mother in addition to all of the other things she had been.

Who knows why she was blessed with such a handsome little baby boy? Was she worthy of such a precious gift of life? From her fragile, slender body worn down by years spent comforting others, she brought forth a miracle. It was her finest moment upon the mortal stage; she gave her best performance: it was the dance of life.

Like the sudden brilliant blooming of a late autumn flower, Angela quickly wilted away while her baby matured into a toddler instinctively searching for balance upon his tiny feet like a miniature dancer. She taught him the flower-dance with its graceful movements that imitated the unfolding of a divine inner beauty. They danced it in slow motion pretending the moment would last forever and ever, world without end, like in a dream or a heavenly prayer.

The moment always faded into the dreary reality of the dingy shack that surrounded them. Yet Angela dreamed on; she saved her final dance, her dream-dance, for her son. He was a blessing. He would make her proud some day. He had the spirit of a samurai. She held his chubby little hand. They danced wonderfully together, an inebriated mother swaying in rhythm to the prancing footsteps of a small boy doing his best to keep step with the music of the spheres. It was exhilarating. She let go of his tiny hand reluctantly and flopped down into a narrow cot adjacent to a round side table on which a beautiful bouquet of flowers still exuded vibrations of hope.

She reached out for the fragrant bouquet of flowers his father – tall, dark, and handsome as ever in his freshly pressed naval officer's uniform – had dropped off the week before, the week before he was scheduled to return to America. He had a penchant for cleanliness, and a weird sense of erotic humor. His dark melancholic eyes twinkled with satisfaction when the little boy laughed and said "Da-Da" in English when he arrived. "I'll send for you both later," he said. "We'll get married." He had noble intentions.

In her heart she hoped, but in her subconscious mind she knew it was hopeless. She waited and waited, and waited. It was a lonely vigil. Paul's desperate cries for attention turned to a whimper. The flowers withered and dried up along with her hopes as she lay there alone in a darkened room, chilled to the bone with a broken heart shattered beyond healing, staring off into space dreaming of the life she could have had.

The flowers smelled just like the kind her dear old deceased grandmother once brought to the hospital. They had a nice scent. It reminded her of a fresh spring breeze blowing out to the ocean. She rode the current. It swept her out to the billowing sea where the horizon touched the sky. She danced on with the wind.

* * *

They say that scent is a powerful trigger on the memory. "Perhaps his real mother appreciated flowers and the scent permeated the shack in which she lived when he was a toddler just beginning to reach out for things beyond his grasp," a social-worker suggested to his adoptive parents who were intrigued by the child's "odd" behavior. According to the information on file at the Court House, Paul's biological mother was discovered by a friend lying on a tiny cot in a shack, exactly seven and a half blocks from "Ichiban's Geisha Parlor" in South-West Tokyo, clutching an old dried-up bunch of flowers as if they were a bridal bouquet. Paul was found wandering about, cold, dirty, and exhausted from crying, on a tiny patch of barren ground that served as a backyard. He could not recall anything about that experience at all. He was probably too young. But somehow he remembered the scent of the flowers, and sometimes when someone brought a pretty bouquet to the hospital – for no reason at all he did a little slide-step across the floor. That was all he remembered of his early childhood. That was all the childhood he had. His adoptive parents always said that as a child he was quiet, somber, and stoic as the day is long.

Over time Paul gradually grew out of that introverted phase, and as he grew older he began to take on his parents' happy-go-lucky attitude toward life. No one knew for sure who his biological father was, or what particular race or nationality he represented. It really did not matter as far as the adoptive parents were concerned; they just wanted a healthy son to love and nurture as if he was their very own. Who could have predicted that that wasted little waif they picked up from the orphanage would turn out to be such a tall, handsome young man with piercing black eyes, dark bushy eyebrows, and smooth shiny black hair that sparkled with highlights?

To the old man Paul looked like a throwback to more primitive times. "Have you ever heard of the hairy Ainu?" he once asked the young Doctor.

"Why do you ask?" the young Doctor replied feeling a little self-conscious

"Because you look like one," the old man stated with conviction.

The young Doctor's adoptive parents were practically middle-aged and had given up all hope of ever producing a child of their own when they picked up their new son from the orphanage. They were surprised at the time to find out that the little boy had a Christian name. They liked it because it reminded them of the famous Apostle who wrote all those wonderful epistles. They were both devout Christians. They had spent countless nights futilely attempting to procreate a child of their own in the so-called "missionary" position; it was a hope and a prayer combined in a fruitless endeavor. And now they had Paul. He attempted to satisfy their biological longing for a child of their very own – which was as deep as the emptiness he attempted to fill in their hearts.

Unfortunately his adoptive father, who was an innovative and congenial school principal, passed away when Paul was in grade eleven. However, his mother lived to see him graduate as a Doctor of Medicine. It was without a doubt her proudest moment. She beamed with such deep appreciation when he hugged her with cap and gown still on immediately after the photo-op, that he felt that he too would burst with pride: pride for achieving his parents' dream. "Imagine, a Doctor!" his plump little mother would tirelessly reiterate whenever he returned home for a visit thereafter.

When his mother passed away soon after her sixty-ninth birthday, Paul felt like he was an orphan, an orphan left on the doorstep of opportunity. It was an opportunity provided by the love and sacrifice of his adoptive parents: two total strangers who took him in and raised him like their own son when his future was as bleak as the barren backyard of a run-down old shack in southwest Tokyo.

"You have a melancholy about you today, my son," the old man said, while staring empathetically at the young Doctor with compassionate eyes. "I know the feeling. I know it very well. Unfortunately it never passes. It makes its home in the very bottom of your heart, and there it tosses and turns with a restless yearning as fathomless as eternity."

Never had the young Doctor heard anything so intuitively insightful. He instinctively clasped the old man's bony hands and held them apprehensively. He did not know what to say. For some strange reason a somber mood engulfed him. It felt something like the loneliness that accompanies a funeral, and he was paying his last respects to his adoptive father – or was it the biological father he never knew? He stood there until the feeling passed, and then with bowed head he said, "God bless you," and when he said it he felt as if he were greeting a long lost relative.

"Happy birthday!" The chief cook followed by the head nurse and an entourage of other service staff surged into the old man's tiny room preceded by a cart on which sat a beautiful cake with candles ablaze. The young Doctor beamed with satisfaction.

"Happy birthday, Dad," he blurted out.

It was just a term of endearment. But it made the old man's day.

CHAPTER TWO

The head nurse stretched, yawned, and got up from her comfortable office chair. It was time to check up on her patient once again. She glanced at her wrist-watch to verify the time. She had taken a shine to the old fellow ever since he first arrived and insisted on placing those derelict old samurai swords at the foot of his bed. It was against hospital policy. They'd had quite an argument back then. The old codger just would not take no for an answer. He went over her head and called the hospital administrator. What could that lap-dog do but acquiesce? Money talks, especially big money and endowments. So the old man got his way. He apologized later. What got to her was the way he apologized. He placed his hands together in a prayerful fashion and spoke in the most humble and contrite manner possible.

"Please forgive me if I have offended you for the sake of these old relics. They are my family heirlooms. We belong together. I thank you for being so understanding."

She forgave him. She even helped to locate and carry in the white metallic table at the foot of his bed upon which they were displayed. She was a slave to his gratitude.

Although the samurai swords were ancient, she had to admit that they had a special quality that made them particularly alluring. The scabbards were weathered and brownish-gray with age. The black silk threads on the handles were frayed and worn smooth from sweaty hands – and yet they commanded a certain degree of majesty. Nearly everyone who came into his room asked the old gentleman if they could unsheathe them. They desired to see what lay inside those battered old scabbards. But he always refused.

"Those swords," he would say, "are only to be drawn by one who has the spirit of a samurai." And so the swords remained in their sheaths, their deadly blades hidden from the curious eyes of those who had no inkling of the fact that they were gazing upon swords that once were wielded by the hands of a man who was crucified on Nishizaka Hill in 1597 by order of Toyotomi Hideyoshi.

It is interesting how things are passed on down from one generation to the next like the genes of one's ancestors. The present only exists because of what has been passed down through time. The present follows the past as the future follows the present.

"We are all hand-me-downs," the old man thought as he stared absentmindedly at his swords, "old relics with a veneer of newness to give the impression that we exist on the cutting edge of the future, instead of the cutting edge of the past. It is the past that is embedded with meaning. It is our karma to enlarge that meaning by becoming more aware of it with each enduring breath of mortality."

He drew in a sobering breath and struggled to reach down to the foot of the bed. He grasped the handle of the two-handed katana with his right hand, and with a graceful sweep of his arm removed it from its sheath. Was not he too a Miki? Tutomu Paul Miki? The steel blade gleamed in the morning sun, as it had gleamed in the hand of Mikisan when he decapitated the man who had sent his father to his grave. "Who shall I leave these swords to?" he wondered, cognizant of the fact that during his youth excessive exposure to radiation had rendered him sterile, along with hundreds of other victims of the deadly radioactive fallout.

The question had been weighing heavily upon his mind of late. The precious swords had been handed down within the Miki family for generations. Was he to be the last? The last link in a chain that began when the Magician of Kogi presented Handayu Miki with swords that looked more like works of art than lethal weapons? Perhaps it was time for a change, the beginning of a new tradition. "Who would be a fitting candidate for these precious old relics?" he pondered. "Who would be worthy of them?" He thought of the Fearsome Foursome. He thought of Penny's son, Jerry. He thought of Jerry's twin sister, Sherry. He thought of Penny's three older brothers. He thought, "Too bad I did not have a son of my own." And then he thought of the young man he called "my son", the Doctor.

He scribbled some notes on a piece of paper from his bedside table, then carefully brought the great sword down and slowly inserted the deadly blade into the battered old scabbard, just as Mikisan had done in 1567 after wiping the blade clean on a silk bandana with brownish-red blotches.

* * *

What is it that makes one reflective as death draws near? Is it a sense of déjà-vu combined with melancholy that makes one so nostalgic for things past? For those little things, those poignant moments that make life magical and worthy of being taken for granted? "Keats was right," the old man confirmed to himself, "'Truth is beauty and beauty truth'. Famous lines like that last because they are authenticated by personal experience." He sagged back against the pillow and stared up meditatively at the ceiling. Attached to the rounded edge of the ceiling light, the remnants of a wispy spider's web, barely noticeable against the white stipple, undulated on an invisible current of air.

"Ah so," the old man sighed regretfully. "What is it that makes some of us so insecure and blind to the beauty all around us? What is it that drives a man to blindly accumulate more and more and more without reaching a satiation point? What emptiness or hunger can feed upon its own emptiness, and hunger for more? What sets a man upon a pathway through life that forever leads him away from himself to dwell in some far off isolated place where nothing is manifested as everything?"

Perhaps the answers were there just below the surface, entangled in the intricate web in which he had been caught like a tasty morsel for a ravenous appetite. It was the "spirit of capitalism" that had besotted his father after he had returned to Japan and formed the web of intrigue in which he had become ensnared.

"Let me tell you something about my father," the old man said with an enthusiastic nod of his head while propping himself up on his elbows. "He was a samurai at heart. He loved to wear his old samurai swords on ceremonial occasions, and from time to time when he thought he was alone in the house he would get out his swords and practice a few deft moves. He was a very good swordsman. I certainly would not have wanted to tangle with him! After one such occasion he once told me a story about a mongoose, a fig, and a bird. 'Beware of appearances'; he warned me, 'The samurai is forever vigilant'. That story has served me well.

"The Yakuza recruited my father a few years after the war ended because of his samurai mentality. They actually began supporting us soon after we arrived because my Dad's uncle was a staunch member right from the beginning. What do you know about the Yakuza?

"The Yakuza initially were just frustrated samurai who had no real role to play in an industrializing society. In such a time it seemed natural for frustrated samurai to look for a new structure within which they could maintain their identity and preserve the samurai's code of Bushido. A subculture that was loosely modeled upon the samurai tradition evolved and later became known as the Yakuza. In the early years mainly dockside workers and employees in the construction industry were recruited. Under the surface they dabbled in gambling and other nefarious activities which attracted a certain criminal element who gave the Yakuza a very bad reputation. People began to identify the Yakuza with heavily tattooed subversive, mafia-type characters. There were certainly many who fit that description in the decade after the war.

"That was one of the reasons why my father did not join right away. As I said before, he was recruited because they were trying to change their image. They needed men like my father who were trustworthy and honorable if they wanted to legitimize themselves and participate in the political process. In the fifties and sixties there were big opportunities for the Yakuza in a developing democratic society. The Yakuza were organized and they had the underlying adhesion of the samurai's code of conduct. That was a huge advantage in an environment where the American model of rampant capitalism was promoted, and a selfish objective like getting filthy rich was considered to be a most honorable goal.

"Imagine, samurai capitalists! No wonder Japan's economic miracle flourished. I was fortunate to be a player in that miracle. It was mainly due to my father's influence that I became such a great success. He had become an important figure in the Yakuza subculture.

"The Yakuza were astute capitalists. Hard-line capitalists. You just did not cheat the Yakuza! Underneath all their business dealings ran an ethic based upon the samurai's code of honor. Believe it or not, that honor was even more important than money. It linked the present to the past. Big corporations honored their commitments to their workers even if it cost them bigger profits. Allegiance to the corporation replaced allegiance to the Shogun. Modern capitalism with a samurai's mentality was a formidable player in the international game of no-limit poker.

"As you know, amongst capitalists, wealth equates to power and prestige. The biggest and wealthiest corporations held the greatest positions of prestige in the international community of economic power brokers. Clear and amicable communications at this level of interaction was, and still is, essential. The language of communication was, for the most part, English, and I, by quirk of fate, spoke fluent English. I was groomed, so to speak, to play an important role. Do you think I became a multi-millionaire on my own? Not a chance. Like the mongoose, I got the bird because my father presented the fig."

* * *

And now, long after he had become "too late smart", the old man realized that all that wealth and glitter that he had spent a lifetime accumulating was worthless. "Fool's gold!" he exclaimed out loud. It meant nothing to him. He could not take it with him. He had no offspring to leave it to. What had he been trying to prove? It was out of character. That was not the real him. The real him lay on a sanitized hospital bed and peered out at the world through eyes weary with age that reflected an emptiness so deep and an insecurity so profound it required a very long lifetime to be realized, to be realized for what it was: his miserable life! It was not a matter of placing the blame. It was all too easy to find convenient scapegoats. It was simply a matter of acceptance.

The old man sagged back down into the bed and gazed at the electric clock on the far wall. He recalled with a tinge of nostalgia that time in Calgary when Penny kissed him on the cheek and said: "I forgive you". Those words meant more to him than all the wealth and power he had spent a lifetime accumulating.

CHAPTER THREE

The mid-August sun filtered in through the curtained window directly above the kitchen sink where Penny was standing. It was that time once again, time to get out the canning jars and put up the winter's supply of canned peaches. Penny canned peaches every year around mid to late August depending upon when the ripe peaches were available. She began canning peaches when the twins were in grade two and were invited to a classmate's birthday party where they had birthday cake with home-made canned peaches. It was the first time they had ever eaten home-made canned peaches and they were impressed because they were served with home-made whipped cream on top of a home-made birthday cake. Apparently the entire mixture was "dee-licious".

So it was that Penny began to can peaches. Canning was not a new experience for her. As far back as she could remember her mother had canned a variety of fruit in the early fall. It was almost like a family ritual. They usually picked whatever fruit they canned. The entire family trooped out to good-picking spots near the south bend of the Old Man River on Sunday mornings to pick berries, mostly Saskatoon's. Sometimes Joyce made Saskatoon pies which only lasted a day or two because everyone pigged-out on them.

Whenever someone with a van or truck would be passing through from the Okanagan with cartons of peaches and pears, Hideo would arrive home with enough fruit to last all winter and into spring once they were canned. Canning, in those days when she was just a little kid, always seemed like fun. What made it fun was the attitude her mother had toward it. She actually looked forward to the "canning season" as she called it. Perhaps the attitude harkened back to her youth as a Métis child growing up along the northwest coast of British Columbia.

Her mother once said that canning was very important to the Native way of life in those days. In addition to canning fruit, they also canned the salmon her father caught in the river. For some reason she rarely spoke about her Native or Scottish background. It might have had something to do with her identification with her husband's race and culture. As the years passed she gradually became a "Japanese wife". Whenever they went out together as a

454 James T. Sawada

family, Joyce was never asked if she was Japanese. Everyone just assumed that she was. She had a smooth pale olive-brown complexion with shiny black hair which she took to parting down the middle. Actually it seemed as if she tried to make herself look the role she was portraying.

Like the French in old Quebec City, who are more "French" than the French in Paris, Joyce in many ways became more Japanese than the average Japanese, who was ashamed of being a "Jap" during and after the War. She was, as Hideo. once phrased it, "the proudest Japanese-Canadian who was a Métis". Not only that, she had learned to speak Japanese quite fluently. Remarkable, considering Penny could hardly speak any Japanese at all. She knew certain words having to do with the bathroom like *benjo*, *onko*, and *shieko*, but little else.

Larry wandered in from the living-room where he had been reading in his comfortable swivel-rocker. He bellied up to the counter, plugged in the stainless steel electric kettle and asked, "Care for a cup of coffee?"

"I'd rather have tea."

"Good day for canning peaches, eh?" Larry commented as he got out the jar of Taster's Choice 100% Columbian instant coffee and spooned a heaping teaspoon into his red porcelain mug with Dad on the side and placed a tea-bag of herbal green tea into the green mug with Mom on it. "You are a woman of many talents," he remarked.

"I try," Penny said humbly. "My mother was much more talented than I am. She could do just about anything. Of course in those days you had to be very versatile in order to survive."

"You know we human beings are really good at selling ourselves short."

"What do you mean?"

"I'm reading a book on human potentiality and it really is amazing how inadequate we are considering our latent potentiality as compared to other less well-endowed species."

"You mean we have the potential to achieve at a much higher level than we presently are?"

"Yes, we have this unlimited potentiality, and yet by our behavior you'd think we were just plain stupid. What other species kills its own kind out of spite, and, pardon my English, shits in its own nest?"

"Don't get carried away, dear," Penny replied as she unplugged the electric kettle, filled the mugs with an appropriate amount of boiling water, opened the fridge and poured a dab of Creamo into the red mug, stirred it, and handed it to her husband.

Larry sat down at the kitchen table and pulled out a chair for his spouse. "Take a break," he suggested as Penny sat down. "Have you ever heard of the Russet Red Knot?" he asked

"No. Why do you ask?"

"Because that tiny little bird can do something that none of us highly intelligent human beings can do, because it is not impaired with a negative mindset and therefore is able to utilize the potential it was born with.

"You mean hatched with," Penny corrected. She slowly sipped her tea when her husband lapsed into a momentary silence which he occasionally did from time to time whenever he felt she was being picky. "Sounds interesting; please elaborate," Penny encouraged.

"Hmm," Larry pondered, attempting to refresh his memory. He blew on his hot coffee and drank down a mouthful. "Well, Pen," he began thoughtfully, "like I said, there is a tiny bird, a russet called the Red Knot that, unlike us intelligent human beings, is not limited by any negative attitudes or beliefs that stifle its freedom to achieve its true potential. Each year it flies more than nine thousand miles one way from the northern islands of Canada, stopping briefly at Cape Cod and Delaware Bay until it reaches the beaches of Tierra del Fuego on the southernmost tip of South America. The amazing thing about this journey is that after the young birds are hatched in northern Canada, all the mature birds who have made the trip before, including their parents, leave the young juvenile Red Knots behind, and begin the flight south around mid-July without them."

"How are the juvenile Red Knots that have been left behind, and have never made the trip south before, going to find their way all the way to Tierra del Fuego, a journey of nine thousand treacherous miles? It seems like an impossible task."

"Fortunately the juvenile Red Knots are not told that it is an impossible task!" Larry grinned smugly and looked over at Penny. "After fending for themselves for over a month, they bravely set out around late August."

"How do they know where to go?" Penny asked, her curiosity mounting.

"The flight plan for this incredible journey is impregnated into the DNA molecule of the fledgling Russet Red Knot."

"So?" Penny responded, raising her eyebrows.

Seeing an opportunity to show off his knowledge on this subject Larry spouted off like Old Faithful, "As you know this molecule is shaped like a spiral staircase or double helix. The side rails, so to speak, consist of linked sugar and phosphate molecules while the treads or stairs are paired molecules called nucleotides."

"Amazing," Penny remarked, which only encouraged her husband to elaborate further as was his tendency when in the presence of a good listener.

"There are only four kinds of nucleotides called Adenine, Guanine, Cytosine, and Thymine. For simplistic purposes they are identified by the first letter of their name. 'A' always pairs with 'T' and vice-versa, and 'G' always pairs with 'C' and vice-versa resulting in four kinds of treads along the double helix: A-T, T-A, G-C, and C-G. It is the sequencing of these treads that makes up the genetic code. In each cell in the Red Knot's body there are identical strands of DNA which when unraveled might reach an average arm's length. There are several billion nucleotide pairs in an arm's length of DNA. This would equate to several sets – not volumes – of encyclopedic knowledge written into the genes of a single Russet Red Knot. Because the Red Knot does not have the impairment of a negative mindset, it just instinctively flies nine thousand miles over uncharted territory as if it were the natural thing to do."

"It is natural. What is unnatural is the way we limit ourselves with our negative mindsets!" Penny expostulated.

"Like the Russet Red Knot, everything Man needs to know is impregnated or stored in his DNA," Larry continued. "Every human being who has passed this way and reproductively participated in the linkage of the Great Chain of Being has made a microscopic contribution to the whole which has been passed on generation after generation to the Now. This is not a static process. It is constantly evolving."

"It is much like karma," Penny noted insightfully.

"Yes, indeed it is. It is everything we need to know to realize our true potential, just like the Russet Red Knot."

"Except, unlike the Red Knot, we are unable to realize even a fraction of our true potential," Penny lamented.

"Scientists have estimated that there is enough DNA in one single human being to reach to the sun, which is ninety-three million miles from earth, and back, about eleven or twelve times, if it were stretched out in a straight line!"

"Compared to the Russet Red Knot's which is about an average arm's length, we are certainly endowed with fabulous amounts of potential, are we not? If we could realize the true potential that is available to us, perhaps the accomplishments of the Russet Red Knot, and the sockeye salmon which is another example of this sort of marvel, would seem vastly less miraculous," Penny added after taking a sip of green tea. "With such a vast potentiality, what has happened to homo-sapiens that places such great limitations upon them?"

"An excellent question. I've thought about that very question myself for quite some time."

"And?"

"You know of all the species, except perhaps the porpoise, Man has been gifted with the most complex and creative brain. Unfortunately this large brain has been acting as a damper upon his freedom to achieve his true potentiality."

"Instead of enhancing Man's freedom, it is diminishing it," Penny chimed in.

"Exactly. The Red Knot acts or behaves mostly upon instinct which allows these little birds with their tiny brains to freely tap, without inhibitions, into the potentiality encoded into the DNA strands of each cell. However Man, over the evolutionary history of his existence, has gradually become more and more reliant upon the fabulous rational powers of his large brain which over time began to control, and to a great extent override and restrict, the natural instinctive potentiality available in his vast strands of DNA."

"Why is that so limiting?" Penny asked, furrowing her brow.

"Another great question. The information encoded in Man's DNA is based upon a continually evolving experience passed on from generation to generation down the Great Chain of Being. What each generation experiences becomes encoded in the strands of each person's DNA. The longer the limiting behavior persists the more profoundly it is "hard-wired", so to speak, into the cellular memory of our DNA per se. The information we have been inculcating into the memory strands of our DNA is filtered through the existential experiences which our large brains accept as being significant and meaningful. Over millennia this recently encoded information has acted as an inhibitor or damper upon our ability to realize our full potentiality. This is an ongoing and continuous process."

"So for the last several thousand years, Man has been irrationally utilizing his greatest advantage, his marvelous brain, to his own disadvantage!"

"You hit the nail right on the head. Instead of using his intellectual faculties to enhance his ability to realize the vast potentiality encoded in his DNA over millions of years of evolution, Man uses his brain as a restrictive filter! It is as if he is consciously attempting to obscure the light of his natural instincts with the pollution of his mind."

"What pollution?"

"Well, for example, within the last two millennia Man has developed this notion that his natural instincts were something to be overcome as he conceived of himself as being naturally flawed. Consequently he rationalized his behavior accordingly. In short he placed limits upon his freedom to realize his vast potential using his greatest gift, his marvelous brain."

"What an irony! The larger the brain, the more it is potentially capable of limiting and restricting."

"It is very difficult for the average person to appreciate the magnitude of our self-imposed restrictions. Compared to the Russet Red Knot's potentiality and brain size, Man should be able to fly to the outermost stars of our galaxy and back as easily as the Red Knot flies to Tierra del Fuego and back to Northern Canada. How far are we capable of flying at the present time? Why can't we tap into our true potential like the Red Knot?"

"It is interesting to note," Penny replied while finishing off her tea, "that some people using techniques developed by Oriental gurus over the centuries are able to use various methods of meditation to still the thoughts and cut through the mind pollution that limits and restricts us. Meditation may be the universal methodology by which Man may be able to realize an inkling of his true potentiality. What do you think?"

"I fully agree. Meditation may be the easiest and best way to cut through the mind pollution, and as such may be part of the solution to the predicament we find ourselves enmeshed in."

"I can feel the polluting influences suffocating me like a wet blanket."

"It is not just you; we are all in the same boat. We do not trust our instincts like the Red Knot to take us over vast, uncharted territory. We would never attempt such a trip, would we?"

"We should at least try!"

"Most of us just look at the Red Knot, shake our heads and marvel at what that tiny russet is capable of doing with his arm's length of DNA."

"We have such a negative conception of ourselves. We think we are naturally flawed or sinful and that our instincts are not to be trusted. The implications are mind-boggling."

"We see through a glass darkly – when we do not need to. That is the most frustrating part," Larry lamented. "It is suffocating. Suffocating!" He shook his head vigorously as if attempting to shake loose the obscurity. He picked up his red mug and drank down the last dregs of his coffee.

"Why can't we realize what the Red Knot naturally realizes with its tiny brain?"

"It seems our negative attitudes and beliefs are preventing us from realizing the miraculous potential that is our birthright. Our reality should resonate harmoniously with the fabulous visions of beauty and truth within – instead look what we are manifesting: pollution, disease, starvation, malnutrition, poverty, injustice, inhumanity, terrorism, and war. Human beings are doing this to themselves, as if they do not have any other options."

"You said a mouthful there! You're beginning to sound like a real guru," Penny complimented her husband. "We must attempt to maintain a positive attitude in spite of our predicament."

"Yes, I'm beginning to see things more clearly now, in spite of my upbringing inside the box of this mindset. Our vision is limited by what we fixate in our mind to be true, i.e., by our beliefs. For example, before we can manifest anything like drawings, sculptures, pyramids, skyscrapers, anything, we must first visualize it in our mind's eye. But if the visionary criterion in our mind's eye is restricted in advance, then it is limited by and operates within those pre-set or prejudiced conditions or parameters."

"We too are ensconced within the parameters of this mindset," Penny followed up. "However, even though we ourselves exist within the box, so to speak, of this collective negative mindset, we can think outside the box; by doing so perhaps we can change the level of awareness of those residing inside the box. The Buddha said, 'All that we are is a result of what we have thought'. If we change the thought, the results will follow."

"We'd better get back to work on that handbook then."

"Sounds like a good idea," Penny replied as she rose to her feet.

"Follow me," Larry headed for the computer room. "The way and the path beckon."

V IDENTIFICATION

(1) The Way and the Path

The Three I-s of Identity

When you say, "I exist," who are you referring to? Are you referring to the Eternal I, the Immortal I, the Mortal I, or all three? Who is it that is existing now, and whose existence has endured until this moment, and will continue to endure? Would it be too simplistic to say that all the Mortal I-s are a material manifestation of the Immortal I-s, and the Immortal I-s are a spiritual manifestation of the Eternal I? And furthermore, would it be a vast over-simplification to say that the three I-s telescope into One from the Many? One constant Eternal I, and many pinpoints of awareness?

These pinpoints of awareness are as finite as the sum total of all the Mortal I-s. The relative awareness created from the point of view of each existent pinpoint gives the illusion that each Mortal I is the one and only existent "I".

The Light, the Pin Holes and the Reflections

For clarity, a concrete analogy might be helpful here. However it is important to keep in mind that it is only an imaginative metaphor attempting to describe the seemingly indescribable! Consider a single light bulb enclosed inside a large opaque ball perforated by a finite number of unique pinholes, surrounded by a holographic screen:

(a) The pinholes of light reflected upon the screen represent the Mortal I-s;

(b) The unique pinholes in the ball represent the Immortal I-s; and

(c) The light-bulb represents the Eternal I.
It is evident that there is only one Eternal I and that there is a direct connection between the light, the pinholes, and the pinpoints of light reflected on the screen.

This notion of a holographic screen is analogous to the known universe. It may sound like a new idea but it is as old as the Vedas of India where it was poetically described as "Indra's Net":

There is an endless net of threads
Throughout the universe.
The horizontal threads are in space
While the vertical threads are in time.
At every crossing of threads
There is an individual
And every individual is a crystal bead.
The great light of absolute being illuminates
And penetrates every crystal being.

And every crystal being reflects not only the light
From every other crystal in the net
But also every reflection of every reflection
Throughout the universe.

In the universe of the holographic screen it is evident that each separate pinpoint of light energy has a purpose of its own: to light up that particular spot on the screen. No other pinpoint has that unique function or purpose. Each pinpoint of illumination can be differentiated from all the other spots on the screen, and its individuality can be traced back to the one and only unique pinhole in the large opaque ball from which it was created by the light bulb shining within. Therefore it could be said without equivocation that: each manifested spot of illumination was created in the image of its pinhole from the energy of the light.

Thus from one light, many pinpoints of light are created. Each Mortal I exists in the light of the paradox of the One and the Many. Each individual is one of the many. Each person has an identity and a unique personality.

The Essence of Personality

The Light in the center of the perforated ball represents freedom, freedom to be; this freedom is unrestricted. The light of each human being, with its unique name and identity, is a reflection cast from the unique pinhole through which the light has passed. The light is the energy source of an infinitude of potentialities, the uniqueness of which are manifested upon the screen as the personas of the various pinpoints. Each pinpoint of light energy vibrates with its own unique potentiality which manifests it own specific vibration or personality. That is why personality per se exists. That is why the Source Light can be personified as being omnipresent.

Because the reflection of each pinhole is manifested upon the holographic screen, it exists as such, and because it actually exists in the relative context of that reality, can be identified or known as that particular essence with its unique persona or personality. But it is only a reflection of the Essence (or existent source as represented by the light bulb) without which there would be no reflection or persona. Since the reflected persona on the holographic screen exists and can be identified or known, the originator of the persona must also be knowable since the one is dependent upon the other. That is why, in this roundabout fashion, the persona or essence of the Existent Source can be known. For lack of a less ambiguous label the combination of existence with essence can be referred to as the Existent-Essence or God. And because the essence, God, can be known, everything there is can be known. This explains why there is such a mysterious thing as knowledge. What is knowledge? It is being aware, i.e. to know. The knowing emanates from the Knower. That is why the Knower, i.e. God, is characterized as being omniscient or all-knowing.

Because God is omnipresent and omniscient, it is often assumed that God is also omnipotent. Paradoxically, God is not about power per se. God is about being, knowing, and empowerment which provides God with infinite potential. God is powerless without the myriad of creatures and life-forms with which God SHARES THE LIGHT. It is the selflessness of God that allows Man to have free-will, and to create like the Creator, to participate in the Light, and to have a unique persona. It is the ultimate application of the Golden Rule. It is through selflessness that God is able to reflect back to Himself what it is that He could be. The potentiality of what God could be is represented by everything there is. This selfless ongoing process of empowerment is called: SELF-REALIZATION.

The Way

In the previous illustration, the Eternal I is represented by the light bulb. The light bulb also represents Oneness, Wholeness, and Unity. In terms of human experience the way to this realization of Oneness or Enlightenment is known as the path. Frequently the terms "way" and "path" are used interchangeably, but in general they are distinguished according to context and usage.

There are many ways that lead to the Path of Realization. In fact there are as many ways as there are pinholes or individual human beings. Each way is the dharma of the person concerned. It is unique to his/her natural inclinations relative to an eternity of karmic development. All human beings who presently inhabit planet earth are here, now, because their karmic evolution provided sufficient conditions for their manifestation or incarnation at this collective level of awareness. All mankind is one humanity: a unique existential status called the human condition. We have everything in common.

Our human condition imposes a commonality, and although we ultimately go our separate ways as represented by the unique pin holes in the perforated ball, the ways that are well traveled and end up at a common destination become identified as Paths. For example, suppose one's destination is the North Pole. There may be many convoluted ways to get to the North Pole; some ways are better than others. It depends on where you are starting from: the moon, the South-Pole, the center of the earth, your bathroom, etc, and what you believe: a flat earth or a round one, polar-shifts, Santa Claus, String theory, and so on. Is it possible to get to the North Pole in the microcosm of your mind while meditating in the comfort of your vibrating swivel-rocker with heated backrest?

The Path

Although there are many paths, two basic paths have emerged over the centuries. Human experience upon Earth since human life became established has diverged into two general ideological and spiritual directions. There are as many ways that lead to these paths as there are individual seekers. All human beings have free will.

They are free to choose as they like. Naturally, it is important to choose wisely if one wishes to realize one's true potential during this incarnation.

The two basic paths are (1) The Path that is life-negating and diverges from the light; (2) The Path that is life-enhancing and leads to the light.

(1) The Path that is Life-negating

This path is currently quite popular; it is associated with the extrinsic view. Many intelligent and well-meaning people have chosen this path because they were born and raised in cultures in which this path has become a paved highway. From birth they were ensconced in a society that primarily condoned and promoted attitudes and beliefs that pointed in the direction of this path. One way that leads to this path is based upon the strongly held belief that Man is a flawed or sinful life-form. This concept of Man's nature has resulted in a religious outlook that is commensurate with this belief. Because it is based essentially upon a negative conception of Man's nature, this path leads away from the source of Man's true potential i.e., away from the pinhole and the light, and the further it diverges the more it deviates and distorts. There are at least three somewhat similar ways that lead to this path. In general they share the following three characteristics: (a) a justification of the sinful nature of man; (b) a justification of the separation of the few from the many; and (c) an ultimate justification for a rationale of salvation, with dire consequences for those who are not "saved", which necessitates the existence of an otherworldly setting separate from planet earth. It is difficult to explain, but this path, for better or worse, resonates strongly at this particular moment in history, within the collective consciousness of billions of human beings who nevertheless – in spite of their life-negating religious mindsets – will be able, each in their own particular (or seemingly convoluted) way, to eventually return to the path that leads to the light.

(2) The Path that is Life-affirming

This path is natural and associated with the intrinsic view. Strange as it may seem, not everyone chooses this path even though it is natural – perhaps because there are no dire consequences for those who do not chose to go in this direction. The way to this path is premised upon the notion that all life is sacred and divine. It therefore has a natural affinity that attracts it back to the source of the divinity i.e., back to the pinhole and the light. The way to this path is self-evident to some and obscure to others. It is essentially a matter of becoming aware or awakened to the source of the light reflected upon the screen of reality and following it back to the pinhole and then to the light bulb. ·However, since there is a vast diversity of levels of awareness commensurate with cultural, social, and religious conditioning, this realization is not immediately apparent to everyone.

Over the centuries the Enlightened have compassionately attempted to devise clever techniques that might help the unaware become aware or awakened. Through the use of various kinds and levels of meditation and the use of a variety of koans like the famous, "What is the sound of one hand clapping?" written by Hakuin (1685-1768), a breakthrough may result that opens the doorway to the path that leads to the light of enlightenment. Being natural, this path relies more on reason and common sense than on the dogma and orthodoxy of religion. At the present time there are at least two world-class religions, with many off-shoot sects, that condone and promote ways that lead to the path that is commensurate with gratitude, love, compassion, and Enlightenment.

The Other Hand

The analogy regarding "the Light, the Pinholes, and Reflections", requires further elaboration. It should be mentioned that in the universe represented by the holographic screen, space is curved as Einstein proposed, and curves around to form a whole. Consequently everything is interconnected. The Light, the Pinholes, and the Reflections are One. What is the sound of one hand clapping? What is the sound of awareness? The sound of knowing? It is the vibrant sound of unity, of coming together that resonates as oneness. All paths eventually lead to awareness and knowledge. Everything that is necessary to one's karmic evolution, to one's greater awareness, to one's self-realization, is available. Sometimes the long and convoluted path can be illuminating: imagine for example how much more significant heaven must be to those who have spent some time in hell! And how can those who went directly to heaven, by-passing hell, truly appreciate the difference?

All paths eventually lead back to the light. Some paths are long and indirect, while on the other hand, some are short and direct. Perhaps many who are now on the short and direct path were on the long and convoluted route in their previous incarnation and were aware enough to learn from their mistakes.   All paths represent freedom of choice and expression, freedom to expand one's limited knowledge and awareness in ways not yet conceived of. All choices and expressions enable God, the Existent Source, to be "everything that can be realized," and the potentiality for what can be realized, even in a finite universe, is infinite.

Perhaps to some, aspects of this explanation may be somewhat disillusioning and perhaps even upsetting, but that is because they are not aware of the "other hand". The "other hand" is the invisible hand of God. God is always clapping and cheering us on toward His greater self-awareness.   It is the sound of God's infinite Love, Gratitude, and Compassion that resonates throughout the soul of the universe and is heard in the cellular memory of the silent chambers of the heart as the solitary sound of... one hand clapping.

CHAPTER FOUR

Larry returned from the kitchen with a glass of orange juice and tomato and lettuce sandwiches for Penny and himself and set them down on a TV tray adjacent to the computer desk. "That pinhole analogy in the last section is a good example of our endeavor to apply the KISS formula in our handbook," he appraised.

"We need to keep things as clear and simple as possible for our own understanding of our own existence," Penny commented, helping herself to a glass of juice and a sandwich. "Simply put, the concept of 'I' is synonymous with human existence per se; 'I' is existence."

"And existence is here," Larry added.

"And here is where 'I' is."

"And where 'I' belongs is called home," Larry concluded.

"And home is where the heart is," Penny sighed, "Don't you agree, Larry?"

"That old cliché has been around for some time and I'm sure it will stick around for some time to come."

"For some reason it made me think of the sockeye salmon," Penny said with a bemused smile.

"Most people would have thought of something like a cozy room in a cozy house with cozy people."

"Funny the way my mind works, eh? However, let me explain my rather unusual response, and then you will find it really is not that far out."

"Please explain," Larry urged.

"First of all, imagine that you are a tiny fry. You've just been hatched from a salmon egg on the gravel shores of a small tributary of the Adams River which flows into Shuswap Lake. You and dozens of your siblings swim about near the gravel in the fresh water, eating and growing until you are big enough to leave your home. You swim downstream to where the little stream flows into the Adams River, and from there you follow the Adams River down until it empties into Shuswap Lake. You swim into Shuswap Lake and rest and feed some more, and soon you are big and strong enough to tackle the Thompson River that flows into the Fraser River that flows past Steveston into the salty waters of the mighty Pacific Ocean. You spend nearly four years growing, living and traveling as far north as Alaska.

"And then, after four wonderful years of unmitigated freedom exploring the northern reaches of the world's mightiest ocean, you become homesick. You have an overpowering instinct to return to the place of your birth, mate and reproduce your species. It is an urge so strong it overrides everything else. You return to the mouth of the Fraser River and spend some time acclimating to the fresh water near the Steveston estuary. You stop eating because you are so anxious to get to your destination. You slowly fight your way upstream eluding predators, fishermen, and every possible hazard of man and nature. You struggle past the Hell's Gate Canyon via the fish ladders and bask in the waters of the Thompson River. Here fishermen and poachers of every kind line the river banks hoping to hook, gaff, net or snare you as you swim by. You are battered and bruised, but you cannot give up. You must summon up the last of your cunning and courage and move onward to your destination: you must get home!

"You methodically swim up the Thompson River into Little Shuswap Lake near Chase, and from there into big Shuswap Lake. Now you must find the entrance to the Adams River. Where is it? You clearly recall swimming down it four years ago; the route is etched indelibly into the DNA of your genetic memory. You locate the entrance and struggle upstream searching for the exact tributary in which you were hatched. At last you find it, a shallow little creek flowing next to a viewing platform constructed of chemically treated preserved wood to make it last for many more major salmon runs.

"Hundreds of excited sightseers from one touring bus after the other crane their necks forward, their eyes bulging with amazement. Some have video cameras, some have ordinary cameras, and some are just there to see one of nature's natural wonders: thousands of scarlet red sockeye salmon with olive green heads with hooked snouts swimming upstream in unison in search of their homes. You ignore all the distractions and forge on up the little creek and there it is: a placid backwater, near the pebble shoreline with overhanging boughs; this is where you were born. You have returned to your roots. You are dying to reproduce your species.

"You find a mate, dig a shallow bed in the loose gravel with your frayed tail, and with a sigh of wondrous relief you lay your precious eggs. Your mate gratefully fertilizes them with sperm. Your entire life has been one prolonged existential orgasm. At last you are spent and sexually satisfied. You drift leisurely downstream with the current. You see thousands of other salmon swimming past you, frenetically searching for their homes. You are content. Your home is where your eggs are and your heart is there too. You have been very fortunate. You are one of the blessed who has realized the completion of your life cycle. You feel as empty and exhausted as an imaginary zero. You float contentedly downstream, belly-up. The world has turned topsy-turvy: it feels like you are on the other-side. It feels like home."

"Now I understand why the phrase 'home is where the heart is' reminded you of the sockeye salmon. You were not that far-out; in fact you were right on!" Larry ejaculated. "I don't think I'll feel like eating sockeye for a while. I know it is just a fish, but fish are as precious as any other life form. It is a shame to disrupt their life cycle," Larry empathized.

"Especially since they only get one opportunity to reproduce their species, just one chance to engage in the reproductive act. It is too bad they have to die right after," Penny commiserated.

"Imagine how our attitudes toward sex would change if like the sockeye we had sex once and then died?"

"A good note on which to review our work on Human Sexuality, eh?" Penny replied with a wry grin.

(2) Human Sexuality

The Mortal I is one of the Many, a part of the Whole. Her desire is to relate to her immortal persona, and ultimately to the Eternal I. Her sexuality represents this instinctive response; it is commensurate with her natural impulse to heal and nurture, and her omnipotent will to live.

Wrapped in the finite trappings of mortality, her longing for immortality is biologically manifested as an overwhelming desire to survive: to reproduce the species, to procreate, to pass on life, to extend her mortality. The satisfaction achieved from the momentary satiation of this instinctive urge is one of Mortal I's greatest pleasures. In the omniscience of her orgasmic convulsions, she attains a mind-boggling sensation of zero-ness, from which intimations of immortality are realized in an inkling of pure potentiality.

The miraculous four-year life cycle of the sockeye salmon epitomizes this innate urge to perpetuate the continuity of the species in a finite cycle of life and death. If the cycle cannot be completed the species faces extinction. Like the sockeye, Mortal I realizes her immortality through her mortality. The great reproductive Chain of Being which has its sexual roots in antiquity connects Mortal I link by link to her immortal beginnings. Although Mortal I realizes that she represents the newest link in the Great Chain of sexual reproduction, she is seemingly unaware that the life force that animates her mortal existence is as old as life itself.

Sex and Sin

It is most unfortunate that the life force that provides Mortal I with one of her greatest pleasures has been religiously defiled by neurotic Man. This neuroticism has swept around the world in an insidious fashion affecting the health and well-being of billions of human beings. Sinful Man is conceived in sin, born in sin, raised in sin, and sinfully indulges in the very process that creates more sinners and more sin. What sinful man reifies, i.e. makes manifest, both within and without, is symptomatic of his individual and collective neurosis. Such a reality, inner and outer, reflects this inculcated notion of being born with a flawed nature. Because it is unnatural, a sense of dissonance is created at the deepest cellular and spiritual levels of the existence of such persons who reflect a reality, both inner and outer, that is commensurate with their flawed self-concept. To Mortal I this is felt as a deep-seated feeling of personal embarrassment which consequently triggers the life-negating symptoms of the illness. The symptoms manifest the illness, which, because it is self-inflicted, is relatively immune from the healing impulse.

This life-negating attitude has turned a natural, instinctive, and powerful reproductive response into a psychological "neuroticism" fraught with sadism, masochism, and depravity. This certainly is not natural. To blame it all on a vengeful external God is also unnatural. However one looks at it, it cannot be said to be in Man's best interest, nor does it contribute to the health and well-being of the species. Yet this negative attitude persists as a prurient interest in all things sexual. Shame, guilt, and a sense of doing something forbidden, unclean, and beneath the moral dignity of guilt-ridden man is still very prevalent.

This negative attitude is exemplified in the derogatory manner by which seemingly intelligent men and women refer to their sexual genitalia. The terminology we use is a reflection of our common neuroticism. The neuroticism extends into practically all areas of sexual behavior. For example, when dissatisfied young couples experiencing problems with "making love" consult a counseling psychologist, the first thing the astute psychologist feels it is his/her professional duty to do is to dispel their romantic notion about "making love". Sinful man due to his bestial nature is incapable of "making love". The young couple must be delusional or in a state of denial. They need to be informed of the unvarnished psychological truth: in Western Christendom, males and females only "fuck". That four letter word has become one of the most expressive, versatile, and frequently used words in the vernacular.

Here are the basic clinical facts regarding the female and male genitalia. The female organ is called the vulva (sometimes mistakenly referred to as the vagina) which is composed of the labia majora (the outer lips), the labia minora (the inner lips), the clitoris (embedded in the apex of the minora), and within the inner lips the urethra (the urinary opening), the vaginal opening, and the vagina. The vulva contains about 8000 nerve endings about half of which are concentrated in the clitoris. The male organ is called the penis which is composed of erectile tissue which constitutes the shaft on which the glans (or head of the penis) is attached and in which the urethra opening is located. The penis contains about 4000 nerve endings, the majority of which are embedded in the glans. When the erect male penis penetrates into the female vulva the resultant interaction is known as sexual intercourse or coitus which is part of the reproductive process, but in the human species is frequently indulged in strictly for the sense of pleasure, well-being, exercise, and good health associated with it.

The vulva contains as many nerve endings as two penises combined. Yet in spite of this biological capacity for sexual stimulation and gratification, the female is inhibited by a paralyzing blanket of chauvinistic taboos, thou-shalt-nots, and socially inculcated attitudes and expectations, from deriving much pleasure from her sexual organs (which, according to the story in Genesis, were non-existent until Eve was belatedly created from Adam's seventh rib, along with the establishment and proliferation of the notion of Original Sin). What a difference the concept of sin has made toward fostering our attitudes and neuroticisms regarding sex!

The purest and most virtuous, who possess these negative attitudes and neuroticisms, do not participate in any activities that require the stimulation of their sexual organs; they remain celibate. This is the only way a human being can remain completely free from any taint of sin. What would happen to the human race if such a virtuous being had the power to force them to remain celibate for their own moral good? Humankind would become extinct in one generation. Fortunately the natural instinct to reproduce is as strong in the human species as it is in the sockeye salmon.

The Healing Impulse

The healing impulse is a natural and inclusive aspect of human sexuality. All healing and sexual energy comes from within as the human body per se is a unique composition of vibrating cells that resonate in harmony, resulting ultimately in the unique identity accorded to each individual. The "health" of the body is an indication of the degree to which all the body cells resonate harmoniously as a whole and enable the species to reproduce and survive. The body instinctively tends toward a state that is commensurate with good health.

Unfortunately, in the case of the creature with possibly the largest brain, the thought creations of the brain have placed many neurotic tendencies and restrictions upon human sexuality and consequently upon a powerful natural process, i.e. the healing impulse. Healing is an instinctive and subjective endeavor. However at the present time the *extrinsic view* dominates the healing sciences yielding an *outside-in* approach to healing combined with sinful man's neurotic obsession with filthy lucre. The following illustration should help to clarify this rather general statement.

The Making of a Drug Dependent Society

At the present time medical science is still considered to be an objective science, the practice of which is supported by the pharmaceutical industry worth billions of dollars. It is a symbiotic relationship essentially based upon good intentions and the making of money. Sometimes the making of money is reinforced by greed and the good intentions as well as reason and common sense are left by the wayside. Is it common sense to decree that only pharmaceutical drugs can cure disease and sickness? If this is so, then ergo, it must naturally follow that the only way to rid society of sickness and disease is by the manufacture and sale of drugs from which incidentally, billions of dollars have already been made and the prospects are excellent for trillions more to be made… creating a sick, diseased and DRUG-DEPENDENT SOCIETY. The irony thus created amounts to this: if drugs actually *cured* sickness and disease, the pharmaceutical companies would be bankrupting themselves! Think about that. Consequently they produce drugs that *treat*, but do not *cure* diseases.

What about all the proven, natural, non-drug related products and practices that trigger the body's intrinsic healing impulse and actually cure or prevent sickness and disease? Billions are spent each year by drug companies brainwashing the general public into believing that such products and practices are bogus, deceitful, and dangerous to one's health. Why? Because healthy people who utilize these products and practices require far less medical attention and consequently fewer *prescriptions* to purchase expensive patented drugs. The pharmaceutical companies are not stupid!

The government's regulatory agencies have tremendous power and authority in determining what is or is not good for the gullible public. Huge profits can be realized if new drugs can be demonstrated to effectively treat specific diseases. In order to protect a gullible public the pharmaceutical companies must prove to the regulatory agencies that their drugs are safe and effective and that the side-affects are not worse than the cure. One popular method commonly utilized in demonstrating the efficacy of a given drug is called a double-blind test. The new drug is administered to one of two separate groups; one group (the test group) is given the actual drug – while the other (the control group) is given a benign, identical looking substance or *placebo*, and told that it is the actual drug. The reason it is important that a placebo be given is that frequently the placebo group does just as well or better than the group receiving the real drug, indicating that the tested drug was not all that effective. The fact that the placebo often triggers the body's natural healing impulse is dismissed as being worthless from the pharmaceutical point of view.

However, the much denigrated "placebo-effect" IS THE REAL HEALING IMPULSE! Real healing comes from within, although it may be enhanced by some drugs. Now this is a dicey problem for the healing sciences! The efficacy of the placebo effect has been proven over and over by the double-blind tests. The placebo-effect works – even when the drugs don't! And it is natural, safe, and available to all, free of charge! At the present time powerful mindsets and commercial interests block the way to the realization of this natural, innate, and instinctive capability.

The Real Healing Impulse

There is a great deal of controversy as to what the placebo effect is, and how it can be triggered. The main stumbling block to the widespread use of placebos as healing devices is the public's negative attitudes and beliefs toward them; consequently they only seem to work if the person using them is fooled into thinking they are not placebos! Medical Doctors have known this for a long time and have been known to dispense authentic looking sugar-coated pills with the instructions: "These will help." As long as the patient is fooled the pills seem to work. THE MIND IS THAT POWERFUL. We have the innate capacity to heal ourselves, as we routinely do whenever we are afflicted with minor cuts or scrapes, or suffer from colds or illnesses that do not require patented drugs or a visit to the medical clinic.

It has been suggested that over half of any drug's healing efficacy can be attributed to the placebo effect. This even applies to powerful pain-killing drugs. The drugs work because the patient consciously or subconsciously expects them to work! If the patient does not expect the drug to work, the "nocebo effect" results where the drug is ineffective. The important question is: How can we, with our negative mindset, "fool" ourselves into triggering the placebo effect when it is needed to heal ourselves, or to perform a "miracle cure"?

There is no simple answer at present. Ask any medical doctor; they are intrigued by the irony of this paradox. For the interested, there are five basic sensate avenues that may lead to the enhancement of an intuitive rapport with one's natural healing impulse. The healing impulse is as natural and as powerful as our impulse to good health, reproduction and survival. Each individual is a unique resonating manifestation of the Light of Life: energy vibrating harmoniously to form a whole. The tendency is always toward harmony and wholesomeness. When disrupting and discordant vibes intrude, sickness and disease often result. Through our five senses we can tune-in to our cosmic instincts for good health and survival. Imagine that we have the following:

(1) Cosmic Hearing: this allows us to hear ourselves through cosmic ears. We hear the resonating harmony, and the discord, and like the grand Maestro we orchestrate the harmonic and healing symphony we would like to hear.

(2) Cosmic Smell: this allows us to inhale and exhale the air that fills our lungs and provides oxygen to the blood. We can smell the freshness or the staleness of each breath of life, and like the great Hunter we sniff the atmosphere and follow the fresh and healthy scent.

(3) Cosmic Touch: this allows us to feel the textures of the body via the central nervous system and become sensitive to its well-being or sickness, and like the master Gardener, tend to the health of every cell in need with a reviving massage of healing vibrations.

(4) Cosmic Taste: this allows us to taste the ebb and flow of life as it pulsates through the body in crystal streams of consciousness. When pollution contaminates the streams and dulls the senses, like the master Chef we prepare a healthy, nutritious, and satisfying meal.

(5) Cosmic Sight: this allows us to see ourselves through cosmic eyes. We see the perfection, and the imperfection, and like the grand Artist we visualize what it is that we would like to see, and we make it manifest.

We have the healing power, triggered innocuously by the placebo as evidenced in the control group every time medical science conducts a double-blind test. Apparently we can fool ourselves into healing ourselves. This business of "fooling" ourselves is a real conundrum! If we are not fooled into believing that the placebo is not a placebo – then the placebo cannot produce a placebo effect. Make sense? The baffling question is: What is preventing us from consciously triggering this healing impulse? Pause for a moment and give that question some serious thought.

Reason and common sense tell us that it is indeed possible to heal ourselves. It has been suggested that over half of the healing efficacy of any patented drug consists of the placebo effect. Belief appears to be a triggering mechanism. That appears to be the bottom line. "Believe, and you shall receive!"

The healing impulse, which is an intricate aspect of human sexuality, is innate, natural, and instinctive. It is as miraculous as life itself. If it was not, the survival of the universe would be in jeopardy. And the Grand Creator is just not as short-sighted, or as sinful/flawed/neurotic as we pretend to be.

The Ultimate Orgasm

Life routinely celebrates its birthday with each birth of its miraculous identity which occurs whenever the Three I-s telescope into One, creating a fusion known macrocosmically as the "Big Bang". This is the ultimate orgasm. It is experienced in microcosm on earth in the tingling synapses of the cellular memory of man's vertebrate nervous system during the act of procreation when the Mortal I experiences immortality in an instant of eternity. It is a wonder of wonders taken for granted as if it were nothing. There is a movement... and a rest.

And once again the soul awakens from its dogmatic slumbers as if wrapped in a cocoon of mortality from which finite dreams can be fashioned from strings of vibrant energy dancing in the twinkling of an immortal eye, eternally grateful that from One can come the Many.

"That must be one of the most non-sexual treatments of human sexuality on record," Penny observed.

"We have attempted to place human sexuality in its proper perspective."

"It is certainly an appropriate subject for a handbook on life. It is a topic of universal significance... given the present status of the global village in which we are ensconced."

"It certainly gives one pause."

"Do you think we have possibly been a little too cerebral in our approach to this topic?" Penny asked feeling a slight twinge of self doubt.

"I don't think we need to worry about being triple X-rated," Larry laughed.

"There seems to be enough sexual explicit literature in the marketplace without us adding to it," Penny justified.

"Sexual exploitation is perhaps one of man's most decadent weaknesses in conjunction with just plain unadulterated greed. The combination of the two, along with the naked use of power, has resulted in a great deal of injustice right here in North America," Larry responded.

"Duh?" Penny stared inanely at her spouse. "There you go, making a mental leap again," Penny complained. "Are we on the same page? What are you alluding to? Are you thinking of the sex trade, the slave trade, or the treatment of the aboriginal peoples, or what?"

"Sorry," Larry apologized sheepishly admitting to a tendency of his to suddenly change horses in mid stream. "I was thinking about the aboriginal people right here in British Columbia. I've been reading up on some of the early history of the Native tribes and finding it quite interesting. Unfortunately, in those earlier days racial prejudice was not uncommon, to say the least."

"I must admit the province of British Columbia probably has had more than its fair share of narrow-minded bigots!" Penny exclaimed, feeling personally tarnished by the actions of those who condoned and perpetuated such unsavory behavior.

"You know," Larry continued, warming up to the subject, "before the extrinsically-minded Europeans arrived in B.C., the Coastal tribes had a sharing ceremony called the Potlatch or Bah'lats. The word itself, which may have been derived from the Nootka word pachitle, is a Chinook jargon-word that means 'to give'. From their point of view the earth was sacred and the good things that flowed from Mother Nature were perceived to be an out-flowing of good will. Man himself being of the earth could exemplify this outpouring of good will. The good will came from within and flowed outward. It was a matter of sharing the good will. It was a sign of reverence and unselfishness to be able to share one's bounty as Mother Nature shared hers with them."

"Our concept of material wealth colored our notions about the meaning and significance of this so called pagan rite," Penny commented.

"To the Getskan it was celebrated as 'The Feast', and the Cowichan referred to it as the 'Great Deed'. It was a concept foreign to the mentality of the white foreigners who coveted their land and material goods."

"What a wonderful term: 'Great Deed'. It conjures up heroic images of self-sacrifice."

"The host and guests participated in the 'Great Deed' in a wonderful ceremony adorned with colorful masks, rattles, coppers, magnificent robes and other ceremonial regalia. It was a literal feast of sharing the bounty. The more one had, the more one was able to share. The wealth was intrinsic; it sparkled like diamonds in the eyes of the bestower of the good will. The more one gave away, the wealthier one became. The wealth was not material; it was immaterial. The host, even though he impoverished himself materially, felt psychologically and spiritually enriched, and was considered by his peers to be a magnanimous person."

"And the 'Great Deed' went on for two or three weeks?"

"Indeed. It was a time of sharing and bearing witness in public. Marriages, births, deaths, and other changes in one's status were announced. Information was shared, food was consumed, and everyone participated with an unselfish attitude, something like that which occurs at a pot-luck supper where everyone shares. The ceremony culminated with the host presenting gifts to every guest in a manner which was commensurate with their social status. Gifts could include canoes, carved dishes, eulachon oil, and other valuable items available during those times. The more 'wealth' bestowed the greater the prestige conferred upon the host."

"No doubt the Catholic Priests were flabbergasted by this type of pagan behavior – eh?"

"When the Europeans came along and witnessed this Potlatch of unrestrained sharing, this ceremonial giving away of earthly goods as a sign of intrinsic self-esteem, they were indeed flabbergasted. What were these ignorant heathens doing? Did they not understand that civilized man takes and takes, and hoards and hoards great abundance for himself in accord with God's laws? That even in the midst of utter poverty, destitution and pollution caused by his own greed, he must continue to accumulate more and more, because it was a sign, a sign that God had 'blessed' him."

"It was hard evidence that the favored were amongst the Elect," Penny chimed in.

"Did these savages not understand the ways of God?" Larry continued, beginning to sound like a preacher of old. "How could any God-fearing person give away his precious earthly possessions as if this were a sacred act of benevolence, an intrinsic outpouring of good will, a celebration of life? This pagan ritual had to be staunchly and firmly eliminated for their own good."

"The good old Indian Act to the rescue!" Penny chimed in once again like a church bell on the upward swing.

"In 1884, thirteen years after British Columbia joined Confederation, the Federal government in its parochial wisdom outlawed the Potlatch ceremony. Still, the Native Peoples persisted as it was an integral part of their cultural identity. The lawbreakers were arrested and sent to prison and their children institutionalized in Parochial schools where they were immersed in the proper view of Man and God."

"Ah-men," Penny concluded, acknowledging Larry's tendency to pontificate once he got on a roll. "Perhaps this would be a good time to review that section on Wealth and Freedom. What do you think?"

CHAPTER FIVE

It was beginning to get dark outside when the section on Wealth and Freedom appeared on the computer screen. "We have been lucky," Penny admitted. "We are reasonably wealthy and free: wealthy and free while millions suffer from fear, starvation, disease, and premature death in a world where material abundance is hoarded by a privileged few."

"A handbook on life would not be complete without a rudimentary understanding of the sufficient conditions which have given rise to the phenomenon we presently experience as Modern Capitalism," Larry added.

"And here we sit like a couple of guilt-ridden capitalists rationalizing our good fortune," Penny pointed out. "Isn't that ironic?"

"Yes, but it has allowed us the freedom and creature comforts required to write this handbook – is that justification enough?"

"Justified or not, here we are attempting to make sense of the economic reality in which we find ourselves," Penny replied sheepishly staring at the computer monitor.

(3) Wealth and Freedom

Wealth is not an easy term to define. What may be wealth to one person may simply be a burden to another. The word "wealth" denotes (a) affluence or riches, (b) large possessions or resources, (c) property that has monetary or exchange value, and (d) an abundant supply or profusion of all objects or resources that man desires. Two of the key words involved in this definition are "affluence" and "desire". The third, of course, is "man". Wealth is that which accrues to man because he desires to become affluent. Why does he desire to become affluent? Because it reduces his insecurity and enhances his freedom.

Basic Needs

In the beginning, man's most basic desires were dictated by his need to survive. These basic desires became known as his "basic needs". They are: air, water, food, and shelter. Intelligence, which gave rise to reason and common sense, was man's greatest asset in his quest to simply survive in a world that was at times a rather daunting place to live, and for the vast majority, still is.

At this time when the ozone layer is not completely unstable and the smog levels are still tolerable, air is not considered by most human beings to be an essential factor in their continuing state of well being. In general man in his reckless search for greater profits still takes his need for unpolluted air for granted.

Water, or the lack of it, has not been a major problem either for most of mankind except in seasons of extreme drought. With his ability to somewhat control his environment by reshaping the natural contours of lakes and rivers, man has been, for the time being, unperturbed by the abundance and quality of the water he needs for survival; this short-sightedness on his part could come back to haunt him.

Food always has been, and perhaps always will be, the one basic need that man deems to be essential to his well-being, mostly because it is the hardest to come by, and its availability on a regular basis, uncertain.

The fourth item, shelter, became more essential as man disbursed into cooler climactic zones, and unlike the beasts of the field, suffered immensely in adverse weather conditions. So it was that shelter also became one of man's basic needs.

In times of scarcity man must compete with others, like all other life forms, in order to secure his basic survival needs. This leads to a competition called the survival of the fittest, so ably documented by Charles Darwin. The outcome of this competition is always in doubt, and this doubt has become man's trademark because of all the life forms in existence, man is the only species who is able to anticipate the future. It is existentially manifested by everyone who has ever drawn breath, drank water, ate food, and sought shelter, as Insecurity.

Insecurity

In a primitive world where man was free to do whatever he wanted, freedom was tempered by the improper use of it. It was a "dog eat dog" world. Life, according to the philosopher Thomas Hobbs, could be "short, nasty, and brutish." The intrinsic feeling of insecurity this created was magnified out of proportion to the existent conditions of the supporting environment. Insecurity made the extrinsic world look like a place where security could only be found in places and things over which one had control. This anxiety-driven desire to overcome one's intrinsic sense of insecurity by gaining control over some or all of one's basic needs led to the behavior which became entrenched socially as "ownership". To be able to possess and control something that enhanced one's survival made one feel less insecure. The more of these possessions one had control of the more secure one felt. These possessions became one's own. They were "owned" by the possessor and defended to the death.

Death was the least desirable method of relieving oneself of this obnoxious feeling of insecurity.

Social Contract

According to the philosopher Thomas Hobbs, the desire for security and control over the basic needs for survival in the natural state of nature pitted every individual against every other individual. Limited though his intellectual faculties were in those early days, man could plainly see that although the selfish hoarding of essential goods for his own use provided a certain degree of comfort, they did not lessen, but ironically increased, his fear of being bashed over the head by someone who coveted his stash. Therefore, it was natural and even reasonable to expect that for the greater security of all concerned, some sort of common agreement should evolve. And it did. Some degree of freedom was exchanged for security. It is referred to by historians and political scientists as a *social contract*. Essentially it was an unwritten understanding arrived at by individual families and clans and then extended to tribes and larger and larger social units. They agreed to give up the freedom to bash each other over the head and steal each other's property in exchange for a modicum of security.

Basic Rights

Eventually, as man formed larger and more complex social units, he was able to trade and barter the things he owned for things someone else owned. Soon small markets flourished where men and women could come together and freely trade and barter, but the insecure fear of being robbed or killed still persisted because the social contract was only an unwritten understanding and not a right. The social contract needed to be much more clearly delineated and enforceable. Man would give up his freedom to rob or kill anyone he wanted in exchange for the creation of basic rights: the right to life and the right to keep his own property. These rights were agreed upon by all members of the social group, and it was up to the head of the group, or the group collectively, to enforce these rights. In a short time man's life changed from being short, nasty, and brutish, to being somewhat civilized.

Social Order

Civil-man now had the unprecedented opportunity to re-create a new social order based upon the rightful ownership of goods and services without the imminent fear of being robbed or killed. With the advent of writing, man was able to codify the social contract and carve it into something relatively permanent like sandstone, granite, and marble, as the "law". The law, such as it was in those days, was always written in the interests of the social group it represented, since it was their sense of insecurity it was addressing. The written law created more certainty in a world where doubt, like the ever present shadows, always lurked behind the scene.

In spite of the certainty of the law it was impossible for man to lose his psychological feeling of insecurity and doubt, because as an individual he still had to compete for and secure his own share of the property available. Competition, of course, created an insecurity of its own within the circumscribed social contract. Freedom to compete within this framework became rationalized much later as "free enterprise". There were no ethical/moral rules of fair play in those days. Anything was permissible as long as one did not bash one's competitor over the head and steal his property. Between those broad parameters, larceny, cheating, and deception were considered to be civilized modes of behavior. Consequently man felt driven to create a social order based upon various degrees of authority where he would be able to rationally control more and more of the uncertain aspects of competition and thereby further lessen his personal doubts and insecurities. This need for greater control and authority was omnipresent in every situation where insecurity and doubt lurked in the minds of the participants. This developed into a kind of psychological driven-ness motivated by fear and greed. Greed that led to greater security was good. Soon strongholds of security flourished around the camps of the excessively driven and fearfully-greedy who by cunning and luck had become rich and powerful, and subsequently gave themselves authoritative titles like Chief, Lord, King, Queen, Emperor and so on.

Currency

In a few thousand years, cities and nation states arose, and the means of trading and barter were expedited by the introduction of facsimiles of goods and services called "coin of the realm" which represented an agreed upon value reflected by actual goods and services, which eventually resulted in a commodity based currency regulated by the sovereign state. Trade and commerce flourished, man lived much longer, and the overt feeling of doubt and insecurity receded beneath a veneer of opulence. The greater the share of the goods and services one controlled or owned the more one felt insulated from the uncertainty of not having enough.

Since this system enhanced survival and reduced man's sense of insecurity, it naturally expanded beyond nation states to include entire continents. A flexible and broadly accepted mode of economic exchange was needed. Eventually currency became based upon precious metals like gold and silver which maintained a high "possession value" by man because they were relatively scarce everywhere in the world. Gold and silver were hoarded by the nations and governing powers concerned, and gold and silver coins became popular.

As trade further expanded it became evident that an even more versatile currency was needed. "Paper currency" was issued backed by the respective gold or silver reserves of the issuers of the paper currency. Soon it was common to be on the gold or silver "standard". For example, the United States of America and Canada were on the gold standard, while Great Britain was on the silver standard. However, as trade expanded to include the entire world, an even more versatile mode of currency was required that would allow those countries that did not have any gold or silver reserves to participate.

The Gross National Product

Success breeds more innovation and more success, and soon every civilized country of the world was participating in this economic system of trade and commerce. When gold and silver grew scarce, currency was produced based upon the Gross National Product (GNP) or the total value of the goods and services of a country. This meant that any sovereign country could issue its own paper money. For example, a Canadian or American dollar was no longer worth a dollar's worth of gold, but a dollar's worth of the value of their respective GNP. If the value of the GNP rose or fell relative to how it was assessed by the international trading community, the value of the dollar rose or fell on the international money markets according to its trading value. Obviously this economic system left plenty of opportunity for those at the apex of the world economic miracle to manipulate the system according to their own personal agendas. The rich got richer, and the poor were marginalized.

Modern Capitalism

Modern capitalism is a relatively recent development. The combination of greed with a religious fervor to accumulate great material abundance as an unmistakable sign that one was personally favored by an all-powerful extrinsic "God" provided the motivation to hoard far beyond one's personal basic needs. It is this obsessive behavior that makes capitalism such a daunting and powerful economic force in the global village today. The development of modern capitalism is astutely described by Max Weber in his brilliant work entitled: "The Protestant Ethic and the Spirit of Capitalism".

The impact modern capitalism has had on the modern world is unprecedented. The conscious and subconscious motivation provided by the combination of the spirit of capitalism with the Protestant ethic has become secularized as "the material way of life" or the "pathway to glory". Individual greed became glorified, legitimized, and magnified in the amoral persona of the "corporation" whose sole motive is to make as much money as possible for its individual stockholders: the more, the better.

The Global Marketplace

The notion as to what constitutes wealth and value has become more and more difficult to fathom as value per se expands beyond the bounds of the GNP of any single nation and becomes integrated in international trade agreements with complex financial arrangements that cross the boundaries of continents and encircle the world. Many large multi-national corporations have assets greater than the GNP of many smaller countries. Suddenly, in a matter of decades, the simple has become extremely complex. This complexity has introduced more uncertainty and more insecurity into a system initially entered into because it enhanced man's security. It has become oxymoronic.

For the majority of mankind this economic system has produced a vast disparity between the "have" and "have-not" nations. The few so-called "have" nations control the system for their own benefit to the detriment of the third world countries which are exploited for their cheap labor and resources. Still there is reason to be hopeful, because now there appears to be enough material wealth created that if it were shared unselfishly, there would be plenty for everyone!

Economic wealth is no longer limited to gold and silver. Knowledge per se has great value; ideas can be patented. Wealth suddenly has become something that exists in the desires of its creators. Billionaires have replaced millionaires, and the value of something as tiny as a micro-chip is worth trillions in a world with an expanding population with newly minted appetites for more and more of whatever is created, adroitly marketed, and accepted as necessary. All of this requires energy to produce. And as long as there is a source of energy, and the negative effects like pollution are not overwhelming, the reification of what we call "material wealth" will probably continue to be manifested. Why?

Because, after all is said and done, such material wealth is just an illusion, "fool's gold" one might say, substantiated by our vanity conditioned by our attitudes and beliefs. The illusion will last as long as there are enough human beings who believe it is real. And who can deny that it is real? Just two centuries ago most of this - these ivory towers of fool's gold - did not even exist! Where did it all come from in such a short time? It was not even an idea, let alone a blueprint, in the wildest dreams of the most creative inventors and architects. Who could have dreamed that human beings in a span of less than two hundred years would expend the energy necessary to create the conditions sufficient for all of this to become manifest? From the horse and buggy age to this! And after man has vainly decimated and polluted the earth in order to create mountains of fool's gold – in the absence of human beings, would the other forms of life find all of this '"wealth" to be valuable, life enhancing, and of great worth?　The great pyramids of Egypt stand as mute archeological evidence of man's vanity, manifested from the desert sands into shimmering mounds of fool's gold reified from the life-energy of thousands of discarded slaves by a powerful few obsessed with delusions of grandeur.

Beyond The Money Game
　　The objective of those playing by the rules of the game called "modern capitalism" is to accumulate the greatest amount of "fool's gold" possible in a single lifetime.　Playing the game can become an end in itself providing a purpose and direction to one's life.　Winning becomes an obsession and success is handsomely rewarded with mounds of fool's gold.　The problem with this approach/goal is that after one's lifetime is over, one must leave all of one's fool's gold behind!　What is the difference between one million and one billion, or between one billion and one trillion?　Three zeros.　What is zero worth?　Nothing.　What are three or three billion zeros worth? Nothing.　Is it all just an illusion, fool's gold?　It is the *one* in front of the zeros that is important.　However, believe it or not, one exits the world as one entered: without any zeros attached.　One will exit the world as naked as one was born into it.
　　How can the spirit of freedom rise to truly appreciate the wonders of this glorious planet when it is weighted down with the dross of one's desires for more and more fool's gold?　Is not real "personal wealth" that which you can take with you, that which is life-affirming to both body and spirit, that which is life-enhancing and glorifies the natural beauty of Mother Nature?　We have freedom of choice, and apparently we have chosen *this*.　We were not forced to create this tragic problem called global warming.　Nor were we forced to create this mess of insecurity, inhumanity, terror, and war, combined with disease, malnutrition, starvation, and poverty... in the midst of plenty!
　　Is there not a better way to meet our basic needs and provide security for all?　All we need is clean air, clean water, uncontaminated food, adequate shelter, and compassion for our fellow man.　That is essentially all we wanted from the beginning.　Where did we go wrong?

"Whew, some sensitive stuff there," Penny reacted, "I hope we don't alienate anyone."

"We always feel we have to tip-toe around anything the slightest bit controversial!" Larry responded in an uncharacteristic tone of frustration.

Penny lapsed into silence, shocked by Larry's emotional outburst. She looked over at Larry. He had been somewhat uptight since her return from the Medical Clinic. It seemed as if he had a premonition about something that he was keeping to himself, something that he had no control over and the anticipation was making him edgy.

"Are we really that intimidated?" she asked timidly.

"Pardon me. Forget I said that. It just slipped out," Larry hastily replied forcing a grin. "I did not mean to upset you."

"It's all right," Penny replied, "I know this waiting is hard on both of us."

"It must be much harder on you," Larry stated empathetically. "I guess I'm just feeling a little apprehensive." They lapsed into a sobering silence that dwindled on and on until it began to feel slightly uncomfortable. Larry loosened the belt on the denim cut-offs he was wearing and drew in a stomach-expanding breath to relieve the tension.

"Thinking has been my way of finding solace," Penny remarked, "thinking about all the creative ideas and subjects we have discussed in preparing for and writing the handbook. It keeps my mind constructively occupied. This project has been rejuvenating."

"It has been a fabulous project," Larry concurred as he pushed back his chair and stretched out his legs with a sigh of relief.

"You have much more hair on your legs than I do," Penny observed as if intrigued by the difference.

CHAPTER SIX

Early spring had such wonderful potential. The tiny buds were just breaking the ground and all around in every nook and cranny new life waited anxiously for the first warming rays of spring sunshine. It was the time of year when Penny and Larry loved to stroll leisurely through the flower garden with anticipation. They could see fabulous growth and vibrant colors where others only saw dried up leaves, barren branches, and un-worked soil. It was, as they say, all in the eye of the beholder. What a difference a positive attitude can make!

"Ah, spring!" Penny enthused with relish. "A world of new life is just waiting to burst forth in all its majestic glory. Every little seedling, every little fibrous root, after resting in a winter bed of rejuvenating dormancy, is ready to sally forth."

"Look how these tiny buds barely poke their heads up. It is as if they are shy little kids hiding behind Mother's earthly apron."

"You are waxing poetic this morning, dear."

"The world feels poetic with potential." Larry brushed off the ornate garden bench with his brand new imitation-leather gloves he had purchased the day before at Zeller's winter clearance sale, and invited his wife to join him on the bench.

"Boy, did you get a deal on those gloves," Penny remarked as they sat down.

"Seventy percent off," Larry stated proudly. "What about your new spring jacket?"

Penny was wearing her comfy new hunter-green spring jacket with detachable pull-string hood. "Only fifty percent off," she said, "but I like it, don't you?"

"It suits you, and green is a spring color."

"There is something about 'newness' that gives one a certain sense of satisfaction," Penny observed.

"Ah, yes," Larry agreed, and after a moment's hesitation added, "but at the expense of all those poor exploited souls in third world countries dying of starvation, and disease. They just want clean water and enough food to eat – while we want newness."

Penny remained silent in ponderous thought, then perked up and added, "Yes, we even build obsolescence into our products so that the consumer is continually obliged to buy, buy, buy. New fads, new styles, new models, new and improved with limited shelf-life; consume, discard, pollute."

"It's not sustainable, and we know it. But who cares about the sustainability or the upcoming generations who will have to suffer for our self-indulgent ways, so long as profits are made and the shareholders are happy?"

"What is wrong with this picture of the global village? It is precisely like that story your buddy Linc sent us in his Christmas card."

"The proper question is: What is wrong with us? We are the ones doing this. Are we just plain stupid or ignorant, or both?"

"Like our dormant garden, we have the potential to manifest a fabulous reality, one where the entire global village is a healthy, beautiful and sustainable ecosystem. With our present technological advances we have the potential to realize heaven on earth. Instead we are well on our way toward creating a reasonable facsimile of hell. Why is that?"

"It is our neurosis. You know, haven't we discussed some aspects of this previously?"

"Yes, I believe we might have. Anyway, carry on," Penny encouraged her spouse by reaching over and giving his left hand, which was enclosed in his new imitation-leather glove, a gentle squeeze. "Nice gloves – eh?" she remarked.

"Seventy per cent off," Larry reiterated with appropriate pride once again emphasizing the shrewdness of his purchase. "Ah, now where were we?"

"Your short term memory isn't getting any better," Penny noted. "Have you been taking those vitamin-B supplements I purchased last week?"

"No, I forgot. Must be my short term memory," Larry laughed. "But don't worry, we were discussing our mindset, the state of mind that causes us to behave in this atrocious manner," Larry stated proudly as his short term memory lit up his face with a rejuvenating smile. "Over the last two millennia we have inculcated certain attitudes and beliefs that have created a powerful stereotype which limits our potential with life-negating behavior. We do what we do because we are manifesting what we believe we are."

"And what is that?"

"Don't laugh – tragically flawed human beings: sinners. This self-concept contaminates most of us with a life-negating outlook. Look at our present behavior. Is it rational to plunder and waste our precious non-renewable resources, pollute the earth with our excessive garbage, and dissipate most of our surplus wealth manufacturing weapons of mass destruction so we can terrorize and kill each other in order to protect and preserve that point of view?"

"Why are we not spending those trillions of dollars feeding the starving, clothing the poor, and eliminating disease?" .

"Now that is truly a stupendously important and illuminating question!" Larry acknowledged with a nod toward his spouse. "We should be - but we are not doing it, are we? That is how powerful this mindset is. It is like a restrictive mental-box that limits our true potential, a debilitating life-negating neurosis that blinds us to the flawed behavior that is a consequence of our collective belief in our flawed nature."

"How can we overcome this frame of mind?"

"As we have mentioned once before – although we too reside inside the box, so to speak, we must 'think' outside the box to realize our true potential."

"In terms of thinking outside the box," Penny reflected shifting to a more comfortable position on the bench, "I've been thinking," she paused to slide the hood of her new polyester jacket over her head, and as she did, her inquisitive mind slid back to the time Larry had mentioned the marvelous feats of travel and navigation the tiny bird called the russet Red Knot was capable of. "You know?" she asked with a funny look on her face that her spouse had seen many times before – just before she followed it up with an animated, "You'll find this rather hard to believe but…."

"Try me," Larry butted in impatiently, knowing that his wife was about to launch another of her seemingly intuitive, yet profoundly insightful observations across the horizon of his incredulity.

"I've been thinking, ever since you mentioned that matter about the fledgling russet Red Knot instinctively flying over nine thousand miles of unfamiliar territory, all the way from Northern Canada to Tierra del Fuego situated on the southernmost tip of South America."

"You have?"

"Yes, indeed. And based upon reason and common sense, it seems to me that over the generations we human beings with massive amounts of cellular memory locked within our DNA – enhanced/restricted by the largest brain of any living creature save the porpoise – have in many ways been our own worst enemy."

"Please elaborate," Larry urged as he usually did in such situations where intellectual discussions seemed on the threshold of orgasmic possibilities.

"It's like you said; our fabulous brain which sits astride our medulla oblongata like an absolute dictator can be either a restrictive tyrant or a benevolent benefactor. We as a species are only in the fledgling stage of our evolution, and already we are moving down a slippery slope that could lead to our premature extinction."

"I presume you are implying that the human species with its present mindset could be considered to be an endangered species if it continues down the road we are currently traveling without due regard to all the warning signs that have already been posted?

"A species that kills its own kind and shits in its own nest on purpose is not enhancing its chances for survival."

"Why do you think we as a species are behaving in such an ignorant and life-negating manner?"

"It's like you intimated before; we use our greatest asset, our wonderful brain, to our own detriment."

"How so?" Larry responded enjoying his role as the enabler.

"Like the tiny Red Knot, our bodies contain all the information we need to instinctively perform life-affirming deeds far more miraculous than anything the Red Knot is capable of. Sometimes in desperation or by sheer fluke we instinctively allow ourselves to do what the Red Knot does without thinking. When it happens, we call it a blessed miracle."

"In the field of medicine alone there are many stories of miraculous cures that defy rational explanations," Larry contributed.

"Somehow we have brainwashed ourselves into believing that we are incapable of healing ourselves and can only be cured by the extrinsic application of ointments, drugs, radiation, transfusions, electric shocks, inoculations, massage, and a variety of other medical therapies," Penny commented following up on her husband's line of thought. "When these cures fail we give up and acquiesce ourselves to our ignominious fate. Why? Because our magnificent brain over-rides our instincts like a tyrant and dictates according to the inculcated attitudes and beliefs that have persisted for so long they have, unfortunately, become stored in the outer fringes of the hard-drive of our memory banks and passed on from generation to generation, preconditioning our brains to act like governors on our innate storerooms of freedom, freedom to fly beyond the horizon of our present limitations."

"We need to use our fabulous brains to help us to delve beneath these negative mindsets, beneath these layers of restrictive, life-negating attitudes and beliefs, and tune-in to our real potentiality."

"Yes, we are fully capable, like the Red Knot, to fly beyond the horizon, the horizon of our self-imposed limitations. But our negative mindset has grown so powerful over the millennia that now it is our nemesis."

"How can we overcome it?" Larry asked, genuinely perplexed.

"That is the very question I have been cogitating on for some time."

"And?" Larry prompted.

"What is it that enables the fledgling Red Knot to accomplish the seemingly miraculous?"

"It is instinct, natural, unfettered, and innate that allows the Red Knot to routinely do what to us human beings seems to be so miraculous. Instincts are very useful and extremely powerful."

"Our most powerful instincts are associated with survival, with life-enhancing behavior, as is the case with all other species of life," Penny added. "One of the most powerful life-enhancing behaviors is the reproductive function. Consider the life-cycle of the sockeye salmon. In all life forms, reproduction of the species is of paramount importance – except in the case of .the species with the most marvelous brain: civilized man. Activities related to reproductive behavior have become layered with *learned* attitudes and beliefs that over generations turned natural instincts into something quite unnatural and even life-negating. This mindset unfortunately has become associated with other natural biological functions such as breast-feeding, urination and defecation. All bodily functions related in the mind with the reproductive act have evolved into an unnatural, all consuming obsession known as *sex*."

"You said a mouthful there!" Larry expostulated.

"This unnatural obsession is symptomatic of our collective problem, or should I say neuroticism. It has spawned a lucrative industry known as pornography." Penny paused to draw in a sobering breath as if to underscore the gravity of the situation at hand. "Perhaps, just perhaps, the way to get back in touch with our instincts, our innate potentiality, our ability to heal ourselves, our life-enhancing freedom to fly beyond the horizons of our restrictive attitudes and beliefs, is to expose and come to terms with the genesis of this concept of man's flawed nature."

"Makes sense," Larry concurred.

"As you know, powerful institutions like the Catholic Church have within a very short span of time been able to popularize the ancient Judaic belief regarding man's tragically flawed nature as described in a section of the Old Testament, called Genesis."

"Yeah," Larry interjected, tuning in on a topic that he had studied numerous times in his youth while in Sunday school. "That really is just a myth, you know, a fable or legendary story about creation metaphorically personified to explain the conundrum of how Absolute Freedom could become Relative Freedom, or how Cosmic Consciousness became subjectively aware."

"Or a fairy-tale about how the Judaic God labeled 'Jehovah' created something out of nothing," Penny resumed. "The genesis of the problem occurred when, according to this fable, Jehovah created a personification of His Cosmic Consciousness called 'Adam', and he turned out to be a naked homo-sapien with testicles and a penis commensurate with an innate instinct natural to their function and use. Perhaps he should have been a hermaphrodite, but he was not. It appeared to be an oversight."

"No kidding," Larry chimed in, playing his role, "In spite of being endowed with the necessary reproductive organs – how could Adam go forth and multiply?"

"This certainly was a serious problem. According to this fable, in an attempt to rectify this problem a companion with ovaries, a womb and a vulva was chauvinistically created out of Adam's DNA or seventh rib, and called Eve, who soon became the apple of Adam's desire. Carnal knowledge was symbolically represented by the tree of knowledge which Adam and Eve were forbidden to partake of – if they desired to retain their innocence and remain in the paradise of their ignorance."

"What a predicament! Why create male and female and then make it impossible for them to mate without committing the first or 'original sin'?"

"Only the original fabricator of this story can answer that question. Was it really 'God'? Or was it someone pretending to be god?"

"Probably some pious old ascetic with a celibate's prosaic bent for metaphorical imagery religiously rationalizing his slavish predicament in the barren desert of ancient Egypt...."

"...while dreaming of paradise lost," Penny completed her husband's thought. "Anyway the story got changed and embellished over the ensuing centuries by the chauvinistic male scribes who copied and re-copied it over and over until it became basically nonsensical, and now it is so far from representing the word of God that it needs to be preserved as dogma in order to retain any religious veracity."

"And yet, you know, I find the story quite fascinating as a metaphor."

"So do I."

"I suppose, because like other mythical tales concerning our origins, it attempts to explain the seemingly unexplainable: the origin of all creation. And by necessity it had to be told in a personified imagery pertinent to the times."

"In some ways it seems like a primordial bedtime story for sleepy adults lounging about their ancient campfires in the still of the darkest night, mesmerized by the glowing red embers, and enraptured by the hypnotic voice of the omniscient story-teller.... *Thus it came to pass that as Eve lay reclining innocuously on her right side, naked as the moment she was created, Adam was overcome by her proximity and her sensuous charms. From an overhanging bough of the symbolic tree of knowledge/good and evil, Eve casually plucked a beautiful red apple while Adam watched as if spellbound, and took a healthy bite from the forbidden fruit. What was she thinking? Before Adam could say, 'Spit it out!' she swallowed and smiled with delight as the sweet juice of the apple titillated her taste buds. And then she turned unselfishly toward Adam with the delicious partly eaten fruit in her out-stretched hand and coyly invited him to partake. What was Adam supposed to do? Was not Eve created out of his seventh rib? Was she not his flesh and blood? Did Adam really have a choice? In order to go forth and multiply did he not have to be disobedient? For the very first time he had to exercise his free-will and exert his independence. Was this God's way of setting Adam free?"*

"'Was this God's way of setting Adam free?' Excellent question!" Larry exclaimed, his face shiny with excitement. "Yes indeed; it makes sense. That is probably what God, in his mysterious way, was attempting to do."

"Too bad Adam was not aware of this."

"Poor Adam, like a celibate priest he could urinate, defecate, and masturbate – but was forbidden to fornicate! What a nasty predicament to be in." Larry glanced up at his spouse with a boyish grin.

"Adam and Eve, if they desired to reproduce their kind, had to copulate," Penny joined in on the rhyming, "just like all the other common beasts of the field. Like you said, what a predicament! Think about it: just like the other beasts of the field! Naked males and females connected by their genitalia, grunting and sweating in heat, convulsed in the throes of orgasmic pleasure. Was this what the sublime creature called Man, made in his God's lofty image, had to lower himself to if he desired to be free and procreate? Adam had free will, but did he want to be free? What a dilemma! It was a classic approach-avoidance conflict. Was there a solution to this diabolical predicament?"

"Well, was there a solution? How did Adam, or should I say the omniscient narrator of this tale, deal with this situation?"

"In the primordial depths of a new born Genesis, why not create an alter-ego, an imaginary 'patsy', a fall-guy to take the blame, and let this *satanic* personification of every fear, dread, and evil imaginable talk you into doing what you desire? Blame it all on the Devil!"

"Ingenious!"

"In a paradoxical moment of gullibility Adam sinned, lost his innocence, became self-conscious, and fell from grace as a flawed specimen dimly aware of the duality represented by good and evil, into a miraculous four dimensional state of reality experienced as mortality. Apparently it was the price of subjective freedom. Zero became one," Penny explained.

"God certainly works in mysterious ways."

"However, in retrospect, the 'piously righteous', after familiarizing themselves with this remarkable fable – unlike Adam – are apparently able to virtuously control themselves and remain sexually ignorant. They endear themselves to their God by remaining celibate, and therefore free from the embarrassment of participating in the supposedly sinful and beastly act of fornication. This in a nutshell, aside from all the complicated rhetoric proclaiming more sublime motives, was and is the righteous attitude of the Catholic Church toward sex. Consequently all artificial means of preventing disease, pregnancy, stress and worry that might possibly enhance man's pleasure and desire to participate in the reproductive act are frowned upon. Total abstinence is the recommended course of virtuous action. In a world suffering from overpopulation, could this simplistic approach prove effective? Perhaps the human race will become decimated by AIDS or other sexually transmitted diseases by non-celibate converts adhering to the Pope's condemnation of the use of condoms as being: *unnatural?*"

"Throughout the world supporters of the Vatican have echoed the Pope's sentiments; for example, during carnival season in Brazil when sexual activity was at a peak, the Auxiliary Bishop of Rio de Janeiro, Rafael Llano Cifuentes reinforced the Pope's point of view regarding the use of prophylactics by informing his congregation: 'I have never seen a little dog using a condom during sexual intercourse with another dog.' Are dogs not concerned about contracting AIDS?" Larry wondered aloud.

"The biblical concept of Original Sin has been, perhaps, the single, most powerful negative influence upon humankind over the last two thousand years," Penny stated soberly, unmoved by Larry's attempt at humor.

"It is amazing how this simple fable about Adam and Eve has managed to warp monotheistic man's natural sexual instincts into something dirty, sinful, unnatural, and flawed. No wonder you have given this... uh-uh chauvinistic matter so much thought!"

"Not as much as Sigmund Freud, Jung, Adler and a host of other brilliant thinkers who have struggled to make sense of our neurosis. We need to get beyond the negative mindset that restricts and debilitates and keeps us in the straightjacket of our own ignorance."

"We need to conceive of ourselves – not as sinners or tragically flawed creatures – but as mortal manifestations of divinity."

"Perhaps then our outer reality will mirror our inner potentiality, and like the russet Red Knot we will be able to fly beyond the horizon of our current limitations."

CHAPTER SEVEN

Insecurity is a strange feeling. It plagues all human beings from time to time. There is something innate in the constitution of intelligent life forms that makes them feel insecure. Perhaps it is totally justified when one considers how vulnerable life is to a thousand "slings and arrows of outrageous fortune", to paraphrase Shakespeare. That life exists at all is a miracle beyond the understanding of even the most gifted intellectuals. Who knows? Perhaps feelings of insecurity are perfectly natural from time to time. So it was that when Jerry and Sherry were about to graduate from high school and had their hearts set on going to the University of Victoria, that both Larry and Penny felt pangs of insecurity.

It was not that they were poor; it was simply a matter of not wanting to sacrifice what they had for something intangible. Sure, they could re-mortgage the house but it had taken them years to pay off that darn mortgage. Their home had appreciated a great deal over time since they lived near UBC. It was only a modest home compared to others in that area, and the thought of re-mortgaging it gave them a feeling of insecurity, not because they could not afford the mortgage payments, but because it undermined the security of one of their basic needs: shelter.

The insecurity sat there and gloated like a sadist while they suffered like indulgent masochists enamored by the prospect of having the opportunity to make an altruistic sacrifice. And they would have done it too. There was no way they were going to allow their precious twins to be encumbered by tens of thousands of dollars worth of student loans in order to get a post-secondary education when all that was required was their signatures on a piece of paper, and a depleting set of numbers would vanish from their bank account every month just like magic. However, they never did get to experience how unselfish they would have felt had they been able to make that sacrifice. It was just one of those fortunate things that sometimes come to pass when you are not expecting it.

A few years back, when the twins had graduated from junior high, Penny had proudly had a family photo taken with the kids wearing fake caps and gowns. It was premature but hey, what harm could it do? On a whim, Penny sent a note to her cousin in Japan along with a copy of the family portrait. She had scribbled something like, "We would like to share this moment with you. We are very proud of our children; they represent the upcoming generation of enlightened citizens of the world," and signed it, "The Fearsome Foursome".

Just before Easter when the twins were gearing up for final exams and high school graduation activities, Larry received a card in the mail informing him that he had a registered letter waiting for him at the post office. "Who could be sending me a registered letter?" Larry asked, holding up the card, when the family sat down for supper.

"Perhaps you're being sued for something," Jerry offered.

"Don't be so pessimistic," Sherry admonished, "Perhaps Dad's getting a special recognition award from the Lieutenant Governor for being a fabulous father."

"Flattery has always been your strong suit," Jerry rebutted sarcastically, "and look where it has gotten you? Nowhere."

"Enough squabbling," Larry interjected. "And what do you think?" he turned toward his wife.

"Let me see that card," Penny reached over, procured the card from her husband, and held it up to her forehead.

"It's just a card of notification – not the letter," Sherry pointed out, "so that probably won't work."

"Never underestimate your mother's extra-sensory powers," Larry responded in Penny's defense.

"Ah," Penny sighed, "I feel a vibe coming in. It's from a long way away… a long way away… and it is making me feel… ah, ah… it is making me feel secure and happy."

The next day Larry drove down to the post office and picked up the registered letter. He brought it home unopened and after supper was over he produced it at the table with a flair of showmanship. Theatrics was something that Larry was quite good at, especially at home before a captive audience. He presided over the opening of the envelope like the presenter at the Academy Awards ceremony. Using a clean table knife he slowly slit the manila envelope open. Inside was a one page letter accompanied by an official-looking certificate. The letter was addressed to Larry. He read it out loud.

"Congratulations on raising such outstanding children. By my calculations they should be ready to graduate from high-school. The world's future depends upon such youngsters. I know the cost of post-secondary education is prohibitively high these days. Educating one child is burden enough, let alone two at the same time. Good fortune has made me extremely wealthy. Money is nothing unless it can be put to good use. It would be a very great honor to me if you would allow me to assist with the formal education of your children, Jerry and Sherry. Perhaps you could establish a trust for the post-secondary education of your children with the enclosed funds. Please give my kind regards to your wife." The amount of the funds was embossed upon an International money order. The embossed number was: two hundred and eighty thousand Canadian dollars.

"That's one hundred and ninety dollars each!" Jerry calculated.

"You mean one hundred and ninety thousand dollars each," Sherry corrected.

"We must be sure to send a thank you note," Jerry said gratefully.

"Who sent us the money?" Sherry asked.

"Your mother's cousin."

"Some cousin you have, Mom," Jerry said thankfully.

"Yeah, Mom!" Sherry exclaimed with deep felt gratitude, "some cousin."

Penny said nothing, but she seemed on the verge of tears.

* * *

A fortnight passed and it was 1:30 p.m. when Larry answered the phone. It was the receptionist from the Medical Clinic. She apologized for taking so long to get back to them. "We had the results double checked just to be sure," she explained. "Dr Lee would appreciate it if you both could come in today. Is 3:30 p.m. okay?" Larry consulted Penny who nodded her assent.

Nothing much needed to be said. They drove to the clinic and sat quietly in the waiting room. In a short while a nurse ushered them into Dr. Lee's office.

"Have a seat," Dr. Lee said politely, while looking intently at some papers on her desk. She removed her reading glasses and gazed searchingly at both Penny and Larry. She drew in a deep breath and said, "I know you'd want me to be candid and forthright. I am very sorry to have to inform you that the samples were malignant. I've had them double checked to be sure," she paused and drew in another breath. "You have cancer," she looked down at the report on her desk and hesitated as if she was unwilling to say more. "It has spread to both lungs. It is treatable but not curable."

Penny found it difficult to breathe. She smiled feebly for no reason. She was feeling light-headed and faint. The only thought that kept crossing her mind was: "If only I hadn't been so gullible, so stupid, so ignorant."

It was Larry who cried. He could not help himself. The tears just kept welling up and running down his cheeks. They would not stop. It was as if he was crying on behalf of the world; the entire world was crying because the world knew something was wrong: Penny had terminal cancer; the quiet humble little person who wanted with all her heart and soul to help make the world a better place for all humankind was going to die.

In the weeks that followed, Penny had to face the prospect of her imminent demise. The cancer treatments had started a week after the fateful diagnosis and were scheduled to be continued as needed. The specialists had been optimistic: "Just hang in there," they said encouragingly, "Chin up... with chemo, who knows how long you could last."

Terminal cancer from a medical perspective is just that – terminal. There is no way out except death. It is a lingering death, a living death; it could go on and on and on.... There is no wonder drug, no cure in spite of the billions spent searching for one – just expensive treatments, one after the other. There is only diminishing hope accompanied by depression, acceptance, courage, and fortitude. The cancer is relentless.

Solace, if it can be found, comes from within, along with the healing impulse. Sometimes for no reason the cancer goes into remission and death is postponed. Sometimes there are miracle cures that baffle even the most brilliant doctors. The degree to which one suffers depends upon one's attitude. Penny had a positive attitude based upon her belief that one did not "die", one just "passed on"; it put a happy face on a mortal being struggling to complete a Student Handbook on Life.

"I could have passed away when I was an infant," Penny told her husband, "I'm thankful for all the precious years I have been given."

"I'm thankful too," Larry replied.

"You will need to finish what we have started," Penny reflected. "The second draft is all there. It will just be a matter of final revisions, proof-reading and editing."

"Don't worry," Larry responded, "I'll make sure the handbook is completed. You just rest."

Penny sat back on the couch. The chemotherapy had devastated her immune system in the attempt to destroy the cancer cells, sapped her strength, and made her look like a survivor of the Holocaust. All her hair had fallen out and she wore a toque to keep her head warm. She was deathly pale and shrunken to a shadow of her former self. Still she struggled on dauntlessly. What else could she do?

"All mortal beings must pass away," she consoled herself, "and now it is my turn. Now I will really be able to enjoy each moment as if it were my last!" In this frame of mind, Penny carried on each day in a cheerful and happy manner. "Look!" she would exclaim when Larry was least expecting it, "how perfectly the sun filters through the curtains and illuminates the room with an aura of golden grace. Don't you feel blessed?" Every waking moment of life was a blessing to Penny. Everything seemed to be touched by the grace of perfection. It was too much at times; the beauty overwhelmed her.

"And yet the rest of us healthy mortals do not appreciate it enough," Larry lamented to himself sadly.

Because of her illness, Penny moved into the second bedroom. She could tell that her husband needed his own space as much as she needed hers. He stayed up late at night writing and re-writing the manuscript. Sometimes she could hear him talking to himself as he worked into the wee hours. "Penny's really going to like this!" he'd say out loud as if to confirm his own appraisal. He worked tirelessly. It was as if he had to get the manuscript completed while she was still alive, so she could approve of the final result.

Although it was a joint project, he considered the handbook to be her legacy of undying inspiration to every student of life. It was tangible evidence that she had indeed trodden this long and winding path; that she had been here and left her tiny footprints on the dusty road traveled by all the nameless ones who had preceded her down the mortal pathway that led beyond the known horizon.

PART NINE

REALIZATION

God is always being realized
Or manifested as something else
In the instant known forever
As now.

CHAPTER ONE

Who knows why we do certain things? Why had he called it, "A Story of the Times"? Why had he sent his cousin a copy? Perhaps it was an attempt to salvage something by sharing, an attempt to salvage a bit of dignity in his senior years?

The simple writing of it had clarified and resolved the dissonance that had clogged his mind. He had written about himself as if he were someone else; perhaps that was the subjective secret of objectivity. Anyway, he had written it and there was no taking it back! What was done was done. Period. Somehow he knew Penny would appreciate the effort. She was that sort.

The old man rolled his eyes upward and concentrated on the spot referred to as the third or "all-seeing" eye. His breathing gradually slowed until it was almost nonexistent and his heart slowed to a steady lum-dum-pesh... and there it was in his mind's eye, almost exactly as he had written it.

Once upon a time there lived a young man named Tutomu. He lived with his hard-working and frugal parents on the northern island of Hokkaido. After his father was recruited into the Yakuza they moved to Tokyo to be near the center of trade and commerce. His parents wisely invested what little income they had saved into stocks that everyone said would be a solid and safe investment. They heeded the advice they were given and established a portfolio of stocks in a few of Japan's more successful post war companies like Mitsubishi, Sony, Toyota, Panasonic, Subaru, JVC, Honda, Cannon, and Nissan. It was not much to start with, just a conservative smattering of stocks here and there that showed promise. Who would have thought they would have become so successful in a post World War II economy where anything that was labeled "Made in Japan" was automatically ridiculed as being of the lowest quality? Maybe it was the samurai mentality that drove those companies to overcompensate. Who would have thought they would have become so successful? Perhaps it was just dumb luck, a change of fortune for all the bad luck Kasuzimo Miki and his family had already endured.

Because his parents were late-blooming investors with big dreams for their only son, a great deal of invisible pressure was placed upon him to eventually become a successful player in the capitalistic money markets of the world. Therefore his schooling had been meticulous and he graduated near the top of his class with a much coveted degree in Business Administration, with a major in Economics and a minor in Accounting, from the prestigious University of Tokyo.

There were nothing but rising expectations in front of him and millions of yen to support those expectations. The Yakuza had connections. His father vouched for him. He spoke impeccable English. The biggest international trading companies needed well-educated young Japanese men who could speak English as well as or better than any foreigner. So Tutomu donned his three-piece suit and set out to justify his existence.

Because the mere thought of failure sent shivers of fear shooting up and down his spine, he resolved to work very hard to live up to the expectations that were placed upon him. And he did. He worked tirelessly day and night. His peers, and especially his boss who worked very hard himself, were amazed by his attitude and his fortitude. No one worked harder, and no one had a more positive outlook.

"For one who is making a handsome salary and is already very wealthy, he works like a horse," the Senior Vice-President confided to Tutomu's parents one evening between sips of Johnny Walker's Scotch Whiskey. They beamed with pride, thankful that their one and only son was proving to be a real credit to the family name and to the company.

So it was that Tutomu, a child of destiny, rose up through the corporate ranks to become CEO of one of Japan's largest and most influential trading companies. Tutomu had lived up to every expectation. He was a corporate shogun. He swore allegiance to Japan Inc. He guaranteed job security to every dedicated worker and treated all of the employees with respect and dignity; and in return they pledged him their undying loyalty. Wherever he walked on company grounds the employees greeted him with deep bows of respect and reverence. It always made Tutomu feel somehow inadequate, as if to say: 'Who am I to deserve such adulation?'

In his rare moments of leisure during his busy day, as a mental break from the tediousness of office life, he often thought of one of his student friends with whom he had associated during the war years. His best friend back then had been an easy-going, quick witted and interesting fellow named Noburu Takehashi. For some unknown reason everyone called him by his last name. He had been born and raised on a small island just off the coast from Nagasaki. When he was a small boy his grandparents occasionally took him to the only Catholic Church in Nagasaki for Mass. His grandparents were known as Kakure Kirishitan, and at that time their religious faith still retained a forbidden stigma, even though religious freedom and tolerance had long been the accepted practice. Takehashi's own parents were not very religious and he himself had no particular religious affiliations. He was a free spirit of sorts, jovial, easygoing and always of good humor.

By luck, during the war they were both posted to work in a factory on the outskirts of Nagasaki to help with the war effort, as domestic workers were hard to come by. As they had been acquainted as students, the familiarity became a bond of friendship amongst an assembly line of strangers. "God bless his soul," Tutomu usually said to himself whenever he thought of that day the atomic bomb fell on Nagasaki, "God bless his fortitude, his courage, and his compassion."

Many years later when Tutomu was an established CEO he heard that Takehashi had fallen on hard times, a victim of the economic recession. When he found out that Takehashi was unemployed and looking for any type of gainful employment, Tutomu offered him a job as senior clerk in the filing and storage department. Takehashi accepted with humble grace and dignity. It was one of the better paying jobs at the firm. Who else would hire a cast-off in his early sixties? Takehashi was grateful. He considered himself to be very lucky to have such a considerate and wealthy person like Tutomu as a personal friend.

As CEO, Tutomu had taken a merely wealthy company and made it fabulously wealthy. He had sacrificed everything in order to meet and beat the expectations that constantly rose in front of him. His reputation was well earned. He was known as the capitalist's capitalist or C.C. for short, a nickname that also stood for his favorite drink: Canadian Club Whiskey. Frequently when he was playing his coveted role as CEO it gave him a natural high that no amount of alcohol or drugs could match.

He was privileged to be Japan's most influential representative at the word's top secret summit conferences of financial power brokers. At the top of economic power the protocol is very cool. Civility is everything because there is very little room at the rarified heights near the peak of the economic pyramid to get "pushy" – the fall is so great! Tutomu was always amazed at how quickly they could all agree not to "rock the boat" too much, and how to manipulate the world's markets to coincide with their private view of Man's purpose on this planet. They were not exactly greedy. Strangely enough, they were very conservative. When one is at the top of the mountain, any unexpected change of the status quo could be disastrous. One had to develop a fine sense of balance and accommodation. There is only so much room to maneuver because from the top all paths lead downward.

"My short term memory is atrocious," Tutomu recalled with regret at the last secret conference he had attended. "If the names had not been written down I could have easily slighted some very rich and very powerful person whose ego is as fragile as-as..." there he had it on the tip of his tongue and now it was gone already! The most outspoken group was usually from the United States, followed closely by the European Common Market. The Common Market was a brilliant coup by that group to consolidate their power, and the North American Free Trade Agreement should eventually lead to a common dollar in that instance; of course the next step would be what his American friends surreptitiously referred to as their manifest destiny, which is to control all of North America.

What a power block that would be, with Canada with the second largest land mass in the world and a huge hinterland of scarcely tapped resources, combined with the industrial might and ingenuity of the U.S. It was enough to make one green with envy. "We've got to do more to bolster the Far East Block, but that won't be easy unless China and India become major players." When he thought about it, Tutomu became animated. "It's just like a game," he once thought, "It's the closest we'll ever get to playing God."

And yet in his old age all that money and all that power could not prevent him from lying on a narrow bed covered by white linen with an ulcerated stomach and a face contorted by a lifetime of constant worry and stress. Rubber I-V tubes fed measured amounts of life-sustaining minerals and vitamins into his paper-thin veins. An oxygen mask hung ready at hand just above his head. There he lay, nearly comatose, a useless old derelict on his death bed.

This might have been a fitting end to the story had it ended here – but it did not. Why? Because in the mind of the omniscient narrator there were still mistakes to be revealed and vital lessons to be learned and shared as if it was a categorical imperative of some type akin to that morally espoused by the German philosopher Immanuel Kant: *...act only by that maxim whereby you can at the same time will to be a universal law of nature.* It is a heavy existential responsibility and the story must continue until there is at least a chance that through acceptance and forgiveness the "part" can momentarily harmonize with the "whole" to provide a semblance of happiness.

The clatter of trays caught Tutomu's attention and he turned his feeble head slightly to see what had caused the noise. On the bed adjacent to his he noticed through the parted curtain that an old man was sitting upright. The old man turned toward Tutomu as if drawn by the charisma of his presence, and smiled graciously. It was none other than his old colleague and co-worker Takehashi-san, the senior clerk. He was recuperating after a bout of minor surgery to remove an unsightly wart from the left side of his face that he had always fretted about. He had been moved into the same room as Tutomu during the late afternoon while Tutomu was convalescing. He was leisurely feasting upon teriyaki salmon with marinated tofu, green beans in soy-sauce, a bowl of steamed white rice, with a pot of green tea cooling on the side.

Tutomu stared at his friend for a long time as if transfixed while a nurse set up a tray on his bed and set down his supper: a bowl of watery-thin miso-soup with flakes of seaweed floating decoratively on top. It was all his stomach could handle. "Nagai koto..." he sighed, which meant something like a long time has passed.

"It is a great honor to be in the same room as you," Takehashi said with reverential respect. "What are you doing in a common room like this? You should have a private room."

"I did not want to be alone. All my life I have been so lonely. I am so glad to see you," and as he spoke his face was transformed by a radiant smile of appreciation. He paused to take a slurp of his watery soup and said, "Isn't it ironic that you, a retired employee from my firm, feast upon such delicacies – while I the millionaire CEO dine upon a thin liquid that passes for soup?"

"No doubt you deserve much better!" Takehashi exclaimed.

"It is karma," Tutomu responded. "I have been given a great deal, and now it is time for me to give back. We must share! It is more blessed to give than to receive." He gazed expectantly toward his old friend. "I have been thinking. I want to set up an international peace foundation of some kind, a charitable foundation to help the victims of war and to promote world peace," he asserted enthusiastically.

"I would be happy to assist you in such an altruistic undertaking," Takehashi volunteered. "It will give me something worthwhile to do with all my spare time."

"Thank you so very much. You are such a kind and unselfish spirit compared to me. In hindsight it is easy to see one's shortcomings. I know I have been so selfishly myopic in my ways; I should have taken the time to reflect upon my-my ignorant behavior. I should have done something like this years ago... years and years ago."

"What is the value of a lifetime spent if one has not advanced spiritually? It has been said that you can only take with you what you have given away," Takehashi sympathized.

"And what have I given away?" Tutomu wondered aloud. *"What personally have I given away that has advanced me spiritually?"* he pondered. A look of alarm seared across his face. *"Wasted!"* he uttered in a loud voice. *"I have wasted my life."*

Takehashi stared at his old friend for a long time. Neither said anything. They just sat in silence and looked at each other, two old comrades connected by a current of empathy. And as Takehashi watched, the starchy paleness slowly faded from Tutomu's face as he brought his trembling hands up to his cheeks. A surge of blood turned his face beet-red and he suddenly cried out in a shrill voice that startled his friend.

"I am so embarrassed! All this time I have thought of myself as a-a 'body'… energized with a spirit. I-I foolishly wasted my time being a foolish busy-body. Now I realize that I had it all backwards! I am actually a 'spirit'… a soul endowed with a body. Forgive me; I am so deeply embarrassed. I can hardly stand my ignorant self!" He writhed with anguish and discomfort. The I-V tubes pulled from his veins.

Takehashi rang for a nurse and sprang from his bed upsetting the pot of green tea that had been cooling. He rushed over to his old friend's side and with his tea-soaked hands soothed Tutomu's fevered brow. *"Be still, my friend,"* he whispered, *"be still."*

Tutomu quieted down although his face still remained flushed with embarrassment and his breath wheezed in and out in desperate gasps. *"I have done little to make the world a better place,"* he admonished himself. *"I was given a wonderful opportunity to be of service, but in my ignorance I-I have wasted my life!"* he stared at Takehashi as if looking for confirmation.

"Be still, my friend," Takehashi repeated. *There is no statute of limitations on unselfish acts of kindness. I will begin work on your charitable foundation as soon as possible. It will be up and running in no time,"* he asserted compassionately. *"Remember, it is never too late. Never!"*

So concluded the story that began with, "Once upon a time…." Was it just a fairy-tale without a fairy-tale ending? Or perhaps it was not a fairy-tale at all, and the ending… was still pending? Only the old man knew for sure. Was he not the omniscient narrator?

"Ah so," Tutomu sighed as though acknowledging the answer to a rhetorical question, "Ahhh so." He shook his head as if rattling around old memories that he was attempting to piece together into a meaningful jig-saw puzzle that looked familiar. There were always pieces that were incongruent, pieces that did not quite fit. It was frustrating, especially when one's memory was as fleeting as the latest piece of the puzzle that looked promising. But all of the edge pieces were there and most of the easy parts were in place. What was left was the hard part, the part that required a greater awareness of what was being perceived.

The old man shook his head once again and as he did the pieces representing "acceptance" and "forgiveness" turned right side up. "Why did I not turn those pieces up sooner?" he admonished himself. There, in the center of that morass of vagueness and ambiguity he could discern a certain familiarity that harkened back to long forgotten memories so ancient they could be considered to be primordial. He squinted to improve his acuity while tentatively searching for a likely looking piece. In his mind's eye certain pieces exuded extra potentiality. He hesitatingly picked one up and after rotating it three hundred and sixty degrees set it back down. Instinctively he picked up another and held it aloft. He examined it carefully in the light of the new possibilities. Would it fit?

Who has not gratefully placed a strategic piece into an intricate puzzle without it being accompanied by a fabulous feeling of accomplishment? A half-smile approximating a self-satisfied smirk slowly spread across the old man's wizened countenance. In the total scheme of the grand design it was amazing how something so trifling could make him so happy.

CHAPTER TWO

"It is never too late," Penny reflected, "to learn the simple lessons life has to offer." Both Penny and Larry considered themselves to be life-long learners. Even in retirement they read voraciously and kept abreast of all the latest world developments. They were aware of who they were and what they were attempting to do. They were doing their best to make the world a better place for their children and for mankind in general.

"Every single day is another golden opportunity waiting to be realized for what it is: a miracle filled with the grace of God. Sometimes when I wake up in the morning," Penny revealed over breakfast to her daughter, "the sun is streaming into the room in golden shafts of illumination... I realize then, as profoundly as I am sitting here, heaven is all around me! And the enlightened words of the intrinsic Christ are revealed with such clarity: 'the kingdom of God is within you and all around you.'"

Sherry reached over and placed her hand on her mother's. "You have a heavenly state of mind, Mom," she said.

"Thank you. That was a gracious thing to say," Penny replied as she picked up her herbal tea and carefully made her way into the study to join her husband who was just getting ready to proofread the section on Buddhism.

VI REALIZATION

(1) Buddhism

Background

Buddhism is as much an ethical philosophy, in so far as it is amenable to reason and common sense, as it is a religion. One does not have to be religious in order to appreciate the teachings of Prince Siddhartha Gautama (563-483 B.C.), the wealthy son of King Shuddhodana Gautama of Kapilavastu and his Queen, Maya. He was born to the Shakya clan at Lumbini in the Himalayan foothills. Even as a young boy he demonstrated a keen intelligence and an uncommon affinity for spiritual matters. When he became of age the

King found him a beautiful wife named Yashodhara, a princess from a neighboring kingdom who bore him a son.

Being a very compassionate and sensitive spirit the young prince was overwhelmed by the suffering of his fellowman. In spite of his comfortable surroundings Siddhartha left his wife and son to find a resolution to the three signs of suffering that seemed unavoidable: sickness, old age, and death. While meditating under a tree near Gaya, he attained Bodhi (Illumination), and thereafter became known as the Buddha, the fully awakened one, and the tree became the Bodhi Tree. In addition to the Buddha, Siddhartha is sometimes called Shakyamuni (Shakya sage) or Amitabha (Infinite Light) or Tathagata (He Who Has Arrived At Perfection).

Siddhartha was educated in India and consequently was taught Hinduism which incorporated the wisdom of the Vedas written by the Aryan people who migrated from Persia and Russia to India around 2000 B.C., and the Upanishads which were brought to India between 800 and 600 B.C. These two ancient scriptures provided the yoga of mind and body that taught the people how to direct their everyday suffering toward a nobler or higher plane of consciousness. These seeds of Hindu wisdom made the teachings of the Buddha all the more profound.

The teachings of the Buddha spread through adjacent countries like China and Korea, and eventually made their way to Japan where they seemed to resonate with the people. There, two major approaches to the teachings of the Buddha evolved. Hinayana (or Theravada) Buddhism emphasized a purity of spirit and an ascetic approach which required withdrawal from worldly life. Mahayana Buddhism provided a reasoned and commonsensical approach that was applicable in everyday life and therefore was better suited for the masses. It is this latter approach to Buddhism that has resulted in its current popularity in the West.

Buddhism as a Concept

There are some important notions about Buddhism that should be clarified at the outset. In Buddhism there are no coveted ideas, dogmas, doctrines or prejudices worth killing or dying for. Buddhism is only a particular means by which truth/enlightenment can be approached – it is not the absolute truth per se. It is simply a way and a direction; its simplicity makes the path very wide and deep. The Buddha himself once said: "My teachings are like a finger pointing toward the moon. Do not get fooled into thinking that the finger is the moon. It is because of the finger that your gaze is moonward."

The Four Noble Truths

There are many paths, but the "middle path" or "golden mean" consists of the four noble truths. They are noble truths because they are ennobling as well as illuminating and uplifting. Carefully consider the following four statements in the light of your own personal experience:
(1) Be aware that there is suffering, and realize that it is your own
(2) Recognize that suffering is an effect of craving, and recognize that the craving comes from within
(3) Understand the dependency of suffering upon craving; without craving the suffering disappears
(4) Be aware of your craving, and follow the "Eightfold Path of Right Action" that will lead to the cessation of your suffering.

The Eightfold Path of Right Action consists of eight right actions that must be diligently practiced as an interrelated group. They are as follows:
- Right Views
- Right Aspirations
- Right Speech
- Right Behavior
- Right Livelihood
- Right Effort
- Right Thoughts
- Right Contemplation.

By following the Eightfold Path your craving will be replaced with the emptiness of Zen and the fullness of Enlightenment.

The Three Main Tenets

The three main tenets ingrained in the Buddha's teachings are best defined in English by the words: Impermanence, No-self, and Nirvana. The three concepts are interconnected in an intricate manner. Impermanence alludes to time or duration where everything is indeterminate and in a constant state of flux, while No-self alludes to space. The combination yields space-time.

Impermanence and No-self are the conditions that lead to their true nature or authentic state of being called Nirvana. Nirvana is a state of awareness or self-realization where there is no fear, no death, no suffering, only being-ness.

When we look deeply into No-self the impermanence of all things becomes obvious. Consider the following illustrations. When a gas called hydrogen combines with another gas known as oxygen, a liquid that is essential to all life-forms on earth is manifested. Where is the gas hydrogen? Where is the gas oxygen? They lose their identity as gases in the water. And the water loses its identity when it is transformed into ice or vapor, and the vapor forms clouds, and the clouds disappear into rain or snow that blankets the earth as moisture essential in all plant and animal forms; and on and on go the observable manifestations of two hydrogen atoms combined with one oxygen atom. Beyond the manifest in the arena of Quantum Mechanics even the hydrogen and oxygen atoms per se can be split and transformed into smaller and smaller particles that disappear into tiny vibrant strings of energy. The "energy" is always there metaphorically as No-self, transforming and changing as if by magic. And witnessing the impermanence of form and matter, an insightful human being said: "Nothing is created or destroyed, only transformed or changed"; and this reasoning became enshrined in Physics as the first law of thermodynamics. The Buddha was not given credit for this amazing insight. He was way ahead of his time.

When one experiences Nirvana, it elicits such a profound feeling of gratitude and Oneness that in the aftermath one cannot but feel One with all mankind and a great depth of compassion for all those who have not been blessed with such an experience. This sense of overwhelming compassion is rooted in our essential humanity. The result is a desire to share one's blessings with one's fellow human beings.

Meditation

The Buddha practiced and advocated meditation as a practical approach to achieving illumination. Through meditation it is possible to eliminate the mind pollution that leads to cravings and hence to suffering. It is essentially a technique whereby the mind itself assists in putting itself in harmony with the rest of the body. In order to facilitate this harmony of mind and body, the body must be stilled and the mind emptied of all disparate thoughts. When this is achieved the artificial separation of mind and body is transcended and unity results. The whole is greater than the sum of the parts. This experience has been called Zen. It is that simple.

The Buddha is mostly shown practicing sitting meditation. However, for busy people and for novices as well as experts, walking meditation is a popular and perhaps the most enjoyable form of meditation. It can open the door to the path that leads to one's true inner nature. It is also literally in accord with many of the metaphorical analogies utilized in Buddhism like path, way, direction, impermanence, continuation and no-self. When you utilize walking meditation you realize that the concepts fundamental to Buddhist thought are experiential.

It is important when utilizing walking meditation that you match your pace to the serenity and tranquility of your surroundings; therefore it is best, but not essential, to select a serene and tranquil setting in which to practice this technique. If your mind is racing it is impossible to be tranquil. Place your mind in neutral and idle the body's engine to suit your pace. Relax. Enjoy being in harmony with Nature. Smile. Smile. Smile. Let your inner state reflect your outer state. This is not a matter of going into a trance but it is important to look deeply into the nature of things. Be mindful of your breath as breathing is essential to the clarity of your mind. Let your mind be as clear as the breath-of-life you inhale and exhale in harmony with your measured gait.

When your mind is in neutral and your body is idling, the Eightfold Way of all Existence beckons:

(1) no coming,
(2) no going,
(3) no sameness,
(4) no difference,
(5) no birth,
(6) no death,
(7) no being,
(8) no non-being.

The Eightfold Way is like a finger pointing. Where is it pointing? To Nirvana?

It helps immeasurably, of course, to have the right attitude when practicing any method of meditation. Without the right attitude, an attitude of openness, tolerance, and acceptance, the light struggles to penetrate the darkness of ignorance. Remember to be open to the light that shines within you, the light that has never been extinguished. When conditions are sufficient, the light of enlightenment will illuminate even the most polluted of minds, as the awakening dawn reveals what the darkest night has hidden.

"I hope we have done justice to the teachings of the Buddha," Penny noted. "In our attempts to simplify the complex, we may have tended to overcompensate."

"We kept it simple, stupid," Larry joked, alluding to the KISS formula.

"So we did," Penny laughed. "However, in a simple handbook like this we need to include other popular views as well."

"As far as possible we need to provide a balanced approach."

"Hopefully the following section will provide some balance, and proportion," Penny replied, turning to face her husband who was, if anything, overly conscious of his Christian upbringing.

"The teachings of the Buddha and the teachings of Jesus are both certainly worthy of being included in a handbook on life."

"I'm glad you insisted upon the inclusion of this next section, in spite of my reticence," Penny replied.

"Your reticence was understandable. It has been my personal experience that Christians in general are very sensitive about their religious beliefs, far more sensitive than Buddhists or Hindus for example. However, that does not mean that they are not open-minded."

"Wouldn't it be wonderful if all Christians were just as open-minded as you," Penny added with a smile. "We must dare to share, if we really care."

"I take it that you have overcome your reticence."

"It was just that so much has been written about the life, times, and teachings of Jesus of Nazareth that to attempt a brief summary utilizing the KISS formula seemed at the time to be a daunting, if not nearly impossible task," Penny admitted.

"Yeah," Larry reflected. "What made it so difficult was that most of the written material presented an extrinsic view of Jesus commensurate with the dogmas and doctrines developed since the

Council of Nicaea in 325, when all contrary points of view were discouraged and nearly all written documents not in accord with the established view were destroyed."

"It was refreshing to discover," Penny elucidated, "that of late more and more historical evidence and research is beginning to provide theologians with a much more believable and down to earth portrait of a man who in the symbolism of his times was aware of 'the Light, the Pinhole and the Reflection'."

"Yes, good point," Larry commented, "He used his own metaphors. There is no doubt Jesus was aware of his own divinity and his relationship to the Light of Divinity."

"The Holy Ghost represented the Reflection, the Son represented the Pinhole, and the Father represented the Light."

"The Father, Son, and Holy Ghost, an apt personification of the Light, the Pinhole and the Reflection," Larry commented.

"A neat analogy for the times, a time when his own people, the Jews, conceived of themselves as being flawed sinners devoid of the light of redemption."

"And Jesus said: 'Follow me... be like me, and do as I do'. He had such an overwhelming compassion for his people he was willing to die for them. He healed the sick and uplifted the downtrodden. He invited the common folk to join him in the open air and sunshine on the mountainside to break bread and drink wine. He was a man of the people. He dared to share!" Larry pontificated.

"It was indeed a new and uplifting view. It was a view that connected the 'Reflection' to the 'Light'. It was the intrinsic view!" Penny exclaimed rising from her chair with animation.

"Jesus personified this view in a cultural setting and at a time in which it was very difficult for the people to conceive of themselves as being anything other than fearful sinners beholden to an omniscient, omnipresent, and omnipotent external God. In the land of such a vengeful extrinsic God, who would dare to chase the money-lenders out of the temple and compassionately urge the sick, the downtrodden, and the sinners to 'follow me' to freedom?"

CHAPTER THREE

(2) The Intrinsic Christ

Preface

There are currently many controversial and diverse works of scholarship written by religious historians regarding the foundations of Christianity ranging from allegations that the Bible has been concocted from ancient Egyptian myths, to assertions that Jesus of Nazareth was resurrected in physical form, as opposed to being resurrected spiritually and thus ascended in human form directly into heaven. The latest rather startling information to be uncovered – which is being strenuously disputed by Christian authorities the world over – occurred on February 23rd 1980. On that date as construction workers were in the process of excavating for the foundation of a new building in the industrial park area of a Jerusalem suburb called Talpiyot, the earth caved in exposing a 2000 year old tomb containing ten ancient ossuaries, or limestone bone boxes/caskets.

According to the Israel Antiquities Authority, six of the caskets contained discernable names along with the remains, i.e. bones, of the deceased. Following years of intensive scrutiny the names were finally and unequivocally identified as: Jesua son of Joseph, Maria (Jesua's mother), Mariamene (Mary Magdalene), Mathew, Jofa (Jesua's brother James), and Judah, son of Jesua (indicating Jesua had sired a son with Mariamene). Claims have been made based upon the collective evidence amassed through DNA tests, archeological findings, and biblical studies that the ten coffins belonged to none other than "Jesua" or Jesus of Nazareth, and his family!

Skeptics, on the other hand, say that although the timeline and the existence of the ossuaries cannot be disputed, the names inscribed were just common Jewish names that were popular during that era, and therefore to make such an extraordinary claim is simply outlandish speculation. However, defenders of the claim point out that the mathematical probability of finding six of the biblically significant names, relevant to the historical identity of one particular person, all together in a family tomb is conservatively less than one in 30,000! This recent controversial discovery could have profound implications for those who believe that Jesus was the celibate and immaculately pure biblical character who was raised bodily into heaven and declared to be "homoosius" with God in 325 by the Bishops at the Council of Nicaea, rather than the enlightened human being who humbly referred to himself as the "son of man" and whose bones were interred along with his wife's and son's in a family tomb near Jerusalem.

The point of view offered in this section is an attempt to expand the dialogue regarding the portrait of Jesus of Nazareth to include a point of view overlooked by most religious scholars. In a Student Handbook on Life, it is important to offer a balanced view of the life of a person who has had such a major impact upon the social, psychological, economic, and political development of Western Christendom.

The "black hole" in the biography of Jesus, which occurs from age twelve to age thirty in which Jesus simply disappears from the face of the earth, is downplayed and passed over from the traditional view as if it were of little or no importance in determining who the individual was who, after a ministry lasting a scant three years, became deified in the minds of his followers as "The Christ." Take any deceased thirty-three year old individual and remove the eighteen vitally significant developmental years from age twelve to age thirty, and claim to really know who he/she was, is an impossible task. But that is precisely what has been done: fait accompli! There is no argument there, just a resounding silence.

What is arguable is what point of view Jesus espoused after returning from this prolonged absence from the scene. Attitude and point of view are major factors in the development of anyone's outlook on life. They play an important role in determining who we are and how we behave. There is little hard historical evidence to indicate to scholars what attitude and point of view Jesus had developed during the eighteen critical years of his maturation from a child of twelve to a man of thirty. Why was this information destroyed? Was it detrimental to the Catholic view of Christ that emerged after the Council of Nicaea of 325?

Every attempt has been made since 325 AD by religious scholars to "flesh-in" the missing years and to develop a religious image of Jesus commensurate with the traditional Occidental view – even though such a view seems oddly incongruent with the existential qualities of the charismatic healer and teacher who taught that the "kingdom of heaven is within you, and all around you". There is an alternate view of Jesus that is emerging that is much more believable, and perhaps even more appealing to open-minded Christians. It does not contradict anything Jesus said or did. It just places everything he said or did in a new light based upon reason and common sense – rather than dogma and doctrine.

Biographical Timeline

What do we actually know about the identity of one of the world's most influential, prominent, and respected religious personalities, Jesus of Nazareth? We know that much valuable historical information was intentionally destroyed by the Bishops who had gathered at the council of Nicaea in 325 in order to eliminate any evidence that contradicted the sanctioned version of the "gospels" being concocted at that time. We also know that the powerful Roman Catholic Church has done everything in its power to preserve the sanctity of the Creed established under the guidance of Constantine the Great. Any new discoveries that did not support the Catholic Church's official pronouncements, dogmas and doctrines were suppressed. How is it possible that the most crucial information regarding the developmental years when Jesus was being educated and maturing from a child of twelve into an enlightened man of thirty – those vital years that led to the development of the attitudes and beliefs that he exemplified during his brief ministry which lasted a scant three years – could simply disappear without raising an eyebrow of suspicion? Jesus of Nazareth's biographical timeline looks something like this:

8 – 4 BC (Birth)	- Born in a "manger" near Bethlehem - Son of Mary, betrothed to Joseph, a carpenter from Nazareth - Illegitimate child - Biological father unknown
4BC – 8 AD (Childhood)	- Visited by three Wise Men from the Orient - Provided with wealth by the three Wise Men - Circumcised as a Jew - Brought up in the knowledge of Judaic Law - Confirmed in the Jewish faith

8 – 26 AD (Missing)	- Left his homeland and went "somewhere" - Between the ages of 12 to 30 he simply disappears - Some evidence indicates that someone from the Middle East spent some time in a spiritual retreat in Northern India - All written data for this period either destroyed or missing - Developed an enlightened point of view
26 – 29 AD (Ministry)	- Returned from "somewhere" to Jerusalem - Displayed a new and refreshing attitude - Baptized by his cousin John the Baptist - Withdrew to the "wilderness" to prepare for his mission - Conducted his inspiring ministry for three years (spreading his innovative message and healing the sick) - The high priests became alarmed by his success - Charged with blasphemy and disturbing the peace - Sentenced by Pontius Pilate - Crucified

Strange as it may seem, in all of the information available from that era, apparently no one thought to ask Jesus where he had been during his long absence. Not once is the question asked: "Where have you been for the past eighteen years?" Wasn't anyone the least bit curious? Certainly this information must have been known at the time but was deliberately left out of the Gospels for reasons that can only be speculated upon. Unfortunately, based upon such scanty information it is certainly possible that this great man could have been misunderstood and misrepresented in the decades and centuries after his demise. The following point of view is included here in an attempt to illuminate and reveal the enlightened attitude of a compassionate individual who deserves to be better understood and credited for what he was trying to accomplish – rather than what has been concocted after his demise.

The Three Wise Men

Jesus was born around 5 BC in a "manger" just outside of Bethlehem. A census was being taken at that time. Jesus was the son of Mary and the illegitimate son of Joseph, a carpenter from Nazareth. As an infant Jesus was visited by three wealthy men from the Orient who realized that this child was ordained for greatness. Very little is said about the indisputable presence of these three wealthy men – except that they are always portrayed in every Nativity scene as illustrious personages who came bearing expensive gifts. What were their expectations of this child of destiny?

These three wealthy men are also described as being very wise. What advantage would the support of three wealthy men, full of Oriental wisdom, be to a young child recognized by them to be very special? They cared a great deal because they were looking for a child born under special circumstances, just as the Tibetan Dalai Lama is selected after a very thorough search by intuitively wise persons, and then educated in a manner commensurate with his spiritual status. Would the three wise men just abandon such a special child and leave after making such a long journey of discovery?

Jewish Heritage

There is considerable controversy regarding the accuracy and authenticity of the Biblical account of the origins and exploits of the tribes of Israel. Although the Biblical version contained in the Old Testament has not been supported by archeological evidence, it is the account that most Christians and Jews "believe". According to the Biblical account that was written as a religious saga rather than an historically accurate document, the story begins with a man called Abraham who originated in Ur, in Mesopotamia, and made his way to the land of Canaan around 1750 BCE. Abraham settled in a part of the hill country known as Hebron; his son Isaac resided in Beersheba, and Abraham's grandson Jacob lived in a region called Shechem. During a famine his grandson, Jacob, also known as "Israel", and his twelve sons, the founders of the "tribes of Israel", migrated to Egypt. Through a series of unfortunate circumstances, the newcomers were subjugated and enslaved. Generation after generation after generation of Jacob's unfortunate descendents were born and raised as slaves in Egypt. How many generations does it take to comprise four hundred years? Finally in about 1250 BCE their god, Yahweh (transformed and personified during their 400 year sojourn as slaves in Egypt from the Canaanite god El) took pity on them. Under the inspired leadership of Moses the tribes of Israel escaped by crossing the Red Sea. After wandering around in the wilderness for forty years in search of the Promised Land, they arrived at the border of Canaan. Under the command of their fearless leader Joshua, the Israelites invaded Canaan, destroyed the Canaanite cities and towns, slew the inhabitants, and took possession of the territory. Was this the "Promised Land"? And, more importantly, were they free at last from the oppressive physical, psychological, and existential effects of over four hundred years of abject slavery?

As an intelligent child growing up until the age of twelve in a Jewish community, Jesus quickly developed a profound understanding of the religious doctrines and dogmas of his forefathers. The implications of their slave background were reflected in their religious beliefs and attitudes. As slaves in Egypt his ancestors had no recourse but to develop a religious view that would justify the pitiful quality of their slave existence. There had to be a reason for this existential plight. There had to be a just explanation as to why they had to suffer while their masters enjoyed the fruits of their labor.

An intrinsic view that placed God and the responsibility within was not viable or credible in such circumstances; neither was the idea of Karma. There had to be a better explanation for their existential plight, one that justified their suffering and ennobled their self-concept. An extrinsic point of view was needed, one that placed the responsibility *outside* the self. This belief was needed for personal survival. This belief was imperative for a people born into slavery generation after generation. This belief was necessary to provide them with hope in a hopeless situation. Their salvation was not to be found on this cruel god-forsaken earth, but somewhere else out of reach of the powerful and the unjust. This belief was their salvation; it justified their existence and enabled them to persevere, because God was *out there*, and God was on their side.

The Chosen People

This *extrinsic* God became an attitudinal projection of all their rationalizations. He had to be vengeful enough to punish their evil and powerful masters. He had to be forgiving towards those like themselves who gratefully acknowledged His existence. He had to be righteous to justify Himself as being the one and only true God, because if He was not the one and only God He would be irrelevant and beyond the power of those who believed in other gods, like their masters who had their own gods. He had to be judgmental in order to insure that in the end justice would be done. Fear of such a "God" was the beginning of wisdom – woe to the fearlessly ignorant!

This Almighty God resided in a paradise called Heaven, and puny man resided down here on earth, because ungrateful man had forsaken and turned away from his Maker and was no longer worthy of Paradise. Man was a craven sinner and the earth where he lived was a god-forsaken place. In spite of this, God had not forsaken the tribes of Israel. In his mercy, God had given them a chance to redeem their sinful selves if they were repentant, servile, and humble.

God, in His own mysterious way, was testing the tribes of Israel. This explained their wretched slave existence. They were actually the chosen people, the ones who because of their wretchedness were being given the opportunity to atone for their sinful nature while on earth, because it was pleasing to their righteous, vengeful, judgmental and forgiving external God who looked down upon them as a Father looks upon his wayward but penitent children.

This extrinsic view of God enabled Jesus' ancestors, the tribes of Israel, to survive under the harshest conditions of slavery and provided them with the fortitude and the hope to carry on day after day – because in the end it would be worth it. (For similar reasons the Old Testament appealed to the Africans bound in slavery on southern plantations in the United States of America.)

The Burden

When they were delivered out of slavery by Moses and were free, the descendents of the tribes of Israel still retained this deeply inculcated religious mindset which was manifested in daily life as a "slave mentality". They still thought of themselves as being "sinners", even though this self-concept was no longer necessary for their survival. In fact the burden of Original Sin had become a detriment to their rehabilitation as a free people and to the natural dignity and instincts of the Israelites as human beings. This willingness to suffer needlessly, to atone, to do penance, to view the world as a negative place, and to view the self as "sinful" was counter-productive to the real needs of a free-spirited people no longer in the chains of slavery. How could such a people rise above their existential predicament?

This archaic perception of self did not reflect the natural, positive, life-affirming attitude of a child not born into slavery. It was suffocating and stifling – yet the powerful High Priests continued to keep the people subjugated to outmoded dogmas and doctrines that kept the people bound in the religious chains of a slave-mentality that was no longer needed and detrimental to their well-being. A religious belief that was once essential for their survival was now an incredibly potent tool with which the High Priests could control a free people no longer bound in the chains of slavery. Why would they want to change the status quo?

As a sensitive and intuitive young Jewish lad of twelve, Jesus had spent many of his days discussing and challenging the archaic views of those entrenched in religious positions of power and prestige. Young as he was, it became apparent to those who came into contact with him that he was "inner directed" and this was reflected in his enlightened attitude. It became evident to his parents and to those charged with his development and upbringing that in such an environment – where any views to the contrary were considered blasphemous and the owner of those views a heretic – it would be necessary for Jesus to leave the stifling atmosphere prevalent in the land of his birth in order to pursue an education befitting a child three wise men had traveled so far to pay homage to. In order to prepare himself for his seemingly impossible dream of freeing his people of their existential burden, and to discover his true identity, it was important that the next eighteen years of his life be spent in an appropriate environment.

Preparation

For eighteen long years Jesus patiently and meticulously prepared himself for his ultimate role. It was his dharma. Like Siddhartha, he followed a path that eventually led to his enlightenment. The child that the three wise men from the Orient had journeyed so far to discover lived up to the expectations placed upon him. He shed the "slave mentality" of his forbearers and sought the divine light that cannot be extinguished. It was a miraculous awakening, a re-birth into purity, an immaculate conception.

He ventured forth with an extrinsic Jewish outlook, and after eighteen years of search and introspection he returned with an enlightened view.   He manifested his enlightened view.   He personified his enlightened view: "My Father and I are one," he said. It was the *intrinsic* view.

Corroborating Evidence

It is interesting to note that in December of 1945, near Nag Hammadi, at a spot approximately three hundred miles south of Cairo, Egypt where the Nile River flows from east to west and is bordered by a railroad line, a well preserved leather bound papyrus was found secured in a large reddish urn which was covered with a bowl and sealed tight with bitumen.   The leather bound papyrus purportedly written only a few decades after the Last Supper by Saint Thomas, or "doubting Thomas" as he is Biblically known, describes a fundamentally different Jesus than the one depicted in the New Testament.

According to the *Gospel of Saint Thomas*, Jesus espoused the apparently intrinsic view that "the kingdom of God is within you and all around you", a view that would have been considered to be blasphemous in his day and could have led to the charge eventually brought against him by the High Priests.   The discovery of this document raised a great deal of consternation amongst the "converted".   The consternation was well founded because subsequently the consensus of most Biblical authorities indicated that not only did the Gospel of Thomas pre-date the New Testament gospels, but it expressed a more accurate and relevant description of the "real" Jesus of Nazareth as he existed at that historical moment in time.

The Gospel of Saint Thomas, had it been discovered prior to the Council of Nicaea of 325, would probably have been destroyed along with the countless other irreplaceable documents that lit up the night with a bonfire that lasted for days.   Saint Thomas, who apparently spent the years from A.D. 50 to 70 in India, describes a down- to-earth, humane young man caught up in the ferment of an epoch rife with political and religious unrest.   Consequently he couched his message in inoffensive parables that would not unduly offend those ensconced in traditional bastions of religious infallibility – but would appeal to a people suffocated by an antiquated notion of Original Sin and yearning for a breath of fresh air inspired by a new-found sense of self-respect and existential freedom. There is a noticeable difference in the demeanor and attitude of Jesus, the "son of man" that Thomas refers to, and Jesus the "Son of God" who is described in the New Testament. Which is the authentic Jesus?

The Return

It is interesting to speculate as to why Jesus returned after eighteen long years to the land of his ancestors. Perhaps like the wise man in Plato's Allegory of the Cave, once he had seen the light, he had to return back into the shadowy realm of the cave and dare to share his illumination. Perhaps he realized during his long absence how profoundly difficult it would be for his own people, due to their strong religious views, to free themselves of their inhumane burden of innate sinfulness. It was an attitude so profound it was like a self-perpetuating psychosomatic illness condoned by an infallible priesthood. What could one single interloper, who had been absent for eighteen years, do to change such a powerful mindset?

Talk of self-realization was redundant because they already were fully aware of who they were: "sinners". Was there a cure for this collective social neurosis? What would it take to free his people of such an archaic notion of sin? Did not the enigmatic Confucius say: "Determined people and humanitarians will not seek to live by means that would injure humanity, but they would kill themselves if that would perfect humanity"?

Mission

Jesus was prepared to sacrifice his mortal life in order to free his people. He wanted his people to be like him, free of the burden of Original Sin. He felt a great compassion and empathy for his Jewish kin. As a Jew he understood with profundity what non-Jews do not fully appreciate: that being Jewish was a very special thing; it meant a sincere and deep-seated historical and religious appreciation for life in spite of every conceivable kind of adversity. He admonished them over and over to "follow me" out of the darksome synagogues, out into the open air, out into the natural surroundings of the mountainside where they could affirm life and celebrate their new-found freedom by breaking bread and drinking wine. He taught them the Golden Rule: to do unto others as you would have them do unto you. He attempted to avoid the misunderstanding and confusion that people long conditioned to an extrinsic view experience when attempting to understand the intrinsic view – by personally personifying the intrinsic view. His "immaculate" conception symbolized Man's natural state of purity; it was a powerful metaphor for the times. He was the Father (External I/Light), the Son (Immortal I/Pinhole), and the Holy Ghost (Mortal I/Reflection). He brought Divinity down to earth from way-out-there, and placed it inside himself, and inside all mankind. It was a new and refreshing attitude toward life. It was an attitude that challenged the status quo. He simply said "follow me"; be like me, a free spirit no longer bound like a slave to outmoded dogmas and doctrines. He led by personal example. He was an inspiration to the multitude who aspired to be like him, free from the dogmatic chains of a slave mentality.

Blasphemy

This was, of course, blasphemy to the High Priests who naturally coveted and protected their positions of power and prestige. Consequently they saw Jesus – not as a noble Jew attempting to unburden his fellow-Jews – but as a competitor, a rabble-rouser who was corrupting the youth and undermining the status quo. From the Biblical view the charges (blasphemy and disturbing the peace) brought against Jesus by the High Priests may seem to be unwarranted and even frivolous, but when understood in terms of a conflict between a prevailing extrinsic view and a new and innovative intrinsic view, the charges reflected the dissonance.

The Establishment had a great deal to protect. The High Priests could sense the power and attraction of the uplifting message being shared and the enlightened attitude exemplified by the charismatic young man who had recently returned after a prolonged absence. What Jesus was espousing was extremely unsettling and disturbing: a new untainted concept of self, free from sin! The curious were leaving the synagogues and following the "son of man" out onto the mountainside where they broke bread, drank wine and shared in the spirit of freedom and fellowship offered by the teacher. Something had to be done to put an end to this. They wanted the upstart, heretic

Jew crucified, and they had the power and the influence to make their opinions blatantly clear to the Roman Procurator, Pontius Pilate.

Jesus could sense the tide of prevailing attitudes turning against him. His positive and uplifting view that "the kingdom of God is within you and all around you", was being deliberately subverted by those who understood the power of his message; and to those who just could not tolerate any other views; it was just blasphemy. But there was still a chance, a long shot that if it worked, might enable him to accomplish his objective. If he took the sins of the Jewish people upon himself, then perhaps his death would psychologically and symbolically represent their release from their historical burden of Original Sin. It was a courageous gamble by an enlightened young man willing to make the ultimate sacrifice in order to free his people from an archaic concept no longer relevant or necessary to their survival or well-being.

The result is clear. It was the ultimate gamble that failed, because the prevailing attitudes were so deeply entrenched that from the established view, he was just another heretic Jew on a messianic mission.

Irony of Ironies

Thus it came to pass after the crucifixion that one of the greatest ironies of all time became manifest. Instead of freeing his people and his followers from the onerous burden of sin – they became even more burdened! What is the greatest sin that can be conceived of by sinful man? Killing God. And if man has killed God's only Son, is that not ultimate proof of his innate. sinfulness? Such was the beginning of the irony that later became established as the foundation of a new and powerful religion that would spread the concept of Man's flawed nature throughout the world.

There is a world of difference between (a) needing to be saved, and (b) being free – from sin. The first, i.e. (a) gave immense power and control to those usurping the power to "save" in the name of the deceased – while the latter (b) empowered the individual with the spiritual freedom, or *Christ Consciousness*, to realize his/her own true divinity/identity. It is the latter concept that the enlightened human being known as Jesus of Nazareth dared to share with his fellowman. He did his best. What more could he have done?

"I know what you're thinking," Larry said as he set the computer to standby.

"You do?"

"Yup, I can tell by your face and body language."

"Your psychic powers must have improved a great deal in the last hour. Pray tell, what was I thinking?"

"You were thinking, about thirty seconds ago that, ah... you were thinking: 'I hope we haven't offended anyone'."

"Gosh Larry, that was very close. Close but no cigar I'm afraid. What I was thinking was that there needs to be a distinction made between the old fashioned or extrinsic Christians, and the new or intrinsic Christians."

"How about just Old Christians and New Christians?"

"Hmm, that might be okay. It brings to mind the difference between the Old Testament and the New Testament, biblically speaking."

"The New Christians would be people who are attempting, in their own way, to follow in the footsteps of the Intrinsic Christ," Larry suggested.

"The distinction makes a big difference."

"Huge! Like night and day."

"It might possibly make Jesus proud to be called a 'New Christian'."

"That would be nice," Larry responded with a smile that lit up the room. "He would actually be a New Judaic-Christian, wouldn't he?"

"On second thought," Penny ruminated, "does he need a label? I guess he could just be himself... couldn't he?"

CHAPTER FOUR

"Could there possibly be a connection between Original Sin and Global Warming?"

"What?" Larry responded, baffled by Penny's question.

Penny poured her husband a second cup of coffee and returned to the kitchen table to finish eating her vitamin enriched organic cornflakes. "I've been thinking that the problem of excessive global warming that now threatens the entire world with dire consequences is to a great extent a man-made condition. On the surface it seems to be an irrational, random occurrence unconnected to anything except man's ignorant behavior, but if we look carefully it becomes apparent that much of what may seem to be just plain ignorant behavior is actually behavior that is consciously, subconsciously, and unconsciously conditioned by certain deeply held beliefs."

"When did you think of this?" Larry asked still feeling slightly baffled.

"Last night when you were snoring so loud I could hear you through the open doorway. I think my hearing has become more acute since you moved into the next room."

"It is nice to hear that you are improving."

"It was just after you stopped snoring and mumbled something like, 'It is self-evident', when it came to me. It came to me just as if it were self-evident."

"Hmm, self-evident you say?"

"Perhaps it was your idea and in your nocturnal slumbers you somehow passed it on to me. Do you remember dreaming last night?"

"No, I don't remember anything at all."

"Anyway, let me elaborate. Beliefs affect our behavior in powerful and unforeseen ways. For example, if I believe my house is about to be burned down, I would feel that it would be a waste of my time to replace the roof and siding and remodel the interior. My attitude toward my house is conditioned, so to speak, by my personal beliefs."

"I get it; if we believe we are sinners then it follows that we can expect to act like sinners. The ramifications as to where this could lead could be horrific!" Larry exclaimed.

"My, I do believe your psychic powers have improved! Yes, the moral ramifications could be far-reaching, and as you say, horrific. Sinful man does not have the moral integrity to prevent himself from doing sinful acts; consequently he needs the intervention of an all-powerful external God to "save" him. Since this external God is not of the earth, this makes the earth as god-less as its sinful inhabitants."

"I'm beginning to see your logic," Larry replied. "Since the world is god-less and prophesied to be ultimately consumed in flames, it may as well be exploited, plundered, and polluted because it is slated for destruction anyway."

"Why worry about the looming crisis of global warming when the destruction of the world is prophesied? Why bother to waste the taxpayer's hard-earned cash attempting to reduce deadly carbon emissions and work toward saving the good earth when the earth is doomed?"

"Why bother to repair your house if it is slated to be burnt down!" Larry pronounced as an alarming sense of incredulity flashed on inside his head like a warning signal. "Why bother to sign the Kyoto Accord and take steps toward reducing carbon emissions on a global level? Why not just blithely carry on, like Australia, the United States and other non-signing countries, polluting the very same atmosphere which everyone else is unselfishly struggling to purify for the sake of the next generation and all the generations to come?" Larry groaned as if in serious mental pain.

"The United States is a staunchly Christian nation. When one believes that one is already "saved", what is there to worry about? The world needs to end – otherwise there is no need to be saved. That is why the word 'self-fulfilling' makes sense when attached to the Prophecy of Doom."

"Religion is the opium of the people," Larry pontificated, quoting one of his favorite one-liners from Karl Marx. "It is like they are drugged. How else can you explain such self-destructive behavior on such a massive scale? It is frightening!"

"Imagine how all the non-Christians who are not "saved" must feel. This is a moral issue that affects everyone no matter what their religious views may be. It is an issue that must be dealt with as if it is Man's Moral Imperative to save this miracle planet!" Penny announced with such conviction it sounded as if she were swearing an oath.

"Moral Imperative, I like that," Larry agreed getting into the spirit of the moment. Christians the world over need to be reminded that their Lord and Savior gave up his life to free us from this life-negating affliction that makes us act like worthless sinners: like 'cut-off bits of hay or the spittle from cattle'," he paraphrased from the Old Testament.

"The crucifixion was a powerful moral statement. It was a moral statement of universal significance: a moral imperative. Jesus sacrificed his life to save the world – while some Old-Christians are willing to save themselves and sacrifice the world."

"Yes, irony of ironies," Larry lamented, "Ironically, soon after Jesus' noble sacrifice a new religion labeled Christianity emerged that, rather than freeing, further enslaved man in the mental chains of Original Sin. It set in motion a tidal wave of events that swept around the world and soaked it in the secularism of the Protestant Ethic and the Spirit of Capitalism, which has brought us to this sorry state of affairs where global warming threatens us with ecological disasters of gargantuan proportions, while we sit back and 'wait and see'."

"There. You've said it quite succinctly. That is what I was getting at when I asked: Is there a connection between Original Sin and Global Warming?"

"Perhaps it is too late already," Larry responded in a subdued tone, "but I'm still hopeful that there is a chance that we can turn this around. I know that most of the scientific data indicates that due to our ignorance and unwillingness to take preventative measures, global warming has now accelerated to a point where there will be dire consequences in the immediate future. We are teetering on the brink of unprecedented catastrophes. There is no question the most powerful nation in the world needs to take a leadership role and set a proper example."

"You will always have a soft spot in your heart for the country of your birth," Penny replied as she reached over and clasped her husband's hands. "I wish all Americans were more like you."

* * *

Retirement had brought Penny and Larry the leisure time to sit back and reflect upon the past from the perspective of senior citizens.

It was a position and a perspective they had always associated with "old people" – not themselves. In their own minds they had not aged that much. They probably appeared old when they looked in the mirror, but in their mind's eye they had not aged much, until of late. The aging process was much more evident on Penny's once youthful countenance than it was on Larry's.

The ravages of time were there, etched in the tiny crow's feet around Penny's eyes and the wrinkles across her forehead. They were evident in the Monday morning light as she sat at the kitchen table eating her certified-organic porridge with a sprinkle of dried raisins as she usually did on Monday mornings. The sight shot a shiver through Larry like a chill of winter in mid-summer as he sauntered into the kitchen. There she was hunched over that white ceramic bowl with a black woolen toque on her head, a reminder of her last chemo treatment. The stainless steel spoon in her right hand was poised just above the bowl as if frozen in time. It would have made a great photo, a photo of the disparity between how Larry saw his wife in his mind's eye, and how she really looked. Penny looked old. "Old", the thought registered starkly as Larry blinked.

It was just a moment. It passed when Penny looked up and said, "About time you got up."

Larry got out a white ceramic bowl and helped himself to his share of the porridge that was warming in a stainless steel pot on the stove. "How are you feeling this morning?" he asked as he spooned up a tablespoon full of mushy porridge which he had doused with maple syrup and 2% milk.

"A little tired. You know that deep-seated feeling of fatigue that robs you of the exuberance and vitality you once possessed – and no amount of sleep can restore?"

"Take it easy today. Okay?"

"I'm tired of taking it easy. I think I'll bake today… nothing too strenuous. I'm going to bake you a banana-cream pie. Would you like that?"

"How can I refuse?"

Penny got up and began getting the ingredients together at the counter. There was a frozen pie shell in the freezer which she removed and set out to thaw. "These frozen pie shells are a baker's delight," she commented. "It makes it a lot easier to bake a decent pie."

"I tried to make a pie crust once when I was a kid. I was going to surprise my mother on her birthday. She always loved apple pie with ice-cream."

"How did it turn out?"

"The filling was fine but the crust was like plaster. My dear old mother said it was the best pie she ever ate."

"You were lucky to have such a thoughtful mother."

"I know. In many ways you are somewhat like her. She was almost perfect, like you."

"I know I'm not perfect but what was your mother's flaw?"

"She believed in Original Sin. She acted like a sinner. Once after she had baked a perfect lemon pie I said, 'Quit acting like a sinner, Mom and admit you are proud of what you have accomplished.' And guess what she said?"

"What?"

"A proud Jew? ...that's an oxymoron."

After Penny finished making the banana-cream pie and had placed it on the counter to set, they retired to the living-room with two mugs of healthy herbal tea which Larry had made.

"We have such a cozy living-room we should use it more frequently," Penny remarked.

"Yes, we should," Larry agreed taking a sip of his tea. "You know, I'm half Jewish," he remarked and fell silent.

"It seems to me that this business of being Jewish has been as sensitive an issue with you as being Japanese has been to me."

"It has sensitized me to all types of racial prejudice; it is such a gross indecency. When will we ever learn that every human being deserves to be treated with respect and dignity?"

"The lessons of history seem to be repetitive," Penny reflected sagely. "You know, ignorance has always been the catalyst that spurs man on to his greatest follies... and his most profound insights." She paused to let her husband cogitate upon this obtuse juxtaposition.

After a while Larry responded, "How so?"

"Well let's see, if we apply our rudimentary knowledge of Hegelian logic to this, it is possible to discern the historical patterns of thesis, antithesis, and synthesis."

"With the synthesis becoming the new thesis that will in time spawn its own antithesis."

"Yes," Penny agreed with a sigh, settling back into her chair and staring meditatively at the ceiling. She clasped her hands together as if in prayer and a quietude settled upon her that was serenely peaceful. The vibrations of the moment resonated up and down her spine like the kundalini of ages past, stimulating the seven chakras with a tingling that set her in a reflective mood. "Always be mindful that we are living in Western Christendom," she began soberly. "All that we have been discussing is real and relevant within the context of the historical consciousness that has so manifested itself over the last two millennia. Do you think that if our friends the Germans had been brought up as Hindus or Buddhists that the Holocaust in Europe would have occurred?"

"Good question," Larry responded and avoided a direct answer by pointing out that, "In Western Christendom we like to blame the unfortunate deaths of over six million innocent Jews upon the Germanic people. It enables us to wash our hands of any complicity, just like Pontius Pilate – whom we loath.

"It had very little to do with being German per se, and everything to do with Germany being a staunchly Protestant nation." Penny looked over toward her husband with compassionate eyes. Their eyes met in a moment of consolation.

After a prolonged silence Larry cleared his throat and said, "Anti-Semitism only makes sense in Western Christendom where the masses have been conditioned to relive the crucifixion of Christ every Easter."

"How can it be forgotten? Every year the schools are closed and chocolate bunnies and eggs are sold by the millions all because Jesus was crucified…."

"…at the hands of the Christ Killers!" Larry completed the sentence, "a label filled with latent hostility and resentment. It is evident that over the centuries the Jewish religion has come to represent the nemesis of the authenticity of the Christian religion. Did they not proclaim that the man crucified upon the cross was not the Messiah?"

"Not that he ever claimed he was," Penny interjected.

"And to this day people of the Jewish faith are still looking forward to the coming of the true Messiah. How does this make every Old-Christian feel? Who is the man symbolically represented by the empty crucifix hung in almost every Protestant Church? If he is not the Messiah, then who is that long-suffering soul hanging upon the cross that they been praying to over the centuries in the fervent hope of being saved?"

"A most disturbing question to Old-Christians," Penny observed.

"Since Saul's conversion into Saint Paul the Christian Church has blossomed into the modern world's most powerful religious institution. And yet Judaism continues to flourish in spite of all the persecution, as a constant reminder to Old-Christians that the man crucified upon the cross and the person biblically resurrected in 325 at the Council of Nicaea and deified as being 'homoosius' with his Father... is not the Son of God. In short, even though it might have been historically and religiously advantageous – and gratuitous as far as the Old-Christians were concerned – for the Jews to claim one of their own native sons as being the long awaited Messiah, they have steadfastly clung to their staunch belief that the real Messiah is yet to arrive upon the scene."

"Now that's a convoluted statement if I every heard one," Penny replied. "And the dissonance this apparent disagreement created upon the world stage is obvious throughout Western Christendom where the latent hostility emerged as anti-Semitism and manifested itself during the Second World War as the Holocaust."

"And now look at what is happening in the Middle East. What is at the basis of the conflict between Muslims, Christians, and Jews? Is this the will of God or simply willful acts of ignorance? When has terrorism and war ever been beneficial to mankind? How will it all end?"

"In Western Christendom we choose not to ask such questions, nor to confront ourselves with our latent feelings of hostility and resentment because it makes us feel uneasy," Penny commented.

"Nevertheless those feelings have been there, submerged in our subconscious and festering for hundreds of years, and every once in a while anti-Semitism rears its ugly head, and we all stand back and point accusing fingers and disclaim any responsibility for fostering it while attending Easter Mass with our friends."

"We really do not want to know what we have allowed ourselves to become, and are becoming."

"Ignorance is bliss," Larry stated sadly, "and anti-Semitism lives on," he added with a hint of exasperation thinking of his Jewish mother who had survived the Holocaust.

"Unfortunately that seems to be the case at this time," Penny agreed, "but we must remember that ignorance and wisdom go hand in hand like the foreground to the background, or the Yin to the Yang, or the Thesis to the Antithesis."

"It is important to see the whole picture."

"Indeed, if we could only step back and see the grand vista of historical change from a cosmic perspective, perhaps we would become aware that reality is a manifestation of our collective karmic destiny and we, each in our own way, are personally responsible for what we are becoming."

"Profound, but slightly vague," Larry commented. "Please clarify."

"Hmm, let's see, how can I put this as simply as possible without being too esoteric?" Penny pondered out loud. "Consider cellular division," she began tentatively, not certain how this approach would develop. "When the tiny sperm penetrates the ovum and cellular division begins, who can predict what the result will be? However, it is all there in the DNA which has been subject to evolutionary change. The collective manifestations of all such cellular divisions with sympathetic vibes give rise to Leviathans of collective consciousness that grow, evolve and resonate on a grand scale upon the world historical stage."

"You're talking about the collective will, conscious, subconscious and unconscious, of all the like-minded human beings on the entire planet, right?"

"Right. The collective will of billions of human beings throughout this planet represented by these Leviathans resonates upon the super-symmetric unified field of quantum gravitational, electromagnetic, and strong and weak forces that constitute the known universe. The dimension of probabilities crackles with opportunities! However, the growth and development of these Leviathans is contingent upon one simple, taken for granted, cosmological constant: freedom. This freedom is manifest in human beings as free-will, and the meaningful expression of free-will is contingent upon one's level of awareness. The greater the awareness the greater the freedom of expression."

"And the more diminished the awareness the greater the ignorance which stifles the freedom, right?"

"Right," Penny affirmed. "The natural tendency is to grow in the direction of greater freedom."

"This means that if a particular Leviathan was a prisoner of its own limited awareness or ignorance the tendency would be to move in the direction of diminished freedom."

"In the context of our present predicament perhaps it is symptomatic of the irony of all ironies."

"How so?" Larry asked while drinking the last drop of tea from his red mug.

"The irony of it all, in Hegelian terms, is the recognized historical fact that a dogmatic and entrenched Leviathan based upon an obsolete concept of Original Sin spawned its own antithesis."

"Judaism spawned the Christian and Muslim sects," Larry insightfully added. "And the synthesis?"

"Armageddon!"

They both lapsed into total silence. The realization was too much. Sometimes it is better to view the cosmic scene one frame at a time; that way it does not seem to be so prophetic.

"There is still time," Penny whispered as if sharing a secret so vital it had to be spoken of in hushed tones. "It is never too late. Never! People are free. Free to make wise decisions."

"We must have faith in the goodness of the human heart and soul."

"We must become more aware."

"As long as there is awareness… there is hope."

"And there is a growing awareness."

CHAPTER FIVE

"**W**hat if you were God?" Penny asked her spouse one evening as they sat in the living-room relaxing with a couple of lager beers which helped them to resonate with a mellow vibe. "And you had a very important message to deliver to all mankind. How would you deliver it?"

"By Canada Post," Larry joked. "I'd send out an anonymous form-letter. Or perhaps I could post it on the Internet."

"Most of the junk mail ends up in the garbage can unopened, and who is going to log on to a crackpot's message from God?"

"You," Larry laughed out loud. "But on second thought you might not. I think I'd have to deliver the message myself!"

"How?"

"I'd pretend I was Larry Petitjean."

"Why would you have to pretend? Couldn't you be Larry Petitjean?"

"Well, I guess I could but who wants to be Larry Petitjean?"

"Okay, so you are pretending to be someone you're not."

"I could be you, but as you know God works in mysterious ways. So in this case Larry is my man."

"How does God pretend to be you?"

"Easy. He puts thoughts in my head which I share with the people."

"Wouldn't the people think that those thoughts were your own thoughts?"

"What difference does it make? The message is out there, and that is the important part. The messenger could have been anyone, anyone at all."

"Some messengers are more believable than others."

"That is why I chose Larry."

"What if the people gave you credit for God's message and deified you as God? And prayed to you and asked you to forgive their sins and to save them?"

"I guess I'd have to do my best to help them, wouldn't I?"

"You could level with them."

"I could?"

"Tell them that it is the message that is important. The messenger could have been anyone."

"Then they might think I was a fake, a false prophet. Perhaps they'd get mad at me and... and kill me."

"Tell them God was only pretending to be you, that you are really and truly just good old Larry Petitjean."

"Do you think they would be enlightened enough to believe that?"

"I hope so."

* * *

(3) Toward Enlightenment

Monotheism

Monotheism implies a belief in one all-powerful, supreme God. There are three major monotheistic faiths that cater to about half of the Global village's religious believers. These three monotheistic faiths have played major roles in the development of the modern capitalistic world as it is presently constituted. They are in order of descending age: Judaism, Christianity, and Islam.

In Western Christendom the youngest of these monotheistic religions with over a billion adherents world-wide is probably the least understood even though it is a direct theological descendent from the two older forerunners. A rudimentary understanding of this latter religion, founded some 570 years after the birth of Jesus, should help to broaden our perceptions and attitudes toward it, and hopefully lessen the hostility and animosity that comes from ignorance and misunderstanding.

What is Islam? Islam is the youngest of the three world-class Monotheistic religious faiths. Its adherents, called Muslims, do not regard the prophet Mohammed (or Muhammad or Mahomet) who was born in Mecca in 570 CE and passed away at the age of sixty-three at Medina, to be the founder of a "new religion", but rather to be the last in a long line of distinguished prophets of the "one true God" (Allah in Arabic). It is the contention of the followers of Mohammed that over the ensuing centuries the original Monotheistic Faith of Adam (and Eve), Abraham, Moses (the Torah), and Jesus of

Nazareth (the Gospel) had been insidiously contaminated, misinterpreted, and corrupted by various self-appointed spokespersons. Therefore the least corrupted and purest monotheistic faith was the most recent: Islam, as revealed by the most recent prophet of the one true God, Mohammed.

Mohammed was "called" to prophesy by Allah in a cave near Mount Hira, north of Mecca at the age of forty. The essence of his message was very simple: obey and believe the One True God (Allah) and obey His Messengers. Like the prophets who came before him he preached about the greatness of God and the humbleness of man. For the last twenty-three years of his life Mohammed received revelations from Allah delivered through the angel Gabriel while in a trance-like state reminiscent of a seizure. The contents of these revelations were carefully recorded by Mohammed's followers and compiled into a single volume shortly after his death. These revelations are known as the Qur'an or Koran, and along with various revered aspects of his life, form the basis of Islamic theology.

Islam, Christianity, and Judaism have six major dogmatic beliefs in common. They are as follows:

(1) Belief in one (extrinsic) God;
(2) Belief in all of God's messengers;
(3) Belief in the holy books sent down to prophets of God;
(4) Belief in the existence of angels and life after death;
(5) Belief in the Day of Judgment, and Heaven and Hell;
(6) Belief in divine Decree.

These dogmatic beliefs associated with Monotheism, as practiced by billions of believers the world over, have a powerful effect upon our perceptions and attitudes wherever we may reside in the Global Village.

Perception and Attitude

Everything we perceive with our five senses and even our extrasensory perceptions is colored by our attitudes. In accord with the third law of motion our attitudinal actions and reactions reverberate between the perceiver and the perceived in much the same fashion as the image reflected in two diametrically opposed mirrors is reflected back and forth at the speed of light. The attitude that is projected is reflected back, perceived and reacted upon by the perceiver which changes it ever so slightly, and this altered attitude is reflected back and forth. Therefore every act of perception (as in the Uncertainty Principle) is relative to and altered by the attitudes and perception of the perceiver. The importance of attitudes is reflected in the concept of embarrassment.

Embarrassment

Embarrassment is a natural reaction. It is an instinctive reaction to an attitude initiated by a perceiver that is difficult to describe because it is deeply personal. It is self-inflicted. The self reacts and changes according to an intrinsic reciprocity between primary and secondary self concepts. The perceiver's attitudes are manifested as the "personality/ego" of the Mortal I and give the Mortal I a unique Identity, manifested like secondary attributes in a primary substance. The dissonance that results from the lack of resonance and harmony between primary and secondary self concepts results in a feeling of embarrassment. For example if a normal heterosexual male imagined himself wearing a dress, he might feel embarrassed. However, if a transvestite imagined himself wearing the same dress, he probably would not feel the least bit embarrassed. The depth of embarrassment felt is dependent upon the depth to which the offending attitudes penetrate the core of the substance of one's identity. Whenever these attitudes manifested by the ego are contrary to or at odds with the Mortal I's self-concept the perceiver will be superficially embarrassed. If the attitudes manifested by the ego are contrary to the Mortal I's and the Immortal I's combined self-concept, the embarrassment will be felt much more acutely as it resonates at a universal level which could lead to various degrees of depression. And if the attitudes manifested by the ego are contrary to the Mortal I's, the Immortal I's, and the Eternal I's collective self concept, the embarrassment could be so spiritually devastating it could lead to suicide.

Embarrassment is a built-in self-tuning defense mechanism whereby attitudes, no matter how deeply entrenched, can be intrinsically transformed or changed in accord with the first law of thermodynamics and the third law of motion. An attitude adjustment is frequently all that is needed in order to alleviate the problem. Each embarrassment is a signal to the perceiver that relative to his dharmic health, which always tends toward harmony and unity, his Ego is out of sync with one or more of the 'Three I-s'; and if he is wise he will examine the origin of his inner feelings of embarrassment.

Embarrassment is Man's instinctive reaction to his self-concept and the path he has chosen. It is relative to the level of karmic awareness and sensitivity of the individual concerned. It is a signal to each individual, making the perceiver personally aware that something is out of sync with his/her nature; for example, *Original Sin* is one of contemporary man's greatest embarrassments. In this sense embarrassment is essentially a healthy human emotion. It spurs Man on to greater self-awareness and enhances his ability to heal himself physically, mentally, and spiritually. It is necessary in Man's natural evolution up the spiritual ladder toward unity and harmony. Without it his humility might be buried beneath the vanity of his egotistical conceit. Fortunately he is able to embarrass himself. It is an existential sign that somewhere in the germinating kernel of his identity he might be intuitively aware of the Generic Faith that illuminates the Secret of the Ages.

Generic Faith

Billions of people the world over believe in an Eternal Spirit or "God". The word "God" is a proper noun with a spiritual meaning. It is the existent-essence of Generic Faith or the genesis of religious faith. Generic Faith is to religious faith what humanity is to the various secondary attributes that constitute race. Differentiation amongst the various races and religions has in the past led to intolerance, prejudice, bigotry, animosity, and war. Little has changed up to the present time. A clear understanding of this notion of Generic Faith may lead to a much more enlightened attitude. Following is a very simple analogy which hopefully will make this rather esoteric notion a lot more palatable.

Consider for the sake of clarity the common, mundane, but delicious Generic Burger. It is a hamburger, and as everyone knows a hamburger is a hamburger: a patty of cooked ground beef sandwiched between the upper and lower halves of a bun. This Generic Burger has been transformed into the Whopper, the Big Mac, the Mama/Papa burger, and a host of other well-known types. People can develop their own burger at home to suit their own taste – but if they want a Whopper they must go to Burger King, or if they prefer a Big Mac, then MacDonald's has the franchise, or if they desire a Mama/Papa burger, then they must visit the A&W. These are all hamburgers. No one has the one and only authentic, genuine burger. We all know this. No one has been killed and no wars have been fought over who has the one and only true burger. We even have a new variety called the vegetarian burger. No one said it was a sacrilege.

In this world we currently have several universally recognized Religious Burgers. They are the Hindu Burger, the Muslim Burger, the Christian Burger, the Buddhist Burger, the Judaic Burger, and many other famous name brands. They are all looking for converts to their particular product. Choose the one that suits your palate or make your own customized religious burger. Enjoy your burger, and let others enjoy theirs. Let us not make hasty value judgments, call names and issue put downs because someone else has a different preference than our own. Let us respect each other's freedom to choose and to believe.

The Faith that underlies all faiths is known as the Generic Faith. The origin of this Generic Faith is associated with the *Divine Essence* known as "God". Is it possible to prove that the *Divine Essence* actually exists? The famous French philosopher Rene Descartes implied that it was when he said: "I think therefore I am", placing essence (thought) before existence (being). The Existentialists, on the other hand, insist that he should have said: "I am therefore I think," placing existence prior to essence. It is a profound ideological argument reminiscent of the age-old question: *Which came first, the chicken or the egg?* Is there a resolution? The combination of existence with essence yields: *Existent-Essence*, the genesis of an abiding "faith" that makes everything-there-is possible. It is an abiding faith that transcends rational comprehension; that is why it is called *Faith*. It is the Generic Faith that underlies all religious faiths and spiritual experience; it is the Faith that gives rise to the *secret of the ages.*

The Secret of the Ages

People in general love to be let in on a secret. It gives one a smug sense of satisfaction to be "in the know". What if there was a secret so grand that everyone wanted to know what it was? However, if everyone was told what the secret was – would it still be a secret?

It has been said that in the beginning there was the "word" and the word was "God". That is how powerful and magical words are. Words give wings to the imagination.   The imagination is the free will being free. It is what allows one to pretend. Pretending is based upon what one knows or is aware of. What one knows is stored in one's DNA and one's memory which is continually being embellished by the stimuli received via one's five senses. All of this knowledge, symbolically reified as words, provides the elemental potential for our imaginings. By combining words we can fill the libraries of the world with the fabulous creations of the wonderful process we all love to indulge in, called "pretending".

Pretending is freedom incarnate. What is more miraculous than pretending?   It enables Zero to equal one.   Pretending allows something to be something else. It is magical. Little children love to pretend. It is natural. Some astute thinkers refer to such fantasizing as "the law of attraction": like attracts like and in like manner we can fashion mansions-in-the-sky (or on earth). Children can revel in the fairy tale world of make-believe where the fantastic becomes as real as the imagination is limitless.   Walt Disney created such a fantasyland for children and called it Disneyworld.

When children grow up and become more aware they realize that fairy tales are *unreal*. Many replace their childhood fairy tales with more socially acceptable ones commensurate with their level of karmic vibration, awareness, and maturity. At the four dimensional level of resonance/awareness achieved by all humankind where the intellect is inundated with the sensate stimuli from their five senses, the simplicity of fairy tales is replaced with more complex imaginings, some of which have become institutionalized in the collective consciousness of many as "religion". This opens the door to the wonderful world – not of Disney – but of the supernatural where adults can pretend to be sinners, saints, demons, angels, witches, devils, gods, etc. and live in the heavenly Kingdom of God, the burning fires of Hell, Paradise, and other such imaginary places. Sometimes people get confused and forget that they are just pretending – then they become neurotically ego-centric and start self-righteously reifying a reality commensurate with their attitudes and beliefs. They dramatize their beliefs upon the planetary stage. What could have been a comedy is turning into a tragedy. Sometimes they really get carried away and ignominiously pollute and desecrate the earth, and terrorize, torture, and kill each other. Sad isn't it? It has been going on for centuries and centuries and centuries. We are *Great Pretenders*, are we not?

Via the analogy of the Light, the Pinholes and the Reflections it is possible to comprehend the gist of this pretence, and to expand our level of awareness accordingly. The Eternal Soul or light of life modified by the immortal pinholes of pretence is reflected in a four dimensional reality as mortality. Think about this question: How can the Eternal Soul become a mortal soul? Think really hard. There is only one answer: *By pretence.*

By passing through the pinholes of *pretence* the Eternal Soul can experience what it is to be mortal. This is an essential experience for the Soul because it is the experience of being mortal that gives meaning and significance to being immortal and eternal. It is the existence of mortality that enables the soul to reflect back to the "Existent-Essence", everything it is possible for the Eternal Soul to be. The possibilities are infinite; consequently the process of self-realization is ongoing. What is the Self realizing? *Everything it is possible to be.* How long will this take? *Forever.*

What is the Secret? The secret is a mystery that is forever unraveling. Somewhere in the echoing synapses of our questioning minds, in the tingling memory of our cellular constitution, in the vibrant strands of our primordial DNA bolstered by an infinite wisdom profoundly tempered by an eternal solitude – *we know.* We know the "secret" buried in the existent-essence of our soul. What is the secret? It is difficult to explain using simple logic; it can best be apprehended via the use of a fairytale.

Once upon a time there lived a beautiful Princess. She was the incarnation of beauty and truth personified. She lived all alone in the universe of her mind. It was a lonely existence being the one and only, very lonely indeed. "Just me, myself, and I", she thought, "just me, myself, and I, forever and ever... world without end." Over an infinity of eternity the Princess grew so lonely she longed in her soul of souls, and heart of hearts for a miracle that would allow her to pretend! Then she would no longer be lonely.

How does one "pretend" if one has never done it before? How indeed! "Hocus-pocus" aside – it just happened as if it were natural: the beautiful Princess gazed into the magical mirror of her mind and to her amazement there she was manifested in a four dimensional reality membrane as if she really existed there!

What did she spy in her mind's eye? A wrinkled old woman hoary with infinite age. Instantly she was overcome with such heartfelt compassion and empathy the old woman was transformed into a "beautiful princess"... just like herself.

On the other hand what did the wrinkled old woman see when she gazed into the four dimensional reality membrane in which she was ensconced? She saw a beautiful princess. Instantly she was overcome with a mortal surge of vanity, conceit, and righteous indignation. She was not beautiful enough! Her beauty was flawed by a tiny blemish barely noticeable on the lower side of her left cheek. In that mortal moment the tiny blemish – instead of being a beauty mark – became an unsightly mole from which sprouted a profusion of coarse stubbly hairs, and the beautiful princess was transformed into a "selfish old hag"... just like... just like... well, you know... or perhaps you'd rather pretend... that you don't?

Embarrassing? Close your eyes and imagine that you are in the universe of your mind where beauty is truth and truth is all you know, where serenity and peace becomes you and you become One with everything-there-is. "Who am I?" and "Where am I?" you wonder...

> *Here I am*
> *Just me, myself, and I*
> *Alone in the here and now of my own creation*
> *Pretending that I am not pretending*
> *To be mortal*
> > *For an instant*
> *To be real*
> *To live, love, laugh, cry*
> *To confront the paradox*
> *To be born to die*
> > *And always*
> *To dare to share*
> *To really care*
> *Before the after*
> *And after the laughter*
> *In the space of time*
> *In a life of rhyme*

To bask in the ignorance of youth
To be withered by wisdom and freed by truth.

Larry shut down the computer and with a prolonged sigh pushed his chair back, stretching out his hairy legs. "I think that just about does it, eh?" he queried.

Penny pushed her chair back even with Larry's and turned sideways. She gazed solemnly at her husband. "At long last," she said quietly, "it is finished."

The statement seemed final. They sat there together in the silence of the study and stared solemnly at one another as if in awe of their accomplishment. There was exhilaration tinged with sadness. It was a sadness associated with the completion of a project that was both a challenge and a joy. It had brought a purpose to each day that stimulated their creative juices and filled every minute of each hour with happy vibes that resonated in their hearts as gratitude. Gratitude for the opportunity to be of service, to be able to sit together side by side month after month writing a student handbook on life that might someday be read by someone other than themselves. And now that it was completed they were left with a vague feeling of emptiness, as if there was nothing left for them to say or do.

"How are you feeling?" Larry asked, turning his head to look at his wife.

"I was just about to ask you that question. I guess we're both feeling a bit ambivalent. We're finished, but we sort of wish we weren't."

"I'm feeling nostalgic already," Larry empathized.

"I remember when I gave birth to the twins, and parenthood descended upon us with the dependent cries of those two helpless babies. It was a wonderful nurturing and sharing experience. Writing this handbook has likewise been a nurturing and sharing experience. We've just given birth to a literary brainchild. Once again we have become parents because we have dared to share," Penny stated proudly.

"We have dared to share our innermost thoughts and bare our intellectual souls," Larry added resolutely as if making a declaration before a panel of skeptical judges.

"We stand naked before our critics!" Penny declared with a tinge of embarrassment. "We have nothing to hide," she added with a laugh, injecting a touch of humor.

Larry was going to say "We stand exposed," but the thought of such exposure filled his mind with such ludicrous images that he paused, momentarily overcome by his inhibitions. "Some handbook!" he exclaimed with a comical smile.

"You said it," Penny retorted, "Some handbook, indeed!" They laughed in unison. When their moment of hilarity subsided Penny turned the computer back on and solemnly declared, "There is one more thing we need to do."

The last page of the Handbook appeared on the computer screen. The last page of a labor of love bequeathed to those who would follow in the footsteps of those who went on ahead.

"My cousin would be happy," Penny reflected, "the seed he planted has produced this brainchild. Perhaps in some small way it will contribute toward the realization of his dream."

"I hope so," Larry commented. "I can't think of anyone else who had such a profound effect upon you, except perhaps your parents."

Penny smiled to herself as she slowly typed the heading on the next page.

DEDICATION

Dedicated to an extraordinary individual, Tutomu Miki, who provided the inspiration that led to the writing of this Student Handbook on Life.

CHAPTER SIX

Tutomu Miki frequently dreamed of the special moments of his life that were spent in Canada. The older he got the more his mind harkened back to the "good old days". Some of the days weren't so good but in retrospect they always gave him a good feeling, a feeling of youthful vibes filled with youthful dreams and aspirations.

"Speaking of Canada," Tutomu rose to address his omnipresent audience, "I have five cousins who live elsewhere in this global village. I think most of them are still living in Canada. I only got to know one of them though, and that was because she had written to me requesting some information about her roots. What was her proper name? Old age sometimes plays tricks on my memory. It was a strange sounding name that started with 'P' and seemed to end with 'pee'. Penopee or something weird like that. A real hakujin type of name. I can understand why she insisted that I call her Penny. Anyway, I did my best to locate the information she was looking for, partly because it pertained to my own roots and satisfied my own curiosity.

"She wrote back after I sent the information, to thank me. She said she'd like to come and visit me some day so we could get to know each other better. My father, who could not pronounce her name either, informed me that she was the one that nearly bled to death soon after her birth. How he knew that, I don't know. It was probably contained in one of the early letters from his brother that arrived soon after we arrived in Japan – before he started saving and reading them aloud. Apparently my Dad's younger brother, Hideo, had, in his youth, astounded my Dad by demonstrating the abiding courage necessary to resist the prevailing prejudices of the times, and marry a beautiful young woman who was snidely referred to by the unenlightened of the day as 'that Métis girl'. Who knows? Perhaps it was divine preference because apparently all of his children, according to my Dad, seemed to glow with a natural aura of hybrid vigor. 'Japan is too ingrown,' my Dad used to say, 'We need more foreign blood'. I think there is quite a bit of American blood floating around since the occupation.

"Anyway, guess what my father said? He said 'Why don't you get up off that futon and go visit your Canadian cousin?' Once he got that notion into his head he kept egging me on. I think he really wanted to go back to Canada himself – but he would never admit it. He had an abiding sense of honor.

We had a bundle of correspondence from Canada that nearly filled a small suitcase in the corner of our living room just under our miniature Buddhist shrine. It represented most of the letters accumulated since our arrival in Japan. Whenever a new letter arrived from Canada it piqued the interest and curiosity of the entire family. In the evening we would gather in our small living room and my Dad would read the letter as if it were the latest installment of a continuing saga that always kept us on pins and needles. Sometimes he would let my Mom read aloud portions of the letter that pertained particularly to her. It felt like we were still back there suffering along with those we left behind! We probably knew as much about what was happening following the evacuation as the individuals who were writing to us. My Dad had a lot of old friends who respected him and sought his advice. Sometimes it took days for him to compose proper responses to letters of anguish... so-so filled with hopelessness and bewilderment you could just weep with empathy. The wretched lumber camps, the horrid sugar beet fields, the backbreaking labor, the brutal prejudice, the contempt, the loathing, the poverty, the despondency, the stoic suffering....

"At first I lounged about lethargically as if I wasn't interested in going to Canada, perhaps out of respect for my Dad's decision to leave. You know, prejudice leaves deep scars. You have to rise above it. I talked myself into going back. You know how it is; you convince yourself you are doing it for someone else's sake: 'Okay Dad,' I said, 'I'll take two weeks off from work and go back.' He smiled as if he was remembering that far off time he and his younger brother Hideo had stowed aboard an old Chinese steamer bound for Vancouver.

"I must admit I was anxious. As the date set for my departure drew closer I was filled with a mixture of insecurity and excitement – even though I was a mature adult by that time. Yeah, I must admit, I felt just like a kid. I got on a big turbo-prop jet and off I flew like a fledgling bird on a migratory journey."

"I was one of those typical Japanese tourists with a Japan Airlines bag slung over one shoulder and a Nikon camera over the other. I've seen those types of tourists, and it always amazes me how they manage to fit the stereotype so accurately. Mind you, it was difficult to see myself, except in my mind's eye, as I emerged from the arrivals gate of Calgary International Airport. Penny was holding up a great big cardboard sign. On it she had printed a single word: 'Tutomu'. That is how I found her. "I'm Tutomu," I yelled over the din.

"She stepped forward gingerly and shyly shook my hand. She was wearing a beige trench-coat with wide patch-like pockets. 'Glad to make your acquaintance,' she said.

"If my memory serves me correctly, she had a comfortable one-bedroom apartment somewhere over on 14th Street North-West. It was on the ground floor of a four story brick building with underground parking. Just around the corner was a convenience store where I stocked up with all her favorite snacks. We practically ate them all the first two days I was there. Once we lost our natural *enyo* we really pigged out. You get hungry when you gab on and on late into the night.

"Did I tell you she was the single most profoundly intelligent person I have ever met? She had read books on philosophy, religion, and a wide assortment of esoteric subjects. It seemed to me she was searching for something to fill – or should I say satisfy – a longing as deep as eternity. I could sense it every time she sighed, and said nothing. I could relate to that.

"Poor thing, she was infatuated with her boss at that time. I think she said his name was Jim. She did not say much about it, but I could tell he was on her mind. The way she mentioned it to me was like, like an aside. It was like she was talking to herself. She said wistfully as she left for work in the morning, 'I wonder if I'll see Jim today.' When she arrived home in the evening, I'd politely ask her, 'Did you see Jim today?' 'No,' she'd usually reply, 'he didn't come down today.'

"Have you ever been infatuated with someone? If you have, then you will probably have some idea of how she felt. I tried to cheer her up as much as I could. She loved to talk about all manner of things after supper. It kept her mind off of Jim, I suppose. Like I said, poor thing, she was so melancholic. It made me sad to see her leave each morning with such hope, and return looking so forlorn. I felt like calling up Jim and telling him to wise up; how could he be so blind and insensitive? Sometimes it even made me downright angry. But I was just a guest. Who was I to be butting my nose into her personal affairs?

"She tried to be the perfect hostess. It was her Japanese heritage. My mother was like that. The guests were always treated like royalty. She did everything: made breakfast, left lunch in the fridge, cooked supper, and cleaned up after me. I may as well have been staying at a four-star hotel with full catering service. Whenever I attempted to tidy up she scolded me saying: 'Leave it, I'll do that later.' I felt guilty just lying around while she did all the work.

"When Penny was at work I'd take the bus downtown and wander about. The place I ended up spending most of my time was at the public library. I'd look up stuff I thought Penny would be interested in. It made her think I was smarter than I actually am. I guess, in my own way, I was trying to impress her. Sometimes, I must confess, I felt very protective toward her, like an older brother. Being an only child perhaps made me feel extra responsible for her well-being, never having had anyone else to fend for but myself.

"I was so happy for her when years later she sent me a letter announcing the fact that she had gotten married to an American citizen. 'An American citizen,' I reflected. For some reason I pictured that young naval officer I mentioned earlier. She must have been in her thirties by then. 'God bless her!' I thought.

"I can't remember exactly, but I think I sent them a wedding gift. I must have, because they sent me a thank-you card saying: 'Thanks for the lovely gift'. It was signed, "Larry and Penny Petitjean". Now there is a weird surname if I ever heard one."

"I never got married, although I had a few girlfriends who wanted to marry me..." the old man paused suddenly. A strange look seared across his face that manifested a combination of fear, anxiety, dread, guilt, and uncertainty. It was a mixture of the many emotions that had become a plague in the aftermath for the survivors of the atomic bombings in Japan.

"You know," Tutomu continued cautiously, "in post war Japan a curious thing happened in the wake of the atomic blasts. The victims, that is, the survivors like myself, became stigmatized: we became the war-lepers, the unclean, the tainted, the contaminated." The old man lapsed into silence overcome by an emotional surge. He wet his parched lips, shook his head sadly, and expostulated, "We survived hell-on-earth and in the aftermath we were treated like - like residents from hell! We were the only human beings in the history of the world to survive an atomic blast, and as such we became specimens to be stared at, studied and probed like experimental rats who had been exposed to some dreadful disease, grotesquely misshapen and deformed creatures who had become national and international objects of curiosity. Who would want to marry a ghoul who had crawled out from under a radioactive cloud like some kind of a miraculous freak?" he paused and let the question dangle. "Who?" he demanded with such vehemence that it caused his face to darken and his eyebrows to curl. Tutomu paused, inhaled slowly through his open mouth, and waited for a reply. Hearing none, he calmed himself down by folding his hands gently across his abdomen and continued in a contrite manner, "I-I pretended I was uh, uh... normal – but I knew I wasn't."

"It embarrasses me to say this: I am sterile. Like dozens, perhaps hundreds, of survivors of the atomic holocaust, I became sterile. My sperm are impotent. What can I say? I love children all the more because I cannot have one of my own. I could have adopted, but I became too engrossed in business matters to take on parental duties." Tutomu brought his bony hands up to his face to hide his embarrassment. "I guess my greatest disappointment is not having a family of my own. Why did this have to happen to me?

"Sterility is a very intimate and personal matter. I can only speak for myself, but I can assure you that it is much more than an inability to have children. It can affect your self-esteem; it limits your sense of destiny. Your mortal destiny ends with you. Your future looks as sterile as you feel. The divine light burns dimly; you work like a dog to compensate. You cannot have children of your own, but you can own everything else. I was married to my job. In many ways I am much like a dedicated Catholic priest; although I am not celibate, I may as well be. I had to compensate for my shortcomings. I hope you understand my predicament. What would you have done?

"I never told Penny. She had worries enough of her own. Perhaps I should have. She had a way of making you feel worthy. It might have changed my attitude and my life." Tutomu sagged back onto his bed as if demoralized.

* * *

Thoughts of sterilization and impotency brought a sudden and dramatic change to the old man's demeanor. He glanced furtively upward toward the ceiling and with a fearful cry grabbed his pillow and held it over his head. From a dreadful sky, black rain poured down like a sheet of darkness. It pelted off the flimsy piece of tin like a death rattle. The old man cowered fearfully under his pillow shivering with fright. He closed his eyes tightly to keep the black rain from blinding him. He was cold and exhausted. When the awful rain stopped he tentatively opened his eyes and glanced furtively toward his vast audience. Where were they? Had they sought shelter somewhere? Or had the dreadful rain taken its toll? He dropped the pillow and pulled the sheets up to his chin. They were nowhere to be seen! He glanced about anxiously, his body rigid with expectation. After a while he relented and sank back into his bed despondently. He blinked his eyes and stared out with diminishing hope. All that he saw was a vast wasteland of destruction and desolation. In the distance the charred hulk of praying hands reminded him of his impotency and sterility.

"Haagh," the sound vibrated through Tutomu's lips like dying hopes vanishing into a great void of despair. He sagged back like a limp doll onto the starched white sheets and soft pillows, his face a wrinkled mask of disappointment. "Haaaagh," the sound resonated throughout the room with a chilling hollowness like a resounding echo inside a cold, empty morgue.

A deep-seated feeling of worthlessness enveloped the old man in a despairing cocoon of hopelessness. He had no wife, no children, no family... no one! He had nothing more to say, nothing more to share. He just wanted to sleep and sleep and sleep. Minutes turned to hours, and hours into days. He refused to take his medication and refused to eat as the days crawled by like a never-ending occupation.

He probably would have passed on sooner, except he could hear the head nurse and young Doctor whispering in urgent tones about him.

"Your audience is waiting," the nurse said when she thought he was listening.

"What audience?" the old man roused himself from his doleful slumbers.

"You can't let them down!" the Doctor demanded.

"They have been so patient," the nurse pointed out.

"What kind of psychology is this?" the old man scoffed, rising to the bait by perking himself up. Depression always made him feel extremely doubtful and distrustful. "I know what you're trying to do."

"You do?" the young Doctor asked.

"Yeah, I know. There is no fool like an old fool. You're just trying to fool me."

"You think we are foolish enough to attempt to fool you?" the nurse asked with a smile.

It was her smile that did it. It was such a coy and demure smile verging on the self-conscious. It was irresistible. "Get me some coffee," the old man said as he rose half-heartedly to a sitting position.

* * *

Tutomu stared out at the void where his imaginary audience used to be with a bewildered expression on his face. He peered out through bleary eyes and shook his head vigorously. All he could see was the round electric clock with the shiny chrome trim staring back at him. "What happened to all the people?" he wondered. All those people who night after night sat there so patiently and listened so attentively as if – as if what he had been saying was worth listening to and as if they were really there! "Where are they?"

He rubbed his eyes with the back of his right hand, blinked his eyes several times and stared back out toward the electric wall clock. It was still there on the far wall. A thin red hand rotated around the face ticking off the seconds one by one. "*Nagai koto – neh?*" he said to himself. Yes, it had been a long time, a long, long time since the black rain fell like a shower of death and robbed him of his potency. "*Nagai koto,*" he reiterated. The words lit up the long forgotten passageways of his memory with renewed hopes as he dozed off with a half-smile blending into the weary lines written on his parchment face that told the story of his life.

The setting sun streamed in through the west window of the old man's sterile hospital room and filled it with an optimistic ambiance. Tutomu's hands were clasped meditatively across his chest and his eyes were fixed upon the electric wall-clock. The second hand was about to go around for the thirty-eighth time when a soothing feeling of acceptance radiated throughout Tutomu's wizened old body as if he had suddenly been immersed in a relaxing bath of warm water. He had been patiently counting the revolutions of the "edge of duration" as it revolved around the face of the clock one enduring second at a time. The effect was mesmerizing; his eyes closed momentarily in anticipation of the thirty-ninth revolution. Perhaps it was the anticipation of the inevitable: the acceptance and the letting go, because when he opened his eyes expectantly and looked out – by god, there they were! Every single one of them. His audience was still there! He rolled over and turned on the bedside lamp to augment the light. It cast a radiant glow over every face. Silent tears of appreciation stained the starched white pillow with damp spots.

There they were just as if they had never left! "Where have you been?" a timid voice asked plaintively. "Us kin folk have to stick together you know," a woman's voice admonished. "We're all in this together," a third voice affirmed. "Welcome back!" a chorus of voices rang out.

It was almost too much. The old man's heart pulsed with such excitement his chest resounded like a snare drum. His mouth hung open and his breath wheezed in and out while his eyes bugged out of his head with amazement. He hadn't noticed before. How could he have been so unaware? They were more than just an audience; they were his family! The vast universal Family of Man. Every single human being who ever drew breath and trod this path before him. What a wonderful family of every color, race, nationality, and religion! Tutomu was overcome with emotion. These were his kin, every single one of them. His chest swelled with elation and pride: his very own family. He felt very protective. 'Whatsoever ye do unto the very least of these, ye do unto me,' he thought in Christ-like fashion. A lump formed in his throat as additional tears of appreciation and gratitude began to ebb from the outer corners of his glistening eyes. He felt the compassion resonate up and down the Great Chain of Being that linked them all together. They were his family. He was one of them, the one who had nearly wasted his life, the one they had sat patiently hour after hour and listened to, because he was the one who needed to share. Never in his entire life did he feel so grateful.

He was not alone. He never had been alone. They were always there for him, appreciative of every word he shared. Every single word. They knew what it was like to be human. They had walked, limped, crawled and run down this mortal pathway. They knew exactly how it felt to have to bear the unbearable. They had infinite patience, kindness, and understanding. They were there for him – even when he was unaware. After all, they were his next of kin, his family.

"Thank you so very much," Tutomu said humbly. "Thank you for letting me share." He turned off his bedside lamp and closed his eyes. A serene smile of satisfaction settled upon his face revealing an inner kindness that radiated a depth of gratitude, love and compassion for his fellow man that was all-consuming.

CHAPTER SEVEN

The restorative powers of sleep are truly remarkable especially for those who are blessed with the ability to sleep like a baby. Tutomu was one of the blessed; perhaps that was one of the reasons he had lived so long. He lay curled up on his right side facing the window. The room was deathly quiet except for the rhythmic sounds of his shallow breathing. Under his closed eyelids his eyes darted about indicative of the rapid eye movements associated with REM sleep. After a few minutes he began to dream his favorite dream.

He dreamed he was back in Canada. He was a small boy going fishing with his father in the new boat his father had built with his own two hands. His father was very proud of that boat and he was too because, small as he was, he had helped almost every day. What a beautiful boat that was! The elation he felt the first day they put it in the water was only exceeded by the joy he experienced the first time they actually went fishing in it. His mother always came down to the landing to greet them at dusk when they returned with a boatload of fish of every kind. During the salmon run they usually caught their share of the salmon which they sold to the canneries for a tidy income. His father always gave him pocket-money; it gave him a sense of being economically responsible.

His mother used to smile a lot in those days. She was a demure little woman with a very big heart. She just naturally shared whatever came her way. Perhaps if he and his father had been more like her, and less vain, things would have been different. On the other hand it probably would have made little difference, because on December 7th of that year, about two months after his father had declared him responsible enough to take the boat out by himself, they heard over the radio that Pearl Harbor had been attacked, and he and his parents became "Japs", inscrutable enemy aliens, and he had been so proud to be Canadian.

When does a dream turn into a memory? Or a memory into a dream? On December the seventh a lot of things changed: dreams became memories and memories became dreams, and some of the dreams verged into memories of nightmares.

Tutomu pictured himself sitting in his desk at Lord Byng School, the only desegregated school in Richmond, proudly wearing the dark blue Toronto Maple Leafs hockey sweater he had received on his sixth birthday. He was in grade two and his teacher at that time was an attractive young lady called Miss Steves. Every morning they stood at attention and sang, "God save the King" followed by a recitation of the Lord's Prayer. Sometimes they sang "O Canada". He always sang that song with gusto. Even in a class of forty-two his voice rang out. Once Miss Steves said, "Tutomu, you have a very pleasant singing voice". After that he always sang "O Canada" with great pride. In later years whenever he heard the playing of "O Canada" during the Olympic Games, it always sent shivers up and down his spine.

His father, Kasuzimo, often took him for a morning stroll along the boardwalk on Sunday. There was something special about those Sunday strolls that reached back to the sense of discovery and joy a young child feels in the crisp cool of the early morn when the sun rises slowly over the eastern horizon and colors the sky with the first signs of glory. It was a feeling like no other as they ambled along that rickety old boardwalk listening to their footsteps echoing off the roughly hewn cedar planks that constituted the main street that snaked along between the wooden houses which lined both sides. Sometimes Tutomu and his father would stop and sit on the main wharf alongside the majestic Imperial Cannery with their feet just dangling, and watch the ripples wash in and out, just the two of them and the rising sun next to the mighty Fraser. It was awesome. It made Sunday feel spiritual. No one could erase such poignant memories.

When the seagulls started screeching they would get up and start walking towards the sun. Just he and his Dad walking hand-in-hand past the Japanese Duplexes, Takayaki's Store, and the Britannia Shipyards toward the Hong Wo Store in the distance. Sometimes his Dad bought him a sweet at the Hong Wo Store if it was open. On the return trip Tutomu recalled such familiar places as Marumoto's, Faruya's, Murakami Boat Works where once or twice a year the newly made gill-netters slid down the rails into the river, Hirokawa's Shed, the Richmond Boat Builders, and Shiozaki's. How could he forget those weathered clapboard buildings perched upon piles to keep them high and dry during high tide when the water rose to within inches of the lower level floor boards. It was indeed a unique place to have spent one's childhood, sandwiched between an earthen dyke and the river's edge on a marshy wonderland.

He remembered his father informing him during one of those Sunday morning strolls that he had been born on the other side of the dyke at the Japanese Hospital. Only Japanese and other non-white children could claim to be born there. Segregation was the official practice in more populated areas. The people who ran the provincial government were not very enlightened. There were plenty of outspoken racists around. Unfortunately they wielded the power to make the lives of the non-white population quite miserable. In Steveston the population in general seemed to be a little more open-minded – but they were just a small enclave in a vast wilderness of prejudice that warped pleasant dreams into weird feelings of anxiety.

Tutomu rolled over in bed and clearly enunciated "*Nagai-koto-neh?*" out loud. His breath became slow and ragged and a serious look of consternation settled upon his countenance. It was a tumultuous time he was ensconced in, and the feelings and emotions that rippled through his memory caused his body to tremble with apprehension. He mumbled something incoherently, and it was not clearly evident whether he was still dreaming or half awake. He coughed abruptly, opened his eyes, stared unseeingly toward the wall-clock, and drew in a staggered breath. When he exhaled, his voice spewed out in a hoarse whisper that was barely audible. He spoke in a rhetorical fashion to his imaginary family.

"The RCMP confiscated all our property: our lot, our new house, our beautiful boat, and everything we owned that could not be stuffed into a couple of suitcases. The government officials gave us a choice: we could either go back to Japan, or go to a concentration camp. It was nice to have a choice. 'What have we done?' my father asked angrily. 'Have we broken any laws or done anything unpatriotic?' The government official said, 'I'm only doing my job – give me a break!'

"I remember my Dad once telling me that 'In Canada there is no Emperor, or King or Czar, or Dictator; in Canada the people are free from oppression. It is the most tolerant country in the world. Did you know they had even operated the Underground Railroad that helped those enslaved on southern plantations in the U.S. escape to freedom?'

"But that was back then – and sometimes things change for the worse. And now we were being treated like enemy aliens. Where in the world could one find freedom from oppression? It was the most difficult decision my father ever made, but he held up his head and said with quiet resignation: 'We will go back to Japan where at least we will be free from this persecution.'

"My mother wept. It was the first and last time I ever saw her cry in public. She wept on behalf of every 'inscrutable yellow Jap', on behalf of every person who ever felt the indignity of racial prejudice. And in her heart I know she also wept on behalf of the ignorance of those who participated in, justified, and perpetuated such indignities. She wept on behalf of the human race." Tutomu blinked his eyes several times, as if he was attempting to see past the limitations of time-space, past the wall-clock into the reverie of memories unraveling as if on cue.

"It was a time of great insecurity, of overwhelming depression, of utter hopelessness, but as they say, life goes on. We were rounded up like cattle and housed in cattle stalls awaiting our eventual fate. No one knew for sure what was going on. The dread of the unknown hung over us like a hangman's noose, and we were standing on the trap door. Fear glistened in every eye day and night. An empathetic RCMP officer informed us that since we had agreed to go back to Japan 'voluntarily' we would not be treated as harshly as the people who had decided to stay. It was hoped that others upon witnessing the preferred treatment we were receiving would change their minds. I am ashamed to say that some did.

"I can honestly say that I wish we had stayed. It is a wish that never goes away. It lingers and lingers deep down inside me and sometimes when I sigh it comes out as a whimper. My heart bleeds for our acquaintances who were sent to places like New Denver to work in the lumber camps and for others like my father's brother and his family who were placed in boxcars and herded off to Alberta to work on the sugar beet fields. I wish I could have gone with them, lived with them, worked with them, suffered with them, and died with them.

"Instead we eventually ended up in Greenwood for a short time before we were returned to Vancouver for deportation. In spite of our so-called preferred treatment we were not even treated like human beings. They just wanted to get rid of us. We had been degraded to the status of farm animals being sent to the slaughterhouse. That made it easier for one human being to maltreat another. We did our best not to smell of the cattle dung that had been hastily swept from our stalls at the Exhibition grounds.

"Who could ever forget such inhumane treatment? I am not a poet, but I wrote a poem. It was an outpouring of empathy. I started writing it on tiny scraps of paper in a dingy, crowded hole on the derelict ship bound for Japan. I'm not ashamed to say that I shed a tear or two while I was writing it. It was cathartic; the words just flowed like molten lava pent up within a trembling volcano. By the time we got to Japan it was partly finished. I have rewritten, modified, updated and extended it several times since then. I became the embodiment of every Canadian who had to endure the sting of being called 'a good for nothing Jap'.

"Poor Penny, born in the midst of such misery! During my visit I recall asking her how her family was treated. She visibly wilted before my very eyes like a fragile flower under the hot sun, hung her head and quietly responded as if sharing a shameful secret: 'Not good'. That was all she said; her body language spoke for her. 'I am so sorry,' I commiserated at the time. I can still see her sitting despairingly on a folding metallic chair staring off into space with a withered look on her face, a sensitive and beautiful face that unfortunately had been too often marred by the racist slur 'Jap' uttered like a malicious slap, and then – poor little thing – being forced to impotently grimace and... *turn the other cheek*. She looked so forlorn, so vulnerable, so small, so solitary. Someone with a compassionate heart and empathetic soul needed to give her a warm embrace, a great big bear-hug. Someone! But alack, I just sat there... and the moment passed.

"The poem kept evolving with the passing years. Each rewriting was therapeutic. I kept it to myself until the year before my father passed away. When I showed it to my Dad he read it with bowed head and heavy heart. He showed it to my mother who sadly said, 'We should have stayed.' It made him weep. He placed it in the black lacquered cabinet that served as a Buddhist shrine in our home. As far as I know it is still in there. I know it by heart. It is called: 'Born Canadian'."

They did not trust me…
                    In the dread of night
Covered by sheets of darkness
They took my family
My home
My years of toil
And stripped me naked
To the soul
                    Still trembling in the spotlight
Cast upon flimsy suitcases
Hastily stuffed full of questions
Anxieties and dreadful anticipations
                                        They tested me
With silent train rides
And hostile eyes
Filled with loathing and contempt
For the pure and innocent
                            They said
Worthless
Undeserving aliens
When little children cried
With hope still in their hearts
They placed dog tags in their hands
And sent them to the compound
Where I heard a Good Samaritan say
Pity those little ones
Whose identity has been stripped away
With their pride
And self-esteem
                    Who will pray for them
When in the harsh mining camps
The lonely sugar beet fields
The crude lumber barracks
They lie exposed?
                    These simple human beings
Silent and stolid
Herded here and there
In frightened camps
With no regard

They tested me
With years of quiet pain
Disdain
Nasty names with the cruel weight of guilt
For crimes committed elsewhere
By other people
And layered upon my conscience
Like a confession
With each vicious verdict
Reserved for those without rights
Without moral support from religious quarters
With the sway of majority government
Suffocating every breath
Did I struggle along
In this unsolicited tragedy
                                    They tested me
With probing questions
Unsubstantiated data
Hearsay
Innuendo
And indecent assault
Upon my character
                            Checked and rechecked
Filed and cross-filed
Classified
To find me out
To prove beyond a reasonable doubt
Did they scour my humanity
                                        Still
They did not shake my faith
In this magnificent land
Where I find my strength
My sustenance
My hope and vision
Of breathless landscapes
Endless skies
And freedom to believe
                                Here
I have grown

As a seed upon honest soil
And my humble roots have hungered
For every morsel
Of truth and dignity
                    Clung
With desperation
To the substratum of human decency
When the gardener's hoe
Hacked and dissected
And the sunlight of justice
Shone feebly
                    In this existential crucible
Where I have grown old
With intrinsic patriotism
And infinite patience
While the shadow of doubt
Disappeared
                    In the clear light
Of authentic reality
Someone important nodded
When I said
                    I am Canadian
I was born Canadian
I am proud to be Canadian
I can be no other…
                    Trust me."

PART TEN

EPILOGUE

Dare to share
If you really care.

CHAPTER ONE

"Trust, how it can fill one with feelings of worthiness and significance in the eyes of one's fellowman. Without it what is there? Suspicion, fear, insecurity and doubt." The old man nodded his head sadly as old memories coursed through the cellular memory of his withered old body bringing a slight reddish flush to his face.

"Ah, it is amazing how imminent death makes one so lucid," Tutomu remarked to himself. "It refreshes the memory with old thoughts that have a certain relevancy that keeps them current. To be truthful, I thought I had said enough, that I was finished, but there is something more I'd like to share with you, something that happened a long time ago, back in '45, less than three years after I arrived from the land of my birth, Canada. What was a Canadian like me doing there?" Tutomu asked, shaking his head as if in disbelief that such a thing could have happened. "In Nagasaki of all places!" he added in exasperation. "I should not have even been there, but nevertheless, there I was as if – as if there was some purpose in it." He paused, nodded sagely to his audience, and drew in a desperate breath so deep that it seemed as if he was on the verge of exhaling a lifetime of stale air that had been suffocating his soul. "There is nothing like a good deep breath," he commented. "What is more important than breathing?" he asked as if justifying his actions while hyperventilating. He stared out expectantly at his omnipresent audience looking for some reaction.

"Ha," a mischievous grin appeared on his face, "So you caught me breathing again!" he joked, and laughed hilariously. When his mirth subsided he leaned forward and said, "As I was saying... what was I saying?" A look of momentary confusion dulled the clarity of his vision. He paused to collect his thoughts. "I might have mentioned it in passing some time ago," he continued in a serious tone, "but it bears repeating because important lessons still need to be learned – otherwise, God forbid, it could happen again." Tutomu pulled his pillows further upright behind him on his hospital bed. "It could happen again!" he repeated in a louder voice sitting upright on the bed. He wore a white cotton gown that was open at the back, and the tubes dangling from his body gave him the appearance of a living puppet.

"I have always kept this matter to myself because it was so deeply personal and politically incorrect to air such views in post-war Japan. The war had to be sanitized so that, as one protester aptly put it, 'war could continue to be glorified by the warmongers', but all of us survivors just wanted to get on with our lives and to put the past behind us. Still, as you know, the past is not behind us; it is a valuable lesson that lives on through us.

"Like I said before," the old man reiterated, "I have been somewhat reluctant to share personal experiences – but like a cousin of mine liked to say, 'We must dare to share if we really care'." Tutomu sagged back against his upright pillows and whispered, "*Nagai koto – neh*?" which he occasionally mumbled under his breath as if to remind himself of the relentlessness of time. Even though so many years had passed that it seemed like another lifetime the old man was resolute: "It is never too late," he said with quiet determination, "Never!"

* * *

In a long lifetime of forgettable moments, there was one unforgettable experience that Tutomu had shared with his friend, Takehashi-san, when they were considered to be pampered students helping out with the war effort on the outskirts of Nagasaki, a busy coaling station and shipbuilding center on the western shores of Kyushu. Tutomu and his friend were assigned to work in a factory where the interior finishing of ship's cabins and living quarters were prefabricated. As young students they were required to help out on the assembly lines at a time when labor was in very short supply as nearly every eligible male over eighteen had been conscripted into the army by overzealous generals with delusions of grandeur.

They were both there, slaving away in that sweatshop during the summer of '45. "August the ninth," Tutomu reflected, "three days after Hiroshima." How could he ever forget? He and his friend Takehashi-san had both been there in that flimsy metal building on that August day when the occasional drone of airplanes was heard as they flew overhead on their way to victory and the glory of Imperial Japan. They had no way of knowing at that time that those planes were actually American bombers and that Japan was actually losing the war! The thought was unthinkable. The Japanese people were descendants from a divine race; just like the Emperor they were invincible.

"The Generals told us we were invincible," Tutomu stated with a laconic grin, "to keep our spirits up, I suppose. We did not know any better at the time. I was just standing there at the assembly line minding my own business when someone shouted 'Bansai!' when they heard the far-off drone of an unknown aircraft. No one knew that the Imperial Airforce was all but non-existent at that time. It was not one of the Emperor's planes. It was actually a U.S. Superfortress B-29 bomber!"

In retrospect sometimes things often take on a dream-like quality, but this particular dream always turned into a nightmare, a real nightmare. "Yes, yes, I understand," Tutomu reminded his audience, "General MacArthur said that even in the short run it saved lives, and in the long run it weighed so heavily upon the collective conscience of the free world that vast amounts of aid poured into war-torn Japan, and like a miracle Japan rose from the iridescent ashes of two atomic bombs like a bionic phoenix with U-238 in its veins. An economic revival began that made many cagey entrepreneurs ridiculously rich, especially those who, by happenstance or quirk of fate, could speak good English.

"The American occupiers rationalized all of this behavior by saying they needed to build up Japan as a bulwark against the demonic evils of Communism, and they wasted many precious lives in Korea and Vietnam afterwards justifying the rationale behind their *rationalizations*; it was a game of strategy the Generals loved to play. It justified their existence and gave new meaning to Darwin's notion of survival of the fittest in military terms.

"It was not the survival of the fittest at Nagasaki. It was 'survival of the unfortunate', as Takehashi phrased it at the time. Never in our most horrendous dreams had we witnessed such utter hopelessness, such devastation as in the aftermath. Some American once made a popular horror movie called 'Night of the Living Dead'; that title evoked memories of the macabre that self-conscious western reporters, and self-effacing Japanese journalists affected with postwar amnesia, failed almost entirely to communicate to the world at large. There was huge guilt on both sides. Both sides. Neither side really wanted to tell it like it really was. It was easier to pretend that it was somehow justifiable behavior. If you were not there, you missed it.

Somehow a valuable opportunity to learn from our mistakes was squandered."

"It was only a moment, just a tiny moment in the long history of the world. Perhaps one went to the bathroom, blew one's nose, drank down a mouthful of green tea, or just raised one's head to gaze out of the grimy windows that lined the metal walls near the roof. It took just a moment; that is all. Just a moment.

"Whatever eternity is like, I know it can exist in a moment. In a moment the walls blew in and, and – there is a dreadful little word that Christians so love to use? I never could comprehend its precise meaning before. Now I know exactly what it means. The word is 'Hell'. The hills surrounding the port city created a natural bowl-effect that prevented the shock and heat waves from dissipating quickly, as at Hiroshima. As a result the devastation was Hell-on-earth.

"We were lucky because we were on the outskirts and the flimsy walls afforded enough protection to save our miserable lives. But those at the epicenter or anywhere near it evaporated without a trace. It was as if they never existed. They were perhaps, as my good friend Takehashi-san said, 'the lucky ones'. The unlucky ones found themselves in Hell.

"Hell does not discriminate. Age and sex make no difference. It is just like the Christians say: the fire burns and burns and re-burns. It is not like an ordinary fire where the heat burns only once. Radiation burns like an invisible acid that no one knows is there. The pus oozes and oozes and oozes, and whatever skin is left floats on a sea of endless pain.

"Strange as it may seem, there are no colors in Hell except a surreal ashen gray. Reality is an after-image burned into the landscape, an X-ray of something that used to be. In such a wasteland there is no hope. There is no self-deception in Hell.

"The Devil is not red. The Devil is a ghostly apparition reflected in the iridescent ash, an eerie presence as frightening as the emptiness that fills the void with moans and groans that pierce the silence with a kind of anguish that knows no respite.

"There is no redemption. There is no remorse. There is only a facsimile of mankind reduced to his lowest common denominator of existence. It is impossible to believe that this was an act of God or the work of the Devil. Impossible. In Hell there is no self-deception. This was the wrath of Man against his fellow man.

"There is one thing I want to point out to every war-mongering General, Dictator, Prime Minister, President, or King: ONCE YOU HAVE VISITED HELL, IT IS IMPOSSIBLE TO BE ANYTHING BUT A PACIFIST. Remember that."

"Ah, life is a mystery from beginning to end," Tutomu sighed and shifted to a more comfortable position on the bed. "Too bad something like a guidebook on life had not been available; as it is everyone starts from scratch and fumbles along in the dark feeling their way through the Braille that impinges upon the senses like meaning upon a word. What is that saying? Too late smart. A perfect summary of Man's quest for knowledge.

"Ah, but if only I knew at twenty, or even sooner, what I know now, I would not have wasted my life like I did pursuing all those tangible things that I cannot take with me. Someone should have taken me aside and said: 'Hey stupid, you can only take with you what you gave away'. And what is it that I can take with me? Only the persona that I have wasted a lifetime becoming. That is all. I wish I had given away compassion, gratitude, charity, goodness, and love. You know? You can only give away what you have," Tutomu sighed with regret. "You cannot give away what you don't have; consequently most of us just give away the qualities that we embody like greed, selfishness, and fear," he clarified. "If only someone had written a lucid handbook on life that had been compulsory reading in one of my boring Business Administration classes, I would have learned something worthwhile, something that would have given me a different orientation, a different dharmic path, a different karmic destiny, a different life. But life goes on and on, does it not?" Tutomu took a sip of water from the glass on his bedside table and inhaled deeply.

"Now, where was I?" he asked apologetically, gesturing to his imaginary audience with a bony arm so thin it was amazing it could hold the needle-end of the tube that was inserted in it. "Oh yes, there I was in that flimsy building with the grimy windows near the roofline. I can still see those grimy windows in my mind's eye. Funny how you remember incidentals like that.

"After the walls blew in an eternity passed. Out of the debris Takehashi and I miraculously emerged crawling over shattered glass, dead bodies, powdered concrete, and crumpled sheet metal. We staggered to our feet disoriented and in a state of shock, like zombies covered with dust, and began walking toward the epicenter. We walked just like the dead in 'Night of the Living Dead'. We walked toward the epicenter instinctively like homing pigeons, while streams of walking dead filed by in the opposite direction like ghosts in the eerie light where the sun casts a white halo through a fog of ashen-gray smog. We walked toward the epicenter to help – that was it, to help the less fortunate.

"After a while from a sky that once-upon-a-time was crystal clear, a canopy of darksome vapor gathered creating an ominous mood of heightened dread and anxiety. The wails of women and children, charred and seared black by the terrible burning winds that followed, pierced our ears with inhuman sounds of suffering. They cried out for water. 'Water! Water! Water!' Desperate pleading voices... begging!!! Who had water?

"We passed by stagnant pools of water where dying hoards had gathered to sooth their awful burns. The ones on the bottom were drowned by the masses of writhing bodies on top desperate for a drop of cooling water. We did not stop. We kept walking.

"We saw one charred woman with shards of glass painfully impaled into her blood-stained body like porcupine quills. She was attempting to crawl somewhere. We stopped and removed as many of the shards as we could, and then moved on with bloody hands.

"An hysterical mother begged us to stop and help her dig into a mountain of rubble. She could hear the feeble cry of her son from deep inside. 'He is only three,' she wailed, 'Have mercy!' We dug with our bleeding hands until they were raw, but to no avail. After a while the whimpering faded into silence. The mother stared up at the sky and emitted such a mournful screeching sound it shattered the pane of silence into invisible shards of glass that pierced our eardrums.

"And then.... And then, God have mercy! The black rain, as black and opaque as a darksome vision of doom, began to fall. The surreal became a living nightmare. Only in nightmares can such awful things occur, such unimaginable horror! Black rain, black as tar, began to fall like a dreadful shower. Huge black droplets rained down upon us streaking our faces into horrifying masks, as if we were inmates in a purgatory so horrible we needed to frighten each other with ghoulish faces. It was too much! TOO MUCH! It was insanely hilarious. Black rain!

"I laughed hysterically while many went stark-raving mad. They danced about and threw their arms up to the heavens and gave thanks for the pitiful rain. They drank in the filthy liquid with blackened dry lips. We shrank away and watched them flounder about in grotesque herds with their gaping mouths open to the sky and their parched throats gargling with death.

"As if by instinct Takehashi and I covered our heads with our tattered shirts and looked for shelter. We found a loose piece of tin and cowered under it. Black rain and more black rain pelted down upon the tin like a death rattle. To be truthful, the black rain did feel cool and soothing on our blistered skin, and except for a few drops that moistened our lips we did not drink any. Thank God! We found out later that those who drank it or were immersed in it developed ugly purple patches and welts all over their bodies. They suffered horrendously. It was worse than the initial blast of burning gases because it lingered and lingered while their bodies rotted away. It was a new disease no one had anticipated. It destroyed the white blood cells and devastated the immune system, leading to a slow and terrible death. They called it radiation poisoning.

"When the black rain stopped the hot drying winds blew in. There was no respite. In less than an hour the moisture had evaporated leaving a dark stain over the landscape. Takehashi and I left our tin shelter and moved on taking care not to step on the grossly misshapen forms, many with missing body parts, eyes sunken in and fused shut, blackened, bloated, half-nuked bodies that littered the way like unwanted garbage.

"Who could do such an inhuman thing... on purpose? Someone playing god – or the devil? 'God help us!' I whimpered. We moved on for the sake of moving on. We lost track of time. In a living nightmare time moves on with an alarming imperceptivity.

"I noticed Takehashi was weeping. He wept and wept – was it minutes, hours or days? Whenever I looked at him he seemed to be weeping. He did not seem to be aware of it. It seemed natural. Everything felt so hopeless, so utterly hopeless. 'It is best to keep moving,' I said. Somewhere there had to be an exit. Somewhere!

"Have you ever had a nightmare so horrible you just knew it was a dream – but you could not wake up? You keep trying with all your might to wake up. It is an intolerable sensation. You can't stand it, but you have no way out. You feel….

"'Why are you crying?' Takehashi demanded with a frown as if perturbed by my behavior. 'Why do you ask?' I responded. He wiped his eyes with the back of his dirty hands and just stared at me inanely.

"'This is just an unimaginably bad dream,' I kept thinking while plodding along behind Takehashi. 'This is insanity. How could anything like this happen in real life?' I asked with a reasoned modicum of self assurance. 'Soon I will awaken, and find myself safe and secure in my comfortable bed!' This thought gave me a glimmer of hope and kept me sane in the midst of so much madness. It was the one and only explanation that made any sense, at the time. As one of the fortunate survivors I am in retrospect able to verify that it was definitely not a dream, because as we all know: atomic bombs are real!

"There is so much more I could tell you… so much more. But who wants to hear a litany of horror stories? I have been trying to forget them – unfortunately some things are just unforgettable. You have to learn to accept… accept and forgive. Did you get that? I said 'ACCEPT AND FORGIVE'. There is no other way."

Tutomu yawned and slowly rolled his head clockwise and then counterclockwise to loosen up the tension building in his neck and shoulder muscles. He was beginning to feel fatigued but he sat up straighter and glared out at his silent audience. He could see them there sitting on the edge of their seats and straining to catch every single word. How could he deny them? He moistened his lips and continued.

"As we trudged stoically through a surreal scene of utter devastation, Takehashi suddenly paused and remarked with a sense of mounting apprehension, 'There used to be a church, a magnificent Catholic Cathedral somewhere around here!' How he knew that was beyond me.

"'I don't see anything,' I said, my senses piqued by his expectant tone as we stumbled along. For some reason I shivered as if caught in a sudden chill as we slowly moved on in silence, mindful of the utter desolation that surrounded us. The air was dry and iridescent with fine particles of black and white ash. It filled the sky and whooshed in and out of our lungs. Tiny drops of perspiration beaded our foreheads, dribbled over our eyebrows and seeped like acid into our bleary eyes. We squinted and rubbed our eyes with the backs of our blackened hands. The mascara made us look like ghouls. 'You look scary,' I said to Takehashi. 'So do you,' he replied.

"We sat down back to back on a powdery mound and rested for a moment blinking our eyes to wash away the sting of perspiration. When our vision cleared we gazed about attempting to get our bearings. 'Look over there!' Takehashi exclaimed as if awestruck, pointing toward the hills behind where I sat. I turned, and my breath exhaled as if into a vacuum of incredulity. It left me breathless! I beheld a scene that remains indelibly carved into my memory like an engraved etching upon a leaden plate.

"There on a distant knoll, stark against the whitish sky, was a charred spire that reached up to the heavens like a petrified pair of hands, hands desperately clasped together as if in prayer. I felt light-headed. I could hardly breathe. What a tragic reminder of the impermanence of all things worldly! There, on the fringe of a vast wasteland of devastation: Praying Hands! Was it a sign?

"'That used to be a beautiful Cathedral!' Takehashi despaired as he dropped to his knees and crossed himself. 'I once took communion in that Church,' he added as I dropped to my knees beside him. We stared at the blackened remains of the grandest Church of God in all of Japan.

"After a prolonged silence I murmured, with a dry lump in my throat, 'That used to be the Church of-of a distant relative of mine... Saint Paul Miki, one of the Martyrs of Japan.' I gazed up at the heavens and whispered, 'Blessed be the Kakure who have passed on here before us.' And then amidst the angst and confusion an immense sorrow descended upon us that stilled the heart and withered the soul with a sickness unto death.

"'God have mercy on us all,' Takehashi added solemnly.

"I respectfully murmured, 'Ah-men,' as we rose with a deep sense of foreboding and slowly made our way toward a distant cluster of tent shelters. 'Who would have thought,' I muttered between breaths as we hastened along, 'that when Francis Xavier landed at Kagoshima, it would eventually come to this?' As soon as I asked the question I felt a tingling run up my spine that made me quicken my pace.

"Takehashi remained silent for about fifty paces and then he soberly replied, 'You mean Saint Francis.' No sooner had he uttered the word 'Saint', when a gust of wind swept up a cloud of white ash that powdered us from head to foot like a baptismal dousing.

"'Perhaps he heard you,' I said."

CHAPTER TWO

"**W**e spent a lifetime in Hell helping the less fortunate to survive, especially the children and babies. It was worse than a death sentence because a death sentence is final. Who knows how or when this will end or what the ramifications will be? All I know is that we were very lucky because our eyeballs had not exploded, and our skin was not charred and peeling relentlessly, and our lungs were not burnt out from searing gases, and even the hair on our heads had not been singed to a frazzle. Miraculously we were still recognizable as human beings, real living, breathing human beings. We were perhaps the luckiest people in Hell.

"In Hell time and space are synonymous. Einstein, as usual, was correct; it really is space-time, not time and space. When there is no exit, space becomes a measure of time and vice versa. Duration is all there is, personified as endurance. Months passed, although it seemed like a lifetime, and then the 'occupiers' began to arrive to help with the relief effort.

"In war there is usually a winner and a loser. To the victor go the spoils of war – and to the loser? Loss of face, loss of pride, loss of dignity, loss of self-worth, loss of all the intangibles that make winning so important. And in a country like Japan it was doubly humiliating to be not only defeated, but occupied by the victor and have to deal bowed-head-to-face with the winner, with the humility and grace as was befitting the progeny of the divine.

"Perhaps we were only receiving what we had given away: it was karma. 'And these things too will pass,' I said reverently to those beyond hope, to those to whom passing was the only thing that could be looked forward to, passing away with dignity, serenity, and acceptance. After all this was 'occupied Japan', and they had lost the war. It was more than enough to change even those veterans with battle-hardened notions about the glories of war, and give them a pacifist's view of the world order. It was indeed a bitter lesson hard-learned.

"I often find myself speaking about my countrymen as 'they', as if I was not one of them, as if I were somehow different. It is a curious quirk of my fate that makes me who I am: a Japanese-Canadian living in the mysterious Orient with the ability to speak English. It defined the particular path I traveled, paved it with gold bricks one could say. However, as everyone knows, all that glitters is not gold; but in postwar Japan I was the golden-boy because it is important, even these days in the hardcore capitalistic world of business, to be able to speak good English.

"Knowing English afforded me the unique opportunity to gain intimate knowledge of the humorous aspects of the occupier's psyche. As a manner of relaxing, they frequently would sidle up to me and speak to me as if I were a confidante. They could tell me stuff they probably would not share with their own comrades, just to get it off their chests. One good thing about smoking in those days was that it allowed you to just stand around and 'shoot the shit'. I shot a lot of shit and smoked my share of American cigarettes.

"Surrounded by so much unavoidable misery it was necessary to interject as much levity into the situation as possible in order to take one's mind off an absolutely humorless reality. What intrigued me the most was the degree to which sex was considered to be a topic of great amusement and hilarity. Perhaps it was my own prurient interests that emboldened the bold to share their jokes and ribald stories with me.

"One particular incident remains fixed in my mind even after all these years. It involved a young American naval officer; his particular rank is not important. What is important is that he was usually quite considerate toward me in spite of my youth, and demonstrated the kind of understanding that indicated a wisdom beyond his years. It was from this American naval officer that I learned a great deal about women in general and their sexual habits – providing the information thus gleaned was accurate. One of the stories that most intrigued me had to do with the number sixty-nine. I was good with numbers; that is probably why I remembered it." Tutomu smiled shyly at his vast audience and felt a tinge of embarrassment as he recalled the story.

"One drab evening the naval officer sidled up to me with a bemused look on his face and asked, 'Ever done sixty-nine?'.

'Sixty-nine? What is that?' I responded.

'It is one of my favorite sexual techniques.'

'What about the other sixty-eight?' I asked my curiosity mounting.

'Six and nine,' he emphasized, ignoring my question, 'or as the French say, seex et neuf. Get it?'

'Seex et neuf, you say,' I repeated. 'C'est bon!'

"He smiled at my attempt at French and continued. 'What I like about the Japanese people is that they are very clean. They have ofurros everywhere. Did I pronounce that right?'

"I winced and replied, 'Just say baths,' and steeled myself to hear another offensive joke about the infamous geisha.

"Instead, the American said, 'The Japanese women like to keep their entire bodies clean, but in England,' he stated matter-of-factly as if he were the world's leading authority on the matter, 'the women are not very clean from the waist down.' He made a face and stuck out his tongue, 'and you know in sixty-nine cleanliness in that particular area is very important.' He paused to let me reflect upon this astounding revelation.

"It was not the role of the occupied to be argumentative, but I surprised myself by saying, 'On the contrary, the English strike me as being very fastidious and the English women in particular to be very hygienic.'

'Believe me, boy,' the naval officer replied condescendingly, 'I speak from personal experience.'

'Ah-so,' I acquiesced, giving way to a man of much greater worldly wisdom.

'Ahh, but the French women are the most accommodating. They are... what was that word you used?'

'Fastidious.'

'Yes, very fastidious about the cleanliness of their private parts, and that is very important because as you know the distance between a woman's genitalia and her rectum is about this far.' He held up his thumb and forefinger to indicate the size of the gap.

'I guess you would know,' I murmured suddenly feeling somewhat embarrassed for some unaccountable reason.

'Give or take half an inch,' the American continued authoritatively. 'And you know, men should be equally as fastidious.'

'Of course.'

'The cleanest part of my body is my dick.'

'Your dick?'

'That is slang for penis.'

'Is it?' I replied and laughed in spite of myself. It struck me that there was something indelicate about this macho brand of humor that might be distasteful to women in general – therein lay its puritanical appeal.

"The naval officer slapped me on the back and said, 'You know, you're all right. You're just like one of us,' and then he paused, reflected a moment, and in the most contrite tone of voice that sounded almost apologetic, made an off-hand remark that has reverberated in my mind ever since. He said, 'The most important thing this damn war has taught me is that a human being is a human being... is a human being. It really is just that simple. Isn't it incredible how profoundly ignorant we can all be?'

"The comment caught me completely off guard. I stood there dumbfounded by the speed with which this naval officer could shift from the ridiculous to the sublime. It was totally unexpected from one so... so American.

"The naval officer stepped back, fished a pack of cigarettes from his shirt pocket, offered me one which I humbly accepted, lit both cigarettes, inhaled deeply, and asked with a mischievous smile while holding up his thumb and forefinger. 'Did you know that the distance between heaven and hell is only that much?'

"It was a rhetorical question. I could have laughed and let it pass. Instead, without hesitation I replied, 'Yes, and it is up to us pacifists to mediate on behalf of the maintenance of that precious gap.'

"I can't explain it, but he just puffed on that cigarette and stared at me inanely as if I had just said something cosmologically astounding. Thereafter he always treated me with a special kind of deference. I don't know why. I understand that many years later, to his everlasting credit, he became one of those original long-haired pacifists who traveled around North America preaching: 'Make love not war.'"

The strain of sitting up and lecturing before such a vast audience took its toll upon Tutomu. He flattened out his pillows, and just before he lay back he said, "Intermission. Take a break. I'll be back. You can count on it." He snuggled into the pillows fetus-style and slept as soundly as he had slept in days. He snored as rhythmically as a cross-cut saw slicing its way through a cedar log and awoke when his bladder indicated that it was time to get up.

It was after eight-thirty when the old man shuffled back from the bathroom and reinserted the connecting ends of the intravenous tubes into his own arms. He refused to use the bed pan. He was not an invalid – yet. He fluffed the pillows up, leaned back, and composed himself before the impatient audience. The intermission had taken longer than he had expected. He rubbed his hands together in preparation. "I'll tell them about the game," he thought, "Yes, that was an important by-product of the occupation."

"Remember the naval officer?" he began. "One of his passions that he and his buddies left as a legacy of the occupation was their love of base-se-bowl, as the Japanese say. It may seem trite to point out, but there is much more to baseball than may be evident to the average fan. Baseball, by its structure and format as a team sport, demands fairness. Even in occupied Japan the game demanded fairness. When a Nihongee became a baseball player and he made a great play, he was recognized as being a great player. Are you beginning to understand why baseball became so popular in Japan?

"Like I said, baseball demands fairness. The role of the home-plate umpire in calling balls and strikes fairly is crucial, and the roles of the base umpires require strict objectivity because the fans as well as the players can see every call, and favoritism by an umpire just cannot be tolerated; it undermines the integrity of the game, and the Americans just will not stand for that because it is their National game.

"Nine men are strategically scattered over a large playing field, and each in turn must step up to the plate and face the music. There is very little body contact to inflame the situation. Every great play or miserable error is on display. Skill and grace under pressure are paramount. There is no place to hide. It is indeed a test of character. However, playing the game well does not always lead to the ultimate goal: winning. Luck is important and is openly catered to. One swing of the bat in the bottom of the ninth inning can turn pending victory into despair. As Yogi Berra once said: 'It ain't over until the fat lady sings'.

"What can you say about the people who play baseball with such passion? They have a noble sense of fair play. There is humility, patience, understanding, and compassion woven into the fabric of every uniform. Under every baseball cap is a rugged individual who knows that it is the emphasis on skill, good sportsmanship, and fairness that has made America's National sport into Japan's most popular game. I am glad they introduced that game to the Japanese; it gives them something in common."

Tutomu smiled as if pleased with his presentation and sagged back against the pillows. The slightest exertion seemed to easily fatigue him. He coughed and said, "Come back tomorrow. I'll still be here."

In the morning the head nurse brought in black coffee and breakfast on a beige-colored melamine serving tray. "And how are you this morning?" she asked cheerfully. She had taken a shine to the old fella in spite of his occasional obstinacies. It was reinforced by his personal opinion that she was the most "elegant nurse" he had ever seen.

"I feel rested," Tutomu replied as he poured skim milk over the hot cereal.

"I'll be back to check on you around noon," she said as she took her leave.

"Don't worry about me," Tutomu asserted feeling a little embarrassed by the extra attention that she was bestowing upon him. "That young Doctor takes good care of me."

After he finished his breakfast the old man returned to his audience. "I'm back," he announced. "Didn't I say I'd still be here? Well here I am." He removed the breakfast tray from the bed and set it on the side table. "Now where was I?" He cupped his right ear and thought he heard someone say, "Base-se-bowl."

"Ah, yes," he recalled, "baseball. You know yet another admirable quality the occupiers had was their penchant for pulling for the underdog. This is perhaps, in my opinion, the singular quality the Japanese most admire about Americans. Of course when the overseas relief workers first arrived they were shocked by the vast scene of devastation and unending misery that greeted them. Who wouldn't be? Their first reaction was usually not very heroic; it was to hold fast to their conditioned response. It was basically a self-righteous – perhaps that is too strong a word – let's just say it was simply a matter of placing the blame. This seemed to be of the utmost importance to most of them, a matter of conscience. They felt a lot better about helping with the relief effort and witnessing such a vast scene of human suffering, knowing it was not their fault. The host nation was responsible for the tragedy which befell them. It seemed that during this initial stage they never tired of explaining how the dropping of the atomic bombs was entirely a pragmatic matter; it was done only to end the war and save lives – there were no other less flattering motives. One Army Medic pointed out to me that if they had not done it the stubborn Japanese people with their samurai mentality would probably have fought to the last man to protect their Emperor and beloved homeland. To hear him tell it, it was almost as if they had done us a favor. I find it personally very difficult to be completely objective about this matter, but I must admit there could be an element of logic in what he said.

"Like the naval officer said, 'a human being is a human being is a human being,' and the longer they worked with us the more they were able to sympathize with the unfortunate victims of the aftermath and empathize with the situation. There are many examples of this I could relate but two should suffice to illustrate this point. One sensitive army volunteer confided to me just after throwing up from the putrid stench of the stagnant latrines, mounds of rotting corpses, and endless streams of oozing pus from the living dead: 'You did not deserve this! No one deserves this!' You had to be there to truly appreciate that remark. An American scientist, a middle-aged fellow who wore bifocal glasses, told me he had been sent there to 'monitor the effects of the experiment', as he put it. He whispered to me as if in confidence, 'This must never be allowed to happen again. I hope they understand, never again!' His voice, bolstered by an undercurrent of exasperation, rose to a crescendo as he added, 'If only the people back home knew what we have done!'

"Views such as these may seem to be unseemingly melodramatic – even today, but at that time it took considerable courage to stand up and be counted, when it would have been so easy to acquiesce and say nothing, like I did. I cannot say I was a coward, but neither was I heroic. When you are young and easily intimidated by those with loud and arrogant voices, you naturally tend to look up to those in control who pull the strings that make the puppets dance. I was a very good dancer in those days. Now that I am on my deathbed I realize that the truth rarely is spoken with an arrogant and self-righteous tone, but resonates with humility and grace. Just listen carefully, and you can usually hear the truth when it is spoken.

CHAPTER THREE

At noon the head nurse dropped in just as she said she would. Practically everyone referred to her simply as the "head nurse", but she had a pretty name; it was Kinko. She was a meticulous young lady.   Not really young – to become head nurse required a considerable amount of experience. But compared to the old man she was, relatively speaking, young. She wore her hair long which was unusual for nurses for sanitary reasons. Her hair was always neatly brushed and looked so soft and shiny the old man was often tempted to reach out and touch it. She had a long nose for a Japanese which in concert with her long hair and slender build made her look quite elegant, even in that starched white nursing uniform she wore so proudly.

"You look extra beautiful in the noonday light," Tutomu remarked and waited to see what effect the flattery would have upon the nurse.

It had the desired effect. She blushed. A pink glow came to her cheeks as she busily moved from one side of the bed to the other straightening the bedding and tidying up whatever needed tidying. "You don't look so bad yourself," she responded.

"How is everything?" They both looked toward the door as the Doctor entered and walked to the foot of the bed to examine the old man's chart. "Hmm," he intoned. "It says here you're still insisting on going to the bathroom unassisted."

"I'm no baby. I don't need a diaper!" the old man snorted indignantly.

"He is doing remarkably well," Kinko chimed in, supporting her patient.

"Wonderful," the Doctor said cheerfully as he moved up alongside the nurse.

"Doesn't she look beautiful in the noonday light?" Tutomu asked hoping to get a positive reaction from the Doctor. Kinko blushed from head to foot but all they could see was her smiling face. Unknown to the old man was the repressed romantic interests of a not-so-young therapeutic nurse that blossomed forth unseen and unappreciated every time the young Doctor appeared in her presence. It was there submerged in the reticent behavior of a mature woman whose heart palpitated with longing and whose breath had to be controlled by a professional understanding of such personal matters. "Pay him no mind," she said calmly.

The Doctor looked at the head nurse approvingly. "Tutomu is right, as usual," he said, "You do look beautiful."

Kinko's face seemed to flush several degrees above normal. She brought her hands up to her cheeks to cover her secret enchantment. "Pay him no mind," she repeated as nonplussed as possible and quickly turned about as if to adjust the old man's pillows.

"Just leave them; they're fine," the old man protested. He glanced up toward the young Doctor and requested in a serious tone. "If you have a minute there is something important that I would like to ask you."

"Ask away," the young Doctor replied cordially.

"I was wondering," Tutomu began slowly, "upon the event of my demise, if you would do one last favor for me?" He paused to give the Doctor time to consider his vague request.

"Anything, just name it," the Doctor replied reaching forward to touch the old man's right hand.

"Would you mind taking over as President of my International Peace Foundation? As you know it is a charitable organization dedicated to looking after any surviving victims of the atomic bombings, and to the promotion of world peace. Everything is running smoothly thanks to my good friend, Takehashi-san – you know the old guy who periodically drops off books for me to read? He is Vice-President. It won't take much of your time." His dark eyes were glued expectantly upon the young Doctor's face.

The young Doctor was stunned into silence. The old man had mentioned some time ago that he was looking for a President for his Peace Foundation. 'Do you know of anyone?' he had asked timidly at the time. 'I'm afraid not,' the Doctor had replied while scratching his head. The old man had just stared at him and smiled.

"What a great honor that would be!" Kinko spontaneously reacted in support of the idea. She gazed admiringly at the young Doctor.

"It-it would indeed b-be a privilege to carry on your good work," the young Doctor stammered overcome with deep-felt humility.

"To the best of his ability," Kinko tagged on as if reading the Doctor's mind.

"That takes care of the President," the old man gleefully announced confirming the acceptance.   However, our current Secretary is retiring next month.   Bless her soul, she deserves a rest. Shall I appoint you Secretary?" the old man asked turning to face the head nurse.

"Of course," the young Doctor replied on behalf of the nurse.   "I can't think of a more competent person."

"I – I..." the nurse stammered modestly.

The young Doctor reached over and gave the head nurse a compassionate pat on the left shoulder as she nodded her consent.

"What a team!" the old man pronounced rising upright on his bed with enthusiasm.   "I shall arrange for my lawyers to get all the papers ready for your signatures."   He clasped his hands together in a prayerful fashion, looked up at the young Doctor and head nurse and quietly said, "Thank you, thank you very much."

* * *

The audience could not be kept waiting.   As soon as the nurse and Doctor left his room the old man heaved a sigh of relief.   That business relating to the Foundation had been bothering him for some time.   And now it was taken care of.   "What a lovely couple they would make," he thought, "I wonder if the young Doctor likes her?" In some ways the head nurse reminded him of the tall Canadian nurse he had encountered during the relief effort at Nagasaki.   It was probably her long hair and slender build.   Anyway that is what he wanted to share with the audience, his encounter with that nurse.

Tutomu peered out into the vastness of his invisible audience and did his best to tune into their vibes.   "There is just one more example that had slipped my mind earlier that I think you'd be interested in," he began.   "It has to do with a Red Cross volunteer, a nurse.   This was prior to '67 so Canadians did not have a distinctive symbol like the red maple leaf that they have now to identify themselves.   At first I thought she was British because of the Union Jack on her bag, but as soon as she started talking I knew she was Canadian because of her accent.

"The encounter took place immediately after a new arrival had once again felt the need to justify the dropping of the atomic bombs, and I had interjected succinctly in English: 'I understand. It was done to save lives.'

"The Red Cross nurse who had overheard me, sauntered up to the tent where I was standing and sympathetically remarked: 'You would have thought that one unholy atomic blast would have sufficed, eh?'

"It was a very good question, I thought, but remained silent. She sidled up to me and spoke as if she was glad of the opportunity to share her thoughts with a Nihongee who understood English.

'You know these Americans can justify just about anything,' she confided.

'They can?' I asked surprised by her attitude.

'I am a pacifist,' she said as if apologizing for a weakness.

'So am I,' I replied.

This response encouraged her to ask, 'Was all this necessary?'

'Well, according to our American friends, the U.S. President, Truman, apparently had issued an ultimatum: either surrender unconditionally or else! The Japanese wanted to surrender, but not unconditionally. It was our fault entirely. All of this could have been avoided if Japan had immediately acquiesced to his demands.'

"The nurse listened attentively. 'You have been appropriately brainwashed,' she declared. 'The U.S. President had many other options. He knew Japan was on the brink of collapse. Food staples like rice and soy beans were exhausted, the air-force and navy were non-existent; all that was left was a rag-tag army of poorly equipped and demoralized homeland defenders. And most importantly, the Emperor *wanted* to surrender in spite of the stubbornness of some of his Generals. The situation was desperate. Overtures were hastily being made to the Europeans and other Allied powers regarding conditions of surrender. After Okinawa fell, the Japanese islands could easily have been surrounded and held captive. There was no need for haste or a perilous invasion. Time was on the Allies side. Japan was a sitting duck ready for the plucking. As I said, the much maligned Emperor *wanted to surrender*. A lot of innocent lives could have been saved. It was a no-brainer! Of course, in retrospect, the conscience-stricken Americans would have you and the world-at-large believe otherwise. All that business about *saving lives* is just a pre-meditated excuse, a rationalization for using the atomic bomb.'

'Seems to makes sense,' I confessed, and then added, 'but by acting decisively at least Truman kept Stalin out of the picture.'

'He had other options,' she repeated. 'It is a grave moral issue in the West where ethical matters are the foundation of justice.'

'I agree, it is a grave moral issue. Let me apologize on behalf of my countrymen. Japan is deeply sorry and remorseful. Like the Emperor said: *We must bear the unbearable.*'

'I don't think you quite understand what I am saying. I am saying that the U.S. President had other options... that he did not have to drop those dreadful bombs!' She paused and stared at me as if to say: *How can you be so dense?*

'But it ended the war,' I replied.

"The nurse shook her head sadly as if disappointed by my response. She started to walk away, and then unexpectedly she stopped and came back. She stood directly in front of me and glared boldly down into my face. I must have had some pathetic look about me that emboldened the occupiers to speak frankly.

'Not only did he have other options because the war was nearly at an end and Japan was virtually defeated,' she lowered her voice and looked around to see if anyone was within earshot. 'Forget that baloney about saving lives – it was just the opposite. They had to drop those bombs before the war ended, while they still had an excuse. It was purely vindictive, vindication for Pearl Harbor!'

"It took real courage for her to say that, albeit to a nobody like me. It encouraged me to respond in kind. I said, 'I have heard other Japanese whispering something to that effect amongst themselves. No one dares voice such an opinion to the occupiers. We are the losers, our opinions are worthless – but someone like you...' I left the phrase dangling there while I looked up at the nurse sympathetically. She was very tall for a woman. When she remained silent I continued, 'I would advise you to keep such dangerous opinions to yourself, for your own good,' I suggested compassionately.

"She stared at me wide-eyed as if in disbelief, turned about and left without saying another word. Somehow I had become the object of her contempt. I wanted to run after her and apologize. What had I done to offend her? It was like the Emperor had said; we had to bear the unbearable."

CHAPTER FOUR

Some painful memories just seem to linger on and fester until the injustice is brought out into the sunlight and exposed to the light of reason and common sense. Sometimes it seems as if the greater the political injustice, the greater the reluctance to admit to it, and deal with it. Such are the foibles of socio-political reality. In Canada, the Liberal governments, whenever they had the opportunity to correct the errors and injustices of past Liberal governments, were loath to admit that Liberals could make such grievous errors. 'It was the law', they said, 'not us'. And so they did nothing. It was much easier for a Progressive Conservative government with the support of the New Democratic Party to right a Liberal wrong.

It is very difficult to get Federal governments to admit to an error, let alone correct one. It is even more difficult when money is mentioned. In 1984 in order to appease a vociferous group of Japanese Canadians seeking redress, the Mulroney government frugally offered them a token group settlement of six million dollars on a take-it or leave-it basis. It was left. In 1986 the respected accounting firm of Price Waterhouse revealed that the economic losses incurred by Japanese-Canadians for wartime property confiscated, was conservatively estimated to be in excess of $443 million.

On August 10th, 1988 US Republican President, Ronald Reagan, (with whom Brian Mulroney sang "when Irish eyes are smiling...") smiled for the cameras as he signed redress bill HR 442 into law compensating each re-located Japanese-American, whose west-coast property had been held in trust and returned after the war, with a token payment of $20,000 as an apologetic gesture. It set a standard of magnanimity that their northern neighbors who had treated their Japanese citizens a lot worse, would find difficult to emulate.

Across the 49th parallel in Ottawa on August 27th, 1988, after years of discussions, a redress settlement was finally hammered out after seventeen hours of intense negotiations. (The negotiators were sworn to secrecy and the government insisted that the documents be held in secret for the next twenty years – until 2008.) It was agreed that each individual Japanese-Canadian directly wronged was to be given a token compensation of $21,000. Unlike their American counterparts the west-coast properties in British Columbia had been confiscated rather than held in trust, and sold to pay for the internment of the dispossessed, and consequently could not be returned. It was the government's recognition of a longstanding injustice, along with the public apology, and the conviction that such a travesty could not happen again in Canada that made up for the lost property.

Aside from individual compensation the Redress agreement provided for the following:

(a) A $12 million fund for rebuilding community infra-structure,

(b) $24 million for a Canadian Race Relations Foundation,

(c) Provision of Canadian citizenship for those wrongly deported in 1946 (after the war had ended) and their descendents,

(d) Provision of pardons for those brave few who protested against the War Measures Act and were incarcerated. (In July of 1988 with input from concerned Japanese citizens the *War Measures Act* had been repealed and replaced with the *Emergencies Act* which made it much more difficult for such injustices to occur in the future.)

The official copy of the Redress document was signed by the Prime Minister on September 22nd, 1988. Years of hard work and perseverance by the National Association of Japanese Canadians led by President Art Miki, had at long last brought a semblance of closure to an injustice perpetrated by the government upon a small visible minority living on the West coast of Canada during and after WWII.

Shortly after the Redress document was signed, Tutomu read about it in a Japanese newspaper. He could have missed it if his friend Takehashi had not called and told him about it. It is not often that something that is said in Ottawa makes the Tokyo news. When he first read it Tutomu found it difficult to breathe. His first thoughts were about his mother and father. "This is for them," he thought, "too bad they are deceased, but better forty-four years late, than never."

The Prime Minister of Canada was quoted verbatim. "Nearly half a century ago, in the crisis of wartime, the Government of Canada wrongfully incarcerated, seized the property, and disenfranchised thousands of citizens of Japanese ancestry...." The message vibrated in every cell in Tutomu's body. Who would have thought such a thing would actually come to pass? It was a sign of a resilient Democracy, a sign of conscience and moral maturity. Honorable MPs like the Minister of State, Lucien Bouchard, had diligently worked behind the scenes in parliament persuading and egging-on reluctant members. It was a sensitive issue with many war veterans and those brainwashed by Hollywood movies and cartoons depicting the "Japs" as untrustworthy, inscrutable, buck-toothed, slant-eyed, near-sighted enemy-aliens responsible for the so-called "Day of Infamy". It was because of the support of many open-minded and conscientious members of the Progressive Conservative Party, along with the urging of the New Democratic Party, that Canada's eighteenth Prime Minister, Brian Mulroney, was able to achieve his greatest moment on the humanitarian stage of Canadian history.

He rose up patriotically in the Commons like a truly great statesman, stalwartly bolstered and supported by Mr. Ed Broadbent, leader of the New Democratic Party, and said: "Error is an ingredient of humanity. So too is apology and forgiveness. We all learn from personal experiences that, as inadequate as apologies are, they are the only way we can cleanse the past so that we may, as best we can, in good conscience face the future...." He noticed that Mr. Ed Broadbent, whose first wife had been of Japanese origin, was overcome by the emotion of the moment and was crying.

Shortly afterwards the Prime Minister received a letter from Cardinal Carter of Toronto which read in part: "*...I wish to commend you most highly as a humble citizen of this country for your historical gesture to our Japanese fellow countrymen. For better or worse, I was old enough at the time... I understood the distress and the war hysteria under which we all laboured, even at that juncture I felt a great hurt and a deep sadness. If there ever was a collective miscarriage of justice and a condemnation of persons as guilty without proof this was it... I love my country. I have seldom been ashamed of her, and this one exception is now expunged by your gracious and timely intervention....*"

The Progressive Conservative Prime Minister had done what no Liberal Prime Minister since World War Two could bring himself to do: admit to a mistake, and apologize for it. The Prime Minister spoke on behalf of the future of all Canadians who live in the "true north strong and free." It was only a communication as fleeting as a speech given in the Commons, but that simple speech, unlike most of the others, had the profound sound of freedom.

"Ah so," the old man sighed rousing himself with a shake of his head. "We must learn to accept and forgive. It is such a simple lesson, yet how tenaciously we cling to past transgressions, slights, grudges, and injustices that suffocate the spirit with feelings of being hard-done-by! We must cultivate a more charitable attitude."

The recollection of a wrong belatedly corrected synchronized in Tutomu's mind with a recently uncovered "truth" about Pearl Harbor. It required the passage of over half a century following the infamous surprise attack of December 7th 1941, before it finally became permissible to let the public in on a long protected secret: it really was not a surprise attack after all!   And moreover, the duplicity, the hostility, the secrecy, the inscrutability, and the outright deceit, in short all the negative descriptors so assiduously projected onto the "Japs" - were a reflection, a reflection of the behaviors required for the implementation of a secret plan executed to near perfection by a handful of the most trusted and powerful government bureaucrats and military officials a free democracy could produce.

When a great untruth has been perpetuated upon an unsuspecting nation (as well as the rest of the world) for such a long time and glorified in Hollywood movies, newspapers, and heroic war stories – the real "truth" feels as disappointing to the deceived public as it might feel to a small child when told for the first time that the man wearing the Santa Claus outfit really is not Santa. Usually there is a sense of disillusionment followed by sadness. A few stubbornly remain in a state of denial as if it is their patriotic duty to maintain the status quo. Eventually most people, children and adults alike, learn to accept the truth; it is a growing up and maturing experience.

Since their joint sojourn at the hospital, good old Takehashi-san, the Vice-president of his charitable foundation, frequently dropped by the old man's room with newly published books that he thought would interest his old friend.   Two books in particular had illuminated and saddened Tutomu, and at the time of reading had inspired him to exclaim, "God bless the truth!"

A tenacious investigator, a World War II veteran and research-fellow at the Independent Institute in Oakland, by the name of Robert B. Stinnett, who had served in the United States Navy and earned a Presidential Unit Citation along with ten Battle Stars, had long been intrigued by the plethora of information available that seemed to indicate that something was seriously amiss regarding the "official account" of the events leading up to the tragedy that culminated on December 7th 1941 at Pearl Harbor. These rumors persisted but were summarily dismissed as being unsupported and unverifiable until Robert Stinnett, after sixteen years of dogged determination, finally achieved, via the Freedom of Information Act, what no other researcher ever had: access to long-classified Naval Documents. He published the results of his research in a scholarly work entitled: *"DAY OF DECEIT: THE TRUTH ABOUT FDR AND PEARL HARBOR."* The book was hailed as being the "definitive account" of the trail of deceit that ultimately led up to the "day of infamy". It was a hard and disillusioning truth to accept, especially for those Americans brought up to believe that FDR was above such Machiavellian machinations.

The simple publication of such a book in the United States is a tribute to the fundamental ideals of freedom and equality upon which the nation was founded, and to the resilience which enables such a democratic nation to accept the truth, even if the truth is a bitter pill to swallow. Who knew that just prior to their entrance into WWII the President of the United States, Franklin Delano Roosevelt, a man much revered for his public dedication to the ideals that made America great, had done everything within the realm of his Presidential power to deliberately manipulate and provoke an overt act of aggression from the only non-European member of the Axis alliance? And after it happened as planned, secretly cover up the "false flag" operation?

President Roosevelt's deceitful behavior was most likely prompted by a powerful desire to somehow arouse an isolationist America into entering the European conflict. (This seems to be the most plausible grounds upon which such devious behavior can be pragmatically "justified.") It was premised upon an ingenious plan meticulously devised by Lieutenant Commander Arthur McCollum, head of Naval Intelligence. Arthur McCollum had a unique background that made him particularly suited for formulating a practical strategy that, if properly implemented, would provoke resource-poor Japan, a small, expansionist country bent upon creating an economic sphere of prosperity in central and south-east Asia, into making an overt act of aggression against the United States and thus catapult a reluctant nation into WWII. At the time of formulation he had no idea that one of the tragic consequences of his "eight-action" plan would be the eventual atomic bombing of the city of his birth.

McCollum had been born in the beautiful port city of Nagasaki in 1898. His parents were Baptist missionaries dedicated to the Christian pursuit of saving pagan souls in the "Land of the Dolls". Did they know they were following in the footsteps of Saint Francis Xavier, Saint Paul Miki and the Martyrs of Japan? Had they set foot inside the magnificent Catholic Cathedral where the Kakure Kirishitan after hiding out for over two hundred and forty years revealed themselves as Christians to Father Bernard Petitjean? How many pagan souls had they baptized and "saved" in the name of their Lord and Savior?

Young Arthur was immersed in the intricacies of the Japanese culture; he even learned to speak Japanese before he spoke English. He spent his youth living in various Japanese cities which gave him a profound understanding of the Japanese mentality. During this time could he have developed a subconscious resentment against the "pagan empire" which had previously been suppressing Christianity? Following his father's demise in Japan the family returned to America where at the age of eighteen Arthur attended the Naval Academy, and four years later after he graduated he was posted to the U.S. embassy in Tokyo as a naval attaché. With such a background Lieutenant Commander McCollum had a keen insight into what particular provocations would be most irritating and threatening to the Japanese. In October of 1940 he sent a confidential memorandum containing his *eight-action plan*, detailing how Japan could be goaded into an overt act of hostility, to two of his superior officers hoping it would reach the Commander-in-Chief, President Franklin D. Roosevelt.

In summary, the confidential memorandum indicated that because it was evident that public opinion was strongly against America entering the war against the European members of the Axis powers, that is, Germany and Italy, Christian nations with considerable numbers of immigrants residing in the United States – it would require a precipitating event, such as a hostile act from the only non-white and non-Christian member of the Axis powers, to inflame the American people and patriotically galvanize them into entering the war. McCollum suggested eight specific actions that America needed to undertake in order to provoke a hostile attack from the Land of the Rising Sun. When questioned about his plan Commander McCollum confidently replied: "If you adopt these policies then Japan will commit an overt act of war." FDR secretly adopted all eight of the proposed actions for provocation. The plan could be pragmatically justified: if it worked, America would gain access to the war on the European front, through the back door, so to speak.

One specific aspect of the plan of provocation nearly led to the desired outcome as early as July of 1941 when the President authorized what he called "pop-up" forays into busy Japanese territorial waters hoping to draw hostile fire from some irritated trigger-happy patriot on a Japanese gunboat. To Roosevelt's dismay, Japan demonstrated tremendous reluctance to retaliate, and instead diplomatically protested strongly to U.S. Ambassador Joseph Grew about American "interference". It would take all eight of McCollum's proposals to eventually incite Japan to commit what President Franklin D. Roosevelt declared to be a "day of infamy".

Due to the fact that the brilliant U.S. cryptologists had successfully broken Japan's secret code for transmitting highly confidential information, key personnel in Naval Intelligence and the U.S. President had advanced knowledge of the specific details regarding the strategic movements and deployment of Japan's powerful navy in the south-east Pacific Rim area. It also enabled Naval Intelligence to surreptitiously monitor the effectiveness of the secret eight-action plan of deliberate provocation. This vital information gave the U.S. a tremendous advantage over the Japanese military strategists, and long before December 7th, 1941 the President knew whether or not McCollum's ingenious plan would lead to the desired outcome.

Three aspects of the eight-action strategy of provocation were very important to the success of the plan. The biggest obstacle to the plan's success was Japan's resolve not to antagonize the "sleeping giant", to do everything possible to avoid hostilities and confrontation. It was just common sense: Japan needed America's cooperation and natural resources to help fuel her wartime economy. How could this political resolve on Japan's part be overcome? First a hostile political stance that would irritate, aggravate and thwart all

Japanese efforts to avoid confrontation had to be implemented. Commensurately a comprehensive embargo around the islands of Japan had to be deployed that would undermine Japan's wartime economy by depriving her of the essential natural resources she desperately needed, like iron, coal, lumber, gas and oil. In addition Roosevelt prevented Japan from using the Panama Canal, thus forcing all of her Atlantic shipping to navigate around the southern tip of South America. The cumulative effects of all the provocative acts, both economic and military, practically choked off Japan's ability to survive as a resource-poor nation, and amounted to an unspoken ultimatum: either attack us and attempt to secure your access to these strategic resources – or give up your military ambitions of developing a sphere of prosperity in central and southeast Asia. Japan was exactly where Roosevelt and McCollum wanted her: between a rock and a very hard place.

Secondly the Pacific Fleet anchored along the protected inlets of California had to be moved out into the middle of the Pacific and deliberately exposed at Pearl Harbor as a tempting military target for Japan's powerful navy. Until then, as part of the strategy, the President had been allowing Japan to purchase oil from the West coast refineries in order that the Imperial Navy would have ample storages of fuel to mobilize the naval fleet. With sufficient amounts of fuel in storage, Japan had the capability to widen the scope of her operations.

Somehow Japan's military leaders had to be enticed into an aggressive act of self-preservation that if successful might enable Japan to survive the crippling effects of the embargo and provide a two or three year window for continued military operations. If McCollum was correct, given the opportunity, Japan would attempt to weaken the means by which the embargo was enforced and by which they could be attacked, i.e. the Pacific Fleet. Motive and opportunity galvanized Japan into a vain act of desperation: attack the sleeping giant! However surprise, surprise, the sleeping giant was only pretending to be asleep. Japan was being enticed like a sucker about to be ensnared on a barbed hook, and the President had control of the rod, line and reel.

At the time, Admiral James Richardson, Commander of the Pacific Fleet, was strongly opposed to relocating the fleet to Pearl Harbor as it was apparent that such a move amounted to deliberately placing the fleet in harm's way. When he expressed his concerns to FDR, the President promptly relieved Admiral Richardson of his command. Reason and common sense gave way to a higher authority. The Pacific fleet was promptly relocated to the mid Pacific as *bait*.

Thirdly, the new Commander, Admiral Kimmel, as well as General Short who headed up the army in Hawaii, both had to be kept entirely in the dark or out-of-the-loop regarding the plan of deliberate provocation, in order that the naval base at Pearl Harbor remain completely defenseless on the expected day of infamy. Every effort had to be made to make it appear as if the attack was completely unexpected, as if they had been caught by surprise. Information regarding the imminent attack had been received and compiled by naval intelligence and radio operatives located at Pearl Harbor. However, this vital information was routed to Washington and deliberately kept from Kimmel and Short who were just a stone's throw away. It was a sacrifice: 2,896 casualties of which 2,117 were deaths resulting from the bombing of the mostly outmoded twenty-seven year old WWI battleships – the newer battleships having been strategically moved elsewhere in advance. It was a sacrifice the President was willing to make in order to get America into the war. No one knew for sure that it was a "sacrifice" – until Robert B. Stinnett, after the passage of over fifty years, was able to gain access, via the Freedom of Information Act, to the appropriate Classified Documents. The Classified Documents were "classified" because they contained the unvarnished truth about a cover-up that reached all the way to the Oval Office in Washington.

Admiral Kimmel, unfortunately, had to take the brunt of the criticism for not being adequately prepared, for not mounting a stronger defense, and for the needless casualties incurred at Pearl Harbor on December 7th 1941. It was difficult for the general public to believe that the well trained and well equipped American military installation on Hawaii could have been so utterly unprepared for such an attack. How could such a massive *floating armada* travel halfway across the Pacific unnoticed? All shipping routes that might have intersected with the floating armada had to be deviously re-routed; planned naval reconnaissance activity by sea or air had to be surreptitiously postponed or re-directed to other areas; everything had to be done to insure that the invading force would go unnoticed.

Of course it was not unnoticed; it had been carefully monitored and assiduously tracked ever since its build-up, and the Naval Secret Service and the President knew exactly where it was and where it was heading... and why. No one bothered to explain to Admiral Kimmel why certain ships had to be moored at Pearl Harbor like a bunch of sitting ducks. In the aftermath what could Admiral Kimmel say in his own defense? "I'm sorry."

Was it surprising to anyone that after the disaster at Pearl Harbor Admiral Kimmel was officially demoted? It was a public disgrace knowingly foisted upon an innocent individual in the guise of maintaining military honor and the promotion of national security by a group of powerful political bureaucrats in Washington. Some *patsy* had to be singled out, and blamed for allowing this infamous day to happen. In all such "false flag" operations, in order to deflect public criticism, someone usually is set up in advance to be the fall-guy.

Fortunately in October of the year 2000, Congress belatedly *exonerated* Admiral Husband Kimmel. However, President Clinton in defense of his deceased Democratic colleague stubbornly refused to sign the document exemplifying the kind of attitude which makes it difficult to retrospectively rectify such past errors of judgment and to learn from such mistakes. Had not Admiral Kimmel suffered enough for a "day of infamy" for which he was not responsible and which he could not have prevented? The public exoneration was a tribute to a patriotic family who had worked long and hard to remove a completely unjustified black mark against the family name. At long last the record was being set straight and the truth uncovered.

"About time," the old man intoned reinforcing the tenor of his own thoughts as he turned his mind to the other book Takehashi had brought him.

In the light of the U.S. government's involvement in conspiring to cover-up the truth about the so-called "surprise attack" on Pearl Harbor and other subsequent "false flag" operations, a revealing publication aptly entitled *The New Pearl Harbor*, written by David Ray Griffin, raised some very disturbing questions about a much more recent "day of infamy". Was 9/11 (destruction of the Twin Towers of the World Trade Center in New York) also a similar kind of *sacrifice*? Was it a conspiracy by a powerful group of government insiders, a false-flag operation? The similarities are uncanny.

The implications of such a possibility are so horrific it is all but unthinkable for a patriotic American public to give serious consideration to such a conspiracy theory even though the cumulative evidence is difficult to refute. For example, it is indisputable that Tower Seven of the WTC was "imploded" immediately after the "collapse" of the Twin Towers that were hit by passenger-planes. One passenger-jet which was countermanded by its passengers crashed into an open field. What was its intended target? It is also indisputable that Tower Seven was not hit by an aircraft – however if it had been hit would it have appeared to have "collapsed"? Were the Twin Towers likewise actually "imploded" (evidence for such a scenario abounds) after being struck by the planes? How is it possible that the most security conscious air-defense system in the world was caught totally off guard? Why didn't the Investigative Committee carefully look into the events surrounding the implosion of Tower Seven? Hundreds of unanswered questions persist just as they did during and after the "day of infamy". (If such disturbing questions pique your curiosity simply Google: *Collapse of Tower Seven WTC 9/11, 2001*).

For the general public it is much more convenient and reassuring to believe in the "official story" as confirmed by the Investigative Committee appointed by the U.S. President. Was there a cover-up? If there was one, it was very thorough, just like at Pearl Harbor over half a century earlier. Without a doubt it is a gargantuan question that raises the hackles of every patriot, as well it should. Who would have believed, in the decade immediately following 1941, that Pearl Harbor was a "false flag" operation, especially after Roosevelt's five-man board of inquiry headed by Owen J. Roberts more or less whitewashed the official story concocted by the Government? In a milieu fraught with insecurity and a patriotic mindset unwilling to challenge the "official version", David Griffin, an eminent theologian and Professor of Philosophy and Religion at the Claremont School of Theology in California, presents a compelling case for what could turn out to be, in the most diabolical sense, a "new" Pearl Harbor.

Usually in such grandiose schemes cloaked in secrecy and clandestine activities with far-reaching consequences, it is very difficult to "cover-up" all aspects of such treacherous trails of deceit. The evidence is usually there, hidden by gag orders, threats, and classified documents, just as it was there in 1941 when a courageous and forthright Admiral James Richardson denounced the Robert's Commission's Report by saying: "It is the most unfair, unjust, and deceptively dishonest document ever printed by the Government Printing Office. I cannot conceive of honorable men serving on the commission without greatest regret and deepest feelings of shame." Who at that time would have appreciated Admiral Richardson's sentiments?

"I would have," the old man asserted vehemently, "if I had known then what I know now." He raised his left hand to his mouth to wipe the spittle that had spewed from his lips, "I would have," he repeated indignantly forgetful of the fact that at that time he was only a young boy living on the shores of the south arm of the Fraser River in Steveston, British Columbia, looking forward to going fishing in the sleek wooden boat he had taken such delight in helping his father build.

False flag operations are by their nature extremely secretive, and because they are carefully covered up at the highest levels of political power and influence, are usually not uncovered, if they are uncovered at all, until decades later. The most worrisome aspect of these false flag operations to citizens of the US and even those living beyond the borders of the Global Village's most powerful and influential capitalistic nation with the greatest arsenal of weapons of mass destruction, is that it appears as if an invisible power-elite with vast capital resources, motivated by power, greed, and self-interest, is able to deviously manipulate public opinion by insidiously controlling the mass media to the degree that a well organized political party primed with biased information, can democratically elect politicians who condone such activities. Unfortunately, such a self-serving power-elite (driven by extremely "selfish genes") is capable of undermining the integrity of a precious form of "freedom", hard won by revolution and self-sacrifice by the people, and for the people.

When – if ever – is it permissible in a genuine Democracy for individuals, trusted by the people to uphold and to represent the highest moral standards of honesty and truthfulness, to deliberately manipulate, mislead, lie to, and secretly cover-up clandestine activities that otherwise would be categorized as criminal or perhaps even treasonous? It takes honesty and courage for the citizens to confront such unsightly blemishes upon the psyche of a democratic nation. Sometimes it takes a long time for mistakes and serious errors of judgment to be recognized, belatedly corrected, and the truth appreciated.

"It is one of the fringe benefits of living to a ripe old age," the old man sagely reflected as he struggled to place his life in the context of the passing parade of recent historical information that intruded like missing pieces of an intricate puzzle into his cognitive understanding of what actually happened. It was difficult to reconcile himself to such startling revelations at his advanced age. The ramifications of such goings-on flooded his weary body with conflicting emotions that made it next to impossible to get a good night's rest. "Who would have thought it?" he asked himself incredulously. "Who would have even considered such a possibility?" He threw up his hands in a gesture of futility and slowly allowed his rigid body to relax against the two pillows he had puffed up behind him – and as he did a weary smile crept across his countenance symptomatic of a degree of acceptance.

"Poor old Delano," he mumbled to himself, "once he set foot down the deceitful path of deception there was no turning back. He had to follow the treacherous path wherever it led. What else could he do? He had to pretend he was telling the truth with every lie... so many had to pay the price... even those who admired and trusted him like Admiral Kimmel. Sometimes we do or say things that we regret. Sometimes in our loneliest hour we think about what we have done and the embarrassment is just too much... too much! I know how it is," the old man commiserated. He looked up to the ceiling and blinked his eyes rapidly as if gazing into the vastness of the universal mind, "You can only take with you what you gave away," he whispered sympathetically, "Didn't you know that?"

Tutomu yawned and composed himself comfortably upon his pillows. "Hmmm," he pondered lost in the existential ramifications of the thought provoking question: "What if... what if FDR had not passed away unexpectedly on April 12th, 1945, leaving the remainder of his last term in Office in the hands of a humorless, estranged Vice-President eager to prove his mettle, named Harry S. Truman – would the atomic bombing of Hiroshima and Nagasaki have come to pass?"

The old man was cognizant of the fact that according to the. *Public Papers of the Presidents (Harry S Truman, 1945, p. 197)* – a scant three weeks after the first successful trial detonation of a plutonium device on July 16th and less than four months after taking over as the Commander-in-Chief, Truman, invigorated by his participation in the Potsdam Conference (17th July to 2nd August, 1945, which called for the "utter destruction" of Japan if demands for unconditional surrender were not promptly met), hastily authorized the only use to date of the dreaded atomic bomb on civilian populations; and following the destruction of the city of Hiroshima on August 6th (exactly four days after the conclusion of the Potsdam Conference), and the port city of Nagasaki on the 9th of August, 1945 – President Truman gloated: *"The Japanese began the war from the air at Pearl Harbor. They have been repaid many fold."*

"At least he was right about the *'many fold'*!" Tutomu exclaimed with a sigh of resignation as the doubts, worries, and insecurities accumulated over half a century spent under a foreboding cloud of anxieties vanished with an air of acceptance and forgiveness into a universe of unlimited potentialities as he raised his chin to draw in a sobering breath. He shook his head vigorously as if to let the reality of what had happened during the war-years filter down to a more acceptable level of credulity. The inanity of it all! To realize that the "official story" had been a fabrication, a deliberate lie, a lie so great it had passed for the "truth", a "truth" that for over half a century had hung around his neck as if he were the *Ancient Mariner* who had shot the innocent albatross.

"Acceptance and forgiveness," the old man sighed as he nestled down into the comfort of his saggy bed, "it makes the unbearable… bearable."

CHAPTER FIVE

"I hope we have been up to the challenge," Penny remarked as she rolled her computer chair sideways toward her husband who slouched against the back of his chair with his legs spread-eagled and his arms dangling as if he was preparing to do the backstroke. Penny leaned back and imitated her husband giving rise to what has become known in the vernacular as a photo-op or a snapshot in time.

It was the atypical posture of two spent literary athletes who had just engaged in the Olympics of the mind and spirit, and were basking in the relative merits of their accomplishment. Gold, silver or bronze? Did it matter? It was the performance that counted. The performance was critical; who could say that it was lackluster? It was certainly an achievement for two ordinary people with Master's degrees in Philosophy and no other credentials of any note. Perhaps it was the teamwork that did it? It had been a team effort, two individuals meshing as one yielding a whole greater than the sum of its parts, like two battered and bruised sockeye salmon worn out and mortified by the culmination of their life-cycle. After achieving the ultimate orgasm, they now floated downstream, serenely happy but exhausted. In the aftermath of such an all-consuming experience, the two old spent retirees felt like rolling over and swimming on their backs for a little while.

"Do you know how to do the backstroke?" Larry asked out of curiosity.

The manuscript was finally complete. It was their gift to the world. Three days after its completion the authors celebrated the birth of their literary brainchild with a delicious home-cooked feast. Larry had prepared Penny's favorite meal: Atlantic lobster and potato salad with hot buttered dinner rolls. After a candle-lit supper Penny jovially declared that she had been privileged to be the world's "most fortunate person" and that she would like to pass on this great privilege to someone else. She asked Larry if he would like to have it. He said he would like to share it with the world, and although he was smiling with gratitude, a shiny dampness appeared below his eyes.

The entire house seemed so calm and quiet that night. Jerry and Sherry had spent as much time at home as they could spare during the year out of consideration for their mother's illness. And while they were around Penny had been so cheerful it was hard to believe she was terminally ill. Having the two "kids" around – who were actually grown-up mature adults – motivated Penny to rise to the occasion. "Take it easy!" they both cautioned her over and over. But how could she take it easy when she was their mother? She just naturally wanted to nurture them as she had always done.

"Miracle cures do occur," Larry had reminded everyone at that time, and at that time the unbelievable seemed believable. Penny actively attempted to heal herself physically, mentally, and spiritually. She believed in being an active healer rather than a passive victim, and indeed in spite of the dire prognostications by her Doctor, she began to gradually improve. She lived well past the most optimistic parameters any of the medical experts she visited had given her. The predictions changed from two months to four months to six months to who knows? Penny's hair grew back in; she put on some weight and began to look somewhat like her normal healthy self.

Once again she began staying up late to complete work on the manuscript. It became an even greater obsession than ever before. "I've got to live long enough to get this work finished," she'd say with dogged determination. So against his better judgment, Larry acquiesced and let her stay up late, and they worked side by side to complete their life's work. And the very day Larry had ordered the Atlantic lobster all the way from Charlottetown, Prince Edward Island, in anticipation of their "completion celebration", Penny suffered a mild relapse. It was as if she had momentarily let down her guard and the cancerous cells were just waiting for such an opening. But the Doctor who still seemed to be baffled said she might as well stay home because she did better there than in the hospital. She gave Penny a new prescription for some stronger painkillers and said, "These will help. Take them as needed with a glass of water."

Larry did a lot of praying. He prayed silently in his thoughts all day long and sometimes he thought, "My whole life is a silent prayer." At night when the house was quiet he liked to lie back on his pillow and wonder how he could help make the world a better place for all. "When Penny passes on the whole world will be diminished," he thought with a suffocating sense of loss. "The world needs Penny," he reflected soberly, "it is a better place for all because she is in it." He sadly recalled her father's sentiments on their wedding day, "More precious than life."

* * *

It had been a gorgeous late Indian summer. The leaves had turned dark red and brilliant yellow, and with the continuing fall warmth Mother Nature had clothed herself in a mosaic quilt of amber hues. The multi-layered earth tones were an indication of readiness. Winter was knocking on the door anxious to change the landscape.

Penny had stopped wearing her woolen toque because her hair had grown so quickly it was almost back to its former length. Her heart beat on valiantly bringing much needed nutrients to every hungry cell. The gaunt, emaciated look was camouflaged with a secondary layer of clothing. The will to live was undaunted by the challenge; even in the late autumn of her life she had hung on tenaciously, long enough to complete the Handbook. It seemed like a miracle.

During the night the first snowfall had blanketed the garden in a cocoon of fluffy whiteness. The precipitation had cleansed the air; it smelled clean and fresh. Tiny tracks from Penny's footprints remained plainly visible in the morning light. They were an indication that she had passed that way, a momentary reminder to those following of the impermanence of all things.

There is something in the cool crispness of such a winter wonderland that speaks with an all-consuming silence of things past, and of the inevitable. Larry saw those footprints; they looked so solitary. Compassion plucked at his heartstrings with trembling fingers. He knew that his wife had gotten up in the early morning light, put on her forest-green parka with the furry brown trim, and in her quiet fashion had wandered meditatively amongst the dormant flowers that brought her such delight - spring, summer and fall. Larry followed the footprints. They wound around the outer fringe of the garden and ended where they began. She had completed the circle.

In the afternoon Penny wanted to go outside because the sun had broken through the clouds and the reflection off the melting snow was dazzling. Larry joined her. The joy of seeing little kids with toboggans, plastic carpets and sleds, sliding, yelling and screaming with delight brought reminders of the times Sherry and Jerry had done the same.

"Things change in order to remain the same," Larry commented as they walked hand in hand down the sidewalk taking in the winter revelry.

"Winter comes every year," Penny remarked, "spring, summer, fall, and then winter. And every year the first snowfall seems refreshingly new, even to older people like us seniors." She laughed, stooped, made a snowball and threw it at her husband.

The snowball hit Larry on the buttocks. He retaliated by running ahead, scooping up a handful of slushy snow as he ran and firing back toward his wife. She danced aside and the missile missed its mark. She quickly replenished her arsenal and fired back.

Back and forth the snowballs flew amidst guffaws, laughter, and bragging rights. It was very stimulating, but exhausting. Finally Penny held up her hands and yelled, "I surrender." The words echoed down the street and passers-by turned to look.

The evening had a special ambiance of its own. Larry had bought some fresh-cut flowers from the local flower shop and had arranged them in a crystal vase on the center of the dining room table. The red, yellow, purple and white flowers added a touch of elegance to a regal occasion: a celebration of the first snowfall of the year: the coronation of Mother Earth.

Larry had spent most of the afternoon shopping for the ingredients for the evening meal. He had gone out of his way to purchase the seasonal fruits and vegetables that delighted Penny's palate. He slaved over the hot kitchen stove whistling a song that Penny had written the previous winter that seemed appropriate for the occasion. It made him feel really happy to be of service to one so special. "How many more 'first snowfalls' will we celebrate?" he asked himself as he sauntered over and turned on the gas fireplace. The amber flame and warm glow spoke of romance.

What a sumptuous supper it was, topped off with a special herbal tea and fresh fruit-cup for dessert. Larry had once again out-done himself. He was, touch wood, in excellent health for his age, and it pleased him to be able to share his vibrancy with Penny in any way that delighted her. It was nice for him to be able to reciprocate after all the years she had humbly serviced his every need.

It was ten-thirty by the time Larry had cleared up the supper dishes and tidied up the kitchen. He had sent Penny off to bed because it had been a long day for her since she had gotten up so early. He sat down with a sigh of relief in his swivel-rocker after turning on the new twenty-six inch flat panel television set Penny had purchased for his last birthday, and caught the tail end of the sports news. The Canucks were on a three game winning streak. Miracles never ceased.

It was eleven thirty-five by the time Larry finally made his way to his bedroom to retire for the evening. When he opened the door he was surprised to see Penny curled up under the blankets. "Are you awake?" he whispered.

"I have been waiting for you," she responded.

"Sorry I took so long. I didn't know you were in here," he replied as he strode into the ensuite bathroom to brush his teeth and prepare himself for bed. He returned with gusto and slid into the downy softness of the queen-sized bed that seemed too large when Penny was not in it.

"You must be extremely horny by now," Penny smiled.

"You know me," Larry grinned boyishly, "I'm always horny." It was Larry's opinion that as they aged the sex act became more and more an act of sharing and communion. "It is a natural biological provision that allows the male and female to join together to form a whole, like Yin and Yang," he had pontificated.

"Could you rub my back?" Penny requested hunching herself up.

They spooned together. "Ah, what a marvelous connection," Larry swooned, feeling the flow of the emotional current.

"It's nice to be connected," Penny sighed. "I can feel your energy."

"The circuit is completed."

"The light has come on."

"Thank you for everything." Larry reached out and began to gently massage the area along both sides of Penny's spine that made her shiver with delight. Some of her body mass had returned and he could feel the resilient warmth of her body's response to his caresses. He imagined his energy flowing into her body like an electric current healing and rejuvenating. They were one, a whole, a single unit of life resonating together for a mortal moment. He wanted so to share his life-force with her enfeebled light, like a battery charger that brings new life to a dying battery.

"You make me so happy... by just being yourself," he said gratefully.

"I'm glad," Penny responded humbly.

Larry patiently massaged his wife's neck, shoulders, and back until she fell asleep from total relaxation. She had become such a shrunken little person since the onset of that dreaded disease. "Will they ever find a cure?" Larry asked himself as he continued to rub his spouse's back methodically, attempting to keep the circuit completed and the energy flowing.

"I love you, Pen," he whispered into the night and held her close feeling the fragility of her nakedness against his own. He held her like one holds on to mortality, for dear life. And then he fell asleep, and the Yin separated from the Yang.

"Larry!" He heard the voice like a gun shot in the dark. It was clear and distinct. A command shouted with great force and urgency. Penny was not beside him. Larry bolted upright and leapt out of bed. He could see the light shining under the bathroom door. He rushed to the bathroom and pushed the door open. Penny stood leaning against the sink. She held a clear plastic drinking cup in her right hand. She started to sway. Larry grabbed her from behind. He felt the weight of her limp body sag against him; she seemed as soft and light as an angel. And then he heard that sound that he would never ever forget, that crisp, hollow sound that resounded in an empty space against the edge of time, as he stood there frozen in the fourth dimension. He could see it in slow motion: that clear plastic cup falling, falling, falling, falling from her outstretched hand and slowly plummeting into the sink with a sharp, hollow rattle that reverberated for an eternity.

Penny never heard that sound. That sound was reserved for the living, the living who must carry on and live with their memories. That sound was locked forever in Larry's memory. His wife had passed on and the vessel he held in his arms was as empty as the plastic cup that lay in the sink. "She's gone!" Larry uttered in bewilderment. It was so sudden, so unexpected. He was more astonished at his own shocked disbelief than he was at her death. He did not cry. He did not feel depressed. He felt a profound sense of gratitude and love. It was hard to explain: he intuitively felt her sense of release, her wonderful sensation of freedom. She was gone but deep within she was still there, where she had always been, a wonderful beacon of radiant light transfixed with happiness and shedding tears of joy for the living.

Larry looked in the mirror. His face was wet with tears. He had not cried. These were not his tears!

They were comforting tears of love, gratitude, and compassion from someone who cared, someone who dared to share; an angelic soul who wanted him to know... she had not died – she had just passed on.

CHAPTER SIX

Tears were streaming down the old man's face. A crumpled mass of tissues lay discarded beside the pillow. He stared out at the vast imaginary audience through bleary eyes and waved a bony hand feebly. "Pardon my self-indulgence," he excused himself and blew his nose into a damp tissue. "As I said before… if only you could have known her while she was still alive, you would more fully appreciate my sentiments." He drew in a shuddering breath and blew his nose once again. "She was my cousin, you know," he reminded them. "She was special, if you know what I mean. I only wish you could have known her while she was still alive," he repeated. "I just know you would have loved her. Who wouldn't have?"

He gazed out at the audience compassionately and under his breath he mumbled "It is all about acceptance and…" he paused, bowed his head humbly and in a solemn voice uttered "forgiveness," before he lapsed into silence. Tutomu clasped his hands together so tightly his knuckles gleamed with tension, and slowly raised his head. He seemed to be ruminating as if there was something he might have forgotten to say. "Yes," he began in a hoarse whisper, "sometimes there are deeply personal experiences that are so devastating and so painful they cry out to be repressed and forgotten, to be relegated into the dead hand of the past, so to speak, as if they never really happened." He paused and shifted uncomfortably upon the bed, "Yet they must be shared because they are not just our own experiences, they belong to everyone, to every human being who ever stumbled, ran, walked, limped, or crawled down this path that unravels before us, on our behalf you might say, so we can all be the wiser for their passing," he explained, "Isn't that right?" A momentary look of indecision flashed across his face, "Isn't that right?" he repeated in a contrite tone as if expecting a negative response. He gazed off apprehensively toward the far wall where the circular clock with the shiny chrome trim stared back deadpanned while continuing to tick off the seconds one by one as if to say: *time waits for no man.*

"How time flies!" Tutomu exclaimed with alarm. "Perhaps I may have waited a little too long," he berated himself. "But I-I just wanted to be sure of myself," he rationalized, "I wanted to get past the selfish resentments and recriminations that make it impossible to learn from our mistakes. I wanted to rise above all the pettiness that diminishes the grandeur of the human spirit. Is it possible that I may have waited too long? Could it be too late?" he asked sheepishly feeling intimidated by the implications of his own inquiry.

"It is never too late!" he admonished his kin-folk rising up from his bed in righteous indignation. "How many times do I have to repeat that?" he asked in exasperation. "There is still plenty of time, plenty of time if we all work together. We can make a real difference." He brought his hands together as if in prayer and sighed, "We must dare to share – neh?" The vast audience nodded in unison as if they were fellow travelers who had once traveled down this very pathway ahead of him and understood exactly the sentiments he was attempting to convey.

Tutomu half closed his eyes and sagged back into the stoic comfort of his thirty-nine inch hospital bed. There were glassy tears in his eyes that reflected a kaleidoscope of past images that drifted by with a tinge of disillusionment, sadness, and nostalgia. He visualized himself standing by the railing of that old freighter bound for Japan and waving goodbye to the rugged rocks, the spiky evergreens, the shiny tin roofs on the wooden houses that dotted the shoreline of the land of his birth. The pathetic look of bewilderment and confusion etched upon the face of an innocent young boy who rode the waves of destiny back to a war-torn Japan, remained submerged beneath the withered countenance of a feeble old man whose youthful glow of potency and innocence had been tragically tarnished when Fat Man plummeted from the bowels of a Superfortress B-29, and enveloped Nagasaki in a radioactive cloud that left him sterile and impotent. Tutomu writhed as if in mental and physical discomfort, and rhetorically mumbled, "Who could have made up such a fantastic story: a story of prejudice, deceit, persecution, suffering, compassion, perseverance, acceptance, and forgiveness? Who would have dreamed that such a tale would actually come to pass as if – as if it were real?"

Memories, memories, and more memories crowded into the dreamy dimension between then and now and brought a healthy glow to Tutomu's parchment cheeks. It had been a long journey across an ocean of dreams, hopes, and bitter disappointments.

* * *

The little ship bobbed and dipped upon a billowing sea of fantasy that spanned the space between past and present. An aged old man stood by the ship's railing with his white hair blowing in the wind. He gripped the rail, braced his legs, blinked his eyes and stared off into the unknown.

The winds of change blew in from the deep blue firmament above the azure Pacific and filled the moment with a fabulous feeling of freedom. Tutomu gazed up at the heavens, the omnipotent heavens that reflected, like a vast concave mirror, all that transpired below, and reciprocated a state of mortal awareness commensurate with that pertinent to each pinpoint of realization. "It has been a long life of longing," he thought, "Yes, a very long life of longing, and longing." It was like a prolonged movement without a rest. "Was the restlessness a reflection of the longing?"

The old man drew in a breath so deep that when he exhaled it amplified the heavens with his thanks. "Thank you," he breathed with such profound humility all those who had preceded him to that moment and whose reflections were mirrored in the infinity that constituted the heavens, took one step forward, to make room for one more kindred spirit.

A translucent glow radiated through Tutomu's circle of awareness yielding a fabulous rainbow of colors from sunrise to sunset. The entire sky was aglow with such a depth of vibrant hues the landscape itself was swallowed up in the brilliance. And there he was, vibrating with perfect health in the center, surrounded by every known color of happiness.

It was hardly noticeable at first, like a speck of dust in his eye. It was there and then it wasn't and then it was, a tiny speck approaching him from sunrise to sunset. Or was it sunset to sunrise? Did it matter? He could feel the dissonance of its mortal vibes impinging upon the colors of his happiness. They lapped over him like waves from a distant shore infusing the moment with a spiritual presence. What, in heaven's name, was it?

It was not dressed in a wispy white gown. It did not have wings, yet it floated like an angel. It was approaching him with what appeared to be, welcoming gestures. It looked all-the-world like, like P-p-pen... Penelope!" he articulated succinctly.

"Just call me Penny."

"Wha-what on earth are you doing here?" Tutomu stammered.

"I guess I could ask you the same question."

Tutomu stared at his cousin as if he were looking at a ghost. He was completely dumbfounded. He could not believe the evidence of his senses, yet he desperately wanted to. "Just accept it," he told himself, "let it be," he mouthed the words, "Just let it be." He blinked his eyes in disbelief. "JUST LET IT BE!" he repeated so loud he could feel the words reverberate in his eardrums like a mantra of hope. He stared at the holographic specter in silence trembling with apprehension, hoping it was real, and that it would not simply vanish like a figment of his imagination.

"When did you get here?" Penny asked breaking the silence.

"Well," he began hesitatingly heeding his own advice, "it is difficult to say exactly, but I think it was when I became aware that I was able to accept and forgive." The response felt like a feeble rationalization but he continued on anyway. "It was a gradual dawning of awareness. It didn't happen overnight. It took a lifetime I suppose." He glanced up at his cousin with a sheepish grin. "I kind of lost track of you for a while there, but it feels good to be on the same page again."

"I'll say, and in the same story too!" Penny exclaimed with a smile extending the metaphor.

"I love your literary sensibilities."

"Remember when you said 'zero equals one'?" Penny asked brightly.

Tutomu scratched his head and pondered. "I recall saying that to a young Doctor. Why do you ask?"

"That mathematical analogy is what places us on the same page of karmic awareness. I suppose you could say that is probably the reason we are both here."

Tutomu scratched his head again. "Ah – so," he reflected. "I always suspected that the dissonance created between the Zero and the One resulted in the energy which produced the freedom to become manifest or aware," he responded feeling compelled to elaborate upon the analogy as if to justify his presence. "In the manifestation-of-the-aware, the awareness is an ever evolving flow of energy created from a Freedom attempting to reconcile the dissonance between Zero and One," he theorized.

"Succinctly stated," Penny nodded, staring wide-eyed at her cousin.

"All life forms are manifestations of the dissonance between Zero and One," Tutomu continued sagely, "of the freedom that represents the diversity that exists between the infinitude of zero and the finitude of one," he paused to draw in a much need breath, and then doggedly rattled on as if driven by some existential sense of insecurity that gave rise to an irrational need to substantiate his existence before his cousin's steadfast gaze, "and being representatives of the dissonance each respective life form is a microcosm or reflection of the divine Freedom: the freedom to be manifest and to be able to manife..." he stopped abruptly, suddenly conscious of his verbosity. "Confusing eh?" he asked, looking up at his cousin with expectant eyes.

"Perhaps the reason we are both here now is to attempt to further clarify the confusion," Penny declared further authenticating the surreal moment.

"Could it be that we are stuck in the 'gap' between Zero and One and it is our karmic destiny to attempt to make some sense of it?" Tutomu suggested with a hopeful air while flashing a bemused smile that masked a waning sense of incredulity.

"Some destiny!" Penny exclaimed and laughed with a joviality that added a light-hearted ebullience to the moment.

"It's nice to have the proverbial last laugh on your side," Tutomu offered.

"On *our* side," Penny corrected.

"Yes, our side," Tutomu affirmed feeling somewhat relieved. "Ha, perhaps that is our mutual karmic destiny!" he added with a chortle.

They laughed joyously together bonded and warmed by their joint appreciation of their existential predicament. "Isn't it wonderful that we can laugh?" Penny grinned.

"A unique human quality that enables us not to take ourselves too seriously even though we are manifestations of the Divine Light of Freedom," Tutomu pointed out with a humble bow.

"We are miraculous manifestations of a primordial Freedom, a freedom to imagine what it is like to be everything-there-is," Penny chimed in, "to have the innate ability to pretend... that zero can equal one! We are tiny sparks of that original Pretence, of that dissonance that gave rise to Freedom incarnate. It is a tiny spark of something so divinely miraculous that in quiet moments it stills the heart and mortifies the soul with intimations of immortality."

"Your words have the beauty of poetry," Tutomu swallowed a lump in his throat and gazed admiringly at his Canadian cousin, "...a tiny spark of something so divinely miraculous," he whispered as if she personified the statement, "that in quiet moments... stills the heart and mortifies the soul with intimations of immortality. You are a credit to the highest level of human thought. Genius," he commended.

Penny lapsed into silence inwardly humbled by her cousin's unexpected praise. She cleared her throat and began with a cautious temerity symptomatic of one not wanting to undermine one's newly acquired sense of intellectual merit. "Does it not make it possible through self-realization, for us egotistical mortal manifestations of the finite-oneness, to realize that as a single spark in an infinite universe, we each in our own relative way help to create the Light that manifests everything-there-is?" she asked hoping the question was worthy of someone recently appraised as being *genius*.

"You have a marvelous way of expressing esoteric concepts. Yes, that would be a natural outcome; it gives our individual 'free-will' or ego a purpose. When we realize all-that-we-can-be as homo-sapiens or mortal-beings, we enable the Divinely Miraculous to be everything-it-is-possible-to-be."

"Awesomely phrased," Penny breathed, impressed by her cousin's astuteness. "When we realize all that we can be, we enable the 'Eternal Spirit' to be everything it is possible to be," she paraphrased. "And who knows what that is?"

"Perhaps it is the Freedom to rise to the sublime heights... of beauty and truth, of excellence and perfection, of serenity and peace, of joy and happiness, of love and... of every possibility that could ultimately lead to unity and harmony."

"And we are manifestations of that possibility," Penny added insightfully, "of that miraculous potentiality," she hesitated momentarily and glanced expectantly toward her cousin.

"From time to time in free moments when we are not aware of our egotistical selves," Tutomu added sagely, "in those precious moments when our vanity is held in abeyance, so to speak, unity and harmony in the presence of a mortal dissonance is experienced divinely in the human species as happiness."

"I have never thought of happiness in that way before, as an intrinsic ego-less expression of our divine nature. You have become inordinately enlightened for an old codger," Penny laughed with an inner sense of satisfaction. "We have plenty to talk about," she paused reflectively and slowly inhaled as if savoring each miraculous molecule of oxygen.

A wholesome silence rained down upon them with a splendid serenity that filled the moment with a freedom so profound that it resonated harmoniously in their souls as the magical sound of *one-hand-clapping.*

Tutomu stepped back and stared at his Canadian cousin. She glowed with an aura that glistened with vibrant health. "Such a rare intellect," he thought. "What is an old has-been like me doing here, talking to her?" the question raised disconcerting possibilities in the incredulous realm of his cognitive domain.

"By the way, have you heard from Larry or the kids?" Penny asked, suddenly changing the subject.

"Larry, Jerry, and Sherry are all doing just fine, as far as I know. It was a struggle at first, but I understand that Larry's hanging in there. I guess they are the fearsome threesome, now."

"Good for Larry. It's tough being the one left behind."

"I hope he doesn't get stuck in a rut like I was."

"He has to learn to let go and let be."

"Don't we all," Tutomu replied humbly. He cleared his throat and shuffled his feet self-consciously. The conversation was beginning to sound too authentic. "Just let it be," he reminded himself, "Just let it be."

"Remember that time you visited me in Calgary?" Penny queried, her eyes as deep and as mysterious as the heavens from which she had materialized.

"That was a very long time ago."

"Seems like a lifetime – eh?"

"It was a lifetime."

"Remember that handbook we discussed?" Penny asked staring at her cousin with such a penetrating look it joggled his memory.

"That handbook on life?"

"It has been written, thanks to you."

"By whom?"

"By Larry and me," Penny replied proudly. She paused and humbly added, "We were just scribes following in the footsteps of all the great thinkers who preceded us down that path. I guess the book is really just a signpost indicating the path we took."

"I'm flattered you took my advice. I didn't mean to burden you with that task. It was just that I knew you could do it. God bless you both."

"As you know, writing is one thing, getting published is quite another. I was going to send you a photocopy for proof reading, but I got sick. Cancer."

"I understand," Tutomu replied empathetically.

"We needed to get together. I had to let you know. It was your brainchild. It was imperative I let you know...."

"I know, I know," Tutomu interrupted.

"You know what?" Penny asked somewhat surprised by her cousin's assertiveness.

"My life force, my life energy has been no more than a tiny spark, the spark needed to ignite the flame. You have been the flame that has produced the illumination required to write the handbook," Tutomu confessed. "You give me too much credit."

"We have dedicated the book to you."

"God bless you both," Tutomu repeated once again with humble gratitude.

"The handbook is simply the manifestation of an act of sharing."

"You have dared to share," her cousin stated matter-of-factly. "What more could anyone do?" It was more of an affirmation than a question.

The golden rays of the setting sun bathed their faces with a blissful radiance. They lapsed into a comfortable silence that resonated with compassion, love and gratitude. There was nothing more to be said. The loose ends had nearly come together to form a whole. There was a tinge of embarrassment. So close and yet so far!

Tutomu took a half-step, hesitated, and then with measured strides walked slowly toward his diminutive cousin. From his

perspective she looked so small, so singular…so solitary. He wanted
to give her a great big bear-hug. She looked so-so… huggable. His
scrawny arms reached out in anticipation.

* * *

The tubes pulled free from the old man's veins and sprang
upward toward the plastic drip bags behind which, on the far wall,
the face on the round electric clock with the shiny chrome trim
indicated that it was time. The old man's shiny black eyes reflected
an omniscient presence, and from that point of view he could see that
the sunrise was setting in vistas of endless happiness. Such a
wonderful moment of splendor he had never in his entire lifetime
beheld. It took away his breath and stilled his feeble heart. The
conditions were perfect. Tutomu's skinny arms were extended as far
as he could reach, and the tips of his bony fingers beckoned.

CHAPTER SEVEN

The sunlight diffused across the eastern sky like a wash of amber paint upon an awakening landscape. With broad strokes the Grand Artist had imbued the heavens with crimson fingers of light. Where heaven and earth met a thin dark line emerged as the horizon. A spectrum of subdued radiance blended from pastel shadows of purple to scarlet red where the watercolors faded and ran together. It was a magnificent sunrise. So beautiful, the crisp morning air shimmered with serene delight.

It was all in the eye of the beholder. The young Doctor drew in a deep breath of appreciation. The windows of his brand new Toyota Solara were rolled all the way down to allow the clean air to greet his nostrils with the sweet scent of morning dew. He could taste the freshness. His left hand gripped the leather covered steering wheel, while his right caressed the smooth porcelain knob of the manual five speed. The engine purred contentedly like a kitten curled up on his lap. Ahead he could see the dark outline of an overpass looming up like a gigantic bridge spanning the edges. It was all there, sight, sound, touch, taste, and smell, woven into one awesome moment of omnipotent beauty. His entire body tingled with the sensations of heightened awareness. It subdued the young Doctor with a profound feeling of reverence. It started with a coolness at the base of his skull where the medulla oblongata connected the spine to the brain stem, and shivered down his spine with a tingling sensation that awoke every nerve ending to the miracle of the rising sun.

The Doctor felt very privileged. To bear witness to such grandeur on such a mundane Monday morning while driving to the hospital was overwhelming, especially when contrasted with the dingy halls of the Geriatrics ward where he spent most of his day traipsing from one eight by twelve room to the next. What had he done to deserve such a wonderful greeting to the first working day of the week? It felt poignant and full of promise. It was unmistakably brighter, fresher, cleaner. There was an extra sensation of freedom floating about. And there it was, spread out before the windshield in 3-D, a supernatural vista of hope zooming toward him as he sped down the road toward his destination.

The mottled firebrick façade on the west wall of the hospital loomed up before him. He pulled into Staff Parking stall number twenty-nine, and switched off the engine. A somber quietude fell over him as he hastened up the walkway toward the side entrance. It was so quiet. Too quiet for such a glorious day. He opened the door and walked briskly to the change-room, where he removed his brownish-gray Harris Tweed sports-jacket, and replaced it with a short, white Doctor's tunic. He liked wearing that coat along with the dangling stethoscope because it reminded him of his role. As he was admiring his Doctor's image in the mirror beside the closet, someone knocked at the door. He stepped around a wooden stool and turned the handle. The head nurse pushed the door open. She looked anxious.

"You'd better come with me," she said tersely. "One of your patients has died."

He could see by her face that she seemed to be under some stress. "Just a sec," he said and grabbed his black medical bag. It was a habit he had developed whenever one of his patients died: just in case. He was the only Doctor on the Geriatrics ward that did it. "It shows he cares," the head nurse once pointed out to a young intern when he raised his eyebrows.

He followed her up a flight of stairs and down a maze of corridors to room number 309. With a flourish she swung the door aside and entered the room with the Doctor hard on her heels. The nurse paused just inside the open door and allowed him to proceed ahead of her.

"He finally passed on," she whispered solemnly. "I found him when I started the morning rounds. I checked for vitals and informed the office. I'd say he passed away sometime earlier this morning."

The Doctor proceeded to the bed and set down his medical bag. He glanced up at the electric wall clock which had stopped and noted the time for no particular reason. "He was awake when he passed on," he commented as he reached down and closed the old man's eyes. "Looks like he was reaching out for something."

"Probably reaching out for those old swords he was so fond of," the nurse surmised.

The Doctor stepped toward the rear of the bed, gingerly picked up the scabbard containing the ancient katana and held it firmly in his left hand. With his right he drew the great sword from its sheath with a majestic sweep of his arm, and as he did he pivoted gracefully upon the ball of his left foot carving an invisible circle in the air.

Fortunately the head nurse had kept her distance. "Wow!" she exclaimed in surprise, "What was that?"

"I'm not sure," he replied as if he was just as amazed as the nurse. "It just seemed natural." He stood there for a moment frozen by the solemnity of the occasion. Pinpoints of sunlight danced upon the gleaming blade as in days of old when the Magician of Kogi examined his handiwork with a critical eye.

"What a beautiful work of art!" the nurse breathed.

With tender care, the Doctor placed the worn handle of the great katana in the old man's right hand and laid the burnished steel blade diagonally across his withered legs. "Leave it there for now," he said looking up at the nurse.

The nurse nodded her approval, "He looks so-so ancient with that old sword in his hand," she observed. "Two old relics, reminders of ages past and the relativity of time," she commented sagely.

A shaft of morning sunlight slanted across the room engulfing Tutomu from head to foot. It highlighted the look of supreme happiness reflecting from his countenance. The nurse bowed respectfully as she stooped to pick up the dog-eared clipboard that hung from the frayed string attached to the foot of the bed. She scrutinized it with renewed interest. "It says here that he was actually born in a place called Steveston, in British Columbia, Canada. Imagine that. You spent quite a lot of time with the old fella..." the nurse let the statement dangle and looked up at the Doctor.

"Yes," he responded with a quick intake of breath while staring intently at the nurse. A weird expression akin to incredulity seared across his face. The reaction seemed somewhat incongruent with the situation at hand. But sometimes such inexplicable things just happen. Just like that. It was as if he was seeing the head nurse for the first time, in a new light. The highlights on her silky black hair sparkled like diamonds against her creamy white skin revealing an exquisite beauty far beyond anything such circumstances warranted. There she was. A gorgeous flower in full bloom – and he had not noticed, before. She was looking up at him with such trusting eyes of – was it admiration? "Yes," the Doctor continued feeling much more self-conscious than he had felt only a moment before. "Yes," he repeated himself for the third time, "it was a privilege. He was a courageous spirit."

"How so?"

He could feel those black eyes glued upon him. "He never gave up. Didn't you ever hear him say, 'It's never too late'?"

"Yes I heard him mutter that under his breath. He'd say 'Never!' as if his life depended upon it."

"He had a lifetime to salvage. Not only his lifetime, the lifetime of the whole generation he represented: a generation of mistakes made, opportunities missed, and lessons unlearned."

"He was so earnest," the nurse pointed out.

"Time was running out, and he had so much to share." The Doctor stepped back from the bed, clasped his hands together, bowed his head and said a silent prayer. He noticed the nurse follow suit.

"Ah-men," he concluded feeling that word to be appropriate.

"Was the old fellow a Christian, Buddhist, Agnostic, or Atheist?" she asked out of curiosity.

"He tended to avoid labels like those. He once said, 'Man is born free, but everywhere he is enslaved by dogma'."

"Especially religious dogma," the nurse felt the need to clarify.

"But," the Doctor continued, "there was one label he probably would not have minded."

"What is that?"

"Good."

"Why good?"

"Because goodness is a universally aspired-to virtue, with a universally agreed-upon meaning. A good person is kind, tolerant, understanding, and compassionate. You do not need to be religious in order to be a good person."

"Like the 'good' Samaritan."

"Precisely. Tutomu would be happy if all that was written on his tombstone was: 'Here lies a good man'."

"In the end do you think he found happiness?" she asked pensively.

The young Doctor looked up at the ceiling as he pondered the question. "He once told me that there is a world of difference between vanity and happiness. Many of us confuse happiness with vanity. It took a lot of soul searching, but in the end I think the old man realized the difference. It was a difficult lesson to learn in one mortal lifetime."

"Most of us never learn it," the nurse pronounced soberly, "We're too vain!"

"Many of us think we are amongst the chosen, the elect, the saved, the special few that are destined to be happy in the hereafter. We postpone our happiness until such a time. In the meantime we righteously let our vanity prevent us from being happy here and now. It is an extremely powerful mindset to overcome in this milieu. The old man was probably ahead of his time."

"Do you think he passed on in a state of happiness?"

"I hope so."

"So do I."

The Doctor turned and with ponderous gait made his way to the open door. He paused and waited for the nurse. She dutifully picked up his black medical bag and followed him to the doorway. "Let's go outside for a breath of fresh air. It's a beautiful day out," he suggested as the nurse brushed past him.

"If you like," she concurred. "Did you learn anything else from him, Doctor?" she asked respectfully as they left the old man's room and sauntered down the dimly lit hallway.

"Please call me Paul."

"And you may call me Kinko," the head nurse quickly responded.

"Yes, I learned quite a lot," Paul continued.

"Anything important?" Kinko asked, flashing a smile so radiant it lit up the his heart.

Paul shyly returned Kinko's smile as he opened the glass door that led to a staircase that wound its way to the ground floor. "Let me think," he began as Kinko latched securely onto his left arm for balance as they made their way down the stairs to the lower level. When they reached the ground floor Paul graciously swept open another glass door that opened into a short, well-lit hall.

"There was one thing that stuck in my mind," he continued as they walked arm in arm down the hallway. At the end of the hall they came to a heavy grey metal door with a self-closer marked "Exit". Paul pressed on the latch and gave the door a push. It seemed stuck. He placed his right shoulder against the door and exerted just enough pressure to hear it grudgingly groan as it slowly opened, letting in a brilliant shaft of light. He graciously held the door ajar while Kinko passed through ahead of him.

The glorious morning sun showered them with rejuvenating vibes. A refreshing feeling of freedom that seemed to radiate from a higher dimension effused the moment with just a hint of the grandeur of the human spirit. "Like the old man said," Paul slowly began as if sharing a confidence in the presence of the sacred.

"Yes?" the head nurse prompted, gazing intently at the young Doctor with eyes that sparkled with curiosity, as the heavy metallic door slammed shut behind them.

"We must dare to share… if we really care."

NOTE

The reader is to be commended for demonstrating the intelligence, patience, curiosity, and fortitude which has enabled him/her to complete the reading of this historical novel. Due to the unique format of this work and the esoteric content of some of the chapters, it may be beneficial to look over parts of it a second time. Like fine-tuning the acuity of a telescope or microscope, perhaps what was once a little fuzzy may become a little less fuzzy.

DISCLAIMER

This is a work of historical fiction, and although it contains a great deal of accurate historical (and scientific) data, the characterizations are fictional.

APPENDIX

APPENDIX A

Historical Facts Re: Christianity in Japan
Timeline of Events

Year	Event
1506	- April, Francis Xavier born at Xavier Castle in the Kingdom of Navarra, Spain
1527	- Francis Xavier, age 21, enrolls at the College of Sainte-Barbe, Paris, France, to study Philosophy
1528	- Francis meets Ignatius of Loyola
1530	- March, Francis graduates with a Masters Degree in Philosophy
1537	- June 24th, Francis ordained as a Priest in Rome
1540	- Society of Jesus officially recognized
1541	- May 6th, Francis Xavier arrives in Goa
1547	- Francis Xavier's guide, Angiro, advises him to visit Japan
1549	- Chinese Captain, Avan, sails for Japan from Malacca with Francis Xavier and two Jesuit companions, and lands at Kagoshima, Kyushu, Japan on August 15th where he is received by the Lord of Satsuma, Simazu Takahisa, and allowed to establish Japan's first Christian mission
1550	- Francis Xavier's friendship with Zen Buddhist Monk Ninshitsu, noted in the many enthusiastic messages sent back to Church Officials during this period (citing his immense success in converting pagan souls to Christ)
1551	- December 3rd, Francis Xavier falls ill during voyage to China and passes away on Sancian Island
1562	- Paul Miki, son of military leader, Handayu Miki, born at Tsunokuni, Japan
1563	- Jesuit missionary, Luis Frois arrives in Japan, and later writes, *Historia de Japam*
1579	- Supervisor of Jesuit missions in Asia, Alessandro Valignano, arrives in Japan where the number of converts has mushroomed to over 100,000 souls, including six Daimyos, indicating the growing popularity of Christianity in Japan

1582	- Four Christian Japanese boys sent to Rome for an audience with Pope Gregory XIII
1587	- Toyotomi Hideoshi issues an edict expelling all Christian missionaries, but the edict is mostly ignored; Toyotomi undermines his own edict by allowing Spanish Friars in, giving rise to a rivalry for converts between Jesuit and Franciscan Orders increasing the number of converts to well over 200,000
1596	- Toyotomi Hideoshi confiscates the Spanish Galleon, *San Felipe* and its rich cargo, after it founders off Shikoku resulting in differing Jesuit and Franciscan views regarding the incident; Toyotomi initially sides with the Jesuits, but after being informed by a Spanish Sea Captain that the insidious function of the Missionaries is to prepare Japan for Portuguese or Spanish domination, he views both Orders with increasing suspicion
1597	- February 5th, Paul Miki and twenty-five Japanese and foreign Christians are crucified on Nishizaka Hill in Nagasaki by order of Toyotomi Hideoshi; besides Paul Miki, the others consisted of two Jesuits (John Goto and James Kisai), six Franciscans (Peter Baptist, Martin-de-Aguirre, Francis Bianco, Francis-of-St.Michael, Philip-de-las Casas, Gonsalo Garcia)), and seventeen Japanese lay converts; they are known collectively as the "Martyrs of Japan"
1598	- Toyotomi Hideoshi passes away; at his death the number of Christians is estimated to be about 300,000, mostly concentrated around Nagasaki in South-Western Japan
1612	- Ieyasu Tokugawa, founder of the Tokugawa Shogunate, issues directives aimed at restricting the spread of Christianity in Japan
1614	- Christian "exclusivism" and its unwillingness to tolerate other religions arouses widespread resentment resulting in a nation-wide ban
1622	- Fifty-one Christians put to death in Nagasaki
1624	- Persecution intensifies; fifty Christians burned to death in Edo (now Tokyo)
1627	- September 14th, Paul Miki beatified by Pope Urban VIII
1629	- *Fumie* for testing a suspect's belief in Christianity begins in Nagasaki

1633	- First *Sakoku* of four National Seclusion edicts (1634-1636) issued; and thirty missionaries executed
1640	- Office of Inquisitor (*Shumon aratame yaku*) instituted
1665	- Daimyo ordered by Shogun to appoint Inquisitors charged with the yearly scrutiny of Christians
1790	- First of three Christian persecutions in Urakami (also in 1849 and 1859)
1860	- First American Baptist missionary, Jonathan Goble, arrives in Japan
1862	- June 8th, Paul Miki canonized as a Saint by Pope Pius IX
1865	- A group of Kakure Kirishitan (Hidden Christians) come out of hiding and reveal themselves as Christians to Father Bernard Petitjean in Nagasaki
1866	- Approximately 60,000 Kakure Kirishitan discovered in all, in spite of the anti-Christian laws which were still in effect; many were jailed or exiled
1873	- Meji government withdraws religious sanctions against Christianity
1879	- Ainu Missionary, John Batchelor, publishes an Ainu-English dictionary
1898	- Nagasaki: American Baptist missionaries, Rev. and Mrs. McCollum, celebrate the birth of their son, Arthur H. McCollum (author of the *eight-action plan of provocation* that resulted in the attack on Pearl Harbor)
1904	- Francis Xavier proclaimed "Patron of all Missions" by Pope Pius X
1908	- An estimated 980 Protestant missions flourish in Japan
1920	- Professor Tagita, first academic to research Kakure Kirishitan
1932	- Japanese Christian History Library established by J. Laures
1941	- Formation of a Union of thirty Protestant Churches
1945	- August 9th, United States drops atomic bomb on Nagasaki destroying its oldest and largest Catholic Cathedral and decimating the largest enclave of Christians in Japan
1990	- Since the conclusion of WW II Christianity has made a significant comeback in Japan, numbering some 1,075,000 in a religiously diverse, peaceful, and tolerant nation.

APPENDIX B

Who Was The Real Paul Miki?

Paul Miki was born in 1562 at Tsunokuni, Japan. He was the son of Handayu Miki, a tolerant and wealthy military leader. Early in life Paul felt the call of religion. In 1580 he attended Jesuit colleges at Azuchi and at Takatsuki where he studied to become a Jesuit priest. Soon thereafter he became a devout member of a growing Christian community which had begun when the Jesuit missionary, Francis Xavier landed at Kagoshima in 1549. Paul became an eminent preacher and a successful evangelist for Christ.

By 1587 the Christian community had grown to well over two hundred thousand devout souls. The rapid spread of Christianity was viewed with suspicion by Regent Toyotomi Hideyoshi. His fear of Christianity was greatly augmented when he heard the Captain of a Spanish ship say that the growth of Christianity would aid the Spanish or Portuguese to eventually dominate and conquer Japan. Subsequently the political climate toward Christianity in Japan became quite hostile. In spite of this, Paul Miki decided to continue with his Jesuit ministry in an open and courageous display of religious dedication.

In 1597 Hideyoshi felt that an example had to be made that would retard the rapid rate of conversions to Christianity. Twenty-six Christians were summarily arrested. Amongst the twenty-six was Paul Miki. They were marched on a six hundred mile journey to Nagasaki. Along the way they sang the Te Deum while being displayed and scapegoated.

On 5th February 1597, the twenty-six Christians reached their destination: Nishizaka Hill in Nagasaki. All twenty-six were fastened to wooden crosses by cords and chains; iron collars were fixed around their necks. The crosses were raised and set upright in holes about four feet apart. Each martyr had an executioner beside him with a lance ready to pierce his side. They were allowed to make their confessions to two Jesuit priests who were on hand. At a given signal the executioners raised their lances and all twenty-six martyrs were killed instantly. This was the Japanese method of crucifixion.

Before being pierced by the lance, Paul Miki gave his last sermon while hanging on the cross. He was beatified on 14th September 1627 by Pope Urban VIII, and canonized on the 8th of June, 1862 by Pope Pius IX.

All twenty-six crucified Christians are known collectively as the Martyrs of Japan. After the crucifixion of Paul Miki and his companions, Christianity was officially suppressed in Japan. Many Christians went into hiding to escape persecution. They became known as the *Kakure Kirishitan*. The memory of the martyrdom of Paul Miki and his brave companions provided them with the will, inspiration, and fortitude to remain hidden for over 240 years. In 1865 a group of *Kakure Kirishitan* publicly revealed themselves as "Christians" to Father Bernard Petitjean at Nagasaki.

APPENDIX C

Source For Photos

Two authentic photos are available on the Internet at: http//www.historyplace.com/worldwar2/timeline/abomb2.htm

The first photo was taken moments after the atomic bomb was dropped by a U.S. B-29 Superfortress. It depicts a mushroom cloud formation rising over 60,000 feet above the city of Nagasaki.

The second photo is a stark picture of the wasteland created by the atomic bomb. In the upper left hand quadrant adjacent to the hill is the charred remains (praying hands) of a once magnificent Catholic Cathedral.

For further information (photos and videos) of the aftermath of the destruction of Nagasaki go to the Internet and "Google" the following: *Nagasaki atomic bombing August 9th, 1945.*

About the Author

James T. Sawada was born in Pincher Creek, Alberta in 1941. He is a Nisei, or second generation Canadian of Japanese ancestry. He holds a Masters Degree in Interdisciplinary Studies. He is a retired school teacher, school principal, philosopher, and writer. He is married with two children. He resides with his wife, Norma, in Steveston and Eagle Bay, British Columbia, Canada.

PLEASE SHARE THIS BOOK WITH AS MANY PEOPLE AS POSSIBLE

Original Owner: _____

	DATE	READER'S NAME	BRIEF COMMENT
(1)			
(2)			
(3)			
(4)			
(5)			
(6)			
(7)			
(8)			
(9)			
(10)			
(11)			
(12)			

"THANKS FOR SHARING"

ISBN 142511423-7